His Blue Moon Princess

Silver City Series Book 1

Jenny Fox

ISBN: 978-1-8381097-0-7

Dedication

A ma maman,
Qui a fait naître & grandir ma passion pour les livres.

Contents

Acknowledgements

Thanks to April, Aura & Wynnie, my Editors, who believed in my stories and His Blue Moon Princess first.

Thanks to my Author friends, for helping me and advising me through this journey.

Thanks to Morgan & Wendy who were very patient advisors and readers, and helped me, without whom this Story wouldn't have improved so much from the first draft.

Thanks to my friends and family, for being in my life, bringing me so much every day and supporting me in everything I do.

And finally, thanks to you, dear reader, without whom His Blue Moon Princess would still be an idea without words.

Thank you.

Introduction

Running Away

I'm running as fast as I can.

I'm running for my life, through the rain and the cold. I'm so, so cold. But it doesn't matter right now. I keep running, the farthest I can, the fastest I can. Tears run down my cheeks, along with the rain.

"Come back here! You whore!"

I can hear his voice behind me, and fear makes me run even faster. He is chasing after me, shouting like crazy, calling me terrible names in the night. How can he do this? How could he do this to me? What did I ever do to deserve such a thing? He is my brother!

I take a right turn down a narrow street, looking for a place to hide, but unsure where to go. Can I really escape? The pouring rain is my only ally, as I know it will cover my scent. I keep running, barefooted on the asphalt, running for my life as I try to escape my only family member...

Don't make a sound. Don't cry, don't move.

I cover my mouth with both hands. I won't even breathe. I'm curled up next to a garbage dumpster, closing my eyes and trying to stop my erratic sobbing. I'm so scared, I'm shaking like never before. I close my eyes and pray. Please, don't let him find me, please, please, please...

My heart is pounding so loudly in my ears; I'm deaf to anything else. Even the downpour seems almost quiet. Never have I been so scared in my life before.

This time, he will kill me. I'm dead if he finds me.

Moon Goddess, mother, please, don't let him find me...

As I can't hear him yell anymore, I sneak a peek behind my hideout. Is he gone? Did he go somewhere else?

"Gotcha! Come here, you whore!"

I scream.

He grabs my hair, and the first blow is so violent, I fall to the ground. The pain is terrible. My vision goes blurry, and tears flow. I scream again, out of fear, trying to protect myself. He punches me again and gets on top of me, pinning me to the ground.

He keeps hitting me, one punch more violent than the previous. I keep screaming, crying, begging, but he won't stop.

I'm going to die.

"Stop! No! Please, stop!"

I keep screaming, but Alec won't stop. My pain and supplications never made him stop before. And he was never this mad. My head hurts; my entire body hurts. My arms feel so weak that I can barely hold them up while trying to protect myself.

"I'm not done with you, Nora! Stop resisting! Die! Die! I'm going to kill you!"

No, no, no, I don't want to die! Please, make it stop! Won't anyone help? The rain covers my screams. Alec is beating me so hard; I can't take it anymore. I'm going to die here on the asphalt. I feel each of his punches on my face, my ribs, my stomach. His fists just mercilessly hit wherever they can reach.

He stops.

Is he done? Oh, Moon Goddess, I hope he's had enough... This pain is killing me. I can taste my blood in my mouth and feel some running on my face, too.

Suddenly, I feel his hands on my neck. He is... He's choking me! I try to fight him, push him away, but his grip is tightening so hard around my throat. I can't breathe! Let me breathe! Black spots start blurring my vision, and my head hurts. I gasp helplessly, but nothing comes; his hands won't let go. My hands try to push him away, but he won't budge. I see the look in his eyes. He will really do it.

I feel my consciousness give up; I can't see anything. The headache overtakes it all.

I can't...

"Hey! What the hell are you doing!"

Chapter 1

"Nora!"

I tremble in fear. The voice calling my name from next door freezes my hands immediately. He walks in with his bloodshot eyes, and I can guess what is coming. I bite my lip. The small kitchen seems way too narrow at this instant, and I instinctively step back as he approaches.

He raises his hand, and before I can say a word, slaps me.

"Don't run away when I'm calling you!"

I can feel the burn on my cheek and do my best to keep my eyes down. If I look him in the eyes, he will get even madder. He unleashes at me, his voice echoing with anger in the room.

"Why is the food not ready, huh? Everyone is waiting because of you! Do you feel you can make everyone wait? Are you happy to make us wait? You useless trash! The Alpha is mad at me because of you!"

The slaps keep coming before I even get a chance to talk back. He doesn't care for my explanation. Why is it so unfair? It isn't my fault! Rory and Bill came late with the groceries they were supposed to bring hours ago! I had to start later than planned, and despite that, I tried to get it done as fast as possible, I really did! But it was just an impossible task. Why do I get a beating?

My brother doesn't care; he won't listen to me. He is just a mad, angry beast. I can only try to cover my face with my arms as the blows keep coming.

"Brother, please, stop!" I beg as my tears run down.

"Who are you calling your brother? I have no useless trash sister like you!"

But I am his blood sister! How can he say that? His words are as painful as his hits. Alec used to care for me. He used to love me and play with me. But that was a long time ago, in our childhood. Everything changed for the worst when our parents died. He was twelve, and I was seven.

He found us late, on a stormy night, in a bloodbath. I remember it all. The horror on his face, the shock in his eyes, and how he ran away from the scene. His attitude changed completely after that.

He finally stops hitting me, out of breath, but still red from anger. It hurts so much. I keep my arms up around myself, just in case, but he steps back. "Hurry up! I'll kill you if you don't hurry! You useless thing!"

He leaves the room, and I slowly lower my arms, still shaking. I try not to cry, but I can feel tears filling my eyes. I get up, ignoring the pain. I need to resume cooking...

I try not to touch the painful areas. It hurts so badly. New bruises will add to the ones I already have. Sometimes it hurts for days, and the pain won't let me sleep. Can I ever escape this? Sometimes I fear he will really end up killing me.

I finish cooking and bring the plates to the dining hall. Many pairs of eyes follow my every move. Some pack members smirk after me, and some pretend I don't exist. I prefer the latter. I keep my eyes down and put one plate on the table after another, hoping no one is in the mood to mess with me today.

I'm almost done serving when I can feel something on my thigh. A big hand is gripping me! I get away from the disgusting touch with a shiver and realize it's Marcus. He is more than twice my age and a real pervert. I can't hold a squeak of disgust and step back hurriedly.

At the end of the table, our Alpha, Vince, hits the table with his fist as soon as he hears me, making me jump. "Nora! Shut up and get out of there! Who wants to see your face when we are about to eat! Get out!"

I run away from this room filled with looks of hate and disgust. Some members of the pack even smirk or whistle when I walk by them. I quickly cover my scar with my hair as I exit the room.

I can only breathe again when I finally reach the empty kitchen. Grabbing some leftovers from the fridge, I hurry downstairs. I don't want to be there when everyone comes out of the dining room.

The basement of the main house is a large, dusty room, filled with overused furniture, broken things, and old stuff no one wants. And me.

I retreat to the yellowish rundown old couch and sit to eat my cold lasagna. This place is where I feel the safest. No one comes here, and no one knows I live here. Yes, this is my room. It has been for the past nine years... I tried to sort it to make it comfier, but I can never get used to it. It's dusty, no matter how many times I try to clean it, and there is just one small window. It doesn't have any heater. The winter nights are almost unbearable, even when I gather all the old clothing and blankets I can to cover myself.

Facing me, a large, broken mirror shows my shattered reflection.

The scolding from the Alpha comes back to me. I had forgotten about my scar. I must have put my hair behind my ear without thinking while cooking. I don't like it either. She runs from my eyebrow to my jaw in an irregular, vivid red line. I brush my hair with my fingers, trying to hide this hideous scar with my dark curls.

I find the girl in the mirror so pitiable... She's scrawny, petite, and pale. I look like a sickly kid when I'm already seventeen. I envy the other girls from the pack. Girls like Jessica or Amber, with their feminine looks, curvy bodies, and confident attitude. They are the same age as me, but we are nothing alike. All I can do is try to live as quietly as possible, avoid my brother's wrath, and the pack members' mean looks. They all hate me.

Suddenly, I wake up, still on the couch. Oh, Moon Goddess, did I fall asleep here? My brother is going to kill me! I get up as quickly as I can and run up the stairs, but as I exit the basement, I can already hear him.

"Nora! Useless freak! Where are you hiding! Wait 'till I get you!"

I freeze next to the basement stairs. What time is it? I try to think of something to explain my absence, but nothing comes to mind. Alec is yelling again, from outside. He must be looking for me, thinking I went to the forest. Our pack is on the outskirts of the city, making it easy for us to take a run whenever we want to. For those who can shapeshift...

I take a few steps in the kitchen, hesitating. Should I try to go to the dining room and start cleaning up like nothing happened? Or I could try going upstairs to hide in one of the rooms...

A wave of pain violently hits me from my scalp. My hair is violently grabbed from behind, and I lose balance as I'm forcefully pulled.

"Found her!" Says a feminine voice. "Alec, I got your bitch sister!"

It's Amber, not letting me go no matter how I try to escape her. My brother storms in and hits me hard–so hard that I hit the floor.

"I'm sorry! I'm sorry!" I beg, sobbing already, "Alec, I'm sorry, I just..."

"Won't you shut the hell up! Where were you hiding, you bitch! You thought the chores would get done by itself? Or were you hoping someone would do it for you, huh?"

"Why the hell is the Alpha keeping this girl, again? She's so useless and dumb!" Says Amber.

"I'm sorry, I'll do it right away! Sorry!" I sob.

I get up to reach the sink and run the water to start washing dishes, trying to keep my tears in. My brother and Amber keep growling, but at least he has stopped hitting me. He won't get too violent whenever someone else is in the room, especially a girl.

"If you run away or hide from your chores again, I will kill you!" He swears as he exits the room, followed by Amber, who can't resist smirking at me.

...I'm so sick of it.

When will this stop? This is my hell, day after day. I've tried running away. I did. But Alec is faster than me, and I got the worst beating ever when he caught me. How could I outrun any wolf when I can't shapeshift myself?

I wish they just let me go, but where would I go next? I don't have any other relatives and no friends. I'm penniless too. Where would I go...? Don't cry, Nora. Stop. It's useless.

"Give it to me, I said!"

I shake my head, confused. "I don't have anything, I swear! He didn't give me anything, Alec, he really didn't! You know he gives it all to you!"

He growls in anger, but it's true. What is wrong with him? I just got back from work, and he started searching, even emptied the content of my bag on the floor. Now he keeps asking me for the money. But what money? He knows Robert gives him all my salaries! I never see a single cent I work so hard for!

Even the customer's tips, Robert just takes it from me as soon as my shift is over! I could never hide any of it! And Moon Goddess knows I wish I could!

"Why do you ask? Do ... Do you have money issues again?" I ask.

He glares back at me, furious. "Again? Isn't that your fault I'm ruined! You are just a damn waste of money! Can't you work harder? How am I supposed to make it through with this measly paycheck you get?"

I'm astounded by his words. How dare he? I work like a slave all day and night! The Alpha makes me do all the chores for the pack, from cooking to laundry to cleaning the whole house, everything on my own. And Alec got me this job at the local pub when I was fifteen, making me work those crazy shifts for half of the night! I can only get a few hours of rest at night, and it is never enough.

He, on the other hand, has never had a proper job. He is twenty-three, but Alec says he doesn't need a job because he must focus on the pack, for when he will be chosen as the next Beta. As if that would ever happen. Even I know there is no way my brother will ever get that position. No decent Alpha would ever appoint someone so lazy and self-centered as a Beta.

However, Alec is convinced otherwise. That only makes him act even more unreasonably. He just spends money whenever he wants and shows off in front of his friends while I must watch. That money is what I earn with my sweat, and yet Alec is the one who spends it. How can he pretend I'm the one he uses it on? I don't own anything but a few clothes! I don't even have a bed, and I can only eat leftovers if there's any.

So why is he now interrogating me like I'm some thief?

"Anyway, you will be working tomorrow night," he says.

"What? But I haven't had a day off in weeks! And the Alpha wants me to make dinner– another pack will be visiting! I won't make it in time if..."

"I don't care!" Alec yells. "It's your problem, not mine! You will go to work, and I'll kill you if you don't! And the Alpha better not be mad at me because of you!"

I stand there, shocked, as he exits the room. What's wrong with him? He has never told me to do anything that might upset the Alpha, and now he wants me to go to work? At least he or the Alpha will be mad at me!

I take my head in my hands. What do I do now? The Alpha was so adamant about me preparing all this dinner! Some people from the Blood Moon pack are coming, and that is big for our pack; he will never forgive me if I don't help him welcome them.

Our Jade Moon pack is one of the oldest werewolves Clans of Silver City and the best located, but we are also one of the smallest and humblest.

We are nothing next to the Blood Moon pack.

I only know what I heard from other people, but it's enough. The Blood Moon pack, despite being only a few decades old, is the strongest in the area, and unrivaled. Even the Sapphire Moon or Gold Moon packs are no match.

But it's not about their numbers. The Blood Moon pack is fearsome because it is wealthy, hungry, and ruthless. Some say the Alpha leads with an iron hand, and no mistakes are permitted. They're scary, but they are like royalty to this City's werewolves. Our Jade Moon Pack is on neutral terms with them, so far. I don't believe any Alpha leader would willingly become their enemy.

So, what will happen if I ruin this dinner? I could ruin relationships between the two packs and lead ours to a disaster! The Alpha will banish me, or worse. I try to sleep, but I'm too worried.

What is wrong with my brother? I have seen him in need of money, but now he acts like he has gone crazy! And his bloodshot eyes... He was down here in the basement when I came home, looking for money. I even heard him ask Amber for cash. What kind of trouble did he get into this time? I don't like this.

What will I do tomorrow? I can't do both! My shift starts at four, and the dinner must be ready at nine. Should I do as Vince said and skip work, or obey Alec? Neither of them will let me off.

Vince hates me as well, and I fear his beating more than I fear my brother's; he is way too strong.

Either way, this won't end well for me.

The next day is a nightmare. My brother is already after me when I'm making breakfast for everyone, threatening me non-stop. "You'd better not let me down, Nora. I want this money, you hear me? You are going to work as long and as hard as Robert wishes you, and you better come home with that paycheck in your hand! Or else you're going to regret it, I swear!"

He doesn't stop until the Alpha comes downstairs to eat. Vince glares at me, and I lower my head, as submissive as I can be. A few other pack members enter after him to join the breakfast. Among them, Marcus sends me a lewd glance, making me shiver with disgust.

"What are you waiting for, you stupid girl?" Says Amber. "Won't you hurry up and serve us the food? Do you want the Alpha to starve or what?"

To add to her words, Vince growls. I can feel my wolf whimper inside, afraid. I can barely feel her nowadays. I serve breakfast as fast as I can, feeling the glares on me. My wolf whines continuously inside. She doesn't want to be there, and I don't either.

I'm about to leave the dining hall when the Alpha calls me again.

"Nora. Tonight's dinner is essential for our pack. If you make any mistake, you will be banished from this pack for good, you hear me?"

I glance at my brother, sitting away from the Alpha, but he acts like normal. Alec will blame me in any case.

"Nora!"

I jump. The Alpha got impatient from my silence. I nod slowly, and he growls once more before starting his breakfast.

I leave the room and exit the house for fresh air. What do I do now?

My eyes set on the forest. This green, vast, and beautiful forest. My wolf wants to go; she wants to run among the trees, feel the fresh cold air. The autumn's fallen leaves, the gentle breeze of the wind, the smell of the grass. I know. How I wish I could let her out, too...

I bite my lip. I wish I could be a free wolf. Free of my brother, free of my pack, and free of those painful memories.

It's so tempting, and I can almost feel my wolf who wants to run there too. But I can't, I can't...

"I won't go," I say.

I'm shaking, but it's been two days, and I won't change my mind. Alec stares at me with a furious look. I ignore him. I may be afraid of him, but the Alpha's wrath is even scarier.

"What, did you say you won't go? You just shut up and go already; I am not asking for your opinion! You bitch!"

I bite my lip and clench my fist, holding the spoon. I try to focus on those appetizers, ignoring the angry eyes of my brother. Alec starts yelling at me, as I expected. I can take his insults. I am no bitch, no whore, no slut. I have never once done anything that could make me deserve these names, but he keeps going on and on. Why would he call me such things? I've never even been kissed before or been with a man!

Hang on, Nora. This is not something he's never done before.

He slaps me, but I don't care. I ignore the pain and keep making those toasts. A new slap, and one of the appetizers falls on the floor. Don't look at him, don't. Keep going.

"You are going to go to work right now!" He yells in the kitchen.

No, I won't. I know it's no use talking back, so I don't. Even my wolf is proud of me. She is being fierce, showing her teeth, sharing her strength with me. We won't submit to him. If I don't make this dinner successful for the Alpha, the whole pack will be mad at me. We all know how merciless the Blood Moon pack can be. Everyone still vividly remembers how they destroyed the Snow Moon Clan two years ago. They didn't just fight them; they killed all of those who didn't pledge allegiance to the Blood Moon emblem.

Compared to that kind of threat, those of my brother are not as fearsome.

He keeps the yelling going, but I ignore him. He slaps me a couple of times, pissed, but that won't work. When he suddenly stops, I raise my head, surprised. The Alpha, Vince, just entered the kitchen.

"What's going on here?" Vince asks. "I can hear you all the way from my office, Alec, keep it down."

"Nothing, Alpha. Just telling this eyesore to work faster..."

"You mind your own business! I need your sister working, stop hindering her work. You want to be useful? Go help upstairs. And shut up!"

Alec glares at me but has no choice but to obey and leave. Vince looks at me with disdain, peeking a glance at my work so far. It's not much, but it's not even 4 pm yet, and I know I'm going to be ready on time. Without saying anything, he exits the room. Apparently, he recognizes I've been working diligently and won't get mad. I let out a sigh of relief and go back to my task. At least now I know Alec won't dare to come back here.

The hours go by, and I can feel the tension rising within our pack's building. Everyone is anxious about this meeting. Vince came down to check on my work five times within the last two hours. But I am proud of everything I have done and even feel somewhat confident about the dinner.

"Nora! Stop daydreaming!"

"So... Sorry, Alpha. But I'm almost done!" I defend myself, showing the completed dishes.

Vince nods, but won't compliment me. Then, he looks at me and clicks his tongue. I glance down. I spent all afternoon cooking, and thus, my clothes were dirtied. They weren't pretty, to begin with, but now... I look like a beggar. Even my hair is messy.

"I will change into new clothes as soon as I'm done."

"Whatever. Just go to your room, and don't you dare come out tonight. I don't need the Blood Moon leaders to see your... face."

His eyes are set on where my scar is, behind my hair. I was careful to braid my hair the right way so my curls would hide it, but it's no use, he knows it's there. I avoid his gaze and lower my head.

At the same time, a group of pack members walks by to go to the recreation room, laughing and jokingly pushing one another. Alec is among them, and he stops as soon as he sees me. He goes from a smile to a pissed-off look in no time and keeps glaring at me. I know my brother still thinks about this shift, but it's way too late now. I wonder why he wanted tonight's money so badly. Is he having money issues again?

But he can't say anything right now; Vince is still facing me and watching my every move like a hawk, making sure I finish in time. I feel, however, that this will only delay Alec's punishment for opposing him...

An hour later, I'm in the kitchen with my completed dishes, giving instructions.

"...And this is called *crème brûlée*. All you need to do is burn the sugar on top a little when you serve it like I just did."

Jill and Maria are frowning, trying to remember it all. They will be the ones to serve tonight, as Vince doesn't want anyone that is not part of the pack to see me. Jill and Maria are my age, but they are way prettier, though they are not really smart.

"Wait, why did you have to make a Russian dessert?" Asks Maria while playing with her blonde hair

"It's not Russian, it's French! Vince said the Black Family is originally from France, so..."

They give me suspicious stares, but I don't care. All I need is for them to remember a few names and how to serve it!

Thankfully, about ten minutes later, I think they finally get it. I hope so... They leave upstairs to get ready, and I can finally clean the kitchen.

It's almost time. Everyone is ready, and it is time for me to go hide in the basement. I'm so exhausted from cooking all afternoon, I just lay flat on my familiar couch. I'm about to fall asleep when I can hear it. The people from the Blood Moon Clan are here!

I get up, totally awake, and run across the room to the small window. I climb on top of a rundown drawer to reach the opening. I need to stand on my toes to get to see something. My eyes are at ground level, and, for a while, all I can distinguish are feet and paws. But I can clearly hear Vince's voice.

"Welcome! Welcome to the Jade Moon Den. I am Vincent Greene, and this is my Beta, Peter."

I can distinguish his big brown boots among the crowd, and Peter, in his wolf form, next to him. Actually, a few members of our pack shapeshifted, too, before the guests' arrival, just in case... I suppose both sides can't trust the other.

However, facing them, the Blood Moon pack members are easy to recognize, even from my position. All of them are in human form and wearing dark suits and classy black leather shoes. Look like some mafia gang has arrived! I'm shocked not even one of them is in their wolf form. Are they that confident? Or just trying to act arrogantly? One of them replies with a gentle voice I didn't expect.

"Thank you for having us. You have a lovely turf indeed... How lucky of you to be able to enjoy a run in the forest anytime you want."

His tone is peaceful, so why is it his words seem so... menacing? I feel like he is threatening instead of thanking! Vince must be tense, but he won't show it.

"Oh, we are very attached to our land. My family has protected it for generations. But the forest is everyone's, of course, so please do not hesitate to come whenever you want to escape the city!"

I don't believe they would wait for permission...

Vince finally invites them in, and I leave my spot to go put my ear against the door. The basement is next to the kitchen and close to the dining hall. I can hear all the chatting as they go by, with Vince introducing some pack members and showing them the way. He is the only one talking; none of the Blood Moon can be heard. I wonder what they look like...

I listen to them enter the dining hall, and then the kitchen goes quiet.

Meanwhile, I change quickly into some clean clothes. I grab a clean pair of jeans that I have left in the old wardrobe and put on a dark blue sweater that's too big on me. At least I feel clean.

I'm putting my messy hair into a low bun when I hear some steps coming from the kitchen. Jill and Maria came to take the first plates, chatting as always.

"Gosh, I could barely breathe in there; everyone is so tense! If only they would relax a little," says Maria.

"Oh, I wish I could relax with that Nathaniel guy. I'm sure he's a wild beast behind the pretty boy look..."

"Keep your paws off, girl. Amber already is eyeing him. That girl is such a slut... But even without her, I wouldn't go near one of them. Those Black brothers are scary. I mean, those guys killed their own father and Alpha!"

"And it's only two of them here. But I heard the oldest brother is the worst; he is the crazy one. Okay, you got everything?" Jill whispers.

They go back, and the kitchen goes silent again. Did they really kill their Alpha and father? I didn't know that part! No wonder everyone is so afraid of them... Jill and Maria come and go again in the kitchen, but the chatting is reduced to them trying to remember what they are serving. It's nerve-wracking to hear them struggle when I'm just behind the door, but I can't disobey Vincent's orders just to help those two!

Thankfully, it seems the dinner goes well. I can hear everyone exiting the dining room, and the voices reach me again when they go out.

"... was impressed. It's been a while since we've enjoyed some authentic French cuisine," says the guy from earlier.

They liked it! I find myself smiling and let out a sigh of relief.

"Glad you enjoyed it! It was our honor to have you here tonight."

"Who knew the Jade Moon Clan had such cooking-skilled

members... By the way, you have some exquisite ladies here."

Vince must be overjoyed. This is the same as saying they would agree to let our packs members court each other, right?

"Hey. Is that all your girls?" Says a voice I haven't heard before.

Judging from his arrogant tone, that must be the other brother. What's with his question? He sounds so disdainful!

"Hmm, well, yes. You've seen all our young girls who have yet to find their mate tonight..."

"Never mind. Let's leave."

They exchange a few greetings and soon leave. I can hear some of our pack members letting out sighs of relief.

"What's with this attitude of his? Are we not pretty enough now?" Growls Amber.

"Anyway, that went well. We should be content with that alone. I don't want any issues with the Blood Moon Clan. Their brother is pissed at the Sapphire Moon Clan these days and trust me. No one wants to take their place..."

I step down, as Vince is now just giving orders for the patrols. What a night... Even without being in the room, I was still on edge because of this dinner. Again, I wonder why the Blood Moon bothered to come all the way here. They own half of the city and scare the other half. Are they interested in the outskirts of the city now?

I just keep thinking about the dark rumors surrounding those three Black brothers and slowly fall into a deep sleep...

Something's wrong with my brother.

Since the dinner with the Blood Moon Clan and me not obeying him, Alec has been acting weird. I thought he would come and punish me afterward, but he didn't. For some reason, he just keeps watching me from afar.

Even today, as I am working, he is standing at the bar, watching my every move and drinking without saying a word. Robert frowns, unsure about what is going on. At some point, he grabs my arm, almost making me spill the beers.

"Hey, what's with Alec? You did something? Looks like he's pissed at you or something'."

"I don't know. Now let me go, customers on table six are waiting for those," I just answer and shake his arm off.

He may not be pleased with my answer, but I really don't know. It's his fourth beer already, and he hasn't said a word for hours! It's almost scary how silent he is.

Knowing he is watching, I keep working. It's not like I'm bored, anyway. Rob's bar is crowded tonight, and the orders keep coming in non-stop. Liz and I have been running around all evening. Elisabeth, Robert's daughter, is the only member of the pack who's kind to me.

I'm cleaning a table for the next group when someone loudly orders more beer from across the room. I nod and go behind the counter to pour the drinks, and Liz joins me, grabbing a towel.

"Those drunkards spilled some of their damn beer on me! How am I supposed to go party after this if I smell like a barrel of beer!"

"It should come off with just water and soap from the ladies' room," I say.

"Really? You better be sure because I'm not going like that!"

I nod, and she runs off to the bathroom. Liz isn't bad. She's just a bit self-centered and still acts like she's sixteen instead of twenty-six sometimes. But I like her. Sometimes she gives me some of her clothes she won't wear anymore, even if it's just because she is too lazy to throw it out. Thanks to her, I can wear something new sometimes, as Alec won't ever leave me any money to buy anything.

I keep working, and the bar is so full, even Robert seems in a good mood. Liz and I run around without stopping to keep up until about 11 pm.

Now the groups are paying and exiting the bar one after another, going to find some more fun somewhere else. I can clean the tables without stopping every time to take a new order, and even Robert went outside for a quick smoke. I realize Alec is still there; only he isn't alone anymore. Why is he talking with Marcus?

I don't like this. This pervert is leering me, whispering with my brother, who doesn't seem very happy. Alex's fidgeting. I wish I knew what they're talking about...

"Nora! If you're done, come clean the glasses, girl!"

Liz has decided she's done for tonight. She takes her apron off and waves me good-bye before heading to the back exit. She probably was waiting for a chance to go while her dad is not watching.

I take over behind the sink, and I'm almost in front of my brother and Marcus now. They immediately stop talking, and both stare at me.

One is looking at me with disgust, the other with lust.

"Hi, Nora," says Marcus

I ignore him and keep washing one glass after another. Even if I concentrate on my hands, I can feel his gaze piercing me. It's so unsettling.

"Playing hard to get? That's not what this pretty skirt says, you know."

Won't he stop? My own brother is sitting in front of him, and neither of them minds his trashy talk! This man is so disgusting. My wolf is growling inside, annoyed, too. Can't he just drink and leave like everyone else?

"Isn't your sister good at this, Alec? She's a freak, all right, but a hot one..."

The freak doesn't want any attention, you pervert. There are so many hot girls in the pack, why is he always after me? I'm not pretty, I wear ragged and oversized clothes, and I even have a scar across my face! Is he blind or what?

Suddenly, his hands go over the counter, and he grabs my wrist.

"Hey, don't run away, sweetheart. Come on; I just want to chat a bit."

Let me go! I struggle to break free, but he won't let go. He is grinning and holding as hard as he can until it hurts.

"Let me go!"

"Oh, here's your pretty voice, sweetheart. Do you have any idea how enticing it sounds? You could..."

"Enough!" Robert is back, and his yell surprises Marcus enough that he loses his grip, and I can free myself. I massage my painful wrist and step back. Marcus looks pissed, but he won't win against Robert's angry face.

"Marcus, why the hell are you annoying her when she's working! Get out!"

Marcus grunts, but he knows who the stronger wolf in the room is. He pays and leaves, to my relief. That was close... He's gotten physical a few times before, but these days, he really is pushier than usual.

Alec, still silent, gives me an annoyed look and leaves behind him. I see him catching up with Marcus outside, a pissed-off expression on his face, talking to him. Robert starts counting today's tips while looking at them across the window.

"Tsk, this guy is such a pain... And you, hurry up with the cleaning. I'm tired."

No need to tell me twice.

The bar is located downtown, thirty minutes away from our Jade Moon territory. I don't mind the walk. Most people don't even notice me, and I can enjoy the quietness of the night. And it's mid-October, so it's not too cold either.

Though Silver City can be dangerous at times, we cohabitate peacefully with humans. They don't meddle in our pack situations, but it's different between the werewolf clans. We get into fights with other packs sometimes, but the Jade Moon Clan never looks for trouble willingly. We don't want to upset a bigger, stronger Clan by mistake.

I finally make it back to the main house, but surprisingly, someone's still up. Rory and Bill are talking in the kitchen over some drinks. I just head right away for the basement, but they call me when they see me.

"Hey, freak! Come here for a second."

I'm in no mood to entertain them now... I want to flee to the basement and get some sleep! But they insist with a hand gesture, and I guardedly enter the dining hall.

"Oh, come on; we are not going to eat you or something'." Says Rory, seeing me so defiant.

I don't trust them. My brother's friends can be quite vile and cruel when they're bored. They've locked me out a few times, for example...

I stop a few steps after the door, within a safe distance from them.

"Hey, where's your brother? We've been looking for him all day!"

I frown. What, so they were just waiting for Alec? I shake my head. "I don't know... He came to Robert's Pub with Marcus, but they left together before I did. I really don't know where he went..."

"Tsk. This dumbass is evading us!" Growls Bill.

"He can't keep it up for long, anyway. Even Peter's looking for him. Bet that idiot was actually stupid enough to borrow some money from the Beta, too."

"Alec borrowed money from you and Peter?" I ask, nervous.

Bill slams his glass on the table, making me jump.

"Hell yeah, he did! And we've had enough of it! That idiot brother of yours owes half of the pack and smokes it away!"

Not good... Alec doesn't win any money on his own! All he has is my salary and the inheritance from our parents. Why is my brother going around borrowing money? There is no way he can pay them back! Rory keeps complaining, but he's obviously drunk and gabbling. I can leave the room without either of them noticing.

Back to my familiar basement, I'm exhausted. Why is Alec so... reckless? He won't get a decent job; he just pushes all his chores on me and beats me up when he's upset.

What was that talk with Marcus for, anyway? Is he trying to borrow some money again?

That night I lay on my old couch with an uneasy feeling...

The next day, my brother isn't in the dining hall for breakfast. And I am not the only one concerned about his absence: Peter comes to me to ask about his whereabouts, but I'm just as clueless as he is.

Borrowing money from the Beta and his friends, what was he thinking? Peter could have Vincent banish him from the pack for this kind of thing; our clan is not easy on troublemakers...

I try not to think about it too much and just focus on my chores for the day. But after cleaning the breakfast dishes, doing the laundries, and cleaning the first and second floors, I keep wondering where he could be. No one has seen him all day, I heard Vincent and Rory complain about it.

I wish I knew where Alec was, too! A lot of people stared at me suspiciously as they came for dinner time, and I realize he might have borrowed money from more people. Wait, he wouldn't have run away, right? My hand freeze on my sponge. Could he? No, it's just been a day; maybe he's...

"Nora, come here."

"Alec!"

My brother is here! He's in the kitchen, fidgeting and looking at me with a weird look. I approach him cautiously. He looks sober, but his bloodshot eyes... Suddenly, he hands me what he's been holding in his hands. Isn't that one of our mother's dresses? I recognize the beautiful embroidery and the lace on the back. I didn't even know he had it!

"I found this. Just put it on."

Is this supposed to be a... present? He's frowning and won't look at it. I am not sure about what to do. Isn't this dress too thin and too big? Why would I put on such a pretty and daring dress here and now?

"Just put this damn thing on, I said!"

He violently slaps me, making me step back. I don't answer and flee down to the basement to obey. I don't want to get hit a second time.

I get dressed in front of the mirror, but my reflection is... unsettling. This dress is pure white, it doesn't look too good on my pallid and bruised skin. And it's mother's...

"How long do you need to put on a damn dress!"

Alec comes down without warning and looks at me, visibly pissed. Seeing that I'm done, he runs up to me and grabs me by the arm without a word. I try resisting, but he's way stronger. He takes me out of the house and starts walking toward the city.

"Wait, Alec, stop! I can't go out looking like this! What are you doing? Stop!"

He stops, and I get a new slap, a second, a third, one after another.

"Will you shut the hell up! I don't fucking care! Just shut up and walk!"

I don't dare to say a word anymore. I don't want any more hits, but where are we going? I'm barefooted, and he makes me walk looking like this in the open! I am starting to get really scared of what's coming now. He makes sure we avoid the rest of the pack, making us take the long way around the houses. Everyone is having dinner, is that why he only came now? To avoid others? I don't like this...

Twenty minutes later, we finally enter one of the buildings on the outskirts of the city. I know this one: It belongs to our Jade Moon Clan, so a few pack members live here. Who are we meeting, then? Without a word, he pushes me into the elevator and finally lets my arm go. I'm freezing, and my arm aches...

"Alec, what's going on? Why are we here?" I ask.

"Settling my debts."

"What, how?"

He doesn't answer and pushes me to the sixth floor. He grabs me again as he sees me hesitating and pushes me. I trip and almost fall on my knees as we enter one of the apartments. When I raise my head, I see Marcus.

Marcus, staring at me with a grin, half-naked.

"There you go," says Alec.

"Wait, what? Alec, what is this?" I ask, panicked.

Oh, Moon Goddess, no, no, no. Marcus won't keep his hungry eyes off me, and my brother looks so... detached.

"I told you we are settling my debts. Marcus will do that."

"Exactly, sweetheart. Now you are going to be a good girl and let me have my fun, and your brother walks out with all that money he needs. How great is that?" Exclaims Marcus, with a broad smile.

Have they gone crazy! I don't want to spend even a minute with this lecherous dog! And now he wants to sell me to this old pervert for money? What the Hell!

"No, no, I'm going," I say, turning back to the door.

But Alec is in my way and grabs my arm forcefully.

"Stop it, Nora! All you have to do is let him fuck you, and our money problems will be over! What, are you going to say you don't want to? You think I give a damn about you? But look, we need that money, so you're going to be a good girl and..."

"And screw you, Alec!" I explode. "What money problems? You're the one who got in trouble in the first place! Why do I have to do this! I don't get a single cent for myself! Now you want to make me pay for the money I earned, and you stupidly wasted? No way I'm doing this!"

He hits me violently —a full punch, throwing me on the floor. I land painfully on my arms, letting out a cry.

"Shut the hell up! Whose fault is it I'm broke in the first place! Who made me an orphan, huh? You freak! Who gives a damn about what you think!"

He grabs me by the hair, forcefully making me stand on my knees, and looks at me with those crazy eyes.

" You're going to do it, Nora. You're going to have sex with Marcus. And after that, you better not complain, not a word, to anyone, because if you do, I will kill you for good this time, you hear me?"

He lets me go and storms out, slamming the door behind him.

He has gone mad. I'm shaking all over, from the panic and the shock combined. What nightmare is this?

"Well, well... It seems like you have your orders, now. So, let's be a good girl, Nora. I'm paying your brother a good sum to have my way with you, so don't you play hard to get now."

Hell no.

I don't want this pork anywhere near me, and there is no way I'm going to let him touch me in any way. My wolf is growling like crazy inside, ready to defend herself.

No way.

Chapter 2

It hurts...

My throat is so painful, every breath feels like a raging fire. I feel so numb.

My body aches all over, and I feel so tired... I can't even find the strength to move or open my eyes. I just lay here, listening to the regular beeping of a machine, and those unknown voices.

"... consciousness already. We just grabbed her and ran here. She was so... He would have killed her. Too bad we lost him."

"How did you know that was her?"

"We didn't..."

I hear a growl, and someone's agitating the soft sheets around me. So, I'm in bed... A real, comfy bed. I can feel someone's breathing close to me.

"Well, she's better. That shouldn't take too long for her to wake up, now."

"She'd better. Our brother is making everyone freak out since that girl's here. Looks like he's about to murder someone or something..."

I've heard that voice before. Where was that? I can't remember.

Why am I so tired? I feel like going back to sleep...

I'm half-awake again. This is such a weird sensation... My body is too tired to fully wake up, yet too tired to go back to sleep. I find the strength to open my eyes, but I'm in the dark. No, wait... It's nighttime. I can figure out some furniture in the room. Some small lights are blinking on a machine next to me, too.

A large window lets the weakly gleaming moonlight in.

The sky is cloudless, and I can see a bit of the moon and stars. I feel a cold breeze coming through. Oh, that fresh air feels so good... But, more important, a tall silhouette stands alone against the window frame.

Two cold silver eyes are staring right at me. I'm mesmerized.

Those eyes are scary and... attractive.

What is this? I can feel it stirring me up inside like something's suddenly blooming. What is this sensation? It's nothing like I've ever felt before. I can hear my wolf, she's... crying? Her voice is so faint, I don't know what's going on.

I'm too tired, too weak. I can't hear her. So sleepy...

I slowly open my eyes.

Such a high ceiling... Where am I? I turn my head. I'm in the biggest bed I've ever seen. I'm surrounded by medical monitors, and it looks like a hospital bed, but... Brick red walls, wood flooring, and fancy furniture? The room is so huge, thirty people could fit in. But there's only three. A man and a woman are chatting on the sofa. There's one younger guy too, playing with his smartphone.

"Oh, I think she's awake!"

A tall woman gets up from the sofa and comes to me once she realizes I'm awake. She has honey-colored skin and two very long, dark braids. Her fingers gently examine me, although she doesn't look like a doctor at all. She looks young, maybe twenty-five or so. She's a bit muscular, wearing a sports bra, tight leather pants, and high heeled boots.

"Okay, her blood pressure's still a bit too slow, but at least she's awake for good. Can you hear me, baby girl? How do you feel? Drowsy?"

I shake my head and try to answer her.

Gosh, my throat hurts! Breathing's so painful, let alone uttering a word. Even while breathing from my nose, I almost tear up just from the pain. There is no way I can talk right now. I try to touch my neck and feel a thick bandage around it.

"Oh yeah, sorry about that. Your throat is damaged, so it might be difficult for you to talk for a while. Don't force it, okay? It will get better, don't worry. You think you can sit?"

I nod, still a bit shaken up by everything that is going on. That woman helps me sit up and puts some big cushions behind me for support. It feels unreal. I don't know these people, or where we are. I look down. I'm perfused and linked to several medical machines. Someone even put me in a hospital gown. Seeing me so confused, she starts explaining.

"It's okay. This is the General Hospital. You were in a coma for about five days. We found you in the eastern district, and someone was attacking you. My brother and I intervened, but you collapsed right away."

I realize there is one more person in the room I hadn't noticed before. A huge golden-brown wolf is lying at her feet against my bed. I can only see him now that I am sitting up. But still, I have never seen such an imposing beast before–he looks like a bear rather than a wolf!

"Yes, that's my baby brother, Bobo. I'm Tonia, by the way."

Bobo? Is that his actual name? Tonia gives me a reassuring smile but won't introduce the two other people in the room. One of them suddenly gets up from his chair, looking irritated. He's most likely in his teens, with dark, messy hair and a dozen piercings in his ears. He grabs a backpack and puts his hands in his pockets, looking annoyed and ready to leave.

"Great, can I go now that she's awake?"

He is not asking Tonia, but the last person in the room. A man in his twenties, wearing a very elegant black suit, waits a few seconds and nods.

"But don't come home late, Liam. I don't want to have to send people to fetch you again."

"Yeah, yeah..."

The teenager exits the room, and Tonia shrugs and focuses on me once more.

"Don't mind this brat. Okay, can you show me the parts where it hurts?"

Now that I glance down, I've got bruises all over, and I can tell my right eye is probably not good either, judging from the pain. I still feel weak, too.

Trying to think about where I feel the worst, I point out my throat, my right flank that is still aching badly, and my arm. Tonia explains to me that I had surgery for internal bleeding, but I am recovering well.

But why? All this medical care can't be free, and I don't think they are just nice to me out of charity. While Tonia comments on my wounds some more, the man behind her is staring at me non-stop. He has a gentle look, with blue eyes and thin facial features. Now that I observe him some more, he looks a lot like the teenager from earlier. Are they brothers? He seems taller, though, and his hair is blonde.

"If you feel dizzy, just lay down, okay? That's perfectly normal, considering you had surgery and lost a lot of blood. And you are way too skinny. By the way, how old are you exactly?"

I raise my fingers to show her. She looks surprised.

"Really? Seventeen? You look younger! I would have said fourteen or fifteen. Well, that's not too bad then."

What is not to bad? I frown, but she doesn't notice my perplexed expression as she suddenly turns towards her brother. The huge wolf sits up and puts his head on her lap. They stare at each other for a while.

"Oh, right. Bobo asks, what's your name. I should have asked earlier, too."

I realize the siblings must have been using telepathy since they are most likely from the same pack. How nice... I never succeeded mind-linking with my pack, since I've never shape-shifted.

I can't talk, so they hand me a notepad and a pen. I write down my name.

"Nora Bluemoon," The man reads out loud. "A pretty name."

He looks like our fated mate...

Wait, what now? What was that? My inner wolf? How would my inner wolf or I know he does? It makes no sense... How would we know that man looks like our mate?

While I'm trying to understand, some vague memory of a pair of silver eyes flashes, and I realize this guy as almost the same eyes. Only his are not exactly silver, but more of a blue-ish grey. Was that just a dream? Or did someone else really come to visit us while I was unconscious?

I grab the pen once again to write my questions and show them to Tonia.

"Why are you here? Well, you were in horrible shape when we found you."

"I don't think that's what she means, Tonia."

The man addresses me, standing still next to my bed. "The hospital belongs to my family, so that's why Tonia brought you here. And we believe you are someone special for my older brother, so we got you this VIP room."

How am I unique? And how rich must his family be to own the General Hospital? I didn't even know hospitals could be bought!

His gentle voice really has a way to make people feel calm and weary at the same time. Why does it look so familiar?

Oh, Moon Goddess.

I know where I've met him before. He was at the meeting with the Blood Moon Clan! He's one of the Black brothers! And saying I'm special to his older brother means...

Suddenly, I can feel it. A loud pounding, like a warning. I tense up. My whole body knows.

He's coming near. He's coming here. I shiver.

We hear a step outside the door, and I can barely breathe. Is that what it feels like? Feeling my mate being close to me? That is indescribable. I feel apprehension, and at the same time, I want to see him so badly... My heart's going crazy.

The doors open quickly, and everyone in the room immediately focuses on Him.

I'm seeing him for the very first time, so why does he feel so... familiar to me? Like I've known him forever. Like we've been waiting for him forever.

The whole atmosphere surrounding him gives off an oppressive feeling. He's very tall and immediately dominates the room without effort. I was right, I've seen those ice-cold silver eyes before. He stares at me as soon as he comes into the room and walks up straight to me.

No, don't approach. Yes, please come.

I'm going crazy! This inner turmoil won't let me think for one second, and my wolf won't hold still either. The beeping next to me suddenly speeds up, but no one says a thing. I couldn't care less. For now, all I can think about is this man coming up to me. His swift steps bring him to me in seconds, and I can't even prepare myself before he sits on my bed, facing me. I barely notice that Tonia immediately shifts back and takes a few steps away.

His face is so close to me. I can barely breathe, but he won't show any expression. Am I the only one in that helpless state? Is it my wolf only that finds him so handsome? No, he really looks like he was carved in marble. A chiseled face, with a strong jawline, a five o'clock shadow, and thin lips. I just can't take my eyes off him, and those two diamonds won't leave me, either.

Without warning, he lifts his hand to come and very gently caress my cheek. His fingers feel so warm and pleasant against my skin...

"How do you feel?" He asks, in a low and deep voice

I just nod, so intimidated. I can't take my eyes off him, as if I wanted to engrave all his features in my mind.

"She just woke up. She can't talk yet, but she's definitely better." Says Tonia.

"Her name is Nora," says the other man.

"Nora..." he repeats softly.

Why does my name sound so beautiful when he's the one saying it? I feel so shy and helpless, never have I been in such a turmoil of emotions before. Thankfully, I'm lying on a bed, because I'm sure I couldn't have faced him on my own two feet, otherwise.

"What else?" He suddenly asks, not taking his eyes off me.

"Nothing much, Boss. She told us she is seventeen, but that's it."

Tonia calls him "Boss"? Now that I think of it, both she and her brother reacted to his presence and stepped back. They're behaving differently since he entered the room, being respectfully still and quiet.

I can tell his Alpha aura is such that it won't be ignored, and any wolf would most definitely submit right away and show respect... It can't even be compared to Vincent; he's on a whole different level. I don't even get how I can stand looking at him in the eye for so long. Is that a mate thing to be somehow immune to him? Only the other man, who must be his brother, is still standing next to my bed, smiling confidently. He's the only one that won't lower his head while talking to him.

"She really just woke up, Damian. We only asked her a few things before you came. How did you know?"

"I felt it."

So, his name is Damian. Damian Black, I suppose... It suits him, his jet-black hair, and his elegant dark suit, like his brother. I bet his wolf form is black, too.

Looking at his collar, I realize he has a large tattoo on the side of his neck. A black crescent moon, adding to his imposing aura.

"Who did this?"

He's asking me.

His hand goes down from my cheek to my neck, and his expression subtly changes into something frightful. His commanding tone means to know who attacked me. And his eyes... scare me. I can feel the cold anger in his voice as he stares at my injury. I try to think of an answer, but when I try remembering, it's so blurry...

I remember my brother dragging me out of the main house of the Clan. The suggestive white dress. Walking to the city, entering a building...

The fright all comes back to me. Alec pushing me in front of Marcus. The lewd smile and his eyes on me. My brother abandoned me there. I unconsciously start quivering. Oh, Moon Goddess, I can't remember what happened next. I just feel terrified as soon as I try. Wait, I think I remember. Yes, the disgusting feeling of his hideous paws on me, holding me while I struggled to escape, pushing Marcus away. It's so sickening, I feel nauseous again. The tremendous fear as I tried to resist him, and...

Blood. Lots of blood.

Oh my gosh, what did I do? I start panicking, unable to remember the rest. I glance down as if I could see the blood-stained dress again. I just remember all this hideous red, on my hands, my legs... So, so much blood! What could have happened? I don't... I feel like I did something terrible, but why is it that I don't remember what happened!

All that comes to me after that is pouring rain, the cold, and my running away in a deserted street. The voice of Alec calling me, chasing me. His cold hands on my neck, tightening, choking me.

"Nora, Nora, calm down. You're gonna be okay now, baby girl." Says Tonia, worried.

She approached my bedside again, worried by my panic state. I realize I've started shaking and tearing up while remembering this horrible night. I hurriedly wipe it off with my sleeve. All of this is so upsetting, and now I wake up in this unbelievable hospital room, like a dream. I don't want to reminisce right now. I'm exhausted, scared, and confused.

"Boss, I think she just needs a bit of rest. It won't be good for her recovery if she gets too agitated now."

I see him hesitating. Is he going to leave? My wolf is whimpering. Stop it! I met him like two minutes ago. Stop confusing me and making me want him to stay. This is so... disturbing. He looks very angered. Is it my fault?

But I can't just tell him about my brother. He gives off a killing aura like he is about to murder someone as soon as I give him a name. My instincts are telling me I should fear him, be wary of him. I know. Even if he is my mate, I know he still is a Black brother. Dangerous. I don't want to get Alec killed like this! He's my only family...

"Nora. Who was it?"

He asks again, but I just shake my head and avoid his gaze. I just can't. I can't.

I see him clench his fists. He's definitely angry now. He suddenly gets up and storms out of the room without a word or a look for me. When he reaches the door, we hear him from outside.

"Nathaniel!"

His imperious tone leaves no room for refusal. His brother, who has been patiently waiting, sighs, and winks at me.

"That's my time-to-leave call. Don't you worry about a thing, and rest well, Nora."

So, the second brother's name is Nathaniel. He follows Damian, closing the door behind them. I can finally relax a little. He was there for only five minutes, but it feels like I just got off an emotional roller-coaster...

Moon Goddess, he really was my mate! I lay back on the cushions and let out a sigh of relief. I just woke up; how can I feel so exhausted? I close my eyes, so shaken up.

"Nora?"

Tonia came to sit next to me, and the wolf-bear, Bobo, is sitting right by the bed, his big black eyes looking at us. They don't look as tense now that Damian is gone. She helps me get in a more comfortable position.

"You need to stay hospitalized for a few more days to recover fully. But don't worry, baby girl, you are in the best hands, okay? Like I said, your voice will get back to normal after a bit of a rest, so don't use it for now. I know it's inconvenient, so just use the notepad if there is anything. Bobo and I are here to take care of you, and we won't leave you."

I grab the pen to start writing again. "Is it really okay for me to be here?" I show her.

Tonia rolls her eyes. "Yes, it is! I told you, this whole hospital belongs to the Boss. You're his Luna, so of course, he won't just leave you anywhere. He went crazy when he saw what state we found you in! Trust me, the medical team will remember it for a long time. You got other silly questions?"

His... Luna... It feels so odd to hear. I grab the notepad again.

"Are you part of the Blood Moon Clan, too?"

"Yep, Bobo and I both. So, you already know about the Blood Moon Clan. Nora, we have to ask you, do you have a pack, too?"

What happens if I answer this question? I remember Damian's angry eyes... Like for Alec, will the pack be in danger if I mention the Jade Moon?

Tonia might be kind to me for now, but she still is part of the Blood Moon Clan. And my instincts tell me she is no way near clueless. Even if Damian is my mate, and seems to care for me, is it safe to trust them? His actions from earlier might have been gentle, but his eyes... Those are the eyes of a killer.

Tonia takes my silence for an answer and frowns.

"You won't tell us, I guess... That's okay. You might as well concentrate on your recovery for now. Well, don't worry, Nora, okay? If there is anything, you just tell me, baby girl."

I nod.

But exactly how safe am I here? I am not that oblivious that I would forget about the Blood Moon. And Damian and Nathaniel act friendly with me, but... This hospital suite, Tonia and Bobo guarding me, the anger in Damian's eyes. Everything about this is unsettling.

After a few days of being hospitalized, my throat is still horribly sore and painful, but my bruises are slowly disappearing, and I feel less tired. I remember the terrible look I had when Tonia helped me to the bathroom. I never considered myself as pretty, but now I really looked horrible. I had a small cut on my lip and a large blue bruise covering my eye and cheek. Alec really beat me up badly...

The siblings really don't leave me all day. Tonia only goes out occasionally for a few minutes when she needs to discuss something with the medical team or to get me something. She watches my every and won't let anyone else near me. I haven't seen any nurse or doctor since I've been here. She even brings in the meals herself.

I've realized the room is actually locked 24/7, which had me wonder why. It's locked from the inside. Are they afraid I might run away? Tonia doesn't seem too worried about that, but I've noticed that Bobo is a light sleeper. If I wake up in the middle of the night and get up to fetch water or go to the bathroom, he instantly wakes up and watches me.

I wonder if he's guarding me. He has never shifted into his human form yet, which is a bit odd to me. I have never seen someone stay in wolf form so long! When I asked about it, Tonia said he's just more comfortable in his wolf form, like this is nothing unusual for him.

I wonder what the Jade Moon Clan thinks of me disappearing. Did Alec leave too? What did he tell them? And what about his debt?

The thing I'm most worried about is the part that I can't remember. What happened in that apartment? Whenever I try, this disgusting feeling of Marcus' hands over me comes over and makes me panic. I know for sure I tried to defend myself, but the blood... I can't remember, and I'm not sure I want to.

"Nora? What do you think, baby girl?"

Tonia is showing me a dark blue sweater dress, brand new. Today, I can finally quit the hospital gown, and she got me new clothes for the occasion. I couldn't bring myself to ask what happened to the white dress.

I nod. It's pretty and looks really comfy, too. Tonia seems happy with my approval and takes out some more clothes from the shopping bag. She got me black tights, a belt, and camel leather boots.

"Great! Now go change so you can show us how pretty you are!"

I blush and take the clothes to go change in the bathroom. Thankfully, the bruise on my face has faded. After the hot shower, I'm facing my reflection, and I don't really like what I'm seeing. I am so thin, and I look pale, too. Annoyed with my frail body, I put on the new clothes Tonia got for me. I'm a bit embarrassed that she bought me underwear, and it's a bit sexy, too. I have never worn such lingerie before! Well, I like the pastel blue color, and it's exactly my size, but it really makes me look... Sexy? I just forget it and put on the rest of the outfit. I really like it.

I brush my curly hair and do a braid so that it will hide my scar, as usual. But as soon as I get out, Tonia clicks her tongue.

"No, Nora, what's with the stupid braid? It hides half of your face!"

That's actually the point! Didn't she notice my scar? Anyone would find it ugly! But Tonia won't have it. She does my hair all over again and gives me a messy low bun, with an elegant but simple look. I really love it, especially with my curls and the two strands of hair that escapes at the front, but what about my scar?

I point it with my finger to show it to her, but she just frowns.

"Oh, stop it, Nora. Yes, you got a scar, so what? You are a pretty girl! So just show your pretty, little face and stop trying to hide behind your hair."

I'm not pretty... But I can't argue anymore. Let's forget this, Tonia won't let me win this fight anyway. And at least I'm glad I get to wear this outfit. I haven't dressed that pretty in... forever! I point out the door to Tonia, to ask if we can go out now that I'm better.

But she shakes her head.

"Not yet, pretty girl. You have to stay here for now..."

What? Why? I'm much better already; I can walk and everything now. Sure, my throat is still not healed, and my right flank hurts a bit sometimes, but I still thought I would be well enough to go out now.

I grab the notepad.

"Can't I even take a walk? I've been locked up here for two weeks! Please?"

"No. I'm sorry, Nora, but these are the orders."

What, orders? Does she mean from Damian? He hasn't come back here ever since... Why is that? I was kind of... waiting for him. My wolf misses him. Doesn't he feel the same? And what's with him having me stay here? I ask Tonia again.

"Yes, it's the Boss's orders. I'm not going to go against it, Nora, sorry. Do you want me to get you a new book? Or we can order a movie!"

She's trying to be enthusiastic, but I don't buy it. Tonia did provide me anything to keep me from getting bored. I've read a few books, and we can watch as many movies as we want on the room's TV. It was nice when I couldn't get up, but now I want to go out and get some fresh air too. It's like I'm a prisoner here!

I shake my head and keep pointing at the door. Tonia looks sorry, but when she was about to answer, Bobo suddenly gets up from the couch and comes to my side. She frowns and stares at him for a few seconds, meaning they're telepathically talking. It lasts a while, but then she suddenly sighs.

"It's on you if anything happens! And yes, I am texting him about *your* idea."

She takes out her phone and types for a while. I exchange a look with Bobo. What is this idea of his? A ring announces a reply text, and

Tonia reads it.

"Lucky for you, brother, he says it's okay, as long as we're with her. Nora, Bobo just got you a tour of the hospital. It's not much, but there is an indoor garden, so you will actually get some fresh air!"

It's not much indeed, but I can't help myself and smile. Fresh air at last! I thank Bobo with a big smile, then tuck my notepad and pen under my arm to take with me, but Tonia just laughs and takes them away from me.

"Don't bother with those, baby girl, I'll let you type on my phone if you need it, okay? Come on, let's go."

Getting out of my VIP room really seems like a big step. It's silly, but I just feel so happy to get to walk a bit. Bobo is literally stuck to me, keeping so close I could feel his fur against my leg with every step I take.

I did have doubts for a moment that I was not in a hospital, but really a hotel with some medical equipment, but this is a hospital indeed. We walk by lots of rooms, patients, nurses, and doctors. And no one seems surprised to see the enormous werewolf walking by my side. Shouldn't it be... not okay somehow?

Tonia just keeps texting and silently walks behind us. Turns out, she doesn't look so worried about my little outing after all.

I might be just walking around in a hospital, but... It's nice. I feel like I'm in a dream. I've been having this feeling since I woke up. All of this is so different compared to the last ten years of my life. Now I just have a walk, and I don't fear that someone might hit me or get angry at me for not doing my chores. I don't have any chores anymore! I just get meals every day without having to prepare it myself or sneak it out. I laze all day, sleeping, reading, and watching movies.

Bobo takes me to some ample outdoor space. This really looks like a garden! There are even a fountain and a few benches where patients are sitting to enjoy the sunshine. Bobo guides me to an empty one.

"Thank you," I mimic on my lips.

He just lays down and starts dozing off. Tonia finally puts her phone away and comes to sit next to me, putting her feet on him like he's some stool.

"So, how do you feel now?"

I smile and nod happily. This feels great. I am a bit disappointed we are not really outside, but this is still really enjoyable. Feeling the warm sunshine on my skin, smelling the fresh air.

"Good, you could use some more tan, baby girl. You're white as a sheet."

I agree. I've always hated my pale skin, but I guess that's what you get from living in a dark basement. Tonia sighs and turns out to me. She hands me her smartphone, with the keypad activated.

"Okay, I understand there are some things you don't want to talk about. But I have to say, Nora, we know nothing about you. We couldn't find where you come from, what happened to you... I get that you've had a hard time, but..."

Bobo suddenly raises his head and starts growling. Tonia pushes him with her foot.

"You, shut up. I'll say it if I want to. Listen, Nora, the Boss is really... mad about what happened to you. Nathaniel's got him focused on other things for now, but he won't let it go. Someone attacked you, and I can tell you know who it is. So, won't you tell us?"

I shake my head slowly. No, no, I can't. Even more, if Damian is going after my brother next. Tonia scratches her head and just nods.

"Okay, so you really don't want to. So, how about you tell me what you can, huh? Even stupid things, okay? Tell me about... I don't know, your family? Your friends?"

I hesitate a little. I'm not sure how much I can really say without endangering anyone. I take Tonia's phone, and slowly start typing. She reads out loud.

"Your parents are dead, okay. I'm sorry, baby girl. Oh, you have a brother. Is he older? …Okay. And no friends... Well, you got us now!"

I smile and nod shyly. That's right, but... Tonia looks at my question, surprised.

"Oh, you want to know about us?" She chuckles. "Okay, so what do you want to know, let me think... So, Bobo and I have an older brother, Neal, who is the Beta to the Blood Moon Clan, actually."

Is their brother Damian's Beta then?

"We have our mom, but basically, we don't have many friends, either. To be honest, the Boss kind of... picked us up when we were in big trouble, let's say. The pack is everything to us now."

I nod. I suddenly remember something I heard.

"Why you don't smell like a werewolf? We were kind of curious about that, too... What? You've never shapeshifted? Are you kidding?"

I shake my head and bite my lip. No, I haven't. Tonia frowns.

"That's really unusual. Most werewolves turn for the first time when they're around ten. Of course, some earlier, some later but... You're seventeen. You... Can you feel your wolf? When did you start feeling her?"

I nod and show her my fingers to answer.

"Seven? Nora, that doesn't sound like a late bloomer. More like... some barrier or something."

I nod. I know... I know I should have been able to shapeshift long ago by now. But... I just can't.

"Do you have some sort of trauma? I know it is bizarre to ask, but... Wait, you do?"

I keep nodding slowly. Well, I don't know if it can really be called a trauma for real, but... I put a few words down and show her, but she frowns.

"...From when you were seven? And what happened? Can you tell me?"

I hesitate a bit, not because I don't want to tell her, but because I'm afraid. It's not exactly a happy story, and I've never told anyone before. It just makes me so... sad and miserable. And how much can I really tell her without revealing too much? I hesitate a while and end up giving her back the phone. She reads it and sighs.

"Your parents were... Oh, I see... I'm sorry, baby girl. Did they belong to a pack?"

That question again. Somehow, I feel that's what Tonia really wants to know. If I belong to a pack, and if that's the case, which one. I'm pretty sure it's Damian who wants to know where I come from, and I don't like it. Why does he want this information for? Before I can answer, Bobo suddenly gets up, turning his head in a new direction. I thought there was something, but as I follow his gaze, I realize it's Nathaniel Black coming to us, with his usual gentle smile. He has a motorbike helmet under his arm. Since his shirt is slightly unbuttoned at the top, I can see the crescent moon tattoo he wears on his chest, the same as Damian. I figured it's a common thing within the Blood Moon Clan, since Tonia has one, too, though smaller, on her arm.

"Hello, guys. I took a small detour to come to check up on you. How is our princess feeling today?"

I give him a smile as an answer. It's not the first time Nathaniel has come to visit me since I woke up. He never stays long, but he always displays a friendly smile and will talk to me about anything but himself. I have noticed that he just likes to inquire about my tastes, like my favorite colors, or my personal tastes. Like today, he hands me a small carton box, and when I open it, it turns out there are four delicious-looking French canelés inside. I love those!

"Glad you like it, princess. You really have a thing for French cuisine, don't you?"

I nod and thank him silently. Somehow, I'm a bit more comfortable around him now. Maybe it's because he's always acting extremely nice to me, bringing me gifts like these and all, but I somehow got used to talking to him, forgetting who he is.

"Really? Well, next time I'll invite you to my restaurant then, you can try it all to tell me your thoughts on our menu. Deal?"

"Oh, the Boss will love the idea," says Tonia, with a mistrusting look.

But Nathaniel doesn't seem intimidated at all. He just winks at me, as if we were now sharing some secret, making me blush. Gosh, why is he so handsome, too! His mid-length hair gives him a wild and juvenile look, and his blue eyes must have all the girls fawning over him. He may not be as breathtaking as Damian, but he still is very attractive–and yes, I do realize my judgment is most likely totally clouded by my wolf-self. But he's more angel-like beautiful, while Damian is the devilishly handsome type.

"Nora, I actually came to tell you that you'll probably be able to leave the hospital soon."

What? Really? That's great! When will that be, and why do I have to wait again? I frown to show him I'm a bit curious about this delay since no one will explain to me.

"Don't worry, I assure you it will be pretty soon. I..."

But then he stops talking and grabs a smartphone. Oh, it must have been vibrating. He answers it in front of me while I take one of my canelés to start eating it. This is so good!

I take one to give it to the siblings. Tonia frowns and declines it - I've learned that she's not too fond of anything sweet or sugary by now-, but Bobo happily gulps it all in one go.

"Yes, yes, understood. No, wait, brother. I'm actually with Nora, do you want to talk to her?"

I suddenly raise my head. Damian? Is that Damian on the phone? I look at Nathaniel with eyes full of hope, but he suddenly gives me a sorry look and hangs up. Wait, what?

"Sorry, Nora, he is... busy. But you'll see him real soon, okay? I have to go now. Tonia, Bobo, take good care of the princess, okay?"

He puts his phone back in his pocket, and he just leaves like that in a hurry. But while watching his hand, I saw it.

A stain of fresh blood on his sleeve.

Back into my room sometime later, I'm still thinking about it. Was that real blood? Gosh, I know it was, I've seen blood like a million times; how could I be mistaken about that? But I just can't help but wonder about it. Like, how did he get it on his shirt; what was he doing before coming here?

I'm not naive. I know werewolves get into fights, and it's not pretty. But the Jade Moon Clan was never very aggressive, so I've seen very few fights so far. We usually stand our ground and stay away from trouble. But everyone knows how bloody the Blood Moon pack is... How could they have gone from the shadows to domineering half of the city unmatched? They have wiped out an entire clan overnight.

And the leader is Damian Black.

I usually try to not think about my mate, as he is still a big, intriguing mystery to me. We barely talked, and I know next to nothing about him. Do I want to know more? I can tell from my only meeting with him that he is as frightening and dangerous as the rumors say. Any werewolf could tell he is the ultimate Alpha material, made to dominate people into submission. Tonia calls him the Boss, and even Nathaniel acts differently around him. They are very clear about this position toward him. What about me? How do I fit in this picture as his mate?

"Nora? Everything okay, baby girl?"

I'm sitting against the window, lost in my thoughts. I completely forgot about the book on my lap. Tonia seems concerned, and even Bobo won't pretend to sleep. I just nod and smile faintly before resuming my reading.

It's been a few days now.

Bobo takes me every day to the small courtyard, but we didn't hear from Nathaniel or Damian anymore after that day. My throat is a lot better, as I can now make some sounds and speak in a soft voice. Almost all of the medical equipment has left my room now, and I should do the same sometime soon.

Then, one night, I suddenly woke up.

I just felt it. That state of nervousness, grasping me from the inside. I instantly knew he was near. The room was completely dark, but I knew it. Sitting up, I reached my hand out in the dark, and I felt his fingers grasping mine.

"You okay?" He whispers with that deep voice of his.

I shiver. That's really Damian, his warmth close to me. My wolf instantly relaxes–she missed him. A lot.

"Ye...Yes."

It feels so weird to be able to touch him at this moment. I feel like I might still be asleep, dreaming, I'm not quite sure. But I know. This feeling is so unreal, I couldn't invent it on my own. I sit up and try to figure his traits in the dark as my eyes adjust. I find the pair of glowing silver eyes right away.

"What are you doing here?"

"We're going."

"I'm leaving the hospital? Now?"

But... It's the middle of the night! Before I can say a word, I suddenly feel him lift me up, and I'm in his arms, carried like a princess. Gosh, thank god we're in the dark, I must be totally red right now! So embarrassing and intimidating.

What is this feeling of emergency? I can tell he's tense, and I immediately pick up something's wrong. Why would I have to sneakily leave the hospital in the middle of the night, otherwise? At least I'm not wearing anything too childish or revealing, just a long, silk slip dress. I grasp his shirt hesitantly.

"Damian, what's wrong?"

But he won't respond to me. Instead, I feel him walking away, taking me across the room. What about Bobo and Tonia? What's going on? The door suddenly opens in front of us, and we're in one of the hospital's bright hallways. I can finally see him.

He looks so serious, and his eyes are ice-cold. I don't dare to ask again and just hold on to him as he takes me away. I realize Bobo is just ahead of us, leading the way and walking fast, looking around as if he's looking for some sort of threat. They're both so tense, it makes me worry. Where is Tonia?

Everyone lets us pass as soon as they see Damian. Some even show a scared look before running off, but he doesn't care. He carries me all the way to the elevator, where Bobo chases some nurses with a growl. The machines go down, and I find being in his arms even more embarrassing now.

"I can walk..."

"No."

His tone makes it clear we are not discussing this. I bite my lip and don't dare to argue anymore. What time is it, anyway? I still feel so sleepy... I lean my head against his shoulder, trying to forget all this tension. I feel his shoulders relaxing a little from my touch. Is he reacting to me because I'm his mate? He won't show any expression, though... Now that I'm close to him, I can smell him for the first time. He's wearing some cologne, nothing too strong, though. Something that really suits him. It's fresh and cooling like the sea, though, wild and strong like a pine forest at dawn. I really might get addicted to this...

The doors of the elevator open in a garage, and Damian takes me to a big car. Tonia's there! She smiles at me and opens the door for us. Damian carries me inside and won't let me go even as we are sitting. Instead, he takes off his jacket and covers me with it. Tonia takes the driver's seat and starts the engine.

"What about Bobo?" I ask.

"Don't worry, baby girl, he's following us. We will meet him there."

But where is "there"?

Tonia starts the engine, and we exit the parking lot. While leaning against Damian's chest, I look out at the window, drowsily staring at the skyscrapers and lights of the city. I love watching the city at night... So beautiful and mysterious.

I fell asleep while gentle fingers stroke my hair, surrounded by this soothing and relaxing smell of his.

Chapter 3

I wake up slowly, feeling the sunshine on my skin. That is so amazing...

When I open my eyes, I realize I'm not in the hospital room anymore. Where is this? I sit up and try to analyze the room around me. Is this a bedroom? It's even bigger! I'm in a ridiculously large canopy bed, with a dozen cushions. Two large windows illuminate the room, with some of the sunlight falling directly on me.

And the view! I can view the whole city from here, like from one of those skyscrapers. I get up to approach the window and realize I indeed am in one of those skyscrapers! This is insane. I step back and turn around.

Someone left a silk kimono on my bed, and I take it to cover myself. There are two large wardrobes, a dressing desk in front of my bed, and an entirely stored bookshelf. The book I was reading at the hospital has been placed on the bedside table. I open one of the wardrobes and recognize some of the clothes Tonia bought me, while some are clearly brand new.

I exit the room, a bit confused, and as soon as I open the door, I almost trip on some huge mountain of fur.

"Bobo!"

The big brown wolf gets up to greet me. Does he ever get into his human form at all?

"Bobo, what is this place? Where are we?"

Of course, he won't respond, but he leads me to another room. I smell something burning as soon as we enter. In a big and modern kitchen, Tonia is busy cooking, with a frown on, but smiles as soon as she sees us.

"Hi, baby girl!"

"Tonia, what are you doing?"

The smell worries me, so I go over to where she is indeed burning some sausages. What a mess... I take over by reflex, and she only seems too happy to let me.

"Sorry, I wanted to make breakfast, but I really suck at this..."

"It's okay, I can do it. Can I borrow some things?"

"You can take whatever you want, Nora, go ahead."

I quickly grab a few things I can find in all the cupboards and the fridge and decide to make an omelet with mushrooms and the sausages I could save from Tonia's attempt.

Bobo hungrily watches me through the whole process.

"If you start drooling, Bobo, I'm not cleaning!" Tonia says.

While the siblings argue, I can only enjoy this fantastic cooking space. Everything is brand new and top-notch material, too! I've never cooked in such a big kitchen before, though I'm only cooking for three. I'm done soon enough, and we can finally sit to enjoy it. I was kind of hoping Bobo would shift to eat on the table with us, but as usual, Tonia just puts his plate down on the floor for him.

"Go ahead, you piggy. Thank you for this, Nora. I knew you liked cooking, but I didn't know you were that good! Where did you learn?"

"My father taught me when I was young. I just loved cooking with him, and after he passed, I just kept cooking for the pack, so..."

I drop my fork. The pack! How could I be so stupid and mention the pack now? I was so happy with my cooking, I forgot to stay on guard. Tonia looks at me, shocked.

"So, you do belong to a pack!"

I gasp, not knowing what to say. Of course, it's too late to lie now. Gosh, I'm an idiot! Even Bobo stopped eating. He starts growling. At first, I think he might be angry at me, but then Tonia slams her fist on the table, making me jump. Why couldn't I shut up...?

"What sort of pack is this! Nora, I examined you; you were abused for years! And your fucking pack never helped you?"

What can I say now? I just stay quiet and bite my lip, confused about what I should do. I can't tell her that my pack was abusing me! She looks so mad, and I'm terrified about the consequences if Damian knows about this. But Tonia is all agitated now, and Bobo won't stop scrutinizing me either.

"What's the name of your pack? I got two words for your Alpha!"

"Tonia, I... I'm okay!"

"Okay? Don't tell me you're okay, Nora, do you have any idea how long your medical chart was?"

I shake my head. "It was because I was attacked the night before, Tonia. Otherwise, I'm okay, it's just... I got scolded a few times, that's it."

She suddenly gets up and exits the room, not the slightest calmer. When she comes back, she has a couple of pictures in her hands, and she shows me. They're pictures in black and white, and I recognize the entrance of the hospital I was at. The caption is yesterday's date. Were these taken from surveillance cameras?

"Who is the guy at the help desk, Nora? He was looking for you; he gave your name to the secretary but ran when we arrived."

I look more closely at the photos. That individual is wearing a dark cap covering his face, but I can recognize the cap itself. It's my brother's. Is that really Alec? The size and shape of the silhouette look about right. Alec was looking for me? Why? Was he concerned, or...? I shiver. Tonia is waiting for my response, and so is Bobo. I sigh and put the pictures down on the table.

"That's my brother... I think."

My answer surprises Tonia, but she calms down a little.

"Your brother? Oh, you did mention you had one. Well, it seems like he is looking for you. Do you want me to find him so you...?"

"No!" I screamed. The siblings were startled, but now they're both looking at me with surprise. I don't want Alec to find me. That's the main reason I agreed to stay locked in this hospital room before–I was scared.

"Nora? Nora, what's going on?"

"Tonia, I don't want my brother to find me. I... I ran away."

That's not totally a lie, is it? At least I don't need to tell them Alec was the one that tried to choke and kill me. Tonia looks a bit confused, and I can tell she's thinking hard right now. She turns her head to Bobo, frowning, and after a while, I understand they're arguing. But soon, Bobo starts eating again, ignoring her. Tonia eventually sighs.

"Okay, I get it. For now. To be honest, we moved you out of the hospital for that reason, anyway. We were worried about having some unidentified guy looking for you... I take it that you're hiding from your pack then?"

"Yes... Sort of. Can we... just not mention it for now?"

Tonia frowns. I can tell she's not happy with my response and is still thinking long and hard, but she doesn't ask any more questions. So I just concentrate on eating my omelet, and that's it.

After a while, I'm done, and we are both silently drinking -tea for me and coffee for Tonia- while Bobo finishes his third plate. It looks like his stomach doesn't mind the burnt sausages.

"Tonia, where are we?"

"Oh, this is your apartment."

I almost drop my cup of tea from the shock. What does Tonia mean "my" apartment? Did she make a mistake?

"What? Tonia, I don't have an apartment. And surely not something as... impressive as this!"

I wouldn't even dream of having such a large place to live in! The whole basement could fit in the bedroom alone, and everything looks so new and modern, and high-quality, and... And now I am enjoying some fragrant tea by a great glass-wall, with a full view of the city. A month ago, I was used by my pack like a slave, doing chores all day, and my brother was ready to sell me to cover his debts. I don't own anything, nothing at all.

But Tonia just smiles.

"Well, you do now. The Boss arranged this place for you. The whole apartment is yours! Oh, of course, you can tell us if there is anything you don't like, and we can always have it replaced..."

"Tonia, I can't have an apartment out of the blue, this is ridiculous. You have no idea how poor I actually am. I really appreciate you trying to help me, but this is... This is too much."

She rolls her eyes with an exasperated look.

"Nora, for someone so cute and tiny, you can be unreasonably stubborn, you know that? Listen now, baby girl. You're the Boss's mate. You got nowhere to go as far as I know, and for some unknown reason, you're hiding from your useless pack. Now, the Boss is the most powerful man in this city, and trust me, buying an apartment like this is nothing for him. I mean it. Just consider it as him lending you a room, okay?"

It's not okay, even if she says it like this, but... Indeed, I don't have much choice either. Where would I go otherwise? I really don't have anyone I know that I could trust...

But being here doesn't feel right either. Everything is too... too much. I feel like I'm stepping in a shoe that's way too big for me.

After breakfast, Tonia gives me a tour of the place that I'm now supposed to live in, temporarily, as I insisted. I'm glad there are not too many useless rooms like in those huge luxury houses. There are three bedrooms, the biggest one occupied by me, and one of the tinier rooms by Tonia. Apparently, Bobo sleeps wherever he wants, but I suspect he's guarding my room, anyway. There's a big kitchen where we had breakfast and a dining room for eight people. Then, Tonia takes me to another place: a study! With a desk, a computer, and more bookshelves! I can't help but take a tour to see all the books, making Tonia laugh.

"You give her a latest-generation, super cool computer, and all she cares about are the books. You were born in the wrong century, baby girl."

"I don't really care about computers; I just love reading!"

"I can see that. Well, you can always use the computer if you want more. Come on, there's one more room."

The last room turns out to be... a living room. I stop at the entrance. There's a large sofa with multi-colored cushions, a large TV, a game station, and even a stereo with a shelf full of CDs and DVDs.

"Oh yes, Bobo and I didn't know what kind of music you like so... Nora, what the hell? Why are you crying?"

I just can't stop.

It's all coming back to me. I could never even step into the Jade Moon's main house living room before! And now I have a full room I can use all I want?

"I'm... I'm okay. Sorry, Tonia I just got a bit... overwhelmed for a second."

She looks at me suspiciously, but I'm just busy wiping off my tears. Bobo rubs his head against my leg, trying to cheer me up.

"Okay, Nora, stop crying. You're making me want to punch some people, and I don't have names yet, so I can't. You know what you need right now?"

I shake my head, confused.

"What is it?"

"You, baby girl, need to sweat it out."

Tonia makes me change into a workout outfit. This is my first time wearing one, and I'm surprised how comfy it is. After braiding my hair quickly, I join Tonia at the entrance of the apartment.

Apparently, the building has a gym upstairs for its tenants, and Tonia, having changed clothes too, takes me there. As usual, Bobo the wolf-bear follows us like a shadow, and once we're in the elevator, I can't help but ask him.

"Bobo, do you change into your human form sometimes?"

Tonia laughs and answers in his stead, "He likes his wolf form much better, actually. You know, he shapeshifted super early for the first time, when he was just five! I remember our mom thought it was Neal. She totally freaked out when we found out it was him, and he was big already."

"I didn't know we could shapeshift so young!" I say while looking at her brother.

Tonia shakes her head and fondly scratches her brother's head. "Oh, this is a rarity! Most werewolves turn around ten or twelve for the first time. He's a natural, I guess... But honestly, this doesn't change much from where he's on two feet. He's not a chatterbox in his human form, either."

I can't really imagine what Bobo looks like as a human. He is so dog-like, it's hard to remember he's a werewolf sometimes.

"What about your big brother?" I ask, curious.

"Neal? No, Bobo's the only one who thinks he is a house dog. Neal likes his human form. He's a copy of Bobo, just a bit smaller."

"And what about you?"

"Hm, I think I'm a tiny bit darker than the guys, and my size should be the same as Neal's. We are still pretty big, anyway. The giant size runs in the family. I'll show you sometime."

I nod, a bit happy to know more about them. We finally reach the gym, and I suddenly remember a question I had in mind for a long time after meeting them, though I never actually dared to ask.

"Tonia, can I ask how old you are?"

"Twenty-four. Neal is twenty-six, and Bobo is nineteen."

Wait, Bobo is still a teen? I thought he was much older than me! It turns out he's not even two years older. No wonder Tonia treats him like a big baby! How funny. I'm looking at my bodyguard in a totally different light now. He doesn't seem to care at all and leads the way in front of us.

The gym is empty, despite being so big. There are two rows of machines like treadmills and elliptic bikes, free weights disposed on shelves, colored mats, and a few punching bags.

"Come over here; let's get started," says Tonia.

She makes me run for twenty minutes, putting me on the treadmill. She uses another one right next to me and watches how I do. Compared to me, Tonia is incredibly fit. Now that she is wearing this kind of outfit, I can see she is slightly muscular, not a once of fat. How lucky. I envy her tan and tall body. When I look at myself in the mirrors, I just look... petite and skinny.

After what she calls the warming-up, she takes me to a boxing ring and makes me put on two boxing gloves. A bit perplexed, I search Bobo for help, but he has started a nap on one of the benches and couldn't care less about what we're doing. I'm pretty sure he's snoring.

"Ok, baby girl. Now that you are better, it's time to get back in shape. Punch this."

She's wearing some big, weird cushion-glove, waiting for me. I try to hit it, but she gives me an annoyed look.

"Nora, you call that a punch? Come on, girl, do it seriously. Again, and don't hold back."

I'm not holding back! I try punching a few more times, but every time, Tonia won't budge. It's like hitting some wall. She looks at me like I'm some fly. A very weak fly.

After a while, she rolls her eyes and asks me to stop.

"Nora, you're holding up. Trust me. Even a five-year-old kid can punch harder than that."

"I'm not used to this! I've never hit... anyone before." I defend myself, blushing

I'm usually the one receiving the hits... Tonia shakes her head.

"That's my point. Learn how to throw a good punch, and next time, you can defend yourself. Come on, try again. Get angry."

I put my fists up as she shows me and go at it again. This time, I'm trying to get angry, as she says. It's easier than I thought. I just think of all I've endured these last few years, how wrong and unfair it was, all of it, and it's coming to me. More strength, more anger, and I put it all into my fist before I punch.

"Good! Much better. Again, Nora, keep going."

One after another, I start punching harder. This time, Tonia has to use her strength to block me. I'm getting the hang of it. Tonia keeps directing me, and I'm sweating, but it surprisingly feels incredible. All this anger I never knew I had in me, all of it comes out and hits one punch after another.

Suddenly, my wolf starts growling. She's with me, getting all her anger out, too. She's being fierce and stands firm. I've never felt her this way before! I smile, happy to feel her.

By the end of our little seance, I'm feeling great. I'm all sweaty and exhausted, but it is such a thrilling feeling! Tonia seems happy, too. She even showed me how to stand and block to defend myself against an opponent, wolf or human. After that, she had me train on a punchbag while she exercised on the treadmills.

"How do you feel?" She asks.

We are sitting on the living room's sofa after a well-deserved shower, and we both changed to new clothes. Tonia is wearing jeans and an oversized jacket over a sports bra, while I picked up a wrap midi dress from my wardrobe.

"Much better, thank you, Tonia. And, I felt my wolf a lot."

"Do you not hear her usually?"

"Not always. Just when I'm really scared, or sad, or when... when Damian is there."

I blush a bit while saying this, but it's the truth. Tonia laughs and shakes her head.

"Don't be embarrassed about it, baby girl. Anyway, it's great you connected with her better. I'm going to keep training you. I feel like you need it."

"I think so, too. I never really expressed myself before. I was always keeping it all to me."

"You know, that could be part of the reason you've never shape-shifted, Nora. Our wolves are like our real selves. They reflect what we want and what we feel deep down. If you're used to staying silent, never saying what you think and ignoring what you feel, it's no wonder you don't feel connected to your wolf."

Could it be? It's not that I never felt close to my wolf before. But she always seemed so... weak. I could only feel her in emergency situations, like when I got a beating or when I was scared. But it never felt like she wanted to take over, though. As if she always thought it was... worthless.

"Tonia... Where's Damian?"

I've meant to ask all morning. I'm sure I fell asleep in Damian's arms last night. It's as if I can still feel his touch, his smell on me, despite the shower and all. It just lingers on me like some warm shadow. And it makes me want more. But Tonia just shakes her head with an apologetic look.

"He's... busy for now. I'm not sure where he is exactly, to be honest. He didn't stay long last night. He put you to sleep, and he left right after that."

Why is it like this? Am I the only one craving his presence? It seems like he won't stay every time we see each other. I felt so safe and serene in his arms... I want to see him again. So why is it that he's never here? He'll provide me a VIP room in some hospital, now a fancy apartment, but he just comes and go. We remain strangers.

I might be wary of his background, of his dark history, but whether I like it or not, he is my mate. All my instincts push me into his arms. My wolf yearns for her counterpart. At the hospital, he visited me twice, and I was half-sleeping. Now, when I thought he had finally come back, he just lands me here and leaves again?

I just stay close to Bobo and spend the afternoon watching a movie with him snoring loudly beside me. Surprisingly, Tonia went out for a couple of hours, saying she had to run a few errands.

When she comes back, I'm in the study, with Bobo sleeping at my feet. She laughs from the doorstep, surprised I'm using the computer instead of reading some of the books.

"Well, someone has remembered she's living in the twenty-first century! I'm even surprised you know how to use it!"

"I'm not that clueless!" I protest, a bit offended.

"If you say so, baby girl. Now, tell me, what are you doing? Getting more books? You couldn't have finished reading the whole library in one afternoon."

"Stop making fun of me. I'm just looking at job offers."

"Wait... You are looking at what?"

Uh-oh. Judging from Tonia's expression, this is not going to end well...

She crosses her arms, looking visibly pissed at me. What, are we also going to argue about this now? This is ridiculous!

"Are you trying to make my job difficult? Why do you have to work?"

How can this be a real question! We agreed earlier that I was just... borrowing this apartment for now, but that also means I don't intend to live here forever!

I must think about when I'll have to leave eventually, and when that happens, I don't want to be as hopeless as I was before. I almost died by the hands of my brother, and I let my pack step all over me. I'm not taking chances a second time. But I can't tell her any of this for now.

"Tonia, I need a job, I need money. I told you, I don't want to feel indebted or anything. Staying here is already too much for me."

"Will you stop with this stupid money issue? You haven't been here for 24 hours yet, and you're already talking about leaving!"

"Because that is the correct thing to do, Tonia! I've never relied on anyone, and I don't want to!"

Tonia lets out a growl of frustration, but I don't care. How am I just supposed to accept this dream life and let myself be sheltered like a kid? Life is no fairy tale! I appreciate what Damian's been doing for me, but I don't want to stand back and do nothing. I'm done with fearing my own shadow. I need to learn to speak and live for myself. And it starts with getting a life on my own. And a job.

"Bobo, say something!"

I doubt her brother will step in to help her. He didn't stop me when I said what I was about to do. Even now, he's pretending to sleep under my chair, even though we all can tell he's just ignoring his sister.

"Nora, I don't think you realize your situation. You're the Boss's mate. From now on, you are going to be in danger 24/7. Do you think you're here just because he is nice to you? Well, there's that, but this is also for security reasons. I thought you wanted to get away from your pack. Just consider that now you have to avoid all the other packs!"

As far as security go, yes, I did notice the 200-pounds wolf following me around all day... But I bite my lip as I realize she's a bit right, too. I know how far Damian's reputation goes, and it's nothing pleasant. If anyone wanted to harm him, they could try and attack me. We may not be an official couple or have mated -yet-, but what I've experienced of our link so far tells me we would feel it if something happened to the other. My wolf agrees, too, she doesn't want to part with him or let her mate be hurt. I don't think she cares about the "getting a job" part at all. That's human stuff. I turn to Tonia.

"How many people know I'm his fated mate?"

She looks a bit surprised by my question and stops frowning to think about it seriously.

"Not many, for now. We tried to keep it to a minimum. Only like, ten or eleven people perhaps, including the Boss's brothers and mine."

So they're basically concealing my existence. Not that it bothers me; I also prefer it that way.

"But nobody needs to know, right? Tonia, I could find a job far from my Clan's turf, act normal, and no one would know I'm related to him in any way."

"No."

I can feel some tension in her voice, and somehow, I think there's something else. Something she doesn't want to tell me. But what could it be? Is it that I'm really in danger, more than I thought? But neither Tonia nor Bobo really seem to be on guard. And Tonia did leave us for a couple hours earlier, something she never did when I was at the hospital.

After a long silence, both of us doing our own thinking, Tonia lets out a sigh. "Gosh, when you were mute for a few weeks, I never imagined you could be that stubborn, baby girl. You know what? If you want to work, I get it. I really do. But please, talk to the Boss before doing anything. He'll definitely be against it, and very mad."

I really hope Tonia's wrong. He wouldn't get mad over something so trivial as letting me get a job, right...? I try not to think too deeply about it and just nod at her answer.

"Okay, then. I will ask Damian first, I promise. But do you know when I can see him again?"

She hesitates.

"I asked him earlier, but... he's busy, Nora."

The busy excuse again. I get that Damian is an Alpha and must be quite busy with such a large pack to handle, but I'm getting tired of it. He's out there doing werewolf stuff while I'm stuck here cooking and reading books, and I hate it.

"I'm sure he'll find time to visit you real soon," says Tonia with a sorry look. "But meanwhile, no more talking about you getting a job, okay?"

"...Okay."

I can see the relief on her face.

So, I did wait.

To be honest, living in the apartment wasn't as dull as living at the hospital. Maybe Tonia trying to keep me busy had some effect, too, but there was a lot more to do here. Every morning, she would take me to the gym and guide me through a proper workout. She insisted on how I should get healthier by doing so and gain some more energy. It certainly did help me get more confident and stronger, I think. Then, I would prepare lunch for them, my favorite part of the day. Tonia and Bobo are no picky eaters, and I can cook anything I want.

After that, the afternoons were... long. Watch a movie, read a book or two on the terrace, play video games with Tonia, or study.

The days went on, and I had yet to hear from Damian. The worst thing is, Tonia would have him on the phone about three to five times a week, and he never wanted to speak with me no matter how many times I asked.

After two weeks, I got to the only conclusion I had left: he wasn't busy, he was avoiding me. And I'd had it. We were on the couch, and Tonia had just taken the call in the middle of some old sci-fi movie I wasn't really interested in anyway.

"Tonia, let me talk to him."

But she quickly hangs up, ignoring me. She shakes her head, and when I see her open her mouth to answer me, I go first before she even gets to speak.

"Not the 'he's busy' excuse again, Tonia! It's been days! And at the hospital, it went on for a full month, too! Let me talk to him. Please."

I see her hesitate, turning the phone in her hands, again and again, confused about what to do. But I've made up my mind. I'm done waiting for nothing. Bobo, who was at my feet, suddenly jumps between us on the couch and takes her phone to hand to me. His sister protests, but it's too late. With Bobo keeping her from taking it back, I quickly search through her contacts, and though she has a lot, I finally find him, simply registered under "The Boss." So mafia-like.

I breathe in and press the green phone button. The first ring isn't even over yet when someone immediately picks up.

"Tonia?"

I'm surprised; I didn't expect to hear someone else! It takes me a few seconds to recognize this voice.

"...Nathaniel?"

"Oh, is it our princess? Hello there. What is it? Everything all right?"

"Yeah, I just... I just wanted to speak to Damian. Is he there?"

"Sure. Damian, Nora is on the phone, she wants to speak with you."

I finally hear Damian's voice over the phone, but he's not talking to me. I can listen to both brothers speaking in what must be French, and I suspect they're arguing. Though Nathaniel sounds very calm as usual, Damian sounds angry. It goes on for a few seconds, and I'm biting my lip, anxious. I wish I could understand French...

In front of me, Tonia is also tense and scrutinizing me. I get up to avoid her gaze and go stand by the glass wall.

They stop arguing eventually, and after a short silence, I finally hear Damian's voice on the phone.

"Nora."

I skip a heartbeat. How can the simple sound of my name with his voice through a phone feel so good?

"What is it?" He asks, making me realize I didn't say anything.

"I... I wanted to talk to you. When can I see you?"

"I'm busy."

I roll my eyes. I'm really getting tired of this sentence.

"Why won't you see me? Don't say you're busy again, please."

He stays silent, and I don't like it. I hate it. Why can't he give me a proper reason? I'm sure he is avoiding me; I just wish I knew why. Even now, I'm suspecting the only reason I can talk to him is that Nathaniel talked him into it. I wait a bit more, but it's still silent on his side, though I hear some sounds in the background. Otherwise, I would have checked to see if he didn't hang up. I decide to give it a go again.

"I need to discuss some things with you, please."

"Are you okay?"

His question surprised me. Did my tone get him worried now? I nod unconsciously and start nervously playing with my hair.

"Yes, everything's fine. It's just, I something I want to discuss with you."

"You can't discuss it with Tonia?"

No, I want to talk to you! Gosh, he really is unwilling to see me! What have I done that he will avoid me at any cost? This is so infuriating. Am I the only one with a whimpering wolf who longs to see her other half? He can't be that cold-hearted that he would ignore his own instincts!

"No! Damian, please. I want to see you."

I wait, praying he won't say no or hang up without warning. I can feel the siblings staring at me from the couch, but I try to ignore their gazes and wait for Damian. I fiddle my hair with my fingers for what seems like forever. Then, I suddenly hear him.

"Okay. I'll come tonight. I might come late, though."

"Sure, I'll... I'll wait for you. Thank you."

He hangs up.

I take a second to breathe deep. I'm seeing Damian tonight!

My wolf is acting crazy, jumping around like some happy pup. I turn to Tonia with a smile, totally ecstatic. She, on the other hand, has gone pale from all the anxiety.

"Tonia, he said yes! He is coming here tonight."

"What? Really! Thank Moon Goddess, now you can stop harassing me."

I stick my tongue out to her, but I don't care. I've gone from anxiety to happiness in just a few seconds, with one word from him. That's crazy.

...And now I'm all nervous again. Damian's coming. My fated mate is coming. Here! He's coming here! And this time, I'm not half-conscious or sleepy. Get a grip, Bluemoon!

"Nora, you're bright red, baby girl. Bobo says it's cute. And he wants to know if we can have lunch now."

I'm anxious all afternoon after that. I keep looking at the clock on the wall, waiting for hours to pass.

Knowing my mate is coming is the most terrible feeling ever. It's like I've become someone else, not controlling my own body. My wolf is acting crazy all afternoon, and I think I might have been just as insufferable for Bobo and Tonia. I felt feverish, anxious, and clumsy.

What was I thinking?

Now I realize how bold I've been. Damian Black is the Alpha of the strongest pack in Silver City. No one is more powerful than him for miles around. He's controlling the Blood Moon Pack, and anyone who doesn't belong to that pack should fear it. And here I go, the seventeen-years-old Nora, not even a proper werewolf on some aspects, commanding that he comes to me. Tonight.

Since when did I get so brave?

So here I am, at almost eleven o'clock, waiting for him.

I'm curled up on the sofa, in my silk nightgown, trying to get interested in that random book while Bobo is happily and loudly snoring next to me. He's taking advantage that Tonia went to bed already to sleep on the couch.

I have no clue about when Damian will come. Tonia didn't hear from him after that. I've been anxious all day, but it just won't get better until I see him. Leaving my book aside, since I've been trying to read the same page for twenty minutes, I think of everything I've been waiting to ask him.

Why is he avoiding me? Why leave me in the apartment? Why can't I work? Does he... Gosh, I think I might need to make a list.

I sigh, and pet Bobo without thinking, but he doesn't complain. I'm hoping I won't fell asleep, but the apartment is so quiet, it's unsettling. Rain is pouring against the glass wall, but I can barely hear it. The view is stunning... The skyline of Silver City by night, like any major city, is full of artificial lights from buildings, streetlamps, and cars altogether. So lively and pretty.

If I look far enough, I can even see part of my Clan's turf on the outskirts. I never really realized how remote the Jade Moon was. There are a lot more different packs living in the city, and I only know a few of them. The Gold Moon, the Blood Moon, the Sapphire Moon, the Rising Moon, the Violet Moon, the White Moon, the Pearl Moon, etc... All those clans do their best to coexist peacefully while also defending their turfs. Some are part of more prominent packs or have old alliances, and some can disappear overnight. Silver City has always been full of werewolves and humans.

Suddenly, Bobo gets up next to me, and I stop petting him. Did I wake him up?

"Sor..."

No. It's Him.

Something stirs me up inside, and my heartbeat quickens without warning. My whole body knows before I do. Even the way I'm breathing slightly changes. My wolf is all ears, waiting. I'm so tense!

Bobo silently leaves the room, but at this moment, I couldn't care less. I'm frozen on the couch, my eyes on the door, waiting for him. How is it that I can sense him before I can see him? Are all bonds that strong? I can tell he's standing behind the door for a few seconds. What is he waiting for?

Then, the door opens, and he takes a step in. Moon Goddess, he is so handsome I can barely think straight anymore. He gets rid of his leather jacket, leaving it on the floor, and walks into the room with this simple t-shirt, showing off his broad shoulders and muscular build.

Before I realize it, Damian's already in front of me, standing a few steps away from the couch. He won't come close, but he looks... exhausted. He lets out a sigh and brushes his hair with his hand.

"Are... Are you okay?" I ask, concerned by his worn-out look

"Yeah."

So why is he avoiding my gaze then?

He's looking anywhere but at me. It's awkward, and I don't even know what else to say. Thank Moon Goddess, the room is quite dark because I must be red right now. I can't help but touch my hair nervously. Try and remember your list, Nora.

"Thank you for lending me your apartment. "

"It's yours," replies his deep voice.

And here we go. I shake my head.

"It's nice of you to let me stay here, but this... this isn't mine."

"You don't like it?"

"No, no, I... I do like it, but that's not the issue. I just can't afford to buy such a place, and if I can't, then I can't say it's mine."

I'm so nervous, I can feel my voice trembling. Damian is so intimidating! He's standing a few steps away from me, and neither of us can bear to look at the other. What kind of conversation is this?

"It's a present then."

"No."

I can tell his silver eyes have gone ice-cold. Oh no, he's definitely mad. He crosses his arms but won't add anything. What does this silence mean? This distance between us is so infuriating! I can barely contain my wolf who wants to run to him, so why is he so distant? He looks like he doesn't want to be here and doesn't want to see me. Does he have any idea how awkward this is for me? And quite intimidating, too. I feel so tiny facing him. He's right there, standing totally quiet and imposing, domineering the room effortlessly. I get up from the sofa, tightening my kimono around me.

I couldn't tell where I find the courage to stand in front of him. I'm trembling. "Why you won't let me work?"

"It's dangerous," he says in his ice-cold tone.

"But I need the money."

"No, you don't."

What does he mean? I can't expect him to shelter me indefinitely! That would be way too optimistic of me.

His short answers are annoying. And scary, but still irritating. It's like his aura suddenly turned the room darker. I want to step back, but my wolf won't have it. Something is chilling down my spine, something I can't describe that has to do with my instincts. My werewolf instincts.

But I'm still hopelessly attracted to him, and that makes his rejection attitude even more painful. I nervously bite my lip, trying to think of what I can do, what I could say. Why is this so difficult? I wish I could trust him; I wish I knew what he's thinking right now. But here he is, indecipherable, cold, and barely talking. Doesn't he want me? Is he rejecting me? My body grows cold just from that scary thought alone.

"I need to work. I want to."

"I said no."

"Look at me!"

Oh, Moon Goddess. I just screamed.

Why am I like this? I'm shaking, I'm tearing up, but I don't care. This whole situation is so impossible! And I'm tired of it! Tired of waiting for a sign from him, tired of his distant attitude. I know we're basically strangers, I know I'm not pretty and not mate material, but still!

My cry finally made him look at me, and he seems shocked. Okay, I am surprised by my own reaction, too. I wipe the beginning of a tear with my hand, trying to act tough like I'm not refraining a sob. Calm down, Nora. I take a second and look at him in the eyes.

"Why are you avoiding me like this? I... I know I'm not the girl one would wish for as his mate, I get that. But I..."

"Stop it, Nora."

I obey immediately, I can't help it. Damian is an Alpha, giving me a direct order. Stupid wolf instinct...

I turn my head to the window, avoiding his gaze this time. Is this it? Will he reject me now? I put my arms around me, feeling colder than ever. My wolf is whimpering continuously, and I feel like crying, too, but I won't.

I hear him sigh, and he steps closer. I shiver, unable to raise my eyes up. I feel him coming. I want to step back; I want to run. But I stay, frozen and terrified. His smell again, and I can feel him facing me, dangerously close.

I hold my breath. Damian stopped right in front of me, so close I can feel his warmth. What is he going to do now? Scold me? Hit me? Hideous flashbacks come to me, and Moon Goddess, I don't want to remember.

He raises his hands and slowly puts them around my neck.

But... Not in a forceful, threatening manner like my brother. No, Damian's touch is incredibly gentle against my skin, his thumbs caressing my cheeks. Before I can even realize what's going on, I feel his lips, very softly, kissing my forehead.

...What is this feeling? I feel a wave a warmth flowing through my body, starting from my forehead. I close my eyes and breathe again. His lips linger on my skin, and I raise my hands to put them on his wrists, as if I wanted to keep him there, close to me.

This simple kiss chases away all my worries. I feel so many things right now, I'm overwhelmed with emotions. I want to stay like this forever. The two of us, so close, in this dark room, with only the sound of the rain.

After a few seconds, he stops and stares at me in the eyes. Our faces are so close, I feel hypnotized by the silver in his. I can see my reflection in it, and I suddenly remember my horrid scar. I turn away and try to hide it with my hair, but he grasps my hand to stop me.

"Nora, don't hide it."

"But, it's..."

"Don't."

I look up to him, embarrassed. He really doesn't mind it? He sighs, and caresses my cheek once again, on the side where my scar is.

"I don't want any other mate than you, Nora."

How can I believe him? Anyone would want someone prettier than me as a mate. I'm ridiculously weak. I've done nothing but tremble in fear for the last ten years of my life. Yet his gestures towards me are so gentle...

"Why didn't you want to see me?" I whisper.

Damian sighs and takes his hands off me. Why is he stepping back now? Did I say something wrong? He looks at me, and I can't tell what he's thinking. I see him crossing his arms on his chest, and he seems to hesitate. He looks at me again, seeming hesitant. What now?

I'm about to ask him what's wrong when he speaks up again, looking straight at me. "I wanted to see you, Nora. I wanted it so badly, I could barely contain my wolf the past weeks. I'm... containing myself. I don't think you realize how much self-restraint I need right now."

...Oh.

I turn entirely red as soon as I understand. How stupid am I! Well, I suppose it is to be expected that his wolf-self would make him desire me... And he is a fully grown man, too. So embarrassing! I really didn't expect that.

And suddenly, I remember Marcus. He wanted me, too. I know Damian's not the same as that pervert, but I... I start shivering when I remember. His hands, his disgusting breath close to my ears. I unconsciously step back, and Damian notices it.

"Nora?"

"I'm okay, just... Just give me a minute, please."

I breathe in deeply. Damian is not Marcus. Calm down, Nora, you know you're safe here.

But what am I supposed to say now? Damian was clear he wants me... That way. And I get it is werewolf nature, how our instincts want it. But I'm not ready for that. And there are so many things that should come first. How should I do this? I don't want to refuse him point-blank! I should be so happy that he won't reject me. And it's not like the idea completely disgusts me, either. I'm just... I still can't get used to the thought of doing this kind of thing yet. I know nothing about men, nothing about dating!

"Damian, I don't... I'm not sure I'm..." I stutter.

He shakes his head.

"Nora, I don't want to force you. I do want you, and I am barely restraining myself from taking you right here, right now. But I won't."

Oh my gosh, why does he have to be so blunt! And with his poker face, too! I'm the only one blushing so much that I have to look somewhere else. I'm feeling so hot right now, this is ridiculous! I try to get back to a normal heartbeat, but It's hard to look at him after hearing that kind of thing. Should I thank him or something? How awkward... And I can feel him staring at me, too, waiting for my reaction.

Unable to come out with a proper answer, I just nod stupidly. "...Can we talk?" I ask.

My question seems to surprise him, but it did come a bit out of the blue. I'm fidgeting a bit, but...

"We've barely exchanged more than a few words before, so... I thought that maybe we could... get to know each other a bit more?"

"...Okay."

He comes to sit on the sofa with me, though we each sit in the opposite corner, making sure we are not too close. I just hope he is not too tired. He lays his head to rest on the back of the sofa and closes his eyes. I just grab my cup of tea, feeling embarrassed now that we were supposed to talk but don't. But what could I ask? With that dark background of his, there are lots of questions I wouldn't dare to ask... Like what it is to be Alpha, or how did he get so rich. I didn't feel comfortable about asking stupid stuff like his hobbies or his favorite movie, either. After pondering for a while, he surprises me by being the first one to talk.

"...You look better."

I let out a shy smile, happy he noticed the changes.

"Ah, yes... I feel much better now. Tonia's watching me. And she's teaching me a bit of boxing, too."

"You're still too thin."

I couldn't disagree with that, so I just nod a bit and take a sip. I still have a long way to go to be as healthy as girls my age. But for some reason, I feel so relaxed now that my mate is in the same room. He's not any less intimidating to me, but his presence is something that my wolf needs.

"Thank you for all of this," I say, realizing I didn't have a chance to thank him so far.

When I look back at what my life was before, I would never have imagined such a thing happening to me. Before that, every day was a nightmare. I would work all day long, fearing someone might scold me or hit me for any reason. The days were long, exhausting, and straining. I had no friend, no one that would care for me. All I could do was pray the sun would set soon so that I could hide back into the dark basement...

Even now, I seldom wake up from a nightmare, thinking I'm back in that cold and frightening place, on that yellow couch. I never dare to say to Tonia how cold I feel sometimes.

"The siblings are the ones that saved your life."

His voice has suddenly gone colder. I look at him, and he has that terrifying, angry look again. Is he thinking about the day they found me? I don't want to remember it... I can still feel my brother's hands on my throat, tightening, tightening, tightening so much while I struggled to breathe.

He would have killed me. He really would have, had Tonia and Bobo not found me. How did you get so despicable, Alec...?

"Tonia said you wouldn't tell us which Clan you're from."

I stay silent. They may have been cruel to me, but those people are still my pack. I don't want Damian's wrath to unleash on them. Some of the pack members are not that bad, and no matter what, I still owe the Clan somehow...

And I'm afraid of what Damian is capable of.

"What will you do if I tell you?"

This time, it's his turn to remain silent for a while. The room stays quiet for a couple of minutes, and I take my gaze to the glass wall. It might be past midnight now, but the rain isn't stopping at all.

"Did they hurt you?"

Yes.

"No."

"Nora."

He knows I'm lying, we both do. But I just can't say it. I can't.

He suddenly turns to me, scaring me a bit. But he looks serious, not angry at me. Gosh, how can he be that intimidating when he's only sitting?

"If I let you work, can you tell me?"

"No!" I reply, shocked by his bargaining.

I'm not going to trade my pack's lives just for the sake of letting me work! All of this is wrong in the first place. I shouldn't even have to ask him!

"Just let me work; I will be cautious, I promise."

"You don't need to work."

"I do! I need money. I don't have anything."

"What do you need money for?"

Why did he suddenly get angrier? He's looking at me with such a menacing look, I feel like he might shred me to pieces if I give him a wrong answer! I can't help but crawl back a few inches on the sofa. What is wrong with him? What is he thinking now?

"You're scaring me..."

"I asked what you need money for, Nora."

Stop looking at me like this! I'm shivering all over already!

"I just... just don't want to be in need again," I stutter anxiously.

He keeps looking at me for a while and finally stops glaring. He doesn't look so angry anymore, I can relax a little. Moon Goddess, what was that? What answer was he thinking of that would make him so furious?

"...You won't."

I look at him, still shaken up from what just happened. He doesn't seem to realize what state he got me in. I do understand how people can fear him so much now. Even when I angered Vincent in the past, he never scared me to that level. What's going to happen with Damian from now on? He is my mate, and I can't get out of that. But what if I make him mad someday?

I catch my breath again, trying to regain some of my composure. I run a hand through my hair with my fingers, getting to relax a little with my tea.

"Damian... What did you think I was going to say?"

I didn't really want to ask. But I thought, maybe if I knew, I might get to understand Damian a bit better and get closer to him somehow. After all, I had no idea why he was angry. And we barely know each other, so how would I get to know without asking?

"Nothing."

Is he playing the silent one now? I sigh. We have so many secrets to keep from each other... I wonder how long this will last. We might have been the worst people to be picked to be each other's mates if I think about it. Aren't we opposites somehow?

A long silence follows, but I don't really mind.

I grab one of the large cushions to put on my legs and observe him. He does look tired. His black hair is disordered, and his shirt is slightly wrinkled. I guess he didn't entirely lie about the being busy part.

"How is it? With... the Clan?" I ask.

"Annoying."

I frown at his weird answer. He doesn't look like a very enthusiastic Alpha, for someone at the head of such a large pack...

"What about Nathaniel? Why isn't he your Beta?"

"Nathaniel is an Alpha; he rules his own part of the Clan. My family wolves are not Beta materials..."

I suppose that can happen, too. Being an Alpha usually runs in the blood, and considering how intimidating Damian is, he probably couldn't submit to anyone. But I thought Nathaniel to be a bit less dominating. I suppose their pack is big enough for them to split the work... That's not unusual among large packs, as sometimes they have way too many members for one Alpha to handle, so they would divide between smaller packs and have other wolves be Alphas to handle it better.

"What about your younger brother?"

"Liam is too young. He's just training as Lead Hunter for now."

Too young? He looked like a teen around my age when I saw him. He may be young, but he could perfectly be an Alpha also... Maybe he seems older than his real age is, then. Or he's too immature for now. But if he is already Lead Hunter, it means he must already be well respected within the pack.

Talking about Alpha stuff, I wonder why the Moon Goddess chose me to be his mate. We have nothing in common, and I don't really see myself as an Alpha material either... How could I ever stand as equal to Damian? Surely his pack would see me as a joke. I was the lowest on my previous pack, and now I must prove myself to the Blood Moon Clan? Was there a mistake somewhere? There should be hundreds of other women more prepared and ready to take the job! Being the mate of the Alpha leader would mean I have to be above all other wolves!

How could that wolf ever be... me?

I wake up a bit later, and I realize I'm in my bed.

Damian! Did I fell asleep on the couch? I panic a bit, but after a second, I realize he is sitting just next to me. I feel his hand gently caressing my hair. Behind him, I can see it's still dark outside.

"What time is it?"

"Almost two in the morning. You fell asleep, so I carried you here. I didn't mean to wake you."

I realize he has his jacket on, and frown.

"Are you leaving?"

"I have to."

"When will you come back?" I ask immediately

He sighs and leans over to kiss my forehead again. "I don't know. Soon."

How soon is soon? My wolf whines, she doesn't want him to go, but my human self knows he has other responsibilities. He caresses my hair a few more seconds and exits the room as silently as a shadow. Tiredness and the sound of the rain pull me back to sleep as soon as the door shuts.

Chapter 4

The next morning, I can still feel his lips against my forehead, like traces of a burn. I stay in bed for a while, thinking it over and over. The whole evening felt so unreal. Damian exuded this aura of untouchability, yet he was so close to me. I could also feel his wolf, so noble yet dangerous. As mysterious as his human self... I can't fully understand him, but I sure want to.

I feel something moving on my bed, and notice Bobo's head looking at me at the end of the mattress, his tongue sticking out.

"Good Morning, Bobo."

It's a bit late for training, so I take a quick shower, and I can't help but remember Damian's scent. Is it so enticing because he is my mate? Or do other female werewolves feel it, too? My wolf growls loudly. Yeah, I don't like the idea either. I choose a pair of dark jeans and an oversized grey t-shirt and pull my hair up in a messy ponytail while exiting my bathroom. Bobo is right there waiting for me.

Tonia, however, is absent from the apartment that day. She just left me a somewhat mysterious note, saying: "Pack Business. Will be back in the afternoon." I read it and just cook breakfast for Bobo and myself. I wonder what's going on. A Rogue attack? Or from another Clan? I heard the Purple Clan is quite aggressive...

I can't help but leave my thoughts to drift to my own Clan during breakfast. Am I still part of the Jade Moon? I wish I knew what happened. It's been weeks now. December is coming, what could Alec be doing now? Did he manage to pay his debts off?

"Bobo, can we go out? Please."

The wolf ignores me, his massive head still on his plate. I get up and go back to my bedroom to grab a white hoodie that seems warm enough, get a pair of sneakers, and head for the entrance.

But once I push the handle, it won't open. What? I've seen Tonia go in and out about a dozen times! Did she close it after leaving? Bobo probably knew I wouldn't be able to go, so he didn't bother to stop me. Great!

Annoyed, I go back to eating my breakfast, trying to think. Is there a spare key somewhere? If we are locked inside, they must have a plan in case an emergency arises? I try to convince Bobo a bit longer, but he ignores me as usual, even when I threaten to stop cooking. How can he be even more stubborn than Tonia!

I try to keep myself busy, but all I want is to exit the apartment and at least take a walk in the city. I know how crazy it is after what he's done to me, but I can't help but worry about Alec. He is my brother, after all. And there is the matter about Marcus...

I still can't remember clearly what happened that night, and it worries me more than anything. I see bloodstains everywhere each time I try, and I'm scared I've done something terrible. They got rid of my dress when they found me, but every time I picture it, she's not white anymore...

Bobo doesn't care about what I do all day. I guess he's confident I won't be able to find the spare key -if there is one- anyway. As soon as I start innocently reading one of my study books, Bobo resumes his favorite activity: sleeping. It doesn't take five minutes until he starts snoring.

Usually, when he's napping, Tonia takes over in watching me, and she won't leave the room I'm in. This time, however, Tonia's away, and I may have two to three hours of no-surveillance time. After a few minutes, I get up to grab a cup of water in the kitchen, checking if Bobo will wake up and follow me. But he doesn't. I can hear him snoring peacefully, and I don't know if I should be glad he won't wake up or a bit annoyed that he is that confident in me not being able to leave.

Taking my chance, I tiptoe to the entrance and look at the keyhole once again. Can I try and force it with a hairpin, like in movies? I don't feel too confident about the idea... And all the clicketing might wake up my bodyguard. I try to force the handle a couple of times as quietly as possible, but of course, it won't just open. So frustrating! I was about to turn around and give up when I hear steps from the other side. Is Tonia coming back earlier than planned? Someone abruptly opens the door, and to my surprise, it turns out to be a teenager with a hoodie and a backpack.

"Liam?" I ask, surprised to see the younger brother here.

He puts an index on his lips, mimicking to shut up with a pissed look. It seems like he is a bit... anxious? Is he avoiding someone? He looks at me from head to toe, then whispers softly.

"You alone?"

"No, Bobo is sleeping in the salon, but..."

He makes a grimace. Did he think I'd be alone? He is about to close the door behind him, but I put my feet in between. He frowns.

"What are you doing?" He whispers.

"I was about to go out!"

"What? Alone? Why? My brother knows?"

Why so many questions? I'm pretty sure the "Brother" he's thinking about is Damian, and I can't help but hesitate a second, biting my lip. Will he report me? He understands my reaction and shakes his head.

"You can't! He is going to get really mad!"

This time it's my turn to make a "stay quiet" gesture. We can still hear Bobo snoring, but I'm pretty sure he will wake up if he hears something suspicious, and I'm running out of time.

"What about you?" I ask.

He shrugs and shows his backpack.

"Skipping school. Nath's going to beat the shit out of me if he grabs me."

"Okay. I won't tell if you don't tell." I suggest.

Great, now I am bargaining with a school-skipping teenager.

"No! Damian will kill me!"

It looks like he is much more worried about his older brother's reaction than Nathaniel's. I thought I was lucky that he chose today to try and sneak here, but now turns out he is focused on making me stay! As if dodging Bobo wasn't complicated enough!

"Please!" I insist. "I only need a couple of hours, Tonia is away, and Bobo is sleeping like a baby!"

His eyes light up suddenly, and he makes a sneaky grin.

"Right! The meeting! There was a meeting with the Gold Moon Clan, earlier this morning, so they are all at the Office! I forgot about that stupid thing."

A meeting with the Gold Moon? Why would they meet? Vincent mentioned once that the Blood Moon Clan was looking for more allies, but... Is that happening at their office? The Black Corporation has its headquarters in a building, from what I heard... is that where they are now? My wolf instantly asks if we can go meet our mate, but before I can even think about it, I feel my wrist grabbed, and Liam pulls me out of the apartment.

I'm a bit shocked, but before I can say anything, he carefully closes the door behind us.

"How did you get in, by the way?" I ask.

"It's an eight digits code: 20071203. I just found it by chance after trying a few times. I've seen my brother use that one before."

How funny, it's the date of my seventh birthday. I wonder if something happened to Damian that day. I follow Liam to the elevator, as I don't remember coming to the building. While the elevator gets down, I realize what I just did. I escaped the room! I feel bad for Bobo, but hopefully, I will be back before he even wakes up.

Next to me, Liam seems a lot less nervous now that he knows his brothers are busy. He looks more like Damian than Nathaniel. The youngest of the three has messy dark brown hair, not as black as his brother, but his eyes are almost the same as Damian, a dark grey. He is a bit smaller and thinner, though. We are probably the same age if he is in high school now.

"What?" He asks suddenly, noticing that I was staring.

"Sorry, but it's kind of the first time we see each other properly, so..."

He rolls his eyes.

"Oh, I got plenty of time to look at you when you were in the hospital. But you look better now, not like a skeleton."

He is as straight-forward as I remember... I wonder why his brothers made him look after me, too, when I was hospitalized since he doesn't look very responsible. Maybe he was just being watched at the same time.

We finally get downstairs, and I can't help but take a deep breath when we exit the building. Free at last! It may only be a couple of hours before I go back to my golden cage, though.

"Okay, what now, princess? Where do you want to go?"

"You're going to follow me?" I ask, surprised.

"Hell yeah. I don't want my ass kicked when we get back just because you stupidly tripped and hurt yourself or something. I'm sticking with you, so tell me where it is we are going."

"We're going east, then."

I start walking, but he just looks at me as if I was doing something stupid.

"What?" I ask, dumbfounded.

"What, are you waiting for me to shapeshift? Aren't we supposed to get there fast?"

I shake my head. "I can't... shapeshift. I've never done it before."

He stares at me for a few seconds, shocked. "Wow, you really are as useless as you look. Okay, never mind then, let's walk like useless humans. But you better walk fast!"

We did walk for quite a while. I hadn't realized how far we were from the Jade Moon turf. At some point, we even took the subway when Liam realized where we were headed, and he paid the tickets for both of us. Surprisingly enough, he doesn't ask me anything. He even took his headphones out to listen to some music on the way and asked me if I liked any music in particular. I didn't, but he kept talking to me about his favorite groups, telling me which songs I should listen to and about the concerts he wanted to go to later that year.

"Liam? Can you tell me about your brothers?"

He looks a bit surprised by my question but put his headphones back into his backpack. We are walking through the last streets of the city now, a few minutes away from our destination. I probably should have asked earlier.

"What do you want to know?"

"I don't know, things like... What do they do for a living? And where do they live?"

"Just that? Well, I'm not sure about what Damian does... He is a CEO, and busy with Alpha stuff most of the time. But he owns five or six buildings and some establishments in the city. Like the one you live in."

What? I thought he earned the apartment, not the whole building!

"Nathaniel is mainly at his restaurants and clubs. He likes it, so Damian lets him runs all the resorts we have when he's not busy with the Clan."

I shouldn't be so surprised... The Blood Moon Clan is the wealthiest and largest of Silver City. Even I know a few places they own and about how big their turf is. No wonder they have to split the work.

"My brothers run the Blood Moon Clan since a few years ago... Since they got rid of our Father."

I'm stunned by how casually Liam can say such things. Is this really a thing to say out loud? And talking about Nathaniel, too, I can't imagine him killing someone as simple as that; it sounds so... coldhearted.

But then again, they are the Blood Moon Clan.

As we get closer to my Clan's turf -if I'm still part of it somehow-, my thoughts are no longer about the Black brother's bloody history, but about my own dark past. I'm genuinely scared of what might happen. Will they reject me? Am I considered dead? Or as a Rogue?

I decide to head for Robert's bar first, as it's one of the Jade Clan's only establishments in the city, and far enough from the main house. Moreover, if I can talk to anyone first, I would pick Elisabeth. She's the only one I ever considered to be a friend. Liam is walking next to me, and I can see him frowning, unfamiliar with that territory. The streets we are in now are a bit too poor to be of any interest to anyone, so it's hard to say whose turf it is.

I stop a few steps before entering the bar and try to hide my hair a bit as I put my hood on.

"The Jade Moon Clan? Seriously? You're from this Clan of weaklings?" Scoffs Liam.

"Yes, now please, I don't want them to notice me for now, okay?"

He rolls his eyes as he lets me enters first. Honestly, I have to say, having Liam with me is really reassuring. He is one of the Black brothers, and I'm pretty sure he can warn one of his brothers through their mind-link if anything goes wrong. Which I hope won't happen.

At this early hour, the bar is entirely empty, as usual. And behind the counter, it's only Elisabeth, cleaning glasses while whistling. She probably partied again last night, as I recognize her familiar messy bun, tired eyes, and jean jumpsuit. She notices us entering right away.

"Hello, what can I... Oh, Moon Goddess, Nora? Is that really you?"

She looks so shocked; she stares at me blankly for a few seconds before running to me. She pats and examines me as if to see if I'm real. Liam stays silent, but he's looking at her like she's some annoying fly.

"Hi, Liz..."

"Don't act like this! You crazy girl! I thought we would never see you again after what happened!"

She's almost yelling at me, and I feel awkward. We haven't seen each other for weeks, and I have no idea what to tell her. For now, she just looks like she's still in shock from my returning and sighs while looking at me.

"Oh girl, you have to tell me what happened, okay? Sit down, you can tell me all about it."

She pushes us to one of the nearest tables and brings three bottles of soda from the bar. I don't feel too comfortable being here, but it's better than being at the main house. I'm still afraid one of the pack members might suddenly walk in but having Liam next to me is kind of reassuring. Liz barely looks at him, too busy focusing on me.

"Gosh, girl, you really have to tell me what happened. Things got crazy after you killed Marcus, you know."

After I... what?

Beside me, Liam raises an eyebrow and gives me an interrogating look, but I couldn't care less. I didn't kill anyone! As far as I know... I shake my head. I have way too many things left unknown until now, I need to start filling in the blanks.

"Liz, please tell me what happened since I... I was gone."

She sighs a bit too dramatically, and I can tell she's happy to gossip. Even when she mentioned Marcus' death, she didn't seem sorry. She starts talking while playing with some of the sparkles on her nails.

"Well, the Alpha noticed you and your brother were gone for a while, so he sent people looking for you guys. But Alec returned alone in the middle of the night, looking like hell. I was there because I had just come home from work. He had a giant bite mark on his face, and he acted so weirdly! He said you had gone crazy and killed Marcus! And that you tried to kill him too!"

What? Alec was the one that tried to kill me! How crazy is that story! Even though I can't exactly remember what happened with Marcus, Alec left me to die, Tonia and Bobo barely got there in time! Is Bobo the one that attacked my brother? To chase him away? I'm so shocked, I can't speak for a moment, but Liz doesn't notice. She starts checking her nails. Next to me, Liam is watching my reaction, but I just ignore him.

"And Vincent believed this?"

Elisabeth shakes her head.

"Not really. A lot of people didn't. To start with, Alec was obviously attacked by a huge wolf, and we all know you can't shift. You couldn't possibly be that big, anyway. And Marcus' body? Nowhere to be found. Dead or alive, he disappeared the same day as you. The guys said his apartment was a bloody mess, though. None of us really knew what to believe. You had disappeared, and your brother kept saying all this weird stuff! Some thought you might have gone crazy for real, but I didn't, of course. I know my girl. Oh, and Vincent and Peter didn't believe Alec either, so they told everyone to shut up until we were sure about what was going on."

Marcus is missing? Is he dead? I know the "bloody mess" part is real, I can remember some of it now, but I'm unclear about what really happened... And it's scarier than before, with what Elisabeth said. Did I really kill him...? I can't remember anything but him trying to rape me, and then Alec pursuing me. But what if he is alive? Will he leave me alone? The idea alone is terrifying...

In front of me, Elisabeth's mind has already jumped somewhere else.

"Hey, tell me what happened to you now! You look all better, girl! And I know the brand of your hoodie! Is it real?"

Elisabeth is in girl's gossip mode, but I'm miles from it. How can she be smiling right now? It's like she doesn't care about all that happened. I know she wasn't there, and she is not close to Marcus or Alec either, but... Am I the only one who thinks this whole story is crazy?

"What about Alec?" I ask, ignoring her questions. "Is he still there?"

She frowns and scratches her head, looking a bit hesitant.

"Uh... Not anymore. Things kind of got messy the week after your disappearance. Vincent was, like, super angry at him for not properly explaining what happened with Marcus and you, and a lot of people started accusing him of borrowing lots and lots of money. It seems like he even stole stuff from the main house to sell it! Can you believe that? Peter unleashed on him one day, it was crazy. He beat him really bad, and eventually banished him."

"He did what?"

My brother got banished from the Clan? And a month ago, to boot?

I'm not surprised that Peter beat him–Alec was never strong, to begin with. But where in the world could he be now? No one wants to be a Rogue! All they can do is live like beggars, stealing from other wolves, and sleeping outside all the turfs. Every pack always outcasts Rogues and won't let them on their territory. It would be hard for him to even be in Silver City now. Did he escape to the wild like others? They say some even go back to completely wildlife and forget they were humans once.

No, wait. Alec was spotted in the hospital days after that. So why was he looking for me? Did Alec know who had rescued me? Or was he pushed to the wall and tried to find me to help him? And there is still the Marcus matter...

"Nora, who's the kid?"

I turn to Liam, but he is growling already. Guess the "kid" part didn't please him... Liz immediately avoids his eyes, reacting to his Alpha aura. He may be young and not have a proper pack yet, but no one can deny Liam's authority. He has the same dominating presence as his brothers, and Liz is just a regular wolf. He finally stops, and Elisabeth decides to address to me instead of him.

"Why did you bring a stranger to our turf? Do you want Vince to be mad as soon as you come home?"

I raise my head, shocked. To go home? Am I still considered part of the pack? I thought they might have excluded me as soon as they did for my brother! But before I can answer, Liam surprises me by being the one to raise his voice for the first time since we entered the bar.

"To be mad at her? What do you mean? Does this stupid Alpha of yours knows what's coming to him?" He says with a·mean grin.

Now Elisabeth's smile is completely gone, and she looks petrified. I can tell she's trying hard not to gaze into Liam's direction and focuses on me solely.

"Nora, what does he mean? What is coming?"

But I turn to Liam and give him a "hush!" look. "Stop it. You're not saying anything, we agreed!"

"Whatever. My brother's going to find them, anyway. Sooner or later, your weak former Clan will be destroyed," he shrugs

I don't like the sadistic smile he has on now, and I can see Elisabeth has started shaking. And it's not my "former" Clan, I'm still part of the Jade Moon, it seems! But Liam doesn't care; he's having fun right now.

He is intentionally scaring her and using his aura. I don't like how he is cruelly making fun of her.

"Liam, stop it!"

He stops but gives me an annoyed look, like a kid who just got his favorite toy confiscated. I don't care. I point my index at the door, ignoring that pissed teen attitude of his.

"If you're going to make things difficult, you can wait for me outside."

"Tsk... Weakling." He growls while exiting the bar.

Elisabeth seems to relax as soon as he's out.

"Nora, who is this guy? And how can you not be scared! I had to fight all I can to keep myself seated; my wolf was going nuts with this guy here."

Now that I think about it, it's true I should have been just as scared as she was. But I've never been really affected by an Alpha's aura. Vincent, Nathaniel, Liam, none of them intimidated me. Only Damian could scare me, but only when he was furious. And now even his little brother could make a grown wolf shiver so much within seconds?

I, indeed, must have some immunity of some sort because of my mate. I don't know how to explain what happened any other way.

"Don't mind him, he's just a... friend."

And Liam Black, my mate 's youngest brother, but that I won't tell her. I feel like I'm desperately trying to prevent two worlds from colliding. I run my fingers through my hair, trying to relax a little. This is way too much information for me to take all at once. I sigh and take a sip of my soda, but Elisabeth can barely contain herself.

"Now, will you tell me? I'm dying here, girl! You've been away for weeks!"

"Sorry, Liz. I... Someone attacked me, and I was taken to the hospital. I stayed there a full month, and then a friend took me in."

She looks at me suspiciously, apparently disappointed by my lousy explanation. So far, I didn't say anything that wasn't true. I just made sure not to mention any names. Even if he's outside, I'm pretty sure Liam can still hear us, and I don't want him to hear anything bad that could reach Damian's ears. Elisabeth ponders for a while, then points an index at me. I've seen her do that before. She is about to fire all her questions at once.

"Who attacked you?"

“I don’t know,” I lie.

“How did you escape?”

“My friends intervened just in time. They chased my attacker away and took me to a hospital.”

“How long? In the hospital, how long did you stay there?” She asks.

“About a month. I was in a coma for a few days, and they asked me to rest after that.”

“And now, where are you staying?”

“I told you... at a friend’s place, in the city.”

“A friend?”

I know she won’t believe me, simply because I never had any friends. Not until I met Tonia and Bobo, and Elisabeth knows that. I sigh, annoyed by this endless examination.

“Listen, Liz, I just happened to meet some good people, okay?”

“People who gave you branded clothes...” She mutters.

I see her thinking, and she looks at me suddenly, with a big, excited smile.

“Oh, Moon Goddess, Nora, you have a Sugar Daddy!?”

“What? No! Are you crazy!”

Moon Goddess, how can she say such things? I’m bright red from the embarrassment, and her stupid idea is really vexing! Elisabeth knows I’m a virgin; she used to make fun of me for it! I’m not even sure about what a Sugar Daddy really is! That is so humiliating, I can’t help but growl at her when she starts laughing out loud.

When she hears my growl, she suddenly stops to get up and steps back.

“What the hell, Nora!”

I stop and put my hand on my mouth, realizing I growled out loud for the first time! And with quite some effect, too. Liz is looking totally freaked out.

“Liz, I’m... I’m so sorry, I didn’t mean to...”

“So, you really can shape-shift!” She suddenly says, shocked. “I thought you were totally unable to shape-shift, but you really can growl like a big girl!”

She’s right. Growling requires us to use our wolf-form throat, and hence, slightly shape-shift. And it turns out, I can do it now!

“Nora, that’s amazing!”

I know. I... I did it without thinking! I'm not even sure I can do it again, now that my anger has vanished. I massage my throat, still a bit surprised. Am I really getting closer to shapeshifting? Can I ever let my wolf out someday? I must try it.

"But you didn't really kill Marcus, did you?" Asks Elisabeth, returning to her seat.

She probably asked because of my slight demonstration, but we both know that's nothing compared to going into my wolf form. I shake my head.

"I haven't, but... I don't know. I'm not sure what happened back there, Liz. Everything is so confusing about what happened on that day. All I get are some random and blurry flashbacks."

She stares at me for a while. Elisabeth really has stopped the gossiping now. I can tell she's serious. She plays with her bracelets, seeming hesitant for a while, before finally speaking out.

"Nora, you can tell me. ...Marcus assaulted you?" She whispers.

I avoid her eyes. I don't want to talk about it, I really don't.

"That dog did what?"

Oh, no. Liam just came back and is standing on the doorstep, close enough that he probably heard what Elisabeth just said. Oh, this is not going to go well. He runs up to us and looks at me with a furious gaze.

"Nora, what the hell is that girl talking about? Who did what to you?"

He may not be Damian, but I can see a lot of resemblance between the two, especially when he is angry like that. Liam has the same ice-cold stare and furious look as his older brother. Why is he so angry? I thought he didn't really like me. Is it because I'm his brother's fated mate? He's menacing, but I'm not scared like I was yesterday with Damian, maybe because it's not directed at me.

But how am I supposed to handle this...? Elisabeth won't say a word now that Liam's back, and I don't want to talk about that topic either. Not to my mate's little brother! I just shake my head.

"It's nothing, Liam."

"What, nothing! Nora, if my brother knows..."

"Don't, Liam! Let's not talk about this now, okay? I really don't want to. Not now."

I try to be as convincing as I can, but I can tell he's seriously hesitating. I can almost hear him debating inside. Then, he glances at

Elisabeth and lets out an annoyed growl.

"Okay, but only for now. Later, you tell me what this is about!"

"I promise, but you won't tell him a thing. Agreed?"

He looks at me with a sullen look for a while, but finally lets out a low growl of agreement. It seems like Liam and I keep bargaining today. At least I managed to have him let go of the annoying subject for now. I'm not sure he will really keep his promise not to tell Damian, but that was the best I could do.

Elisabeth's eyes go from me to him and back, and she grabs my hand without warning.

"Nora, come with me. We have to tell Vincent you're fine."

But I take my hand out of hers, filled with worry. Elisabeth seems confident, but I'm not sure everyone in the pack will be as happy to see me as she was. Did she forget how they treated me? I was no better than a slave back there, and I don't want to go back to that meaningless life of mine. I glance at Liam, but he is waiting for my decision. Wasn't I the one who wanted to come back here, after all?

Sure, I wanted to see what happened after my disappearance, but having my brother gone changed a lot of things. And I may still be part of the Jade Moon, but I refuse to be insulted or hit again. I ponder for a while, but no matter what, I must go somehow. One day or another, I will have to face my Alpha about what happened and decide what to do.

"Could you accompany me?" I ask Liam.

"Sure. But I warn you, if those guys do anything to you, I won't let it slide. I was at the hospital when the doc examined you. I'm not dumb. And trust me, you should be glad it's me rather than one of my brothers."

"I know. I just need to settle things with them."

"Okay, then. Don't be a weakling."

But instead of heading for the door, he goes behind the bar and starts undressing. Once he's naked, he stuffs everything inside his school bag and changes to his wolf form. His transformation is extremely quick.

The youngest Black brother has a somewhat standard size for a wolf, but his big paws indicate he might not have reached his final size yet. He is dark, but not just black. He has some dark brown-red hair here and there, on the collar and below his ears. He comes up to me and gives me his backpack, and I turn back to Elisabeth.

"Okay, let's go, then."

Elisabeth gives me a happy smile and comes with us, closing the bar behind her.

I am in a terrible state of nervousness. If Liam wasn't walking beside me, I might have turned around already. We walk up until we can finally see the main house. I know the Jade Moon members can already smell us if they are in their wolf form, and there are always some guarding the area.

As expected, as soon as we approach, several wolves start following us, growling with a menacing tone. But most of them recognize Elisabeth and me, and no one approaches us. I suppose they are most cautious of Liam, who is a stranger, stepping on their turf. But he just keeps walking by my side, ignoring them.

"Alpha is coming," says Elisabeth next to me.

She probably is talking with some of them telepathically right now. I wish I could, too. I wonder what everyone is saying right now. We are a few meters away from the main house when I stop. I don't want to come in, and Vincent is coming anyway. He looks stunned, and his eyes keep switching between the black wolf now sitting at my feet and me. Liam acts like he doesn't care, patiently waiting, but I can tell he is watching what's going on very closely. Peter comes out right after Vince, and Liam growls lowly as they approach us.

He lets out a menacing bark when they're a few steps away, and they stop, aware it's a warning. Vincent looks at me, dumbfounded.

"Nora... I really didn't recognize you from afar. What happened? We looked for you!"

Did they really? Damian mentioned Alec as soon as my brother was spotted looking for me, but I realize now that I haven't heard from the Jade Moon Clan at all. Moreover, since Damian and Nathaniel were actively looking for which Clan I came from, I doubt they would have missed people asking around for me. The Jade Moon most likely already considered me dead and didn't bother to check.

"Hello, Alpha. Beta." I salute without averting my eyes. "Sorry I disappeared. Lots of things happened."

"Lots of things? Nora, you better have a good explanation for why you were gone for..."

But before Peter finishes his sentence, Liam is growling loudly beside me, and everyone understands he's most likely warning him to watch his words. Peter glares at the black wolf and turns to me.

"Who is this?"

"A friend."

"From which Clan, Nora?"

I hesitate. Is it okay to reveal my new connection to the Blood Moon Clan now? I'm not sure if it's a good thing to do. After all, I have no official connection to them yet, and I'm not supposed to be here either. Neither is Liam. Will Damian be mad if he knows? I don't care about the Jade Moon, but I would rather not take chances with him. I decide to ignore Peter's question and turn to Vincent.

"You exiled Alec?"

"Yes, about a month ago. Your brother had become too troublesome. He stole from his Beta and kept borrowing money from everyone. Peter confronted him, and we decided to banish him."

"Do you know where he is now?"

"I don't know, and I couldn't care less. But you are not in a position to ask questions now, Nora. We need to discuss this. Come in."

They turn around and start walking to go to the main house, but I don't move. I am not going into that house ever again. I feel like I will be back in prison if I take a single step closer. Next to me, Liam hasn't moved either, but he is still growling at the other wolves circling us. Now I realize this situation is not so good either. I may have decided to not give in anymore, but that won't hold Vincent from getting mad at me. What if he decides to punish me and attacks us? Liam is probably very strong since he is the Headhunter of his pack, but he is alone, and I can't shift.

I exchange a glance with the black wolf, he doesn't seem worried one bit.

"What are you waiting for?" Growls Vincent. "I said come in."

"We can discuss from here."

"Excuse me? Who do you think you are now?"

He growls again, but this time I can growl back, too, and I do. He will not force me to submit again. For some reason, I feel stronger and more confident than ever. My wolf agrees with me–she is done with this nonsense. She won't let me down on this one.

Me responding to the Alpha like this causes everyone else to fall silent from surprise. But suddenly, everyone starts threatening us back, loudly. Gosh, I really hope nobody is going to attack. I don't like how things look. Even the sky is getting darker and menacing. I focus on Vincent, perfectly aware that no one will dare to do a thing without a word from him. I can tell he is hesitating. His eyes went from shock to anger, but now he is considering the dark wolf and me.

"What is this, Nora? You disappear for weeks, and now you come back and actually dare to disobey your Alpha?" Says Peter.

"Why is nobody asking about my disappearance then?" I ask.

"We said we will talk about it inside. And without strangers," replies the Beta, glaring at Liam.

"No, I'm not going anywhere, and neither is he. I will talk here, or I'll go."

"Don't bargain with your Alpha!" Growls Peter.

But he isn't scaring me anymore. I'm scared about the twenty or so wolves surrounding us, but the Alpha and Beta's authority won't work on me. How is that possible? Did they already banish me? Or is the fact that I'm getting closer to my wolf, allowing me to stand against them?

I can really feel her. She is with me, standing her ground and growling to show she's no pushover anymore. They always considered me a fake, weak, useless wolf, but things are different now. I may be more vulnerable and unable to shapeshift, but I'm done being a slave for them to use. That doesn't mean I'm not scared. I do my best to appear strong, but my hands are slightly shaking, and no confidence can take away all that I have endured these past years. I may not give in to the Alpha's authority, but I'm still very aware of how painful a wolf attack can be. I'm not going to provoke them and get myself killed today.

They look at me, probably gauging me all over again.

"There is still the matter of your attack on Marcus and Alec," suddenly says Vincent.

"I did not attack them!" I yell back, annoyed.

"Then why did you go that day? People saw you going with your brother."

He was dragging me out! But Liam is here, I'm not sure what I can tell.

"I did not attack Alec," I say. "He forced me to follow him."

"You liar!"

I turn around. Amber just arrived, looking furious, and pointing her finger at me. What does she want now? That woman was always acting like my brother's girlfriend, and Alec probably thought so, but everyone in the pack knows Amber used to cheat on him as she wanted. She's popular, with her honey-blonde hair and curves, and loves the attention. I could name at least five guys she's been sleeping with without thinking! She joins Peter and Vincent, looking at me like I'm some pest.

"She had Alec follow her, pretending she could solve their money problem. Then, she tried to kill Marcus to take his money! Everyone knows he was loaded!"

What is this crazy story? Where did she make this up from! I'm so shocked I can't even find the words. Peter turns to her with a frown.

"That's what Alec said, but you weren't there when it happened."

"No, but he told me!" insists Amber. "Oh, come on! Do you think Marcus disappeared on his own? And Alec hurt himself? This bitch did it! You know how much she hated them!"

"I did nothing! Alec lied!" I try to defend myself.

"Oh, really? Then why did you disappear for a month? And now, you come back looking all good and dressed up in fancy clothes? How dumb do you think we are, you murderer!"

"Shut up!" I yell, infuriated.

How can she say such things? She knows nothing, she just hates me! But now both the Alpha and the Beta are looking at me and my clothes with a suspicious look. Liz sighs.

"Oh, please! Vince, this is Nora we are talking about! Nobody believed Alec when he told that story, and now you're going to actually listen to that whore?"

"Liz! Shut up and go back inside! Why are you getting yourself involved in this?"

Robert, who had been standing by until now, comes and grabs his daughter, taking her away. Elisabeth protests, but he's much stronger. I can only watch as she is taken away to the side, still yelling at Amber. Now Vincent seems hesitant and Peter's eyes keep going from Amber to me.

"Amber knows nothing, Alpha," I say. "I was hospitalized, and someone helped me out. But I didn't kill Marcus or took his money. And I didn't do anything to my brother, either."

But I can tell they don't believe me. The mysterious friend helping me out of nowhere is a big loophole, and I know it. I glance down at Liam, wondering what to do. He is fiercely growling at other wolves, and about twenty Jade Moon wolves are only waiting to jump at us. How did I get into such a situation!

Peter takes a step and reaches his arm out to grab me. "Okay, that's enough. Nora, you are coming with us. Tell your friend to go away, or we will attack him, too, if..."

But before he can finish his sentence or even touch me, a huge shadow jumps over him, and we hear bones getting crunched.

I see Peter's arm hanging under Bobo's enormous fangs. We hear a scream before I can even realize what just happened, as I'm still in shock. The Beta's shoulder is bleeding in an endless flow where his arm was still attached a second ago.

I can barely keep myself from throwing up. Other people start screaming in shock or fear. In front of me, Bobo is standing like a massive barrier between me and the trio. Peter has lost consciousness between us, but the other two have stepped back.

"Looks like you guys are going to need a new Beta," sighs a voice behind me.

I turn around and see Nathaniel standing there, smiling scarily.

I can't believe what's happening. Everyone has gone totally silent, and all eyes are set on Nathaniel. He is walking calmly to us, and it takes me a few seconds to realize a dozen menacing wolves are following him. Among them, I notice a big one, and I realize it's probably Tonia, as her fur is slightly darker than her brother's, like she depicted.

Vincent looks even more shocked than I am. He is staring blankly at Nathaniel, his mouth open, looking totally lost. I know this is precisely what he always feared. Provoking a stronger pack. I can remember how stressed out he was about the whole dinner thing. He won't even look at Peter lying in a bloodbath next to him. He just stares blankly at Nathaniel, trying to understand what's going on. Amber has gone white as a sheet, and she is shaking from head to toe. No one dares to say a word.

Nathaniel slowly walks up to me, and I'm totally lost on what to say. I feel so bad. About all of this. But he gives me his usual gentle smile.

"Nora, you should have just told us, you know. Now I had to come all the way here and hear all this nonsense."

"I... I'm sorry, I just..."

But before I can figure out how to explain myself, Nathaniel reaches out his hand to gently caress my hair and shakes his head with a gentle smile.

"It's okay, princess. You should save it for when you see my brother. He is... not very happy about you sneaking out."

Oh, my Goddess, Damian knows. He is going to kill me. He must be dead furious now. And right after he finally came to see me, too! Nathaniel turns to Liam, crosses his arms, and sighs. His little brother just avoids his eyes like a kid who knows he is about to get scolded.

"You can't help yourself, can you, Liam? Not only you skip school, but now you must help Nora run into trouble, too?"

He waits for a second, still looking at his younger sibling, and I realize Liam must be talking back to him. But Nathaniel shakes his head.

"Oh no, don't even start trying to use our princess as an excuse, Liam. We are going to have a serious discussion once we get back. And yes, little brother, you're grounded."

Liam just lets out an annoyed growl, but apparently, he won't stand up to his brother. The hierarchy is evident between the three of them.

Nathaniel now walks past us and stands next to Bobo, looking straight at Vincent. He is not smiling anymore. As all the Blood Moon Clan wolves are now growling fiercely, the Jade Moon ones have slowly started taking a few steps back. Even though some of them still try to keep growling, too, they clearly are frightened. Nathaniel's wolves make it very clear who has the upper hand. Tonia walks up to me, standing opposite to Liam. I try to whisper a "sorry," but she is ignoring me. I guess I'll have to deal with this once we get back...

"Prin... Princess?" Mumbles Vincent.

He seems to have realized who the black wolf that was accompanying me is by now. He is looking at me as if he's seeing me for the first time, trying to process everything.

"Well, now I would love to hear an explanation," says Nathaniel.

"Ex... Explanation? About what?" Stutters Vincent.

"Yes. An explanation to know why you guys hid and mistreated our precious princess."

Nathaniel's words are a cold shower for everyone here. Some members of the pack are looking at me with terrified eyes, probably reminiscing about when they last hit me or were rude to me in some manner. And it's not just two or three people.

"What? We didn't hide her..."

Suddenly, I remember the dinner night. Liam's voice asking, "Is that all your girls?" before he and Nathaniel left. That intriguing sentence angered Amber, but back then, I didn't really think about it twice. But what does it have to do with me? Nathaniel makes it sounds like the Black brothers were... looking for me. But how could that be?

"We asked you if we had met every girl from your clan, and you said we did. You had no one looking anything like Nora at the dinner. So now, let me ask you, how could we possibly have missed her if she was indeed one of your pack members?"

Vincent looks completely lost. He had me locked up in the basement that night. He didn't think I was worthy of meeting them, and honestly, how could he have imagined such a day would come? The weak, pathetic, hated, and disfigured girl turns out to be the most feared Alpha's mate. That's not something Vincent would ever imagine, not even in his worst nightmares. He looks at me, still trying to make a connection, unable to face the truth.

"How could this girl be of any... any interest to you? She's just a... a stray!"

Nathaniel is smiling, but I can tell he's not the slightest happy. I would say he's only getting even angrier. His eyes look like ice, and that's a frightening look I've seen before on both his brothers. Two grey eyes staring at Vincent like he could murder him on the spot. And I bet he could.

He takes a menacing step towards Vincent, and for a second, I think he really is about to kill him right here. All the blood seems to have left Vincent's face. When Nathaniel speaks, his voice is just as menacing as if he was holding a knife next to the Alpha's throat, and his sharp and cold voice gives me a chill.

"That 'stray' girl you are talking about is my older brother's fated mate."

A chilling silence follows his words, and all eyes turn to me. For a few seconds, Vincent looks like he is about to collapse as he staggers, white as a sheet. He looks at me, so shocked he can't even utter a sound. But Nathaniel suddenly speaks up again, and takes a new step closer, making Vincent stagger and fall on his butt in front of him.

"So, now. Would you tell who is responsible for her scars? My brothers and I are really, really eager to know."

I hear several people from the pack gasp or let out a whimper. Bobo is growling very loudly, and that's a frightening sound not three wolves together could make. He still has Peter's arm, and the blood is still leaking out in a gruesome manner beneath him. Vincent suddenly shakes his head, looking panicked.

"No, no, no, it's... it's not that. We... we really didn't know, she... Nora was..."

I look at him, disgusted. What, that the Alpha I used to fear all the time? He is blabbing nonsense, trying to come up with excuses. How could I ever fear such a pathetic man? Nathaniel stands there, emotionless, while Vincent is struggling pathetically.

"We... we welcomed them to... to our pack a few years ago. They were just... just homeless kids, they... She had nothing. We gave her food and shelter!"

"...Food and shelter?" I can't help but repeat, shocked.

Both Nathaniel and Vincent turn to me, surprised to hear me speak out. But I shake my head, glaring at my pathetic Alpha. "You put me in the basement. You made me work from dawn until dusk, and never let me eat with you. You never even considered me a part of our pack."

Liam starts growling again after hearing me, but I ignore him. Vincent is apparently not as scared of me as he is of Nathaniel and tries to defend himself.

"Everyone has to work to earn their living! You... you would have died in the streets if it wasn't for me, Nora."

I look at him, taken aback by his nerve. How can he still be standing there saying such things to my face? To earn a living? I was not even nine years old when the Jade Moon Clan took me in! For almost nine years, they only let me live to work for them as a slave, giving me scraps!

"Nobody else would have helped you, but we did! Doesn't that count?" Asks Vincent.

I know he is trying to beg for his life. He's aware Nathaniel only cares about me and won't hesitate a single second to kill him and all the others. His Beta is dying in a blood pool at this very moment. Vincent is basically begging me to spare the rest of them. But I'm in no mood for his excuses.

"You never really meant to help me, did you? All you saw was a helpless child, a free slave you could make use of. I was young, and you know no one would protect me. Nobody would care no matter what happened to me. You never did."

The hurtful words I could never say out loud are now flowing out, with tears, and I can't stop it. All the suffering resurfaces. All those bitter memories that I can't stand anymore. I'm giving up on any hope I had left in this Clan. This is the truth, and it has long waited to come out.

"You are not my Alpha! You never acted like one to me. You never protected me or considered me your family, not in the slightest. All you did was use me, like some tool you could throw away anytime. I was broken, and all you did was break me even more."

I gave the last nine years of my life to this man, to this pack, and now I realize what a mess they have made of it. I was never meant to be that pitiful or weak, but they pushed me to the edge day after day. Whether they abused me or stayed as bystanders, no one in this pack ever gave me a hand. None of them ever cared about me, and they were content with it. Living their everyday lives, keeping their eyes closed and ignoring all I endured like it wasn't their problem.

"No, Nora. I didn't do it. I never laid a hand on you, did I? I even tried to keep Alec off your back, sometimes, I..."

"You didn't do anything! You let others do it for you, and that was it! You saw what they did to me, and you closed your eyes a million times! A million times, you could have put an end to it with a single word, and you never ever did! You are worse than any of them! You are not even worthy of being called an Alpha!" I yell, bursting with anger.

"I... I..."

But he has nothing else to say. He knows I'm right. Never saying anything doesn't mean I don't remember. Vincent shakes his head, trying to find something else to defend himself, but I am done with this. I turn around to wipe my tears, exhausted by all of this. Nathaniel is looking at me, and he seems impressed by my sudden burst, but I just feel angry and exhausted by all this yelling. But as I turn around, a voice suddenly arises.

"You wench! You should just shut up and be grateful the Alpha accepted a cursed, damn freak like you! No one wanted..."

Amber's words die in her throat when Liam suddenly jumps at her with a loud growl. She has the reflexes to change into her wolf form to defend herself, but the battle is cut short. Within two seconds, his fangs lacerate her neck and face, and the golden wolf dies before our eyes before she even has a chance to fight back.

I cover my mouth, speechless. I can't believe Amber just died as quickly as that. Liam leaves her corpse to go back to his brother, but his mouth covered in fresh blood is still growling angrily. Nathaniel looks straight into Vincent's eyes, and this time there is no smile.

"This was the last time I hear one of you talk like that about Nora ever again. We will leave behind as many corpses as necessary for that."

The Alpha is so stunned about what just happened, he can't help but nod with a totally blank expression. Two of his wolves just died in front of him, and he couldn't do a thing to stop it. And now the lives of his whole pack are hanging. He seems about to say something but doesn't.

Suddenly, one of the Jade Moon wolves, who I recognize as Marc, one of Amber's lovers, leaves the group to run towards us. He is clearly attacking us, but even before he is within reach, two of the Blood Moon wolves jump and kill him on the spot. Right behind him, I see his sister whimper, and she starts running, too. But this time, no one stops her. She runs straight to us, visibly aiming for me.

But the she-wolf is suddenly stopped by Nathaniel's hand. I did not even see him move, but he managed to grab the brown wolf by the throat and holds her at arm's length, her paws not reaching the ground. She whimpers and tries to free herself from his grasp, but he is clutching, and we suddenly hear her neckbone breaking.

Nathaniel's eyes roam the assembly, but no one dares to move an inch anymore. He just killed a wolf with a single move, while still in his human form. He opens his hand, and the dead wolf falls at his feet.

"I warned you. Anyone else wants to try me?"

"Enough, enough, please!" Says Vincent, shaking.

Nathaniel turns to him.

"I have yet to hear any names."

"Nathaniel, stop it."

Surprised, both Alphas' eyes turn to me, but I'm only looking at Nathaniel.

I can't really feel sorry for the Jade Moon pack. I wonder if that's wrong of me, but I just don't. They were about to trust Amber's words instead of mine, and they probably didn't care to know if I was telling the truth anyway. If it wasn't for Nathaniel, I might already be back in the basement getting a beating by now. I can't feel sorry for them anymore.

However, even if I don't consider them my pack anymore, I can't let the Blood Moon just keep killing them without saying a thing. There are innocent families and children among them. I don't want to be the reason for bloodshed and tragedy.

I step up to the man I once considered my Alpha, and Bobo comes to stand close to me, acting like a bodyguard again. He finally spits out the lifeless arm. Ugh, I wish he had done that earlier, that's so gruesome. Nathaniel's wolves all start growling loudly, pushing Vincent's warriors to retreat away from him. I face Vincent, clenching my fist.

"I'm not stopping them because of you. I still hold you responsible for what happened. But this Clan needs its Alpha, and I'm done with seeing blood spilled today."

"From today on, the Blood Moon Clan is hostile to the Jade Moon Clan," declares Nathaniel. "Any of you takes one step into our turf, and you will face the consequences."

This is basically exiling the whole Clan out of Silver City. Even if the Black brothers only reign over half of the City, the remaining Clans won't take risks by having contact with the Jade Moon Clan. Any other pack's turf will now be a potential threat to them. Nathaniel just isolated the whole pack in two sentences. Vincent looks like he is about to cry, but unfortunately for him, this is not over yet.

"In ten days at dusk, I want this whole pack to come to the East Point Ground. If a single person is missing, no matter the reason, we will hunt them down. This is a challenge for the Alpha position."

I stare at Nathaniel, dumbfounded.

A duel to take over the Jade Moon Clan?

Chapter 5

Nathaniel took us back to the city, and a car is waiting for us. Almost all the other wolves have already dispersed one after another, leaving only a few of us. Tonia changes into her human form as soon as she retrieves her clothes from the trunk. Visibly pissed, she quickly puts on her jeans and a tank top and takes the driver's seat without a look for me. Bobo, who was busy licking the blood off his face and cleaning himself, goes to lay on the back seats. Liam takes his backpack back and changes to his human form, too. The whole time, Nathaniel's eyes won't leave him. It seems like I'm not the only one in trouble...

"Nora, you get in the car with Tonia. Liam, you come with me."

Liam and I exchange a look, but we don't dare protest. He rolls his eyes and obeys his brother's, following him to another car. I bet he's going to get scolded...

I take the first car's passenger seat and notice a cream wolf with mesmerizing amber-colored eyes jumping in Nathaniel's car behind us. Aside from Bobo, she's the only wolf left from the ones that came with Nathaniel. She naturally stands close to him, so I assume she is a member of the Blood Moon pack. So pretty... Who is she? I don't think I've ever seen her before.

I try to get a look at the trio, but Tonia starts the engine, and I lose sight of the other car in a few seconds. We drive for a while, clearly aiming back to the apartment, but a heavy silence as taken over the vehicle. She doesn't even put the radio on, and the oppressive atmosphere is unsettling. After a while, I decide to give it a go.

"Tonia, Bobo, I'm sorry..."

"Oh, really?"

She sounds pissed. She must be. I did sneak out of the apartment while Bobo was sleeping... What can I say now? She seems focused on the road, but I'm sure she is boiling inside. Everyone stays silent for a couple of minutes, but suddenly, Tonia explodes and starts yelling.

"Nora, what did you think you were doing! Do you have any idea how mad the Boss is now? Nathaniel could barely keep him from coming! And you know what would have been the result of him coming to get you? Do you know? A slaughter! And you! Do you have any idea how dangerous and stupid of you that was? This idiot Alpha of yours could have hurt you! Or any of those wolves! Do you want to go back to the hospital again? That was a foolish idea to go there alone, Nora!"

"I wasn't alone..."

She hits the dashboard, making me jump.

"Don't mention that idiot Liam! This brat is no better than you! Always getting into trouble, why does it have to be the two of you now? Two weeks ago, he got into a fight with five rogues! And now he is skipping school and helping you in getting yourself killed? If he's still alive once Nathaniel is done, I'm going to teach him a good lesson, too! I'm so mad about you two! What is wrong with teens!"

I'm feeling sorry for Liam. I think I can handle being scolded by Tonia, but I bet Nathaniel might be giving him a hard time right now. Judging by their interactions earlier, he really respects his brothers.

Tonia keeps talking and goes on about my recklessness, but I'm not listening anymore; I'm thinking about what happened today. This is crazy...

My brother made me guilty of everything that happened in the Clan's eyes. Then, Nathaniel's intervention... I see Peter, Amber, Marc, and his sister's corpses. Four people died within ten minutes before my eyes. I knew the Blood Moon Clan lived up to its reputation, but...

I'm well aware this kind of thing happens with werewolf Clans. We are not gentle creatures; our instincts push us to use our strength to mark our territory and fight for more. I've seen people die before. Rogues we killed, other Clans members fighting to death... But now, I know what they mean when they say the Black brothers are ruthless. Nathaniel didn't even sweat or blink while killing Marc's sister. Liam and Bobo both attacked to kill from the start. None of them showed the slightest hint of hesitation.

They have nothing in common with the Jade Moon Clan, which is always avoiding trouble. The Blood Moon takes what it wants. That makes me think about Nathaniel's words. How could they possibly have been looking for me? They couldn't have known who I was to Damian back then! Now that I think about it...

"Nora, are you listening to me?"

"Sorry, Tonia, I was... thinking. But why did you save me that night?"

She looks taken aback by my sudden question, and her angry expression vanishes as quickly as that. She looks at me, confused. Behind us, Bobo stopped pretending to sleep and has raised his head and ears to listen.

"What do you mean? You were attacked and..."

"No, I mean, why me? You didn't know I was Damian's mate. It was cold and pouring, nobody was out in the streets that night, but you guys were there. Not only were you there at the right time to save me, but you also took me straight to a hospital and treated me like... like a princess from the start. It doesn't seem like something someone from the Blood Moon Clan would do at all. Not for a random stranger, some unknown girl you found in the street."

This time, she goes silent. Tonia seems hesitant, and I can see her exchanging glances with Bobo through the mirror. Are they talking using their telepathic bond? Hard to tell. The siblings stay silent for a long moment before Tonia finally sighs.

"Okay, you're right, baby girl. We were looking for you."

"But you didn't know me!"

"No, but... We were looking for a seventeen-year-old girl with blue eyes, black hair, and a scar on her face. We knew you were in danger. Bobo smelled your blood, and we tracked you all the way to that street. It's not just us, Nora, all of the Blood Moon Clan was roaming the streets looking for someone fitting your description that night."

What? How could that be? This is nonsense...

"The Boss knew you were in danger. He felt your panic and sent everyone out to find someone fitting your description. I don't know how he knew precisely what you looked like, Nora. He just said his mate was in danger before we all went."

This is impossible! First, how could he have known I was in danger that night? To know our mate is in danger or hurt, we need to have met him or her at least once and made eye contact, to awaken the bond between our wolf-selves! How could Damian possibly have known I was his mate before having met me first?

Moreover, even if, somehow, he could feel our bond, how did he know what I looked like? The description Tonia gave me is too precise to be luck. He even knew how old I am and about my scar. And why couldn't I know about our bond? My wolf recognized Damian for the very first time as her mate when we were at the hospital. I'm positive she had never felt any connection like this before; she never met him. None of this makes sense!

"I don't get how this could be possible... Tonia, Damian and I met for the first time at the hospital. I didn't even know I had a mate before that."

"Me neither, baby girl. The Boss didn't explain anything, you know. He just confirmed it was indeed you when he saw you lying in the hospital bed after that. He never told us how he knew about your bond. From what I saw, the only other person who might have known about the Boss even having a mate is Nathaniel, since he wasn't surprised at all. He acted as if he knew about you right from the start. I am not sure about Liam, though."

I take my head in my hands, trying to process everything. That is way too much happening in one day for me to handle. Not only everything going on with my Clan, but now even my bond with Damian is... I sigh. Behind us, Bobo lets out a whimper.

"He wants to know if you're okay," explains Tonia.

"I'm fine, Bobo. Sorry again for sneaking out on you..."

Tonia seems about to scold me again, but she exchanges a look with her brother and rolls her eyes.

"He says he's not really mad. He understands you wanted to go out, but he was anxious something might have happened to you. He says next time you ought to bring him, too. And that I... Hey, I don't nag too much, shut up!"

"Aren't you guys supposed to stop me?"

"Well if you're going to sneak out anyway, we would rather come along, though it'd be better for you not to."

I smile at Bobo, thankful to him for being so understanding. He probably felt as trapped as I was in that apartment. I don't get why Damian is so persistent in having me locked in. I'm done with the golden prison.

We finally arrive back at the building, and by the time the elevator takes us upstairs, most of my confidence has vanished like snow under the sun. Liam is standing next to me, pouting and avoiding Nathaniel's gaze. Guess the Big Brother talk really had some effect on him... Now that I see them, it seems like they are several years apart. If Liam's my age, I would guess Nathaniel is around 22 or 23... But he might be even older, I'm not sure. What about Damian then? I need to ask Tonia later.

With the two wolves and four people standing in the elevator, space is quite crowded, but I wish we stayed there longer. As soon as it stops, I feel a pain in my stomach starting. I'm so nervous, I can barely breathe.

The door opens, but only Nathaniel, Liam, and the pretty she-wolf exit the elevator. This is two floors beneath mine. Is one of the brothers living here, too? Or both?

"We will see you later, princess."

The door closes again, and this time, the siblings and I exit the right floor. How can I be so tense already? I feel like a storm is waiting for me behind the door. Tonia opens it for me, but both siblings flee to the kitchen, leaving me alone to face Damian.

I take a deep breath and step in. I take out my sweater to leave on one of the chairs, as it got tainted with blood somehow, and I feel way too hot. When I finally enter the main room, Damian is standing against the glass wall, looking right at me with his silver eyes, arms crossed.

Even when he is fuming like this, I find him breathtakingly handsome. I feel scared, but not as much as I was before. I slowly walk up to him, and his eyes won't leave me. I stop when I'm within arm's reach from him.

"I'm sorry."

"For what?" He asks with that cold tone again.

"For leaving the apartment without warning anyone or saying where I went."

I really am. I should have at least left a note for them to know. I realized it while speaking with Bobo in the car. I only wanted to exit the apartment, but I didn't think about how much it would make Bobo or Tonia worry. Or Damian.

"You could have been killed."

I sigh. "Liam was with me."

"Liam is an eighteen-year-old brat!"

"An eighteen-year-old lead Hunter. And what choice did I have?"

"You should have stayed right where you were!" He suddenly yells with a bang on the wall.

"Don't get mad, please," I whimper, taking a step back.

"I am already mad, Nora! You knew I didn't want you to go out, and you still did! You put yourself in danger, and you told no fucking one!"

His voice echoes on the wall, and I can't help but step back again. This situation is much scarier than the one before. I find myself defenseless facing him, and he so furious right now I have no idea what he is capable of. I have flashbacks, no good memories. Damian breathes heavily, his fists are clenched. Why does it have to be like this?

Well, I'm not giving in to him. I feel like if I don't step up to him right now, I will never be able to express myself ever again.

"You can't keep me locked here forever, Damian. I will go out again, with your permission or not. I shouldn't even need to ask you!"

"Why won't you listen!"

He suddenly steps forward and grabs my shoulders.

"Nora, you could have been hurt or killed! You went out there, and if anything had happened to you... If anyone had put a hand on you, I swear I would have slaughtered each one of that wretched Clan! The only reason I stayed back is that Liam said you were with him, Nathaniel was coming, and you were finally taking them to your Clan!"

I grab his shirt and try to push him back, but he just won't let go. I use all my strength to repel him, but he won't move an inch. Why is he so strong! Though his hands are not hurting me, I hate to feel trapped like this! I can't help but start tearing up, exhausted from everything that happened, from yelling and fighting with him.

"Let go of me! Why are you so interested in finding my Clan in the first place? You don't know anything about me, yet all you talk about is getting to those people! Let me go! I hate this!"

"They hurt you, Nora! Those people abused you for years! I will never forgive them for what they did to you! And they are going to pay for every single time they dared to touch you!"

His voice is so cold I get the chills. Why is he so mad? I try to push him away from me again, ignoring my stupid crying. I understand that he saw my scars, but that's not enough for this murderous intent I can feel from him!

...No, there is something else. I remember what Tonia said in the car, and suddenly, the reason for Damian's anger becomes so clear. I stop trying to push him away, slowly realizing the truth.

"...You felt it."

I look up into his eyes to see if I'm right, and he suddenly releases me, his arms falling to his sides. I stare at him, completely stunned by what just hit me. I would never have imagined such a thing a few hours ago, but now that explains it all. Everything about Damian's actions towards me. His eagerness to know where I come from. His hatred for my Clan, and even his extreme protective attitude towards me. My hands tighten on his shirt, and I whisper in a breath.

"You felt it all, didn't you? Every single time I was hurt, you felt it through our... bond."

A long silence follows my words.

I was right. Damian is avoiding my gaze, but that is way too late. I... I feel like crying again. How did he feel, all those years? I remember each hit I took, every slap I got unfairly. Feeling my pain through his wolf and being unable to do anything about it, how could he endure it? That's the worst feeling!

"I'm so sorry..."

"Don't."

He stops me, putting his hands on mine and holding them tight. He looks down at me, and even if he is still angry, I can tell he is trying hard to hold it in.

"I don't want to hear you apologize, Nora. What I want is to make sure those bastards never approach you again. I'll never forgive what they did to you. That night... My wolf was going crazy. Someone was trying to take my mate by force, Nora! Do you have any idea how I felt back then? Why won't you tell me anything!"

I'm crying for good now, reminiscing what happened. Marcus' grin, his dirty hands on me. My screams, my wolf begging for help. I never imagined my mate could have been... hearing me, feeling my despair. I understand his anger. He is not just mad for no reason. It's not like he wanted any of this. I get it. Damian had to endure it for years. Not being able to do anything, feeling my wolf's suffering day after day. And now, this... He must have been mad, so mad... But not mad at me. At them. Once I realize that, I shake my head. He is boiling with anger, but all I can feel is sadness. I'm feeling guilty that he had to endure all my hardships with me. How can he not hate my Clan? All of this, everything that happened is so wrong! And with what happened... I shiver, overthrown by disgust. Alec tried to sell me to Marcus. I fought all I could, and I escaped somehow. What if I didn't make it? If I didn't protect myself, what if Marcus had...? I would have been destroyed entirely inside, and Damian would have felt it, too.

I'm the one being unfair to him. He's been powerless, in the dark for years, and all I've done is push him away every time he wanted answers. Protecting my pack from Damian's wrath seemed right until now, but they deserve his anger and payback as much as mine. I look up to him and try to stop my frenetic sobbing.

"...Marcus Sickels."

"Who?" Asks Damian with a frown, putting his hands on my shoulders again, more gently this time.

"The guy who assaulted me. His name is Marcus Sickels, from my Jade Moon pack, but... Damian, I think he might be dead."

The fog is clearing up. The blood on my dress, on my hands... Oh, my goddess. I think I... Suddenly, I feel nauseous, like I'm about to collapse. Black and white dots cover my vision. I stagger, but Damian notices it right away, and his hands catch me before I fall.

"Nora? Nora, what's wrong? You... Nora! Nora! Shit, Tonia!"

All my strength has left me at once. I hear rushing steps and panicked voices around me. They grab my wrist, and I lean against someone's chest. Damian's reassuring smell gets to me, and I wish I could get even closer to my mate, where my wolf could feel safe.

"Her blood pressure is low, Boss; she needs to lie down."

I feel him carrying me, and a loud growl. Then, I feel something soft beneath me as he lays me cautiously on my bed.

"Bobo, go grab some of yesterday's leftovers, she needs to eat something. And some water."

"I'll call the hospital."

"No need, Boss, Nora just fainted from fatigue. That's too many emotions for her today, and Bobo said she barely ate anything this morning. She just needs some rest. If anything, you could ask Nathaniel to have something nutritious delivered."

"Okay."

I feel cold hands on my arms, palpating me, and I feel a bit better from lying down. I somehow manage to open my eyes, and Tonia smiles at me. She is putting some blood pressure monitor on my wrist.

"Hey, baby girl. Stay with us, okay? Let's see your tension."

The device makes some weird beeping sounds, and Tonia doesn't look too satisfied with the result while she takes it off.

"Yeah, not in top shape today. You are staying in bed for the rest of the day, baby girl."

I don't feel too good, either. My head is not spinning anymore, but it's like all strength has left my body. I want to close my eyes again, but I'm worried about Damian. I don't know where he is, I can only hear him, somewhere not far, speaking French. I feel something large and fluffy, hopping on the bed next to my legs.

"It's just Bobo, baby girl, he's going to keep you warm."

I manage to nod, feeling a bit better. At least, I can stay awake without too much effort or feeling numb all over. I feel Tonia's hand patting my head, and Damian comes back into my vision field.

"How's she?"

"She is okay, Boss, just tired a bit. Nora, you think you can eat something?"

The three of them help me get a bit of yesterday's dinner, and then Tonia insists they let me rest. I do feel tired...

When I wake up, I immediately realize I'm not alone. Someone's arms are wrapping me, and another pair of legs are on top of the sheets. I feel warm, and this is the first time I ever woke up and instantly felt so secure. I recognize Damian's smell, and vaguely remember collapsing in the living room.

"How do you feel?"

His mouth is close to my ear, I can't help but blush a little. I wish I could hide somewhere, but I feel his chest against my back, and there's no way I could even move a toe without him knowing. At least I'm glad he can't see my face. Is it okay for him to hold me like this? He even avoided seeing me before, and know we are, well, sleeping on the same bed...

"Much better."

It's true. I'm still a bit numb, but my head isn't spinning, and I don't feel too tired anymore. However, I don't really want to get up right now. Lying next to my mate feels so warm, so right, and my wolf is almost purring. I wonder how he is holding up, being so close.

"Is this... really okay?" I ask, hoping he understands what I mean.

"...Don't ask."

I can't help but giggle a little, hearing his grumble. He must be fighting against his instincts like crazy right now. I'm grateful for that.

It feels so good to be lying next to him... Being close to my mate feels like I will never feel incomplete again... And it makes me want more.

I don't want to act greedy now; I know it's not the moment. But that closeness with Damian is something I will want more of again. I remember how I sometimes envied the mated couples of my pack... The girls always looked so loved and happy whenever their loved ones were in the same room. It's so rare for a fated couple to be able to find each other–most werewolves live their whole life hoping to find their mate. Some give up at some point and get married anyway, and others run miles to search for the One. And some just don't get the ending they hoped for...

"What is it?" He asks.

"I was just thinking... You could have rejected me. If you did, our bond would have been severed and ...You could have lived your life normally."

"No."

His firm tone surprises me, and I wonder why he was so set on not abandoning me. I am still missing pieces of this puzzle... A long silence follows, but I must ask.

"Damian... How did you know about me? Tonia told me. It's not only that you felt our bond, but you already knew exactly what I looked like. How come?"

He sighs, and I feel him move to bury his face into my hair, his forehead on my shoulder. One of his arms is under my head, the other around my waist, and both suddenly hold me tighter against him. This closeness makes me blush even more, and I can feel my wolf getting agitated. She likes it, but she somehow wants more. Hush girl, we are talking about some serious stuff right now!

"...We've met before," he whispers.

"It can't be. My wolf didn't feel anything like a bond before I saw you at the hospital, she had never met you."

"That's because you were too young. Your wolf wasn't awakened yet. Mine was. He recognized you right away, even if our bound was one way at that time."

The age gap. I hadn't thought about that... Most werewolves only start feeling their wolf-self for the first time around seven to ten-years-old, a few months before they begin shapeshifting. Before then, we are just like humans. No enhanced sense of smell, no night vision, no mind-linking to our pairs... And no way to recognize our mates even if they're right in front of us. But I didn't know we could bond even if our mate isn't awakened yet. Doesn't that mean the bond is that strong? How impressive...

"How old were we then?"

"I was fourteen... You were about to turn seven."

"We have a seven-year-old difference?" I ask, surprised.

I did guess he was twenty-four or older since he was older than Nathaniel, but still, it's amusing to hear it! He growls, a bit annoyed.

"Six years and three months."

"...You even know my birth date?"

"December third. You told me back then."

Then why can't I remember it at all? Well, I was young, indeed, but... I would have sworn I had never seen his silver eyes before. Moreover, it somehow explains the digit code...

"How did we meet?"

I wait a long moment, but he doesn't answer. Did he fall asleep? I try to turn around to face him, but he stops me, still holding me tight in his embrace.

"Damian?"

"I'll tell you some other time."

"...Why?"

"It's... It's not a happy memory. For neither of us. I just don't want to reminisce now, Nora. Some other time, I'll tell you, I promise."

Not a happy memory? But I want to know! Why can't I simply remember it... I thought my "unhappy" memories started when I was seven, when we lost our parents... I wonder what Damian would say if he knew about that tragedy. My worst memory so far... with Marcus' episode. I shiver.

"What is it?"

"Nothing, I just thought about the man that tried to..."

"Don't worry, I swear we'll get him. Liam sent the hunters to get him, wherever he is hiding. Alive or not, we will find him."

I had forgotten I finally gave Marcus' name to Damian. I am aware that by doing so, I basically condemned the guy to death, but I have no pity for that rapist. And I will feel safer once he's caught. I wish we could at least know for sure if he's dead or alive... The memories from before I fainted come back to me, and I move my hands to find

Damian's. I weave my fingers with his, looking for some strength.

"Damian, I... I think I stabbed him."

"...What do you remember?" He asks softly.

"I tried to defend myself. He grabbed me and tore my dress. I remember scratching his face, and him slapping me. We fought, my wolf was going nuts, and I almost lost control. I think... I think he grabbed me by the hair at some point; he wanted to take me away from the entrance because... because I screamed. I... I think he took me to a kitchen, and I took a... a knife and I..."

I stop, unable to say one more word. I felt Damian's anger on the rise as I was reminiscing, but I didn't stop. I feel like if I didn't tell him now, I would never be able to talk about it again, to anyone. He holds me tight, breathing in with his face buried in my hair. His closeness is the most comforting thing I have ever experienced, but that doesn't wash away the guilt.

Moon Goddess, I really stabbed someone. I'm a criminal. I could be charged for assault, or punished by the packs... Feeling my distress, his thumb gently caresses my skin.

"Nora, it's okay. It's okay. I swear, I won't let anything like this happen ever again to you, Nora. I swear to you."

I feel Damian's lips on my shoulder, but I can't help but cry bitterly. I don't want to be a murderer; I didn't mean to hurt him. I just didn't want him to touch me. I keep crying silently, soothed by Damian's voice, whispering to me until I go back to sleep again.

I drowsily wake up, but it doesn't feel like that much time has passed since I talked with Damian. What time is it? I turn my head to my bedroom window, and it's dusk. I slept the whole afternoon, how embarrassing... And now there's no way I'll go back to sleep tonight. I realize that Damian's gone, but Bobo is there, sleeping on the floor.

"Bobo?"

He raises his head immediately and walks up to me. He puts his big head on my mattress.

"I really hope you brushed your teeth since you chomped that arm, Bobo," I sigh with a frown.

Gosh, that was disgusting to even remember.

Where is our mate?

I sit up, shocked to hear my wolf. I can feel her so clearly now! She is sniffing around for Damian's smell, and I find myself doing the same thing unknowingly. What a sensation... I can read in her as clearly as I can think now. I think she's grey... Or no, maybe even white. She doesn't mind Bobo's presence, she likes him, but she wishes it was Damian. And I can smell Tonia's not far, too. How strange.

Bobo lets out a short, low-pitched sound, and I know he asks if I'm okay. I wouldn't call it a sentence, more like a... feeling. It doesn't come as precisely as if we were mind-linked, but my wolf still understands what he means to say for me.

"I'm okay, Bobo. I... I can feel my wolf!"

He tilts his head to the side, his tail wagging a bit like a curious dog. I just want to enjoy this new range of sensations. It feels different, yet the same. As if I had just awakened a sixth sense, or a second me, no matter how weird that sounds. I breathe in deeply. She is checking out our environment, and I feel it through her. The smell of fresh sheets, and some lavender coming from the wardrobes. Bobo mostly smells like food and dead leaves. No smell of blood, thankfully. She picks up something good ... cold chicken and onion soup? I look around me and notice a closed Tupperware on the nightstand.

Now that I think about it, I'm starving. We both are. But as I reach out to grab the cold soup, something weird holds me back from my ankle. ...Did I just hear a metallic sound?

I frown and push away the sheets to look at my legs. ...What the hell...?

"Damian!" I yell, too shocked to say anything else.

Instead of him, Tonia rushes into the room, alerted by my screaming. She has changed into dark jeans and a sports bra, and her hair is all over the place. She walks to my bed to try and check me with a worried look, but I push her away.

"Baby girl, are you okay?"

"No, I'm not! Tonia, why the hell am I chained to the bed!"

I'm totally panicking right now. A shackle is running from one of the bed's feet to my ankle, with a big leather bracelet holding it up. Why the hell am I chained to this bed? I look at Tonia, trying to get a decent, logical answer to what is going on, but she just seems uneasy.

"Nora, I... Sorry, I couldn't stop him..."

"Tonia? ...Don't tell me this is Damian's idea."

Her silence is more than eloquent for me, but I can't believe it. Is

Damian crazy? Why would he chain me to the bed like a dog! I try to force on it, but of course, it won't go off. He can't do this to me! I get out of bed, only to realize the chain is about ten feet long, just enough for me to reach my bathroom. I take my head in my hands, unable to believe what's happening.

"Nora, are you okay?"

"I'm not, Tonia! Why would he do this? I'm chained to a bed!"

She really looks sorry, exchanging glances with her brother.

"I swear I tried to stop him, Nora, but he didn't listen. He said he doesn't want you out until they have caught that guy, Marcus."

Oh, my Goddess, is it because of what I told him? Did he freak out because I told him the details of when Marcus assaulted me? I remember his last words before I fell asleep. He really meant it. He won't let me out until they have caught him. But he didn't have to chain me to that bed like some animal! I try pulling on it, but Tonia intervenes to stop me.

"Stop, stop, Nora, calm down. You really shouldn't be moving around so much when you collapsed earlier..."

"Tonia, I don't care! I don't want to be chained! Not by Damian or anyone else! Where is he?"

"He had to go back to work. He left about half an hour ago..."

"Call him," I order her with a clear voice.

I won't calm down until I can talk to him. Tonia sighs but takes out her phone. I'm so angry, I'm almost shaking right now. She gives me her phone, and within a minute, Damian is at the end of the line.

"What is it?" He asks coldly.

"Damian, you can't chain me to a damn bed!"

"...I'm in a meeting right now."

"I don't care!" I yell. "You just can't do this! You undo it right now! I can't believe you did something that crazy to me!"

"You are safe where you are, Nora. I don't want to risk you sneaking out on Tonia and Bobo again and getting yourself in danger."

"Damian, I promise I won't do that again without telling you. I swear. But I don't want you to force me like this. I don't want to be chained like a dog!"

"No."

"Damian!"

But he hangs up on me without letting me finish. I let out a scream of frustration. How can he do this to me! I know I shouldn't have snuck out, but that doesn't mean he can go ahead and do something like this to me!

Tonia is nervously playing with one of her braids, visibly feeling sorry about the situation.

"Tonia, do you have a key to this thing? Answer me honestly."

"No, baby girl, I swear I don't. The Boss knows I was against this, so he won't trust us with a spare key."

"Bobo, can you break this bed?"

He lets out a growl and shakes his head. I can't blame him. This thing is obviously too big, but I had to ask. I sigh. I can't believe this...

I need a clear head. I grab new clothes in the closet and head to the bathroom. It really is long enough for me to take a shower with this horrendous thing still hanging on my ankle, but it's a real pain to take my clothes off, even for a dress. I take my time in the bathroom, washing my hair and body with cold water to try and think. I'm too angry to make good decisions right now. I keep thinking about what to do. I can't let Damian do this. I know how stubborn he is, but I just can't let him win. I understand I went too far, but this is not security, this is a punishment.

I get out of the shower and start dressing up. I randomly picked some black lingerie, but I realize this shackle is a nightmare to even put my panties on! I can somehow manage to pass the underwear through the hole, but that means I can't wear pants if I have this thing on! By chance, I choose a sweater dress that I can put on with no difficulties, but I'm still mad!

I glare at my reflection in the mirror, with my wild black curls falling all over my shoulders. I look like an angry lion, but I also realize my eye color has slightly changed. From a natural dark blue, my wolf's recent awakening has given it a new shine, like two sapphires. Even if I like this change, it doesn't minimize my anger one bit. I'm not going to go along with this change. ...But what should I do?

"...I don't understand," says Tonia. "You can get mad like this at the Boss, the most powerful wolf in the City, but you let your pack abuse you for years? What's wrong with you?"

"It's not the same fight," I sigh.

And I know this won't be an easy one either...

"Nora, please."

I keep ignoring him, sitting as far as I can on the bed, watching the sunset outside. It's already been two days, but I won't give in.

"Nora, I don't mind if you give me the silent treatment, but you have to eat. Please."

I'd rather starve than allow this. I need Damian to realize that. I tried yelling, begging, crying, but since putting myself in danger is the only way to make him react... I'm never going to allow this. I need him to understand how mad I am. He hasn't been violent, but this isn't any better than the days I was locked up in a basement.

With Bobo lying behind me, like a big cushion, I feel a bit better despite the hunger and dizziness I'm trying to fight off.

I know Damian is mad at me for doing this to myself. But he doesn't have any right to do this. He's torn between the fear of losing me to someone else, to a pack that wants to hurt me, and seeing me like this.

"Nora, look at me, please."

I finally turn to him, and I can see the horror in his eyes. I've lost weight. More than I can afford. I see him try to breathe, calm himself. He takes my hand, and I don't fight him. I don't have the strength to push him off, to be honest. He brings them closer and slowly kisses my palm. I can't hold back a smile. He's about to surrender; I know it. He understands.

I'm starting to understand how hard it is for him. To let go, to trust me. Damian is a man who controls absolutely everything around him, including his family. But I won't give him that power over me, and it... terrifies him. If he could, he'd probably lock me away just like this forever, in his golden tower. He sighs, and his hand goes to the shackle. He uses his strength and tears it in a few seconds with an annoying metallic sound.

"...Thank you," I whisper.

I caress his cheek. I'm strangely proud of him. I know I should be angry, but I don't have enough strength left for that. I see all the craziness in his eyes. His fear, his anger, his love for me.

"Boss, she needs to eat..."

"Leave us."

Tonia and Bobo exit the room without discussion.

We keep staring at each other for a long, long time. Until the suns sets, until it's completely dark outside. After a long while, I smile.

"Damian, I promise I won't leave again without telling you. But you can't, ever, do that to me again. Don't restrain me. It's like I'm back in that basement all over again."

His eyes darken, hearing my words. I know how much Damian suffered from all that happened to me, but it's over now. He finally nods and leans forward to kiss my forehead.

"Don't do something like that again, Nora. Take Bobo and Tonia with you, and tell me, or Nathaniel."

"So, you are okay with me going out again?" I ask.

Why does this feel like such a victory? I'm so happy, my heart goes wild. I see him frown.

"Yes, I am, if you just promise me to not do such a reckless thing ever again. Don't let these people hurt you again, Nora."

"I won't, I swear. All I want is for you to trust me. Look."

I place a bit more space between the two of us, and focus on my breathing, closing my eyes. I hear my clothes tearing up and slowly, let my inner wolf take over in front of his eyes. I shapeshift completely into this pure, white wolf. He smiles, amazed.

"You're beautiful..." He whispers.

I come closer, using my four paws, and he caresses me. His eyes are on my paws, and slowly, he seems to understand.

"You could have left anytime... If you shapeshifted, you would have been thin enough to..."

I chuckle internally, happy he realized that. I see his eyes widen when he understands this was all on purpose, to show him that if he wants me to trust him, he needs to trust me first. I hesitate a bit before shapeshifting back again, so we can talk. He closes his eyes and hands me his shirt right away. I blush and put it over my naked body quickly.

"Thank you," I say, blushing a bit.

"Nora, don't let anyone hurt you again. You're strong."

I nod, agreeing entirely with him. Things are certainly different now. I have people supporting me, and my wolf finally awoke. I'm no longer defenseless. Damian seems about to say something but, he looks at me again and, before I can say anything, he suddenly grabs my waist and draws me into a kiss.

I can't believe it. Damian's lips are on mine, and he is kissing me so passionately, my breath can barely keep up. And yet, I want more. I respond to his kiss, my hands on his torso, my whole body on fire. His grip on my waist brings me even closer to him, sitting on his lap, and his fingers in my hair are making me crazy. I'm losing control. I need him like I need air, I crave for more each second his lips are on mine.

It's not a sweet, innocent kiss. Damian is passionate, claiming his hold on me, wanting me. Our bodies entangle dangerously, and I can feel a wildfire igniting inside me. I'm... Gosh, I'm going insane. I didn't know I could be so indecent, but here I am, responding to Damian's kiss with all my might. My clumsy hands are on his neck and on his bare torso. It's almost like my wolf has taken over. I'm so... reckless and hot all over. The taste of his lips, his hard breathing, and his hands all over my body are driving me crazy.

Suddenly, he interrupts our kiss and pushes me on the bed, holding my wrists down. We are both panting, looking into each other's eyes.

"Okay, stop, stop, Nora. If we keep going..."

I nod. I know, I felt his wolf going crazy. I can barely hold mine, too. She might be ready, but I don't think I am. I mean... I'm not sure about it. I just know I feel like I went through Hell and Heaven altogether, but I know my wolf is also doing her share, too. She is so excited that I don't know how I feel myself anymore. I need a clear head, and for now, I'm just dizzy. I need to catch my breath. Gosh, I must be so red from blushing...

"Sorry, I..."

But I don't know what to say. Everything's so confusing right now. Damian leans on me and kisses me, a quick, innocent one this time.

"Stay there. You really need to eat something. I'll go get Tonia."

He could just use their mind-link to ask her, but we both know it's best to put some distance between us for now. He exits, or should I say escapes the room quickly. I'm such a mess right now! I must be red from blushing, and I can barely catch my breath. I sit up, pulling Damian's t-shirt down, and put my fingers in my hair to try and brush it roughly.

Oh my gosh, I can't believe what just happened. I feel like I just got off an emotional roller-coaster. My heart is beating like crazy, and my wolf is not acting any more decent either. I can't stop smiling. I'm happy I finally managed to get Damian to understand and trust me, but... I didn't expect what followed! I was so glad to show him my wolf form, but I couldn't possibly have imagined he would... kiss me next!

"Nora?"

Tonia just came back, carrying a table tray. I feel so embarrassed facing her after what just happened, and I just have a t-shirt on! It's big enough to cover up to my thighs, but still! I go to grab a new outfit from one of the wardrobes and run to the bathroom.

"Nora, I know that t-shirt!" She laughs. "You naughty girl!"

This is so embarrassing I could die, though I do try to ignore her laughing while I get dressed up. I grabbed a blue denim skirt and a white top that match my taste. Once I'm a bit more decent, I look at myself in the mirror. My hair is a bit all over the place, and my cheeks are bright red, but it's not that bad.

When I exit the bathroom, I flee straight to the bed and stubbornly concentrate on my lunch to ignore Tonia's amused glances.

"Well, happy to see you feeling better, baby girl. Bobo was worried, too, you know."

At least she doesn't look like she will try to ask difficult questions. I catch a bit more rest in the main room after eating while Damian left to go back to work. He said goodbye with a surprisingly innocent and swift kiss, but just remembering it makes me blush, too. Bobo volunteers to accompany my nap on the couch.

When I wake up again, it's dinner time. Bobo is snoring loudly at my feet, curled up like a giant, furry ball. I get up and join Tonia in the kitchen, but to my surprise, she is not alone. Nathaniel smiles at me as soon as I come in, dressed in a formal shirt and dark jeans, his blonde hair shining like he just stepped out of some magazine. How can the Black brothers be so handsome, all three of them?

"Hello, princess. How are you feeling today?"

"Much better, thanks. Are you staying for dinner?" I ask as I walk over the counter to check what's left in the fridge.

"No, princess, I'm just dropping by. I was hoping we could talk a little."

I frown and close the fridge. What does Nathaniel want to talk about? He may be smiling, but I can tell he's pretty serious. I walk over and sit at the table next to him. Tonia brings us drinks, and I know she wants to listen, too.

"What do you want to talk about?"

"Remember, you mentioned you wanted to work?"

I nod, intrigued. I did more than mention it, considering the argument I had with Damian that night, but I didn't think Nathaniel would be the one to bring that matter on the table again. He gives me a reassuring smile.

"Well, I've discussed this with Damian, and I wanted to know if you would be interested in working at one of my restaurants, *La Rose de L'Aube.* You could have a trial period there and see if you like it."

"Are you serious...?"

I'm so shocked, I can barely breathe. I can't believe Nathaniel is offering me a job! He laughs at my surprised expression.

"Yes, I am, Nora. I happen to be short on staff now, and as we both know, my brother wants you somewhere we can watch you. My restaurant is secure enough for that, and I know you have a knack for French cuisine, so, isn't this perfect?"

"But you've never seen me at work before! And to get such an offer..."

Even I have heard of that restaurant! Of course, I didn't know who it belonged to, but *La Rose de L'Aube* is famous for being one of the top restaurants of Silver City. I only have experience as a waitress in a pub and cooking for a pack! Nathaniel laughs at my confused expression.

"Don't worry, Nora. As I said, just give it a try! No pressure, princess, it's all up to you. You can take your time, and when you've made your decision, you'll give me your answer next week, okay?"

I nod, but I'm still going to need some time to process this. It's like having my dream job served on a plate! It feels too good to be true, and in a certain way, it is. But I know of Damian and his brothers' influence. It is not an exaggeration to say they own half of the city. Liam did mention his brother had several hotels and restaurants to manage. Finding a spot in one of them probably was a piece of cake. But still, it is hard to believe how lucky I am!

"Nora? There is something else we need to discuss."

He looks a bit more serious this time. He puts his hands before him, taking a thinking pose for a second, searching for his words. Then, he looks at me in the eye, not smiling for once.

"We are facing a... rather odd issue. Damian and I looked into the city records, trying to get to know more about you."

When they were searching for my Clan, I suppose. It is probably no surprise, either, that they can freely run through the city's classified documents to get information on someone. It must be as simple as walking in a library for them. But what would be the problem with my legal information? The city records should hold every citizen's data, such as our birth date, the city of origin, and parents. The night creatures like werewolves also can access some information concerning the Moon Clans we are related to this way. But I don't see where there might be an issue on any of these.

Nathaniel frowns, and takes out several documents that I have never seen before.

"When you told us your name was Nora Bluemoon, we started looking for you. My brother knew your birth date, and I originally thought we would be able to discover your background information quite easily. But we didn't."

What? I don't get it. How could they not find a single piece of information about me? I look at the documents scattered. Register of births from 1995 to 2003, list of family names established in Silver City since the eighteenth century, several Clans registers, and a few family trees with names similar to mine.

"What do you mean?" I ask, confused.

"That means there is absolutely no trace of your existence, nowhere, Nora. Legally, you have no records in any of these documents. You should be in at least half of them, but you are not. No girl named Nora was born in 2000 or any of the years around it. There is no family name like Bluemoon registered in Silver City, and you are not even mentioned as part of the Jade Moon Clan!"

I look at him, dumbfounded. How is that even possible? I have never lived anywhere else as far as I can remember, so how can this city records be utterly unaware of my existence? I check the documents he's brought, trying to find some clue, anything to prove he's wrong, but after a few minutes, I have to admit Nathaniel's right.

I don't appear anywhere.

"...How is that even possible?" I ask.

Nathaniel frowns.

"I'm not sure, princess. It seems like your existence has been concealed from the very first moment you were born."

"But why would someone hide her birth?" Asks Tonia, perplexed.

I have no idea... The Jade Moon Clan was simply ignoring my existence so they could use me as a slave and could not have been bothered about it. But I should still have some legal presence somewhere, shouldn't I? If so, then what is this?

"...What about Alec?" I suddenly ask.

Nathaniel frowns.

"You mean your older brother?"

"Yes. Alec was born in 1997, did you find any trace of him?"

"Not in the Jade Moon Clan's registers, but we can find him somewhere else..."

He grabs the 1997 births register, and we quickly go through it, when I finally spot him.

"Here! Born on October 3rd, Alec... Blackwood?"

That's the right birthdate and first name, but why is his last name different? It doesn't make sense. I know my last name! Bluemoon, Nora Bluemoon! I grab the 2000 births register, thinking I may have missed something. Maybe my name was misspelled, or I was registered as... Blackwood, like Alec. But after checking twice, still nothing. No name even remotely similar to Nora Bluemoon or even Nora Blackwood. There is a Luce Norwood, born in early October, and a Janice Bell in January, but those two are the closest I could find.

"Alec Blackwood," reads Nathaniel, who's still looking over the 1997 register. "Firstborn son of Stephen Blackwood and spouse Alice Blackwood, born Alice Frost. It says your parents got married in June the same year."

I nod. Those are the names of my parents! So why am I not registered under their names like Alec? I can't believe it!

"Do you know of the Blackwood family?" I ask Tonia.

"There are a few Blackwood, in the Gold Moon and Rising Moon Clans mostly. It's a rather common last name for werewolves."

Nathaniel and I both grab each Clan's register and start looking. I find it first and show them. My parents and brother are indeed in the Gold Moon's Clan register, along with a long line of ancestors.

"Do you remember living in this Pack?" Asks Nathaniel.

I shake my head.

"No, I was too young. Our parents died when I was seven, and Alec and I lived in the slums until the Jade Moon Clan took us in a few months later... I don't remember much before that."

The trauma of my parents' death is still lingering somewhere in my mind, but I really don't want to think about it now. All of this is unbelievable! How can I be totally omitted from all of those documents? Did my parents not record my birth? If we were part of the Gold Moon

Clan, I should have been registered like any of their pack's children!

Nathaniel sighs and grabs those documents back. He tries to give me a reassuring smile, but I'm too confused right now.

"Don't worry, princess, there must be a logical explanation. For now, let's not focus on this, ok? I will try to look deeper into this. At least we now know your parents' names, and we are still looking for your brother. Maybe he will be able to help you understand some parts of your story you didn't know about."

I nod, but I still don't know what to believe about Alec. I didn't mention to anyone yet that my brother tried to sell me to Marcus. I don't know what Liam understood from my conversation with Liz, but for now, Nathaniel and Damian don't seem to know about it, and it might be best to keep it that way until we find Alec. He is still my brother, after all. I hope he is still in the area, and we can talk things out.

I get up, trying to process everything that just happened, and Tonia and Nathaniel are thoughtful enough to give me a moment. They start chatting about trivial matters, making it visible they are changing the topic on purpose.

I make myself some herbal tea, trying to calm myself.

"Nora? I still have one more thing to discuss with you, princess."

I come back to Nathaniel, my cup in one hand, and he smiles as I sit facing him again.

"About?"

"The Jade Moon Clan."

I had forgotten about that matter. Nathaniel did leave them with an unambiguous warning, and summoned Vincent as the Alpha for a fight in five... No, four days now? This is going to be dangerous. People from other Clans might even come and watch, and the Jade Moon Clan's turf is exceptionally well located, and thus, envied by others.

"You challenged Vincent for the Alpha position. Are you going to fight him yourself? Do you really want to take over our Clan?" I ask.

He has a sneer on for a second, looking at me with a mysterious expression. What is he thinking now?

"No, Nora. I thought you would fight this Alpha to take over the Jade Moon Clan."

...Excuse me?

Chapter 6

I keep punching, aiming right at the targets like Tonia told me. I'm sweating like crazy, as I have been at it for two hours now. But I'm genuinely feeling great. I finally got back to the gym, and I really missed our morning workout sessions. She lets me hit a couple more times the target, encouraging me all along. When we finally stop, I'm panting.

"You're doing great, baby girl!"

"I still feel this is never going to be enough, Tonia. Nathaniel is crazy."

She rolls her eyes and helps me take off the gloves. We are both wearing dark workout outfits, but that makes the difference between us all the more visible. Tonia is one head taller than me, and she shows a lot more muscles under her tan skin. Even if I did gain a few new pounds and can now last longer at training, I still feel like I'm lacking and weak. How am I supposed to defeat a grown man, an Alpha to boot?

"No, it will be enough. It's all in the head, baby girl. What you need is to work on is your willpower, and to avoid being hurt."

Here we go. Tonia and Nathaniel have this crazy theory that I have some Alpha potential, enough to be able to make Vincent submit. I know he is not the strongest Alpha around, but still, I'm just a teenage girl who's only known how to take a hit before! I shake my head.

"Tonia, you overestimate me. I can only stand against Damian because he is my mate, not because I can actually dominate an Alpha!"

"Not only the Boss, Nora. Do you realize you've done it with any Alpha you've met? Even Liam! No one but his brothers can talk back to him like you did. Even I couldn't, and my wolf is pretty strong! But we are wolves, and wolves stick to their ranks. I'm a Beta, and I tell you, you're an Alpha down to the bone, and your wolf should never have submitted to that pathetic guy in the first place."

I feel a growl inside. My wolf agrees with her. She never wants to submit again, and she's quite angry about it. What, you've been hiding for years, and now you're ready to go all claws out against Vincent? I sigh. The new mystery about my birth that unexpectedly arose since Nathaniel came has me thinking a lot, too. I remember my parents. I know I looked a lot like my dad, and he loved me lots. However, my mother was more distant, and we didn't have much in common. They sometimes argued, even if I don't remember what it was about. While thinking it over last night, I remembered something Alec said: "Whose fault is it that I am an orphan?"

What could he mean by that? We both lost our parents most tragically. I still remember that day vividly, but Moon Goddess, I wish I didn't. I've already lost most of my childhood memories before that event due to the trauma... Because of that memory, I can't remember meeting Damian, either.

I haven't seen him since our kiss yesterday, but I understand he's working. I quickly called him this morning to thank him for the job at Nathaniel's restaurant and let him know I was feeling a lot better too. It felt great, being able to communicate simply with him, though I blushed the entire call. He even said I should go out shopping with Tonia. I feel like they have something planned, but I don't mind.

When we go back to the apartment, I take a well-deserved shower, as usual, and take my time dressing up for once, since we are going out. We're now at the end of November, so I go for white pants, a cute-patterned sweater, and some brown leather heels. I'm still inspecting myself in the mirror, unsure about my choice when Tonia comes in. She is wearing her black leather pants and jacket, and a sexy white gym top with only one strap. She whistles when she sees me.

"Hello, baby girl," she says with a playful smile. "Damn, I wish I was as thin as you, you look like some princess from a fairy tale! Oh, wait, you need accessories. Let me pick some for you."

"I look like a child," I sigh while putting on the earrings and bracelets she gives me.

I've always hated my thin and small build. Maybe it's from malnutrition, but I've always been one of those petites, slender girls. I wish I had some more curves and muscles like Tonia. Damian looks so tall next to me! Thinking about his build makes me reminisce about the touch of his hands on me... I get a hot shiver. It still seems so unbelievable. Damian always treats me like I'm some precious flower, yet when I look in the mirror, all see is this horrendous scar on my face...

"Nora?"

Tonia is looking at me, worried. I unconsciously brought my finger to touch my scar, following the long red thread, running from my right eyebrow to my jaw.

"Sorry, I was thinking."

"Your scar... You never talk about it. How did you get it?" She asks while sitting on my bed.

What do I say? An accident? It was not an accident... I bite my lip, trying to look for some explanation that won't leave her too shocked. I really don't want to get into the details, but I don't want to lie to Tonia again, either.

"It was some sort of domestic incident, with a knife. When I was very young. But I don't want to talk about it, Tonia, sorry."

She nods, still frowning. I really don't want to talk about this memory. Not now and not here. I put on a smile and grab a coat.

We head outside, with Bobo following us as usual. I'm starting to wonder if I will ever see him in his human form at all. The elevator takes us to an underground garage, and Tonia heads for a black SUV that looks brand new. Bobo jumps on the back seat while Tonia and I take the front ones, and she drives out.

I'm so happy to go outside again! I aim to open my window, but Tonia closes it as soon as I do.

"No, no, baby Girl. Too dangerous."

I frown. Why can't I open the window? It's not like some sniper is after me! I pout, but I don't want to argue with Tonia when we just barely exited the building. Now that I think about it, the car does seem to have tinted windows. They are not kidding about my security... It's almost like I can see Damian's shadow surrounding us.

"Tonia?"

"Hm?"

"What is Damian's job exactly?"

She thinks for a while before answering me. She put on some aviator glasses and rock music on the stereo. She looks so cool while driving, I'm envious!

"Basically, a businessman. The Boss runs the Black Corporation along with his brother Nathaniel. He is the CEO and main shareholder, so he has to show up to meetings every now and then. He's excellent, but he hates going to those and always says they don't need him. He sends our brother, Neal, to replace him sometimes, but according to him, they all go crazy when the Boss is not there."

"Is that why you always call him Boss?"

She laughs at my question and plays with her ring while waiting for the light to go green.

"Sort of. It's Bobo who started, actually. Since we are werewolves, there are always big internal struggles with the money, deeds, and who gets more power and stuff. It's like a Mafia, and the Boss certainly works that way. He never forgives anyone who oversteps their boundaries or tries to double-cross him. He has them all shaking whenever he enters a room. Thanks to that, it's going smoothly, but trust me, some guys can never sleep well."

This doesn't come as a surprise to me. Saying that it works like a Mafia doesn't only apply to Damian's group, but all the packs as well. It's all about power between werewolves. We learn to respect and submit to the strongest and fight to survive. The territory wars are no joke. Some packs are known to be more peaceful than others, but no one wants to step a foot on the wrong turf.

Considering this, the Blood Moon Pack needs just as many assets to strengthen its power over Silver City. Being a strong wolf means nothing if you have to beg others for money, or don't have a proper place to let your pack live in. From what I've seen so far, Damian doesn't have this kind of problem... I wonder how and when he got that powerful.

Tonia finally parks in front of a colossal shopping mall I've never seen before. She is smiling so brightly, it's almost blinding.

"Here we go! Shopping time!"

Bobo lets out a low growl, and I'm pretty sure he's not as enthusiastic as his sister.

I soon understand why. It was nice for the five or six first shops we visited. Tonia loves to try on lots of different things, dress me up like a doll, and run around to see what she might have missed. Her shopping technique is a bit scary, as I've never seen someone pick out clothes so fast. Only brands too! I feel a bit shy standing in the middle of such high-class items, but Tonia is clearly used to it. I wonder how she gets the money to pay for all that, though she only buys one-tenth of everything she tries. I try to keep her from buying me things, too, as my wardrobes are already full, but Tonia doesn't care. When we leave the tenth shop, I'm carrying more shopping bags than decent, and my feet are killing me. I have to beg Tonia for mercy.

"Tonia, I'm just going to grab something to drink. Can you meet us at the café we saw upstairs earlier?"

"Sure, sure. But stay with Bobo!" She says while looking into a pair of jeans.

"Promise."

The big wolf is only too happy to accompany me to the third floor and escape his sister's shopping marathon. We walk away side by side, and, once again, I wonder how come nobody says anything about the enormous beast walking around in broad daylight. I mean, werewolves are nothing new in Silver City, but he's as big as a bear!

We find a table in a corner, and Bobo hops on the bench. I order two lemonades since I've seen him drink some at home. Gosh, I'm so tired! I don't know how Tonia can run around on her heels all day.

The mall is actually not so crowded. It's a Tuesday, after all, so no surprise there. I like this place, it's all white, rather neat, and clean without being too pompous. There are three floors, the two upper ones being open so we can see downstairs. I like to look around to watch what people are doing. It's mostly early Christmas shoppers, I would say. December is already starting next week, after all.

While I'm lost in thoughts, I suddenly get a chill. My wolf starts growling, and I instinctively get on my guard, too. I feel like someone's observing me. I look around, but aside from us, the café barely has more than a couple of customers. I still can't shake off this uneasy feeling. Something's off.

"Bobo?"

He stood up and has started growling, too, standing against my leg in a protective stance. We wait, looking all around to understand what's going on, but for a while, nothing happens. The uneasy feeling gradually disappears, and after a couple of minutes, I spot Tonia running towards us.

"Nora! What's wrong? Bobo said something was happening!"

"I don't know. I feel like someone was watching me. I'm not sure, and we saw no one." I answer while looking nervously around me.

Tonia looks all around us, too, but everything seems normal. I'm sure someone was staring at me, and it gave me the creeps. My wolf instincts don't lie.

"Whatever it was, it's gone... But I don't like this. If someone's watching you, that's no good, Nora."

"Could it be someone else Damian sent to protect me?"

Tonia shakes her head.

"No. The Boss only trusts Bobo and me for your security. He would have told me if anyone else was supposed to watch you. And Bobo didn't pick up any familiar scent either; it's definitely not someone from our pack."

She sits, still on her guard. But I think whoever it was, they're gone... Tonia then grabs one of the bags and gives it to me. I frown while opening it and turns out it contains a small box wrapped with a Christmas-themed paper. She gives me a smile.

"Sorry, it's actually for your birthday, but they only had this kind of wrapping. An early birthday present, though you should have had one sooner."

I open the present, curious to know what it is. It's a brand-new smartphone! I know this Korean brand, and it's the latest model, too! Tonia even picked a white case and some very girly and shiny stickers so I can decorate it. She shows me how to use it, and in the contacts, she already put her number, as well as Damian's.

Without warning, I can't help but let out a few tears.

"Nora! What's wrong, baby girl, why are you crying? You don't like it? Should I have picked a different model? Or is it the color?"

She is so panicked about my tears that I can't help but laugh at her questions. I wipe out my tears to answer, a bit embarrassed to be crying in public.

"No, no, Tonia, it's awesome, really. I... I just... I haven't received a present in years, so I'm really touched. Thank you so much."

"Oh, Nora, you are so cute..."

She comes and gives me a hug. I really am sincerely touched. Back in the Jade Moon Clan, nobody cared about my birthday–most of them didn't even know when that was. Alec gradually forgot about it, too, since he didn't care anyway.

Tonia orders coffee and enthusiastically shows me some of her favorite apps since it's my first time using one. She suggests I get a mailbox and some games. Apparently, she uses her own phone a lot.

"Does Bobo have a phone?"

She nods and takes a second phone out of one of her jacket inner pockets, a black one. This one is an older version and looks used.

"I keep it for him most of the time. He doesn't like using it too much anyway, except for listening to music. He loves Latino stuff, like reggaeton."

"Really?"

It's funny to imagine that this big, lazy, and aloof wolf loves dancing music! Tonia nods with a smile while petting her brother's fluffy ears. I noticed Bobo really loves to be pet, like a house dog.

"You should see him dancing! It's the only time he doesn't want to sleep. Put the big boy on a dancefloor, and he becomes a real killer. We will take you out dancing someday!"

"I want to see that someday, Bobo!"

We laugh a bit, but then I focus again on the smartphone. Tonia shows me a few more things, and I think I understand quickly enough how it works. She lets me use it for a while as she drinks her coffee, and I even download and try a cooking game for a bit.

"Okay, enough playing Nora. How about trying to make a call?"

Her smile speaks volumes about who I should try to call, and I blush immediately. To call Damian? Out of the blue? What am I supposed to tell him! What if he is busy? I ponder for a while, but I really do want to try calling him. Okay, but if I'm to call him, I need some intimacy! I get up and exit the café to stand in the hall, and Tonia and Bobo can still clearly see me from the glass wall, as I'm barely a few steps away.

I try to ignore the fact that Bobo will probably be able to hear me since he is in his wolf form, and I call Damian. It rings for a while, and I wonder if he might be busy, like in a meeting or something. But suddenly, someone picks up.

"Who is this?"

I frown. It's a masculine voice, but not Damian's. I don't think it's Nathaniel either, and I don't recognize that tone at all. Did Tonia put the wrong number?

"Hum, hello, is this Damian... I mean, mister Black's phone?" I mumble, confused.

"It is. I asked, who are you?"

"Oh, sorry, it's Nora, Nora Bluemoon."

"Nora? Oh, my apologies; wait a second."

His tone changed completely as soon as he heard my name! I hear someone taking the phone, and this time, it's Damian's voice.

"Nora?"

"Damian! Hi... Sorry, I... Tonia got me this new phone, and I wanted to try calling you. Are you busy?"

Gosh, I must be so red right now. Calm down, Nora, calm down.

"No, no, it's okay, sorry about that. Neal usually answers when it's an unknown number. I'll be sure to save it for next time. How are you? Everything okay?"

Oh, so that voice was Bobo and Tonia's older brother! I forgot he was Damian's Beta. What's with him and having others answer his phone, anyway? Last time it was Nathaniel, too. So intimidating!

"Yes, yes, I'm fine. Tonia took me to this huge mall today, so we are out shopping. It's nice to go out. Oh, but Bobo is with us, so don't worry."

"I know, Tonia texted me. Did you find anything you like?"

"A few things, yes. Tonia is good at choosing for me; actually, I don't know how she can pick so many clothes so fast!"

"You should choose things you like, too, Nora. Don't let Tonia do it all for you."

"I chose a few things... But I... I don't really have any money yet, so..."

"Who cares? This mall belongs to the Black Group. Pick whatever you like, Nora."

Ohm Moon Goddess. Of course, he owns this mall, too... That's probably why Tonia picked this one in the first place. For some reason, I feel so embarrassed now. I blush and nod, before remembering he can't see me. Let's just change the topic.

"...Are you at work?"

I hear a sigh on his end.

"I am. Getting ready for a meeting."

"Tonia told me you... scare your associates."

"I do. People work faster and better when they think I will kick their asses if they don't."

I chuckle a bit. We both stay silent for a while, and I find myself brushing my hair with my fingers nervously.

"...I love to hear your voice." He suddenly says, making me blush

"I love to hear yours, too," I whisper, embarrassed. "When can I see you again?"

"I'm busy with work, for now, since I missed a lot recently... And Neal is glaring at me right now, so I guess it will be hard to take some time off. But you can call me anytime."

"Okay, I'll do that, then."

"I have to go. I'll call you later."

He hangs up, and I can't help but feel a little bit disappointed. I know he is busy with work, but still. I feel like we only talked for, like, two seconds. I bite my lip.

While I was about to go back inside the café, my eyes suddenly catch a movement in the corner. I turn around, and I spot him. He is wearing a black cap and a large jacket. He is looking straight at me from across the hall.

Alec.

I can't believe my own eyes. He looks thinner and messy, but it's my brother, Alec. And he is staring at me, too. What is he doing here, of all places? Is he looking for me? What do I do? He doesn't look like he wants to approach me. More like... He is glaring at me.

I run back into the café, panicked.

"Bobo, Tonia, my brother's here!"

Both jump on their feet and follow me outside. But Alec's gone. I run to the place I spotted him, but there is no one. Damn! Where did he go now? I look down at Bobo.

"Did you pick up his scent?"

"He's not sure. There are too many different smells, it's a public place after all... Nora, are you sure it was your brother?"

"A hundred percent sure. Alec was definitely standing there, and he saw me, too, he was watching me."

"You think he was the one watching you earlier?"

I wouldn't be too sure about that. The feeling was... Different. I shake my head, looking at Bobo, who is still sniffing every inch of the floor. Tonia asks me how he was dressed and picks up her phone to give out orders. She is sending out people to look for Alec, but I can't help but feel nervous. I keep looking around, hoping to spot him somewhere among the crowd. I don't like the way he was looking at me, so full of hatred... Even worse than before.

I shiver, and it has nothing to do with the temperature. Bobo notices and comes to lean against me. My wolf tells me he means it's okay, not to worry. I just nod, too anxious to speak. Why do I feel so nervous all of a sudden? I don't like this situation. Something's off.

"Nora? You okay?"

Tonia comes to put a hand on my shoulder, but I shake my head.

"I want to go home. Now." I say, staring where Alec stood.

"Okay. Let's get back to the parking lot, then."

I don't say a word for the whole trip back. I know Tonia keeps glancing at me, but I ignore it. I just feel anxious for some reason, and I can't shake this weird feeling off. I really wish Damian was here. I'm nervously playing with my phone, but I can't bring myself to call him. I know he's busy, and I don't want to bother him for something so trivial. Maybe it's just me being paranoid.

Once we are back at the apartment, Bobo is stuck to me. I know he is trying to reassure me, and I'm thankful for that. For a second, I wonder what to do, but I decided to go change into one of my gym outfits and grab my boxing gloves from my room. Without asking Tonia anything, I just head to the gym upstairs, Bobo following me as usual.

I don't like this feeling. I try to punch it off on the sandbags, irritated. What is Alec planning? He clearly wanted me to see him, so what now? I never know where to stand with my brother... Alec has never acted like a sibling to me. He was the worst back when we were still in the Jade Moon pack, and showed no remorse hitting me. Yet I could never wholly resent him. Because he is my brother and I know what happened to our parents messed him up a lot. Maybe I was blinded all along.

I remember the last time I saw him. He was ready to let Marcus rape me and to kill me. He would have if Bobo and Tonia didn't intervene. I throw a couple more punches, with all my strength. What is wrong with him? Why does he hate me so much? I feel like I'm missing something here, and I can't let it go anymore. I need to settle things with my brother for real. For good.

I keep the punches coming and even fail to notice Tonia entering the gym. I only realize she's there when she starts talking.

"I see someone needed to blow off some steam."

"Did you find him?" I ask, panting.

She shakes her head and hands me a few black-and-white pictures. I take off my gloves to look at it while she puts my hair into a ponytail.

"The surveillance cameras caught him at the west entrance of the mall, but that's all we could gather. What do you want to do?"

This is the first time she is asking for my decision. I take a while to think, but I already know what should be done. I give her the pictures back.

"I need to find him. I need to talk to my brother seriously. You have his full name, and we know he's still in town. Without a Clan, I doubt he would go anywhere on the other Clans' turfs, and I think he is watching me. He's probably somewhere in the Blood Moon Clan's territory."

My wolf agrees with me, though she wants to go find him herself. But that would be reckless, and I promised Damian I wouldn't do anything dangerous. Somehow, I feel Alec is up to no good following me, and I just can't leave it like that. Tonia nods with a big smile.

"Now that's an Alpha talking!"

I roll my eyes. Since we discovered this whole mystery about my secret birth, Tonia and Nathaniel have been going on about my hypothetical Alpha genes whenever they get an opportunity. I don't really want to have to think too deeply about it. This whole matter about my non-recorded existence is already enough of a headache as it is. But, as a matter of fact, I also believe my brother may be able to enlighten me about that. Even more reasons to get ahold of him.

A couple more days pass without any sign of Alec.

It's nerve-wracking. I try to chase my worries away by keeping myself busy, switching between my studies and workout sessions, but it's no use. We can't confirm Alec's location. I have no idea what he wants, but I really want to ask him some questions about our parents and the mystery surrounding me.

Damian barely has any time to call me at all. It seems like he really is as busy as Tonia said. I only manage to have him on the phone a few minutes a day. Apparently, they are about to reach an agreement with the Gold Moon Clan, making the neighboring packs uneasy, and thus, some conflicts are bound to rise.

"My brother said you made your decision," says Damian the next day I have him on the phone.

"Yes. I'm not sure this is a good idea yet, but... maybe it's worth trying. I need to end things once and for all with the Jade Moon Clan."

I'm sitting on the couch, brushing my hair with my fingers while holding up the phone. It's almost midnight, and Bobo is sleeping like a baby against my legs. Damian sounds dead tired, yet he gave me a call, as promised.

"You can do it, Nora. Put that scum back into his place, or I'll come and do it for you."

I can't help but smile. I've noticed Damian is more straight-forward and less polite when he is tired.

"I'll do my best."

"We're still looking for your brother. He really knows how to stay under the radar. Nathaniel even gave the word to our allies, but no one has spotted him yet."

I have been thinking about this matter a lot. Recently, I had an idea about how to get ahold of Alec, but I'm not sure this will work.

"Damian, I think I know when we can catch him."

"Tell me."

"I think he will be there at the duel against Vincent. Alec is rancorous. Peter and Vincent banished him, so I'm sure he will want to be there to see the Alpha being demoted. He will definitely find a way to see the fight, we will have a chance to catch him."

"We can have people watching the grounds. Two days is more than enough to prepare; I'll ask Nathaniel to take care of it."

I leave out a sigh. If Alec has been watching me recently, why is he so cautiously staying away? Does he already know my connection to the Blood Moon Clan? I haven't told anyone that Alec was the one who tried to strangle me that night, and I'm not sure if I should say it. Damian might seriously kill him if he knows...

We discuss a bit longer about what preparations should be made to be sure to catch Alec, but I still feel uneasy. What if we do catch him?

"Damian, can you promise me something?"

"What is it?"

"When we catch Alec... Promise me you won't attack him."

"Nora, what is this about?"

I know he suspects something. He probably wonders why I would be worried about him hurting Alec, but I can't tell him the truth. I can't even be sure that Alec won't talk and spill the beans. Moreover, my brother is always so harsh while talking to me, and Damian is not the most patient person... I must be sure he won't lose patience before I get my answers.

"Just promise me, please."

He stays silent for a while.

"...Okay, I promise."

That's one last thing to worry about, at least. I sigh, tired by all the anxiousness. I rest my head on the sofa and close my eyes for a second.

"I miss you," I whisper.

"...Same here."

"I wish I could see you right now."

"Same here."

I chuckle a bit. He really is tired.

"Are you just going to keep saying that?"

He stays silent for a while, and I'm thinking we should hang up to both catch some sleep, but I hear his voice before I can talk.

"...I want to come all the way over there and kiss you again."

I blush, embarrassed, and hide my face with my hair even though he can't see me.

"...Same here." I whisper.

The next day is the last one before the duel against Vincent.

To be honest, I'm not as worried over the duel as I am about Alec's matter. It feels like my brother has all the answers I'm looking for, and I'm afraid we might miss him again. Even the siblings feel my anxiety and stay next to me all day. Tonia helps me train for a few hours, though it doesn't help me relax.

However, when we get back to the apartment, to my surprise, both Nathaniel and Liam are there. As elegant as ever, Nathaniel is standing still in the kitchen while discussing with his younger brother. Liam is lazily lying on the couch but sits up when I walk in. He casually waves at me.

"Hello, princess," says Nathaniel.

"What are you both doing here?" I ask.

The two of them coming to the apartment doesn't seem like a simple, friendly visit. And I know I can't trust Nathaniel's smiles. Liam rolls his eyes and leans back on the couch, leaving the explanation to his older brother.

"We just wanted to come and see you before the duel. How do you feel?"

"I'm fine," I answer honestly.

It's true. I've been living away from my Clan for a whole month, seeing things differently. Now, Vincent doesn't seem as threatening as he once was. I'm not overconfident about my fighting abilities, given that I have only shape-shifted a couple of times before, but I don't intend to hold back and act scared either. I just wish to settle things for good.

"Good! Well, Liam and I will be there tomorrow, as well. Damian wants to make sure his princess doesn't run into some... unnecessary trouble."

He means if the Jade Moon Clan meddles in. They could try to hurt me before the duel, or even find someone else to challenge me again and again if I win over Vincent. Moreover, during a fight for the Alpha Position, a Clan is usually weakened, making it easier for Rogues and other packs to attack. However, none of the local packs will dare to do such a thing if the Blood Moon Clan is there. With Liam and Nathaniel Black present, the Jade Moon pack members will have no choice but to acknowledge the duel's result.

"Thank you. Did you talk to Damian?"

I'm sure the two of them already discussed the matter of Alec. Nathaniel nods with a smile.

"Yes. Don't worry. We will prepare accordingly to be sure to catch your brother."

"Just focus on your duel, Nora. Trust me, we won't miss him," adds Liam.

I feel better knowing the Black brothers will be there. As expected, Damian most likely won't be able to come, but I know I can trust these two. Even if no one from the Jade Moon Clan will be on my side, they will.

"What of Marcus Sickels?" I ask.

No one dared to bring back that matter on the table for a while, but I need to ask. I'm sure Nathaniel was on it, and I need to know if there is a chance he will show up, too. But he just shakes his head.

"Still no trace, sorry, princess. We are still looking into it."

If I stabbed him, he couldn't have gotten very far without help. And I remember how much blood there was, it was no light wound!

Well, for now, I should just focus on the upcoming duel with Vincent. While I go to sit on the couch next to Liam, Nathaniel keeps talking.

"Your birth matter is still a blur, too. Your parents were indeed part of the Gold Moon Clan, both of them. It's a pack we are on good terms with at the moment, I got some info. Apparently, the Blackwoods got married in their mid-twenties after your mother got pregnant with your older brother. They shortly bought a house to start their family, and it seems like they got less involved with their Clan after that. More importantly, no one remembers them having a daughter."

"To be honest, I don't remember living among another Clan before the Jade Moon, either," I admit.

It's not so rare for young werewolf couples to detach themselves from the matters of their pack to focus on their family. Especially those with young pups.

"What happened to them, then?" Suddenly asks Liam.

All eyes converge on me. I bet Nathaniel already knows... He probably already told Damian about his findings, too. But now that Liam is asking me, and with the siblings there, I can't really hide it anymore. I really don't want to say too much, and my memory isn't too good either. I might as well keep it to what Nathaniel should know, as it is all in the police report. I take a deep breath to answer as calmly as I can.

"They died. About ten years ago. When I was six, my... my mother killed my father and then took her own life."

Liam and the siblings look at me, dumbfounded. Only Nathaniel acts very calmly, going to the kitchen to grab drinks for everyone. Liam is the first one to react after a minute of heavy silence.

"Wait, what?"

"It's as I said. Our mother was... mentally unstable. She was often depressed or anxious. She had been ill for a few months before it happened, and she had a sort of... crisis. She went mad and... aggressive. She stabbed my father."

"The police report did mention that Alice Blackwood was under serious medication for her mental health."

I just nod. I really don't feel like reminiscing any further, so I'm not going to give any detail. This is the darkest memory of my six-year-old self, and I don't want to linger on it any more than necessary. It seems like Nathaniel already dug up all that there was. I take a cup of tea Nathaniel prepared and drink from it, letting everyone stay silent for a while. Bobo and Tonia are looking at me, but I don't want to seem pitiful. Liam, however, is frowning with an odd expression.

"What's with your last name, then? You told us you were named Bluemoon. Isn't that odd you don't even remember being called Blackwood at all? What about your brother? Did you guys ever use either name at all?"

"I never had to. Since Vincent picked us up, I... I spent all my life in the main house. I never had to do any official documents; I just assumed everything already was in order, or that Vincent or Peter took care of it for us. Before Nathaniel brought it up, I never imagined there was absolutely nothing about me!"

"What about the school, then?"

I shook my head.

"I never went to school. The pack just gave me tasks, one after another, and no one ever brought it up. I knew how to read and write, I assumed it was enough. I just studied whatever books were in the basement with me."

They look at me, clearly shocked.

I remember spending hours reading old books no one wanted, like *Wuthering Heights*, *Metamorphoses*, or *Hamlet*. Treasures of Literature with beautiful covers, yet no one ever looked at them. No one cared for the dusty, massive bookshelves since screens and video games were available upstairs. There were also full collections encyclopedias and dictionaries, and I just read them all to complete my vocabulary. I would even pick up history books when I was bored or couldn't sleep.

"...Lucky you." Mumbled Liam, but Nathaniel gave him a tap behind the head

I can't help but chuckle over his grumpy teenager's face. I wonder if Liam skips school often. It feels like his brothers are keeping a close watch on him, and I can't help but feel a hint of jealousy. Nathaniel turns to me.

"I can't believe they didn't even bother to send you to school... It is intriguing, however, how the Jade Moon Clan also never cared about your legal existence at all. I wonder if they know anything about your origin."

"I doubt it... Vincent found us in the streets. I guess he was only too happy to find a useful pair of orphans."

"But he never treated your brother like you?"

I brush my hair with my fingers, absentmindedly, trying to remember our first days with the Jade Moon pack.

"A bit, at first... But Alec just pushed all his chores onto me and seeing I never complained, Vince didn't really care. My brother blended more easily into the Clan, I guess. Vincent scolded him once, and Alec tried running away. He couldn't get past the warriors, but after that, Vincent officially admitted us into the Clan so we wouldn't try to leave anymore. Alec was ecstatic to have joined the Clan, and I... I was compliant, so that was it."

Liam growls, visibly pissed.

"I can't believe you submitted to such a weak Alpha... You should have just let me kill him the other day, Nate."

But his brother shakes his head.

"Don't be so reckless, Liam. After all, Nora needs to get back at him for all she endured. Let her give him what he deserves herself."

"You better kick his ass tomorrow!" Says Liam.

I'm not as enthusiastic as he is. They are all eager to see me get my revenge, but that's not my state of mind now. Sure, I have past grievances over Vincent, but I don't have that thing for revenge. I just want to settle things once and for all and sever my ties to the Jade Moon.

My main objective will be to get ahold of Alec. I really hope we catch him tomorrow as planned. The brothers didn't really tell me what kind of preparations they've made, but it mostly must be asking a lot of people to chase after my brother once he shows up. The more I think about it, the more I'm convinced he will. I just hope I'm not wrong.

"Nora, are you still okay with beginning next Monday?"

I look at Nathaniel. Oh, that's right, I told him I was accepting the job. Ready or not, I do need a job, and I have to give it a try.

"Ah, yes. Do I need to bring anything specific?"

"No, not really. Dress casually, and Liam will come and pick you up to bring you there. For the first day, it's okay if you just stay close to Narcissa, the manager, and watch how everyone works."

"All right, then."

After discussing some more, Liam and Nathaniel stayed over for dinner. Since my future boss was here, I did my best cooking, and everyone seemed to enjoy it. Liam insisted on giving me pieces of advice about the fight, making me curious about how experimented he could be. For a high schooler, he does seem prone to fights. Apparently, he's also taking boxing classes weekly, and was happy to discuss it with me. Obviously, Liam is the most hot-blooded of the three, while

Nathaniel always seems very calm and rational. He stayed quiet for most of the dinner, but I did notice he spent a lot of time texting on his phone. The second brother's face never shows what his real thoughts are. He smiles easily and usually comes as quite charming and polite. However, I won't forget how he was definitely the scariest one back when facing Vincent.

How can I be worried when I know those two will have my back tomorrow? As I go to bed, I look blankly at my phone's screen, wondering if I should call Damian or not. Nathaniel did mention he was busy, and... Well, he knows what is waiting for me.

I wake up early.

The only one who is up before me is Liam, who's having breakfast alone in the kitchen. I salute him when entering.

"Did you have a good sleep?"

"How could I? Bobo snores like a pig." He growls. "I have no idea how you can get any sleep with him in the same room!"

I can't help but chuckle as I grab the tea.

"I'm used to sleeping with a lot of noise. The basement I was living in was directly under the recreation room, and there was always someone to watch TV or make noise until late. I had to get used to it. And Bobo's snoring isn't that bad."

He looks at me like I'm some alien, but I ignore him and sip on my cup of tea. We both stay silent for a while. He is on his phone playing a game, and I'm just watching the sunrise behind the glass wall.

"Nate's on his way." Says Liam out of the blue

"He didn't sleep here?"

They explained to me last night that the apartment downstairs was actually one of Nathaniel's places. He didn't sleep there often unless he had to work until late in one of the close restaurants, so Liam would use it every now and then.

He shakes his head.

"No, he slept with one of his women."

So, Nathaniel is a player... You really can't judge a book by its cover.

"I thought he had a mate already..."

"Not really. Well, he almost had one. An older woman. But she was already married, and Nate was a nobody then. It was before Damian took over the Clan. Nathaniel didn't really have anything, and that woman was with a rich guy, with the dream house and everything. She said he wasn't worth the trouble and rejected him."

What? How heartless! I bite my lip, feeling bad for Nathaniel. How did he endure such a rejection? I can't imagine how I would have felt if Damian had rejected me... I suddenly feel something fluffy on my legs and realize Bobo is up. He casually walks past me to put his head in the fridge.

"Don't tell him I told you, okay?" says Liam. "Nate doesn't like people talking about it. And he's over it now; it's been years."

I nod and take a new sip. Being a player now doesn't necessarily mean he forgot what happened... I feel bad for Nathaniel all of a sudden. Now I understand better why he's the type to hide his emotions. What a heartless woman! I feel angry, just thinking about it.

After everyone woke up and had breakfast without rush, I head back to my room to dress up, picking a comfy and sporty outfit. I will shapeshift and get dirty, no need to pretty up today. I put my hair up in a ponytail and choose a dark sweater with some sneakers.

I want to go upstairs and train some more, but Tonia keeps me from it, saying I should save my energy for tonight. But I don't want to do anything either. It's Liam who ends up spending most of his day keeping me company, as he brought his school backpack, and for some reason, we end up studying together on his homework for most of the afternoon. Solving exercises and copying his lessons had the benefit of keeping me too busy to think about the fight. Around four, we paused our math exercises and get ready to go.

Nathaniel meets us downstairs in the garage, wearing his usual smile. He went for a more casual look than what he usually wears, so I suspect he will be ready to shape-shift at any moment, too. Liam, however, didn't even bother changing and is already in his wolf form, like Bobo. Like last time, we take two cars to go.

I start to feel nervous on the way. Tonia casually talks to me, and I suspect she's just trying to distract me. We discuss the songs played on the radio, what weather to expect for the coming days and clothing brands. None of those really manage to distract me, though, so I do think about the upcoming fight.

I wonder why Nathaniel picked East Point Ground. It's a large plaza in the middle of the industrial area, covered in graffiti and on open grounds. It's a place where skaters or delinquents could gather at night to drink. However, it is not usually crowded, unlike tonight. When I exit the car, I'm shocked. There are dozens of people!

I suddenly get why Nathaniel specifically selected this spot: It isn't part of any turf. Hence, a lot of people from the Jade Moon or the Blood Moon Clan freely came to watch. Duels for the Alpha position are usually private matters inside a pack; however, the Black brothers want to make this one public. Once again, I feel that Nathaniel has a lot more in mind than he let on.

A lot of people are eyeing me as I exit the car, most of them whom I don't know or recognize. With both Bobo and Liam in their wolf forms next to me, I don't feel as intimidated as I could have been. On the contrary, I can't help but look at the crowd.

People from other Clans came to watch the fight. I recognize people wearing markings from the Pearl Moon Clan, the Gold Moon Clan, or the Rising Moon Clan. To my surprise, even a few members of the White Moon Clan are there, too. Don't they have a terrible history with the Blood Moon Clan? But they are clearly harboring the White Moon marking... How odd.

Of course, almost all the Jade Moon Clan is there, too.

Almost all of them are glaring at me. I suppose that's what I should expect, considering the situation. Most of the Clan is here to support Vincent, of course. He is a carefree leader, letting his people do whatever they want most of the time, as long as they don't cause any trouble. He only focuses on his hunters and warriors most of the time.

I finally see him among the crowd. He is discussing with his wife and one of the warriors, probably Peter's replacement as the Beta. He looks tired, has dark circles under his eyes, and his beard is messy. When his eyes find mine, he frowns and ignores me. I wonder if he is having regrets now...

Nathaniel's arrival causes a lot of people to react. They stare at us and move to not be on our way to the center of the plaza. The only ones that didn't move are the Blood Moon Clan's.

I see him smiling. Is he excited about the fight? Or because of the large crowd? I don't understand why they made sure a lot of people could see it... I realize that Bobo is moving his head non-stop, he must be scanning the area, searching for Alec. I had almost forgotten about my brother. I'm still clueless about how many people are actually going to help us catch him. I start looking around, too, but Nathaniel walks up to the center of the plaza.

"Good evening, Jade Moon Clan. I see you didn't dare to run away from this."

"I'm not going to run away and leave my turf in the hands of a brat," growls Vincent.

"We will see that with the outcome of this fight. So, do you acknowledge that if Nora wins, you will let her entirely decide your pack's fate?"

Vincent looks at me, seeming hesitant. He must be wondering if I really do have a chance to defeat him. Honestly, I don't feel too confident right now. I don't trust my Alpha blood as much as Nathaniel and Tonia do. I barely have any experience shape-shifting, and I just learned how to fight. For most people, this would seem a lot like suicide.

However, inside, my wolf is already growling. The battle has already begun, though nobody else can see it. Vincent and I are staring at each other, judging our strength, testing our wolves. I know what his wolf looks like. I know he must be growling just as much as mine right now. It is way too late to back down.

"I will, only on the condition that you guys let us have a fair fight. No interference from your people to help her. She must fight me alone."

Nathaniel puts on a shocked expression, looking a bit too dramatic to be true.

"Oh, you think we would actually cheat?"

He steps closer to Vincent, and I can tell the Alpha is fighting hard against his instincts not to step back. They may both be Alphas, but the difference is clearly showing. Anyone watching can tell who has the upper hand.

Nathaniel whispers to answer him, but somehow everyone can clearly hear him.

"If we wanted to cheat, we would not bother to organize a public fight here and now. If we wanted an easy win, I would have taken my warriors to kill your pathetic lot of dogs the day Nora led us to you. You wouldn't have a chance to answer back, and you wouldn't be standing on your two feet."

Vincent is obviously shaking with fear. The ice-cold look in Nathaniel's eyes is terrifying, even for him.

"So now, you're going to be a good boy and let our precious princess beat you all she wants to settle for everything you have done to her. And I can predict you're going to think this is heaven compared to what my brother and I have in store for you once she is done."

Being in the middle of a crowd is nothing reassuring. It's even worse when you know half the people present are wishing for you to get killed. All eyes are directed at me or Nathaniel. I feel grateful to Bobo for standing close to me. His enormous figure attracts attention, and a lot of people seem surprised by his appearance, too. He is almost twice the size of a regular wolf, and those who are there in their animal form are showing signs of nervousness. I would be worried, too, if he wasn't my bodyguard.

Nathaniel's threats to Vincent are quite efficient. Some of the Clan's warriors have started growling, but I also see a lot of them slowly step back. Liam is walking, circling us while growling at anyone who dares to approach this invisible circle. Tonia is standing at the back, arms crossed, and I notice she now has a wireless earbud in, and she's talking to someone. I wonder who she is talking to.

Now, it's only me, Nathaniel, and Bobo facing Vincent and his new Beta. Everyone else is watching us, waiting.

"She is just a kid. She won't win," says the Beta.

"Shut up," says Vince immediately, annoyed. "Go with the others."

His Beta gives me a mean look, but he can't help but obey. I turn to Nathaniel, too. It's time. He just smiles at me and turns back to join Tonia. I put my hand on Bobo's back, and his green eyes turn to me. I give him a smile. I know he's reluctant to go.

"Don't worry, Bobo. Go."

He lets out a short sound and goes, too, but not without growling at Vincent. He's so loud, the Jade Moon pack's Alpha jumps from surprise. If Bobo had Alpha potential, he would be unstoppable... But I guess it's evident that despite his size and strength, his temper is more Beta-like.

I'm left alone with Vincent. He considers me from head to toe with a sneer. I try to be as unreadable as Nathaniel, hiding my emotions.

"You will regret it, Nora. Did you think you suddenly got big because you have a strong back-up?"

I ignore his remarks. My wolf is growling like crazy, and she's the only one I intend to rely on tonight. I might lack experience, but I know I'm tenacious and strong-willed.

I wonder if I should take off my sweater now, but it's still chilly. We both step back to a ten-foot distance between each other and start walking slowly. Everyone tenses up around us, feeling the battle's about to start. I wish Damian was here. I would be even more confident with him behind me. But he's not.

It's just going to be me and you, girl, I whisper to my inner wolf.

I mentally recite all of Tonia and Liam's advice. Mind the distances. Watch his eyes, the way he moves. I'm weaker, but I'm faster and smaller. Liam told me every weak point I should aim at, for his wolf form and his human one. Duels between werewolves don't really have rules, aside from being one-to-one, and no weapons are allowed. We can shape-shift whenever we want.

I have tried shape-shifting a few times, and Tonia immediately pointed out my strong point: I can shape-shift extremely fast. I have to make use of that. Liam said the best outcome for me would be a short fight. I need to take advantage quickly.

We take a few steps, walking in a circle while observing each other. I tried to guess when Vincent is going to attack. Liam predicted that he would take the initiative to launch the first attack. Vincent won't want this to take long either, as he is worried for his pack.

And he does. I see him suddenly shift his balance and run towards me. Try not to take any hits, said Liam, you are too weak to endure several injuries. I dodge his fist at the very last moment and slide under his arm to stand behind him. I immediately kick behind his knee as Liam showed me.

It works! He can't help but bend and get on his knee. Don't miss an occasion. I go to launch my fist, aiming for his jaw, but before I can reach him, I see a leg expanding, and I'm suddenly kicked in my stomach. He pivoted at the last second, and I couldn't do anything to stop him. I'm ejected a few meters back and fall miserably on the ground. Wow, that really hurts... I feel like throwing up. It's been a while since I've taken such a hit, but Tonia's advice comes back to mind immediately. Never stay down. I get up, ignoring the pain.

"Are you trying to get killed, Nora? What is the point? Do you think you can be an Alpha all of a sudden and win my Jade Moon pack over like this? Or is it that you want us all killed and at His feet?"

"Do you think you can call yourself an Alpha, Vincent?" I ask.

He looks at me, frowning, confused by my question. I take off my sweatshirt and tighten my ponytail.

"What now, are you going to complain about how we treated you again? Are you playing the pitiful girl now that you have found your wealthier pack to lounge at?"

"I'm not talking about myself. You are weak, unable to make decisions, and ready to bow to other Clans anytime just so you can take it easy. You don't control your young ones and let them roam freely and unsupervised. You don't train them. You don't care about others. You mind your own business as if you were a Rogue."

"Careful with your words! Don't you insult me!" He growls.

"Oh, do you really want to have the talk about insults? Mockery?" I shout back.

He growls even louder but doesn't talk back. Instead, I see him look towards where Nathaniel is. But he hasn't moved. He appears very relaxed, standing next to Tonia and Liam, and Bobo is now the one walking in large circles around us. Liam was right. Having the Black brothers watching us will not let him concentrate on the fight. I know I can take my chance. This time, I jump at him while he is still staring at Nathaniel and throw a punch to his solar plexus.

He saw me coming at the last second, and to my surprise, he doesn't dodge. He takes the hit, contracting his muscles. Does he want to show he is more robust than me? I don't care, I still throw my fist as hard as I can, and a second later, he obviously regrets not protecting himself. I've learned how to throw a punch now. His breath is cut short, and for a second, he is choking, falling on his knees, and desperately gasping for air. I hear growls and angry voices rising around us, but I don't listen. I knew this kind of thing would happen, and I trust the others to control the crowd one way or another.

While Vincent is still choking, I take a couple of steps back and get ready to hit again. My wolf warns me just in time. He's shape-shifting.

It takes about two or three long seconds to Vincent to turn into a dark-brown wolf. That is way longer than me, but still. Facing a wolf is way different from facing a human man. I adjust my position and throw a kick at the right moment to send him away. He falls a bit further, but I know I was just lucky his shapeshifting took long enough for me to be able to prepare my kick. Now, I will be facing a wolf, and that's a whole different thing. I need to shape-shift and let my wolf take over, too. But at the right moment.

I take a couple of steps back, and I feel my wolf getting impatient. *Just a few seconds, girl.* Wait for it, wait... And there he goes. As expected, he jumps as soon as he can get on his feet again, running towards me. I stand ready, carefully waiting for the right time. He runs closer, and when he's almost at me, all fangs out, I shape-shift.

I erase my human self, letting my wolf completely take over. It's even shorter than a split second for me. Like going through a wall of fresh snow. I jump on the other side; the sudden change brings my wolf-self right at the perfect spot to attack his exposed neck. She bites furiously, with a newfound rage, and he lets out a plaintive whimper. Her fangs on his throat are powerful, I can already smell the fresh blood. He struggles, trying to kick her off him, but she won't let go. She's clenching her fangs hard, not giving the slightest care for his pain.

Around us, people start yelling loudly, calling me names, or telling their Alpha to free himself. Not a chance. I'm not letting go. We won't. He knows what he has to do, and he just doesn't want to. He tries fighting back for a while, but I can taste his blood in my mouth. He is running out of time. My wolf wants him to submit, or she'll kill him. His pack encourages him not to give up. Are they blind? I'm biting his throat! I could kill him with just a snap, though I don't want to kill anyone. Is he counting on it? I won't. I can control my wolf perfectly; she and I are one. I'm not like some of us who can't resist their beast instincts and attack randomly.

Suddenly, I feel a vivid pain to my flank, and let go by instinct. I don't know what happened, but he probably managed to scratch me deep enough. I feel the blood flowing from my injury, but not enough to worry me. We are not done yet.

I trust my wolf. I know she can keep up a fight now that she's tasted blood. I let her take control. Most of the crowd are now cheering, but others are all stunned by my appearance. I hear comments on my blue eyes and white fur. Liam seems overexcited, leaning forward and growling loudly.

"...Stay with your wolf."

Vincent suddenly attacks, and the voice in my head surprises me enough to almost not see him coming at me. I react at the last moment, throwing my fangs at him.

"Don't let him dominate you!"

Who is guiding me? I listen to her anyway, and start fighting him off. I growl loudly and don't let him take the upper hand. He is bigger, but I'm beginning to understand his tactics. I can dodge some of his moves smoothly and manage to bite him back for every time he manages to injure me. I can see he hasn't fought for a while. He tries to get a hold of me, but I won't let him. I'm careful not to let him too close or get on top of me. I'm starting to get tired, though. It feels like this goes on for a while before I finally see an opening on his flank. I aim for his shoulder with no restraint and bite as hard as I can.

"Take him down."

I use my strength and his sudden reaction to the pain to push him down to the ground, laying ons his flank. He is still fighting me off, but his shoulder and throat are obviously painful for him.

"Go for his neck."

The voice in my head is guiding me all the way, I don't have any time to wonder who is mind-linking with me. I fiercely bite Vincent's neck and hold him down. This time my fangs won't let go, and he can barely move, let alone free himself. I'm smaller, but my front legs are on his back, and the continuous pain is getting to him.

"You got him."

I hope she's right and hold my position. The crowd's getting louder, but I don't care. I'm waiting for Vincent to admit his defeat. I'm tired, I want to finish this soon. His pack keeps encouraging him, but some are starting to yell at him for being weak. The other Clans seem to have lost interest in the fight, the outcome is clear now. They are patiently waiting to see it.

Finally, Vincent submits. He stops fighting, his tail between his legs, and whimpers. This is it. I slowly let go and retreat a few steps back. Tonia comes up to me to give me my sweatshirt so I can cover myself when shifting back to my human form. This is quite embarrassing in front of so many people, even if it's for a split second! Thankfully, Bobo stands in front of me, too, and I suppose the best anyone got was a quick peek at my butt before I got my panties on.

I stand up and look at Vincent. He takes his time to shift back, and his wife brings him a pair of jeans to put on. I wish he would hurry up, I'm freezing with my bare legs... Gosh, while looking down, I just noticed I'm bleeding from under my sweatshirt, probably my flank injury. Some got on Bobo's brown fur, too, as he is standing right next to me. I try to gently push him away, but it's like trying to move a mountain, he doesn't care one bit. He is focused on Vincent, growling at him and his pack, making sure no one dares to come at me. Meanwhile, I see Nathaniel walking up to me. He smirks at Vincent.

"So?"

Vincent growls, but bends one knee and lowers his head, his neck covered in blood... I can't believe I really did this. He is visibly furious, but with so many witnesses, he has no choice.

"I acknowledge my defeat. Nora Bluemoon is now free to lead the Jade Moon Pack if she wants."

A lot of unhappy pack members growl, but they don't have a say in this matter. Vincent raises his eyes to look at me, filled with hatred. I look around. Is that right? I see Nathaniel smiling, but Liam is still fiercely growling. A few pack members have come to gather behind their Alpha.

Vincent might be a lousy Alpha, but his Clan still values him very much, as the Greene Family took over the Jade Moon Clan a few generations ago already. I sigh. What do I do now? I could take over, and they would have no choice but to obey me, but...

"Do it, Nora. Isn't it what you wanted?" Says Vincent.

I realize everyone is waiting for my decision. I turn to Nathaniel, but he's still smiling mysteriously, leaving me to decide. I breathe in.

"I don't want to be your Alpha. That will only be an excuse for you guys to hate me more than you already do, and you will turn against me on the first occasion. I don't want to have to fight every day until one of you gets to kill me."

Everyone is looking at me, surprised. They probably didn't expect me to reach such a decision. I see the beginning of a smile on Vincent's face. Oh no, you won't get away that easily.

"However, I do have conditions," I say.

Now everyone is back to growling again, but other than the Jade Moon pack members, everyone is staring at me, all ears, waiting for it. I look straight at Vincent's eyes.

"The Jade Moon Clan will pledge full and complete allegiance to the Blood Moon Clan from today on. Your turf will become part of their territory, and your Clan members will follow the same rules as theirs."

"What? What kind of condition is that!" Yells Greg.

I glare at him, annoyed by their attitude. I take a step forward, and Bobo follows me, growling loudly at them.

“I just dominated your Alpha, I’m free to do whatever I please with this pack. You guys never cared about training properly, so it’s high time for things to change. Your turf is one of the first grounds outside of Silver City. If anyone launches an attack on the area, you will be the first wall of defense. Do you want to stand on the frontlines being unprepared like you are now?”

They look at me, dumbfounded by my words. I turn back to Vincent.

“And you, you’ll have to finally act like a real Alpha. You will train the young ones properly, watch the border, and make sure everyone in your Clan is treated fairly. Am I clear?”

My apparent calm may have led him to think he could answer back. He growls at me.

“Who are you to decide what kind of Alpha I should be? Aren’t you washing your hands of my pack? You are giving us to Him, and now you get to decide what we...”

“protecting their pack is the duty of any alpha here!” I start yelling. “Stop being so lazy and do what you were named Alpha for! You may have their respect, but you are worse than a dog if you think you can sit comfortably and relax just because of that! Any Clan could overpower yours, and yet I’m giving you a chance to keep your turf and pack and turn them into a proper one! If you don’t like it, all of you leave!”

A long silence befalls on the assistance. I’m fuming, pissed at their attitude, and Vincent’s ignorance. But all of a sudden, I feel an arm around my waist, and a familiar smell surrounds me.

“...It seems like my coming here wasn’t necessary.”

I turn around, facing him. I can’t believe he really came!

Damian is holding me tightly against him, but his silver eyes are glaring at Vincent. I notice that everyone in the plaza has reacted to his presence. A lot of people have instinctively stepped back, shapeshifting to their wolf forms or regrouping with their peers. I’m sure some people even ran from the scene right away.

But the most scared one is definitively Vincent. He doesn’t dare to look up now and is shaking. Honestly, I don’t feel sorry for him; I’m tired of his attitude, and if Damian can finally get him to understand his place, so be it.

"What are you doing here?" I whisper.

"I couldn't sit still while you were fighting this trash. And I have a few things to settle once you're done with him..."

His ice-cold voice is definitely aimed at Vincent. Even his pack members don't seem so sure about staying close to him now, as nobody wants to have a share of Damian's wrath. But I'm not like them; I don't fear him. Instead, I'm feeling even more confident with my mate next to me. I glance at Vincent, too, letting him make up his mind.

He is now looking at me, carefully avoiding Damian's piercing glare.

"We agree to your terms, but we would like to pledge allegiance to you, Nora. I promise to do as you said, and I do recognize that I have lacked as an Alpha."

To me? I don't understand why they would obey me instead of Damian. Aren't they supposed to form alliances with other Clans instead of a single person? Now it's like he is submitting his Clan to me, but I'm not sure I want to be responsible for the Jade Moon Clan... Though in this configuration, it would be more like having ownership while Vincent is managing it, I suppose? When our eyes meet, I think I get it. My earlier words really did have an impact on him. Is it possible that I do have Alpha potential, as Tonia and Nathaniel thought? I exchange a look with Damian, but his eyes are still on my former Alpha. He is clear: I can do whatever I please with them. I turn to Vincent.

"That's fine for me, then."

"All right... The Jade Moon Clan, with me, Vincent Greene, as its acting Alpha, swears a total and willing allegiance to Nora Bluemoon. May the Moon Goddess be our witness tonight."

A few people in the plaza applauds or whistles. Nathaniel and Damian both seem content too, and my mate gives me a swift kiss on my forehead.

"Well done, princess."

I smile and blush, still a bit shy. I think it's the first time Damian called me by something else than my first name... I lean my head against his chest. I'm tired, but his warmth is the best thing right now. He glances down and frowns with an angry look all of a sudden. I forgot the blood running from under my sweatshirt. I shake my head and try awkwardly to lower my clothing on my thighs.

"It's okay, it's not that bad."

Damian is not listening to me, his eyes fixated on the thin trail of blood. I want to say something, but suddenly, both Bobo and I turn our heads in the same direction.

Alec's smell. I'm sure of it. Bobo jumps ahead of me and starts running in that direction. I only take a second to shapeshift, escaping Damian's embrace. I hear Tonia behind me.

"Nora, no! Don't!"

I'm not listening and not stopping. Running on all fours, I'm right behind Bobo, following Alec's scent in the north-west direction. I'm sure my brother was close just a second ago— we can't lose him again. Bobo is much bigger, but I still catch up to him, proving that I'm definitely faster than most. We run side by side, chasing the same person.

I hear, or sense, other people running behind us, too, but no one can catch up to us. We have to act fast; I can't slow down. We chase him for a long time and enter further into the industrial area of the city, running past several warehouses. Is that where he was hiding? This is a remote area of the town; it could make a good hide-out.

I finally spot my brother running in his wolf form ahead of me. He is a mix of light brown, white, and sand colors that I can easily recognize even in the dark. He is fast, too, but not as fast as I am, and I'm catching up. It's only a matter of seconds now. We have arrived at the Docks area, which I am not familiar with. From what I can see, there is nothing but old warehouses on our left and the sea on our right. If Alec keeps going North, we will end up on the Sea Moon Clan territory, though. I definitely don't want to enter there; we will be attacked right away.

I'm almost on him! I realize I ran ahead of Bobo and lost him, but I can't think about it now, and he can't be too far behind. He will probably catch up soon. I have to focus on catching my brother. Without warning, Alec suddenly turns around to face me.

I wasn't prepared for that. I try to slow down as much as I can. Alec seizes the occasion right away and jumps on me. For a second, I think he's going to attack. I realize I'm wrong a second too late. He pushes me with all his strength. I'm already unsteady because of my run, and I can't defend myself. In a split second, I realize what he is doing. He just pushed me in the sea. ...Alec knows I don't know how to swim.

My body brutally hits the surface, and I gulp a lot of water unwillingly. I try to paddle, but I'm disoriented by my sudden fall and the freezing waves surrounding me. I can't believe he got rid of me so easily!

I have to find the surface, but I'm choking, unable to breathe. I panic, trying to fight off the water blindly, desperate for air. I start to feel numb and tired. A dark veil is taking over me, and my head is spinning...

"Hang on!"

Air! I feel myself being pulled out of the water, and I start coughing unstoppably. Someone's patting my back, helping me breathe and pulling my hair out of my face. I hadn't even realized I had shifted back.

"Are you okay?"

That's the voice that was talking to me during the fight! I want to answer, but I'm drowsy and just nod while trying to catch my breath.

"It's okay, breathe. Use the mind-link to talk to me, don't waste your strength."

How do I do that? I try to formulate a clear thought, and I feel my wolf helping me somewhere in the process.

"Thanks."

I feel her shapeshifting next to me before I can take a glance at her. But when I look up, I immediately recognize her creamy-white fur and her gold, mesmerizing amber eyes. I've seen this wolf before. She was the wolf accompanying Nathaniel when I went to the Jade Moon Clan a few days ago.

"Don't worry; they'll be here soon. Bobo got him. Just catch your breath, your mate is coming. I got to go," her voice echoes in my mind.

"Wait! Who are you?"

"I can't stay. I am not supposed to be here. Don't worry, I'll find you again. Don't tell anyone about me. Especially not Nate."

I want to say something, but before I do, she's gone, and I am in no condition to try catching her. I'm exhausted and can only lie on the ground. I close my eyes to try and chase the dizziness away, but an unknown smell suddenly grabs my attention. Other wolves.

I hear growling and try to stand up, but I'm way too tired. It's not good... I look up and see a bunch of unfamiliar wolves slowly circling me, menacing. I'm sure they are from the Sea Moon Clan. This is really bad. I'm lying on the ground, too tired to defend myself, or even return to my wolf form! A guy in his human form goes ahead of his peers with a nasty look on his face.

"Look what we got here... A pretty mermaid just landed on our docks, boys. Are you lost, sweetheart?"

I answer with a growl. That guy is making fun of me. Gosh, why do I have to be defenseless and naked now! He frowns at my growl, unhappy with my response. I wish I could be more menacing than that, but even my growl shows how weak I am at the moment. In response, all of them start growling back and come closer.

Suddenly, a large shadow flies over us, and a young black wolf attacks them without warning. He pins one of them to the ground and breaks a neck in one swift motion. All of the Sea Moon wolves take a few steps back, some getting ready to attack, some afraid. I finally recognize Liam's fur, and by then, another beast comes.

He is pitch black, darker than night. He moves slowly, his fangs showing, the menacing wolf exudes the most dominating aura I've ever felt. He seems even bigger, surrounded by shadows. I gasp. All of the Sea Moon wolves are focused on his presence, obviously wary of him. No one dares to move an inch.

Damian finally reaches me, standing above my naked body, in a protective position. He is guarding me and looking straight at the man who talked to me with killer eyes. The guy gulps, his gaze going from Damian to me back and forth. The terrified look in his eyes says it all.

"I... We didn't know, we just... wanted to check on her. It's..."

Damian's silver eyes are still on him, without blinking. He is not growling or moving, but even I can feel his anger from here. Liam lets go of the neck he had his fangs in and shapeshifts. I try not to look at the naked teen in front of me.

"Hey, I thought you guys wanted to play, what's this?"

Gosh, Liam, you're having way too much fun right now.

"We don't want to cause a fight. We just came to check why intruders were approaching. And you attacked us first!" He shows his injured comrades, still lying on the ground. I can't tell if they are unconscious or dead, but the amount of blood on the asphalt is not okay. Liam doesn't care.

"So what? Do you want to complain? You guys should have stayed put instead of coming to take a peek at my brother's mate while she was vulnerable."

"We did not know who she was!"

But Liam shrugs. Above me, Damian lowers his head, gently

pressing his muzzle against my cheek. He's worried about me. I raise my hand to lose my fingers through his fur. I'm so tired, I feel like I could fall asleep here on the ground. I hear a car coming and steps rushing towards us.

"Nora!"

It's Tonia. She approaches me and covers me with a large coat. Finally, someone bothered about me being naked. Damian has been covering most of me with his body, but still. He gets up, and I can hear him changing back, too. When I look up, Damian already and only has a pair of jeans on despite the cold. I can see his bare torso; I never noticed how muscular he is. I look away, though I'm probably too cold to blush any more.

Suddenly, I feel strong arms pulling me up, and Damian taking me off the ground. It's a bit embarrassing to be carried like a princess against his chest when I'm wearing nothing but a coat! And in the middle of a territory dispute, to boot. I'm soaked, tired, and I probably stink more than I can smell.

"Can't we just go home already?" I ask.

Liam turns to me with a pout, visibly annoyed that I'm ruining his fun. Damian doesn't care, though. He heads back to the car without a glance at the dozen hostile wolves behind him, Tonia behind us.

"What about Alec?" I ask.

"Bobo got him, don't worry."

Behind us, I hear Liam growling. He and the Sea Moon Wolves haven't moved. We reach the car, Damian sits at the back, with me on his lap.

"Liam!"

The youngest Black brother can't disobey, but he still gives a glare to the guy.

"Next time, guys."

He dashes to join us and finally sits in the car while Tonia drives away. I notice a few wolves outside that must have come with them, but they all quickly disperse as soon as the car starts. I try looking for the creamy white wolf from earlier, but I don't recognize anyone.

"What about Nathaniel?" I ask.

"He stayed behind to take care of things with the Jade Moon Clan."

I nod. Why didn't that female werewolf want Nathaniel to know about her presence? I assumed she was from the Blood Moon Clan, but it seems more complicated than that. How could that woman mind-link with me? She is not from the Jade Moon Clan, and aside from that, only relatives or bonded mates can do such a thing!

Unlike I thought, I couldn't fall asleep in the car. I don't know what kept me awake, despite the long trip and my exhaustion. For a while, I just stared at Liam's silhouette against the window and the city's nightlife behind him. Tonia put the heater on, and I'm starting to feel better already. She has some jazz music playing on the radio, not too loud, though. Sitting on Damian's lap, I feel his hands gently brushing my hair. Gosh, I always feel so safe whenever I am in his embrace. I'm cold, soaked, and exhausted, yet I am content being there. What happened in just a few hours seems crazy.

"You okay?" Asks Damian

"Just a bit tired... What about Alec?"

"We caught him. Boyan is taking him to one of our houses as we speak."

"Are we heading there?"

I want to settle things with my brother now. After selling me, and trying to kill me twice, I think it is high time we have a little conversation. Tonia stops me in my reflections.

"No, we are not. We're going to the hospital. Nora, in case you haven't noticed, you are bleeding."

"Well, I know, but I figured I would just... heal."

"I meant you are *still* bleeding."

I realize Tonia's tone was a bit worrying for a reason. I check the cut on my thigh, and it is indeed still leaking a bit of fresh blood. And it stings, thanks to the seawater. It may be deep, but I thought my wolf would have taken care of that by now. Why am I not healing fast? Any werewolf is supposed to do that! That's part of the checklist: Shapeshifting, enhanced sense of smell, mind-linking, night vision, and healing fast! Why don't I?

I try to get to my wolf to explain this, without success. Meanwhile, Damian lifts a bit of the coat, too, checking my injury with a frown. I bite my lip. Okay, this deep cut is worrying. Liam is looking, also, a bit curious until realizing that this is still my bare leg, and thus, his brother is glaring at him. He quickly looks away, but I'm pretty sure he is blushing. Sorry, Liam.

"Why aren't you healing?" Asks Damian.

"I wish I knew... I thought I would heal like any werewolf now that my wolf is fully awake, but... I don't get it. Maybe it's the salt from the seawater?"

"You're not a bad spirit, Nora, salt doesn't affect werewolves..." sighs Liam.

"Maybe a Witch's curse, then?"

"You mean the ones that our father would be stupid enough to keep living in a city full of werewolves instead of exterminating them...?"

I feel Damian stiffen all of a sudden, but Liam doesn't notice it. I knew about their father having chased all vampires out of Silver City years ago. That's not a secret for anyone. He made sure it was... blatant. I don't think I have heard anything about witches, though. Is it the mention of their father that makes him react then...?

"Liam's right, I don't think we have any witches in the area, and anyway, I don't see why a witch would have anything against you. You were under the radar until a few days ago," says Tonia.

Well, I don't have any other ideas. I keep looking at my cut, disturbed, but Damian puts his hand on it, slowing the bleeding. I sigh and rest my head on his shoulder once again. He presses his lips against my forehead gently.

"It's okay, we're almost there, baby girl."

"Thanks, Tonia, but... I don't get it. Why don't I heal? There is already enough going on, with my brother and all the mystery surrounding my birth, and now this..."

Nobody answers, but I feel Damian tensing up. I should have known. If it appears that I am really unable to heal myself, my already very protective mate will probably not like it at all... We finally arrive at the hospital, but no VIP room this time. Damian carries me straight to the ER, and an old lady doctor comes to examine me. She is tall, skinny, with long white hair. She seems acquainted with Tonia, judging how they are openly conversing about my injuries and sharing her notes. Apparently, other than my apparent cuts, I have a broken rib and a few bruises. After a few stitches and the bandaging, I'm only left with some swelling and an ice pack. Liam gives me a wink. "Not bad for a first battle."

"Nana, any idea why Nora isn't able to heal herself?" Tonia asks the doctor.

Wait, what? Does this mean this woman is actually Bobo and Tonia's grandmother? She does look a bit like the siblings now that I think about it... She has the same chocolate-colored skin and Bobo's greenish eyes. Well, that would explain how Tonia knows so much medical stuff without being a medic herself.

"I don't know, sweetie. This is the first time I see such a thing. Well, you are healing a bit faster than a human, to be honest, but a regular werewolf would already be healed by now."

"Then what is it? Maybe a spell?"

The doctor rolls her eyes at Tonia.

"What's this idiotic idea? No witchcraft can prevent a werewolf from healing herself. Trust me, I know enough about black and white magic to know this has nothing to do with it."

I'm even more curious now. Bobo and Tonia's grandmother seems to be acquainted with magic, how cool is that? She smiles at me and shows my banded injury with a comforting smile.

"It's going to be fine. You just have to bear it the human way."

"I can do that. It's not like this is my first time..."

Liam smiles, but his brother is clearly not happy about it. Damian remained silent until the doctor came and was next to me for the whole examination. Now though, I think it might have been better for him to stay outside. He reacts so negatively each time I'm wounded...

We exchange a look, and he exits the room without a word. Tonia's grandma watches him go, but she clearly isn't affected by his Alpha aura.

She is not one of us, whispers my wolf.

Oh, that certainly explains it. I wonder how she got werewolves grandchildren then? After all, she still seems to know quite a lot about werewolf specifics.

"He probably just went to call Nate or Neal," explains Liam.

I nod and turn to Tonia and her grandmother.

"Then, can I go now, doctor? I have spent enough time in the hospital as it is, recently."

"Oh, you can call me Nana or Granny Adriana, sweetie. And yes, just make sure you take your medicine, and you're free to go. Rest well tonight, and make sure you eat enough, sweetie. Antonia, tell your brothers they have to come to see their old Nana sometime."

Granny Adriana gives us a smile and exits the room. Liam and I turn to Tonia with the same smirk.

"Antonia?" I tease.

"Oh, shut up, you two. I hate my first name," she grumbles.

About an hour later, I finally exit the hospital. It is dark outside, but Damian carries me straight to the car despite my protest. I want to see my brother, but the three of them are against it.

"You need to go home and rest baby girl, you heard Nana. Your brother can wait."

"Don't worry, Bobo and Nate are watching him. He's not going anywhere," says Liam.

Damian doesn't say a thing, but he clearly agrees with them. He's barely said a word since the hospital. I wonder what he is thinking. But to be honest, I'm too tired for any deep thinking right now.

Once we finally reach the apartment, Damian carries me all the way to my bathroom before exiting to take a call. I can finally take the hot shower I dreamed about on the road. It was high time; I really do stink after the battle and that short swim. Tonia comes in to help me wash my hair, as I'm too tired to stand after all that. I really have to work on improving my stamina.

When I'm done, I finally feel clean in my blue pajamas. I arrange my hair in a low bun for the night and prepare myself to sleep when Tonia comes back carrying a tray with a three-course meal on it. I frown.

"No, don't you say you don't want it," warns Tonia. "If you do, I can call the Boss and have him spoon feed you like a baby."

I can't really say anything after that. Tonia puts it in front of me on the bed. Well, it does look good. Vol Au vent, pesto pasta, and even an almond cake for dessert. I bet all of this came straight from one of Nathaniel's restaurants.

I start eating under Tonia's close surveillance. We don't really talk since she is busy texting someone, and I'm lost in my own thinking. I haven't forgotten about the she-wolf that helped me during my fight and pulled me out of the water. Seeing how she called him "Nate," I guess she is related to the second brother somehow. But then why wouldn't she want him to know she was there? He didn't seem to have anything to say when she was with us at the Jade Moon territory... I wish I knew her human form or saw her Clan marking. She said we would meet again soon, but how? I don't even know her name!

"Nora?"

Damian came back to the room, followed by Liam. Apparently, I'm not the only one that showered, the youngest brother also smells like soap. I'm not done eating, so he sits in front of me on the bed while Liam walks to the window, standing next to Tonia with his arms crossed.

Damian's silver eyes are glowing scarily, and I'm instantly worried. Did something bad happen?

"What is it?"

"Why does Bobo say that your brother is the guy that attacked you?"

Oh, crap.

I forgot about that. I didn't even think Bobo would be able to identify him, considering how it was raining that day. Still, he did chase after Alec and hurt him. He must have identified him then, and that also explains how he recognized his scent as quickly as I did earlier today. I bite my lip. Damian looks really angry, and Tonia is staring at me with wide eyes, too. I put my fork down. How do I handle this now?

"Nora!"

"Don't yell at me! Yes, Alec is the one that tried to kill me."

They all look at me, shocked.

"I thought that Marcus guy was the one!" Yells Tonia.

"No, the guy you saw that night in the alley was Alec."

"I thought you only wanted to find your brother to ask him about your birth thing?" Says Liam.

"Yes, that, too, but Alec hates me, and yes, he tried to kill me."

Twice, actually, but they don't need to know that. Gosh, Damian looks furious. I feel bad for not telling them the truth earlier, but I'm a hundred percent sure he would have killed him on the spot if he knew everything.

"I knew something was odd about your brother," exclaims Liam. "When we were at the Jade Moon Clan that day, your former Alpha and that weakling girl did mention he had been wronging you, and you said he lied, too."

"No wonder he wanted to avoid us so badly now," says Tonia.

The only one that remains silent is Damian, despite his fuming eyes on me. I try to reach for his hand, but he gets up. Both of his fists are clenched.

"Damian, say something, please."

"Why didn't you tell me?"

"Because I didn't want you to get mad at him."

"Really, Nora?"

Okay, I do realize it is way too late now. Damian is obviously furious and mad at me, also. I sigh, trying to find my words.

"Damian, I need to solve things with my brother. Yes, Alec hates me, and he tried to kill me. But that's my problem, okay? I need to talk to him and solve things with him. I can't do that if you kill him first!"

"I want to kill him, Nora!" He yells. "I don't give a damn about him being your brother! I'll slaughter anyone who touches you, and he fucking tried to kill you! You would be dead if it wasn't for Tonia and Boyan! You lost your voice, and you were in a coma for days! How do you think I felt after I finally found you, and yet I had to watch you while you were unconscious in a hospital bed day after day!"

"I am mad, too! How do you think I feel after my own brother tried to strangle me? Damian, for the last ten years, there wasn't a single day Alec was nice to me! He was the worst, but he is still my only blood relative left, and I need to know why he is like this! I'm not protecting him; I just want to face him myself! Damian, I need you to let me do this!"

He stays silent, and I can tell he is seriously thinking right now. Gosh, why do we always end up yelling somehow? I'm even more exhausted now. And in front of Liam and Tonia, too, though they both seem concerned.

I get up and grab Damian's arm. He ignores me, but I still hold his hand and look at him.

"Damian, please. Alec's attitude changed after my parents' death, and I need to know why. He is the only one that can help me know why my birth was kept a secret. After I talk things through with him, I promise he will be out of my life."

He stays silent for a while, then turns to me, with his ice-cold eyes.

"That's why you didn't want me to hurt him."

"Yes. You promised me, Damian."

"That was before I knew he tried to kill you!"

"Damian!"

He can't go back on his promise now! We both glare at each other for a long time. I'm not going to let him touch Alec. Then, I see his eyes shift slightly, and he points at my scar.

"Is he the one who did this?"

"What? No, Alec has nothing to do with my scar, I swear."

I'm telling the truth this time, and I really hope he will believe me. He keeps staring at my scar, and I hate it. He usually ignores it, so why is he curious about it now? I tighten my grip on his hand, seeing how conflicted he is. Can't he stay here with me? I just want to go to bed, sleep in his embrace, and forget about all this for a few hours. But the anger in his eyes is not reducing in the slightest. I bite my lip.

"Damian, please. You promised me you won't hurt him."

He looks at me again, and all of a sudden, leans in to kiss my forehead, before storming out. I stay there, completely blank. Where did he go now? I turn to the others, but a long silence follows for a while.

"Don't worry," says Liam, "my brother never breaks a promise."

I wouldn't be so sure about that. Damian looked really, really angry. What do I do? I turn to Tonia, worried. What if he really kills Alec? I need him to talk! After staring for a while, she rolls her eyes and takes out her phone.

"All right, I'll call Neal. But I can't guarantee the Boss will listen, Nora."

I nod, biting my lip anxiously. It's better than doing nothing... I haven't met Neal yet, but seeing how mad he was just now, I doubt even Nathaniel will be able to stop him if he really decided to kill Alec. I just need to talk to my brother. Why do I have to worry that Damian will actually slice him or something?

Tonia exits the room to call her brother, and I sit back on the bed, exhausted by all this tension. Liam comes to sit with me, pushing the tray towards me so I can finish eating.

"Your brother is a real piece of shit."

"He wasn't always like that... When we were kids, he was nice to me. My mother never really liked me, but Alec and my dad did. He changed when she died."

"Do you have any idea why?"

I shake my head and finish eating my pasta while thinking. Why, indeed? How did my brother come to hate me overnight?

"He said something like it's my fault we are orphans."

"About your parents' death? You said it's just your mom that went nuts. How could it be your fault? The police report Nate found was the same."

I sigh. I really don't understand either. I was there when our parents died, and that was the most horrifying thing I ever saw. Alec was there, too, we both saw the same thing. So why does it feel like I'm the one missing a piece of the puzzle?

Liam takes a bit of my cake, frowning. He looks a lot like Damian when he does that. The three brothers really look a lot like each other despite their different personalities. Nathaniel is the only one who is blonde with blue eyes, and he's about the same size as Damian. Liam's eyes are a mix of blue and grey, and since he is younger, he still has room to grow, but I bet he can get taller than them in the future.

He notices I'm observing him and frowns again.

"What? Is it because I took your cake?"

I laugh a bit and shake my head. Liam may be the same age as me, but he can be really childish sometimes.

"No, I was just thinking. You guys are close."

He shrugs. "We had to. Our father was... He never gave a damn about us. He was obsessed with his Alpha stuff and never cared about his family. The only one he ever cared about was his mate, our mom, but he changed a lot after suddenly becoming the Alpha. He became more and more of an asshole... And our mom was sick for as long as I remember, but she loved us. She was the best."

Looks like Liam was really fond of their mother... I wonder what she looked like. Did they take after her? As for me, I didn't resemble my mother, nor did I ever feel close to her... She clearly always preferred Alec, but she wasn't cold to me either. Until... Liam takes a new piece of the cake and keeps talking while eating.

"We took it hard when she died... But the worst was our father; he got even more violent. Her death really made him snap."

I frown and get closer. I recognize that dark look in Liam's eyes. I know it all too well. Could it be...?

"He beat you?" I ask softly

He nods, avoiding my eyes. "He beat anyone... any reason was good. Damian and Nate took most of the hits. They always protected me because I was younger. That just made our father even madder. Life with our father was hell. Damian stood up to him every day, despite still being a teen, and even his Beta couldn't stand him. He fought with anyone like some mad dog. He always was crazy about gaining more territory, more power, killing vampires, fighting other clans..."

I didn't know that. Back when I was young, the former Blood Moon Alpha was famous for being ruthless and extremely violent. Still, I never imagined he was even abusing his own children. I remember how people respected him a lot for chasing the vampires out of Silver City, years ago. But I guess none of them knew what kind of man he really was... No wonder Damian got as strong and fierce as he is today if he had to face this kind of monster since they were young. Liam growls and turns his head to me with a frown.

"Honestly, Nora, if your brother is the same kind of bastard as my father was..." He sighs and shakes his head with a disgusted face.

I know. I think I finally understand Damian's anger towards my brother. Moreover, he experienced all of my hardships through our bond, too... He can't ignore it like that. Who would have thought our families had so many similarities?

I finish eating with Liam's help. Apparently, he and Tonia will sleep here tonight. I wonder if Bobo is guarding my brother with Nathaniel. It's a bit weird to not see that big brown wolf following me everywhere tonight. I guess I got used to his presence.

Despite my exhaustion, I have a troubled sleep that night. I have nightmares about drowning, Alec hitting me, and a young black-haired boy crying. Images of everything that happened today keep coming, more vivid and intense. When I wake up in a cold sweat, I am trembling and feeling more tired than I was before going to sleep. It is about five in the morning and still dark outside.

I know I won't be able to go back to sleep. I used to have such nights back in the basement, it's nothing new to me. Instead, I get up and head for my bathroom. I check my injuries while dressing up. Thank Moon Goddess, it does look a lot better than yesterday. I give up and leave my hair as it is after an attempt to brush it and put on a hoodie, as I'm still feeling chilly. Fully awake, I head to the kitchen as silently as possible. However, I didn't expect to find Damian there.

His dark silhouette is standing still, facing the large window with a cup of what smells like dark coffee in hand. He changed clothes and even shaved. Seeing me enter, he frowns and walks up to me.

"Nora? Why are you up at this hour?"

"I could ask you the same thing. When did you come back?"

He sighs and puts his cup down to embrace me. Gosh, it's only been a few hours, and I already missed being in his arms... It seems like his anger has dissipated. The question is, how...?

"Half an hour ago. I didn't kill your brother. Neal called me on the way, convinced me not to. I went to the office to work instead."

So, he just went to work? In the middle of the night? I hope nobody was around to receive his anger on the way to his office... I need to thank Tonia's older brother later. I wonder what kind of Beta he is, but obviously, he knows how to handle Damian reasonably well.

"To work? You didn't sleep?" I ask.

"I did, for about three hours. I have a private loft above my office."

Of course, he does... I don't even want to try thinking about how rich he must be. The less I know, the better. For now, at least.

He puts his hand on my cheek, examining me despite the darkness. I must look tired. It's a bit embarrassing.

"How are you?"

"I'm okay. I just couldn't sleep..."

All of a sudden, he lifts me up to have me sit on the kitchen counter, facing him. He is still taller than me, so I have to look up. Standing so close to each other like this, with him between my legs, is kind of embarrassing. But he doesn't seem to care. Instead, he keeps his hands on my waist and lands a soft kiss on my forehead. Then, he retreats to look at me in the eye with a stern expression.

"Are you worried? About facing your brother?"

I just nod, biting my lip anxiously. I have to admit I am. It's not like we will be thrilled to see each other... And we will have to discuss some really, really painful memories.

"I hope I will get the answers I'm looking for. It kills me to be in the dark, not knowing why Alec resents me so much, why he hated me all this time...Why he hurt me so. I just... I don't know how I can find the strength to face him after everything that happened."

Damian gently brushes my hair and leans to gently kiss my neck. I shiver slightly, but his lips keep going, flying like butterflies from my neck to my jawline, to my cheek, before he finally takes my lips for a sweet, long kiss. I answer his kiss, and a small fire ignites inside. Whenever Damian touches me, it's like the most natural thing in the world. All of my anxiety goes away, replaced by this instinctive desire for my mate. Yet, I don't want to let go of my human self, a bit shy and clumsy. I place my hands around his neck, looking to gather some self-confidence I don't have. It's like Damian's strength is getting to me, and when our lips eventually part, I feel a lot better already.

He looks into my eyes and whispers, "Nora, I won't let him do anything to you anymore. Don't worry. I swear, I won't let anyone touch you, hurt you, ever again."

I smile at him and put my hand on his cheek. I love this man.

I don't know when I realized it, and I don't really care. I just know I do. The way he is so dangerous, yet so protective of those who matter to him. The way his silver eyes look at me as if he could capture me. His warmth, the feeling of his skin against mine, and how he kisses me, forceful yet so tender. It feels so dangerous, so wild, yet so right. It's like I'm a different person, a version of myself I had yet to reveal. Being with Damian can be scary at times, but I still find myself wanting more.

Like this, when I lean to kiss him, despite blushing like crazy. It's thrilling, and I feel a bit proud, being able to show my feelings, too. He smiles softly, obviously pleased by my boldness. Then he takes his turn to kiss me again.

"Oh please, can't you guys get a room?"

I jump, surprised by Liam's voice. Why can't anyone sleep at this hour! He is looking at us with a disgusted face, with only his pants on and his hair all messy. Damian sighs and retreats a bit, leaving his hands around me but still watching his brother's moves. Actually, Liam ignores us and walks to the fridge, opening it with a grumpy face on, scratching his bare stomach. He frowns and turns to me.

"Nora, you guys don't have anything ready to eat here? I'm starving!"

Now that I think about it, I didn't see him have dinner yesterday, aside from my almond cake. I don't know who usually cooks for him, considering that he lives downstairs, but Liam is obviously clueless while looking at the fridge's content. Damian sighs and lets me get down of the counter.

"I'll make something if you can wait a bit."

"Yes!"

He makes a winning gesture with his fist, and I just roll my eyes. I guess it's okay to cook breakfast at five in the morning if everyone is up anyway... Tonia is still sleeping, but she will probably get up sometime soon, too, per usual.

Turns out I was right. An hour later, the four of us are sitting around the table, having breakfast while it's still totally dark outside. Tonia turns to Liam as I'm serving orange juice. "What about the school, kid?"

Liam rolls his eyes and is about to say something, but then his eyes cross those of his brother. In a split second, Liam's attitude changes and he sighs. "I... I'm going. After breakfast."

I can't help but smile. Apparently, Liam can be cheeky with others, but he won't risk it in front of his older brothers... I already noticed it before with Nathaniel. He sighs, but Damian is just quietly enjoying his coffee. Now, Tonia is smirking while Liam is frowning at his breakfast.

I start drinking tea, absorbed by the first rays of sunlight, throwing orange and pink shades into the sky outside. Now that I think of it, we are on the 1st of December. It's already been over two months since I met Damian, his brothers, and the siblings. My life really did change a lot in just a few weeks. So much, it's almost unbelievable. I still feel like I could wake up at any moment, finding myself back in the basement and realizing this was all just a dream.

"What are you thinking about?"

Damian caught me daydreaming, and I blush a bit.

"Not much... When are we going?"

"It's up to you, princess!"

I turn around. Nathaniel just arrived, looking very proper as usual. He walks up to us and helps himself with the coffee. Judging from the large cup, he probably didn't get much sleep either.

"What about Alec?" I ask.

I was almost prepared to see him followed by my brother, maybe even Bobo, but he came alone. Now that I think about it, I didn't even see them catching Alec

"It's okay. Your brother is under tight surveillance and all ears for your questions."

I frown. I don't like the way he said this. He might be smiling, but I still don't really believe it, not with his choice of words. I turn to Damian, hoping he did respect his promise, but he is eating his breakfast silently. I put my cup back and get up to face Nathaniel.

"Okay, let's go see him now, then."

Nathaniel nods.

About twenty minutes later, the four of us are in the familiar white car that I assume to be Nathaniel's as he is driving instead of Tonia. Liam stayed home to finish his breakfast before going to school. While in the car, I feel the anxiousness rise again. I turn to Damian, but he is just looking at his phone, his hand on mine. It seems like he is reading emails, probably working.

I try thinking about something else instead. Looking at Nathaniel in the mirror, I suddenly remember the she-wolf from yesterday. She mentioned him specifically, even referring to him as "Nate." Aside from Liam, no one seems to call him that. Now that I'm reminiscing about her... something does feel familiar. No, it smells familiar! It's her smell, I'm sure of it. Why can I smell it all over Nathaniel's car...?

It's a bit disturbing, now that I'm focusing on it. It's definitely that she-wolf smell... Doesn't that mean she comes in here often? But if she's close to Nathaniel, why would she hide from him that she intervened last night to save me...? What could be between those two?

Moreover, her relationship with Nathaniel aside, I still have to understand how she could mind-link with me. That was my first time experiencing it for real, and it felt so natural, so clear. I wish I could hear her voice again. She said she would find me. How? She sounded confident, but I'm guarded non-stop by either Damian and his brothers or Tonia and Bobo. Is she okay contacting me with them around? Will she?

While I'm lost in my thoughts, the car finally stops in front of a large, modern-looking company building. We have arrived. For some reason, I was expecting something more secluded, maybe a warehouse, like in Tonia's action movies.

Damian opens the door for me and takes my hand to guide me in the building. There's even a middle-aged doorman, and he politely inclines when the brothers walk in. He's not a werewolf though, is he? The building looks pretty standard, against all my expectations. We walk into a lobby, and two ladies welcome us from behind the reception desk. Gosh, this is a bit intimidating... Isn't this an office building? I'm glad I dressed up a bit more than my usual hoodie. I'm wearing a white sweater and a pair of dark jeans, but I wish I had put heels on instead of my sneakers... Well, Tonia is wearing a jean ensemble and her usual sports bra, so I guess it's okay.

There are a lot of office workers despite the early hour, but nobody really pays attention to us. Damian leads us into an elevator. Some people that were queuing to get in immediately step aside to let us through. Why does everybody turn so silent as soon as they notice

Damian? It's like he's some mafia boss; we walk out of the elevator, and once again, a lot of people turn around or politely salute him wherever we go. It's a bit embarrassing. Nathaniel and Tonia don't say a thing, and Damian still hasn't let go of my hand, caressing it with his thumb.

"Is this your office building?" I finally ask.

"One of them," answers Nathaniel. "Damian and I work at the headquarters; this is just a secondary office. We have a dozen like this across the city."

I had no idea... I should really start learning more about the Black Brothers' businesses, I hate feeling so clueless like this. We are now on the eighteenth floor, which looks empty. It's frigid, with grey walls, empty open spaces, and almost no decorations. Nathaniel guides us through several corridors until we finally enter a large meeting room.

I gasp. It's reeking of blood here! I cover up my mouth, feeling immediately disgusted by the smell. But I have more to be concerned about.

The room is almost empty, except for chairs. There are three people already present. A large and tall guy, the exact same skin tone as Tonia, is leaning against a wall, playing with a knife. His hair is completely shaved, he has a ring piercing on his eyebrow, and with his black suit, he could be the protagonist of any spy action movie. He salutes Damian as soon as we enter the room. "Hello, Boss."

Is that Neal? He looks a lot like Tonia and older. Plus, Bobo is there, too, in his wolf form as always, sitting in the corner of the room. He sees us come in but doesn't move. Neal walks up to us, but I don't care.

All I can see is Alec, sat up in a chair in the middle of the room, looking like he just came back from hell.

I'm not exaggerating. My brother has a lot of blood on his face and his clothes. As I noticed back at the mall, he's a lot thinner than before. His upper lip and one of his eyebrows have significant cuts, still open and bleeding, and he has a black eye. His shirt is ripped open, and his chest shows contusions and large lacerations. He's a total wreck. They even actually put a large plastic cover under his chair so all the blood wouldn't stain the floor!

"You promised not to hurt him!" I yell, furious.

I want to run to Alec, check on him, but Damian holds me back. I glare at him, but he won't let go of my hand.

"Oh, Damian didn't," says Nathaniel.

I stop and turn to face him. The second brother is smiling at me with a look I don't like at all. He walks up in front, and he and Neal both raise hands.

"We did, princess. You can be mad at us, but we didn't promise anything."

Who are they kidding? They just took advantage of my own words! I glare and even growl at both of them, furious, but they obviously don't care. Neal has a blank expression, and Nathaniel keeps his annoying smile on. They act like this is some funny joke, but I'm miles from being entertained right now!

"Stop laughing! I didn't want you to hurt him!"

Neal rolls his eyes. "Oh, please. We were already nice, considering what he did to you and how much he struggled. If it wasn't for you, this would be settled already."

I know what he means by "settled," but I'm not scared by their words. I'm too mad right now. Are they telling me they didn't go all the way to kill Alec for my sake? How is that supposed to be a proper explanation for his current state? Before I can add a thing, a laugh starts from behind them.

All eyes turn to Alec. My brother is laughing like a mad man while looking at me. "There she is... My precious little sister! What now, huh, Nora? Don't you want to finish the job and kill me yourself? You must have wished for this all these years..."

Is that really my brother? I look at him, disgusted. He has that crazy look in his bloodshot eyes, in the way he stares at me that makes me really uncomfortable. But I can't step back now. I'm done being intimidated by Alec or his words.

"Enough with this, Alec. I never wanted you dead."

He scoffs and suddenly stops laughing. "Too bad. Because I want you dead."

Damian immediately starts growling loudly while heading towards him, looking furious. I try to hold him, but it's actually Neal that comes and stands between Alec and him. They struggle a few seconds, but with Neal and me holding him back, he eases up a little. Tonia is growling, too, less loudly, and Nathaniel is just staring at Alec like he's observing some curious science experiment subject. Bobo stood up, also, and starts walking in circles around Alec. I know he's ready to attack and kill him at any moment, though he doesn't look agitated at all.

With nobody actually stopping him, Alec keeps talking.

"Mom should have just killed you in the first place. Too bad, she missed!"

"Stop talking like this!" I shout back.

"Why? You don't like it? But it's the truth, isn't it?"

"No. Mom was sick, she..."

"You made her sick in the first place!" He suddenly yells.

I don't get it! What do I have to do with our mother's sickness and our parents' death? Why is it my fault? How can it be my fault? I was six years old! I remember way too vividly what happened, and I had nothing to do with it!

I remember it all too well. It was the end of November, ten years ago. Our mother had started acting strangely for months already. She had always been a very calm and discreet woman. I don't think we had many visitors, her whole life revolved around her father and us. She took care of the house, watched us, and didn't work. Dad was the one always away for work, for days sometimes. I suppose that had to do with the pack, though I don't really remember it.

Our mother never seemed unhappy, but she was clearly happier when Dad was home. I don't think that she didn't like us, but somehow, she was never a very loving and caring mother to me. It seemed more like a job, a mission she had been assigned on since we were born. Alec was the one always looking for mom's warmth. I was okay with her passive attitude. She never scolded us or got angry. All she wanted was for our dad to be with her, look at her. When he was, it was like her whole world illuminated. The entire house was much happier then.

She was a pretty woman, with her long brown hair and dark eyes, but she was like a lifeless doll unless our dad was here. She would always make herself very pretty and tell us to behave when he came back. Those were the best days for everyone, as dad was home, and mom was nice and happy. As time passed, it somehow got worse.

She kept ignoring Alec and me, and always looked for my dad. Mother paid less and less attention to us, as she wondered how to look prettier for him. I remember her spending most days in front of her mirror, talking to herself. She couldn't stand him being away.

Sometimes, when he was away for work, she sat and blankly looked outside the window for hours, not hearing a thing around her. She could get confused about what time it was, or the date of the day. She asked where our father was a hundred times a day. She only ever talked about him. As children, it was complicated to understand what was going on, but Alec and I somehow got used to it. We spoke to her when we felt she needed it, or we didn't. I was just a child then. I had no idea how bad it could go.

On that day, it snowed for the first time of the year, so I got home all happy. I loved the snow because the snow kept my dad home. I don't remember where I was before that. I think I was with a friend... I can't really remember. I just remember how I played in the snow on the way home, jumping around and leaving my little boot footprints on the white coating of powder.

As I walked closer to our house, I started hearing terrible screams. I recognized my mother's voice right away and started running. I had no idea what was going on; I was just worried about my mother. I pushed our front door and followed where the screams came from, completely panicked. When I entered the room, my parents were there, loudly fighting and struggling. Mom, her hair all over the place, had a large kitchen knife in her hands and kept trying to stab my father with it. Dad was holding her wrists, yelling at her to calm down. Alec was there too, crying, begging her to stop. It was the most terrifying thing ever. I had no idea what was going on. Dad was yelling. Mom was screaming, tears running down her face. She looked crazy and... desperate.

I wanted to run away, but I was so scared something wrong would happen to my dad. I walked towards them. I didn't even make it all the way. A slashing sound and blood covered my favorite white coat. I saw my father's chest cut open, and his eyes wide open in surprise. His knees gave away, and he fell on his side, right next to me. I remember how my eyes slowly turned down to him. He was looking right at me.

He muttered my name very slowly. As if he had just realized I was standing there. For a second, the scene froze. My mother's yelling stopped, and she looked at me in shock. I thought it would end, that she would realize what she had done.

The next second, a silver flash, and the left side of my face became horribly painful. My vision went completely red. I saw my mother branding the knife one more time. I am going to die, I thought.

I was pinned to the ground. My head hit hard against the floor. A dark silhouette had come over me at the last second. I cried from the pain, but the fear was even worse. The thing covering me wasn't moving. I couldn't see a thing. I could only listen to my dad's erratic breathing next to my ear. Mom's screams started again, and more slashing sounds followed. His body twitched over and over again.

I was so scared. The side of my face hurt, and I could hear terrifying sounds, yet I was blind. My mother kept screaming. Alec kept crying. It seemed to last for hours. I heard my father's breathing stop right before I fainted.

I take a deep breath.

"When I came back to my senses, mother had stabbed herself, too," I say. "The knife was still there, right in the middle of her chest, and you were crying, Alec. Dad's body was still on me, and I struggled to get up. I really remember it. We spent a long time there, both crying in silence. When you got up and left, without saying a thing, I just followed you. That's how we ended up in the streets, and Vincent found us a few days later."

"Oh, Moon Goddess, Nora... And you were just a kid..." Mutters Tonia.

They are all looking at me with wide-open, shocked eyes. I can't blame them. It's my first time telling this story out loud, and it's horrible for me, too. I really didn't want to reminisce, but it's time to clear this up with Alec.

Damian's hand is still firmly holding mine, thank Moon Goddess, because I'm shaking. All those emotions are overwhelming me, and my wolf is quietly whimpering, too. My parents' death is like a big black hole in my heart; there is no way I can talk about it calmly.

Alec stares at me with eyes of contempt, not moved in the slightest.

"Sorry, was I supposed to cry?"

"You can say what you want, Alec, but I did not kill our parents," I retort with a hoarse voice.

"Really? You think that's it? You're so clueless, it's pathetic, Nora."

"What?"

I want to believe he is the one who is acting crazy and making no sense, but for a second, he looks so composed and sure of himself that I can't help but wonder. Is it really possible? Something I possibly missed in that memory? Something that only Alec? It can't be. I saw it with my own eyes, and I'm a hundred percent sure of this memory.

Alec laughs at my confused expression. "Oh, you can stop thinking, Nora. You have no idea, do you? You're so pathetic... You think you're a victim, that you couldn't have done anything wrong? But guess what, sis. You didn't have to do anything! You did anyway!"

He's crazy. His sentences make no sense. Why do I have to listen to all this? I shake my head. "Enough, Alec!"

"You were freaking born! Here's what you did wrong!" He yells.

What? What is this now? This makes no sense... While I'm lost by my brother's words, Tonia suddenly walks up to him and slaps Alec with all her strength. She looks furious.

"I'm done with your stupid word games! Spill it now, you damn junkie, or I swear I'm finishing you myself!"

"I said it! If she wasn't born, my family would have been perfectly fine!"

"What do you mean?" Asks Nathaniel, getting impatient too.

Alec spits a bit of blood to the ground, probably because of Tonia's hit. She growls and steps back to let him talk. Alec stares at Nathaniel then Tonia before his glare comes back to Damian and me.

"Mom wasn't sick," he says, "she was just in love. She had loved our father for many years since they were kids. They were from the same Clan, and they grew up together. The only one mom ever loved was him, but they weren't fated mates. So, even if she tried, for years, our father ignored her. He believed he might find his mate someday..."

His eyes shift from me to Damian with a smirk. Damian growls again, but I put my hand on his chest to have him wait. Alec annoys me, too, but I want to hear it. Damian's hand covers mine and presses it gently. His growling gets a little softer, but he still glares at my brother.

"As years passed, it became clear neither of them found their mates, so he eventually agreed to start dating mom. A few months later, she got pregnant with me, and they got married. Can you imagine how happy she was? The love of her life finally marrying her, letting her have his children!"

I don't like how he makes it sounds...

"Father was one of the Clan's hunters. He wasn't very good at it, to be honest, and our grounds weren't the best either. Father wandered further and further into the North, apparently to patrol. Every time he was away, Mom disliked it, as you remember. Yet there was another reason. As our dad went away, she started to wonder. What if he was still searching for his fated mate?"

Insecurity? Is that what it was? But our father never found another woman...

"Yet, father always came back home, and every time, Mom's worries disappeared just as easily. For three years, she was all right. She just missed him while he was hunting. She soon forgot about her doubts, because no matter what, dad always came back and eased her. One night, while he had been gone for days, Mom was awakened by a baby's cries. That's how you came into our lives, Nora. A newborn baby, crying on our doorstep."

Wait, what? It can't be. They told me... I mean, I was sure I was born from Mom! And plus, I resemble my father! That's when I suddenly understand. Oh, Moon Goddess, no, no, no...

Seeing the expression on my face, Alec smirks.

"Do you start to understand, Nora? Mother took you in. After all, you were just a newborn baby, and your parents were nowhere to be found. When dad came home, he agreed with it right away! How funny, huh? Mom had no idea back then. She started taking care of you, too, as her own daughter. After all, Dad loved you, didn't he? Do you start to understand, Nora? What sort of bastard our father was?"

I shake my head. No, I don't want to hear it. My dad didn't do that. Alec sighs and smiles.

"So, years passed! Mom was fine, letting you believe you were her daughter since it made our father happy that way. Yet she slowly started to doubt, watching you grow. Because somehow, you looked like me, you looked like Dad. How amazing is that? Whenever dad was away, our clueless, stupid mother was left with the two of us and her doubts. Despite our three years difference, it started to show, Nora. Our nose, like Dad's. Our curly black hair. Even our voices. All those little, but intriguing similarities. Can you imagine how much Mom started to think and wonder? What if? What if you really were our Dad's daughter?"

Tears silently start running down my face. I wish he was lying. I hope this was all a made-up story, something twisted that Alec invented to hurt me. Yet why does it feel like this is the truth? The last, scary piece of the puzzle.

"Years and years to wonder, Nora. She never dared to ask. If she was wrong, Dad might get angry and leave her. That thought alone kept her silent for almost seven freaking years. Can you imagine what it does to the mind, Nora? All this time, every single minute, wondering if you are raising your husband's child, yet knowing it's not yours? But she loved him. Oh, Moon Goddess, she loved him so much she kept her doubts to herself for so long. Until that day."

That fateful day. And all this time I thought my mother just had gone crazy all of a sudden... I had no idea she had to keep it bottled for so many years. How did she feel every time she looked at me? Did she despair inside, yet hide it? She never said a thing...

Alec closes his eyes, and I suddenly see a tear among the blood on his face.

"One day, she finally asked him, Nora, she did. I was upstairs. I heard them yelling... When I came down, Mom was... she was crying. She kept asking him how he could do this? Have a child with someone else and leave another woman's baby on her doorstep? He didn't say a thing all these years, keeping the lie alive! But you know the worst, Nora?"

This time, we are both crying. Tears flow, and I can't stop. Alec doesn't care, he keeps talking, half smiling, half crying. He looks crazy again, and his tone keeps changing. Yet this time, no one is stopping him. We are all listening, stunned by the truth unveiled.

"He didn't even do it for her! It's not because he wanted to keep his marriage! Not even because he was afraid of leaving her, or because he wanted to stay with his family. He lied for you, Nora, all for you. He wanted his daughter to have a normal family, to be able to grow up with a mother and a father. With a Clan to protect her. All his lies, all he did, he did it for you!"

I'm crying desperately, shaking my head. I can't hear it. I can't believe it.

"You did it! Because of you, my father became this man! He drove my mother mad, and he lied to us! Just because of you, Nora! Because of you!" Yells Alec.

I can't hear him. I'm crying and sobbing hard; I don't want to listen to this. My head is spinning. I want to leave this room; I want to forget this. Little black dots cover my vision. I hear Damian's voice, but I don't understand. Strong arms hold me, and I fight the dizziness to stay awake. I blink several times, trying to breathe to calm down. I feel a hand on my back, patting me. Tonia's voice reaches my ears.

"That's it, baby girl, breathe, slowly. Calm down, it's okay. It's okay."

"Nora, Nora..."

I hear Damian repeating my name, and I feel his arms around me. I'm in his arms again, but I still feel colder than ever. I close my eyes a bit to rest against his chest while trying to slow my breathing and stop crying.

"She has a bit of a fever, boss, probably from last night... "

"Let's take her back."

"No."

I don't know where I found the strength to protest, but I open my eyes and clumsily try to stand up again. Damian helps me, and I can rest on him while regaining my composure as I can. I turn to Alec.

"What about my mother, then? My... birth-mother."

He shrugs. "How would I know? I figure the bitch is dead... How about you join her?"

Bobo and Neal both angrily growl as a warning. Damian turns to his Beta. "We're done with him."

"No, stop!" I yell.

After all this, Alec is a victim, too. What happened to our family was not his fault. He was just a kid, also, only ten! He loved our mother so much, and... after what happened, I can't blame him for hating dad and me. I know how awful he was to me, I didn't forget any of it, but... but I don't know what I'm feeling right now, I'm baffled. Too confused to make any right decision. I can't let Damian have him killed. I don't want to regret it later.

Alec laughs at me again with a smirk.

"What, you want to save me, Nora? Play the nice sister? The pitiful one? When are you going to get it? I hate you! And I don't regret a thing I did to you! Every single time I hit you was fucking worth it! I wish I had killed you that night!"

All of a sudden, I lose balance and see Damian rush towards Alec. He's way too fast. Bobo jumps to stop him, but Damian punches him away like a sandbag. Neal steps in a second later, but Damian runs into him with full force. The Beta is projected against the wall.

Damian shapeshifts into a black wolf, his fangs ready to take my brother's throat. I scream.

He's about to kill Alec. For a split second, I see my brother dead. The black wolf rushes towards my brother, and it takes me a couple of seconds to realize there are no two black wolves. I didn't even see Nathaniel jump in. Everything happens so fast.

As soon as he realizes it's his brother, Damian steps back, growling furiously. Yet Nathaniel keeps standing in front of Alec, his pale blue eyes fixated on Damian. The two wolves growl and glare at each other, and for a while, I'm terrified they'll fight.

"Don't worry," says Tonia. "the Boss would never attack one of his brothers. Nathaniel is convincing him to let your brother live."

I nod, fighting the dizziness while Bobo and Neal both get back up. Bobo comes to my side to support me, while Neal walks to his Alpha, probably arguing with him, too. I wish I could hear it. Damian won't stop growling.

After what seems like an eternity to me, Damian turns back to me and shapeshifts swiftly. He only puts his pants back on while I'm shyly looking away. Nathaniel probably shifted back, too, because I can hear his voice.

"Let me handle him, Nora," he says. "Don't worry, I promise we won't hurt him anymore."

When I look, he is putting tape on Alec's mouth to shut him up. I don't know how I feel about this. I want to make sure Nathaniel's not tricking me again, but he speaks before I get to it, guessing my thoughts.

"Don't worry, I'm serious. I will have him put up for a psychological evaluation and rehab, okay? We will keep him under surveillance at the hospital."

I don't really get how they are going to take him to the hospital after they did this to him themselves, but I don't care anymore at this point. I'm still way too shocked by his earlier revelations. I'm still teary and tired. Just when I was about to try and get up again, Damian walks up to me and takes me outside, carrying me away from the scene. Behind us, Tonia and Bobo are ready to follow, but Damian growls.

"Leave us alone."

Tonia frowns, but we are already at the elevator. Damian steps in and turns around. I hear him pushing one of the buttons, and the door closes. He's still carrying me, my head against his shoulder when he softly whispers. "It's okay, Nora."

Just as he says these words, something I was holding up until now suddenly breaks loose. I start sobbing loudly against his neck. I can't stop it. My arms around Damian's neck, I cry like a little girl while he holds me tightly against him. It's unstoppable. I feel so weak, so overtaken by everything I just heard. I can't deal with all those emotions at once. I feel so stupid! All these years, I had no idea what had happened between our parents. How could I be so clueless and naive!

I keep crying, unable to bear it any other way. Damian is walking again, but I have no idea where he is taking me. I just want to exult my pain somehow and keep crying.

At some point, he sits down. His hands move, one to caress my hair, holding my neck against him, the other around my waist. I feel his lips pressed against my temple as he tries to help me calm down.

"It wasn't your fault, Nora. Don't cry..."

I can't. Tears flow, and my heart tightens painfully. My family was destroyed from within, and I was the cause of it. I can't forgive myself for being ignorant all these years. I was the little seed that implanted the madness in our mother's mind. I can't even blame my father! What happened to my birth mother? Why didn't I grow up with her? If Dad had a lover, why did he stay with Alec's mother all these years without saying a thing? Did my biological mother die, as Alec said? I have more questions than I can handle, and so much grief, I can barely breathe.

Damian is whispering softly against my ear, trying to calm me down. I'm shaking in his arms, sobbing uncontrollably.

"You're okay, Nora. None of this is your fault. You didn't know. You were too young. It's okay, you're okay..."

He keeps caressing my hair and murmuring comforting words, leaning kisses on my head or temple from time to time. Despite all this, being in Damian's arms makes it all a little easier. He rubs my back, soothing me. After a while, I lean back a bit, still sitting on his lap but facing him. He brought us to what looks like an immaculate office, probably his. I look at him, still teary and probably looking really messy after all this crying.

"I... I can't believe it. My dad, he..."

"He probably did this to protect you, Nora. I don't know what happened to your birth mother, but he made sure to keep you with him, and he protected you until the end."

"I'm the reason he died! And mother, too! She went insane because of me! Because I existed!"

Damian shakes his head and puts his hand on my cheek, caressing me gently with his thumb, keeping me close to him. "No, Nora. Your parents had issues. Your father should have told the truth, and your mother probably had troubles before you came. Nora, you are not to blame. You were a baby, you had no idea."

"But Alec, he..."

"Your brother took his frustration out on you. He had no right to. Despite what happened, you were not responsible, Nora."

I have a hard time believing it. No matter what Damian says, everything happened because of me, because I was born from my dad's affair with another woman. How do I live with this? What do I do with it from now on? I never knew, but now...

Damian suddenly kisses me, taking me by surprise. His lips are gentle against mine yet passionate as usual. After a few seconds, I answer his kiss, carried by the movement. I don't want to fight it. I need his comforting presence; I need him. His warm hands on my skin, his fingers grabbing my hair. I love this feeling, this wave of heat coming from inside, like a low fire burning within. I grab some air and continue the kiss, my arms around his neck. Is this really okay? After all that happened, it seems crazy to be having a moment with him in this office. It's just the two of us, and everything is quiet. Behind Damian, this fantastic view of the city that makes it look like I'm in Heaven with him...

His lips get more passionate against mine, and I don't say no. Our breathing accelerates, and I feel hotter than before. I shiver, feeling his fingers on my skin. One of his hands is under my shirt, caressing my back and giving me delightful shivers. I gasp and hear him chuckle. Is he amused by my awkward reactions? I'm shy, I can't help it!

I try to kiss him a bit forcefully to make up for it, and I can tell Damian is smiling against my lips. His fingers clench tighter in my hair, and his other hand holds me closer to him until I'm actually sitting astride him. Our kiss gets more intense, and I hear our breath intertwine, echoing loudly in my ear. Our lips part and Damian aims for my neck with ruthless kisses. I bite my lip and find myself leaning on the side to offer him more of me. What's happening to me? I should be embarrassed, but my desire for more overtakes it all. My hands are on his back, caressing his neck and putting my fingers in his dark hair.

"Nora, Nora..."

His voice whispering my name is making me crazy. I seek his lips once again, and our kiss starts anew. His hands progress on my skin, caressing me gently. ...But suddenly, a cold shiver rises.

"...good girl, Nora. ...don't you play hard to get now."

I gasp and stop the kiss, panicked. Damian doesn't notice and keeps kissing me. His hands keep going, and I shiver all the more, but not from pleasure this time. I'm scared.

"Stop, Damian, stop!" I almost scream. I struggle, getting off his arms, stumbling, panicked. He looks at me, shocked by my reaction. He tries to hold me back, still confused, but that only scares me more. I fight him off, and when he finally releases me, I almost fall on all fours on the side.

"Nora? Nora, what's wrong?"

I get up and cross my arms in front of me, tearing up again. I can't believe it. I'm scared. I'm afraid of Damian's touch! He gets up and wants to come close, but I shake my head and retreat. Kissing was okay, but... He looks at me, confused. Oh gosh, I'm so, so sorry... I'm about to cry again. Damian stops and sighs.

"Nora, tell me what is it."

His imperious tone, as usual. But I can't even utter a word right now. I'm scared and horribly ashamed. How can I compare Marcus and Damian? Why now? I shiver and shake my head again, my arms around me like I'm shielding myself. He grabs his phone.

"Tonia, get here. Now."

He sounds so angry. I wish I could hide somewhere. It's my fault. This kiss was intense, perfect, and yet here I am, rejecting him like a crazy girl. As if I needed this now. I thought I needed Damian, so why do I find myself eluding him! I wish I could run back into his arms, ask for his warm kisses again, but I'm terrified. Those cold shivers won't leave me, and I don't think I can reject him twice.

He keeps glancing at me, silent. He must think I'm crazy, maybe he even regrets having such a troublesome mate! That's not the end of my dark thoughts, but thank Moon Goddess Tonia finally enters, followed closely by Bobo and Neal, the later back in his human form.

"Everything okay?" She asks, worried, as soon as she enters. She comes to me, taking my face into her hands. She frowns almost immediately. "Nora, you're burning! I knew you had a fever. Boss? We really need to take her home," she tells Damian.

"Take her back."

Damian is still staring at me, but he won't show his emotions. Tonia, understanding there is something wrong between the two of us, puts an arm around my shoulder and pushes me toward the exit of the office. "Okay, baby girl. Let's get you home now, you need some rest."

I nod weakly, still dizzy and a mess. Damian watches me exit the room, but I can't decipher his cold silver eyes. I feel numb while Tonia escorts me out of the office. As we pass the door, I hear Neal's voice. "Why the murderous look?"

The ding from the elevator makes me jump, and Tonia softly pushes me inside while my mind is still somewhere with Damian. I start sobbing again when the machine starts, and Tonia sighs. "Oh, Nora, you've had a tough day, huh? You have dark circles under your eyes, too..."

She rubs my back, trying to comfort me. Gosh, I just want to go home and curl up in my bed to cry once and for all...

Chapter 7

As predicted by Tonia, I had quite a fever that day. Too many emotions at once... I slept until the next morning, only waking up a few times to take medicine and eat. More than being sick, I was concerned about Damian not contacting me.

I did act as if I was rejecting him, but that wasn't my intention! I was just scared, that's all. I thought about it all night when I couldn't fall asleep. When morning came, I was well-rested and totally awake. Bobo had slept in my room, back to usual, but I was waiting for Tonia. When I heard her knock and enter, I was almost on the edge of the bed.

"Hi, baby girl! How are you feeling?"

"Much better! I think I'm healed. Tonia, what about Damian?"

"Easy, girl, I don't think you've healed already. Let me check your temperature first. Did you forget about your slow-healing thing?"

Is she eluding my questions right now? She sits next to me on the bed and puts a hand on my forehead, but I avoid her.

"Tonia!"

"Looks like you're okay... And yes, the Boss called me last night, to know how you were. I said you were resting, and that's it. I have to give him an update this morning."

"Is he angry?"

"Angry? At you? Of course not, Nora, he's just worried. Now, will you explain to me what happened yesterday? Without the unnecessary details, please."

She has her big sister tone, but that's not necessary. I need to talk to someone about this, and Tonia is the only one I can confide into here. Plus, she is a woman, and older than me, too. I don't know how much she will understand me, but I don't want to keep this bottled up. I sigh and start talking while nervously playing with my hair.

"Yesterday, Damian comforted me. We started kissing and... we got a bit passionate. I liked it, but when Damian started touching me, I...

I couldn't... I got petrified. I felt like I couldn't stand him touching me like that."

She listens to me with a frown, looking genuinely intrigued. After a while, she hesitates, then asks me a question on her own. "Nora, have you ever been... intimate with someone?"

I bite my lip. The only one who knows is Liam, and he doesn't seem like he told his brothers... How do I explain this? I barely avoided Alec being killed yesterday, and now this.

"Not willingly. But I... This guy, Marcus Sickels, he... touched me several times back when I was still with the Jade Moon Clan. Just before Alec tried to... to kill me, Marcus almost..."

"...Raped you." She whispers to finish my sentence.

"Damian knows," I immediately add. "He felt through our bond that someone had tried to force me, and I told him about that guy. But now, sometimes, when Damian touches me, I... I can't help but remember. I don't want to feel like this when I'm with Damian!"

"It's okay, Nora. I think you're experiencing some form of PTSD. It's not your fault, baby girl."

PTSD? A traumatism? It might be... But how do I get out of it? I don't want to feel like running away every time Damian touches me! I get up and head to my wardrobe, looking for something to put on.

"What are you doing, Nora? Come back to your bed!"

"No, I'm done resting. Let's go to the gym."

"Punching sandbags won't solve this! What you need is some time, Nora, and talking to the Boss."

I turn to face her, annoyed. "What do I tell Damian, Tonia? Sorry, some douchebag touched me before you did, so now you can't touch me because I'm traumatized? I hate this!"

She rolls her eyes. I know I'm stubborn, but I don't see anything better to do! I need to blow off some steam. But Tonia gets up and takes the workout clothes from me with a resolute look. She throws them on the floor and crosses her arms.

"Enough, Nora. I wasn't talking about speaking to him about this issue. More like getting to know the Boss and letting him know you better. The two of you might be close because of your bond as fated mates, but the truth is you two barely know each other! I say you need to talk to the Boss, get to know him for real. Maybe this way, you will learn to trust him, and that will help you overcome your fear."

She has a point... The attraction I feel to Damian from the start is probably mainly our bond's work, but what else is there? All I know of him is what I heard from others. I don't know his hobbies, his tastes, his habits, nothing. How can I even describe our relationship, then? And Damian, too, seems to know things I don't, but... when do we ever really interact? He is often busy and only calls me from time to time to inquire how I am.

It's not enough. I want him, but I want all of him. Tonia's probably right. If I get to know Damian better, I will probably be able to overcome my fear, and trust him, won't I?

"Bobo says you should have him take you on a date. Isn't your birthday tomorrow? Ask him then."

I almost forgot about my birthday! Do I want to celebrate it? After what I learned from Alec yesterday, I didn't think about such things, but now it seems a bit unreal. Is it even my real birth date? Dad probably knew... I hesitate a bit, biting my lip. It might be an idea. I look at Bobo, sitting next to my bed. Sometimes I really wish the big wolf would take human form and talk to me.

"You really think so?"

The brown wolf nods. I sigh and turn to Tonia. "Okay... Can I borrow your phone?"

After a few minutes, Damian finally answers the call. "Nora. How are you?"

Thank Moon Goddess, he doesn't sound angry or anything. Is he really over what happened yesterday? Gosh, I feel so awkward now...

"I'm fine. I feel much better. Damian, I... I'm sorry about yesterday."

I hear him sighing softly. "It's okay. I figured out what happened afterward. It's not the first time. I'm the one who should apologize, I got carried away."

"No! No, Damian, it's... it's just me."

It's my fault because I'm damaged. I'm scared, way too scared. And I still don't know how to overcome it, even for you. I nervously run my fingers through my hair, fidgeting.

"I just need a bit of time. I'm still... shy."

Shy, really? It's the understatement of the year! I'm literally terrified by the idea of a man touching me, yet that's all I can tell him? How pathetic, Nora. I need to get stronger. Didn't I promise myself to leave my past behind me? How will I if I let myself be restrained by such things? I need to work on it.

I need to tell him the truth, to Damian, at least.

"...Nora?"

"I'm still scared, Damian. I still think about what happened whenever someone touches me. I swear I don't want to, but it just... I don't know how to handle it for now."

A long silence follows. What is he thinking? Does he regret having such a complicated mate? Or will he search for Marcus once again? Alec only implied he had died, but that's still an unsolved issue for now. When are we going to find the truth? I did stab him, but what happened afterward? If he died, what about his body? I'm still feeling uneasy about this. And it's hindering my relationship with Damian.

"I told you, it's okay."

"But what if... It takes a long time for me to get better? I'm scared."

"Scared of what?"

Scared that you might not want me anymore at some point. It's already a miracle for Damian to be interested in me! I'm not pretty, or remarkable in any way. Compared to Damian, to his brothers, I'm utterly insignificant. And yet here I am, making him wait for me. I hate it, I wish things were different.

"Nora, don't cry."

I wonder how he knows. I'm tearing up a little bit. If only all these nightmares with my parents, Alec, the Jade Moon Clan, Marcus, all this, never happened... It would be so much easier. I could have lived a completely different life, where I might actually be deserving of Damian's affection. I wipe my tears away. Enough crying, already.

"I'm okay. Damian, can we see each other?"

"I can come tonight. After work."

"No, I meant like a... an actual date."

I'm red, definitely red. I wish I could hide somewhere. I stepped away from Tonia and Bobo, but I feel their eyes on me still.

"...You want me to take you on a date?"

"If you're busy, it's okay, I just... It was just an idea, I..."

"Okay. Where do you want to go?"

Oh, Moon Goddess, he agreed! I feel like jumping around the room right now, but I have to control myself a bit. I'm still blushing, though. Where do I want to go? I have no idea; I've never been on a date!

"I... I don't know."

"You want us to celebrate your birthday together? I can take a day off. What do you usually do then?"

For my birthday? Nothing. Back at the Jade Moon Clan, nobody would have bothered to celebrate or even remember which day it was. I would do my chores, like always, and the 3rd of December would pass like any other day. It was a bit different when I was young, though. My parents celebrated my birthday with a cake and a nice dinner. But I can't just ask for a cake from Damian... Can I?

"Nora, tell me."

"An Opera Cake."

"What?"

"I... I want to eat an Opera Cake..." I confess, blushing.

I hear him chuckling at the end of the line. It's embarrassing enough!

"Okay, my Love, an Opera Cake. What else?"

Oh, my Goddess, what did he just call me? Can I get any redder than I am now? So embarrassing! I'm blushing so much my cheeks are on fire. What was that? And Tonia and Bobo are both watching, I must be looking crazy right now! I need to answer, Damian is waiting at the other end of the line.

"I... I don't know. Anything's fine..." I mumble.

"Okay. Let me know if you think of anything else. I need to hang up, I have a meeting."

"I'm sorry, are you going to be late?"

"Neal's glaring at me, and about twenty executives are staring, too, so I suppose I already am."

Oh, Moon Goddess... I stutter a "bye" and hang up as quickly as I can. This is so embarrassing, I could die... His staff heard me requesting a date! And this stupid Opera Cake, too! How could I be so shameless! I'm never, never, never asking for anything over the phone again, this is way too dangerous! I turn around and see Tonia laughing.

"This is not funny!" I protest.

"Oh, hell yeah, it is. Moon Goddess, you are so cute, Nora!"

"I'm not cute, I'm embarrassed to death!"

"It's okay, Nora. You got yourself a date for tomorrow, girl! And for the whole day, too!"

"So you did hear everything!"

"Of course, I did. Now we need to decide on what you're going to wear tomorrow, so let's go shopping!"

What shopping? The wardrobes are already full! I argue with Tonia for a long time before she finally gives up. Instead, she insists on helping me choose my outfit for tomorrow. But the thing is, I have no idea what we are going to do...

I finally find a minute where Tonia is too focused on the wardrobe to watch me and step out of my bedroom, Bobo behind me. I go to the main room to lie on the sofa, and he comes to sit next to me.

I'm happy about going on a date for my birthday, but I can't stop thinking about Alec. Did Nathaniel take him to the hospital, as he said? I hope he didn't lie about that... Thinking about Nathaniel makes me remember something. I was about to get up, but Tonia enters the room carrying three different pairs of earrings in her hands.

"Which one do you like most?"

"I don't know, the white one? Anyway, Tonia, I have a question for you. Who is Nathaniel's Beta?"

"Nathaniel's... It's Isaac Graves. He was their father's Beta's son. Why do you ask?"

I thought the creamy white wolf might have been his Beta, but it seems like I'm wrong.

"I was just curious... You remember when you guys came to get me at the Jade Moon Clan?"

"Excuse me, you mean when we kept you from being killed after you and Liam sneaked out? Yes, I do remember."

When is she ever going to forgive me about that? I ignore her remark and keep going. "There was a white wolf with Nathaniel that day, who went with him afterward. I just wondered if she was his Beta."

Tonia looks a bit surprised, and exchanges a look with Bobo, frowning.

"I'm not really supposed to talk about that, Nora..."

"Why? Is it something you can't tell me?" I ask, intrigued.

"It's not about you. She's... part of Nathaniel's private life. I think they just happened to be together that day, and that's why she came along."

Oh. I think I get it. It explains her smell in Nathaniel's car... but I thought Nathaniel doesn't have a mate? From Tonia's embarrassed look and her words, I suspect she might not be an "official" relationship... Why would she be interested in me, then?

"So, she's not part of the Blood Moon Clan?"

"No. That woman is from a different pack, I don't know which. I don't even know her name, and I've only seen her a couple of times."

Great, so the only person who knows about her is Nathaniel, to whom she doesn't want me to talk to...

I wanted to wake up early the next morning to get ready for my first day of work. I had set the alarm for six o'clock. Instead, I gradually got awoken by noises coming from my bathroom. I open my eyes, making sure I'm not dreaming.

There are sounds of the shower running. I quickly check my smartphone, which Tonia gave me back yesterday. I had left it on the site of my fight with Vince... It is not even 6 am yet! Who is using my bathroom at this hour? Tonia always uses her own. Is it Damian? But we agreed to see each other tonight, and I'm pretty sure he mentioned he would be busy this morning.

It's okay, it's our friend.

Our friend? My wolf doesn't seem worried one bit. Could it be the white she-wolf? How would she get all the way here without being noticed by the siblings, though? And where is Bobo, anyway?

I grab the dark blue kimono lying at the end of my bed to put it on, unsure about what to do. Should I get Tonia? What if it's Damian and I'm alarmed for nothing? I don't think a stranger would be brazen enough to come all the way to my room and take a shower!

While I'm hesitating, the sound of water running stops, and I hear someone putting on clothing. I step back, unsure. Why are you not worried, wolf! But she clearly isn't. Who did she recognize?

The door opens, and to my surprise, a stranger comes out. The first thing I notice, he is really, really tall. About two meters high, I would say. He is quite muscular, too, and he only wears a pair of jeans, so I can't miss the sizeable crescent moon tattooed on his torso. A Blood Moon Clan member?

He sees my empty bed and turns around with a worried look until he sees me. He softly smiles once his gaze meets mine. He looks young, but I wouldn't be able to tell his age. With his large build, his thin black dreadlocks, and soft features, it's hard to say. However, I do feel something strangely familiar about him.

"Hi, Nora. Happy Birthday!"

He has a really soft and low-pitched voice and a warm smile. But it's only when I look up that I finally recognize those familiar dark green eyes. I can barely believe it.

"...Bobo?"

He gives me a big smile and opens his arms. "It took you a while!"

"Oh, my Goddess, Bobo!"

I run into his arms without thinking. I can't believe it's my Bobo standing there! He hugs me back and laughs softly. I never imagined I would get to see Bobo's human form today! It's weird, like meeting a friend after a long time of not seeing each other, but we saw each other literally every day for weeks now! I don't care, I'm happy to be able to finally see the human Bobo. He is as big as his sister said, too! While he hugs me, I feel like a baby trapped in his massive arms. He is still half-naked, though, and I back away a bit to look at him.

"Sorry I didn't shape-shift earlier. Being a wolf is just so nice, you know. But I wanted to be able to wish you a happy birthday, so..."

I can't believe he shapeshifted just for me! I smile back at him, overjoyed. "Thank you so much, Bobo! I like your wolf self, you know. It's just nice to finally talk to you!"

He laughs softly. "Sorry about that. But you can talk to me anytime, you know. Even if I can't answer, I can listen to you whenever you want. I know my big sis can be fussy, so just know you can confide in me, too, okay?"

I nod, and he pats my head. "Good girl. Now listen. There's another reason I wanted to talk to you."

He grabs my hand and takes me to sit with him on the bed. He looks a bit serious suddenly, so I wonder what this is about. He grabs one of my rubber bands and ties some of his dreadlocks to keep it out of the way, then turns to me, speaking softly.

"When we were chasing your brother, Alec. You ran ahead, and I thought you caught up with him. But when I arrived, he was alone. What happened?"

I bite my lip, hesitating. Is it okay to tell Bobo about her? I did ask Tonia yesterday, after all. But that she-wolf acted like she didn't want anyone to know she was there that night. Before I can actually make up my mind, Bobo speaks first.

"Nora, I know someone else was with us. I felt a third presence, someone who was a stranger but not hostile. You didn't mention it to the Boss."

I realize Bobo knew something was off about this chase all along. Still, he never mentioned it to anyone before talking to me today. If not, Tonia or Damian would definitely have asked. I decide to tell him the truth. After all, Bobo has been siding with me every time.

"It was a white female wolf..."

"I knew it. What happened?" He asks, frowning.

"Alec caught me by surprise and threw me into the sea. I thought I would drown, but she came and pulled me out of the water right on time. It was the white wolf I was asking Tonia about yesterday."

"So, I was right. I thought I had caught her smell, but I thought it just came from Nathaniel."

Does that mean he knows her? Tonia seemed to barely know of her existence. How come Bobo identified her smell so quickly?

"Bobo, you know her?" I ask, whispering.

He nods. "Her name is Elena. Elena Whitewood. She's from a different pack than ours, as Tonia said. The Opal Moon Clan, a branch of the White Moon. She's one of their fighters."

Finally, I get more information about that mysterious she-wolf! "How do you know her? Tonia said she doesn't really know her..."

"That's because she and Nathaniel aren't an official couple, so they avoid being together in public, usually. They shouldn't even be together, being from different Clans. My sister isn't really into gossip, especially when it concerns Nathaniel— she never liked him."

I noticed that, too, a while ago now. Tonia and Nathaniel are polite to each other, but they never interact unless it's necessary. She seems more comfortable with Liam or Damian, though I don't really know why.

"...The other day really was a coincidence, I think. Even I only learned by accident that they have a relationship. I know Elena from another place, actually. She likes to go to clubs on weekends, and I've seen her around a few times."

Oh, right, Tonia did mention that Bobo likes to go out.

"So, you met her at a club?"

"Not directly, but yeah, we have friends in common."

"Then, do you know how I can meet her?"

He frowns, intrigued. "Why do you want to meet with Elena?"

I forgot Bobo doesn't know we are mind-linked. I decide to tell him the truth, starting from when I heard her voice during my fight against Vince and everything else Elena and I exchanged after that. He listens, intrigued, but stays quiet until I'm done. I'm glad Bobo woke me up earlier. I feel comfortable sharing this with him, but for some reason, he is the only one I want to tell about all this.

"Interesting. So, you and she are probably related somehow..."

"You think she might have clues about my birth mother?" I ask.

Somehow that's what I have been thinking about since I learned the truth surrounding my birth. The information Nathaniel found about my father and his wife matches what Alec told us about them belonging to the Gold Moon Clan. However, it also raised questions about my birth mother. I'm curious about her. Why didn't I grow up with her? Why did my dad bring me to his wife instead? If that girl, Elena, has more information...

Bobo seems to be lost in his thoughts for a while, then sighs. "Maybe. I'm not sure, Nora. Perhaps Elena already knows why there is a link between you two. I can't say."

"Can you help me meet her?"

He scratches his head, thinking, but shakes his head after a while. "Not for now. I don't think it's a good idea for you to meet her in private at the moment. Nathaniel and the Boss will be watching you more closely from now on. But if Elena told you she will find a way to meet you, I would believe she will. Just be patient, baby girl."

I smile unconsciously. So he picked up this nickname, too. He seems to read my mind because he immediately says, "Sorry, I hear it in my sister's head all day..."

"Do you guys use the mind-link often? I didn't think we could use it so easily in our human form..."

"That's because we are closely related, and I'm very comfortable with my wolf form, so it makes it easier. Except for the Alpha, few people use the mind-link in human form. Too complicated."

"You have to teach me someday. I struggled to speak to Elena."

"I will be happy to chat with you once you join the pack!"

It reminds me that I don't belong to any Clan anymore. I severed all my ties with the Jade Moon Clan if I had any, and I don't belong to the Blood Moon Clan either. I wonder what is going to happen from now on? Will Damian make me join? It's a bit surprising that we never mentioned this earlier now that I think about it. Am I considered a rogue then...?

Bobo notices my worried expression and puts his arm around my shoulders. "Don't worry, Nora. I don't just guard you because of orders. I like you, baby girl. After all, I've been by your side all along, haven't I? There was supposed to be a rotation, you know. But I refused and took the job full-time. I'll be on your side no matter what. I bet you're going to be a great Luna, and I will be right by your side then."

Bobo's words bring me to tears. He chuckles and ruffles my curls, making me laugh. We chat about trivial things for a while, things he couldn't say before, like how much he loves my cooking or his fights with his sister. I don't feel uncomfortable at all being so close to Bobo; it's like I'm chatting with my best friend.

When my alarm clock strikes six, Tonia enters the room with a large bouquet of flowers in her hands.

"Happy Birthday! Look at what came for you this morning!"

Just then, she notices her brother, surprised.

"Bobo, you shapeshifted! When?"

"Just this morning, for Nora," he says while giving me a wink.

"And you actually have some pants on! What a day!"

What does this mean? Tonia looks at her younger brother with a conspicuous look, but Bobo ignores her. She hands me the flowers. There is a card with it, from Nathaniel, wishing me a happy eighteenth birthday. How nice of him, considering he will see me in less than three hours! I get up and take my present to the kitchen to find it a vase, the siblings following me. To my surprise, once I reach the room, there are several gifts on the table! I turn around to Tonia, perplexed.

"What's all this?"

"Your birthday presents, of course!"

All of this? Impossible! I see about a dozen wrapped boxes and bags! And I haven't gotten anything in ten years... Tonia is smiling from ear to ear, waiting for my reaction. I'm speechless! I slowly walk up to the table. There are three birthday cards: one from the siblings, one from Neal, and the other one from Liam.

"Wait... All of this is from you guys, Liam, and Nathaniel?" I ask, dumbfounded.

Tonia nods, excited. "It is! So, considering you are saving your evening for your date, we thought you should open them this morning! Both Liam and Nathaniel can't be here, so it will just be the three of us though, I hope you don't mind."

If I mind? Gosh, Tonia doesn't realize I haven't even celebrated my birthday in years! I'm overflowed with emotions right now; I don't know where to begin. Well, I'm trying hard to hold my tears in, for starters.

"Thank you so much, guys..."

Bobo laughs and gently pushes me towards the pile of presents. I start by opening and reading the birthday cards, and I can't stop smiling all along. Tonia and Bobo chose a pretty one with a winter theme, while their older brother went for a simple one. Liam picked a very girly one with purple and blue ribbons on it to tease me. All of them wrote really simple but touching birthday wishes.

After the cards, Bobo gives me one of the presents.

"But you guys already gave me a present: the smartphone!"

"Oh, stop it, Nora, and open it. You said you haven't gotten birthday presents in years, you can let us spoil you today!" Says Tonia while giving me a large box.

For some reason, Bobo is smiling and waiting to see my reaction. What is this? The box is a pale blue with some golden letters on it, like a chic brand... Not anything unusual from Tonia so far. However, as soon as I open the box, I blush and close it just as quickly.

Oh, Moon Goddess!

She got me super sexy, embarrassing, shameless French lingerie! I turn to look at Tonia, red with embarrassment. Why did she have to go and pick something like this! Even if I glanced at it only for a few seconds, I already know that this... piece of clothing is way too sexy and revealing!

Bobo is laughing out loud, and Tonia is acting innocent. "What? You might need it sooner than you think."

"Tonia! How can you buy me such an embarrassing thing? It barely has any fabric!"

"Well, it's not meant to be worn long, after all..."

"Tonia!"

Is she enjoying getting me embarrassed, or what? I can't believe it! I'm still struggling with having Damian touch me, how could I be thinking about the appropriate outfits for a physical relationship now! I'm already stressed enough about tonight's date as it is!

While the two siblings are still laughing at me, I take a shy glance at the piece of clothing once again. It's a night blue ensemble with a bit of embroidery, laces, and ribbons. I do have to admit that it's beautiful, but I can't picture myself wearing it. I push the box aside, for now, trying to regain my composure.

Bobo holds in his laugh and gives me another big box.

"This one's from me."

I really hope his present his less embarrassing than his sister's... I open it, and to my surprise, it's a brand-new pair of boxing gloves! I can't believe it! I turn to Bobo, and he is smiling.

"I knew you would like it. Next time you need to throw some punches with me, too, okay?"

I nod, delighted with it. I love those new gloves! I try them on, and they are the right size, too! I play with it for a while and put them back after thanking Bobo. Aside from the lingerie, Tonia also found the time to buy me a stunning winter dress for tonight's date. I wonder when she got it. I like it a lot. It looks warm and pretty, too. I'll definitely put it on tonight. Tonia also booked me an appointment at some famous salon after work so I can have my hair and makeup done by a professional. She always complains about how I'm never putting any makeup on, so I guess this was her way of cornering me into this...

Nathaniel's present is a very expensive-looking pair of pretty shoes from a French brand, which I think is supposed to go with my new dress. I am a bit worried about the high heels, but they do make me gorgeous once I try it... It seems like a have another fairy godmother.

Liam, on the other hand, offered me a selection of movies and CD albums of his own choosing. He was a bit surprised about my lack of knowledge in pop-culture last time we talked about it, so I guess it gave him ideas. I really like it, though, since I do feel like I've missed a lot all these years. He even put sticky notes on some of them, stating which ones we should watch together or his personal favorites. I really like that he actually took the time to write these down.

Once I'm done opening all of these, I turn around to thank Bobo and Tonia once again. "This is definitely the best birthday ever!" I say, ecstatic.

Tonia laughs and gives me a wink while pushing me into the

kitchen. "Save that for your date, baby girl! Now let's get to breakfast before you get late on your first day of work."

Bobo agrees with her, and I happily start preparing breakfast. I'm in the best mood today and even put one of Liam's CDs on the music station to play while I'm cooking and dancing around in the kitchen. Bobo happily joins me in my dancing, trying to teach me a few steps of Latino dancing and making me laugh. At the same time, his sister takes pictures of us with her smartphone. I really love my Bobo in his human form. He is not a big talker, as expected, but I find that he does express himself with his gestures and smiles. It's like having a big brother, but a caring one. We get along incredibly well, as we keep chatting over breakfast.

Once we are done eating, I get ready for my first day. I'm quite nervous, actually, but I do want to make a good impression, so I pick an ivory shirt with black pants. It's good that I can choose to wear pants... Robert always made me wear short skirts whenever I was working at the bar, and I hated it. Tonia helps me put on a bit of mascara and lip gloss and styles my hair into a pretty bun. While she goes out of my bedroom to go get her own makeup done, Bobo swiftly enters, while I'm still anxiously examining myself in the mirror.

"Hey, pretty girl."

"It's not too much, is it? I don't want to make a bad impression..."

He shakes his head and walks up to me. "Don't worry, it's great. And it will be perfect with this."

He takes out a small box from his jean pocket and gives it to me. What is this? There's only a tiny ribbon on it. Another present? I look at him, confused. Bobo smiles. "It's another present for your birthday. I didn't want to show it to my sis, she can be naggy about this kind of stuff... Open it."

I take it and open it. It's a pair of earrings! And they are so cute and pretty, too! They are blue and tear-shaped, and about the size of my pinky-nail.

"It's blue topaz, your birthstone. I noticed your ears were pierced."

That's true, my dad had them pierced when I was young because I wanted to wear pretty earrings like mom...

"Oh, Moon Goddess, Bobo, I love it..."

I really do. The earrings are delicate and not too garish, perfectly suitable to wear anytime. I immediately put it on. He smiles and nods, visibly satisfied. “They match your eye color. Really pretty.”

“Thanks, Bobo, I love them lots.”

I hug him quickly as thanks before looking once more in the mirror. Bobo is right, they do look like my own iris color, a deep London blue. My eyes are the one thing I’ve always liked about myself. Their dark blue color is uncommon, but somehow, I still loved it anyway. If only it wasn’t for my scar... I look in the mirror again. As always, the red line running across my face is hard to miss. Bobo seems to follow my train of thought, and lifts my chin up gently, giving me a reassuring smile.

“Hey. Don’t worry about details, baby girl. Okay?”

I nod obediently. Bobo’s right. No matter what, my scar is there and won’t go away, so I might as well cope with it. It’s my first day at this job, so I can’t start with a negative mindset. I need this change.

About an hour later, I’m in the car, nervous but quite excited at the same time. I keep playing with my phone between my hands, and Bobo is observing me with an amused smile but says nothing. While Tonia is looking for a parking spot, my phone suddenly vibrates. It’s Damian! I blush before I even get to answer.

“Hi...”

“Happy Birthday, Nora.”

“Thank you. Are you at work?”

“I am. Trying to get it all done so I can have a date with my princess tonight.”

I blush a bit. Bobo taps his sister’s shoulder, and they exit the car to give me some privacy.

“Please tell me you’re not saying this in front of a lot of people again.”

It’s like I can hear him smiling. “No, I’m not.”

“Good. Because it’s really embarrassing.”

“Not for me.”

Well, it should be! I know he is playing with me, but I still fall for it and blush.

“How’s your day so far?” He asks.

“It’s... Really great. No one has celebrated my birthday in years, you know. But this morning, I woke up, and I had people me wishing a Happy Birthday, birthday cards, and presents all over the place.”

I keep talking, making me realize how happy I really am. Damian listens to me, and we discuss for a few minutes, about things like my presents, Liam's music, and how happy I was to see Bobo in his human form. I love how we can have trivial conversations like these over the phone. I feel a bit closer to him that way. However, there is still this wall between us, something holding me back and making me shy.

"...I got a couple of surprises for you tonight, too."

I smile and bite my lip. What plans did Damian make? We barely talked about our date since last time. We only agreed to both diligently go to work, as I didn't want to ditch my first day, and Damian still has work, a busy CEO. Only at night did we plan to reunite to celebrate my birthday together. I wanted to go as soon as my job was over, but Tonia intervened, saying I needed to pretty up first, and would need a few hours for that. I didn't dare to oppose that. It's my very first date, after all, so I should at least listen to her advice on this.

"I can't wait for it," I whisper. "But I still want to go to work."

"I know. Have a good first day, then."

"You are not going to wish me good luck or something?"

"What luck? I will get rid of anyone who dares..."

"Damian!"

How can he say such things so easily? That is ridiculous! I'm just going to start a new job, what does it have to be a threatening situation for some people? And what could possibly happen? I'm just going to work...

"Okay, I'll call you later. Just let Nathaniel know if there's anything you need. And stay with Bobo."

"I know. Have a good day."

We both hang up, and I sigh. My bodyguard's presence was the only condition Damian refused to discuss. No matter what, if I wanted to work, Bobo had to be there. Even Nathaniel agreed to it right away. I was the only reticent one. Who goes to work with a bodyguard? I'm not some royalty! But no matter how long I argued, no one agreed to let me go to work alone, be it the siblings or the Black Brothers.

I exit the car, and Bobo's waiting for me. Tonia is not supposed to come with us, so she drives away, leaving us alone to walk to the restaurant La Rose de l'Aube. I'm as nervous as one can be...

When we get there, Bobo opens the front door for me, and a gorgeous young woman comes to meet us right away.

"Hello! You must be Nora, right? I'm Narcissa Brookes. Nice to meet you."

We shake hands, and she has this professional smile on all the time. I feel a bit intimidated. Her brown hair is tied in a perfect chignon, and her crimson dress is impeccable as well. There is not a single thing out of place. I'm glad I took the time to dress up and am wearing my new earrings.

"Nathaniel asked me to show you around, so you will be under my wing for today!" She says with a smile

"Thank you for that."

"Please, I am doing my job. So, please, follow me."

Narcissa gives me a tour of the restaurant. I love it. The decoration is delicate, not too fancy. Glass, pale cherry wood, white velvet, some floral elements, and marble. It's big enough to hold about fifty people, and it does look as high class as I heard it is. I can't believe I will have my shot at working here...

Narcissa is the Maître d'hôtel and quickly introduces me to the people already present, the kitchen staff. Most of the team is werewolf and part of the Blood Moon Clan, as expected, and welcome me warmly. All of them seem to know Bobo, though they are surprised to see him in his human form.

"I heard you have a bit of experience as a waitress?" Asks Narcissa.

"Yes, but just in a local pub."

"I see. Then you can grab one of the menus and start learning it. The other waiters will arrive in about an hour or so to get ready, you can join them then."

I do exactly as told, though I find the menu quite easy to remember. Once the rest of the staff arrives, I naturally join the other waiters and help with the dressing. I befriend everyone quite quickly while working, especially two girls my age, Kathie and Elise. Apparently, aside from Narcissa and the chef, no one really knows who I am or how I'm related to the Black brothers. Some question Bobo's imposing presence in a corner, but Narcissa dismisses them.

Truthfully, I feel quite happy to be working and useful. As soon as I show how fast I can learn, everyone looks glad to let me participate. Narcissa protests a few times that I'm only supposed to observe for now, but as the day goes on, I can't ignore it when someone needs help, and step in when I can. As the lunch service starts and goes on, I act as a support to all the waiters, and Narcissa has no choice but to let me do so, considering she gets quite busy herself. Nathaniel didn't lie when he said the restaurant was understaffed. I run all day to help one waiter then another, and even the chefs start asking my help for the service.

La Rose de l'Aube is busy, due to its reputation, but nothing I can't handle. I make sure to clear or set the tables quickly, assist anyone who seems in need, and keep an eye on all the tables to make sure nothing is amiss. The rhythm is quite peaceful compared to Rob's bar... By the end of the service, I'm a bit proud. Everything went well!

However, Narcissa suddenly calls everyone in the restaurant, including the kitchen staff, looking unhappy.

"What was with today? I said Nora should observe! Why did you guys give her your work?"

"I volunteered, Narcissa," I explain, immediately stepping up. "I couldn't just stand aside when I saw some of the waiters struggling."

Narcissa answers with a smile, clearly only meant for me. "They should have been able to handle it themselves, Nora."

I frown. What does Narcissa mean? They are clearly understaffed! Though it was all very professional, everyone was running around until the end of the service thirty minutes ago! How is it their fault? No one made a mistake, they just had too much to handle!

"Oh, shut it, Narcissa," says the Chef, Michel. "The girl did just fine, and she was exactly where we needed her to be. It's been weeks since we had a service going so well. We do lack some waiting staff and everyone's overworked. Let them breathe a little."

Michel is a strong man in his mid-forties and a force of nature, as expected of a head chef. He was a bit surprised to see me come at the pass a few times today but let me take the dishes without saying a thing. Behind him, Elise nods. "That's right. I had to handle fifteen tables by myself, and if it wasn't for Nora, I'm not sure I would have made it so swiftly, Narcissa. But every time I thought I had forgotten something or missed a detail, Nora had already taken care of it."

"And she helped everyone that way, the whole restaurant," Adds Kathie. "I barely noticed her for the full service, but she was always there right to handle things when I thought a problem might arise!"

I start blushing from their compliments, not knowing what to say. Narcissa still seems pissed, but she rolls her eyes and puts her hands on her hips. "All right, if all of you guys are ganging up against me, I won't argue anymore. But I insist that no matter how efficient Nora might be, she is still in training. Nora, you will keep working as a busser for now. Let me know if you have any problems."

Yes! I guess that means my first day went well! Narcissa sighs and steps out with Chef Michel to discuss the menus. Everyone else disperses to start the cleaning. Kathie and Elise run up to me, smiling.

"You were great, Nora!"

"I can't believe you memorized all the menus and table numbers so fast!" Says Kathie. "And you can endure the pressure like it's nothing, too!"

Well, try working for a hungry pack that won't hesitate to hit you if you're late...

"Thank you, guys, but you were the ones that helped me. I couldn't have learned the ropes so fast if it weren't for your help."

They both laugh and disagree, and then Kathie puts her hand in her apron and hands me a bit of money. Elise does the same. I look at them, confused.

"What is that?"

"Oh, come on, Nora, we want to share with you!"

"Bussers don't get any tip, but you helped us so much today, I will feel bad if you don't get your share! Here!"

They put the money in my hands before I get to say a thing. I'm so shocked, I can't say a word for a few seconds. I can't believe they are sharing their tips with me! I start tearing up unwillingly, and Kathie frowns, while Elise puts a hand on my shoulder, worried.

"Are you okay? Nora, what's wrong?"

"I'm okay, I just... This is the first time I earned money for myself!"

I'm so touched by Elise and Kathie's gesture. No matter how long I protest, they insist I take the money, so I eventually accept it, though their kindness means much more to me than the amount. What a great first day! From the corner of the room, Bobo gives me a thumbs up. After thanking my new friends and colleagues, I join everyone to clean the restaurant in a cheerful atmosphere. Everyone chats happily, and some of them seem eager to know more about me.

"Are you a fighter, Nora?"

"Not really... I'm kind of a late-bloomer werewolf."

I'm a bit awkward. From his corner, Bobo is sending me amused looks, not helpful at all. I'm glad everyone in the staff seems accepting of me, but this is a bit... Narcissa quickly intervenes as she comes back.

"Are you cleaning or chatting? Why do I find you annoying Nora? Stop being so curious!"

An hour later, I finish working with a large smile stuck on my face and join Bobo, who was waiting with a large cup of coffee. He smiles when I approach him.

"Hi, there."

"A macchiato?" I guess from the smell.

He nods and finishes his cup in one go. Bobo really has childish tastes... I sit in front of him, watching my coworkers go one by one, all of them saying bye to me.

"You look happy," says Bobo

"I am. It went great! And everyone is nice, too."

He smiles as an answer. I hope he wasn't too bored while I was working, just waiting in a corner. Bobo didn't help at all and barely interacted with others. I only saw him talking with Michel at some point.

"Do you know the staff here well?" I ask.

"Michel's one of our Blood Moon Clan warriors when he is not cooking. So are a couple of others from the kitchen staff. Elise is among our hunters too. She's good."

It's a bit weird to imagine them as wolves when I saw them working all day as a perfect-looking staff. But my wolf did analyze their smell out of habit, and about two-thirds of the team are werewolves. I should learn to be more aware of the other Clan members now, I guess... All the staff slowly leave the restaurant until we are left with only the head chef and Narcissa. They are still discussing menus, but Bobo and I are useless in that, so we just casually chat.

Then, around 3pm, Bobo raises his head, and I see Nathaniel walking in. Narcissa immediately walks up to him with her perfect smile on. From the expectant look in her eyes and her attitude with him, I gather what's going on immediately. She might be trying to act natural, but I can tell she is mindful of her every move and slightly changed her tone, too. I exchange a quick look with Bobo, who nods. She is either after Nathaniel or already one of his "private" relationships. I recall what Tonia and Bobo mentioned earlier. Behind the gentle and smiling face, I guess the angel-like brother really is the player they described, then...

He listens to Narcissa and Chef Michel for a while, then dismisses them and walks towards us. He greets Bobo with a nod and gives me a smile.

"Happy Birthday, princess! How was your day? Narcissa told me you did great."

"Thanks, Nathaniel. And thank you for the birthday present, I loved the shoes! And yes, it went well! Thank you so much for letting me try this job, I truly love it. And the team is great, too."

"I'm glad to hear it. Well, it seems like everyone is happy, so I guess we can think of making this a long-term position for you."

I nod, happy. It would be awesome! A real job, with no pervert customers, my own paycheck, practical working hours, and friendly coworkers, too!

"Let's give it a week and see if it works well for you. You can discuss the details with Narcissa since she's basically in charge of this one. I come often, but I just oversee it and only intervene if I'm needed."

"Okay. But will Bobo have to wait for me every time? It's a bit long for him, and Tonia has to drive me, too..." I can't help but ask.

Nathaniel shakes his head. "That's not for me to decide, princess. Personally, I don't think you're at risk being here, but we both know how my brother can be overprotective. I suggest you bring this matter to him yourself, but I wouldn't get my hopes up if I were you."

Indeed. Damian is stubborn when it comes to my "safety", though nothing happened so far... What is he fearing? Could something really happen? I proved that I could take on an Alpha, so who would attack me after that? There is no point, I don't even belong to a pack as of now! I exchange a look with Bobo, but he doesn't seem really interested in the matter either. Is it because he won't disobey Damian? How could he not be bored after waiting for me all day? I still feel guilty, somehow.

Nathaniel and I discuss a bit longer about my work at La Rose de l'Aube until Tonia comes to get us. I forgot about the appointments she got me...

One thing I have to admit: I'm really not used to people taking care of me. It's like in those movies we watched together, where the lead actress gets a total makeover after going through the hands of beauty specialists and putting on brand-new, expensive clothes. Well, one thing those movies have wrong: it's incredibly long, and there is no entertaining background music. Instead, I need to stay seated and wait for hours while Tonia and the professionals take care of my skin, my hair, and my nails. I refused the massage after the perfumed bath, despite

Tonia's protests. I don't want to lay while some unknown lady touches my bare skin. Bobo's older sister argued for a while, but I said no and stuck to it, I hate people seeing my bareback! In the end, Bobo stepped in to tell his sister to stop insisting. Tonia sulked for a while, but she let me move on to the hairdresser lady.

After two hours and a dozen products being put on my head, both Bobo and I are helplessly bored. Tonia obviously doesn't care, as she keeps discussing with the hairdresser and makeup artist. How can it take so long to get ready for a date? I know I have no experience in taking care of myself, but still! I make the silent promise to myself to learn how to style up my own hair and use makeup from now on.

While she is arguing about going for a braided chignon or styling my curls, Tonia's phone suddenly rings. She frowns and immediately picks up. Sitting next to me, Bobo, who was half asleep until now, sighs.

"That's the Liam-is-going-to-get-scolded ringtone," he whispers.

I listen to Tonia's conversation, and it does seem like it.

"What do you mean he went to the eastern territory...? Why did he have to go there again! That makes it three times this month! Three times! I don't care... No Neal, I'm not going to get him again, I'm busy! Find someone else! I'm done fetching that brat! He... No, I don't care! Just send Erik or someone else! ...So what? He asked for it! Didn't the Boss tell him to stop? He got in this mess himself. I'm done with the Purple Clan, let them kick his ass!"

I frown and turn to Bobo. The Purple Moon Clan? They are known for their rude behavior and constant fighting with others. Out of all the local packs, they are the most agitated and ruthless, always looking for someone to pick a fight with. Bobo doesn't seem worried and shrugs. With that and Tonia's heated conversation, I guess this isn't the first time... I wonder why Liam went to mess with them.

"Why does it have to be me? I said I... No Neal, I told you, let the brat handle his own mess! He... Well, I don't care, he is not my Alpha! ...So what? You can't let me handle this every time! ...Oh yeah? And how long do you think this will work? Lysandra is... Oh, shut up!"

They keep arguing for a while, loudly. Bobo leans to me to explain quickly. "Tonia has ties with the leader of the Purple Clan. She almost joined them before we met the Boss. Liam often picks fights on purpose with their fighters, so she's usually the one to intervene."

From what I know, the Purple Clan as a lot of young members, but I never imagined Tonia almost joined such a reckless pack... Well, I guess the Blood Moon cannot be considered as soft-hearted, either. She and Neal argue for a while on the phone, but eventually, she hangs up, angrily, with a look of defeat written all over her face. Well, I guess she can't really say no to her Beta after all.

"I got to go settle this. Bobo, you stay with Nora. I'll be back quickly."

She leaves angrily, leaving Bobo and me alone in the salon, with the confused hairdresser.

"Ahem... For your hairstyle...?"

"Hair down," I say in unison with Bobo.

Leaving the lady to her work on my impossible curls, I start playing some games on my smartphone while Bobo is reading a magazine. After a few minutes, I hear the entrance bell. Bobo turns his head like a watchdog, and I follow his gaze.

A young woman just entered the room. She walks up to us, confidently, silent as a cat despite her heels. She is wearing a baseball cap, and a men's large denim jacket, making me think she doesn't want to be recognized. But despite her disguise, I find her radiant. She is a bit taller than me and has very feminine curves. Once she gets closer, she takes out her cap, showing off long, honey blonde hair. I immediately recognize her amber eyes.

"Hi, Bobo," she says with a beautiful voice.

I see my bodyguard frown, a bit annoyed. "...Elena. You're not supposed to be here."

"I know. Are you going to stop me?" She asks with a confident smile. They stare at each other for a while, and I wonder what's between them. Bobo did imply they knew each other, but now he seems a bit taken aback by her presence. And Tonia just left, too. Her timing is a bit too perfect... However, Bobo doesn't act defensively at all, making me think he trusts her.

He looks hesitant about what to do now that she's here. After a long silence, he sighs, "Okay. You're already here anyway."

She smiles and takes the seat next to me. How can she act so confidently? She is on another Clan's territory! Isn't she worried about being attacked? But she seems totally carefree, openly smiling to me.

"Hi, Nora."

"Hello..."

What should I say in such a situation? This is too sudden! Elena doesn't let me think before she starts talking. "So, you recognize me, I guess. Sorry, I had to leave suddenly last time, but I don't really want Nate to know that you and I are acquainted."

"Why?"

She shrugs, looking a bit uneasy for the first time. "Personal reasons. Let's just say it would make things a bit more complicated... It made it hard for me to get to you already. Your security is quite tight! Thankfully your bodyguard is a friend."

A friend? That's not really what Bobo said, but judging from his embarrassed expression, I guess Elena isn't exaggerating. She winks at him, and Bobo blushes a little. How is she actually able to make the aloof Bobo blush?

"You owe me one, Elena," he says.

"I know, I know, big boy. I'll talk to him, I promise."

I wonder what and who they are talking about, but before I can come up with any theory, Elena turns back to me and speaks softly. "Anyway. I really wanted to meet with you, Nora."

"Me, too. I have so many questions for you! What happened last time? How can we be mind-linked? I never did that with anyone!"

"Easy, girl. I know you have a lot to ask, but I can't stay long. And I may not have all the answers you are looking for. First, our mind-link suggests we are related somehow, though I'm not sure about the details. When we met on the Jade Moon Clan's turf, I felt it. My wolf reacted strongly to your presence, so I came to your fight against the Alpha to confirm it. That's why I tried the mind-link, and it worked!"

"Yes, I heard you during my fight. And after that."

"Exactly. You did great, by the way!"

I smile back at her, a bit flattered. I love how natural she is while talking. "Thanks. But I still have no other clue about how we are related... I just learned that my father was from the Gold Moon Clan, but I have no clue about my mother. All I know is that I didn't inherit my father's last name. When we searched for it, Nathaniel said the name Bluemoon doesn't appear anywhere."

"Because that is not a last name, Nora! Didn't you notice that it sounded a lot like a Clan's name...?"

Elena looks at me, waiting for my reaction.

"...You mean, like a Blue Moon Clan?"

Elena nods. ...What? But I've never heard of a Blue Moon Clan! Of all the Clans of Silver City, I'm pretty sure I've never heard of that one... I turn to Bobo to see if he knows something about such a name, but he doesn't react, looking just as confused as I am.

"There is no Blue Moon Clan in Silver City," he says.

Elena nods. "To be exact, there is no Blue Moon Clan at all. Not anymore. But from what I've discovered, there used to be one, far up in the North. I don't know why or how, but they were all... killed. The full pack. About eighteen years ago."

That's when I was born... What happened then? Who could have decimated a full Clan of werewolves? Usually, it's settled with a fight between Alphas, or the pack warriors. Still, there are always survivors who would become rogues or submit to join other clans to ensure their survival. For a full pack to be killed... Unless they were attacked by humans or witches? Or vampires?

"Killed? An entire pack? But... how?" I ask.

"I still don't know yet. But you and I are proof that some people from this Clan survived..."

"Wait, you are... I mean, you think you are from this Blue Moon Clan, too? Did you grow up in this Clan then?"

"No, no. Someone saved me when I was an infant, and brought me to a childless couple of the Opal Clan here, in Silver City."

Now that I look at her from up close, it does seem like Elena is in her early twenties, maybe younger... But I never imagined she might be an orphan too.

"The woman who saved me told that a Royal's family had been killed and that she had found me alone in the middle of the... slaughter."

I gasp, stunned. A Royal Family? I've heard of it, but...

Among werewolves, the Royals are the purest! Descendants from the very first werewolves, blessed by Moon Goddess. They have kept their bloodline so pure, staying away from humans and other species, that they are all born Alphas and deeply respected by other werewolves. Some say they have abilities granted by the Moon Goddess herself, but most of those are legends, I didn't think there were any Royals alive!

"Royals? Are you sure?" Asks Bobo.

"For now, I am not sure of anything! I have no memories of surviving a massacre either. I just got pieces of information from the woman who saved me... But I've seen Nora's wolf, and you did, too."

I frown. What does she mean with that? How is my wolf shape related to this Clan...? Both Elena and Bobo stare at me for a while, with complex expressions I can't decipher. I don't get it!

"What do you mean?" I ask Elena.

"You are a pure wolf, Nora. Dark blue eyes and a perfectly white fur. Do you have any idea how rare is that combination among werewolves? It's almost legendary! And you even have a Clan's name as your given name!"

"No, no, you said yourself, it is probably only the Clan's name. Even if I am from this Blue Moon Clan, it could just be..."

"Royal Families do take their Clan's names as a symbol of power, Nora," says Bobo. "They carry it for generations until there is no more descendant, and usually a new Alpha from a dominant but non-Royal family takes over. Any Clan's name can be really old or newly made up, but only the Royals are entitled to carry it. Your father definitely knew who your mother was. Why would he have told you this was your last name otherwise?"

"One does not give a Clan's name to their child!" Adds Elena.

I look at both of them, stunned. No, I can't be a Royal's child! That makes no sense...

"Then why wouldn't that make you a Royal's child too? Aren't we related?" I ask Elena.

She laughs softly and shakes her head.

"We are related indeed, but I don't believe I am the child of a Royal. Not directly, at least. I have gold eyes, and my fur isn't completely white like yours. One of my parents probably wasn't a pure werewolf."

But she is an Alpha, isn't she? My wolf can smell that she could be a dangerous opponent. I shake my head, lost by too much information.

"So, you think my birth mother was...?"

"A Royal, yes."

But my dad was most definitely not... And until now, I thought there weren't any Royals left! Centuries have passed since the very first werewolves. How could we keep the blood so pure until now? I know that there were still some of them a few generations ago. Among Clans, it is known that Royals were treated like treasures because of their pure blood and abilities, and ruled any Clan they were in. By nature, they had to lead and govern; they cannot be submitted. But for me? How many times did I give up while facing Alec or Vince?

Bobo gently pats my shoulder.

"You're probably mixed, Nora. He might not have been an Alpha, but your father's blood was most likely pure enough for you to keep some of the characteristics."

"Not all of them. I can't heal properly, and my shape-shifting isn't ideal either."

"Wait a minute... You can't heal fast?" Asks Elena, surprised.

I shake my head. "No... I still heal faster than a human, but my healing ability is not as good as regular werewolves."

She looks shocked and points to herself. "Nora, I have the same issue! As far as I recall, I never healed properly!"

"Really?"

"Yes! So far, I thought it was just me being weaker than other werewolves, but now..."

She's right. If we are right about being related, and both experience the same problem with our healing capacity, that means it must be an issue with our blood. If we are indeed related to the Royals, shouldn't our abilities actually be more reliable than our peers'? Why are we slow healers? Is it because we are mixed, then?

"Did you experience anything else that's different?" I ask.

"Mind-linking. I'm much better at that than anyone I know, including my own Alpha. No matter the distance, I have no problem communicating with my pack members. I can even communicate with other packs' Alphas."

"Wait, aren't you an Alpha?"

She frowns. "No, I'm not. And I don't want to be."

But she definitely has Alpha potential, like me! I was sure she was her own Pack leader and can't imagine her in any other position. I want to ask her, but she's annoyed by the subject, so I give up for now.

"What about you?" She then asks.

"I can't, for now. I don't belong to any Clan at the moment, so..."

You should try it. With your Alpha mate.

I don't really get how it works yet...

Nora, you're mind-linking. Like, right now.

I look at her, surprised, and at Bobo. Gosh, she's right! I did it without realizing it because she started talking to me that way, and her voice sounded so clear in my head that I couldn't tell the difference. Elena smiles at me, amused by my reaction.

"Don't use it too much on others, though. If you're like me, people might... not really like it."

"Why do you mean?" I ask, intrigued.

"You'll see."

She checks the time from the clock on the wall and frowns. Bobo nods and takes a look at the entrance. "You should go, Elena. Our pack will have noticed your presence by now."

"What? Wait! We are not done talking!" I protest.

I still have so many questions, and Elena is the only person who knows anything about my origins! But she shakes her head and puts her cap back on. "Sorry, Nora, Boyan is right. I already stayed longer than I should. Don't worry, I'll keep searching about the Blue Moon Clan."

"When can we meet again?"

She winks at me. "I will find you, don't worry. For now, don't tell anyone about what we discussed today, okay? No one but Bobo must know, Nora, it is crucial."

What about Damian? I don't want to have to lie to him! Not when we are starting to trust each other! Elena seems to read my thoughts and answers right away.

"Not even your mate, Nora."

"But..."

"If it makes you feel better, you are not the only one with secrets. I wouldn't trust Damian Black so easily if I were you."

"What do you mean?"

"You'll see."

She turns around to head to the exit, ready to leave. But just when she's about to go out, Nathaniel suddenly appears at the entrance of the salon. When he sees Elena, his face has a stunned expression I've never seen him make before. She clearly didn't expect to run into him either.

They stare at each other for a few seconds, in awkward silence. He seems confused, but she's very calm while facing Nathaniel.

"Elena... What are you doing here?"

"I came to see Bobo."

"Bobo?"

He looks in our direction, and Bobo immediately nods. Nathaniel stares at me, too, but I act innocent. I don't know if he buys it, but his eyes go back to the pretty blonde, with an angry expression this time.

"You're not supposed to be here."

"Are you going to kill me then?"

Her straightforward question clearly destabilizes him, and he drops the hostile act. I'm amazed by how composed Elena is, compared to Nathaniel. They stare at each other for a while. Their eyes express so many things, I feel like I'm eavesdropping on a private exchange. They might be mind-linking, but I can't tell. After a while, Nathaniel silently steps aside, letting her leave without another word. He watches her figure go, and I can't help but wonder once again what's between those two...

Once she's out of sight, Nathaniel turns to us, frowning. This is the first time I've seen him looking annoyed.

"Boyan, what was that?" He asks in a cold tone.

"Just as she said."

I feel bad for letting Bobo handle Nathaniel alone, but I remember Elena's words. Nathaniel and Bobo stare at each other for a few seconds, and I wonder if the Alpha will interrogate him again... Against my expectations, he doesn't ask anything else. Instead, Nathaniel breathes in, regaining his composure, and turns to me.

"Sorry about that, princess. Anyway, you look beautiful, and I hope you have a great date tonight with my brother. Enjoy your birthday."

His words sound a bit empty, and I can't help but think that his mind is somewhere else. I had almost forgotten about the salon's staff around us during my talk with Elena. They quietly and swiftly resume working, and Nathaniel leaves. I wait a bit before turning to Bobo.

"That scared me..."

"Don't worry. I doubt he would do anything to Elena, but let's be more careful next time. It might not be Nathaniel that shows up."

I nod. It usually doesn't end well for a werewolf trespassing on another Clan's territory. Elena did seem pretty confident, but I still wouldn't bet she was totally out of danger by coming here. The lady behind me clicks her tongue when I turn my head to talk to Bobo again, but I ignore her.

"Is the Opal Moon territory far from here?"

Bobo shakes his head and scratches between his dreadlocks while thinking. "Not really... They are mostly located in the Art District and around the University Campus. As I said, they're part of the White

Moon Clan, which is even bigger, so they can walk freely on most of North End. They have good bars with live music. They are tolerated on the Blood Moon turf, though, as long as they don't push it..."

Of course. If the other packs' members weren't tolerated on the Blood Moon Clan's turf, a third of the inhabitants wouldn't be able to take a step in the city. Usually, everyone tries to stay on their own land, but we all live in Silver City. There has to be a bit of tolerance between most packs, or it would be impossible for other werewolves to even go downtown. What could raise suspicions is if a strong wolf adventured too far alone and unannounced on another territory like Elena did today. Basically, once on another pack's turf, any wolf is at the mercy of that pack. They don't need a reason to attack; they make their own rules on their domain.

This makes me wonder how Elena will be able to meet me again...

I get lost in my thoughts while another lady comes to do my makeup. As my preparation goes on, Bobo asks if I want a cup of tea, but I politely refuse. I know he is just trying to help me ease my mind, but I still have a hard time processing everything I learned just today.

The child of a Royal? How could that be...? I look at my reflection in the large mirror facing me. Is it even possible? Until now, I didn't even know the Royals still existed in this day and age. Now Elena comes in and states that I am related to such a legend. As a mixed child. Did my father know? If so, why did he take me from my mother? Was she killed along with that family?

Somehow, I feel a hole in my heart whenever I think of my birth mother. Is it because I never really got along with the one who raised me? I wonder if she looked like me. She was probably the one with blue eyes. I want to know more about her, but where to start? And what about Damian? Elena advised to not tell him a thing, but why? If I really am the child of a Royal, I think I should tell him. I want to ask Bobo, but there are too many ears around us for now, so I hold it in. Anyway, this is all too sudden. I need to think about it.

I get lost in my thoughts and forget about the time. When my makeover is finally done, Tonia comes back just in time to witness it. I'm standing in the middle of the salon wearing the beautiful winter dress she gave me as my birthday present this morning, with Nathaniel's shoes. To be quite honest, I love what I see in the mirror, though I can barely recognize myself. With the heels, I don't look so petite anymore, and the dress fits me perfectly, making me more feminine than ever. It is sea-blue, with a silver ribbon and beads around the waist, and stops at my knees. My hair was very nicely done as well, giving my dark curls an elegant but natural look. The makeup is light, too, with a bit of blush here and there, a touch of mascara, and camellia-pink lips.

This girl facing me is beautiful, and I feel a bit embarrassed, staring at myself. Behind me, the siblings are both smiling.

"Very pretty."

"Pretty? She is stunning!" Claims Tonia.

I don't know what to say, so I just whisper some shy thanks. Now I'm starting to feel anxious. Seeing myself all ready and dressed up reminds me that I am about to have a date with Damian. My very first date! I'm both excited and nervous... I have no idea what he prepared. I feel like I barely know him already; how could I guess what plans he made for tonight?

As I suspected, Tonia is driving me to the rendezvous. In the car, I'm as anxious as one can be, and no one speaks. The girls from the Jade Moon Clan always argued about romantic moonlight strolls, going to the movies, or candlelit dinners. It's a bit hard to imagine Damian doing any of these... Tonia puts some music on the radio, and I try to relax.

About half an hour later, it's already dark outside when we stop in a location I can't recognize. It is pretty quiet, actually, except for the sounds of the seashore. Why are we at the waterfront? The last time I came close to the sea didn't end well... But the atmosphere is quite different this time. Tonia covers me up with a large white fur coat, and we walk a couple of steps to face a large boat.

It's actually a superb white yacht with its lights on and elegant wooden floors. Pushing me gently, Bobo helps me get on board while I'm still in awe. I have never been on a boat before! A private yacht to boot! I take shy steps inside, but the siblings don't follow me, staying on the dock, waving with big smiles on. Oh, well...

My wolf detects five... No, six people inside while I slowly walk in, though I don't see anyone. My heart is already thumping loudly. My wolf feels his presence, and that's all she can focus on for now. A romantic song is floating in the air, coming from the deck, so I head that way. This is so intriguing...

Once I finally reach the deck, I'm left completely speechless.

As if in a dream-like setting, the deck is decorated with white flowers and fairy lights all over. On the floor, there is a thin layer of snow, perfectly even and white. In the middle of it, a wooden table was set for two, with white napkins, crystal glasses, and silverware, with a centerpiece composed of candles, sand, and seashells. All of it is arranged in an elegant, but intimate, and unbelievably romantic setting.

Everything is absolutely perfect.

And in the frame of this incredible sight, stands Damian.

I find him more handsome than ever. As always, he is wearing only dark clothes, but this time it is a jet-black suit, with a silver tie matching his glowing eyes. He appears effortlessly handsome standing there, and I find myself falling for him once again. His muscular figure, the marble-chiseled traits, his thin lips... He even got a fresh haircut and a clean, short stubble beard.

...How can one be so handsome? I'm tearing up when I walk up to him. He catches my hand, entangling his fingers with mine as our faces come close. Our eyes meet, and I feel happier than ever. My heart is so warm and loud; I feel like it will explode any time now. Damian's eyes lock onto mine, sheening love on me. How can such an icy gaze make one burn with feelings at the same time?

Before we say a word, his lips find mine, and we lose ourselves in a long, tender, and passionate kiss. He is intense but gentle. I follow his rhythm, answering his kiss with more confidence than before. This taste on my lips is addicting, and I don't want to stop. Ever. I kiss him back, putting my free hand on his chest. I don't need air. I just want this man's lips against mine.

I feel Damian's hand sliding into my hair, his fingers playing with my curls like he loves to. He grasps and holds it, keeping me close enough to melt under his embrace. Winter means nothing. I feel myself burning from this man's delightful kiss, almost like I could get drunk on it.

When our kiss finally comes to an end, Damian holds me close against him, and his lips slowly slide all the way to my ear to whisper.

"Happy Birthday, Nora."

I blush again, uncontrollably, because of those three words. Damian's voice so close to my ear, it makes me crazy. I can even feel his breath softly brushing my neck. How can one endure that! I avert my eyes, the blood rushing to my cheeks. He chuckles softly from my reaction and gives me a quick kiss on the cheek.

"Blushing already, Nora? So cute..."

"You're the one making me like that!" I protest shyly.

"Then I must be doing something right because you look adorable that way," he whispers while putting a slight kiss on my forehead.

I try to push him away from me a little, or I will never be able to regain my composure otherwise. He smiles and stops with the kisses, though he has no intention to let go of my hand. Instead, he takes a step back and observes me from head to toe with a smile. He even raises his arm and makes me take a slow spin.

"You are beautiful tonight..."

I smile at him and step closer to him again. "You, too. I love the beard," I whisper, brushing my fingers against the little spikes on his chin.

"I'll remember it," he says, kissing my fingers when they get close to his lips. "...Come."

Holding my hand, he takes me to the table and helps me to my seat like a gentleman. I take my arms out of the sleeves of my coat, but keep it laying on my shoulders. Next to us, a small brazier is burning, slowly warming up the air around us, but it's not enough. Damian grabs a blanket that was on a side and covers my legs with it. I love this.

We are having a candlelight dinner on the deck of a boat in December! I hadn't realized the ship had started moving, but we are slowly getting farther and farther away from the port. We are headed toward the vast sea, leaving Silver City's night lights behind us. I wonder if we have a set destination? Either way, I'm just overwhelmed by all of this. Even the most romantic movies I've watched with Tonia never had something like this! This is something out of a Fairy Tale, and I feel like I might wake up any minute.

I'm still very much awake when Damian opens up a bottle of French Champagne. Gosh, I hope there aren't too many alcoholic beverages planned. I don't have any experience with it... All I have is the few times Elizabeth made me try the beer at her father's pub, and I hated it. And now I'm being served a glass of fancy Champagne... However, Damian purposely gives me only half of what he pours for himself; he knows I can't drink too much.

He raises his glass, and we clink the crystal glasses together before taking a sip. It's actually quite good! It's a bit sweet, and I love the fizzy feeling on my tongue.

"So, how was your first day?"

"It was great! I loved it. The restaurant is amazing, and the team was really nice, too."

I start telling him about how the day went, from my arrival at the La Rose de L'Aube to the end of the service, so happy to share this with him. I tell him about the service, how I helped as much as I could, and even about a few memorable customers. Damian's eyes don't leave me for a single second all this time.

"So, I take it you want to continue then?"

"Of course! Nathaniel said I could keep working as a busser for now."

"And then? What do you want to do?"

My goal? I never really thought of any professional perspective before... Not that I could dream about any from Robert's dirty bar I used to work in, anyway. But I guess I could start if this is to be my first real job! I think for a few seconds, but the answer is suddenly crystal clear to me.

"I want to learn the ropes about the catering business."

"Cooking?"

"Not just that. How to cook, make menus, plan things, manage the staff, handle customers, and oversee it all. When I was young, I dreamed of having my own restaurant someday. If I can still try..."

I realize he is smiling, and I blush a bit.

"What?"

"...You remind me of my mother."

Wow. This is the first time Damian has ever mentioned their mother. I wait a bit to let him speak. He puts his hand on mine, slowly drawing circles with his thumb.

"She was always a dreamer, despite her sickness. She missed France a lot, so she wanted to have her own restaurant to serve French cuisine there. The flavors of her childhood. Nate gave his restaurant her name."

"Do you mean La Rose de l'Aube?"

He nods. "It means the Dawn Rose, literally, but another word for Dawn in French is Aurore, our mother's name. Roses were her favorite flowers. Nate inherited her passion for cooking."

That explains why he is the one in charge of almost the restaurants of the Clan, though they are not all French.

"What was she like? Your mom?" I ask.

He smiles softly. "The sweetest person you could think of. She always saw the good in anyone, a real pacifist at heart. Everyone in the pack loved her. And she was beautiful, too. Blonde, with blue eyes and pale skin. Her eyes were much lighter than yours, though. She had very soft traits and always looked young. Nate got her blonde hair and blue eyes, but Liam is the one who most looks like her."

Which means Damian takes after their father... I wonder what their childhood was like with such parents. Their dad probably wasn't so violent at the start, like Liam said. What kind of brother was Damian to Nathaniel and Liam?

"Liam said you were studying together," he says, changing topics.

I nod and tell him about all the books I go through at the apartment, how I somehow started taking Liam's homework. I'm only seventeen, after all. Not going to school was really something that bothered me for a long time.

"Don't you want to take classes?" Asks Damian.

"Maybe private lessons... Just so I could get a diploma. It feels too late to start school now, though. It'd be awkward."

"You can think about it, Nora."

I nod, but I'm still not too confident about this...

A young waiter suddenly appears to serve the appetizers. Damian went with an entirely French menu to please me. I wonder if chef Michel participated? Some of the dishes look familiar. Anyway, it's delicious, and we talk about more trivial matters as we eat.

After a while, I notice the boat has actually stopped, and the view is fantastic. We are a few miles away from the coast, and, more importantly, we have the most incredible view over Silver City's night lights. It's breathtaking. Below the starry night sky, all the skyscrapers assemble, shining with colorful lights and neons. Yet, we are far from the noises of the city. This scenery is so peaceful, with the soft ambiance of waves and the piano in the background.

I take a moment to stare at it. My city.

Damian notices that I stopped eating and follows my gaze. How does he feel, as the silent King of this modern realm? No title, yet the most feared wolf in town. Sometimes I forget he is not just my fated mate or an Alpha. He is Damian Black, the most powerful man and werewolf of Silver City.

For so long, I thought I wasn't a good match for him, that we were too different. I had no idea about my Alpha potential or my heritage. If I really am a Royal, then it turns out I might be much more useful than I thought to him. And I want to be. I don't want to leave him to fight on his own. The brothers went through so many hardships already, and who knows what's next? We live in a dangerous world.

"Damian?"

"Hm?"

"What happened to your father?"

He turns to me, frowning a little. He probably never thought I would ask. For a while, he remains silent, and I wonder if he will answer me at all. He might not. I heard about the Black Brothers' story from others, but I don't believe that's something they would spread themselves.

Damian sighs and starts talking while looking at the city. "Our father was never able to handle his Alpha compulsions. Alphas are born to dominate. We have strong fighter instincts and don't react well to orders. That also means we experience stronger urges to fight and are more prone to violence. My father was such a man. If he was annoyed, he would hit. If he was bored, he would fight. The constant fighting with the Vampires made it worse, and our mother's Luna power was too weak to help. He was addicted to this."

He stops for a minute while the waiter takes away our plates. When he resumes talking, his hand is on mine again, though his eyes are fixated toward the city.

"...Addicted to all that violence. It might have been okay if he was only fighting vampires or rogues, but he just didn't know when to stop. He killed ruthlessly, even members of the pack. No one could stop him at the time. He was way too strong. He even beat up some of his closest friends, even the Beta. Even us. His sons were Alphas, so why shouldn't he fight them, too? We were just kids, but it made no difference. Anything that upset him was a good enough reason to hit us."

"What about your mother?" I can't help but ask. "Wasn't she around to protect you guys?"

"No, she was already at the hospital at that point. We never said a thing, but she knew. That made her worse. She couldn't endure being powerless, but her sickness was... Anyway, she couldn't do anything for us. We had to endure it for years, tiptoe around our father or wait for it to pass when he used his fists. I still have so many memories of when he suddenly got crazy and hit anything around him... Even his own children. 'Werewolves are fighters,' he always said. He almost killed me several times. He sent Nathaniel to the hospital once. I had to carry my brother on my back all the way there. He broke Liam's arm when he was just eight. I hated that man so much, Nora, you have no idea. Just the thought of being of the same blood as that asshole made me want to puke. We were too young to fight back, but Nate and I trained. As time went on, we stopped being passive and started hitting back."

I can't even imagine what kind of life they had growing up... And they were only children! It's a miracle the three of them got to where they are today with this kind of story behind them.

"What about Liam?" I ask.

Damian shakes his head. "He was too young. We did what we could to keep him out of it. Nate and I knew how it would end, and we didn't want Liam to be in the middle of this mess, too. I didn't even want Nate to be part of it, but of course, he didn't listen. So we trained, and we waited. We waited for an opportunity to kill our father."

I can't act scared or even shocked by Damian's words. With what the brothers went through, they might have been the ones to die if things had gone differently. Also, I realize that what Damian did was also his way of protecting his brothers. How could he endure seeing his younger siblings hurt for so many years while holding his hatred in? Back when Alec beat me, I had no one to hold dear, no one to protect. Things were different for the Black Brothers. Liam knows his older brothers shielded him from their father's madness, yet he still couldn't escape it.

"His Beta knew what we were planning, but he didn't say a thing to our father. He had come to hate him, too, yet he had to obey. Our father even beat up his son once, to punish him. How could he not despise him? That's when I understood I had more allies than I thought."

A faint smirk appears at the corner of his lips for a split second. He helps himself with a glass of wine while I drink some water. The dishes between us are getting cold, but neither of us cares. I'm too immersed in his story to think about my plate.

"So, Nate and I got ready, taking our time. We allied with rogues like the Mura siblings."

"Bobo's family?"

"Yes. Our father was so harsh, he never wanted to take in new wolves in the pack, even some desperate families that stood at our borders. It was almost too easy. When they saw how strong Nate and I were getting, and our Alpha potential, many submitted without a fight. They didn't ask for anything as long as I wasn't like my father. The pack got so big so quickly, we couldn't believe it. Until then, we had thought we would have to wait for years until we could take my father head-on!"

"Why? Wasn't it only about dueling him for the Alpha position? What does it have to do with the size of the Blood Moon pack?"

Damian stays silent for a while, and I wonder what he is so reluctant to say. Eventually, he sighs and looks at me straight in the eye. "We wanted to be sure that, no matter the outcome, my father wouldn't be able to survive."

"...What do you mean?"

"I wasn't sure to win, Nora. If I died during the fight, Nate and I wanted to be sure someone would finish the job. And if someone did, we had to be sure my father's wolves wouldn't take him out."

It takes me a few seconds to realize.

"...It was about Liam. You wanted to be sure that even if you died, Liam could kill your father and take his place."

Damian nods. "I knew I could hurt him badly enough, but I wasn't sure I could win. Nate came up with that idea. That even if he and I died, we would make sure Liam killed him. We also had to make sure no one would kill our little brother before he could get to our father and that people would support him afterward."

"Hence the Blood Moon Clan. It wasn't just a branch clan; you wanted it to be able to take on your father's pack."

Damian chuckles. The waiter comes back to take away our empty plates. My mate grabs my hand once again, intertwining my fingers with his.

"Back then, it was still called the Black Moon Clan, but yes, that was the idea. However, it didn't even come to a real fight between the two groups. When I turned nineteen, I defied my father while we were alone. He didn't take me seriously and attacked me. We started fighting in his office. We made so much noise that a lot of people came. Nate, Liam, the Betas, and about twenty people each from the Black Moon and Blood Moon Clans. But it turns out, most people from his pack were actually cheering for me."

They once again underestimated how despised their father was. Or maybe people felt Damian already had what it took to be a better Alpha. In any case, I'm not even surprised.

"The only people still rooting for my dad were holding onto the fact that he was the one that had chased all the vampires away. I can't really blame them for that, though. He was an insane and violent man, but as an Alpha, he was still the strongest wolf around."

"But you did beat him," I said.

"Not easily, trust me. People were shocked by how adamant I was about finishing him off. Most of them had no idea about what he had done to us all those years. If anyone tried to intervene, Nate, Neal, or Seamus killed them on the spot."

"...Seamus?"

"My father's Beta, Seamus Graves. I told you, he had our back. He couldn't attack our father directly, but he did kill anyone from the Black Moon pack who opposed us. Lots of people were shocked, but Seamus had made up his mind years ago. When I finally won, I wasn't in good shape, but he killed two wolves who tried to attack me. He was a traitor, the one who helped us the most to take over the Black Moon Clan."

"What happened to him?"

Damian shakes his head. "He left the territory, saying he should have died with his Alpha, but he still had his sons, and he didn't want to do that to them. So, he asked me to banish him. We don't know about his whereabouts. Maybe he joined another pack or is still alone."

I feel a bit sorry about the man. If we look at the bigger picture, he helped the Black Brothers in so many ways, for the sake of protecting his own. Yet it cost him so much: betraying his Alpha and leaving his family. Now that I think about it, Bobo did say one of his sons was now Nathaniel's Beta. Isaac Graves, was it? I suppose the Beta genes run in their family...

"Anyway, after the fight, many other packs that were fed up with the Black Moon tried to attack us. It was chaotic for a few days."

I remember that. The word that the "Black King" had fallen spread quickly, and many packs got crazy, hungry for power. The Black Moon's Alpha had overshadowed so many people for years. As soon as he was gone, many seized the opportunity.

However, the Black Brothers quickly made it known that the Blood Moon Clan could take on anyone and was not to be underestimated. The former pack had become even more significant, and all of that had been done secretly, to boot. Clans that tried to fight were wiped out, and opposing werewolves were submitted in no time. Just like that, the previous territory established by their father got even larger in only a few weeks.

"I can't believe this all happened when you guys were still teens..." I whisper.

"Our mother's death accelerated things. Things got way with our father, and if we didn't act, I was afraid he was going to kill us first."

I nod. If Judah Black had no problem hitting his children when they were young, who knows what it would have been like once they reach adulthood... It's a miracle they survived that far.

Once again, I find myself thinking about their mother. I can't even imagine what she went through, being unable to help her children. Her sons, enduring her husband's insanity. I imagine young Damian, Nathaniel, and Liam living each day in fear while their powerless mother was on a hospital bed. And yet all they did was protect each other and love her.

I silently make the promise to myself to never be as helpless as she was. Not only do I want to stand by Damian's side even more, but I also feel like I should do what their mother couldn't. I want to be that Luna, the one that can protect her pack and her children. I feel my wolf growling fiercely inside, and she's more than up for that challenge.

While I'm thinking, so is Damian. He is frowning, and his silver eyes are fixated on his meat, though it's evident that he doesn't see it. I can almost feel his thoughts echoing mine. I can guess what's on his mind right away.

"You are not going to be like your father, Damian," I say softly to him.

He raises his head, surprised, and this time I'm the one putting my hand on his and doing the talking.

"I know you are afraid of being like he was, because you are both strong Alphas, and I understand. But you two are different. You can control yourself. All you wanted was to protect Nathaniel and Liam. Even now, you are always trying to protect me. And you listen to your brothers, to your Beta. Your father didn't care about anyone but himself. You are a fighter, but that doesn't make you an evil person. Just a strong Alpha."

He stays silent for a while, making me wonder if my words had any effect on him. But after a while, he finally smiles. Then, he brings my hand to his lips, kissing it while looking me into the eyes with a resolute look. "I will protect you, Nora, I swear to the Moon Goddess Mother. I'm not letting what happened to my mother happen to you; I won't lose you. You have no idea how much I need you. I need you to keep me sane, to remind me what's right and what isn't. I've never been afraid to fight, but I'm afraid of losing you."

I smile, but why do I feel like his words have a deeper meaning than what I hear...?

Before I can get any further into my interrogations, the waiter comes back. I blush a little, as Damian is still holding my hand and keeps kissing it shamelessly. He sends me playful looks, amused by my reactions. I feel embarrassed, but the waiter doesn't say a word and takes away our empty plates.

Once he is gone, I click my tongue and try to have my hand back. Of course, he won't let go so easily.

"Stop it..." I mumble shyly.

But Damian ignores me, and instead gets up, leading me to do the same. He puts a hand on my waist and puts my hand he was holding onto his chest. I smile and wrap my fingers around his neck, brushing the baseline of his hair. He slowly starts dancing, small steps that I can easily follow.

For a while, we don't say a word. I let him lead our little dance and rest my head on his chest while listening to the music. It's like we are alone in the world, and for now, I love it. Surrounded by the sea, fairy lights, and Damian's arms. I feel his fingers gently brushing my skin, and the shivers I get have nothing to do with the cold. Can't we pause this moment forever? My eighteenth birthday is a dream I couldn't have dreamt of myself.

Two songs pass, and we can't separate from each other. I feel safe in those arms. Far from all the worries, the mysteries, the secrets...

And I find myself thinking about Elena's words. What did she mean? Why shouldn't I trust Damian? Moon Goddess wants us together, so why is it that I can't trust my fated mate completely? It's not just Elena's words. Something tells me I've only scratched the surface. Getting him to talk about his past was already a big step, yet I still want more. Much more. He is always keeping me away from the real world.

It's like being trapped in a golden prison. I can't go out as I wish, and I have no idea what's going on outside. Why do I need to be so protected? It can't just be related to our bond...

Just for tonight, I close my eyes, and I forget all about my questions. That can wait until tomorrow, can't it? I don't want to ruin this, my first date with Damian. He is gentle, loving, and just for tonight, he is all for me.

I feel him leaning slowly towards the side, and his lips gently land on my neck. Soft kisses, running with a small fire on my skin. Anything he touches burns, and it's addicting. I blush again and close my eyes. Suddenly, I feel his hands leaving me, and I frown. What is he doing? Then, I see him put something around my neck, and I gasp. A necklace! He puts the thin platinum chain around my neck and helps me put my hair back around it. Oh, Moon Goddess...

"You didn't think I wouldn't give you a present, did you?"

I smile and grab the little pendant with my fingers to look at it. It's a magnificent crescent moon, made of a myriad of tiny white diamonds. The design is so elegant and pure, I love it... Though the moon is not too big, it shines like a treasure against my pale skin. I can't take my eyes off it for a few seconds, making Damian smile.

"You like it?"

"Damian, I love it!"

I jump to kiss him, standing on tiptoe and putting my arms around his neck. My gosh, why does he have to be so tall! But it does not matter, as I feel him smile against my lips and bend over to kiss me some more. I play with his hair under my fingers, and he suddenly grabs my waist and hoists me up, before putting his arms under my thighs to carry me while I face him. Our playful kiss goes on, with the two of us chuckling from time to time, trying to take over the other's lips. It's funny to stand a little higher than him for once, and I like the way he looks up to meet my eyes.

I hear the waiter coming back, and I'm red again as he sees me straddling Damian. I try to break free, but of course, the man won't let me go and keeps holding me against him. I hide my face into his neck, too ashamed to face the young waiter. Can't he be a bit more decent sometimes?

"Nora, look."

I frown against his shirt collar. What does he want now? Is the waiter gone, at least?

When I finally turn my head, another surprise is waiting for me. A cake! A small cake is now on the table, with two lit 18-shaped candles on it. Damian puts me down so I can approach it. I can't believe it! He really got me an Opera Cake!

I smile subconsciously, happy to see my favorite dessert. Someone even wrote down a "Happy Birthday" in white chocolate on top of the cake and drew flowers with the icing and spread some gold powder, too. I bite my lip, not knowing what to say. My first birthday cake in forever, and it's so perfect!

I finally turn to Damian, smiling from ear to ear. "You really got me that cake!"

"You can thank Nate for that, actually. I had to ask for his help. So, this Opera Cake you wanted so badly was just a chocolate cake?"

I laugh and shake my head. "Not just a chocolate cake! It's several layers of almond sponge cake, soaked in coffee syrup, with layers of ganache and coffee buttercream! And it is covered in the chocolate glaze," I recite with assurance.

Damian looks at me, surprised. "Sounds like you could do it on your own."

"Maybe I'll try it sometime. I read the recipe long ago, and I always wanted to try it."

"What, so this is your first time eating one?" He asks.

I nod and head back to my seat. I really want to have a taste of it now! Damian chuckles and joins me, putting his chair next to mine. The waiter comes back quickly to serve us some champagne once more. I take a new sip, feeling fine. I'm just a little bit light-headed, nothing wrong with that, and it might even not be to blame on the alcohol...

I lean toward the candles, and close my eyes, trying to think of a wish to come up with. I feel like I can't ask for anything more than all that is given to me now... In the end, I just silently ask Moon Goddess Mother to watch over the people I love for this new year. I blow out the two candles quickly, and my fated mate puts a quick kiss on my head, wishing me a happy birthday once again.

Damian puts his arm around my chair while I grab the little forks. I decide to ignore the plates the waiter gave us and eat directly from the cake. Gosh, this is so good. I take another bite, a bit greedy. We are still facing Silver City, and I'm having an Opera Cake on a boat, with pretty clothes and a birthday present from my fated mate around my neck... If someone had told me that three months ago, I wouldn't have believed any of it.

"Are you going to eat all that Opera Cake on your own, or do you intend to let me have some of it, too?"

I laugh at him with my mouth still full. I was so absorbed into my tasting that I even forgot to hand him his fork... Instead of giving it back to him, I take some of the cake with it and feed it to him.

He makes a frown as soon as he tries it. "Too sugary..."

"You don't like sweet stuff, anyway! Why did you want it then?" I ask, amused by his grimace.

"I was curious about what that cake you wanted so much tasted like..." He grabs his glass and drinks some champagne, probably to take off the taste. Well, it seems like this cake is all mine then!

I keep eating happily, and Damian keeps drinking, watching me stuff myself with a smile. I know he still thinks I'm too skinny. They all do, though I'm pretty sure I'm not underweight anymore.

After a while, I finally stop eating, too full to have any more of it. I lean back and rest my head on Damian's shoulder. "You didn't smoke all night."

"How do you know I usually smoke?"

"The smell. I've never seen you with a cigarette, but you always have this faint tobacco smell on you. How come you never smoke in front of me?"

"I couldn't smoke at the hospital, and the Mura siblings hate it, so... I don't need it that much, anyway."

"Do your brothers smoke, too?"

"I don't think so. Maybe Liam, but he knows we don't want him to. Nate is more of a drinker, but I don't think I've seen him smoke."

I nod. I got that impression, too. And he works around kitchens all day, so I guess he would try to stay away from it.

When I'm about to ask him something else, I suddenly feel him tense up. He stays completely immobile for a minute, his eyes fixated on the horizon. I try to see what he sees, too. Isn't there too much agitation at the north end of the harbor?

"Damian...?"

He suddenly gets up and runs to the back of the boat, yelling orders to go back to the bay. What's going on? I focus on the mind-link from earlier, looking for her...

"Elena!"

"Nora? Where are you?"

"On the sea with Damian. What's going on? There's too much agitation at—"

"North End, I know! I'm headed there now, we're under attack!

"Rogues?"

"No, damn vampires!"

A vampire attack now? That doesn't make any sense! I thought the former Alpha Black had chased them far to the North? And Silver City is entirely dominated by werewolf packs now, so what's the point of attacking us? It's suicide for them!

Damian is still yelling orders, and the boat is now going back full speed to the harbor. He comes back to me just when I am holding the rail not to fall, looking furious. He walks up to me, having no problem to walk despite the boat's speed, and puts his arms around me.

"I'm sorry, Nora," he says, "We have to go back. It's a massive attack."

"It's okay, I know," I answer, nodding against his shoulder.

"You stay on the boat, I will..."

"No, Damian, I'm coming with you."

"No!" He yells, making me jump, though I expected a refusal. I saw it coming the second I decided to go, too. His silver eyes have turned into an ice-cold stare, as he is fixating on me furiously.

"You stay there, Nora, don't you come an inch close to those blood-suckers. I'll handle it."

"You can't put me aside, Damian; I want to go! And it's not even your territory!"

"It's not yours, either! You don't have a territory, for now, Nora!"

Thanks for the reminder. Now it's my turn to glare. I'm well aware that not having a pack makes me a target anywhere I go, aside from the Blood Moon Clan's territory. But this is my city, and I refuse to sit while it's attacked.

Damian realizes his words hurt me more than he thought and shakes his head. "Sorry. But I just want you to stay safe, Nora. You stay there, and that's final." He walks off, taking off his jacket.

I bite my lip. I don't want to stay back! I have to go. What if someone really gets hurt or worse, killed? Vampires might be weaker than us, but they are still dangerous! It took years to chase them all out of Silver City. My eyes go to the harbor, trying to get a hold of whatever is going on there.

"Elena, are you there yet?"

"On my way. But my friends told me there's a lot of them. Really a lot."

"Is your pack okay?"

"For now. The White Moon, is there, too, and some of the Sea Moon pack warriors joined, as well. But those damn vampires just keep coming."

"The Blood Moon is on their way."

"I figured so. Nate's guys just arrived."

"What about the other clans?"

"They have to watch out for the other sides of the city. This might be a massive attack. I just saw some guys from the Gold Moon and Rising Moon packs heading south."

I didn't think of that, but Elena might be right. Vampires are known to be smart— they haven't been around for years for nothing. Those cunning creatures wouldn't attack recklessly like that. Not only must they have an aim, but they probably have a plan, too.

Our boat reaches the shore, and Damian takes off his shirt. He comes back to me and quickly kisses my forehead before looking at me in the eye. "I'll be back, Nora. Stay in the harbor. Bobo and Tonia are coming to get you."

And with that, he turns around and shapeshifts in a split second. The big, jet-black wolf immediately starts running toward the North, growling furiously. Moon Goddess helps anyone who will stand in his way. The guy who served us dinner helps me out of the boat, but my thoughts are somewhere else. Elena's words got me thinking.

Didn't she say she could contact any Alpha? Then maybe I should be able to do so, too. But I only know one personally other than the Black Brothers... Gosh, I really didn't want to make use of this, but this is an emergency. I ought to try.

I feel my wolf inside, ready anytime I need. She's on edge, too. She felt the intrusion on the territory and doesn't like it. She wants us to go and help our mate.

"I know, I want to go too, but there is something else we need to do first," I tell her. Then I call out: *"Vincent."*

"What the... Nora?"

Gosh, it worked! And so quickly, too. I feel like I can almost see his brown wolf, and mine growls immediately, making him submit right away. I was afraid he might try to refuse me somehow, but he shows no resistance to the mind-link.

"Yes. Listen, there is a vampire attack in the North. Right now.

"I know, just heard of it. I was about to give orders for our warriors to—"

"No! Stay there and guard the East forest. The White Moon, Pearl Moon, and Blood Moon Clans are already focusing on the North, but these might be multiple attacks. Our territory is the first line of defense in the East of Silver City, we can't leave it defenseless."

He stays silent for a while, and I feel his wolf being restless.

"...Okay, it makes sense. I'll do as you say and send more sentinels to the East. If something goes through, we'll know."

"If it happens, send a distress signal to the neighboring clans. Everyone is on the look-out, so they'll help."

"Got it. I just sent word to the Pearl Moon Alpha. She'll definitely help."

"Okay."

Satisfied with that, I cut the mind-link. I can't believe I just mind-linked Clark! And it went well, too. I feared he wouldn't listen to me, but it looks like Vincent will keep his word.

I feel a bit better, knowing the other sides of Silver City aren't defenseless. Out of all the big Clans, most are going to defend their position or help somewhere. Though the packs usually fight a lot among themselves, werewolves are quick to gather as one to fend off an enemy.

Still, I feel restless. This attack really makes no sense! The North is the easiest to defend, with the White and Opal Clans there, and they are close to the Blood Moon's territory, too. They are bound to have reinforcement in a few minutes once they request help. Why would the vampires choose this spot to launch an attack? That is suicide! Or are there really many of them, like Elena said? Could they outnumber us?

I'm starting to feel worried. Why aren't Bobo and Tonia there yet? I've been waiting at the harbor for a while now! Did they get held up somewhere? Are they okay? While I'm worried about everyone, Elena's voice echoes again in my head.

"Nora! Some passed through our defense! They are running

through the city!"

"What? Where are they aimed to? They're targeting the humans?"

"I don't know, but it doesn't look like it. They are staying West on the Sea Wolves' turf! Following them now!"

That's just North to my position! I can't stay there. I take off my heels, my jewelry, and my dress, leaving them on the ground. The waiter looks at me, standing in my underwear. Well, I'm a werewolf anyway, and I don't want to rip this dress! And there is no time for shyness or blushing now!

"Okay, girl, time to shapeshift."

I breathe in and let my wolf take over. It's been a while, but it's as easy as closing my eyes. She is only too happy to make her appearance. I'm in my white wolf shape within a few seconds and start running as soon as my paws touch the ground.

Gosh, this is my second time going to the Sea Wolves' territory within a very short time. I hope they won't mind because I can't afford to fight them, too. I keep running as fast as I can, going up the shoreline. It doesn't take long before I start hearing growls and sounds of fighting ahead of me. They got even further into our territory than Elena thought! When I arrive at the scene, about twenty wolves are ganging up on about a dozen vampires.

Those creatures are taller and thinner than humans, with blood-red eyes and pale skin. All of them are dressed in black leather, and some of them are even carrying daggers or swords. I see them glowing in the dark. Those are made of silver! It explains why twenty wolves are not enough to hold them, everyone is cautious because of those weapons.

I immediately jump on the one closest to me, who is about to stab a young grey wolf. Without the slightest hesitation, I bite off the hand that held a dagger. I may not be a warrior, but my wolf knows how to follow her instincts, and she won't show mercy for bloodsuckers. He didn't see me coming and screams in horror. The wolf that was under him seizes the moment and aims for the throat directly. With a third wolf joining in, we finish this creature off, tearing it to limbs. While the other two end the job, I look around. We still have the upper hand, and no one seems to care about me coming there. I need to talk to the Alpha.

It only takes a second to notice him among his own. He is dark-grey, bigger than the others, though he looks old and has a lot of scars all over. I try to focus on him while staying cautious of my surroundings, establishing a mind-link. I see him react, raising his head.

"*Wait... Oy, who is that?* He turns his head around, searching for a while, and his eyes fall on me. *The white wolf? What are you doing here, kid?"*

"I came to help. More are coming."

"I know. My wolves are watching all over the harbor. Those bloody vampires are all headed there. Bet they want to stay close to the sea."

The sea! I didn't think of it earlier, but vampires are excellent swimmers! They don't need to breathe, and their eyes don't mind the water, either. It will make a good escape route if things go badly for them. But then again, what is their aim?

I help another duo to fend off a vampire, and we kill it quickly. Even armed, a vampire is no match for three werewolves. What annoys me is that they keep coming. How is that possible? I wish I knew how Damian and the others are doing in the North.

"Marina!"

I turn around. A young female is pinned down by a vampire. Somehow, she got isolated from the rest of the group, leaving her almost defenseless. Using a wolf next to me, I jump off, and, with a big leap over several heads, I fall on her enemy. My fangs find his neck, but he immediately swings with his dagger to try and shake me off. I feel a sharp pain on my arm, but don't let go. The young she-wolf doesn't miss her chance and furiously bites his shoulder, making him drop the dagger. As we are still struggling, another wolf that has the same fur as hers jumps in and rips the vampire's head off with a single bite.

Ouch, silver really hurts... I feel blood on my paw, but I'm okay, I guess. I'm a slow healer, anyway, so I think this doesn't change much. The young she-wolf comes to me and immediately starts licking my wound. It's the first time someone did this for me... She stops once the bleeding slows down and puts her muzzle to touch mine. I know she's saying thanks. The other wolf, probably a relative of hers, nibbles her ear quickly. We must go back to the fight.

The three of us jump back into the fight, and for a while, we are doing good. Other than me, two other wolves are hurt, but that's it, while numerous vampires who are already on the ground.

"Nora, you were right! Vampires are coming from the East! But we can hold them off, for now. The Pearl Clan's warriors are here, too, and the Gold Moon pack is fending them off in the South."

I don't have time to answer to Vincent, but he didn't sound too worried. And the Gold Moon Clan is one of the strongest, also, so I know they can hold the Southern position for a while. What I'm more worried about is the North. If that many vampires are getting past our defenses, what is going on up there? Are Nathaniel and Damian okay? And Bobo and Tonia are still not here!

This is my very first fight, and I don't have a second to rest. Though we kill many of them, the vampires keep coming. How come there are so many of them? Vincent and the other Clans are doing fine in the South and East, but I wish I knew what's going on in the North!

"Elena! Are you okay?"

"Yeah, doing my best. I'm just a few blocks ahead of your position, but the situation's worse here."

My wolf tenses. *"She's in danger."*

My wolf's right. I would have said so even without hearing her obviously tired tone. Moreover, every time she mind-links me, I feel she is not in her wolf, but in her human form. Why wouldn't she shape-shift now? Did she got hurt by silver or something?

"Damn it! What is he still doing here? Stubborn wolf!"

"Elena?"

"It's Bobo! I keep telling him to go to you, but he won't leave me! His sister is running to you, though!"

I'm a bit relieved to hear about Bobo and Tonia, but what is going on? Damian told Bobo to come to me, so why is he staying with Elena? Though, if she is not in her wolf form, I still feel better knowing my friend is with her. Maybe she's even injured, and that would explain Bobo staying with her. I can do fine on my own here, and the Sea Moon Wolves are cooperating with me like I'm one of them.

After a few minutes, Tonia indeed appears to join the fight here. She isn't injured, thanks to Moon Goddess. She is almost as big as her brother, though she's thinner, and her arrival cheers up the tired Sea Moon Wolves. She jumps to me, and immediately takes a defensive position, growling at the closest vampires. I wish I could ask her about Bobo and Damian!

"Nora, something weird is going on here!"

"Vincent?"

"All the vampires are... I don't know, something is attacking them!"

"What something? Is it attacking our own?"

"No, it's... Whatever it is, it's protecting my injured wolves! The... Shit, I can barely believe it, but roots are growing from the ground to hold the vampires!"

Roots? Like actual tree roots? Is he kidding? Did Vincent hurt his head or something? But he sounds fine to me. What is going on now?

"...It's like the forest in attacking the vampires! They were about to get the upper hand on us, but all of a sudden, the trees have started pinning them down! The trees!"

Our forest is attacking the vampires? What is this now? I hear Vincent exulting in my head, and I close the mind-link. Well, at least now I can stop worrying about the East. Though I really wish I knew how the hell the forest is suddenly stepping into this fight!

We are now clearly getting the upper hand. A few Sea Moon Wolves are injured, but werewolves from another Clan stepped in, I'm unsure which. Anyway, these new wolves are fighters, seeing how they attack the vampires without mercy and take them down one by one. They are now enough to defend themselves here. I leave this part of the battlefield, avoiding enemies to head North. I need to join Elena, Bobo, and the Blood Moon Clan.

Behind me, I hear Tonia growling, but I ignore her. I know Damian told me to stay back, but I never agreed to it. The harbor isn't any safer now, anyway. She follows me, and we soon reach another fighting ground, more into the city this time, somewhere in-between the Port and the Latino District. I spot Elena right away: As I suspected, she is the only one standing in her human form, other than the vampires.

Even so, I have to say, she's obviously a great fighter. She is fighting with some sort of wooden pole, and her moves are like those fight choreographies you see in action movies. Not even one vampire can get close to her, she is fiercely standing her ground. Plus, she has two wolves siding with her: one is Bobo, and the other is a smaller tawny wolf unknown to me.

"Elena!"

"Nora! Are you okay? Moon Goddess, you're bleeding!"

"It's okay. Why aren't you in wolf shape?"

"Don't worry, I can defend myself fine this way."

That's not what I asked! She obviously ignored my question, so I don't ask again. We have more urgent matters at hand. Elena didn't lie when she said they were not doing great here. The number of vampires is starting to grow, and there are only about a dozen werewolves.

I try to defend another wolf who having difficulty, but Tonia is hindering me in attempting to protect me. Can't she let me fight by myself!

Bobo, too, is fighting harder, trying to protect both me and Elena. Is it because of her heritage, because she is a mixed Royal like me? I feel like there is something else. He is also very protective of the other male wolf next to Elena, though this one is doing just fine. Elena and this tawny wolf seem used to fighting together, completing each other's moves like a synchronized dance. At least I can stop worrying about her since she really is doing great on her own.

I, on the other hand, can't say the same. I've been keeping this up for a while now, and the exhaustion is growing on me. I'm glad I stuffed myself up with cake earlier, giving me extra energy for all I'm burning right now. But somehow, more and more vampires come at me one after another. My wolf and I aren't ready to back down, however. I ignore the pain in my arm and jump with Tonia on a female vampire close to us.

"Nora, there is something weird."

"What is it?"

"I feel like they're targeting you!"

"What?"

I look around, and though it takes me a few minutes, I realize she might be right. No matter how hard Tonia and I fight, it's like the vampires focus on our duo. As more keep coming, a lot of vampires do keep the other wolves busy, but I still notice a bunch of them aim directly toward us. That's why we have been doing triple work all along! Elena's right, there are a lot more vampires lying around Tonia and me than anywhere else. I jump to another position, and our opponents ignore Tonia to rush towards me. Why now?

I keep fighting them off, Tonia and Bobo helping me. For my first real fight, other than the duel, I never thought I would be fighting vampires alongside other packs! But there is a mix of Opal Moon, White Moon, Sea Moon, and Blood Moon wolves gathered all around, and everyone is doing their share.

"Nora, we are pretty much done here! The forest stopped attacking the vampires a while ago, but we are finishing the job! We sent a lot of our valid warriors straight to the North to help now!"

Finally! I relay Vincent's news to Elena, who immediately shares it with her own Alpha and the Alpha of the White Moon Clan. Realizing she was talking with them all along, I ask her about the situation in the North while shredding a neck off.

"Not good. Xavier said something odd is going on over there, too. The vampires are using some sort of poison, slowing our people. I know it sounds weird, but our river is attacking the werewolves. Tell the Sea Moon Wolves to stay far from the water, it's attacking the packs!"

Seriously, the water now? I wouldn't have believed her a few minutes ago! I was glad some sort of force from the forest was helping the Jade Moon Clan, but then how come the water is attacking us? The Northern territory is right on a river, too! If this is what the vampires were relying on, it explains why they choose to attack from the North. I use the mind-link to pass the information to the Sea Moon Alpha.

"We're good here, kiddo. No attack from the sea, but I'll tell the guys to be careful!"

Whatever it is, it's only in the North now. But it's powerful enough to let the vampires dominate four packs allied together! Gosh, I hope Damian is alright! I ask Elena, but she says she doesn't know. It's probably too chaotic in the North, so no one can stop and look for a black wolf. I pray to Moon Goddess for him to be okay and focus on my own fight.

Suddenly, Tonia takes a violent hit from a duo who ganged up on her. I want to step in, but I'm already fighting off another one of those bloodsuckers a few meters away. Bobo is also too far away, helping the other tawny wolf. They managed to scatter our group somehow, this is not good. I hear Tonia whimper— she's really hurt. The second I turn my head to look at her is a mistake. I feel a vivid pain, and a kick throws me a few steps back. The pain blinds me for a second, and my wolf whines in response, the distress echoing in our mind.

"HELP!"

"Nora, don't...!"

For a second, all the wolves around me freeze and turn their heads to me. It's like they all heard me, and in a few seconds, they all fight harder than ever. I realize some of them are trying to fight off their opponent to come and help me, but it's useless. I'm too far from any of them. I'm on my back, and that damn vampire as a hand on my throat, pinning me down. He lost his dagger earlier in the fight, so he focuses on trying to hit me. I bite furiously anything that comes close. Gosh, those creatures are damn strong! I need to break free before he breaks my neck!

Suddenly, we hear a loud howl, and everyone turns their heads. A new pack has joined the fight! I hear Elena's cheer of joy in my head.

"It's Lysandra Jones! The Purple Moon Clan!"

It's my first time seeing her, and the dark wolf launches the attack as soon as she's here, starting by the vampire that was on Tonia. Their pack is small, but they are notorious fighters. The fight resumes, and this time no side has the upper hand. Lysandra's wolves are helping others, taking over for the hurt wolves. But they are not on my position yet, and I must keep fighting the vampire on me. Just when I thought he was about to kill me, his hand tightening around my throat, I suddenly hear the vampire next to him, a woman, yelling: *"Idiot, don't kill her! She needs us to take this one alive!"*

What the...? Before I can realize what she just said, a dark form jumps over us, and a loud growl follows. I see a black fur above me, covering most of my sight. The furious wolf bites off the vampire's shoulder, pushing him off me, and attacks again. I struggle to get back on my feet. For a split second, I thought it was Damian, but I notice this wolf is a bit smaller than my mate and has reddish hair around his collarbone.

"Liam!"

He turns to me and helps me get up; his fur tainted with vampire blood all over. I probably don't look any better, either...

"Hey, Nora, what's up?"

"Don't "what's up" me! What are you doing here? Why aren't you with Nathaniel and Damian?"

"Don't yell, I sent them reinforcements already! But my brother was worried about you, so I went to you first. We heard your distress call! How the hell did you do that?"

They heard me what? Oh, Moon Goddess, did they actually hear me all the way to the Northern territory? I just mind-linked without thinking!

I don't really have time to focus on anything else, as, despite our arguing, Liam jumps into the fight right away. I can catch some rest while he fights off my opponents, but I'm too worried about my friend. I look for her on my left side.

For some reason, the Purple Moon Alpha is protecting Tonia fiercely, not letting anyone approach her. However, my friend is trying to push her off. Bobo, too, is busy defending Elena and her friend. I notice the tawny wolf also got hurt, he is limping a bit.

Around us, the fight is slowly dying down. The arrival of the Purple Moon warriors totally shifted the power balance to our side. Liam, too, is exceptionally efficient. It's my first time seeing the youngest Black brother fighting. Still, he's doing great, taking vampires down one after another without stopping. He even scares off a few of them.

"Elena, how is the...?"

"The North is okay; they are almost done! The water stopped attacking them, and the wolves that were hurt are getting back on their feet, too. I don't know what it is, but whatever it was is gone."

We both start mind-linking our sides to check, but it's the same everywhere. Vincent is busy taking care of his injured pack members, and the Sea Moon Wolves are dispersing to chase the remaining vampires on the harbor and hunt them down.

Elena starts to check her friend's leg, frowning. *"You're hurt... I told you to not shield me! Idiot!"*

Though she sounds angry, she seems genuinely worried for her friend. Moreover, I'm observing Bobo, who is walking in circles around them, not coming too close or leaving them, visibly anxious. What is this, Bobo? I wish he would go back to his human form to talk to me, but he just walks up to me once he sees me. He whines a bit, bowing his head, putting his ears down.

Gosh, don't apologize, Bobo. I'm okay, aren't I? I wish I could communicate with him, too, but instead, I just push him off gently with my muzzle. Once she's done tending her friend, Elena starts setting the vampire's corpses on fire, the usual thing to do. To my surprise, the Purple Moon Alpha then shifts back to her human form.

She's a tall, dark-skinned woman with long purple hair and lots of tribal tattoos. She obviously doesn't mind walking around naked, as she helps Elena with the fires. Once she goes back to Tonia, my friend growls furiously, obviously trying to fend her off. Didn't she spend the whole fight protecting her? What's with Tonia not wanting her close? I remember Bobo saying they have a connection, though he didn't get into the details. Well, it's probably not of my business anyway.

Liam walks back to my side. *"My brother is nagging me about you.*

They are coming here."

"Are they okay?"

"Nora, it's my brothers. Of course, they are fine."

Though his arrogant tone is a bit annoying, I'm finally relieved. I look around, and sadly, there are a few dead werewolves from each clan. I bet it's worse in the North... The Sea Moon Alpha joins us, and he shifted back to his human form, though he is clothed. He is an old man, rather short, with a sailor look.

"Jones, you little rascal," he says to the Purple Moon Alpha.

She waves back at him. "Hi, Old Man Seaver. How's your side?"

"It's not pretty, we lost a few good people. How's yours?"

"We're okay."

She won't say more. It must be hard on the Alphas whenever they lose people in a battle like this... And because of vampires, too. The Sea Moon Alpha turns to me. I can't really shapeshift now, I would be too embarrassed to stand naked. Still, it doesn't matter since I can communicate, anyway.

"Thank you for your help, young lady. I almost lost my daughter today, but you saved her. You helped a lot of my boys and girls. The Sea Moon Wolves have a debt to you, I won't forget it."

"It's nothing. I did what I had to."

"No, no, a Sea Wolf pays his debts. Sooner or later. Anyway, which pack are you from? I haven't heard of a pack with a white Alpha."

Oops. How am I supposed to answer that? I can mind-link other Alphas because of my genetics, not because I'm a pack leader... I exchange a look with Elena, but she just shakes her head, telling me not to disclose my origins. I know. But I can't think of what to answer. I'm not the Jade Moon Alpha, and I don't belong to Damian's pack either. Before I can answer, other wolves come running to us.

"Nora!"

Damian runs up to me. He and Nathaniel took the time to shapeshift and put on pairs of dark jeans, though they are still bare-footed, and their naked torsos are full of blood. It's quite a gruesome sight, making them both beautiful and scary, like angels of death. And to say I saw him in a perfect tuxedo not two hours ago... A dozen other wolves come following them, all looking a wreck.

My mate comes to me, putting his hands in my fur, checking for injuries underneath all the vampire blood. He soon sees my arm injury and growls in anger. The two other Alphas tense up immediately.

"Stop it, I'm fine..."

"I told you to stay right where you were!"

"Yes, and if I did, I would have been alone fighting vampires, anyway! They ran through the whole harbor, Damian! I had better chances with the Sea Moon pack than alone."

He growls again but doesn't talk back. We both know I'm right, and this is no time and place to argue. He stands up to face the others. The atmosphere totally changed upon their arrival. All wolves gather behind their Alphas, except the purple-haired woman, who is still by Tonia's side. Elena is also standing with her friend and other Opal Moon Wolves that arrived in the meantime. I notice Nathaniel is stealing glances at her, but she ignores him.

"The Black youngsters," says the Sea Moon Alpha. "I don't like seeing the likes of you on my harbor, but I guess this is what they call an emergency situation."

"Indeed," adds Lysandra. "How is the North?"

"We are fine. The remains are being burnt as we speak, and we chased them far enough. The White Moon Clan is taking care of whatever is left," says Nathaniel.

Once again, he looks at Elena while mentioning the White Moon Clan, but she doesn't say a thing.

"What was that? They attacked at the South-East, too." Asks Lysandra, annoyed.

"They struck the North first. We received the Northern packs' distress calls early enough and went to help them, but there were about a hundred vampires."

"You mean only a hundred? How come the White Moon couldn't get rid of that? Did they get soft or something?"

Elena, her friend, and the other Opal Moon wolves present immediately growl at her, vexed by her words, but she ignores them.

"It wasn't only vampires. Something was helping them. I saw the water from the river catching and trapping wolves. Some were poisoned, too; we had many victims that way. Something was definitely off."

"Sounds like a witch to me."

All eyes turn to the old Alpha, Seaver, who is scratching his beard. Damian turns to him, frowning.

"A witch?"

"Witches are elemental creatures. If a Water Witch was helping them..."

"It would explain how they got past the first defenses so easily..." Whispers Nathaniel.

"Then what drove her off? Did anyone get her?" Asks Lysandra, looking around.

"We didn't even see one. Only vampires. But she could have attacked from further away. I don't know how their magic works."

"Send some people to look at the bodies. See if they find a Witch among them," orders Damian to some of the Blood Moon wolves.

I didn't think of a Witch... I know very few about those, they are by far rarer than other creatures, too. All I've heard is that they look like human women and have mystical powers they use to cast spells and manipulate elements, as old Seaver said. The presence of a Witch could indeed explain what happened. They are our natural enemies, like vampires. But would they ally with vampires?

"What about what happened in the South, then? That time, the trees helped the packs. I don't think a witch would have changed her mind," says Lysandra.

"And they can't change their elements, either. What if there is another Witch left in the South?" Asks the Sea Wolf Alpha.

"If there is, she helped us. She was on our side," says Elena.

All eyes turn to her, surprised to hear someone else other than the Alphas talk, but they don't have time to discuss hierarchy now.

The old man sighs. "I don't like the idea of a remnant witch here."

"Me neither," says Lysandra.

I don't blame them. Who wants to keep a natural enemy anywhere near? I see Elena frowning, exchanging looks with the tawny wolf. Is she worried about a witch being around?

"Let's send people to search for her in the Sou—" But before she can finish her sentence, Liam is loudly growling next to us, making everyone jump. I never heard him so angry before!

"I will take care of it! Let me look for the witch!"

His voice is echoing in my mind, but he is obviously talking to the Alphas. Why is he so adamant about looking for that witch? Damian and Nathaniel both put on the same surprised expression. Obviously, they didn't expect this. They stay silent for a while, but none of the other Alphas dares to speak as the three brothers keep exchanging looks for a while, obviously mind-linking. Eventually, Nathaniel sighs.

"If you want, Liam, you take care of it. We have our hands full as it is with this mess anyway... Just ask if you need help. Don't take on a Witch by yourself."

"...Understood, brother."

He looks enthusiastic about this, but I'm a bit worried. If this witch helped us, whoever she was, is it okay to try to find her? But I can't say it here. I will talk about this with Liam later when things cool down.

After that, the Alphas keep talking, mostly about the casualties and damages. I exchange a look with Elena, who isn't listening.

"Is your friend okay?"

"Yeah, he injured his leg, but it's going to heal quickly. I'm more worried about the rest of my pack... We lost some people, so I want to go there soon."

"Why don't you go now?"

"My Alpha wants me to represent him here, seeing what the other packs will do. It's only the White Moon and Opal Moon Wolves to clean the mess up there now, so we got to make sure we will get some help."

Saying this, she looks to Nathaniel, and their eyes finally meet. I can guess he is asking her if she's okay with his lips, but she soon shifts back, her eyes to the group.

"Nathaniel will help you."

"Nh."

Her response is a bit odd. Why is she hiding so many things now? Not shape-shifting, avoiding Nathaniel... I bet he doesn't know she can mind-link other Alphas, either. I don't want to put my nose in a business that isn't mine, but I feel concerned whenever Elena's involved. Is it because I know we are related?

While I'm lost in my thoughts, the Alphas are done talking. The Sea Moon Alpha, whom someone called Patrick during the conversation, draws back his wolves. He nods in my direction, and with that, the Sea Moon Wolves head back to the South.

Lysandra turns to Damian. "It was nice, making peace to kick some blood-sucker's asses. But don't think I'm going to get nice with you dumbasses because of that."

"Just get the hell back to your turf, Jones," growls Damian.

It seems like the short-lived alliance is over... And the Purple Moon Wolves have no intention to behave well because of what happened, either. Lysandra sends a kiss in Tonia's direction, who answers with a growl, before their pack leaves. Right when I think they will now talk with Elena, I notice she and her pack members are gone already. I didn't even see them leave!

"We are not on our turf either, we should go," says Nathaniel. "And then, Nora, maybe you can explain to us how you mind-linked the whole werewolf population of Silver City."

Oops. I had forgotten this detail.

"Okay, I really wouldn't want to be you right now..."

"Gosh Liam, shush. You are not helping at all."

Chapter 8

I refuse to shift back to my human form while still on the fighting ground and win some extra time to think about an explanation to give to the Brothers. Of course, Liam kept mind-linking me all the way to the apartment, though we both acted like nothing happened. Damian seemed too busy to notice anyway. He stayed silent, but I could tell from his frowning that he was busy mind-linking other people as well. Maybe Nathaniel, since he didn't come with us.

Aside from all of Liam's restless questioning, I'm more worried about what to tell his eldest brother. I know Elena asked me to keep what she had found about us a secret for now, and honestly, until it was confirmed, I didn't want to talk about it either. But now, everyone heard me call for help, even all the way to the White Moon's Clan Northern territory. How do I explain this...?

Once we reach the building, Liam and Damian first go to the apartment downstairs to take a shower and change. Bobo, Tonia, and I aim to do the same in mine. We ruined the cars with all that vampire blood, and truthfully, it's one of the worst smells I ever experienced. I use lots of shampoos to take it off my hair and cleanse my wound, too. Once in my human form, I realize it's not that bad. Just a clean, about five centimeters long cut, and not too deep either, the bleeding already stopped. Silver does sting...

Since it's late already, I change into my pajamas and go back to the main room. Tonia is already there, in a bathrobe, inspecting her wounds. She has a black eye, a cut on her lower lip, several ecchymoses, a sprained ankle, and I would guess a couple of broken ribs. I quickly fetch the first aid kit from my bathroom and come back to help her take care of it.

"This is pathetic," she growls as I put some cream around her eye.

"It would have been better if you hadn't insisted on stepping between them and me," I scold her.

"For the reminder, protecting you is my job, baby girl."

I roll my eyes, but don't argue back. I don't feel like getting into this endless discussion now. Bobo comes back from his sister's room, too, wearing jeans. I'm glad he's back to his human form. Aside from a few bruises, he seems fine. He joins us and looks at Tonia, frowning.

"It's been a while since you've been in such a bad—"

"Don't say it," growls Tonia. "It's embarrassing enough as it is."

Bobo sighs and goes to sit on one of the kitchen stools. He looks exhausted, with his dreadlocks in a mess. He rests his arms on the bar and closes his eyes. Right, it's past midnight now. I hear something vibrating, and he raises his head to take out his phone. He reads a text and smiles. Tonia sees it, too.

"I really want to smash you right now. Stop smiling. You do know the boss is going to kill you, right?"

"Apparently, it was worth it," he whispers with an enigmatic smile.

"You left Nora alone, you selfish brat!"

"It's okay, Tonia, I really don't mind. I did okay by myself, and Bobo did protect me afterward."

"No, he was supposed to protect you, not that blondie!"

Bobo ignores her, and so do I. This can go on for a while with Tonia. So, I just take care of her wounds while Bobo closes his eyes and pretends to rest next to us. I honestly don't mind, though I am a bit curious to know what happened back there. Then again, I trust him. He probably had his own reasons.

A few minutes later, I'm done treating Tonia as much as I can, though I think she should go to the hospital. A couple of X-rays may be useful, but she refuses, saying she will be healed in a few hours. So instead, I decide to cook some late dinner, since the fight basically left everyone tired and famished. I grab whatever I find in the fridge to make up a pile of sandwiches. Liam warns me through the mind-link that he and Damian are coming up.

"What about Nathaniel?"

"He's still there, taking care of the aftermath. I think it's more about his girl, though. Who knows?"

"...Elena?"

"Yeah."

The door to the apartment opens, and they walk in. The two of them picked black t-shirts and jeans, and, as Liam predicted, they both look unharmed and fine. Liam runs to the table to grab some sandwiches and starts eating before he even sits up. I can't blame him; I'm starving, too, and I'm not sure the twenty sandwiches I made are going to be enough to feed all the wolves in the room. Even Damian picks one before coming to sit next to me.

I was a bit afraid of getting into another argument with him, but he gives me a quick kiss on the forehead and sighs. "Sorry for earlier. I was a bit on edge... You did great, Nora."

"Hell yeah, she did. She couldn't even shapeshift one month ago, and now she's fighting vampires like a warrior," adds Liam, his mouth full.

I smile. Indeed, I'm quite surprised with myself in a good way. It seems like my instincts did their job tonight...

For a few minutes, everyone enjoys the silence and my sandwiches. It's been a crazy night, for sure. First, my birthday surprise, then an attack on the harbor, and now I'm having a tuna sandwich at 1 am. I think about the things that I left on the boat. I hope I can retrieve those later; I left my necklace and earrings there...

"There was something weird about this attack," suddenly says Tonia.

Damian nods. "It's like they just wanted to get inside the city no matter what. And I've never seen such a big group of vampires."

"Could it be they had a commander?" Mutters Bobo.

"You're thinking about the witch?" I ask.

"Maybe. It's not the first time a witch would have taken control of vampires. They do partner up sometimes," says his sister, taking a new bite of her sandwich.

"...I think they were targeting Nora."

All eyes turn to Liam. He stopped eating, his eyes far off. He takes a new sandwich and starts talking again. "When I arrived, one of them said they needed to take her alive. Isn't that weird? Why do they care who they kill or not? And there were a lot of them after you, too. If you were their aim, that explains why they rushed to the harbor."

All eyes turn to me. I hesitate for a while, but I can't hide things forever. I turn to Damian. "Liam's right. I'm not sure about being their target, but one of them did say they wanted to capture me."

My mate frowns. "Why would they want you...?"

"I think... It might have to do with my lineage."

"Your lineage? I thought you didn't know who's your birth mother?" Asks Tonia with a confused look.

"I still don't. But... I think she might have been a... a Royal."

As soon as I drop that last word, they look at me with shocked expressions, except for Bobo and Damian. I wish I knew what he is thinking, but as always, his silver eyes are indecipherable.

"...A Royal?" He murmurs.

I nod, waiting for his reaction. But he stays silent, looking at me like he's deep thinking. After a while, I shift my eyes to Bobo, silently asking for help.

He sighs. "Someone from the Opal Clan mentioned it today. A family of Royals got killed in the North about eighteen years ago. And Nora has... well, white fur and blue eyes, so..."

I hope Elena won't resent me for this...

"You think your last name is a Clan's name?" Asks Tonia.

"I'm just saying it could be."

"...That would explain a lot of things..."

I turn to Liam, who is scratching his chin, thinking. He points out his fingers one by one in his free hand, the other one still holding a sandwich. "Clan-like last name. The white fur and blue eyes combination thing. Your dad taking you away from your unknown mom. Your Alpha genes and obvious good fighting instincts. Your altered abilities, like no fast-healing but large-scale mind-linking."

"Yeah, what was that, by the way? Even I heard you!" Says Tonia.

I shake my head, just as clueless. I have no idea what I did! I just panicked and unconsciously asked for help. I didn't think that would result in me sending out a significant distress signal to all the werewolf population of Silver City!

Damian finally turns to me, reacting to Tonia's words. "Did you know you could do that?"

"No, not at all. I just discovered tonight I could reach out to other Alphas, too. It's like a door opened in my mind. If my wolf has seen them eye-to-eye, she can talk to any Alpha, I think."

"Can you talk to me?"

"I can. See? Easy."

"That's interesting..."

Damian smiles, but Liam catches us.

"Hey, no mind-flirting now, you two! We are still in the room."

Damian playfully growls at his brother, but I just chuckle. He is one to talk, we spoke like that for the whole trip to here!

Tonia, too, wants to go back to the serious topic.

"Okay, so now Nora can mind-link any Alpha. That's an Alpha ability anyway, but she mind-linked us, too, tonight. To be honest, baby girl, it was more of a big siren ringing in my head than nice talk."

"Yeah, same for me. Felt like all I could focus on was your voice, it was loud and... mesmerizing," says Bobo.

"It sounded normal for us, Alphas, right brother?"

Damian nods. I remember Elena did advise me not to make use of the mind-linking too lightly. What did she say again? Her pack members found it annoying. Maybe that's what she meant if our voice sounds like what the Mura siblings described.

"I don't think I could do it again now, anyway."

"Well, don't try. I already have a headache. Let's save the testing for another time, baby girl," grumbles Tonia.

"But it's good to know. Now even if Nora is in trouble, she can ask for help by herself as easily as that." Liam winks at me and grabs his fifth sandwich.

He's right. Now not only we confirmed that I can fight for myself, but I can even warn others if I'm in trouble. Damian nods, my mate seems content about this news. Can I hope he is not going to be as overprotective as before now?

"There is still that whole Royal theory we need to confirm," says Bobo.

We exchange a look. I know. Elena wasn't sure of anything, but if we could somehow find a way to confirm it...

"...What about a blood test?"

All eyes turn to Tonia.

Damian frowns. "You think you could check this with a blood test?"

"Wait, you're telling us the girl spent a month in a hospital, and you never checked her blood?" Says Liam.

"Because we didn't think of checking her DNA! We were busy trying to keep her alive, for the record. Analyzing werewolf genes is a specific analysis. But yeah, it's worth trying. If Nora is a Royal, we..."

"A Royal's child," I correct.

"Right, but even as Royal's child, your werewolf genes should light up like a Christmas tree once we check your stats. I can ask Nana to help, I'm sure she would know."

Damian nods, but to be honest, there is something else I would like to check. My eyes turn to Bobo, and he knows right away what I am thinking about. If we can do blood testing, I can even see how closely related Elena and I are!

When I come back with the tea, they already changed subjects back to the attack. Damian left Nathaniel behind to oversee the Northern territory's defense issues with the White and Opal Moon Clans, and Tonia explains the situation at the harbor.

"They were so adamant about getting to the harbor... Doesn't that mean they knew where Nora was right away? Assuming she was her target, anyway."

"She definitely was," says Liam.

"But why? Why would they want Nora, why her in particular?"

"...Maybe it's because of this whole Royal thing?" Says Bobo.

I frown. What would vampires have any interest in a Royal? Royals are specials for werewolves, not for vampires... And it's not like I'm a leader of some sort or anything.

"Or it could be to destabilize my brother? He is known to be the Alpha of Silver City, even if it's unofficial. If they took Nora as a hostage, they could—"

Damian growls, but I put my hand on his to calm him down and shake my head.

"I doubt it, Liam, no one really knows about me. Even tonight, people from the other packs had no clue who I was or which Clans I was related to. The Jade Moon Clan concealed my existence for years, and I only went out a few times in the last two months. Vampires should be even more clueless..."

"But what's their point in catching a Royal's kid?" Says Tonia, doubtful.

"Maybe not for the vampires, but for the witch..."

Once again, all eyes turn to Liam.

"What? Witches can do weird stuff. Maybe she wants to try, well, using Nora for curses..."

"You got to be pretty damn sure of how useful she is going to be if you send a hundred vampires to a city full of werewolves just to get one!" Grumbles Tonia,

Damian growls again. I guess hearing about how a witch could use my body is not to his liking... I need to stop all this thinking before he gets too many ideas.

"Anyway, we are not sure of anything for now. We can only test my blood and see what's right or not about this whole Royal theory."

"And strengthen our defenses. Neal said they didn't find any witch among the bodies, so if there really is one, she might try to attack us again. I'll hold a meeting with all the Alphas," says Damian.

"I think we have some time before that Witch can attack again. It must have taken time to gather so many bloodsuckers, and we killed them all. If it was an alliance, she won't be able to find any Clan willing to cooperate with her for a while. If she subdued them somehow, I would guess it's going to take a while to do it all over again, too," adds Liam.

"Those are just theories. And since when are you a witch expert, anyway?"

I must agree with Tonia. I had no idea Witches could subdue vampires, but Liam seems to know a lot more than I would have thought.

He shrugs. "I have to hunt one down on our territory. I should know the basics, at least."

"Catch her fast, Liam. We ought to know if she's on our side. Otherwise, we have to get rid of her, too..."

"I know."

I yawn without being able to hold back, and Bobo does the same two seconds later.

Tonia sighs. "Well, I guess kids should go to bed. You're getting up early tomorrow."

"Wait, I have to go to school, too?" Says Liam, pissed.

"Yes, you do! Just because you came and fought a few bloodsuckers, you think you can skip? Hell no, brat," growls Tonia.

I forgot about work, too. It's late, but I can still catch some decent sleep if I go to bed now. Liam argues with Tonia for a while before Damian intervenes.

"Liam, enough."

With just those two words, the youngest brother stops complaining right away, though he is obviously pouting. Tonia smirks, and I can't help but smile, too, at his childish behavior.

Damian throws him a key. "You're sleeping downstairs at Nate's place. Tonia, you're coming with me. Bobo, you stay there."

They all agree, but I turn to Damian, a bit disappointed. "You're not staying?"

"I have to go back. The White and Pearl Moon Clans need help, and I can't leave Neal and Nate to handle it on their own."

He quickly turns his eyes to the others, and everyone gets the message; they all exit the room immediately, leaving us alone. He takes my hand and kisses it softly, making me smile.

"Sorry... I know it's your birthday."

"It's okay, my birthday ended over an hour ago. And I had the best one in my life, too."

I lean to kiss him, and he responds to it immediately. I'm getting braver and braver whenever we interact. Maybe getting to know more about his past helped, too. He puts an arm around my shoulders, and we both lean on the back pillows, my head against his shoulder.

"I'm sorry for leaving you behind, but I'm glad you weren't in the front lines. I was worried enough about where you were."

"I know... I'm glad I can defend myself now, but there is so much going on..."

"Don't worry. We can handle a witch or two."

"At least the other packs helped. I didn't think they would."

"Not all the packs. That's another reason I want to talk to them, but you don't need to concern yourself with that."

Here we go again. Whenever it involves the other werewolves, Damian shuts me out. Am I not supposed to become his Luna someday? Shouldn't I at least be interacting with his pack already? But Damian never lets me close to his pack's affairs or members, except for his brothers and the Mura siblings. I don't like being put aside.

Maybe Elena is right, and I should stay cautious...

"You look tired. I should go," he whispers.

I nod, and he puts a quick kiss on my forehead before leaving. I stay alone for a while, lost in my thoughts without really falling asleep. I hear Bobo coming back, and he lays next to me on the couch, his head on my lap, like he always did as a wolf.

"Liam and my sis left. How are you?"

"Tired... How about you?"

"Same. But your sandwiches were delicious."

"Thanks, Bobo."

We stay silent for a few seconds, and for a moment, I wonder if he fell asleep after closing his eyes, but he starts talking again.

"I think it's worth a shot. The blood testing."

"I think so, too... I should ask Elena to do the same."

"Don't worry, she has someone who can do it for her."

"...The tawny wolf?"

I just guessed randomly, but to my surprise, Bobo nods. I hope her friend is okay, though his injury didn't seem too bad. She mentioned they lost friends from their pack... I probably shouldn't try to contact her now. They are probably either tired or busy. I suggest to Bobo we should get to bed, and he agrees. He changes back to his wolf form and comes to sleep on my bed.

I take a while to fall asleep, though. Once again, it was a big day. I would have had an incredible birthday if it wasn't for the events that followed it... I remember my moon necklace and quickly text Damian about it. He replies right away, saying not to worry and that he'll send someone to fetch it. Reassured, I finally lose myself to slumber.

For the next two weeks, things get quite busy for everyone.

I kept working steadily at Nathaniel's restaurant, even if the man barely had any time to come and visit it himself. Since I demonstrated my fighting skills during our battle against the vampires, Damian finally agreed to lighten the surveillance around me. For example, Bobo didn't have any obligation to watch me while I was working at the restaurant anymore. He was now only showing up at the end of my shift. Also, Tonia didn't come to the apartment as often as before. We kept our training sessions in the morning, and she would still sleep over a couple of times a week to have more time to help her brother with his Beta functions.

As planned, she sent my blood samples to Granny Adriana, and now we are just waiting for the results. Liam also took some, though he never said who he would give it to, no matter how I insisted. He did promise he would let me know later, though.

Finally, Elena said her friend Daniel, the tawny wolf, was to run some tests on both our blood samples to see if he could find out about our kinship. Apparently, Daniel is a medical student, though his specialty is psychiatry. But Elena and I barely interacted since the fight. She seems busy, probably still the aftermath of the attack.

Damian, too, hardly has any time to meet with me. It looks like his

Alpha duties keep him running from one place to another after this mess. He never shares with me whatever it is that he was busy with, though. As time passes, I ask less and less but got more suspicious. Not only is he obviously keeping me in the dark, but because of this, I can't trust him, and our relationship wasn't making any progress either.

One evening after work, Liam, like often, comes to the apartment to eat with Bobo and me after his classes. I was starting to doubt that he really is looking for the Witch in Silver City. He just goes to school or skips it from time to time to drop by unannounced, like tonight. However, I'm set on making him spill the beans about Damian. I know he and Nathaniel know more than they want me to think.

"Why do you think my brother lets me meddle in his adult stuff? They both treat me like a kid!" Says Liam, sitting on my kitchen counter and eating cherry tomatoes.

"Don't act innocent when it suits you, Liam. I'm sure you know something and won't tell me."

"If I do, and I don't say I do, I'm not going to snitch. Sorry to disappoint you, Nora, but you are not nearly as scary as my brother."

So, I'm just not intimidating enough now? I roll my eyes while fetching the basil herbs, and take the bowl of cherry tomatoes from him, only to annoy him. "I thought I could trust you!"

"Oh, you can! But still, not going to talk."

He is really annoying sometimes... I turn to Bobo for help, but he is busy texting again. He is glued to his phone these days! I stir up the sauce, trying to think of how I can convince him.

"Liam, I know something is going on, and no one will tell me. All I do is go to work and come home."

"What are you talking about, you do go out sometimes."

"I'm talking about wolf stuff! I'm still without a pack, remember? It's been weeks! I can't just act human, I need to have a pack, hunt with other wolves, mind-link other people."

This is the biggest issue for me these days. I don't get why Damian still hasn't let me join his pack yet. He won't even let me meet them!

"Welcome to my life! My brothers only cared about having me go to school and not get into fights."

"But you do get into fights," says Bobo.

"Yup, I'm a rebel. But that's not the point."

His finger heads to try my sauce, but I slap his hand and glare at him. No answers, no treats.

He pouts. "Gosh, you're starting to learn from my brother. You're almost as good as him at glaring now..."

"I'm going to do a lot more than glaring if you don't start talking, Liam.

He gasps. "Seriously? You're down to threats now?"

"Told you, my patience has its limits."

He frowns, and stays silent for a while, thinking. I leave him to his thinking and set up the table for three. Bobo finally puts his phone aside and helps me bring the food as we take a seat. Finally, Liam comes to sit too and looks at me in the eyes.

"Okay... I can't talk, because I want to die a painless death, but I can give you a hint, as long as you promise not to tell my brothers."

"I promise."

He breathes in and finally says it. "You should go the Black Corp's Christmas Party. There you go. ...Can I eat this plate of pasta now?"

He starts eating right away, but I'm still dumbfounded. "Wait, what Christmas party?"

Liam ignores me and keeps eating, so Bobo is the one to explain.

"It's the Black Corporation annual Christmas Party. They hold one every year for all the employees, including big clients, so a lot of people attend. Most of the Blood Moon Clan will be there, but they also invite people from other Clans."

I had no idea this kind of event happened. I don't think the Jade Moon Clan ever was into any sort of big business like this. I know close to nothing about Damian's company, either.

"So, why would I go to this Christmas Party?" I ask Liam.

"Just go, and you will see what this is all about. I should warn you though, you are probably not going to like it."

Why wouldn't I? What is this mystery that I could solve by attending this party? Is Damian going to make an announcement of some sort? I don't think Liam chose this randomly or is warning me without reason. I should probably go... And not tell Damian about it, though I really don't like the idea of doing such things.

"When is it then?"

"In a few days. December 14th."

"Oh, I got time then."

But Liam chokes and spits out a bit of spaghetti. I hand him a glass of water to help, but he gulps it down before turning to me. "Nora, It's not just a next-door party. You can't go in like that. You are going to need an invitation, an escort, a dress."

Now he is scaring me. I have never been to a party before, but I didn't imagine it would be such a big fuss! For a minute, I'm wondering if he is not exaggerating, but that doesn't seem the case. I turn to Bobo, and he just nods. "Those parties are a pretty big deal. All the rich people of Silver City are going to try sneaking in."

Great... Which means I will be totally out of place there. I sigh. Why must I go through all this? Just because Liam said so doesn't mean I will find what I'm looking for! What if I go there for nothing or worse, just go ridicule myself in front of a bunch of strangers? Liam sees me panicking and rolls his eyes. "Don't start panicking now, Nora. I can be your escort, for starters. They always send me an invite, but I don't usually go. This way, my brothers won't suspect a thing."

"For the dress, you surely have all you need in your wardrobe," says Bobo. "If not, you can just ask my sister to go shopping. She probably won't think it's for the party."

I nod to their suggestions, not happy about it, though. I'm too scared and busy thinking now. Can I really go to that party behind Damian's back? Gosh, I hope it will be worth it...

After dinner, Liam leaves, and I head straight to my room to talk to Elena. Bobo gave me her number earlier since it will probably be less intrusive than mind-linking. I'm on my own since Bobo decided to go to the gym upstairs. Turns out, despite being usually on the lazy side, he does have a thing for training, like his big sister.

I lay on my bed and take out my smartphone to call Elena, who answers after a few seconds.

"Hi, Nora."

"Hi, Elena. Are you free to talk right now?"

"Sure, it's just Danny and me. Is everything okay?"

"Yes, yes, everything is... fine. How is Daniel?"

"He's recovering fast, like a werewolf. Lucky him."

I chuckle. I suppose Elena is thinking about our inability to fast-heal... I hear someone talking to her in the background, but she just answers that she's on the phone with me.

"Sorry, Nora."

"No, it's okay. I just wanted your opinion on something."

"What is it?"

I explain everything to her; How my relationship with Damian is confusing me, his attitude, what Liam told me. It takes a while, but I am finally pouring out everything I held in so far. For some reason, I feel a lot better confiding in Elena. Maybe it's because she is a girl and not part of the Blood Moon Clan. Also, it might be because I hope we are related, but I really feel some connection with her... I'm more interested in confirming that before knowing whether I am a Royal's child or not. If Elena and I really turn out to be related, she would be my only family left, other than Alec...

Once I'm done talking, she stays silent for a long while, then starts slowly laughing.

"What is so funny?" I ask, smiling, too.

"Sorry, it's just... Really, nothing is ever simple with those Black Brothers, don't you think?"

I can't help but agree.

"Are you and Nathaniel...?"

I'm not sure how to finish this sentence. I'm probably not supposed to know, let alone supposed to ask! I blush, realizing a bit late I'm totally intruding on Elena's privacy. To my surprise, she just sighs.

"No... And yes... I guess it's complicated. For now, I need time to think, so I've been keeping Nate out of my life these days."

"...Are you okay?"

"I am. I just didn't think things would get so complicated. That's what relationships do to you, I guess? But don't worry, I'm okay. And I've got Danny supporting me."

I hear him answering her in the background, though I don't know what he says.

"Anyway. To be honest, I would say you should trust Liam on this one."

"...You already know what this is about, don't you?"

"...I have suspicions."

I figured so. After all, Elena was the first one to tell me not to trust Damian to quickly, so she probably had her reasons for that. I guess she will not be the one to tell me what all this mystery is about, anyway. I must figure it out on my own.

"Nora, anything yet on the blood results?"

"Not yet. Tonia said it would take time. Apparently, gene-testing is longer."

"I figured so... Danny said the same thing. But I have something else. Apparently, matching our blood test results is much quicker."

I stop breathing for a second. Is this for real? Already? I'm so not ready! I get up, fidgeting while trying to breathe again.

"Nora?"

"Sorry, I'm just so stressed suddenly! Do you really have it? You know?"

"Yes. Daniel just got the results this afternoon. I wanted to see you in person to tell you, but now that you called me first, I really don't think I can keep quiet until then. But can you breathe first? You're scaring me a bit, and if you collapse, I'm way too far to help."

"No, I'm okay! Just tell me, is it a match? Is it?"

I hear her laugh at the end of the phone, and someone is agitating some paper. Probably our results! Gosh, the suspense is killing me!

"Elena!" I beg, unable to wait anymore.

"Nora, it is! We are related!"

Oh, Moon Goddess Mother.

It's for real. Elena and I are related! I can't believe it! I have another family member that close to me! Moreover, she is related to my mom, to my birth Clan! I feel tears coming up, and I smile like an idiot. While I'm trying to catch my breath, I hear Elena silently crying, too.

"Are you okay?" I ask.

"Why do you ask? You are crying like a baby, too!" She replies, half-laughing and half-crying.

We both laugh and cry for a few seconds, and Bobo suddenly comes back into the room. Seeing me in tears, he runs up to me with a worried look. I shake my head, whispering that I'm okay. I put the phone on speaker, to let him hear Elena, too.

"Nora, there's more."

"What do you mean?"

"According to Daniel, the percentage of matching DNA can indicate how closely related we are, so he brought the full results. You and I have 13.3% of matching DNA."

Isn't that a lot? I must calm my breathing again. I can hear Elena smiling; she is having fun with this suspense.

"Elena, speak!"

"We are cousins, Nora. First cousins! One of my birth parents was your mom's sibling!"

"...Are you kidding?"

"No, I'm not! Daniel just told me this much matching DNA can only be a first-degree cousin! Can you imagine? Your mother is my aunt! We are cousins!"

I can't believe it! I have a cousin! A cousin from my mother's side! I can't help but cry and giggle, and Elena is in the same state at the other end of the line. We don't even look alike, how could I have guessed we were so closely related? I did hope that we would turn out to be distant relatives, but this is unreal!

Bobo is happy for me, and he hugs me as I try to calm down. When I finally do, he brings me to sit with him on my bed. Once I eventually calm down, I can see and think much clearer. So clearly, in fact, that I realize another detail.

"Elena, do you know what this means?"

"Yeah, I thought about it right away. That means if you turn out to be, I would be a Royal's child, too."

"Could it be?"

"Daniel said so. I may not have as much as you, but I do have some Royal characteristics, after all... Probably that my non-Royal parent was less pure or something? I don't know..."

I feel her tense up a little bit, and her tone as changed, too. Why do I feel like something is wrong...? I thought she wasn't really caring about the whole Royal thing? Not that I am, either, but...

"Elena? What do you mean you need to find out?"

"I know I said before it didn't really matter for me, but..." I hear sighing, and she whispers something with Daniel for a while, I don't know what. Bobo suddenly pulls the phone towards him.

"You can tell Nora, Elena. She won't tell anyone."

"Tell me what?" I ask, a bit worried now.

"Nora, I need you to promise me you won't tell anyone what I'm about to say. Especially not the brothers. Not even Tonia, or anyone else."

"I promise. What is it?"

"...I learned yesterday before the battle. I'm pregnant. It's Nate's."

Oh, Moon Goddess...

Chapter 9

The next Friday, even while working, I can't help but think about my conversation with Elena again. A baby... She started crying after telling me about Nathaniel being the father. I was unable to say anything and just felt useless, listening to her. I just found out she is my cousin, and now she is also pregnant.

Eventually, that friend of hers, Daniel, took the phone and said they would call back. I haven't heard from them since then, but I know she probably just needs some time.

I still felt bad for Elena, though. If she is not Nathaniel's girlfriend or anything, how will she handle this pregnancy? It explains why she was so distant from him yesterday, also why Daniel and Bobo were so adamant about protecting her during the battle. A pregnant werewolf can't shape-shift, not without risking the baby's life— the shapeshifting is too much of a struggle on the body after the first few weeks. I wonder how far how along she is?

I'm too busy to think about it any deeper, though. Earlier this week, a garbage boy took a last-minute sick-leave, and I had to replace him for the day. Turns out, Chef Michel was so happy with my performance in his kitchen that day, he fought with Narcissa to keep me there. So now, I must switch all the time between the kitchen and the restaurant, even during the actual service. Not that I would complain, though. I like working in the kitchen so much!

Chef Michel and I are now on a first-name basis. It has become a habit now that I would come and help the kitchen staff in the morning. I am nowhere near the level of the cooks or aides here, but they are always teaching me things and even asking for my opinion at times. It's thrilling to keep up with the rhythm in the kitchen, but I'm doing my best. Once again, everyone was surprised how well I handle the pressure. Truthfully, I'm a bit proud of it. Like any chef, Michel yells a lot, but this is really nothing compared to what I've felt before.

Once the service is done and we start cleaning up, Chef Michel suddenly calls me, sending someone else to take over for me. He is smoking at the back of the restaurant, like always. I don't really like the smell; I just stand a few steps away not to be impolite.

"You called for me, chef?"

"Yes. You did a perfect job today, Nora. Again. And what was that suggestion you made this morning? For the dessert?"

"Using rosemary to flavor the caramel?"

"Yeah, that one. How did you think of that?"

I blush a bit, overwhelmed by the compliments. How do I explain this? I feel a bit embarrassed about my background. Even though I seem to know a lot, I only have elementary experience in cooking. You can't learn it all from books...

"I just really like using herbs and spices while cooking, so... I tried balancing with sweet flavors for a change and found out some pairings work really well."

"Like what?"

I feel like this is some sort of test. I try to think of an answer I would give anyone, not to an experienced chef. "Like basil and strawberries. Or honey and lavender."

I see him smile. "You're good, Nora. You really got a talent for that. Why didn't you apply to be in the kitchen instead of a waitress?"

"I... I have no experience and no training to be in a kitchen."

He shakes his head. "You got the basics, that's all it takes. Good sense of taste, multitasking, and reactive. You're hard-working, and you can handle the pressure. Starting tomorrow, you'll work as an apprentice in the kitchen."

"What? But Narcissa..."

"I don't care what Narcissa says. I'll call the Boss, if necessary. You can start with Sam at the sauces for now. The old man could use an assistant."

I gasp. I don't even know what to say! Being a saucier's apprentice is already more than anything I could have asked for!

"Chef, I..."

"Don't thank me yet. We'll see how you can handle the old man first; he's twice more stubborn than I am, so that should—"

He suddenly stops talking and turns his head towards the end of the alley. I do the same. My wolf is growling, sensing something's wrong, too. Who is that? There's a horrible smell coming from a block away. Chef Michel throws his cigarette on the ground, his eyes not leaving the end of the alley a single second. We both stare at the same spot, waiting to see if the intruder will come closer or not.

No one is supposed to be there. There is a wooden fence at the end of the street, and only the restaurant's employees should be able to come here. That smell doesn't belong to anyone from the restaurant. It's such a disgusting smell! A mix of alcohol, rotten flesh, and cheap cologne, reeking so much I can't even distinguish its owner's scent.

"Who is that...?" I whisper.

"Someone who's not supposed to be here," growls Chef Michel.

I feel him tensing up, ready to shapeshift at any moment. I tell my wolf to be prepared, too. However, the smell disappears. Did they run away? We wait for a few seconds, but whoever it was is gone. I turn to Chef Michel, still frowning. "A rogue?"

"...It looks like it. I must tell the Boss. Let's go back in. Tell Boyan to come and get you. I don't like this."

To my surprise, it's not only Bobo who shows up, but as well. Unlike other days, there is no car, but just a big, black motorbike. I look at the engine, a bit worried. "Please tell me I'm not supposed to get on that thing."

"What's wrong with my bike?"

"I've never even been on a bicycle, Liam!"

He laughs, but this is just plain scary! "Don't be a baby, Nora. You just need to hang on tight, I'll drive safely, I promise. Come on, we have to change quickly before we get to the party, or we'll be late."

Late for what, exactly? I get on the motorbike despite my fear. At least, Liam seems experienced with it. And he's right. We are finally the 14th, and I want to see what all this fuss was about. To think Damian came to dine with me last night, and now I'm going to go to his party behind his back... But I need to know what he is hiding from me. I want to think Damian is being sincere, yet there is this invisible wall between us that I need to take down. And I'll see what kind of wall it is tonight.

Once we get home, I go straight to my room to shower and get ready. Choosing a dress is quicker with the guys than when Tonia is here, mostly because they let me pick it myself. I go for a rather simple empire dress with a silver glitter top and a long white skirt. Elegant yet straightforward— it should be good enough. For my makeup, even if I've been practicing these last few days while getting to read for work, I usually keep it really simple. For tonight, though, I have to make extra efforts. I look at a couple of online tutorials before getting started and proceed very slowly and carefully. The result is alright, I think... I put on a natural peach eyeshadow, a thin trail of eyeliner, some mascara, and a light pink blush. When Bobo comes into the room, I'm putting on the final touch, a rosy lipstick. I turn to him.

"How is it?"

"Very pretty. You look more natural than last time."

"Because I didn't put as much stuff... I can't remember half the names of the products the makeup artist gave me anyway."

Bobo smiles. "Are you going to be okay...?" He asks

"I don't even know what I'm supposed to see, so... Is it bad?"

He stays silent for a second. "...You should get your heart ready."

I stay silent. The more I hear about it, the harder it is to think it's a good idea...

Turns out, Boyan is good at braiding my hair and helps me put it up into a Greek goddess-like hairstyle. It also matches my dress perfectly, so I'm more than happy with it. Once we return to the main room, Liam is desperately trying to do his necktie. He turns to us, but before he can even ask, we shake our heads. I have no idea how to do this... He frowns, and takes it off, undoing his first button.

"Forget it, I'm not going to impress anyone, anyway. Are you ready, my lady?"

Indeed, I am, though I'm shaking a bit... I grab my white coat and put my necklace on. The little diamond moon is shining bright and matches my dress just fine.

"I just hope I'm dressed enough..." I sigh, taking an overall view in the mirror again.

Liam rolls his eyes. "Yes, you are. You're wearing a $5,000 Dior dress and a diamond $2,000 necklace. What else do you...?"

"I'm wearing *what*?" I scream, shocked.

"Oh, get over it, you know my brother is like, crazy rich."

"Liam!"

"Oh, come on, Nora, you should be used to it by now. So, if you are done being scandalized, can we go, please? Trust me, the price of your dress will be the last of your concerns after tonight."

While in the car, I'm still sending annoyed looks at Liam. I hate it when he plays with my nerves like that! And he's doing it on purpose, I know it. Even now, he won't bother to hide his smirk. I growl at him.

Bobo is driving, and no one is saying a word. I'm too nervous to talk, to be honest. I have no idea what to expect. While I imagine several scenarios, Liam's phone rings.

"Hi, Nate. What's up?"

I can recognize his brother's voice, but even with my enhanced hearing, I can't tell what Nathaniel's saying... Liam starts smiling. He lets his brother speak for a while before interrupting him. "Don't worry Nate, I'm on my way. ...Yup. No, I'm dressed as I should be, tuxedo and all. ...No, I borrowed someone's girlfriend to be precise."

His brother stays silent for a few seconds while Liam smiles. I heard my name, but Liam answers before I can say anything.

"Good guess! ...First, we both know Damian would never touch me. Plus, I bet Nora would kill him first. She deserves to know, don't you think? ...Do you really want to have the conversation about managing love relationships, Nate?"

Touché. Though I think that one was a bit mean from Liam... For a few seconds, I think about Elena's baby. Neither of them probably knows about the pregnancy yet. Nathaniel's love life is about to get a lot more complicated...

Both brothers stay silent for a while again, and I wonder if Nathaniel can do anything to prevent me from going. He could probably revoke Liam's invitation, no? To my surprise, Liam starts to smile again. "Really? You're going to help us?"

I hear Nathaniel yell something, but Liam laughs and hangs up. Even if he said otherwise, not doing anything is basically the same as helping us. Though Liam is happy about it, this call didn't make me feel better at all. I wonder if it's too late to turn back, but I don't even know what I'm supposed to fear! When Bobo finally stops the car, I recognize where we are. It's the entrance of the Grand Hotel, a five-star and one of the most luxurious hotels in Silver City. I'm feeling kind of better about my overpriced dress now...

Liam helps me out of the car, and Bobo follows us. It's my first time seeing the two of them dressed up, but there is quite a difference. Liam obviously chose a very luxurious tuxedo, while Bobo's outfit is much more discreet. He looks like a bodyguard with this look and size, and well, I guess that's kind of what he is for tonight?

A doorman guides us to the 32nd floor without even asking for an invitation. Liam winks at me. I guess he didn't need one, being one of the infamous Black Brothers... Once we finally arrive, the doors open on a gigantic Reception Hall.

It's very luxurious and intimidating. The marble floor is so clean and polished, I can see my reflection in it, and it's the same for the walls. Large chandeliers are hanging from the roof, with real candles lit up. On my right, a large bar with five barmen working swiftly, and on the left, a large glass-wall like the one in my apartment offers a breath-taking night view.

The place is crowded. Now I know why Liam said I wouldn't be overdressed. Every person standing in the room is wearing luxurious brand items, jewelry, and outfits. My dress doesn't seem out of place, and it's not the fanciest. Some ladies even have real gemstones embroidered on their dresses, when they are not wearing it as jewelry.

Liam gives me his arm to hold on, and I don't let go. I feel way too intimidated. For the first time, I see him really being a Black Brother. As we walk, people get out of our way, and I hear whispers all around us. A lot of the guests are eyeing Liam yet avoid his gaze. A few steps behind us, Bobo is also definitely making an impression too.

People are staring at me, as well, probably because I'm accompanying Liam. They observe me from head to toe, and they are not even trying to hide it. I feel like I just stepped into a nest of snakes...

"Well, well, look who is there!"

I turn around, and to my surprise, Lysandra Jones, the Purple Clan Alpha, is walking up to us. This time she is wearing clothes, a superb purple combi with assorted jewelry, and gold rings in her hair or as piercings on her nose, ears, and eyebrow. She stands in front of us, with a wide smile.

"Hi, Lysandra," Says Liam.

"You brat... You fought with my guys again this week, didn't ya? How many times do I have to tell you to stay out of my territory?"

"Come on, I thought we were just training? Are they tired yet?"

"Don't be too cheeky... One day I will come myself to give you that kick in the ass you're asking for."

"Any time!" Replies Liam with a cheeky smile.

Though the conversation seems heated, I feel like Lysandra is more amused by Liam's attitude than annoyed. I wonder why he has to go so often to provoke her warriors? Is it because they are strong rivals? She turns to me.

"Nice to see you in human form, whitey girl."

"How did you recognize me?" I ask.

"Blue eyes, a big scar on your face, and those guys around ya? Come on."

Right... I guess my visible scar in both my forms is a big giveaway. I tend to forget about it these days. Now I feel stupid... Indeed, anyone could recognize me, then. Lysandra doesn't mind that I'm staying silent, she starts talking again.

"By the way... I wondered which pack you were from, but seeing you're with these two, I guess you're a Blood Moon?"

I shake my head. "Not really. I'm more of a... free spirit now?"

This is a dangerous thing to say in a room full of werewolves, admitting that I don't belong to any Clan. But Lysandra just laughs. "Nice one! Well, if you ever get past this free-spirit phase, you can come to the Purple Clan anytime. We value fighters in my pack, so you would definitely be welcomed with what I saw the other week."

Wow, I didn't expect that... I whisper thanks, too shocked to think of anything else. Liam growls, though. "Don't dream about it. Nora will belong to my brother's pack."

"Who knows... The girl might change her mind?"

"If so, then you can always join the Sea Moon Wolves, too!"

We turn around. It's Grandpa Seaver! He walks up to us, flanked by two young people. The girl looks about my age or younger, with chubby cheeks and a brownish ponytail. She is wearing a sea-green dress and aquamarine earrings. The young man, probably her brother since they look so alike, is wearing a brown suit and has a large scar across his neck.

"Old Man!" Says Liam.

"Oh, shut up, kiddo. I'm here for the young lady, not you."

Is there an Alpha that Liam hasn't angered out there? They all seem annoyed at him! But he just laughs while the old man turns to me. "So, you're named Nora, are you? Patrick Seaver. Here are my children, Marina and Arthur. You saved both their lives last week."

The young Sea Moon she-wolf waves at me, a bit shy. Her brother just nods, but his eyes are glaring at Liam. Gosh, he really loves messing with everyone...

"It's nothing. We were in the middle of a battle, after all."

"Hopefully, the last one! I'm done with vampires for this lifetime!"

"Don't get your hopes up, old man. Those bloodsuckers will be back. Remember the last Council?" Sighs Lysandra.

"Everyone thinks the same?" I ask.

Lysandra nods. "All those who bothered to show up, anyway. The Sapphire Moon Clan really is a bunch of cowards, I tell you!"

Now that I think about it, among all the big Clans of Silver City, the Sapphire Moon Clan is the only one whose wolves didn't show up at all... They are one of the strongest Clans around, though. I would say they only lose to the Blood Moon, and Gold Moon Clans in terms of power. But other than that, those three are the strongest out there.

"...Even those weaklings from the Jade Moon Clan showed up!"

Liam scoffs. Gosh, I really didn't need to hear this... Seeing something is wrong, Lysandra frowns and asks about it. Liam is only too happy to answer. "Nora is the Jade Moon Clan... how do you call it? Owner?"

"Stop it, I don't own anything..." I whisper, embarrassed. "They just gave me their allegiance."

"Wait, you little girl controls half the east territory?" Asks Patrick.

I hesitate and nod. I guess this is a way of putting it... Lysandra suddenly claps her hands. "Right! The boys did tell me someone kicked Greene's butt a few weeks ago! Well done, whitey!"

...Is she really going to keep on calling me like that?

"Interesting. It seems like the Blood Moon Clan is really working on their connections..." mutters Arthur Seaver.

His father scratches his beard. "Right, son. Can't blame the kid, though. Times are hard. Lots of little mutts are showing up everywhere."

"Who cares about the rogues? What he wants is to contain the Sapphire Moon Clan. If they can't reach an agreement, things might get ugly!" Says Lysandra.

What agreement? I turn to Liam, lost. What is this about? I knew that the Blood Moon Clan and the Sapphire Moon Clan weren't on good terms, but I didn't think things were that bad...

"They are a proud Clan, the Sapphires. I doubt they will ever listen to Black. Though I'm not fond of the Gold Clan, either. Too greedy."

grumbles old man Seaver.

"Yeah, I'm not too fond of the idea either..." Says Lysandra

What about the Gold Moon Clan? Is Damian trying to make them his allies? I turn to Liam, asking him with my eyes what this is about, but he shrugs. The two Alphas change subjects, arguing about the limit between their turfs. Liam gently pulls me to the bar, leaving them. One of the barmen immediately walks up to us with a professional smile.

"What would you like, Mister Black?"

Liam is only too happy to answer to that and asks for two cocktails. I frown. We are underage! Plus, my alcohol tolerance is definitely not cocktail proof yet. But before I can even protest, he hands me a turquoise drink that smells a lot like vodka. I'm wondering if I can give it back, when my phone rings. It's Tonia...

"Nora! Where are you? I'm at your place, and no one is here. Bobo isn't picking up his phone."

Uh-oh. I turn to Bobo, not knowing what to say. He probably turned his phone off on purpose. I have a feeling his sister is going to freak out just like Nathaniel. I hesitate and finally answer.

"Tonia, I'm all right. ...I'm at the party."

"The party... What? At the party? Who told you about the party?"

She yells at the other end of the phone, but I really don't want to argue with her now. I'm mad at her for not telling me about it, too. Liam grabs my smartphone. I bet he is only too happy to make things worse... I ignore them and take a sip of my cocktail. Gosh, this is strong!

Suddenly, I hear a lot of chatter. A young woman just made her entrance. She is stunning, from what I can see before a lot of people run to her like bees gathering around honey. She has gorgeous brown hair, and golden eyes like Elena, though hers are darker, brownish. I'm not particularly inclined to fashion, but her dress is gorgeous. She looks like an actress, wearing a gold gown and a white fur coat.

"It's Alessandra King, daughter of the Gold Moon Alpha," whispers Bobo.

I get the information, but as my eyes follow her, some unease rises in my heart— a pain thumping in my chest. I watch her walk across the room; She has a perfect smile on her face and walks like a queen.

Everyone steps aside to let her through, and at the end of this path, I see Damian. Damian, standing there in a gorgeous black suit. He has a glass of champagne in his hand and is standing a few meters away from me, but I can see his features clearly. He is expressionless, looking at Alessandra. Once she arrives at his side, they slowly bow to each other.

I'm almost choking. My wolf is growling furiously. Something's wrong. Something's out of place. My fingers tremble around my drink, and my mind goes blank. She's putting her hand on his arm. Why does he let her do that? Why do they talk so casually? Why is nobody reacting? Isn't there something wrong with this? I feel sick, disgusted. Someone else is touching my mate! Why is she standing so close to him, their arms are touching!

While I'm running out of breath, watching them with my thoughts going wild, Liam comes next to me and whispers to my ear. "Welcome to my brother's engagement party, Nora."

Damian's... what?

My mind goes blank, yet my eyes can't stop watching them. This couple, standing across the room. Next to each other, a black and gold movie-like scene. I can't think; I just stare like some mindless idiot. I feel so stupid...

In the crowd of werewolves around them, no one is surprised to see those two together. They all know. Except for me. Nobody told me, and worse, they all made sure not to. Foolish, ignorant, blind Nora.

"Nora, are you okay?" Someone asks.

I don't know. How am I supposed to feel? I feel nothing right now. My heart just fell, somewhere really, really low. I'm numb as if my body is covered in ice. I can't even cry. I have both eyes fixated on them, and I have no idea what to do or how to react. Damian is talking to someone else, while that woman is still attached to him, her arm around his like he belongs to her.

"He is mine!"

My wolf is screaming inside, growling and crying her guts out. Her pain hits me like a hurricane. My chest is so painful, I can't breathe.

I take a step back. I want to run away from here. Why can't I stop watching when it's so painful? I can't stay here. Her. With him. The two of them, side by side. My mate and that girl together. I don't want to see that! The more I watch, the crazier my mind goes. Thoughts like a raging fire, burning me from the inside. How long? Since when? Why her? Does she love him? Does he love her? Does he love her more than me? Does he love me at all!

I can't stay here. I take another step back and realize there's broken glass at my feet. Is this mine? When I raise my head again, a lot of eyes are on me. Among them, a pair of silver eyes, wide open with surprise.

"Nora, watch out, you—"

I push them back. I can't take anyone touching me now. Not Bobo, not Liam, not anyone. I want to run from this horrible place, from this world. I turn around and start running. I hear Damian's voice calling my name behind me, and his brother's.

I run to the elevator, and a surprised waiter steps out to let me in. I push the ground level button, again and again, but I hear Damian's steps without looking up. Just as the door closes, he rushes in the tiny elevator space, and I instinctively retreat until my back hits the wall.

"Nora, listen to me. Look at me."

I avoid his eyes. I don't want to talk to him right now. I don't want to look at him. It's too painful! If I look at Damian, I'll see that vision of him with her again! I see his hands coming close, and I scream. "Don't fucking touch me!"

That's when I realize I'm crying. From my scorched voice. I'm crying hard and shaking. His hands freeze just before he touches me.

"Okay, okay. I won't touch you. But Nora, you must listen to me. It's not what you think."

Who cares about what I think? It's what I just saw and heard that matters! And I'm not ready to listen to it again! I feel like my heart will stop beating if I do! I cross my arms around me, shielding myself from him, staying the furthest away I can from Damian.

Why does it have to be me? I can take a hundred hits from Alec, but I can't take this! I trusted him. I knew something was wrong, somewhere in my mind I had that thought, but I still decided to trust him. Why now? Why this? After all this time? I love him, I love this man so badly, and that's why it hurts.

I raise my head, looking at him in the eyes, and between my tears, I hear my own voice. "Tell me it's not true. Tell me you're not engaged, Damian."

Maybe Liam lied. Perhaps I saw it wrong, and maybe that girl is just a close friend. Maybe it's was all just a joke, maybe I'm dreaming, some nightmare I need to wake up from.

I see Damian open his mouth, hesitating, but he stays silent, and this time, he is the one to avoid my gaze. I can't believe it. I cover my eyes with my hand, trying to calm down my crying, but gosh, it's hard.

"Nora, listen to me, please. It's true, I am engaged to Alessandra, but..."

"Shut up."

I don't want to hear her name in his mouth. I don't want to hear anymore. He's been with me for two months now. Yet he's still having this engagement party. I don't think of any good reason for this. He had weeks to call it off or break up with me. I... Who am I to him?

"...I thought you loved me."

He looks at me with scandalized eyes. "...What? Nora, I do! Do you seriously think I don't love you? I..."

"Then why the fuck is she the one you're going to marry! Why?"

"Nora, Alessandra is not the one I love, you are! She will just be my official Luna!"

I look at him, stunned beyond words. Is he mad? Does he have any idea of what he is saying right now? His Luna? What would I be, then? I think of the apartment he gave me. So, he wants to keep me in that tower, like a bird in a golden cage? I shake my head, at a loss for words.

The elevator reaches the ground level and opens. He is still in front of me, barring the exit.

"Move out of my way, Damian."

"Nora, no. You're hurt, and..."

"You're the one who hurt me!" I yell, ignoring all the people in the lobby. "I've had broken bones and a hundred wounds, but never have I ever been in pain like now! You took me for an idiot, Damian! *Now, out of my way!*"

As I yell those last words, he brutally retreats oddly, like he's pushed back or something. I don't even care. I run out in the lobby, with a lot of people staring at me. I must be looking crazy... I try to wipe out my flowing tears, I can barely see in front of me, I'm so angry, sad, and confused. I bump into someone, a man. I try to step aside and go on my way, but before I can make two steps, he suddenly grabs my arm.

"...Queen Diane?"

What the...?

He looks at me, his eyes confused. Who is this guy? I shake my head and elude him, running away. I run to the entrance of the hotel, to outside where it's pouring. I hate the rain... I keep walking anyway. I don't care about the rain or the cold, I just want to put as much distance as possible between Damian and me. I don't want him following me or something.

After a while of walking and crying, I finally stop. Gosh, I have no idea where I am... And Liam kept my phone, too. Who would I call anyway? I don't want to see any of them, they all lied to me all this time! The Black Brothers, even the siblings! Who can I trust now?

Suddenly, I remember Elena. I'm so agitated that it takes me a while to mind-link her, though.

"...Nora? Nora, why are you crying? Are you okay? What's wrong?"

"Elena, can I come to your place? I have nowhere to go."

"What? But what about your...?"

"I'm not going back there."

I know she can feel my distress. I'm tired, cold, and angrier than I have ever been. And even sadder than that.

"Okay, okay. Do you know where you are? We will come and get you, okay?"

After a couple more streets, I finally find the name of a nearby restaurant to give her.

They arrive ten minutes later, in a car. Elena takes me to sit with her in the back seat, covering me with a thick blanket they brought. A blonde guy is driving, probably her friend Daniel. His human form is different from what I expected. He is thin, tall, and has a rather pretty face, with blue eyes and small, round glasses. With his little goatee and fold-over sweater, he looks like a bit of a bookworm. He starts the engine, and Elena turns to me, handing a tissue.

"Nora... What happened?"

"Wait, it smells like blood, babe," says Daniel.

Elena looks down, and we both see my injured feet. Gosh, I didn't even realize I was cut.

"Oh, my Goddess, Nora!"

The broken glass from earlier pierced my shoes and cut me all over. My previously white shoes are now covered in red. Oh... I didn't even feel any pain, I was too angry. Now that I'm staring at it, it does feel quite painful. I sigh, too tired to even react to this. Elena, however, looks deeply concerned.

"Danny, you think you can handle that? Or do we take her to the hospital?"

He looks over his shoulder a couple of times, inspecting my wound, and frowns. Oh right, Daniel is a medicine student, isn't he?

"It should be okay, but we need to disinfect it quickly."

"My Goddess, Nora... What happened to you?"

I start explaining everything. I start crying again in the middle of it, with my chest and heart being painful. Elena and Daniel stay silent. She pats my back, looking deeply concerned. When I'm done talking, we have entered a part of the city that I don't know at all.

"...Men are jerks."

"Not helpful, Danny," sighs Elena. "Nora, I'm so sorry about what you went through tonight, really. But don't worry, okay? Tonight, you can stay at our place, have a good sleep, and calm down. And we can talk about it tomorrow when you feel better, okay?"

"What is there to talk about? She needs to ditch the guy and *basta*."

"Danny, park the damn car and shut up!" Growls Elena.

Once we arrive, Daniel decides to carry me on his back, so I wouldn't hurt my feet anymore, and Elena keeps the blanket around me as we go to their flat.

We enter a very cozy apartment, and I love it instantly. It's small, but full of warm colors, with a small kitchen counter, a sizeable bottle-green couch, and a fluffy carpet. There are three large bouquets of flowers dispersed in the room and a strong smell of coffee, freesia, and citrus.

Daniel helps me sit on the couch and goes behind a door. He comes back with an extensive first aid kit and surgical gloves, and Elena sits next to me while he helps me take off my shoes.

"How is it, Danny?"

"Well, bleeding. I'm going to have to make sure she doesn't have any glass left in her foot, but it should be okay. Not a good idea to run around with your feet in that state, sweetheart."

"Sorry... I didn't realize it."

Daniel sighs, but puts the gloves on and starts taking care of my feet carefully.

"Do you want a cup of coffee, Nora?" Asks Elena.

"If you have some tea..."

"I would love a cappuccino, too," says Daniel.

"I wasn't asking you!"

"Thank you, babe."

Apparently, they are both used to those kinds of arguments because Elena gets up and does take out three cups. Daniel turns his head into her direction and clicks his tongue. “No coffee for you, mama!”

She growls. “Crap, I forgot...”

Right, I forgot she’s pregnant too. Has she told Nathaniel yet? It’s been a week or two now. Now that I’m thinking about it, Elena is wearing a large sweater. She had boyish clothes on too last time, but this one is clearly oversized. Even if there was a baby bump, it wouldn’t be showing with this kind of top on.

While she is pouring some milk in the cup, her phone rings. She frowns when she sees the number and shows her screen to us.

“It’s Nate...”

“...They are probably looking for her. You should answer before the whole Blood Moon Clan rushes to our territory.”

Elena hesitates for a while, but after a few seconds and looking at me, she answers the call. “Yes, Nate? I’m okay, thanks... I know, sorry, I’ve been busy. ...Yes, she’s here with me, at my place. ...Yeah, she’s okay. Well, a bit shook up, but she is safe, and Daniel is taking care of her feet... Not tonight, Nate. It’s not a good idea. Nora is still upset; she needs some time. ...Yes, of course. As long as she needs.”

She stays silent for a while, apparently waiting for Nathaniel’s answer. I hear him talking, though I can’t really get what he is saying. Elena frowns. “...That’s none of your business, Nate. ...Fine, I can ask. ...Nora?”

“Yes?”

“Bobo wants to come and see you tomorrow morning... Is that okay?”

I hesitate a bit. Bobo also kept the truth from me, but... he is still my best friend. I don’t want to see Damian or even Liam, but I guess I can see Bobo. I nod.

“...She said yes. ...Okay. Yes, I’m fine, I told you. Good night, Nathaniel.”

Elena hangs up, a bit too fast to act normal. She sighs and comes back to us with the cups. Daniel is observing her with a genuinely worried look.

“...Are you okay, babe?”

“I am. Anyway, Nora is the one to be worried about.”

“Well, she should be happy, Bobo is coming for *her*.”

Is that... jealousy I hear? Elena rolls her eyes. "Oh, stop being a baby, Danny! Bobo is worried about Nora as a friend! Now drop the jealousy act, or, baby or not, I'm really kicking your scrawny ass!"

Oh my gosh!

"So, you're Bobo's mysterious boyfriend!" I exclaim.

"Okay, it's time you girls both get to bed," he says, blushing.

The next morning, I wake up with a very annoying headache. I'm a bit disoriented, and for a while, I have no idea where I am. Until I remember about last night. The party.

I wish I had forgotten a bit longer. I get up. Oh, right, Daniel gave me his bed. Their apartment only has two tiny bedrooms, so he slept on the couch. I walk into the main room, but it seems like I'm the last one up. Elena is curled up on the sofa, and Daniel is busy making hot chocolates behind the kitchen counter. It's still pouring outside, and so dark I can't tell how late it is.

"Good morning, cousin," she says with a smile.

I can't help but smile when I hear that. It does sound good... I sit on the couch with my cousin, and Daniel brings us the cups.

"So, everyone decided to wake up early," sighs Daniel. "What is the program for today, ladies?"

"Waiting for Bobo, for now," says Elena. "And I'm not going anywhere with this rain and this hellish nausea."

"...How is the baby?" I ask.

She smiles. "Fine, thank you. I think..."

Before she can finish her sentence, the doorbell rings. She smiles at Daniel, who is slightly blushing. He rolls his eyes and gets up to go open the door. Bobo appears, carrying a little paper bag that smells terribly good. Daniel, still blushing, tries to avoid looking at him in the eyes. Still, Bobo grabs him around the shoulders anyway and kisses his forehead. Oh, my Goddess, Daniel is so red, it's like his hair is about to change color, too.

"S... stop it. Just... come in. What's with the ba...bag?"

Next to me, Elena laughs behind her cup. "I never see Daniel stutter like this, unless Bobo is there. Never. It's so cute," she whispers to me.

Indeed, it's too cute and funny to watch. Bobo's eyes are fixated on his beloved with a little smile, while Daniel is clumsily trying to ignore him. However, he's red like a tomato, and his eyes blinking way too many times. He goes to the kitchen, but still stumbles halfway. I can't help but chuckle, too. I didn't know there was someone who could be worse than me around their mate...

Bobo walks up to us, and Elena opens the bag with hungry eyes. "Croissants! Moon Goddess, thank you, Bobo, we didn't get any breakfast yet," she says while taking one.

"It's from Nathaniel, actually. Did you tell him about...?"

Elena frowns and shakes her head. "No, he doesn't know about the baby yet."

"Oh... He was worried about you. You should give him a call."

"Mh."

She doesn't say anything else and starts eating her croissant. Too soon, I guess...

Then, Bobo comes closer and sits just next to me, on the floor. He is so tall that it's doesn't really make a difference, though.

"Hi, Nora," he says with his usual smile.

"I'm mad at you, too, you know," I reply with a pout.

My wolf raises her head, a bit annoyed at me. She likes Bobo; she is not mad at him. I decide to ignore her.

"I know," he says. "I just came to check on you. How are you?"

"Are we talking about my feet or my feelings?"

"Both."

"My feet are fine."

I'm really hurt by their lies, though. I still can't believe none of them told me anything. About Damian's engagement or that woman, Alessandra King, whoever she is. Do I mean nothing in their eyes? Don't I deserve to know the truth? Even Bobo didn't say a thing... I sigh. "I don't know, Bobo, I can't get what Damian's thinking. He... He said he loves me, but..."

My voice breaks, and I feel tears coming. I don't know what to believe anymore... I love him, I really do. Nothing to do with that stupid mate thing. I just love Damian. His silver eyes and the way he looks at me. His voice, so deep. How he treats me like I'm so precious, his hands, and gentle touch. I don't want to lose him.

Bobo puts his large hand on mine. "He loves you, Nora, a lot more than you think. He really does. If you had seen him after you left yesterday..."

"But what about this engagement, then?"

Why would he get engaged to another woman! He knew I existed, that he had a mate, for years! If he was searching for me, what was the point if he planned to marry someone else anyway? I start crying silently, and I hate it. I hate feeling so lost and powerless. I have no idea what to do, what to say to them. Am I supposed to make decisions now? My mind is in such a mess! I don't want to.

Elena starts patting my back. "Hey, Nora, it's okay. Why don't you take a couple of days to cool off, hm? I think you might need a little break to think things over. Stay here with us for the weekend."

I look at Daniel and Elena. Is that okay? I do feel like I really need a break right now. "What about Daniel? You are not going to keep sleeping on the couch..."

"Daniel can sleep at my place," says Bobo immediately.

"You...your place?" Stutters Daniel, blushing again.

"Great idea!" Says Elena with a big smile.

"What great idea! I haven't agreed to it. ...Yet. Maybe I... I like the couch," mumbles Daniel.

"Oh, please. I'm done with you complaining about Bobo staying with Nora all the time, so now you enjoy your man all you want, and I'll spend time with my cousin. Come on, baby, you know you want it," says Elena, pushing him gently with her feet.

"Elena!"

We both laugh at his offended look. Daniel is so red and embarrassed, it's way too cute. Bobo starts whispering something into his ear, and Elena winks at me. A few seconds later, Daniel is red like a tomato again and pushing Bobo away.

"Okay, okay, okay! I'm coming, but please, stop that! Where did you learn to say such... stuff!"

He steps away from his boyfriend and comes to grab a croissant before sitting between Elena and me, who tease him again. I know this whole scene is also to help me cheer up a bit. Bobo comes to joins us, sitting on the floor next to me again.

While Elena is arguing with Daniel about some sweatshirt that she apparently took from him, Bobo comes closer to me. "He canceled the party yesterday."

I stare at him, surprised. "...Really?"

He nods. "Right after you left. He sent everyone home, and he didn't want to see anyone, either. It took a while to calm him down."

I remember Damian's eyes from yesterday. Usually, they shine with assurance, but all I saw last night was confusion, and even fear. He was genuinely panicked. I play with my pendant between my fingers for a while, remembering the night he gave it to me. I finally raise my head to look Bobo in the eye. "...So, he really doesn't love her... Alessandra?"

He shakes his head and gently tightens his hand around mine. "No. Trust me, Nora. I may not be the closest one to the Boss, but one thing I've seen is the way he looks at you. The way he is with you, he isn't like that with anyone else. Before he found you, he was like a machine. The only ones who could approach him without any fear were his brothers. You are immune to his aura, so you don't know, but for anyone else, Damian Black is the most terrifying man-wolf in this city."

It's strange to hear it all from Bobo's mouth. It's like I was blinded for a while. I know how much Damian tried to protect me, but along the way, I also forgot what kind of man he was, and the responsibilities that come with it. And how lucky I've been so far...

Without Damian, I would be dead, killed by my own brother's hands. He gave me everything I needed and more. For two months, I have been living without any worries about where to sleep or what to eat. Compared to the last ten years of my existence, it's... It doesn't change what I saw yesterday, but I can't just blame Damian and forget everything he's done for me either. That would be too unfair of me.

"I need time, Bobo. Thank you for talking to me, but this is still too fresh for me. No matter Damian's reasons... He kept it hidden from me for weeks. He should have told me. I've had too many secrets in my life already. I want to be able to trust my mate. For real."

He nods. "I understand. I just wanted to tell you. Also, um... Liam wants to talk to you, too."

"Liam?"

He suddenly takes something out of his pocket. My phone! Right, I left it at the party last night... I open it. Six missed calls from Damian, and two from Tonia. He also left a message on the voicemail... I hesitate and decide I'll listen to it later. Not now, not in front of these three. Whatever he said in that message, I am not ready to listen to it now.

Liam left me a text, though, so I open it. He apologizes for last night, saying he feels I deserved the truth. He wants to talk to me face to face. "No surprises this time."

I reply, a quick text to say we can meet tonight. I finally feel a bit better now. I take a sip of Daniel's delicious hot chocolate, warming myself up from the outside a little. Elena is right. All I might need right now is a bit of time.

Since the downpour should continue all day, we decide not to go out. Daniel must prepare some exam coming up and surrounds himself with lots of enormous books. Apparently, he wants to specialize in psychology. Elena is a business student, but she doesn't feel like studying today. She goes to shower first, changing into some jeans and an oversized top, then lends me some of her clothes to change into.

Once I come out of the shower, it turns out that she fell asleep on the couch while waiting, despite the radio station playing in the kitchen.

Daniel raises his head from his books. "Don't worry, it's like that since she learned about her pregnancy. She will wake up from her mini-nap in ten minutes or so."

"Is she okay?" I ask.

"Yeah, it happens to some pregnant women. She feels sleepy suddenly, and within a minute, she's napping. Don't worry, she's fine."

I nod. Elena is curled up on one corner of the couch, and they covered her with a blanket. Bobo is sitting at the opposite corner, busy with his phone. I make myself some tea and come back, joining Daniel who's sitting on the carpet, bent over the little table with all his books and a computer. "Can I ask you something?"

"Sure."

"How did you meet Elena?"

He smiles and takes off his glasses to look at his sleeping friend. "When we were really young, like five or six. The same pack, but we didn't really fit with the other kids. I would always get mocked by the other boys for being tinier, weaker than them. Elena was an orphan, so she was ostracized, too, but unlike me, she was the one who would come and beat those kids once they were done kicking my ass." He chuckles at the memory. "She made them cry a lot. She was a real little punk, even picking fights with kids bigger than her."

"So, she helped you?"

"Oh no, she kicked my ass and called me a weakling a lot of times, too! But after that, she would always come and share her cookie with me or something. She was like that. Even when she lost and got beaten up, Elena would never hold it against them. She moved on and trained harder. So, I trained harder, too."

"Pfft... You cried whenever I trained you."

Elena just woke up and is looking at us with a grumpy look.

Daniel sticks his tongue out to her. "That is not how I recall it, mama. And for the record, you were a violent, thick-headed little punk."

"Not going to deny that..."

I laugh. It's funny to witness their interactions. They are best friends, but also like brother and sister, bickering non-stop. I suppose Daniel will always be there for her, even if she decides to part ways with Nathaniel...

Here I go thinking about Damian again. He brought more people into my life than I thought I could ever have. Bobo is like a big, protective brother to me. Liam is a bit of a brat, but he still is someone I trust and like having around. Tonia, too, is like an older sister. I never had anyone like those three in my life before.

Elena was right about the downpour. It rained all day, but despite that and everything else, we enjoyed it. Those two basically listen to music from dawn until dusk and even dance around sometimes. They made me cook for lunch, and in the afternoon, I trained a bit with Elena, while Bobo helped Daniel review his notes. We couldn't do any boxing or shapeshift because of her condition. Still, she did show me some new workout exercises and moves. She also explained to me some meditation techniques to help me interact better with my inner wolf, things I had never tried before. It was like opening a new door, and at the same time, seeing things differently, better.

The training helped me empty my mind for a while. Also, I had no time to be anxious before Liam's arrival, though it came quickly.

As planned, he showed up around eight, alone. "Hi, Nora. Ready for our little date?"

I smile and grab the coat Elena landed me.

"Yes. Where do you want to go?"

"Since you met with the Sea Moon Wolves, how about the harbor? There is a little café by the docks I used to go to a lot when I was a kid, and the lady there makes mean hot chocolates..."

Liam takes his favorite black bike, and since it's only the two of us, we arrive quickly at the docks. As we enter the Sea Moon Wolves' turf, some wolves come, but they recognize us and let us through. As we had fought side by side only a couple of weeks ago, they have no real reason to argue with us. Not today.

Liam finally parks his bike in front of a family restaurant, a large one facing the sea. The building has been built in one of the dock's warehouses entirely renovated to give it a seventies decoration, with leather seats, neon lights, and a retro feel. Once we enter, a few heads turn, mostly sailors and dockers, but nobody says a thing. I guess the word must have been given, as everyone quickly go back to their meal.

A waitress runs up to us, a plump woman in her fifties. She smiles at Liam and opens her arms.

"Liam, boy! It's been a while, sweetie! Moon Goddess, you are so grown up already! How old are you now?"

"Eighteen, Nina! How is my favorite waitress? I missed you!"

"Oh, you little sweet-talker..." They quickly hug, and the adorable lady turns to me. "Did you bring a girlfriend this time? Hello, darling!"

"Hi, I'm Nora."

"She's my brother's girlfriend. I stole her for a date," says Liam with a wink, putting his arm around my shoulders.

Nina laughs and adjusts her red bun before grabbing two menus. "I see, I see, well, come on, I got your favorite table available, sweetie."

She takes us to a great spot, a little table with a view on the ocean. Giving us the menus, she is still looking fondly at Liam. "Oh, sweetie, I feel so nostalgic seeing you there again! You know, darling, this boy used to come here every single day when he was a kid! Oh, Liam, I remember you doing all your homework on this very table, with that little mint diabolo you always had."

"And you would always give me free refills, Nina. Can I get that diabolo today?"

"Sure, you can, sweetie! What would you like, young lady?"

"I'll have the same as Liam."

"Okay! Take your time, I'll come back for your order. Our special today is the fish and chips; I would recommend it!" She takes off quickly, and Liam sighs with a smile.

"She loves you a lot," I say.

"Nina is the sweetest waitress in the world. She didn't just give me refills, you know. Most of the time, she didn't take any money for those diabolos."

"So, you really came here often?" I ask.

Liam nods, but before saying anything else, Nina comes back with our diabolos, takes our orders. I pick the fish and chips, the biggest burger for Liam. Once Nina leaves, he starts playing with his straw and looks at me. "How are you, Nora?"

"I'm fine, I suppose... Better than last night."

"Looks like it. I was a bit worried. Well, a lot actually. I was afraid that might have been a big blow for you."

I frown and push my drink aside to lean closer to him. "Why did you take me there, Liam?"

I want to know what he was trying to achieve. After all, he was the only one among all the others who chose to do so.

He frowns and sighs. "To be honest with you, Nora, I didn't do it for you. I did it for Damian. That engagement is total bullshit, and I don't want him to be unhappy, tied to a bitch like Alessandra King."

He says her name with so much disgust, I do feel a bit better.

"Why did you bring me to the party, then? Couldn't you just talk to him before all this? Liam, now that it's done, I'm... It's just plain painful for me!"

Does he realize how much I suffered last night? Seeing Damian with another woman... No matter the reasons Liam had, I still feel like I was just brought there to watch this nightmare and suffer. Why use me in all this?

Liam stays silent for a while, apparently thinking. After a while, he turns his head to the docks, and a soft smile appears. "...You know, my brother is the worst liar."

What does he mean now? Sometimes I can't decipher Liam. One minute he is acting like a kid, and the next one, he is there acting all mysterious and plotting behind his brothers' backs... He points to the docks, and I follow his finger.

"When I was young, Damian used to work right there. He started when he was ten. After school, I would go see my mom at the hospital, and then Damian would take me to this restaurant. I'd do my homework and drink diabolos while he was working. He worked, on this very dock, for five or six hours straight every day. He carried huge boxes back and forth from boats to the dock. Whenever he stopped, he just came here to check up on me, and he went back right away."

I try to imagine a young Damian, working there, sweating under the weight of heavy containers. It's hard to imagine how his youth was like...

"Those boxes were awfully huge and heavy. It was a job even a lot of adults didn't want because it was hard. Old man Seaver let my brother work there, because he never complained, never took a day off. When he was done, if I said I was tired, he would carry me home. Whenever I asked, he lied, saying he wasn't tired."

He must have been. How could he have not been, after working like that... And Liam and Damian have a six-year age difference. No matter how young Liam was, he must have been heavy for Damian to carry after all that...

Liam chuckles. "He lied all the time. He made me believe for ten years that he didn't like chocolate because our Mom often gave me chocolates for the three of us, and I loved it. So, Damian would say he didn't want it, and I'd eat his share without knowing."

I can't help but smile, imagining a young Liam happily eating chocolate... Our plates arrive, and after thanking Nina, Liam goes on.

"Nate and Damian always hid stuff from me. I learned very late that they had to work because our father didn't give us any money. We ate fish that Damian would bring back from his work. They both dropped out of high school to work full time. Yet, they never let me see any of the hardships. Every time, they made it look like a game."

Now I know why they are so adamant about Liam going to high school properly... They are genuinely caring for their youngest brother. The three of them had to protect each other, but Liam more because he was the youngest. It's a miracle they turned out the way they did, given their family situation... Liam stops eating to play with his fork.

"You know, I suffer from claustrophobia because of them. When I was a kid, they made up a game where I had to sleep in a hole under Nate's bed. Moon Goddess, I hated that game! It was a stupid hole, with just a blanket. Damian took my bed whenever he'd make me sleep in there. With Nate's mattress above, I couldn't see a thing. I thought for years that they were messing with me, the kind of stupid jokes you would play on your younger siblings, you know?"

Liam shakes his head, frowning at the memory. Why would they put him in a hole? I don't see Damian or Nate playing this kind of mean jokes on him just for fun.

"It took me a long time to realize. Every time I was in that hole, it was a night when our father would come home."

Oh, Moon Goddess. Does he mean...?

"Yes, Nora, you got it. Nate and Damian hid me in that hole so our father wouldn't hit me when he was drunk. Most of the time, I fell asleep fast and didn't hear a thing. Only when I grew older, I started to realize Damian and Dad fought when I was in that hole. Nate used the mind-link to tell me to stay hidden until it was over. Then, I would come out and find my brother beaten up bad. Nate, too, sometimes."

Liam looks very sad when telling this. He plays with his fork with a sullen look, bending it and putting it back, with that same frown as Damian when he's conflicted. Suddenly, he looks at me, and from his eyes, I feel like he is holding his tears.

"You know what's worse? The one that dirtbag really wanted to beat up was me. But my brothers never let him touch me, so he would beat Damian instead. He let our father hit him until he was satisfied, because once he had enough, he would go out again and stop looking for me. You have no idea how many times I found Damian soaked in blood, Nora. He was strong, so my father never held up. But Damian never complained, not a single time. Instead, he just smiled at me anytime he saw me, saying he was fine. Lying again, to protect me."

I feel tears coming from hearing this. Liam had already told me that Damian fought with their father and confronted him a lot, but... This all sounds way too real. Liam's voice is breaking. What kind of mess did they grow up in? I hate their father so much! He was a monster to his own kids. Liam wipes away a couple of tears and drinks a bit before going on.

"Damian is that kind of guy, Nora. He never shows how hard it is for him. Do you know why he rarely visited our mom in the hospital? Because most of the time, he had bruises and cuts, all from our father's beating, and he didn't want mom to see it. Damian is doing the same with you now."

I frown. What does he mean with that? Damian's engagement, that whole situation, how is it related to me?

Looking more serene, Liam takes a severe tone. "Nora, you are the most important person in my brother's life. He would do anything, and I mean anything, to protect you. Just like he did for our mom and me. And sometimes, that idiot is willing to make foolish decisions, sacrificing himself for this."

"...Like the engagement, you mean?"

He takes some fries and nods. “Exactly. He accepted the Gold Moon Clan’s proposal because he believed he could protect you, and us, with it.”

I don’t get it. I shake my head. “Liam, you’re going to have to be a lot more precise if you want me to believe that Damian got engaged to another woman for my sake.”

“Nora, Damian has treated you like a little princess, shielding you from whatever is going on in Silver City right now. But trust me, my brother is going to need a lot of help from now on, and I don’t agree with getting it from that King bitch.”

“What are you talking about? What is going on in Silver City?”

Liam smiles and eats another portion of his burger. Why can’t he answer me first before stuffing himself? It’s nerve-wracking! After a few very long and annoying bites, he takes a gulp of his diabolo, and just when I’m about to lose patience, he smiles at me.

“A war, Nora. Forget vampires and witches. Silver City is about to get in a mean, violent, and bloody war between all the werewolf Clans if we don’t do something soon.”

I stare at him, totally confused. A war in Silver City? The last war happened not ten years ago when Damian killed their father to take over the Blood Moon Clan! Why would another one erupts now? I thought the Black Brothers were unmatched in terms of strength, so why would anyone choose to start a war now?

“Liam, I don’t get it. I thought...”

“We were the untouchable Black Brothers? Well, that part is true, but a werewolf Clan isn’t all about its Alpha, Nora. Sure, Damian is the big bad wolf in town, no questioning that. If he had to single out any Alpha in the area, he’d win. Easily. But what if he had to fight fifty wolves at once?”

He’s right... The Black Brothers are feared by many because they win in terms of power, dominance, strength. No one would be stupid enough to force them into a duel. If anyone wanted to overthrow them, it would have to be in a massive attack, with enough people to attack not only Damian but the whole pack. Now I’m worried.

“You’re telling me other packs want to attack the Blood Moon.”

“We are not popular, Nora. Our father’s reputation did a lot of damage, and for most of the population, Damian is just as fearsome.”

“But Damian is not your father! He is not looking to fight the other packs! He—"

I stop, realizing I started yelling a bit too loud. A lot of eyes are now staring at us, and I mumble some apology before turning back to Liam. That idiot is smiling, mocking me.

"So cute... You are so prone to defend my brother; I'm feeling reassured now."

"Oh, shut up! Tell me, who wants to fight the Blood Moon?"

Liam takes three of the sauce pots, placing them in a triangle.

"Right now, the situation is like this: the three main Clans are ours, the Gold Moon Clan, and the Sapphire Moon Clan. In terms of power, number, and wealth, those three clans hold the most power. But those two are still behind us. The Gold Moon is large, but their Alpha and warriors aren't that strong. As for the Sapphire Moon, it's the other way around: they got strength, but they are not as numerous or wealthy."

"If those two are still behind, what is the problem, then?" I ask, confused.

I already know that through the Black Corporation he established, Damian made sure his Clan had the most possessions in Silver City. They dominate about one-third of the City, leaving the other packs to share what's left. Liam moves some fries, placing them behind the sauce pots.

I observe his patterns and take a guess. "The Clan alliances?"

He nods. "Exactly. The other Clans are not going to grow any bigger until years now. However, some of them started to understand that having allies might be much more profitable and efficient than waiting. Guess what the other Clans did once they understood that befriending some rogues and people from the former Black Moon Clan was how Damian and Nate beat our father?"

"...They would start seeking internal alliances," I whisper.

Liam nods.

This is crazy... Werewolves are usually secluded to their own packs. Outside of our packs, we may be "friends" with other wolves, but it doesn't involve any exchange, unless necessary. Like the Jade Moon and the Pearl Moon. I have always seen the two packs being friendly, but we never acted as one. They had their own fights, and we would never interfere. The most we exchanged was information about possible rogue attacks, but we never acted together against them.

I turn to Liam.

"How are things, then?"

He smiles. "You understand quickly. We weren't sure of anything until two weeks ago. We knew the Rising Moon Clan had agreed to ally with the Gold Moon Clan, but we had no idea about the others."

"Until the fight against the vampires, right? All the packs had to react, so the alliances naturally showed."

I start recalling the events. That's right. The Blood Moon rallied the White Moon and Opal Moon in the North, but the Gold Moon Clan headed south with the Rising Moon Clan, confirming those two are allies. Also, the Pearl Moon Clan moved to help the Jade Moon, so Vince probably has an alliance going with their Alpha. Then, I recall one crucial detail.

"The Sapphire Moon. They are the only ones that didn't move."

Liam nods. "Exactly. But the truth is, they are not the only ones. The Violet Moon also didn't make a move, while their branch Clan, the Purple Moon, came to help the Sea Moon here."

"However, the Sea Moon Clan is neutral, isn't it?"

"Yes. My guess is Lysandra acted against her father, the Violet Moon Alpha, to help Old man Seaver. She is not one to miss the action, and I bet she didn't like being told to stay on the sidelines."

"If that's so, the Violet Moon and Sapphire Moon Clan are allies..."

This means that their power would now be equal with the Blood Moon Clan! The Jones family is a powerful line of Alphas, and their Clan holds a lot of people. Not to mention Lysandra's warriors! I've seen them in action, and they are real war machines. I try to make the math in my head, but no matter how many times I try to think of it, the Sapphire Clan, if allied with the Violet Moon, really is more powerful than the Black Brother's Clan...

"...And they hate the Blood Moon Clan".

"Exactly, Nora. Alcott Blue, the previous Sapphire Moon Alpha, had a long feud with our father, and it didn't die with his son William taking over. He wants nothing to do with us and thinks Damian is not the right Alpha King for Silver City. So, he is waiting for an opportunity to overthrow us at any time."

The pieces of the puzzle are finally assembling, letting me see the larger picture. I can't believe I didn't know any of this earlier. How could I be so blind? Seeing all the packs work together to fight off the vampires, I had no idea so many people were making their moves in the shadows. I look up to Liam.

"So, the Gold Moon wants to ally with Damian?"

He frowns but nods, eating the fries he had left on the table.

"Exactly. They were the second most powerful clan after us. Still, now, the Sapphire Moon bested them by allying with the Violet Moon, and the Rising Moon is nowhere as good as the Jones. So instead, they came to Damian with this proposal."

I finally get it now. If the Sapphire Moon is after them, they must change alliances quickly and assert their position to avoid a war. But why an engagement for that? I'm still so mad! I understand that the Gold Moon Clan would be the most powerful Clan to ally themselves with, but this condition is... Gosh, I'm annoyed just thinking about it! My wolf is furiously growling, too. I'm not okay with this!

"Hey, hey, Nora, calm down. Your Alpha aura is scaring everyone, girl," whispers Liam.

I look around. Oh, Liam is right... Everyone is staring at us, and some people instinctively backed away a few steps from our table. Did I do that? My wolf was angry, but I never noticed I could let others feel my aura... I calm myself down a bit, embarrassed. Liam laughs.

"Wow, it's the first time I see you acting like an Alpha. Except for that time with the Jade Moon, I mean. Girl, you do have fangs after all!"

"It's not funny, Liam! I don't even know how I just did this..."

"It's an Alpha thing. If our wolf gets mad, other wolves will feel it and react to our aura. Yours is unusual, even I felt it... other Alphas are usually immune. Guess it's your Royal side acting up, too."

"We are not sure I am a..."

"Oh, stop it, Nora, you know damn well you are by now. Who needs those stupid tests?"

I shake my head. I'm not having this discussion now, and we have more important matters to discuss. I try to think calmly about this alliance with the Gold Moon Clan. Wasn't there any better option?

"What about the other Clans?" I ask.

Liam shakes his head. "We tried, but those who don't fear us, hate us. A lot of the Clans will choose to remain neutral, and it's better they do because we probably wouldn't be their first choice anyway."

"What about the White Moon Clan?"

"Same, Nora, they want to remain neutral. They were grateful we helped them, but they have a long history with the Sapphire Moon, they are not going to betray them. Plus, they hate the Gold Moon Clan, too."

I can't believe it... This situation is impossible. I try to think it over, but for now, I don't see any way to help Damian. The Jade Moon Clan is nothing compared to the others, and I won't bring Damian any help with this.

"So, you're telling me their only way out is for Damian to marry that... girl?"

Liam growls, annoyed. "I don't like it, and Nate doesn't either. We tried to talk Damian out of it, and trust me, our brother doesn't want it either."

"Why didn't he tell me then?"

"Because they were already engaged when we finally found you, Nora! Damian doesn't want you to throw you in the middle of this mess! If the war explodes, guess who they will attack first to hurt Damian?"

His Luna. That's who they would attack first, to weaken the Alpha, especially if that Luna is his fated mate; it will hurt much more. I'm stunned. That explains his words... "*You won't be my official Luna.*" He didn't mean to have me as his mistress, but to hide me from people who would want to hurt him. I'm... I'm nothing but a weakness to Damian now! My wolf whimpers, too sad from this thought. Why are we so powerless!

"I told you everything, Nora, because I don't want Damian to make a decision he would regret. Even if he doesn't want you involved, I think you might be the solution to all this."

I look at Liam, dumbfounded. The solution, me? I'm just a powerless mate! I only have ownership of one of the weakest clans around, what could I possibly bring Damian that he doesn't already have?

Liam clenches his fist and looks at me right in the eye. "Nora, I know it's hard, but my brother loves you. He has loved you, and only you, for ten years. ...Ten years ago, one night, my father came home really, really drunk and angry. He started hitting Damian. Harder than he had ever hit him any time before. I was terrified. It was so bad that Damian told Nate to run with me. As always, Nate obeyed. I struggled to stay, but the last thing I saw was my oldest brother being beaten to death by our father. I was certain he would kill him, Nora. I cried so much because I was so sure Damian was going to die back there."

I see Liam looking infuriated for the first time, clenching his fists.

"When we came back, our father was gone, but so was Damian. All was left was blood, all over the floor, so much blood. We thought he had been killed. Nate panicked; he couldn't feel our brother's wolf anymore. I remember I ran, went through every room of the apartment, yelling his name. He was gone, Nora, and I was terrified."

He stays silent for a while, and, to my surprise, a gentle smile suddenly appears. "For a full week, Nate searched for him, everywhere, even looking for a body. He went through all the territories, despite the risks. Our father didn't come back either, we had no idea what had happened. Suddenly, after eight days, Damian reappeared, looking perfectly fine! No wound, not even scars. I thought he was a ghost, but honestly, I didn't care. My brother was back. Do you know what the first thing he said was?"

He raises his eyes, looking into mine, smiling.

"He told us a little princess with the most beautiful blue eyes had saved his life."

...A little princess with blue eyes? Damian meant me? Is that when the two of us met, during those eight days? I can't remember any of it. How could he come out perfectly fine? If their father's beating was as hard as Liam said.

"What else did he say?" I ask, impatient.

Liam shakes his head. "Not much. Damian never told us the details about your encounter. He just talked about his little princess all the time, his fated mate. I never saw him looking happier than the days that followed. Sometimes, he would just close his eyes to feel you, even if you couldn't feel him, and smile. Though after that, he realized he couldn't find you anymore, and that's when we all started looking for you. He was desperate, Nora. Sometimes, he would get so angry, because he could feel you getting hurt. He became crazy. It's like he was closing his heart all over again. He was obsessed with finding you because he knew you were in pain."

I know. It's all I could think of once I knew Damian had been linked with me since my childhood. Every time I got hurt, he was on the other end, feeling the blow and my pain with it. To think he looked for me for ten years...

Suddenly, I feel the need to be close to my mate. I want to see Damian, to be in my mate's arms again. I want to look into his silver eyes. I don't care for all those power struggles, the Clans tactics, or any battle. I want him.

I fight to calm my wolf and silence my urge. I massage my temples. What is wrong with me? Liam looks at me, intrigued, but I just shake my head as if it was nothing. We resume eating, and I take a few bites before talking again.

"You have a plan, don't you? You wouldn't have sabotaged this engagement party and brought me there otherwise."

He smiles. "It's more an idea than a plan, for now, to be honest."

"Are you going to actually tell me about it, Liam?"

"Are you going to reconcile with my brother?" He asks right back.

What game is he playing? I don't like his little smirk. So, what, he won't tell me anything unless I forgive Damian? How can he toy with my feelings right now! I growl at him, but he ignores me and keeps eating, waiting for my answer.

"I'm still mad at him, you know!"

"I know."

And yet he keeps smiling like some mischievous kid. I really don't like his attitude! He is acting like I'm so gullible! Who said I was going to forgive Damian so easily? He got engaged to another woman, for Moon Goddess' sake! Whatever reasons he had, how am I supposed to get over this, and it hasn't been two days, either!

While I'm fighting with my emotions, my wolf is fidgeting, too. She wants to see our mate badly. She is angry, but she misses him a lot also. *Can't we go see him?* I want to tell her to shut up, but I know she is me, too. A part of me that longs for her other half.

I'm still thinking it over and over when Nina comes to take our empty plates away. This time, Liam chooses the desserts for the two of us without even looking at the menus, and I don't mind it. I'm too busy fighting my inner turmoil to argue over desserts right now.

"Talk with Damian."

I glare at Liam, annoyed at him.

"I'm serious, Nora. Talk to him, at least. You two love each other."

I hate that look he is giving me right now. Why does he have to be always right? And so sure of himself, too.

"I still don't understand how I can help Damian."

"Nora, you are much stronger than you think. You don't realize it yet. I know you; you are not going to let that girl get Damian."

My wolf starts growling. *Hell no, he is our mate, ours!* It takes me a few seconds to calm her down. I wish I were better at taming my inner wolf, but that whole fated mate thing doesn't make it easy.

Nina brings our desserts, crepes topped with fruits and chocolate, with two hot chocolates covered with marshmallows. Gosh, how can Liam eat so much? He practically jumps on his dessert like he hasn't eaten in three days.

I sigh. "Okay, I will talk with Damian. I don't promise anything else."

"Mm," he replies, his mouth full.

I start eating my dessert, too, and though it is delicious, my mind is still lingering somewhere else. What am I supposed to say to my engaged mate? Liam just gave me a lot of information about whatever was going on, but I really need to hear it from Damian. Last night, I lost all trust I had in him, and now, it's like picking up the pieces of broken glass. It's sharp and painful, and I know the cracks will remain. I don't want to go through something like this ever again.

"I've had enough with all the secrets."

Liam raises his head, and I realize I subconsciously used my wolf's voice to talk. He smiles and puts his spoon back on the table. His eyes wander outside, watching the rain and the sea.

"You know, I overheard my brothers' last secret recently," he says.

What is he talking about now? He keeps talking, his eyes still looking outside.

"There was a reason my father hated me, why I was the one he always wanted to beat up. Our mom... She got sick because of me."

Because of Liam? They never gave me details about whatever their mother suffered from, but I know she died slowly, very weakened. Liam's eyes are undecipherable, but he won't stop gazing outside.

"Our father already fought a lot before I was born. Mostly against vampires. There were several Clans here, in Silver City, a few years ago, constantly fighting with us werewolves. One day, he attacked the wrong one. He killed a vampire's loved one, so... that vampire took revenge on him."

"...He attacked your mother?"

Liam nods. "Vampire bites are poisonous to wolves. Usually, we can survive if we don't get too much of their venom, and our wolf form will heal it for us, but when that vampire attacked our mom, he wanted to kill her. Our mother was a strong wolf, though. She should have been able to fight him off, but... From Elena, you probably know that pregnant werewolves can't shapeshift, right?"

So that's it... Their mother didn't die of sickness but from a vampire's venom, because she was pregnant with Liam and couldn't shapeshift to take her wolf form. Hence, she had no choice but to get poisoned. Past a certain level of venom, our wolf abilities can't do anything; it's too late. Their mother was infected…

"You didn't know?"

He shakes his head. "I just thought our mom was sick. They never said a thing, and neither did she. It does explain a lot of things."

It really does... Even their father's hatred for vampires, why he chased all of them out. I think about Liam, and his brothers, hiding him the truth. Why they did it...

"It wasn't your fault, Liam."

He nods. "I know. I already had that talk with Nathaniel. He and Damian chose not to tell me so I wouldn't be hurt or feel guilty. My mom probably felt the same, too. It doesn't change the fact that our father was a monster, but..."

He turns to me, and grabs my hand, looking at me very seriously.

"It made me realize how much they have overprotected me, again. And this time, Nora, I'm not willing to let Damian make all the sacrifices by himself. I want to be the one to protect them, and I'm going to need your help with that. So please, don't abandon Damian."

Much later, I'm back in Elena and Daniel's apartment, though the latter is now gone, off to spend the night with Bobo. I'm left with my cousin, who fell asleep a few minutes ago. I can't sleep at all.

Everything Liam and I talked about today keeps circling in my mind, and I can't shake it off. How many more hardships will the brothers have to face from now on? This war is coming... Damian, how is he going to face it? I keep seeing him, next to that woman. Remembering that scene still hurts, but I am a werewolf. I need to start thinking like one, and that includes everything that is going on for the Clans right now. I need to start taking decisions.

I get up silently, trying not to wake up Elena. In the living room, the clock indicates it's one in the morning. It's still pouring outside... I grab one of the blankets and sit in the kitchen. I take a few minutes, calming myself and observing the rain. This is going to be hard... I finally take out my phone and look for Damian's voicemail to listen. He left it about two hours after I left yesterday. I take a deep breath.

For a few seconds, the message is entirely silent. I check several times if it's really playing, but after a while, I suddenly hear some sounds. Oh my gosh, is Damian... crying?

I feel my heart tightening. It's muffled, but I'm almost sure this is what I think. I feel my own tears running down my cheeks, hearing my mate's pain. He breathes in, and finally, starts talking, slowly, with a broken voice.

"Nora... I'm so sorry, Nora... I'm sorry. I... I know I should have told you, I... I'm such an idiot. Nora, I never know what's the right thing to do when it comes to you. Nora... I want to protect you so much. You're the most important thing to me. I love you, Nora, I love you. I love you so much it hurts because I never know. I don't know how to make you happy, and I don't know how to protect you. I... That engagement, that woman, they mean nothing to me, Nora. They are nothing. I swear. You're the only one in my mind, you've been the only one forever. I... I need you, Nora. I don't care about any of the rest. My Clan, my people, my brothers... I can't do this without you, Nora. I'll go mad, and I... I can't take it. I need you. I really need you. Nora..."

He breathes in, and I do the same, not holding my tears back anymore. But there's more, Damian's voice comes in a whisper.

"...I love you. I love your blue eyes, the way you look at me and make me feel like a better man than I am. I want you, in my arms, every single second that goes by. Nora... I don't want to lose you, and I love you. I... I'm so, so sorry. Please, Nora. Don't leave me, please. I... Can we talk? I want to explain to you. I know it's late, but..."

He goes silent again, but I can hear his breathing, calmer than before. After a while, he chuckles.

"I'm a fucking idiot... And I'm always too late when it comes to you, aren't I? I... I don't want to lose you again, Nora. I can't. I don't know how long it will take, but... I just hope you will forgive me. Tell me what it will take, I'll do it. I just want you back, Nora. I'm sorry. And I'm a dumbass."

I can't help but laugh between my tears when he says that. I never heard Damian pronounce that kind of word. A long silence, again, but I can hear his breathing, so I keep listening until he starts talking again.

"Nora... I hope you'll listen to this. I don't feel stupid, talking alone here. If I just imagine you are listening to this... I already feel better. I know I should feel bad, but I... Damn, I miss you already... I love you, Nora. I should have told you sooner, not in that stupid elevator, not like this... I told you, I'm always too late... But I'll say it again. I love you. I'll say it as many times as it takes, as many times as you want to hear it. I love you, Nora Bluemoon, I love you."

I burst into tears, listening to his voice, whispering those three words again and again.

The next morning, I wake up on the couch. I fell asleep there, listening to Damian's voice. My first reflex is to check that his message wasn't deleted or anything, but it seems like my phone archived it on its own. It turns out the battery is almost dead because it stayed online most of the night. I use the last of it to listen to Damian's message one more time.

It feels so unreal... Every time I hear it, I'm brought to tears. His voice breaking, his words, repeating how much he loves me. It takes me a few minutes to calm down. My wolf, too, is going crazy, begging to see Damian. I have a hard time taming her, and my heartbeat is going wild. Is the room spinning? And I feel hot suddenly...

I hear Elena's voice, calling my name. What is wrong with me? I'm burning, and a bit dizzy... When I wake up again, I'm feeling cold. Elena is next to me, gently caressing my hair. I recognize her living room; I'm still on the couch... What happened? I'm so thirsty! She notices I'm awake when I try to sit up.

"Nora! How do you feel?"

She helps me sit up, but all I can think of is this hellish thirst.

"Elena, can I get some water?" I ask with a raspy voice.

"Oh, sure!"

She hands me a water bottle, and I start drinking like I haven't had any in weeks. Once I'm done, I feel a lot better. Daniel takes the bottle away, and Elena smiles at me and puts her hand on my forehead like a doctor.

"You should feel a lot better now. Do you still feel hot?"

I shake my head, still confused. "Elena, what's going on? What happened?"

"I found you there this morning; you looked very sick. I thought of taking you to the hospital, but it was just a slight fever. Too many emotions these days, huh?

I nod. I didn't think I'd feel sick just from all that... Probably the rain from the other day, too... Elena sighs, "Don't worry, we already gave you some medicine. It works great on werewolves, so you should be fine now."

So that's why I feel a bit cold instead of hot... I don't feel my wolf either; it's like she is half-asleep.

"Thank you, Elena"

She nods and gives me an extra blanket. "It's alright. You can sleep anyway; it's Sunday. Will you be okay about going to work tomorrow?"

Right, work... I can't believe I have to go to work after everything that happened. It feels a bit surreal, but after all, I wanted this job. I nod. I may not be too happy with it for once, but I guess I must. And it's not like Damian will come, anyway.

"Okay. Well, just rest for today, Nora."

I spend the Sunday resting on Elena's couch. I feel cold and a bit drowsy for most of the day, and when I'm not talking to Elena or Daniel, I just sleep. All those semi-naps allow me to take time to think, a lot. About Damian and our relationship. What I want to do next. About the whole situation of Silver City, too. Sadly, I can't come up with any solution regarding the Clans.

Regarding my mate, however, I know exactly what my feelings are. When Monday comes, Bobo brings me some of my clothes from the apartment. Elena lent me hers for the weekend, but she is taller than me, and I need to wear my own clothes for work. I put on a denim skirt and a white top, my earrings and my necklace, and Bobo drives me to work after breakfast.

It feels good to be back to work. There is so much to do that I don't have time to think about anything else. Chef Michel keeps me busy all day, and every other minute, Narcissa is the one giving me chores. During my break, Liam and Tonia send me messages to hear some of my news. Honestly, I'm fine.

I feel better than I have been in a long time. Once my shift is over, Bobo comes to pick me up as promised.

"Are we going back to Elena's?" He asks while starting the car.

"No, Bobo. Can you bring me back to the apartment? I want to take a shower and change. I will go see Damian after that."

"Okay."

The apartment is just as I left it, but colder. Bobo waits for me while I take my shower. It feels nice to wash my hair after a long day of work. When I'm done, I put my denim skirt back on, and pick a white sweater to go with it. Bobo helps me dry my hair while I put some light makeup on.

"How do you feel?"

"I'm okay, Bobo. Talking with Liam was... enlightening. Have you heard about Damian?"

He nods in the mirror, still focused on braiding my hair. "He is not doing well, according to Neal. He didn't go to work today. Only Nathaniel can approach him..."

That doesn't sound too good... I remember his voicemail once again. I know it almost by heart now; I listened to it so many times. It is high time we talk. After a few more minutes, I'm finally ready.

In the car, surprisingly, I'm calmer than I have ever been in a long while. My wolf and I are finally synching our feelings, and it's more peaceful this way. I just want to see Damian for now. It's only been two days, but it feels like I haven't seen him in weeks...

We arrive at the Company building, and Bobo accompanies me to the elevator, pressing the button to the top floor for me. Now I'm starting to feel anxious. I play nervously with my necklace as the numbers grow on the little panel. 24th floor, 25th... Calm down, Nora. My wolf is starting to get restless, too.

When we finally arrive, to my surprise, Nathaniel is at the entrance, talking to someone on the phone. As soon as he sees me, he hangs up, surprised.

"Nora? What are you...?"

"I came to see Damian. Is he here?"

He nods. "He is upstairs, in his apartment, but..."

"Can I go see him?"

It takes a few seconds, but he nods and steps aside to let me through. I don't really know where his apartment is, but I remember his office layout from last time. There was a small corridor with some stairs, and I quickly find the door I'm looking for.

When I enter, everything is dark. All the curtains are down. Didn't anyone at least put the lights on? I wouldn't be able to take a step in if it wasn't for my wolf's night vision. It's not only the room that is in the dark— all the furniture is either black, grey, or dark wood. Very different from my own... This place is much colder, neat, and sober. It doesn't feel like a place to live in.

I leave my shoes at the entrance and walk silently. It's my first time here, but I can just rely on my wolf's instinct to find her mate. I progress slowly in the apartment until I reach the master bedroom. Next to a large king bed, pieces of furniture are scattered, like someone broke them violently. Probably the remains of a bed-side table...

"Nora...?"

Damian is sitting next to the glass wall. He looks like a wreck... He's shirtless but wearing the same pants as last Friday and a three-day beard. He has dark circles under his eyes, and his black hair is in a mess. When I walk up to him, his silver eyes are filled with surprise. I crouch down in front of him, calmer than I expected, despite being so close to him.

He reaches his hand to caress my cheek, and I can see in his eyes he is checking if I'm real. I breathe in, gathering my confidence. "Hi, Damian."

My voice seems to give him a shock, and he suddenly gets agitated. "Nora, Nora, I'm so sorry! I've been an idiot, I... I know I should've told you about all this. I'm so, so sorry, Nora..."

I put my hands on his scratchy cheeks, looking into his eyes, trying to calm him down. Our faces are so close. He keeps shaking his head, whispering excuses with a broken voice.

"Damian, calm down," I murmur calmly.

"I'm so sorry, Nora, I'm sorry..."

He seems to calm down, and without being able to refrain myself any longer, I lean in to kiss his lips. Gosh, I missed this taste... I retreat, and he stares at me, surprised.

"I'm still mad at you," I clarify. "...But I listened to your voicemail. That, and I talked to Liam, too."

"My message... I didn't think you would really listen to it..."

"Well, I did."

He nods and sighs. He looks really tired... Don't tell me he hasn't gotten any sleep since Friday night? It can't be...

"I meant everything I said. I'm so sorry, Nora... I should have talked to you."

"Damian, we can't keep going like this."

He frowns and looks at me in the eye. I need to say this now because I can't take it anymore. I take his face in my hands, talking very seriously now.

"Don't hide things from me. I know you want to protect me, but this is just hurting me more. I don't want to have to learn things from others again. Tell me, Damian. Anything I'm involved with, everything I need to know. You should have told me about the issues with your Clan and this engagement sooner. I can handle it, okay? Stop protecting me so much."

He shakes his head. "I will never stop protecting you, Nora. I don't want you to suffer or be caught in any of this mess."

"You are making me suffer more with those secrets! Damian, I love you too, but if I can't trust you, I can't stay with you."

Damian suddenly grabs me by the waist, bringing me closer to him with an anxious expression I've never seen before. I'm straddling him, but we are both too agitated for any other thoughts right now.

"Don't leave me, Nora. I don't want to go through this ever again," he says, looking more serious than ever.

I put my hands behind his head and look him right in the eye. "Then promise me. No more secrets, Damian. About me, about you, or the Clan. Don't deliberately hide things from me again."

"What if you don't like it?"

"I can handle it. I'm a big girl, Damian, not a defenseless pup."

I see him hesitating, frowning. He is thinking so hard, it's like I can hear his inner turmoil from here. He closes his eyes and rests his head on my shoulder. I instinctively start caressing the base of his hairline, brushing his short hair with my fingertips. His arms slide around my waist, hugging me close.

"...What if you don't love me because of what you are going to hear?"

"Damian, I came back after hearing you were engaged to another woman. Unless you have a wife and kids somewhere, I should be able to handle it."

He chuckles, and I slap his shoulder, annoyed. It's not funny! I'm still mad about this whole engagement thing...

I feel him sigh against my neck. "I'm a fighter, Nora. I've killed people before, and I will do it again if needed. Not only my own father, but I have a lot of blood on my hands. You are so pure and innocent, sometimes I'm scared all this darkness will scare you away."

I know that. I knew from the start that one doesn't become Alpha in a city of werewolves just with relations and money. We live in a world filled with violence. The Black Brothers are not just the three nice young men I know. They hold the lives of hundreds of people in their hands, and many more depend on them. It's a scary world hiding in their shadows. Even if Liam is a teen like me, he is a fighter. Nathaniel, too, fully supports Damian. Lastly, Damian is the King of this city, the most powerful man and the most dangerous wolf. I never forget that. Even now, when he is in my arms.

"You won't, Damian. I promise."

He raises his head and kisses me without warning. A loving, tender kiss. I respond to it, unable to resist. I've missed him so much for those two days... His strong arms holding me, the touch of his hands in my hair and on my waist. His body heat and smell melting with mine. After a few seconds of getting drunk on his lips, I gather whatever is left of my self-control to push him away.

"Stop kissing me, Damian. You didn't promise. Please."

He sighs, playing with my curls between his fingers. When he speaks again, he looks at me in the eye, very seriously. "No more secrets, Nora. I promise."

I smile. Finally! Now that I have his word, and I hope he will keep it, I have to ask a question that has been on the back of my mind all weekend. Truth is, I'm a bit scared. I really hope he will give me the answer I need to hear. I take a deep breath and ask him very seriously.

"Damian, that woman... Did you sleep with her?"

I can't even describe how scared I am right now. It's like my stomach is filled with ice.

For a second, Damian looks perplexed by my question, and after a while, he sighs and gives me a faint smile. "No. I swear, Nora, I've never even kissed her. I don't love her, Nora, you're the only one for me. You've always been the only one."

I want to believe him, I really do. I guess it will just take some time now, after everything that happened. I nod to his answer, feeling definitely better, and Damian smiles and gives me a quick kiss. He makes it look so simple...

Just when I'm about to say something, he suddenly starts searching for something around us with his hand. I see him grab one of the wooden pieces left on the floor. It's small, but triangle-shaped, looking quite sharp. I want to ask what he is going to do with this, but before I can say a thing, he suddenly uses it to pierce his own hand!

"Damian! What the...?"

I grab his wrist to look at his wound, panicked. Why the hell did he just do this? It looks deep, too!

Damian stays very calm, his eyes still on me. "You said no more secrets. So now, I need you to kiss me."

"What? Are you mad? It's not the time for kisses, Damian, you're bleeding!"

He is bleeding! I want to do something, call Nate or someone, but Damian suddenly grabs me by the waist, forcing a kiss on me. I try to push him away. Who wants to kiss at a time like this! But of course, he is way too strong for me. He is so passionate, his forceful lips playing against mine. I'm still worried, but it's like a conditioned response for me to move my lips. For a few seconds, our breaths intertwine, while my mind is half enjoying it and half worried about his injury. I retreat after one or two seconds.

"Damian, stop! You need—"

"Nora, look."

Cutting me in the middle of my sentence, he shows me his hand. His perfectly fine hand... What just happened? There was a deep cut right in the middle of his palm just a few seconds ago! Yet now, it looks completely normal, except for a bit of dried blood around it. Even for a werewolf, healing this fast from a wound like this is insane!

"But, how...?"

"It's you, Nora."

Me? I stare at Damian, confused. What does he mean by that? Does he mean this kiss was for...? I take his hand in mine, rechecking it, making sure I'm not hallucinating or something. A bit of fresh blood is still there, drying already, but the wound has completely disappeared.

"I don't get it..."

"I don't really know how it works, either, but if I kiss you, all my wounds will heal much faster than usual just like this," he explains.

"How did you know...?"

"From our first meeting. You saved my life like this."

I suddenly remember the story Liam told me last Saturday. How badly their father injured Damian ten years ago. Liam did say he thought his brother might actually have died from it at that time. Those were no light injuries. They even thought he might have died, but Damian showed up alive and completely fine a few days later... I blink, stunned by what it all means.

"Damian Black, are you telling me you kissed a seven-year-old girl and magically healed from death-threatening injuries that way?"

He smiles, amused by my shocked reaction. I can't believe him! He knew for ten years that I can do those... weird magically healing kisses, and never said a thing!

"Don't laugh! You knew since the very beginning that I can do this, and you never told me!"

"I had my reasons. First, it's tiring for you, isn't it?"

Now that he says it, I do feel a bit more tired than two minutes ago. Like after a workout or something similar. Not to the point of exhaustion, but I still feel sleepy.

"The first time you did it, you collapsed, Nora. I didn't want to put you in danger this way. Thankfully, this ability only seems to tire you out if I need healing. As you already know, if we kiss when I'm fine, nothing happens to you. I also think this is linked to you not being able to fast-heal. Since you can heal me, it probably takes away a bit of your own ability, and I don't really like that."

It kind of makes sense, in a way... Is it because I'm half a Royal, then? Could it be some sort of secret ability? Healing others instead of myself? But, with a kiss? It's still a bit... odd.

"Do you think it only works on you, because you are my fated mate? Or maybe..."

What if I used it on others? Well, it's not like I plan on going around kissing people to try, but still, I wonder if it's just between the two of us or if it could work on anyone. Damian suddenly makes an angry face after hearing me. Uh-oh.

"Don't even think about it, Nora," he growls.

I forgot how possessive he can be, sometimes...

"Wait a second... Don't tell me that is the real reason why you never told me."

I wait for an answer, but he actually stays silent, avoiding my eyes. What...? I can't believe him! How can he be so selfish and jealous?

Keeping this a secret the whole time was just because he was afraid I would go around kissing other people? Really!

"Damian Black! You—"

Before I can unleash my anger at him, he suddenly grabs me by the waist again and makes me shut up with a kiss. Gosh, this man!

However, my anger subsides naturally after a few seconds. I'm comfortable in Damian's arms, leaning on his chest to answer his kiss. I feel his hand, caressing my cheek, playing with my hair, holding me close. I don't want to part with him. This is where I belong. In this man's embrace, surrounded by his caresses. Moon Goddess, I feel so much better now, pressed against his chest.

After a long while, our lips finally part. We face each other, Damian's arms around me. His silver eyes are glowing in the dark...

"I've missed you..." He whispers.

"I missed you, too."

I observe him. He looks older, with the lack of sleep, and the beard. It's my first time seeing his bare chest, too. I never realized how muscular he was, underneath all the clothes. I can't help myself and slowly follow the lines of his muscles with my fingertips. He has perfectly shaped abs, like a Greek sculpture. I like it... a lot.

He grabs my hand with his. "My Love, I'm happy that you enjoy the view, but if your fingers go any lower, then you're going to make things difficult for me."

I blush a little. Silly, Nora. I kind of forgot which position we are in... He chuckles at my embarrassment, and brings my fingers to his lips, kissing them one by one.

"You work out?" I ask, trying to chase my uneasiness.

"When I have free time. It helps to keep my wolf under control."

The whole Alpha thing. I guess it's like me when I can't manage my anger properly, letting everyone around me feel it. Is that why he stayed here? I look around, my eyes falling on the remnants of furniture.

"Seems like this self-control thing isn't perfect yet..."

He sighs. "Only when it comes to you... I'm the most irrational man there is. Neal and Nate lectured me lots already."

I can't help but feel sorry about all this, too. It seems like this weekend was a nightmare for him...

He leans on my shoulder again, closing his eyes.

"Damian, you should get some sleep, you look exhausted..."

"...Stay with me."

"I will," I answer without thinking.

For a few seconds, he stays silent, and I wonder if he fell asleep. To my surprise, he suddenly gets up, carrying me with him, and take us both to the bed. We land heavily on the dark sheets, Damian still holding me against him. We are so close, his lips are almost touching my forehead. I touch his spiky chin again with my fingertips.

"I like it. Your beard."

"I'll keep it that way then," he whispers.

I hear his breath slow down until he falls asleep. I fall into slumber, too, a while later, soothed by Damian's embrace, the silence around us, and the darkness.

Chapter 10

I feel safe... Something warm is surrounding me. Damian's familiar, reassuring smell. This is where I belong.

I breathe in deeply. Suddenly, a cold chill runs down my spine. I'm... scared. I can't sense my wolf anymore. Where's Damian? I can't feel him anymore! There is a dark, frightening shadow coming closer, reeking of blood. Of sweat. A memory that scares me. I want to run away, but I can't move. I don't feel my legs; I don't feel my wolf!

"Nora, Nora! Wake up, Nora!"

I suddenly open my eyes. Damian's facing me on the bed and holding my trembling hands. What was I...? A nightmare? I'm on his bed, in his room. The sun is rising outside. I catch my breath, slowly coming back to my senses. Damian puts a hand on my cheek, worried.

"Are you okay?"

"Yeah... Sorry, I think I just had a nightmare..."

What was it about? I forget already. I can vaguely remember a chill and something that made me panic. Gosh, this was so intense...

Damian leans to kiss my forehead, caressing my cheek. "You're okay, Nora. Sorry, you were asleep so deeply, I went to take a shower before waking you up."

Now that I notice it, his hair is dripping, and he is wearing a new pair of dark jeans. He is still half-naked though, with a bath towel around his shoulders, and I can see the black crescent moon tattoo on his neck in full. He smells like mint-scented shampoo. I smile.

"I like a clean boyfriend," I say while giving him a quick kiss.

"Noted, princess."

"Can I borrow your shower if you're done?"

"Sure. I'll try to find you something clean to put on."

I go to his bathroom to wash the remnants of my nightmare away. I can't remember what was scaring me so much in that dream... Maybe that's for the better. I realize I just spent the night sleeping with Damian and blush. I felt so great into his arms, I could get used to it. If only I could overcome my fears. I'm all right as long as it's kissing and hugging, but whenever we go past that, I just can't do it; I'm frightened. Moon Goddess, I wish I could get rid of these feelings... Damian is already more than patient with me, and even my wolf is going crazy about it now. What is wrong with me?

I finally get out of the shower, and I have no choice but to roll a large towel around me. When I go back to the bedroom, I find a plain grey t-shirt Damian left for me on the bed.

"Sorry, that's the best I could find. I can ask—"

Damian stops, staring at me in my bath towel, and my bare legs underneath. I didn't realize he would still be in the room! He averts his gaze immediately, and I get all red, grasping the situation.

"Moon Goddess, you're really not making it easy, Nora."

"Sorry... Can you give me a minute?" I mumble, deeply embarrassed.

He exits the room with a sigh, and I run to grab the clothes. How bold can I be? Stupid Nora! You're the one making him wait, and now you walk around half-naked in his bedroom! What kind of torture is this! Moon Goddess, I really need to be more self-conscious around Damian from now on...

I quickly put on my underwear and denim skirt from yesterday, with the new t-shirt. It's obviously oversized, but I remember seeing how Elena wore stuff like this, tucking it in her skirt and all. Once I'm ready, it does look alright in the mirror. I dry my hair quickly, leaving my curls to take a natural shape, and find my earrings. When Damian comes back, I'm busy texting Bobo. He is now wearing his usual black shirt and a dark tie.

"Sorry about earlier..." I mumble, still embarrassed.

"Well, I can't say I didn't like what I saw."

He approaches me with a smile, putting his arms around my waist, and leans a quick kiss on my lips. At least I know he likes my body...

"Let's go get breakfast, I still think I need to feed you a bit more."

"Do you have a kitchen here?"

I don't remember seeing one yesterday while I was exploring his place. He shakes his head, proving me right. "We are going to the Company's cafeteria. It's not Nate's restaurant, but it's decent."

He takes my hand, and we exit his apartment. This time the

windows are all open, and the whole place certainly looks better than yesterday, in the sunlight. To our surprise, Neal is waiting for us at the entrance of Damian's office. He greets us quickly.

"You look better, Boss. Hello, Nora."

"Thanks, Neal. What are you doing here?" Asks Damian.

He sighs. I haven't seen Neal often... He is wearing a dark suit like Damian's, and I notice his wedding ring. So, the oldest Mura sibling is already married... I wonder if Bobo is an uncle?

"Your job. We canceled yesterday's meetings, but seeing how your lady came back last night, I figured you would come to work today. We have a lot to catch up on, and a board meeting in two hours."

He hands a thick red folder to Damian, but my mate frowns.

"I just got up, and I intend to have breakfast with Nora."

Seeing Neal's upset expression, it doesn't seem like those matters can wait... I take the folder from his hand and give it to Damian. Both men look at me with confused expressions.

"You can review this over breakfast, okay? I already feel bad enough that you skipped work yesterday because of me," I explain.

A broad, satisfied smile appears on Neal's face, the first one I've seen, actually. "Now I know why my sister and brother love you so much, Nora. On behalf of the other employees, thank you."

It sounds like he didn't really like me before... Well, I guess he didn't have many occasions to meet me. Now, at least, he seems satisfied. Damian, however, is quite unhappy. He takes the folder but growls at Neal when we walk past him toward the elevator.

"I didn't think you would side with Neal on that one..." He sighs as the elevator goes down.

"I had to. We probably made things difficult for him lately, and you are a CEO. Even I can understand that you have responsibilities."

"My girlfriend is my principal responsibility for now. Neal can do well by himself..."

I kiss him on the cheek to have him drop that grouchy face. He may complain, but the truth is, he has already opened the folder to check its contents. I take a look, too, but it's full of detailed reports, numbers, and graphics that I can't understand at all.

"How is your company doing?" I ask casually.

"Not bad, despite the Sapphire Moon Clan embargo..."

In our time and City, werewolf Clans fight with their fists but also with business deals. The Black Corporation is related mainly to the Blood Moon Clan; thus, what happens to one always impacts the other.

I keep thinking about it over breakfast. As Damian said, it's quite decent for a Company cafeteria, but empty at this time of the day. Which is good, because my outfit is still a bit too casual here, especially when I'm eating facing Damian. My mate, imposing in his dark suit, frowns a lot as he reads his files. I don't dare to speak, but his hand is on mine for the full breakfast, and that's enough for me.

Now I finally feel like we are a couple. Last night's discussion was really an eye-opener for me. I want to stand as an equal next to Damian, not just his scared and weak mate. The vision of Alessandra King is still engraved in my mind. She wasn't just introduced as his fiancée; she was radiating by herself, a strong presence anyone could feel. I want to be the same.

"Nora?"

I raise my head, realizing I got lost in my thoughts, and he noticed it. Damian is done eating and looks at me with a worried expression.

"You were frowning. What's wrong?"

I shake my head and smile at him. "Nothing, I'm good. Can we go? Bobo will be downstairs anytime, and I'm pretty sure Neal will have found a whole bunch of other folders to keep you busy with..."

He gets up and comes to hug me, kissing me passionately once again. Am I getting used to this? I don't feel as shy as before while moving my lips against his... I still get butterflies running wild through my whole body every time we do, though.

When we part, he sighs. "I don't want to go to work... I missed you so much this weekend."

"You have to, Damian, and me, too. I'll see you tonight, okay?"

"You're more reasonable than me. Okay. Stay with Bobo."

I roll my eyes. "Did you forget the whole part about me being able to take care of myself?"

"You may be able to fight, my Love, but you still can't drive! So that gives me an excuse to keep your bodyguard close," he laughs.

A few minutes later, I get in the car, still sulking. Bobo laughs when I tell him the reason. "So, I got promoted from your bodyguard to the driver?"

"It's not funny, Bobo!"

"It's okay, Nora. Even the Boss rarely walks alone; it's too dangerous. He's just looking out for you. Plus, it gives me an excuse to stay with you, isn't it great?"

Well, he's right... I do like having Bobo close, so I can't really complain. He takes the highway, and I stop pouting.

"Bobo, what were you doing before you became my... bodyguard?"

"Some errand boy for the Black Corp, mostly. Neal often made me deliver important papers from one place to another, even when I was in high school, confidential documents. I liked it, too. I only had to fight an ambush once in a while, and I got a good paycheck for really flexible hours. My brother was a bit bossy, though."

"You sound like you were some corporate spy!"

He laughs. "Aren't I a bit too noticeable for that? More like a bodyguard for secret paperwork! I like being your bodyguard much better," he says with a wink.

I smile, pleased by the little compliment. It's good to know I didn't change Bobo's life too much. I would have felt bad if they had him resign from some position to be my bodyguard. Now that I think about it, Bobo should still be aware of the Black Corp's whereabouts...

"Bobo, that engagement with the Gold Moon Clan girl... It would be quite profitable for Damian's company, right?"

He gives me a surprised look and stops at a red light. I can tell he's looking for the right words to answer. After a while, the car starts moving again.

"The King Family owns most of the Gold Financial establishments of Silver City; that's the reason their Clan is doing so well. The only other Clans in the same field are the Pearl and Sapphire Moon. The Black Corporation is mostly in techs and telecoms."

"The kind of field that requires lots of money and transactions..."

Bobo nods. So, being allied with the Gold Financial would be incredibly beneficial for them... I feel a bit depressed now. That Alessandra King really has everything that would make her the perfect wife. A strong Clan backing her, the looks, the power...

"Bobo, could you give me a crash course about those things? What the other Clans specialize in, the big companies they are represented with, and such?"

"Sure, but why?"

"I just feel like it's high time I knew about these things..."

Even if Damian and I are together from now on, I can't keep

walking around totally clueless about my surroundings. It's not all about fighting with my fists, I get that. It may not be my primary field, but I still ought to know the basics. Maybe this way, I will finally be able to find a solution on how to help the Brothers from now on.

Bobo parks in front of the restaurant, and hands me a bag. "As you asked, I brought you some clothes. I took what I could find in your wardrobe, hope that will be okay."

I check the content, but what Bobo chose seems perfect for work.

"Thank you, Bobo. I'll just use the restaurant's changing room."

"And you also have mail."

Mail? But I've never received any mail before. I don't even know my own address! I check the envelope Bobo hands me, it's indeed my name on it... I don't recognize the handwriting. For a second, I thought it might be Liam, but he would have texted me, and this handwriting is obviously a female's. It doesn't seem to be Elena's. I open it.

"Dear Nora,

We have never met yet, so I decided to write to you first. We have many things in common, but first, I believe we both want to preserve the peace in Silver City. I know many people are acting in the shadows to disturb that peace, and I do not intend to let them do so. I figured you might like having a new ally. You will feel suspicious: I cannot tell you my full identity yet, but I am a Witch.

Of course, I am fully aware werewolves and witches aren't always on the best terms, but we might have to. As the only Witch of Silver City, I have no intention to leave, and no intention to let another Witch on my territory either. That other witch who attacked Silver City a while ago, is the one I think about. She might be gone for now, but I believe she will return.

A War between the packs would be precisely the kind of opportunity she will wait to strike again. I do not usually meddle in those kinds of things, but I cannot let that happen. However, I am powerless in that situation. So, I decided to rely on you, Nora Bluemoon.

I will give you my help, if you help me preserve the peace in Silver City. I will not ask for anything else. Keep the butterfly with you, he can be of help. Please, do not talk about my letter to anyone. The contents will hide from any eyes but yours, so you may keep it.

Finally, be careful about who you approach. The Gold Moon Clan may have presented a golden offer to your mate, but they are much more dangerous than they seem, and their interests may lie somewhere else.

Have faith in yourself, Nora Bluemoon.

Sincerely yours,
A Friendly Witch".

I keep staring at the letter, stunned. A Witch? Does a Witch want to ally herself with me? I still can't believe it, this all sounds so unreal! I check the envelope, but there is no name, no clue to who sent this and how. At the bottom of her letter, next to her signature, a butterfly is beautifully drawn. How am I supposed to keep it with me? Shall I keep the letter? While I'm wondering this, I see the drawing suddenly move by itself! The little butterfly flaps its wings twice, and takes off, flying away from the paper. Amazed, I watch the now very living butterfly fly around a few seconds before it comes to land on my hair like some ornament.

What sorcery is this? This butterfly is now very alive and standing proudly on one of my curls.

"Nora?"

Bobo looks at me, worried. I'm speechless, and before I can formulate any thought, I see his eyes drawn to the letter.

"What is this? It's blank?"

Blank? He takes the letter and flips it over several times like he is looking for something. Oh, my Goddess, this is real. Bobo can't see what is written there. It's just as the Witch said. I raise my finger, showing the butterfly in my hair.

"Bobo, do you see this?"

He frowns. "What, something wrong with your hair?"

He really can't see it? This butterfly is bright red, and rather large, too. Anyone would see it right away, but because of some Witch's trick, it seems like I'm actually the only one who can... Is it really okay if I keep it with me? It seems to be peacefully resting in my hair like some ornament. It's not going to attack me or something, right?

"Nora, are you okay?" Bobo looks at me with worried eyes.

I nod and quickly fold the letter to put in my pocket. "Yes, sorry, Bobo, I'm fine. Maybe just a joke, who knows?"

"But—"

"I'll be going before I'm late, okay?"

He nods, and I quickly get out of the car before he can ask more questions. Once I'm in the restaurant's changing room, I change really fast so that I can re-read that letter, making sure I didn't dream it.

The contents are still precisely the same, and anyway, the butterfly is still in my hair. It just seems to fly away when I move around, but it always comes back to me. Is it going to stay there indefinitely? Is it fragile like a real butterfly, or will it throw fire or something if I try to mess with it? My wolf isn't reacting at all to it, so I guess it should be okay. She is much more interested in the letter. There's actually a sweet smell coming from it. Something like an autumn forest after the rain, and wildflowers. Is it that Witch's smell...?

My colleagues arrive one by one, and I start my day as usual. I focus on my chores, though it's a bit harder today, Narcissa is picky. She gets mad over very trivial things, and everyone is annoyed with her.

During our break, Elise keeps complaining about her. "It's not our fault she has issues in her personal life! Why does she have to put her bad temper on us? It's not like it will solve anything!"

"Issues in her personal life?" Asks Kathie. "How do you know?"

"I heard her. Before entering the restaurant, she was having an argument with her lover on the phone. It seemed like a jealousy thing."

"I didn't even know she had a boyfriend."

I nod. Narcissa seems like the type who is married to her job... But I do remember seeing her react around Nathaniel. Was he the one on the phone with her? That reminds me, I should give Elena a call after work. I promised I would tell her how things went with Damian, and I just texted her quickly this morning to say I was okay. While the girls keep talking, my phone suddenly vibrates. It's Damian. I take a few steps to isolate myself while answering.

"Hello, my Love. How is your day?" Damian says.

"A bit long, actually. The manager is in a bad mood... What about you?"

"You were right. Neal found a lot of paperwork to keep me busy for the next three hours, and a lot of executives for me to get angry at in case I would get bored."

I chuckle. "Is it all the bosses who like to terrorize their staff, or just you?"

"I would say it's a personal hobby. And I have to get prepared if I want to cancel that engagement soon."

"Damian... Are you really going to cancel it?"

I don't feel good feeling about it now. It's not just about us. After talking with Neal and Bobo, I realize there is a lot more at stake. People's jobs, business deals, financial issues... Damian's whole company could be in a wrong position because of this.

"What, do you want me to marry her?" He asks, seeming amused.

"Go ahead, marry her. That way, I can crash your wedding like in movies, fight her and kidnap you," I reply back, a bit annoyed.

"I would love to see that..."

I roll my eyes. I know Damian is just trying to make me feel better about this whole thing. I can't help but feel restless, though I don't intend to give Damian up either. He is mine, my mate. Or my mate to be, if I want to be precise...

"Nora, don't worry. I've already made up my mind, and Nate and Liam agree with me, too. I will find another way to reach an agreement with King."

It won't be so easy, I'm sure of it. Isn't there any other way out than allying with them?

"Nora?"

"Sorry, Damian, I have to go. Can I call you back after work?"

"I want to see you after work. I'll come and pick you up."

"Okay. See you later. ...I love you."

I'm red as a beet after those three words. Plus, Kathie and Elise are giving me looks that clearly indicate they heard that. I hang up and scurry to them, trying to calm down my heartbeat.

"Nora, you have a boyfriend? Why didn't you tell us!" Screams Elise.

I try to explain myself to my two excited colleagues, but before I can really get to the depth of it, Narcissa arrives, looking annoyed.

"You three! Your break is long over, go back to work! Elise, table fourteen is waiting for you to take their order. Nora, someone requested you on table two."

Someone asked for me? I'm not even among the waiter's list. Is it someone I know? I follow the girls back inside, and quickly walk up towards table two. When I see who is sitting there, I freeze.

Oh, Moon Goddess. Alessandra King?

She is sitting alone at a table for two, looking very proper in a black dress. You can tell she is from a wealthy background. I may be wearing a diamond necklace, but she is wearing flashy gold jewelry, and her designer dress is probably just as expensive. Gosh, I'm really in no mood to face my boyfriend's fiancée now. When I walk to her, she is smiling like a perfect lady.

"You asked for me?"

"You must be Nora! I recognize your horrible scar."

Seriously? That's how she wants to start, bringing up my scar? When she looks at me, I can tell her eyes are obviously fixated on it, too. Most of the time, Bobo and the brothers act perfectly normal around me, so even if other people can't help but look at it, I feel okay about my scar. However, here, Alessandra's eyes are fixated on it, and it's making me uneasy. I try to ignore it.

"And you are Alessandra King."

"That's right. Damian's partner."

She is doing this on purpose, isn't she? I cross my arms. Obviously, she doesn't want me to take her order. "Do you actually have anything to say, or did you just come all the way to my workplace to annoy me and make me lose my time? I have other customers," I say, not hiding how much she is annoying me

She keeps smiling and takes a sip of her wine. "Don't be so angsty, I just came to talk. I heard Damian wants to cancel our engagement because of his attachment to you. I hope you will help me reason him."

His "attachment" for me? I'm not some damn pet! Moon Goddess, that woman really has a gift for pissing people off just by talking. If it wasn't my workplace and there was no one around, I would be growling at her already. My wolf has been at it for ten minutes already, and though I agree with her, I must fight to contain her.

"Why would I convince *my* man to marry another woman?"

If she wants to play with words, I can do that, too. I may be a pacifist, but when it comes to Damian, I'm ready to show my fangs anytime, you pest.

"Oh, please, Nora, you know there is much more at stake, don't you? Damian Black is not just a common guy who can marry anyone," she says confidently.

"I am not anyone. I am Damian's fated mate. You know what it means, right?"

She starts laughing, a high-pitched and annoying sound. I just hate how confident she acts while obviously looking down on me.

"Do you really believe in that kind of thing? This is so... ancient! This is the twenty-first century, honey. No one cares for that kind of thing anymore."

If she calls me honey one more time, I'm seriously not going to stand for whatever happens next. And "ancient"? Who does she think she is! What are werewolves, then? Does she have any respect left for our Moon Goddess mother?

"I do care, and so does Damian," I reply right back.

"Unfortunately, whatever bond you have with, it's not going to be enough. Are you still a child? Well, you do look like one... Let me teach you something then: If Damian stays with you, he'll lose everything. If he marries me, he will be the King Alpha of Silver City, and no one will be able to resist him."

I clench my fists. I need no lessons from that woman. Yet, she keeps talking, while I feel my anger rise.

"If he marries me, he will have the full support of the Gold Moon Clan. Do you have any strong Clan supporting you, Nora? I doubt it. You are a penniless orphan. You have nothing to bring to him, no financial support, and no power whatsoever. So, you should learn your place right now, before I put you right back where you belong."

...Put me back to my place? Is that bitch threatening me now? My wolf is on all fours, growling furiously already, ready to rip her head off any time. *You're right.* I won't let her speak that way to me. Not to us. She is the one who has no idea who she is talking to.

I slam both hands on the table, looking at her eye to eye. I draw all the strength and anger I can from my wolf for the first time.

"Listen to me, King. I don't care about your money. I don't give a damn about your Clan, either. I don't need a pack, and I don't need support. I don't need anyone but myself. I don't take any threats or orders, not from you, not from anyone. So, don't you dare speak to me that way ever again. If you want a fight, I will gladly give you one. You don't know me. You have no idea what I'm capable of, but you are going to learn that the next time you have the nerve to come to claim my mate. I will give you a lesson you will remember. Are we clear?"

I stop, my eyes still burning with anger.

She is shivering with fear. Alessandra is staring at me with a shocked expression, completely speechless. She stood up and took a couple of steps back by instinct, scared by my wolf, still furiously growling at her. I feel myself surrounded by something hot and fuming right now: my Alpha aura.

"You... You're an... an Alpha?" She stammers.

Hell yeah, I am. That woman clearly wasn't expecting that. Moreover, she probably doesn't get yet that I'm not just an Alpha, but one with Royal blood, too. No wonder she got so frightened, despite being an Alpha herself.

"Surprised? I hope you weren't expecting an easy fight. I'm not the type to submit."

Damian would be proud of me. My eyes are throwing daggers right now. I step forward, and Alessandra steps back right away, not hiding her fear.

"Now, you go back to wherever you came from, and don't you dare show your face around here anymore, because I promise I won't go easy on you next time."

She grabs her bag in a very awkward way, her eyes on me all the time like she is expecting me to attack her. Truthfully, I have a hard time holding back my inner wolf, who is dying to give that woman what she deserves.

"We are not done, Bluemoon. You and Damian will definitely regret this..." She mutters while stepping back.

"Scram!"

She runs off, and I'm still trembling with anger. I can't believe what just happened, and I can't calm down, either. A lot of eyes are on me, but I don't really care right now.

I close my eyes, using Elena's technique to calm down my wolf. I was that close to letting her out when that wretched woman opened her mouth again. But I'm still in the restaurant, in front of a lot of surprised customers. I just can't. Calm down, Nora, calm down...

"Nora?"

I turn around, and Narcissa is standing there. She doesn't look annoyed this time, just a bit wary of me. She points out the kitchen.

"Go, we can handle it here. Take a break if you need one."

"No, I'm okay. Thank you, Narcissa."

She nods, and I flee to the kitchen, getting away from all the stares, including some from my colleagues. When I step in the kitchen, Chef Michel gives me a questioning look, but I just shake my head. I find something to do and try to immerse myself into work to forget it all.

I just can't. That woman's words keep going in circles in my mind, and I'm unable to forget it. At some point, I step out, because I'm unable to calm down, and at this rate, I'm going to make a mistake. I rub my temples.

"Nora, come here."

I walk up to join Chef Michel at the pass and rest my back against the wall while he is checking the orders and passing plates. He gives me a look before placing the order. After a few seconds, when everyone else is busy, he starts talking, keeping an eye on everything else.

"How are you?"

"Not great, Chef..." I confess.

"Elise just told me what happened."

"I'm sorry, Chef."

"Don't be."

He gives a new order that just came into the staff, and I help him arrange the entrees meanwhile.

"You can't always be nice to everyone, Nora. It's not the world we live in, and it's not what we were born for, either. Especially if you're an Alpha. Fight for what you want. Or who."

"But even if I do, that woman, she's right."

We keep working side by side, talking while not even looking at each other, focused on whichever plate we must get ready.

"I don't have anything. That's why I'm so mad. Even if I can fight her, she's still someone who can support my mate better than me."

"What about your mate? What does he want?"

"He wants... me," I confess a bit shyly.

"Then that's all you need to know. Don't let others interfere with your relationship. A fated mate bond is way too rare and precious to give it up because of a stranger."

"It's not just about us... The fate of several Clans is at stake."

He shakes his head and yells to remind one of the chefs about the meat's cooking. I step out a second to give a hand to the sous-chef, who is having a hard time with all the desserts. I quickly get his workspace cleaned up and take away a couple of ready plates. He thanks me, and I return to chef Michel's side.

"Don't think too hard about the consequences, Nora. It's not all about your own decisions, either. Your mate is an Alpha; he can make his own judgments."

"I'm afraid he will make bad judgments because of me."

"Maybe. But that's his call, not yours. Instead of thinking about mistakes, start thinking about solutions. When you cook, do you think about how you might fail or how you should do things?"

The Chef is right... My decision is taken anyway, and so is Damian's. There is no way I would ever let that woman get anything she wants from my mate. I know I couldn't take it, the same way I could never submit to her.

"I get it, Chef. Thank you."

"Good then. Now go and help that moron with the sauces before I get there myself."

I tried to keep the Chef's words in mind all day after that. I didn't make a wrong decision, and I won't regret it. This woman had no right to come here and make a scene. I just put her right back where she belongs. Those thoughts keep me preoccupied for a while, enough for my coworkers to leave me alone. A lot of them even act slightly differently around me now, probably because they discovered I'm an Alpha. When we are done, Narcissa calls everyone for the usual meeting at the end of the day, but I just listen to it absentmindedly. No one mentions what happened with Alessandra King.

When the meeting finishes, I'm the first one in the changing room. My clothes smell, so I change back to Damian's t-shirt and my denim skirt, feeling better in it than in my work outfit. Probably because I can smell a bit of my mate on it, too. I realize the crimson butterfly is still around. I had forgotten about that... If I try to touch him, he doesn't really react, and just flies away, only to come back if I insist. He really acts like a regular butterfly, except for the fact that he is set on hanging around me.

I check my phone. No news from Damian, but I decide to call my mate quickly. It takes a few seconds before he can answer.

"Nora. Are you done already?"

"It's not already, the lunch service ended late, actually. I just got a couple of hours before the dinner shift."

"Really? Crap, I didn't look at the time..."

He sounds preoccupied, but I can guess right away why.

"You're still busy, aren't you?"

"Yeah... I'm sorry. I still got a ton of work."

I knew it. There was no way he would be done by four; he took a full day off yesterday, and Neal looked exhausted this morning. They probably have a lot to catch up now that Damian's back to work; I can't possibly blame them.

"It's okay, I figured so. I'm going to hang out with a friend until my night shift, okay? You can come and get me if you're done by then."

"A friend?"

"A female friend," I specify, because of his inquisitive tone.

"Okay. Take Bobo with you."

"Does Bobo ever get a day off?"

"Sure, when you're with me."

I roll my eyes. Seriously, this man... For a second, I hesitate to tell him about Alessandra and my show-off, but he's probably busy with work right now, and I'm afraid he might drop it all and come here if I tell him. Surely this can wait for later.

"When does your night shift end?" Asks Damian.

"Around ten or maybe eleven tonight. I'm not too sure, we don't have a lot of reservations yet."

"All right, I should be able to get you then. Just text me when you're done."

"Okay. See you later."

"Later, Love."

I hang up, trying to control my blushing. When will I ever stop feeling like this every time I hear Damian's voice...? I still don't really feel too great because of what happened earlier, though. I need some fresh air. I grab my things and exit the restaurant. Bobo is right there waiting for me, phone in his hand and his back against the car. He stops smiling when he sees my expression.

"Bad day?"

"Mh. I'll explain later."

He nods, and we both get in the car. I open the window to enjoy some fresh air. Gosh, I needed this...Getting away from the restaurant helps me finally calm down a little. I still resent Damian a bit about what happened. If only he hadn't gotten engaged to that woman...

Hanging around and having a cup of tea with Boyan makes me feel better. I tell him in detail what happened with Alessandra earlier, and Boyan is proud of me for standing up to her. Overall, it feels great to enjoy a cup of tea while chatting with my friend. For ten years, I never had any friends to hang out with. All I had was my abusive brother and a pack that hated me. Now, I can freely talk about trivial matters, and Bobo will listen. And I have Tonia, Elena, Liam, and even Danny, too.

When Bobo takes me back to the car to head back to work, I feel a lot better already. I'm playing with my necklace, watching the scenery. Bobo, too, is humming to some Latino music coming from the stereo.

"Bobo? How did you meet Daniel?"

I've been wondering for a while now, but with everything going on, I forgot to ask. The big guy smiles at my question.

"In a nightclub, a few months ago. I was working, delivering documents to someone. I noticed Danny just when I was about to leave."

This is the first time I see Bobo smiling so much. It seems like this is a fond memory for him, so I'm even more interested.

"What was it like?"

"...Love at first sight. He was dancing, and I just fell for him right there. It was the first time I ever felt like this. Nothing else mattered; it was as if he was the only one in the room. I still remember it all perfectly. The music, his clothes, everything. I just thought, I wanted this guy, bad, right then and right there. I would have kissed him in the middle of the crowd if we hadn't been total strangers."

I laugh, a bit amused by that last sentence said with such an honest face. That's my Bobo, so straightforward and blunt. He keeps driving, but I want to know more now.

"What about Danny, then?"

He sighs. "It took a while for him to accept me. He didn't want a younger lover, so he tried to ignore me, but it was my first time wanting something or someone so much, so..."

"You were persistent?"

"Quite so. He eventually gave up after a few weeks."

A few weeks? Oh my gosh, Bobo sure is persistent! I chuckle, imagining Bobo's relentless pursuit of Daniel's heart. The two of them are just so adorably cute when they're together... I totally get why Elena teases Daniel so much. He's the only person I know who can blush redder than me!

Bobo smiles at me. "What about you? How is it with the Boss?"

"We are fine, I guess. I just wish I could overcome my fear of physical relationships once and for all..."

Bobo is the only one who knows, aside from Tonia. He was a bit disappointed about me not telling him sooner about Marcus, so I ended up telling him all about what I remembered and my traumatism.

"You want to be with him?"

"Of course, I do. But, every time we start... touching each other, I just get those cold shivers, and bad memories come back. The worst part is, I don't even remember exactly what happened, how far Marcus went, and when I... supposedly stab him. I know he didn't rape me, but whenever Damian wants more, I just..."

"Nora, it's okay. With what happened to you, it's completely normal to be scared. Just take it slow, treasure yourself, and build your trust with the Boss, Nora. Put yourself first. You deserve it, okay?"

I feel tears coming back again. Bobo notices, and parks on the side of the road. Without saying a thing, he hugs me and lets me cry all I want. After a while, I breathe in, trying to calm down.

"What if that woman is right, Bobo? What if Damian was better off with her instead of a mess like me?"

"What, you are going to let King have him now?"

"No way! I don't want to break up with Damian, ever! It's just... sometimes I can't help but wonder how the Moon Goddess could pair him up with someone as powerless as me. I know I am a Royal's child now, but that's it. You know why I was so mad earlier? Because that woman was right, Bobo. I don't have a Clan backing me, no money. I have any way to be useful to my mate."

Bobo sighs and pats my head gently. "Sometimes, you are too mature, Nora. Maybe you don't have all the answers yet. Anyway, you are powerful enough on your own. You are equal to any of the Alphas out there. I don't think King can say the same, and she knows it, too."

While Bobo speaks, something suddenly came to mind. I might not be powerful or anything, but I do have some other options now... Well, one, but that might help a lot.

"Mm... Bobo?"

"Yes?"

"Sorry but, could I ask you to leave me alone in the car for a minute?"

He looks at me, not hiding his surprise. I know my request is odd and coming at a totally unexpected time. How do I explain this?

"Please?" I ask again, trying to look sorry.

He sighs and points out the little café across the road.

"All right, but just a couple minutes. I'll go grab some coffee. You want something?"

"I'm good, Bobo, thank you."

He goes out, and I'm finally alone in the car. I watch him cross the road, making sure he is not looking, and grab a strand of my hair, agitating it. The little butterfly, annoyed at all this rampage, flies away and lands on my hand. My idea might be really, really stupid, but...

"Okay, Magic Butterfly. I hope you can understand me because I could really use some help now. I need to contact the Witch. I'll accept our alliance if she can give me some help. How do I contact her?"

I really hope it understands because otherwise, I'm probably looking crazy talking to a butterfly. I wait for a few seconds, and suddenly, it starts flapping its wings. They turn green. What does that mean, green? Is that a good sign? Does it mean I can talk or something? I suppose a butterfly can't talk, anyway, but I have no idea how a Witch's powers work... Okay, I can try, I guess.

"Witch, if you can hear me this way, I want to ask you a favor. I'm trying hard to stop this war, but I think I just added oil to the fire, so I'm looking for other options. Can you give me a hint, anything? I stood up to King, but I'm not sure that's going to help. If we can't trust the Gold Moon Clan, then who? I tried to think of options, but I don't know where to start! Can you help? You said we were allies; how can you help?"

I wonder what else to say, but my mind is too confused for now. All of a sudden, the butterfly takes off, flying away from me for the first time. Where is it going now? Did I annoy him? Or did he get the message? He flies around for a few seconds in the vehicle interior, but it doesn't make any sense. His wings turn red, then blue, then red again. What now? Did I break it or something?

Just when I'm wondering what I should do, Bobo comes back. So soon? The butterfly keeps flying around, but Bobo can't see it.

"Are you done?" He asks.

I sigh and nod. I don't know what else to do, anyway. I feel a bit stupid now. Bobo starts the car again, and I'm angrily staring at the butterfly that won't stop flying around.

When we are back at the restaurant, a few minutes later, as I step out of the car, the butterfly suddenly takes off. What? I see it fly away, headed to the south. Where is it going? Is it annoyed at me or something?

Should I follow it? It doesn't seem to be waiting for me...

"Nora?"

Bobo is waiting for me, looking confused by my attitude. I sigh and follow him into the restaurant to resume work.

We have more reservations than when I left and, as expected, the restaurant is quite busy. I keep running from one table to another and then to the kitchen, as both Narcissa and Chef Michel keep asking for me. I'm doing fine, though, and it's going smoothly so far.

"Nora, do you know when I can get my desserts for table seven? The customer said twice he is in a hurry... "

"I'll go get them for you, but the table three needs—"

Before I can finish my sentence, a huge racket can be heard from the entrance. A few customers scream in surprise, as a dozen wolves suddenly barge into the restaurant. What the...?

"Nora! Nora!"

It's Damian's voice. I see him running in, still in his dark suit, obviously looking for me. What's going on? I drop whatever I was holding in Elise's hands and run up to him across the restaurant. He is accompanied by Bobo, Neal, and Nathaniel, all in their human forms and looking serious. Damian's Alpha aura is probably going wild right now, scaring everyone who hasn't already left the room at the sight of the werewolves bargaining in.

"Damian!"

When I walk up to him, he finally sees me. To my surprise, my mate runs to me and takes me into his arms, hugging me tight.

"Nora, thank Moon Goddess, you are fine..."

"Damian, what is going on? What happened?" I ask, worried.

Instead of answering, he turns around and starts yelling orders.

"Neal, I want this place empty and closed, right now. Nate, take the staff out, too. Everyone here gets the fuck out!"

The wolves start growling, and the customers run away in a panic, emptying the restaurant in seconds. I watch the scene, completely lost about what is going on. Damian looks furious; I've never seen his eyes so cold before! I grab his arm, trying to get his attention.

"Damian, tell me what's going on!"

Neal who walks up to me, while still watching the wolves taking everyone else out of the restaurant.

"Your apartment was attacked, Nora."

Oh, Moon Goddess. Attacked? Attacked how? By whom? Damian suddenly puts his arm under my thighs and picks me up, carrying me as he walks across the now almost empty restaurant. Before I can say a word, he takes me to the Staff Room. Behind us, Nathaniel and Neal are following closely, while the wolves guard the entrance.

When we enter, Damian puts me down, but his arm stays firmly around my waist to keep me close.

"Damian, calm down, I'm okay. What happened?"

"Liam noticed something was wrong when he came back from school. When he went to check your apartment, he said the door was wide open, and the whole place has been sacked."

Nate walks up to me, handing me his smartphone. I look at the pictures. Oh, my Goddess... I can barely recognize the apartment. Someone splashed every room with a red liquid, and some of the furniture was destroyed. The whole place was sacked, I can't believe what I'm seeing.

"Oh, Moon Goddess..."

The last picture was taken in my bedroom. My wardrobe is on the floor, a lot of my clothes torn apart. Even the bed was shredded. But, most of all, on the glass wall, a message in the red liquid was left: *YOU WILL BE MINE."*

I feel like I'm going to be sick looking at those words. Seeing my shocked expression, Damian takes the phone away from me, throwing it back to his brother and kisses my forehead to comfort me. He is just as agitated as I am, but I can tell he is trying hard to control himself right now, so I keep him close, my hands on his chest.

"It's okay, Nora, I'll find who the hell did this, I swear."

His words are burning with anger, but he is still worried about me. I shake my head, slowly processing everything I just saw and heard.

"I can't believe it... Is Liam okay?" I ask.

"He is okay, Nora, no one was there when he came up," says Nate.

"It happened this afternoon. Everything was normal when I went there earlier," Bobo says.

Bobo is right; he went back to get me clothes only a few hours ago.

"The surveillance cameras didn't give anything," says Neal, looking at his phone. "Someone disconnected them."

"How the hell did they get in?" Growls Damian.

"Liam said the door's lock was... shot. ...He found silver bullets."

I gasp. Oh, Moon Goddess, this is serious. Someone armed with a gun to kill werewolves broke into my place. What if I had been there? Or if they had met Bobo? Or Tonia, or Liam?

"And the blood?" I ask. "Is it really blood?"

Moon Goddess, I hope it isn't. So much of it would be really, really bad news. No one can answer me: Neal is now busy taking one call after another, speaking so fast I can't understand a thing, and Nate is reading texts, too. I turn to Damian, and once again, his eyes are terrifying. My mate looks like he is about to kill someone. However, he can't scare me, so I just lean onto his chest, and I feel his hand in my hair a second later.

"What do we do now?" I ask.

"You're coming with me; I'm taking you back to my place. Neal, find as much information as you can, and get Liam to Nate's place."

"He said he already has a place to crash," says Nathaniel.

Damian immediately growls at him, annoyed. "I don't give a shit, Nate. I want to know where Liam is, and you bring his ass back whether he likes it or not. We are not playing games now. Boyan, you and Tonia go help Neal, too, Nora will stay with me. I want the full Clan gathering in two hours, with no exceptions. Clear?"

Everyone agrees and disperses right away, leaving the two of us alone. I turn to Damian, but before I can say a thing, his arms surround me, and he is carrying me again across the restaurant. I would probably be quite embarrassed if the situation wasn't so urgent, but now is certainly not the time to fight with him. None of this makes sense anyway. I was working just a few minutes ago, but now, it turns out I'm in a life-threatening situation.

Damian takes me to a black sports car and starts driving at full speed across the city. I can't say a word during the full trip. I'm too shaken up, and I wouldn't know what to say. Moreover, Damian takes one call after another on the car monitor. Neal, Nate, and some other people's voices give him more information as soon as they get it, and I just listen. It's not much. The building surveillance cameras went down for two hours in the afternoon, and they are still looking in the neighborhood for some decent footage of the closest streets. No one heard the gunshots, either, but they found a total of eight bullets; most of them were used to destroy the door's lock.

At some point, I stop listening to close my eyes. This is all so unreal like I'm in one of those movies Tonia loves, where they talk about crime scenes and ballistics. I look at the city outside, wondering what happened that it would come to this. At some point, I feel Damian's hand on my knee, and I take it. I can feel his emotions so clearly; my wolf just translates it all for me. Our mate is worried about us and furious. He is on the phone, but we don't need to talk for now. We are next to each other; we don't need any words.

Once we arrive back at the office building, Damian stays close to me, putting his arm around me to take me inside quickly. He only seems to ease up a little when we finally arrive at his flat.

There, he heaves out a deep sigh and hugs me once more now that we are entirely alone. I lean into his embrace, the safest place in the world to me.

"I was so worried something might have happened to you..."

"I know. I'm okay, Damian. I'm fine."

He nods, and for a while, just keeps me in his arms. I feel his shoulders relaxing a little and get on my toes to give him a kiss. I know we are both shaken up. Damian takes my hand, and we both sit on the large grey sofa, facing each other.

"Are we going to tell the police?" I ask.

"Already did, Nate is on it. We are going to need forensics to know who did it."

"The message on the wall... This is clearly someone who is personally after me."

"Your brother is still in the psychiatric ward. The only name I can think of is..."

"Marcus," I whisper.

Damian nods. I really didn't want to believe it, but that's the most plausible answer. I can't believe he is still alive, and after me. How did he even find me? Why now, after all this time? He got to my apartment, with a gun full of silver bullets. The more I think about it, the more I think that all this doesn't look like Marcus at all. He is a rash man, and not that smart either. Leaving blood all over the room and sacking my apartment, that's like him. The message, too. That sicko has been eyeing me forever. But sneaking into the Blood Moon's territory, finding my location, and deactivating the building's surveillance system?

"What is it?" Asks Damian, noticing my frowning.

"Something's not right. Damian, I think Marcus is the one who did this, too, but a lot of things don't make sense. Like, how did he get access to the surveillance system? Or how was he able to find me, and get a gun too? He shouldn't have any resources left in Silver City, so how did he pull something like that? I know him. That psycho is definitely not smart enough for something so elaborate."

"You think someone helped him... But who would?"

An answer immediately comes to mind, but I really, really don't like what that would imply. That person would have the resources to pull this off, and an excellent reason to use Marcus, too. Damian is not going to like this at all...

"...Nora?"

Someone comes in before I can reply. Nathaniel, followed by Liam. The third brother looks exhausted.

"Hi, Nora," he says

"So, you came back after all?"

"Well, I heard Damian was going to spank me if I didn't..."

I chuckle, and Liam comes to sit next to me. Nathaniel is glaring at him but doesn't say a thing. He probably wasn't happy to have to go look for him now.

"So?" Asks Damian.

"The cops took over. The CCTV from the shop across the building showed a man going in and out, exactly in the time slot Boyan and Liam gave us. He was wearing a cap and a large coat, so I don't think we will be able to identify him."

Nate sighs and goes to get himself a glass from the kitchen, some whiskey, judging by the smell. Damian frowns while his brother does so but doesn't say a thing.

"I bet it's Marcus."

"We think so, too," says Damian. "But Nora thinks someone helped him, and she's probably right. That sicko couldn't have gotten in so easily."

"Who then? The Jade Moon banished him, right?" Asks Liam.

"What about the Sapphire Moon? They hate us."

"They wouldn't stoop so low has to help a shithead like Marcus," Growls Damian.

"Guys, I have something to tell you."

All three of them turn their heads to me, and I suddenly feel awkward, but I must tell them. Damian promised not to keep secrets anymore; I should do the same. Moreover, this is important. I turn to Damian, trying not to worry too much.

"Damian, promise me you won't get angry."

"Wow, now coming from you, that doesn't sound good."

"Shut up, Liam. Damian, please."

He looks at me for a few seconds, visibly lost by my request, and retakes my hand. "I won't, but Nora, what is it?"

"I... I had a bit of a fight with Alessandra King earlier today."

"You had what?"

Damian's Alpha aura immediately acts out, and for once, my wolf isn't feeling too great about it. Both Nate and Liam look at me with shocked faces, too, but their oldest brother worries me the most. He jumps off the sofa and looks at me with an expression I can't decipher, something between rage and incredulity. Well, I don't care, but he better not be angry at me now! My wolf remembers the very disagreeable experience and agrees with me.

"You said you wouldn't get angry!" I protest. "Plus, she started it, she came to the restaurant looking for me."

"Looking for trouble, you mean. How typical of King," mutters Nathaniel.

"What did she say?" Asks Damian, in his ice-cold tone.

I tell them all about Alessandra's words and how I stood up to her. Liam can't help himself and interrupts me a couple of times to react, but both Nathaniel and Damian are staring at me until I'm done. Telling them about that stupid fight annoys me again when I have to remember all of Alessandra's words. When I'm done, I'm just as mad as I previously was.

"I didn't want to have to stoop to her level, but she started it, Damian, and I was not going to back off."

A few seconds of silence follow I'm waiting for their reaction. Finally, Liam breaks the silence first. "That's our girl! I'm proud of you, Nora, though I wish you had bitten her, too."

"Well, I'm not going to say you were wrong, either," says Nate. "And King was wrong from A to Z, coming to look for Nora in the first place."

Eventually, all eyes turn to Damian, waiting for his reaction. I get it a second before his brother, through my wolf. *Our mate is mad. Really, really mad.*

In a split second, I see a sudden movement, and the large table loudly breaks in two under Damian's fist.

"That's expensive..." Sighs Nathaniel, rolling his eyes.

"I can't believe the nerve of that woman! How dare she threaten you! And making fun of our bond on top of that? Who the hell does she think she is!"

"I don't care about her threats, Damian. I don't want that woman anywhere near you or telling me if I deserve to be with you or not."

"Well, I care! If the Gold Moon Clan wants war, they are going to have it!"

Oh, Moon Goddess, this is so not what I planned. I get up and grab his arm, trying to have him calm down. To my surprise, Nathaniel and Liam don't move a finger to help me reason with Damian, just watching the two of us.

"Damian, calm down. This is not worth blowing your partnership with their Clan."

"Nora is right, Damian," says Nathaniel. "The current situation is too tense to make such decisions."

"King overstepped her boundaries. She came on our territory to threaten Nora and, indirectly, she threatened Damian, too. And what if she really is the one behind the attack at the apartment?"

Suddenly, I remember the Witch's words. What if the Black Brothers' alliance with the Gold Moon Clan really turns out to be a trap? Does that mean they don't have any reliable allies? The boys start talking about the situation at the border and arguing about what to do with the Gold Moon Clan, but something else catches my attention.

The Witch's butterfly is back! I don't know how it came all the way to Damian's apartment, but it flies all the way to me, carrying something. It drops it at my feet and lands on my shoulder. A business card?

I bend over to grab it, reading: "William Blue, CEO, Sapphire Holdings."

"Nora?"

While Damian and Nathaniel are still talking, Liam catches my expression. Can he see the business card? Probably not. I quickly put it in my pocket and walk back to sit next to him on the sofa, using the mind-link to talk to him without his brothers listening. That ability sure is convenient for keeping secrets...

"Liam, do you know William Blue?"

"Of course, the son of the Alpha of the Sapphire Moon Clan, remember? The guy that hates us to the core."

"You said his father hated your father. Did you guys ever try to negotiate with him?"

"Yeah, Nate and Damian tried to talk to the man a lot of times, but he never wanted anything to do with us. The guy is a stubborn jerk."

"I'm serious, Liam."

"I'm serious, too! Try going into a territory where the pack hates you. I did it, quite a few times in a lot of places I should never have, believe me. But the Sapphire Moon territory? That's a no-go, even for me, Nora. I can have a few fights with the Violet Moon wolves, but the Sapphire Moon watchdogs would kill me on the spot."

So, things are at a dead end. Why would the Witch give me their Alpha's business card then? Did I miss something? There is what I suppose to be their headquarters' address written on the back but going there would be suicide! I know where their turf is, but if I go, there is no guarantee I will come back safe and sound. What is that Witch's plan exactly?

"Hey, what are you thinking about?"

"I'll tell you later."

Liam gives me a suspicious look, but I realize Damian and Nate stopped talking to look at us. My mate comes back to sit next to me.

"What are you guys talking about?"

"Nora was asking me about the Sapphire Moon Clan, just filling her in."

"We can't exclude the possibility that they are the one behind the attack," says Nate.

"I'm still not going to let what that woman did slide," growls Damian.

"What do you...?"

Before he can end his sentence, we can all hear Nathaniel's phone rings again. He takes the call.

"Tonia, you got anything new? No? Then... Oh, really? What, seriously? Are you sure? That's..."

I see his eyes aiming my direction a few times, and I wonder what this is about. He looks surprised. What is going on? After a while, he hangs up, asking Tonia to email him everything. Damian frowns.

"Nate, what's going on?"

"It's Nora's blood test results, they just came out."

"And?" I ask, curious.

I already know the results, and I thought we all did by now, but Nathaniel's expression is a bit off— he seems too surprised. Is everything okay? His phone beeps, and he looks at it.

Damian growls, impatient. "Nate!"

Nate jumps, and shows his phone's screen to Damian. "Seventy-eight point six! Nora has almost eighty percent of Royal genetics..."

My mind goes blank. 78.6%...? That's too much! I thought I would be half Royal at most, because of my dad, but that number is way higher than expected! I can't believe it! Damian and Nathaniel seem stunned, too, but Liam is internally screaming.

"Oh, Holy Moon Goddess mother! Nora! Eighty percent! Nora, you're a freaking princess!"

A princess? What princess? I don't understand. Nathaniel shows Damian the email detailing the results, but I'm just sitting on the couch, not knowing what to think. Nathaniel starts reading out loud.

"According to Tonia's grandmother, common werewolves have above five percent of Royal genetic markers. For Alphas, it goes up to ten sometimes, but this amount is only possible for a Royal! Nora is not a Royal's child; she is a Royal herself!"

"That's not possible! I told you my dad was a normal wolf!"

"If he was your dad, Nora, you don't know about that yet. Maybe..."

"This is nonsense, I look like him, Nate!"

"It doesn't mean he was your father! We don't know what exactly happened between your parents, but I have your blood test results right here, and there is no way this is wrong. Nora, no Royal is a hundred percent Royal, okay? With time, fights with vampires, and mixing with humans, a lot of the Royal Bloodline was lost. Now, any werewolf with about twenty percent of those genes could claim to be a Royal. But you have four times that amount! Liam is right; according to our standards, you have the pedigree of a werewolf princess."

Granny Ariana probably told him all this anyway, so there is no point in arguing anymore. I sigh and cross my arms, a bit annoyed. I don't really care about all that princess stuff, but I'm certainly tired about all this questioning around who are my birth parents or not. I thought this was settled when we interrogated Alec weeks ago!

"Okay, I get it. But I don't want to talk about my father anymore. Can we go back to the main subject, please?"

"You don't seem too surprised, Nora," says Nate.

"Not really, we had suspicions from the start, anyway. I don't plan to change anything just because I'm some werewolf royalty..."

"You could try ordering Nate to wash your dirty socks. Or take over Damian's spot. That would be funny to watch."

All three of us glare at Liam, making him stop with his stupid jokes. How can he be spouting nonsense like this now?

"Anyway. What do we do from now on?" I ask.

Nathaniel scratches his chin and sighs. "Damian's right on one point. King came to my territory unannounced to seek a fight with you. She had no right to do so. The Gold Moon Clan might be powerful, but it would be good for them to remember they are not above us," says Nathaniel.

Damian nods. "Right. I'm sick of her father's pathetic arrogance, too. They are getting bolder by the day, using our name and their money. We might be on good terms for now, but I think a little reminder of who is the real King of Silver City might do them some good."

"I like the sound of that, Brother."

Honestly, I like it, too, but I can't help being worried. Is that really all right? Liam catches my eyes while his brothers start talking about business deals and numbers.

"Don't worry, Nora. That Gold Moon Clan had this coming anyway. And it's not like Damian is going to fight them; this is barely a slap on the hand."

"What if this upsets them? Aren't you afraid they will get back at us or terminate all deals?"

"They won't, they would be on the losing hand. I told you, the Gold Moon Clan is hell rich, but that's it. Their wolves are not powerful, and they really don't want to get on Damian's bad side, trust me."

"Hey, what are you guys talking about?" Asks Nathaniel.

Liam shakes his head.

"Our Princess is scared about the Gold Moon Clan getting mad."

"Don't be, Nora," says Damian. "If we go soft now, we are not wolves. King should never have threatened you in the first place."

"You mean us."

"Same thing."

"So, what now?" Asks Nathaniel.

Damian smiles, but that's more of a scary smile, the kind of smile when someone else is about to get in trouble. Liam and I exchange a look, and I know he is way too content right now.

"Let's make them see how angry we can get. Gather the Clan as we planned. All our Alphas, hunters, warriors, and family heads. I'm going to introduce Nora at the same time and tell them the Gold Moon wolves are no longer welcome onto our territories."

"Got that. Everyone is already assembling anyway."

"Wow, introducing your girlfriend one week after introducing your fiancée. That's what you call bold, Brother."

"Liam's right. Not that I'm going to complain, however. I still despise King, and so does the rest of our Clan. That was a bad idea, to begin with, especially with Nora in the picture, Damian."

Well, I'm happy Nathaniel and Liam are saying this. I glance at Damian. See? You messed up really bad by getting engaged to that vixen. My mate gives me an apologetic look and kisses my hand quick.

"I'll repeat it, I'm sorry. I'm going to make things right about that engagement, too."

"Is that still a thing? I mean, you just drank some champagne and walked into a room together. There is no contract yet, is there?"

"It's more than that, Liam," sighs Nathaniel. "By now, all the Gold Moon Clan will have used this engagement for business issues and consider it as valid. Even if Damian turns out to have a lover, I doubt they will even care. They will most likely just pretend they don't know or pass it off as a baseless rumor. The news of this engagement is too big; the Gold Moon Clan took things to their advantage to put pressure on other companies, saying the Black Corp is backing them up. If we want to stop them, Damian will need to make a formal statement."

So, this is an even more significant issue than I thought. To think a simple engagement could have so many consequences... I remember my conversation with Bobo in the car earlier. Don't waver, Nora. Even the Witch said the same thing. I should have faith in myself. Maybe I will find a way to help Damian later.

I keep thinking about that business card. Maybe I have a chance to turn tables now. This can't just be a coincidence. I bite my lip, thinking about what to do next.

"Damian?"

He turns his head to me, and I point the bedroom.

"I'll get changed before we meet your clan. I'm all sweaty from work. Okay?"

He nods, and I head off to the bathroom. Thank Moon Goddess I still have the clothes from this morning, because I don't feel like putting on anything that was in my room if there is any left. I still can't believe someone did this to the apartment. I shiver just thinking about it. What would have happened if I had gone home during my break? If it was Marcus…

Elena! I suddenly remember my cousin. I haven't heard from her... I'm under the shower but, now that I think about it, I don't need a phone, do I?

"Elena?"

"Nora! What is it, too lazy to use the phone now?"

"I'm showering. Plus, Nate is right next door. You still don't want the brothers to know we know each other, right?"

"No, no. Are you all right, Nora? Your wolf seems all shaken up."

Quickly, I tell her about all the events since we last saw each other, what happened in my apartment, our suspicions, and about the blood tests, as well. I grab a towel as I finish talking and start dressing up.

"Nora, that's a lot of information. I'm not so surprised about the blood results, to be honest, I always knew you were more... Well, more Royal than I am. But what happened at your place? That's really no good."

"I know, I'm totally freaked out, too, though I don't want to worry Damian."

"I understand. But stay close to your mate until they found this psychopath, okay? And you can talk to me if you need help, anytime."

"Thank you, cousin."

Cousin...

I like the sound of that. Elena and I keep talking through the mind-link for a while before I finally exit the room. To my surprise, Liam is waiting for me in the bedroom. I frown.

"Liam? Where are Damian and Nate?"

"They are waiting for us downstairs. Neal and Bobo just came back. So, we have a few minutes to talk before they come back."

"Talk about what?"

"About this?"

Oh, Moon Goddess. Why does he have that business card! I walk up and take it back from him. Don't tell me he took it from my clothes while I was showering? I can't believe him!

"Liam, that's not your business! Don't go through my stuff again!"

"What, you're hiding little secrets now? Why do you have that guy's business card, anyway?"

So, he can see what's written on it. Couldn't the Witch have hidden it from other people, too, like her letter? Apparently not. How do I explain this? I know Liam is good at keeping secrets, but gosh, he is good at spying, too! Moreover, there is no way I'm telling him about the Witch; he is the one supposed to hunt her down.

"Someone gave it to me," I mumble.

"Oh, really? I wonder who."

Gosh, can't he be less curious just for once! And while he's at it, drop that stupid smirk of his, too! I know there is no way he is going to let this go, so I might as well give him something else to think about instead of telling him about the Witch.

"Okay, I was thinking of going over to talk to their Alpha."

His smile drops immediately, and he crosses his arms, looking a lot like Damian when he is unhappy. "Nice. Did you completely forget the part about them killing intruders on the spot? Because I'm pretty sure I mentioned it something, like, ten minutes ago."

"You said they hated you guys. Doesn't mean they will be as hostile towards me."

"They don't like strangers at all, Nora. Do you really think you can just walk in there and try your luck? I think you're a tiny bit overconfident here, Princess."

"Liam, it could be the solution! Moreover, you said it, I'm a princess, a Royal. Maybe that will help...?"

He rolls his eyes. "Nora, even I am not that crazy! And you? You are a Princess, but you are still a 5'2", underweight, eighteen-year-old girl who learned how to control her wolf not two months ago! This is not like an Alpha fight; this is you running into a freaking dead-end!"

I cross my arms, annoyed at him. For the record, I'm not as thin as I used to be, and he knows this isn't a matter of size either. I'm disappointed. I mean, Liam has been one of my most trusted friends since the beginning, and always the first one up for any crazy plan! I mean, isn't he the reckless one among his brothers?

"What, you don't trust me now? Liam!"

"I trust you, Nora, but this is a suicide, and I'm not a big fan of that! Wait till my brother kills me, too, if I let you to go there alone! You think Damian handcuffing you to the bed was unreasonable? Wait until you see how he punishes me!"

"Actually... I thought you could come with me."

"Excuse me now?"

He looks at me with shocked eyes, but I'm still not giving up. I really think this might help. I try to make a pleading face, putting my hands together, and stepping closer.

"Please, Liam? You know Silver City like no one, and all the packs would let you on their turf."

"All except for the Sapphire Moon Clan! And they don't let me in, I just sneak in, Nora. Most of the time. What you're asking me is..."

"What about Lysandra Jones? You guys are on good terms, and her Clan is an ally of the Sapphire Moon!"

Liam shakes his head. "No, Nora. First, we are not friends, she just likes to fight with strong people, and I'm one of those. Secondly, the Purple Moon is only a branch Clan of the Violet Moon. Lysandra doesn't agree with her father, so assuming her pack is allied with the Sapphire Moon Clan is a bit risky. Finally, I'm not even sure, even if Lysandra agrees to help us and an ally of the Sapphire Moon wolves, that this plan would work. That's way too many ifs!"

I know this idea is risky with the way things are now. but with Damian breaking the engagement, I'm afraid the balance of power between the Clans will shift way too fast, and I must act before that. "It might be my only to help you guys."

He shakes his head. "Nora, this is a really, really bad idea. Damian would be super against it, and with all the right reasons for it!"

I do feel bad about acting behind his back, but he would prevent me from going there if I did. I know I'm the one who came up with this "no lies" thing, but I don't see any other way to help my mate. I sigh. "Okay, let's talk again about this later. You think about it, please, Liam."

"You better think about it, too, Nora! Like, as an awful decision you should not make!"

He sighs and turns around to leave the room. I know this is

unreasonable, but this is the only thing I could think of after receiving this business card. I look at the butterfly flying around me while I quickly brush my hair. Is this little thing going to get me killed? The Witch wouldn't let such a thing happen, right?

I try to chase away those depressing thoughts and get downstairs to join the guys. Liam ignores me, but I just naturally walk up to my mate. Damian puts his arm around my shoulders, and it's time to go.

We don't need to get far; the elevator takes us way downstairs. The brothers guide me through a couple of corridors, and we finally walk into what looks like a vast reception hall. Except that nothing is put up for a reception, no decoration or furniture whatsoever. Instead, it is just crowded with a lot of people. It looks more like some shady business reunion. The curtains are closed, and everyone is dressed in dark outfits, mostly black. Most are between their twenties and forties. Some wear suits, others wear some street clothes like hoodies or leather jackets. I finally understand. Neal didn't gather the full Clan, but its lieutenants.

The Jade Moon Clan was not that big, only eighty or a hundred people, so Vince was enough as its Alpha to control it, with the Beta's help. For the Blood Moon Clan, however, that wouldn't work. From what I've heard, this Clan has hundreds, perhaps thousands of members. With so many people, a single Alpha could never oversee it all. Hence, like any prominent Clan leader, Damian, has an organization that allows him to control all the wolves without being himself on the scene.

That's where the lieutenants come in. Those people are Alpha werewolves, but of lower strength than the main Alpha. Just strong enough to control smaller groups. I look around, and that seems about right. Headhunters, top fighters, family heads, gang leaders. Every single person in this room is an Alpha, leading their own smaller pack, but moving under Damian's orders.

As we walk in, all of them react to my mate's presence, willingly lowering their heads in respect, calling him "Boss."

Despite the room being full of Alphas, I can tell none of them are on Damian's level. He has his own aura, on a whole different scale. And here I am, walking next to him, with no idea how to act. Gosh, I can't believe I'm just standing there with a denim skirt and this plain t-shirt! Maybe I should have dressed up a little? I feel awkward facing all the lieutenants with their severe looks in this casual attire.

Damian walks up to a small stage, where all of them can see him.

Taking a quick look, I try to estimate how many people are there. Maybe about a hundred or so? How large can the sub-packs be, then? Some of them look young, maybe my age or so. They don't look childish at all, though, more like punks and street gang people. It really looks like some Mafia gang gathering...

"Hi, everyone. Apparently, Neal already filled you in, so let's go over this quickly," says Damian. "From today on, no more favors for the Gold Moon Clan. They overstepped their bounds, and we are to make them regret it."

To my surprise, most people in the room cheer or applaud, and a couple of them whistle in appreciation. Are they happy about pissing the Gold Moon Clan off?

"I like that, Boss!" Yells some guy with a large beard.

"Let's ditch those money-suckers!"

"Who do they think they are!"

A few more people are heard before Damian growls. Immediately, everyone goes silent again, all eyes focused on him. A woman with a black leather jacket raises her hand.

"What about King, Boss? The engagement? Judging from the young missy next to you, I bet you found better!"

Damian smiles and takes my hand gently before making me face the crowd with a fierce look.

"I found the best one, Vane. All of you meet Nora, my fated mate."

A few seconds of silence follow his words when all eyes turn to me, and all sudden, the cheering starts again, ten times louder this time. People clap their hands, and congratulatory words are flying all over the room.

"Finally! We're so happy for you, Boss!"

"Blessed Moon Goddess mother, a fated partner for the Boss!"

I can't believe all these people are genuinely happy for us. Aren't they disappointed I'm not of a powerful family, or as pretty as Alessandra King? Do they think I have some significant backing they don't know of yet? I blush, embarrassed by so many people cheering for our relationship. Damian pulls me back next to him, putting his arm around me in a showy manner. Once again, the crowd calms down as soon as he gestures it.

"From now on, Nora is my one and only partner. The engagement with King is no longer. Don't let the Gold Moon Clan use it anywhere.

No more favors, no more special treatment."

I see the Alphas wearing black suits all nod. They are giving off a businessman feel. They are probably the ones handling businesses and dealing daily with the Gold Moon Clan. Damian then turns to the side with the most street gang people, the younger Alphas.

"I don't want them anywhere in my territory. Let everyone know they are not welcome anymore. No more coming unannounced, no more going through our territory. If they don't like it, show them it's not up to them."

A young man with red-colored hair nods. "Got it, Boss! I was tired of seeing them acts like they own the place! We will drive them off and make sure they don't dare step in our streets again!"

"Spread the word, Sean. And tighten up the security; from now on, I want more people watching our borders. Some psycho managed to go past our defenses; make sure that doesn't happen again."

"Sure, Boss."

Damian keeps giving instructions to chase the Gold Moon Clan off their territory. Not just geographically, but they also start talking about land property and corporate actions. None of this I can help with. Meanwhile, I notice a few people looking at me with curious eyes.

Well, I kind of dropped in out of the blue, so that would be logical. Everyone probably wonders where I came from, how I met Damian, but surprisingly, no one dares to ask. They listen to Damian's orders religiously. From my perspective, no one seems really worried about what's coming next. All that matters to them is the Boss's orders. A hundred Alphas, all gathered in one place and listening to my mate with no discussion. I feel like this is the first time I'm really witnessing with my own eyes the extent of Damian's influence.

The meeting takes longer than I expected. Damian's orders were clear, and some of the lieutenants left right away. Still, some stayed to ask him about some border issues like the rogues, or how they should handle business deals. I notice a few of the lieutenants still look at me from time to time. I go to sit aside with Liam and Bobo, leaving Nathaniel and Damian to handle the Clan issues. To my surprise, five people shortly walk up to us.

I recognize the woman who spoke earlier, and Sean, the teenager with a large hoodie. Three other guys are with them. One is wearing a completely black suit and glasses, like an office worker. The one next to him has an entirely different look, with a leather jacket and tattoos all over his arms. I'm pretty sure he's a biker. The last guy wears a casual outfit and a beard, but he has a large burn scar on half of his neck.

"Hello, miss Nora. I hope we are not bothering you, we just wanted to pay our respects to the future Luna," says the woman, Vane.

Bothering me? I'm just sitting next to the wall, doing nothing! I get up to salute them. What am I supposed to say? This is a bit awkward, but they act politely and respectfully, so I do my best.

"Oh, thanks. It's nice to meet you all, I'm Nora Bluemoon."

"That's a pretty name, young lady. Nice to meet you, I'm Joshua Hale, in charge of the North highways," says the biker guy. He gives me a handshake with his gigantic paw, and a big smile.

Next to him, the teen just nods, his hands in his hoodie's pockets. "Sean Pierce. I'm in charge of Rock Park, and all the dark alleys a lady like you shouldn't go."

"Hello, miss Nora. I'm Thaddeus Cooper, in charge of the Financial district and M. Black's accounting assistant," says the guy with the office worker look, bowing in a really polite manner.

The last man gives me his hand, too, and a gentle smile. "Isaac Graves. We have met before, but I was in my wolf form, at your fight against the Jade Moon Alpha. A beautiful fight, by the way."

"So, you're Nathaniel's Beta, right?" I ask, suddenly remembering where I heard his name before.

He smiles and nods. "That's right."

"And I'm Vanessa Brookes, in charge of South Main Street and the southern border. You can call me Vane, everyone does."

I shake hands with the woman. I feel like I've heard her name before. Her face reminds me of someone, too, but I can't remember who. She is tall, with her brown hair falling on a red leather jacket. She gives me a warm smile. "We are happy you're here, miss Nora. The Boss has been looking everywhere for you, you know, so we were curious. It's good to finally see you in person."

"You guys know about this, too?" I ask, surprised.

The biker guy, Joshua, laughs loudly. "Everyone here knows! The Boss gave orders a few years ago. Find a teenage girl, blue eyes, black hair, a scar on her left eye. And here you are!"

"Thank Moon Goddess. If the Boss really married that King, I would have killed that whore," grumbles Sean.

"Well, you won't need to get things that far, it seems like the Boss will take care of things after all," says Isaac.

"I was surprised earlier. Are you guys all against that woman? I mean, this alliance with the Gold Moon Clan should be full of advantages..." I say.

They look at me with surprised eyes. Sean rolls his eyes, but Vane gives him a slap behind the head right away, telling him to watch his attitude.

It's actually Thaddeus who clears his throat to answer me. "Putting the financial benefits aside, miss Nora, the Gold Moon Clan is not a popular choice for the Clan. Their wealth is mostly due to a long history in Silver City, not smart business decisions. If I may say so, their wealth went up naturally, but they're poorly managed. The Alpha is..."

"...A nutjob who just got lucky," mumbles Sean.

"Well, you may also put it that way," says Thaddeus.

"It's as the guys said, miss Nora. The Gold Moon Clan may be rich, but that's it. They are not good fighters and not smart either. They just act like they are. The same goes for Alessandra King, she acts as if she owns every place she goes, but that only if she got her purse in hand. If anything, she is the queen of disrespect, and nobody here likes that."

I nod to Vane's words. So, therefore everyone was so happy about Damian's announcement concerning the engagement's cancellation.

Joshua smiles at me once again. "We may have submitted to the Boss, miss Nora, but we are not ready to accept anyone as the Luna. But you look like a fine young lady, and if the Moon Goddess chose you as the Boss' pair, I'm all for that."

"That's right. We already know you're a decent fighter, too. A lot of us heard about that fight, even if we didn't go. I like a Luna who's not a wimp."

This time, it's Joshua's turn to slap him behind the head. "Watch your words when talking to the future Luna, punk!"

"Don't touch me! You want to fight, fatso?" Growls Sean.

The two of them start growling at each other, but Vane grabs them by the collar and pushes the two guys away like kids.

"Okay, enough, you two. If you want to fight, take it outside. Sorry, miss Nora, those guys tend to get excited quickly. We will leave now, but if you need anything, don't hesitate; you can count on us."

She takes the two guys, still bickering at each other, away, trying to separate them, and Isaac and Thaddeus follow behind. I feel Liam coming up to me, and he gives me a quick smile.

"They're good guys. And super loyal to my brother, too."

"They all look very different."

"Well, Damian gathered a lot of people from different places. Isaac, Thaddeus, and Vanessa's families used to belong to our father's Clan, but they sided with us as soon as we rebelled. Joshua is a former rogue, but he is a good guy, so my brother allowed him in the pack."

"What about the young guy? Sean?" I ask.

Liam shrugs, still looking in their direction. Joshua left, and Sean is sitting next to Vane, his hood hiding his eyes.

"Sad story. He grew up in the streets as an orphan. No one knows where he came from, but he's a real little punk. A good fighter, too. I think he looks up to Damian a lot. He is the only one Sean listen to, with a couple other people."

"Like Vane?"

"Yeah, she's like the big sister of the group. She was one of our first lieutenants, so..."

It's interesting, getting to know the dynamics of Damian's Clan. So many people are counting on him now. I understand more how the whole Blood Moon Clan works. A lot of them are either people who turned against the former Alpha, or outsiders, strays. Werewolves the other Clans wouldn't have wanted. Especially Alphas. The natural reaction for any alpha werewolf is to consider other Alphas as their rival and push them off. It's a common situation in huge packs— they would try to chase off any potential threat.

However, Damian didn't do that. Instead, he let those Alphas lead smaller groups and gathered them around him. It wouldn't have been possible if he wasn't strong and charismatic enough himself. Would I have been able to do this?

While I'm still thinking, a few more of them come to salute me. I try to remember the names and areas they are in charge of, but before I get any rest, more than twenty lieutenants have come and gone, and I'm a bit lost. I hope I will be able to remember most of them, though. I share my worries with Liam, but he laughs at me.

"Don't worry, Nora, you'll have plenty of time to get closer to them! Plus, even I don't know everyone here, there are too many faces!

Just do it like me, and if you're unsure, ask us with the mind-link."

Oh, right, there is this solution, too. I never thought of that before. How convenient.

"Nora?"

Damian is back, and he takes me in his arms right away. "Sorry, that took a while. Are you tired?"

"Now that you mention it..."

It's true. I don't know what time it is, but it's late, maybe past midnight, even. I look around and realize almost everyone left, aside from a few groups of people talking here and there. Nathaniel arrives behind Damian, looking exhausted as well.

"I'm going home, guys, I'm dead tired."

"Home? You're actually on your own again tonight?" Asks Liam with a smirk.

To my surprise, Nathaniel glares at him. Judging by his reaction, I would guess Elena is still avoiding him... Without saying a word, he turns around and leaves.

Damian frowns and turns to Liam. "What's wrong with him?"

But the youngest brother shrugs. "Don't ask me, he is the one with relationship issues..."

Damian frowns, but I act like I don't know about it. After all, this is Nathaniel's business, not mine. I just hope everything would settle down with Elena. Unfortunately, that's not my place to interfere.

"Can we go, Damian?" I ask, trying to change the subject.

Thankfully, my mate nods and takes my hand. Bobo, Neal, and Liam follow behind us when we walk back to the elevator. I'm feeling so tired, I'm almost sleeping against Damian's chest already. The elevator stops, and the Mura brothers exit first a few floors below Damian's place. Does Neal live here, too? That wouldn't be too surprising. To my surprise, Liam follows us to Damian's apartment.

"All right, I'm going to bed. Good night, guys!" He says, leaving towards what is probably a guest room.

As soon as he is gone, Damian carries me like a princess, taking me to his room to land me on the bed. I yawn irresistibly, and he laughs.

"You're so cute when you are tired. I should make you stay up more often."

"No way, I need to go to work tomorrow..."

Gosh, work. Can I go back to work after what happened? Damian doesn't discuss it, and I wonder if he heard me. He exits the room for a minute, and I head to his vast wardrobe. I pick a sleeveless shirt, big enough for me to wear to sleep. I understand why Elena loves wearing oversized clothes so much. This is so comfy! When Damian comes back, only wearing pajama pants, I'm already in bed, and drowsy. He smiles and joins me. He puts his arm around me, holding me close against his bare chest.

"How do you feel?"

"Just tired..."

"You're getting stronger. I thought you would be more shaken up by all that happened today."

I know. It's been a long day. The Witch's letter, Alessandra King barging to my workplace, the attack at my apartment, the Blood Moon Clan's gathering... I sigh. "I won't get used to it, but... It's not like I can sit in a corner and cry either. I promised myself to get stronger."

I feel his lips pressing against my forehead. "You're doing great, Nora. I'm proud of you, my Love."

I like it when he calls me that… I wish he'd say it again, but I fall asleep to quickly to ask.

Chapter 11

I open my eyes suddenly, feeling completely awake. I'm still in Damian's embrace, and it's still nighttime behind him. What time can it be? I wonder why I'm awake so early.

I don't feel like moving, though. It feels so warm under the blanket, and I'm surrounded by my mate's smell. We are so close... When we are next to each other like this, I'm not scared at all. On the contrary, I feel totally safe. So why do I get so scared when Damian wants me?

It's our mate.

Very softly, I caress the dark tattoo on his neck. The Blood Moon Clan's black crescent moon. Once I'm officially his mate, will I get one, too? Yesterday, a lot of the lieutenants had it where I could see it. I wonder where I would do mine. Liam, Nathaniel, and Bobo all have it on their chests, and Tonia has hers on her arm.

My fingers go down on his torso, careful not to wake up my man. Sometimes I forget he is six years older than me. He is a full, grown-up man while I still feel like a child. I don't find myself desirable. I'm thin, with barely any curves, and small breasts. Not to mention my scar...

Maybe that's my main problem. I don't see how Damian, or any man, can find me attractive. Marcus considered me like a toy, an object for sexual satisfaction. Somehow, am I afraid Damian is the same?

While lost in my thoughts, I sense Damian moving next to me. He takes my hand that was wandering on his chest and brings it to his lips to kiss it without opening his eyes.

"Sorry. Did I wake you?"

"No. What are you thinking about? I feel your wolf is... worried."

I don't know how to say this... And I don't want to worry him, either. We both stay silent for a while, and I would think he went back to sleep if it wasn't for his thumb, gently stroking my hand.

"Do you think you would have loved me if it wasn't for our bond?"

"Yes."

His immediate and definite reply takes me by surprise.

"But we were just kids..."

"That's not when I fell in love with you. I liked you as a child, I cherished you, but I really fell for you at the hospital, when we met again. As a man, attracted to a woman. How strong and fragile you were at the same time. I loved that," he whispers gently.

"Really?"

"Yes. I told you. I can wait, but I still want you, Nora."

"I thought that I'm... I'm not... desirable."

He opens his eyes and moves, shifting to stand on his arms above me. He leans to give me a long, deep kiss. Slowly, his lips take mine over, and I respond unconditionally. When he stops, he is smiling again.

"Moon Goddess, you *are* desirable, Nora. That's why I want you so bad."

He goes down, landing soft kisses on my neck, and I feel one of his hands grabbing my waist gently. I let him do so without moving, just closing my eyes and enjoying this. Is it because it's Damian that this feels so good? I'm shivering under his lips, but it's from pleasure this time. I don't feel any fear, just this slow fire burning on my skin wherever he touches me. I can tell he is hesitating, watching my reactions, but I really am not afraid the slightest this time. So, I put my hand on his neck, gently stroking his hair while his kisses keep coming.

I feel his large hand adventuring lower. He caresses my leg, my bare skin shivering under his fingers. Damian is deliberately acting gentle and cautious, and I love it. That fire under my skin is not calming down. I caress his cheek and come to claim a kiss from him. He seems a bit surprised, but he doesn't resist. His fingers go up again, shifting from my leg to my waist, under the shirt this time. I gasp. I can barely breathe; this is so intense and thrilling. I claim more of Damian's lips, and I feel his hand hesitate a bit before he starts fondling my breast. Oh, my gosh... Damian's hand is really touching me this way, and I like it, I really do. So much that I hear my own breathing accelerating on its own, and my heartbeat quickens without warning. This is how it is supposed to be. Thrilling, intimate. Something we both really want. I gather my courage and start kissing his neck, right where his tattoo is. I can feel his reaction: a shiver of pleasure. His hand runs through my hair, grabbing it and playing with my curls between his fingers. The other hand leaves my breast, to adventure further down...

"Damian! Nora! Time for breakfast, guys! I'm starving!"

We both freeze, startled by Liam's yelling. I completely forgot he slept here, too! This is so embarrassing! I blush uncontrollably, but Damian growls and takes his hands off me.

"I might really kick his ass this time…"

I can't help but chuckle a bit at his annoyed expression. Liam is so... Oh, well. I still kiss Damian's cheek quickly to stop his frowning. My mate growls a bit, but he eventually sighs and kisses me back.

He doesn't get up right away, and instead leans on the side to look at me, his fingers still playing with my hair.

"You looked okay."

I felt more than okay. I nod, playing with the little spikes of his beard with my fingers." I think I'm getting there..."

"That's good to hear, then. Stay in bed a bit longer. I'll take a shower real quick and then we can feed that annoying brother of mine."

"Okay."

He gives me another kiss before going, a proper one this time. I can't go back to sleep now, I'm still way too awake and excited! Instead, when Damian leaves the room, I reminisce about what just happened. I can't believe we just almost...! If it wasn't for Liam's stomach!

The places where Damian's hands touched are still hot. Is that what making love is all about? It felt like my heart was about to burst out! Yet, I think I wanted more, and it would have been okay not to stop there. Gosh, since when did I became so confident?

"Nora, Bobo's here!" Liam yells. "He got you some clothes."

Oh, right! I almost forgot about yesterday's events. Most of my clothes must have been ripped out back then. Did Bobo manage to find something he could save? I get up and check myself in the mirror. Aside from being a bit red, I guess I look fine. The wrinkled t-shirt and messy hair can be attributed to the sleeping, anyway. I get out of Damian's bedroom and find Liam and Bobo in the salon.

"Hello, sleepyhead. Hey, what's with those rosy cheeks? Don't tell me you and my brother got naughty so early?"

Gosh, that idiotic and nosy Liam! I ignore him and walk up to Bobo. He is in his human form, wearing some baggy pants and a hoodie. I go hug my best friend, happy to see him.

"Hi, Princess. I got you some new clothes."

He hands me a large bag with some brand's name on it.

"New clothes?"

"I figured you wouldn't want anything that sicko might have touched, so Tonia did some shopping for you last night. You can just text her if you need anything else."

He is right on that one... I don't even feel like I could step into that apartment ever again. I inspect the bag's content, but Tonia knows my tastes well. All those clothes are ones that I would have picked myself.

"Thank you, Bobo, this is perfect."

I grab a set of underwear, a winter dress, and thick black tights to go with it, and head back to Damian's bedroom.

"What about me? I don't even get a morning hug?"

"Have you changed your mind yet about going to the Sapphire Moon Clan?"

"Nope. I still think this is a terrible idea."

I had hoped he may have thought it over overnight. It seems like I was wrong. When I get back, Damian is out of the shower and busy buttoning his shirt. He gives me an interrogating look since he probably heard Liam's yelling.

"You're giving him the cold treatment?" He asks with a smile.

"Just for a while. Liam is too annoying, sometimes."

"I can only agree with you on that..."

I take a quick shower and get dressed. I put on my favorite jewelry, the earrings Bobo got me, and Damian's necklace. Once I'm ready, I join Damian, and we both head to the living room. Liam is busy playing on his smartphone, and Damian takes it from him.

"Hey! I was about to finish that level!"

"Liam, listen. You are accompanying Nora to work this morning. You just have two hours of classes, today, right?"

"Yeah. Can I skip those?"

Damian clicks his tongue, and Liam forgets about skipping.

"After you drop Nora off, you go to school, and then you head back to Nate's restaurant. Got it?"

"What, I'm playing bodyguard now?"

"Exactly. We are still looking into what happened in that apartment and the intruder. So, for today, you are watching Nora too."

"Yeah, yeah, got it..."

I am a bit surprised that Damian decided to ask Liam to watch me, too, but I don't say anything. I don't believe he would make any compromise, anyway. Moreover, this way, I can have Liam with me all day today and not raise any suspicions.

The four of us have breakfast downstairs in the Company cafeteria, like last time. I hope this doesn't become a routine; I miss cooking for the guys. At some point, Damian's phone vibrates, and he frowns.

"I have to go... You two, don't leave Nora. See you later, Love."

He gives me a quick goodbye kiss and runs off upstairs to his office. As soon as Damian is out of sight, I turn to Liam.

"Liam, please."

"I said no, Nora! This is way too dangerous!"

"What is it?" Asks Bobo

I explain my plan to Boyan, though I don't mention the Witch on purpose. It's not hard to ignore the butterfly on my shoulder since Liam and Bobo can't see it. When I am done, Bobo is frowning.

"I don't like it either, Nora. This is risky."

"Thank you! That is what I have been telling the Princess for two days now!"

I growl at Liam. Why does he have to be such a chicken now!

No matter how long I plead in the car when Bobo drives me to work, Liam is not changing his mind at all. When we arrive, I'm kind of mad at him, but it's his turn to ignore me. So, I go to work as usual, while he goes to school.

The restaurant surprisingly functions just as usual despite yesterday's events, just with a bit fewer customers. Meanwhile, I'm still thinking about how to go to the Sapphire Moon territory. I have a location, but I am not confident at all about crossing at least two werewolf territories to go there on my own. That's why I was really hoping Liam would help me. When it's finally time for my break, I go to the changing room, and, to my surprise, I get a text from Liam.

"All right, I will take you there. But be ready to follow my terms. This is going to be super dangerous."

He said, yes! I re-read Liam's text, but even with those conditions of his, that won't stop me. I'm tired of being useless and overprotected. This time, with the Witch's help, I can finally do something.

However, Liam is right. So far, I barely know anything about the Sapphire Moon Clan. I am not going to be reckless a second time, going there without any information. So, when I resume work, I try to interrogate Elise and Kathy as we keep working.

Fortunately, both girls' act as usual despite what happened yesterday. Most of my co-workers had no clue about my background until now. After yesterday's events and Damian barging in the restaurant yelling my name, some of the staff changed their attitudes towards me. Apparently, being the Alpha King's fated mate is something scary enough that some of them don't even dare ask anything of me anymore. I don't really mind, though, since Chef Michel and Narcissa have no problem ordering me around as usual. I don't feel like I'm working less or privileged, just that some of the staff members are wary of me. I try not to mind; it was bound to happen eventually.

Elise and Kathie didn't hide how surprised they were, but that was it. A bit of questioning and gossip, and the day resumed as usual. So, as we are busy cleaning the tables, I try to ask them about the Sapphire Moon Clan, without really giving them the real reasons for it.

"Well, they are a very secretive Clan, you know," says Elise.

"That is right. I heard they don't really like interacting with other Clans... It is hard to approach them," adds Kathie.

"That is what I heard. But don't tell me no one knows a thing about such a big Clan?"

I grab a few dishes to bring back to the kitchen, and Kathie follows right behind with a handful of dirty napkins. While we walk, she keeps talking, trying to remember all she can think of with a cute frown on.

"My father said they came to Silver City when he was a kid. It was before the Black Moon Alpha, when the Snow Moon Clan was still around and the strongest Pack. Apparently, they had to fight a lot to finally find their place in Silver City. That's probably why they don't like the other Clans."

"But they do get along with the Violet Clan, right?"

"Now that you mention it..."

We place everything we are carrying for the garbage boy to take care of, but instead of going out of the kitchen, Kathie takes me to the staff's meeting room. Some guys from the kitchen staff are there, chatting and laughing around cups of coffee and some leftovers.

"Hey Mickey, you got a second?"

One of the guys raises his head and gives her a smile. "I even got a full minute for you, sweetheart."

He stands up and walks up to us. Mickey is one of the sous-chefs usually in charge of cooking the fish dishes; I've helped him a couple of times. He stands at the door with his coffee.

"What's up, ladies?"

"Mickey, didn't your sister marry into the Violet Moon Clan? Nora was curious about the Sapphire Moon Clan; do you know anything?"

He frowns, a bit taken aback by the question, and turns to me. "What do you want to know?"

"Why do they hate the Blood Moon Clan so much? Or even the other Clans? I heard the Violet Moon Clan is the only one they trust, is that true?"

Mickey nods and takes a sip of his coffee before answering. "I don't know the details, but my big sis said the Sapphire Moon came from the North about fifty years ago. They came here with a large pack, and though they had a lot of wealth, most of the Clans here treated them like rogues and made it hard for them to establish themselves here."

"Except the Violet Moon Clan?" I ask.

"That's the thing. The Violet Moon Clan was three times smaller back then, and they were struggling, too— fighting a lot with the others and everything. That's how they grew to be damn good fighters. So, the only ally they found was the only Clan that was having it harder than they did. Both Clans helped each other and grew stronger together. The Sapphire Moon had money; the Violet Moon had warriors. You can do the math."

Of course. Those two are the most important things for a werewolf pack to survive. If they had it, no doubt the Sapphire and Violet Moon Clans could make it. It also explains a lot their attitude towards the other Clans, if they resented them for giving them a hard time. Is that why they hated Damian's father so much?

"You got business with them, princess?" He asks.

I jump hearing Mickey calling me that, but then I remember this is just what he usually calls me when we are not working. He is quite the sweet-talker and has a nickname for every female staff member here, except Narcissa. How ironic it is that mine turned to be that one...

"Maybe. I was wondering if I can get to talk with them..."

"That might be hard, they are as hard to approach as the rumors say. I get you are not a member of the pack yet, but I suppose they would consider you as a rogue with no background, and those guys value blood over anything else. My sister said they are acting kind of mighty, with the Royals and all."

Oh, Moon Goddess, is that for real? I try to stop my hands from shaking. "What did you say? The Royals?"

"Yeah. You know, the werewolf purebloods? The Sapphire Moon is totally into that stuff. I heard they are loosely related to Royals, so they are really into it. They respect blood purity over anything else. It's kind of old school, but..."

"That's great!"

They both look at me with surprised eyes, but I'm so happy right now. This is exactly what I was looking for! Kathie and Mickey exchange a look before turning to me.

"That's great?" Ask Kathie, looking lost.

"Sorry Kathie, I guess I will explain later. But thank you, Mickey, that is exactly what I needed to hear!"

I give him a quick thank-you kiss on the cheek and run off, leaving the two of them stunned. I go back to the changing room and try to calm down. The Witch's butterfly acts just as excited as I am, flying all around me. Did he understand what Mickey said, too? I look for my wolf internally, and it's not hard to feel her; she raises her head as soon as I do. She is so in sync with me these days, I forget she is even there sometimes.

"Liam! Liam, I just heard the greatest news! The Sapphire Moon Clan totally respect the Royals! Do you hear that?"

"Great. Now we can go, and I am the only one who is going to get killed. Awesome."

I growl at him. Can't he be a bit more enthusiastic?

"Liam!"

"Don't yell in my head! This class is giving me enough of a headache as it is!"

"Are you still not done?"

"In ten long minutes. Anyway, when do you want to go to let's-all-get-killed land?

"As soon as you can come? I don't want to delay this any longer. Plus, I don't work tonight, and Damian will probably be stuck with work until late."

"You mean until he realizes we are gone."

Well, I guess Liam is right despite his pessimism. Damian is really going to get mad at us… I won't tell him that, though, so after I make him promise to come straight to the restaurant after school, I call Bobo.

He is not happy about my plan either, and clearly concerned about my security, but he doesn't stop me as long as he can come along.

When my shift is finally over, I'm kind of worried, because Bobo has arrived with the car, but Liam is not there yet. Why would he be late now? His class ended long ago, and his high school is not that far either. I'm nervously playing with my necklace pendant while waiting. Bobo is acting as usual, texting, probably Daniel.

"If he is not here in ten minutes, we should—"

"No can do, Princess!"

I turn around, and to my surprise, Liam is finally here! I notice he doesn't have his backpack or anything. He walks up to us with a confident smile.

"You are late! Where have you been? Did you go home to leave your bag?" I ask.

Liam shakes his head. "No, I dropped by my girlfriend's place to leave it."

His what...? I stare at him, dumbfounded. Even Bobo's jaw drops!

"Since when do you have a girlfriend?"

Liam tilts his head, trying to look innocent or cute, I can't tell. "For a while, actually. What, I can't have one?"

"You never said a thing about having a girlfriend!"

"I never said I didn't have one! It's just that you and my brothers don't ask!"

So, both Damian and Nathaniel have no idea either? Liam is even sneakier than I thought! I stare at him, not knowing what to say. I can't believe this guy has a girlfriend and never said a thing!

Bobo frowns, really surprised, too. "Since when?"

"A few months, but don't ask anymore, my lady is really shy."

"What, so you won't introduce her to us? You could at least tell us more!"

I have to admit, I'm feeling all curious now! Liam pretends to ponder for a while, a bit annoyingly I should say, then he gives me a wink. "I can't, sorry! Anyway, didn't you want to hurry up just a while ago, Princess? We should get going, the sooner the better before Damian unleashes all hell on us for this suicide mission you got for us!"

Despite my curiosity about Liam's girlfriend, there was no way I would delay our trip to the Sapphire Moon Clan to learn more about that. We are running against the clock on that one. So, I give Bobo the address on the business card the Witch gave me, and he heads the car to the southwest. This is a part of Silver City I am very unfamiliar with. With the Jade territory being in the East, and the Blood Moon in the center, I never had any reason to head West until now. Judging from where we are headed, the closest I probably ever got to that part of town was probably when fighting with or against the Sea Moon Clan, located in the southwest.

"The Gold Moon Clan is located in the West, right?" I ask Bobo.

He nods. "Right. Their territory is not that big, but they have several establishments in the city, too, on the Rising Moon Clan's turf."

I really need to study this kind of things more carefully, but now I have a rough idea of how Silver City and its suburbs are divided between all the big Clans. Obviously, the Black Brothers and their packs are located at the center, owning quite a lot, too. In the East, my Jade Moon Clan, with the allied Pearl Moon more to the North. Elena's Clan, the White Moon, dominates the North area, with the Latino and Artsy districts, but some parts like the Silver University premises remain neutral, of course.

The South, on the contrary, is larger and divided between the Sea Moon Wolves, focused on the sea border, the Violet Moon, and the Sapphire Moon. Of course, the borders are not definite and precise, more like a general idea of who is not supposed to go where. But our wolf instincts clearly tell us when we are somewhere we are not supposed to be.

Like now, when the highway takes us further away from the Financial District, the buildings getting smaller behind the car's windows. This is a different landscape. More like the old part of the city, with historic buildings and brand-new skyscrapers popping out of nowhere. I can't decide if I like it or not. This is really different from the Silver City Damian brought me to, all made of glass, neon lights, asphalt, and steel. The Blood Moon turf is more uniform, urban and concentrated, while the Sapphire Moon Clan looks like a mix of old and new, wood and marble next to steel and glass. As we keep driving further, I notice the car slows down, while more and more wolves and people suddenly surround us. Their eyes are all following us without blinking, and we can't ignore them. Bobo has to pull the car over, and we get out. We are probably just at the entrance of it but driving any further into their territory would have been too imprudent.

As we step down, a lot of the wolves that were following and a few people immediately rush towards us, all of them growling loudly. A sturdy woman comes forward, looking very pissed. "Are you kidding me? How disrespectful is the Blood Moon Clan to actually step into our territory unannounced! Are you prepared to get killed!"

Bobo instinctively comes to place his large body in front of me, growling very loudly in a threatening manner, warning anyone who would try to harm me. Sometimes I forget how large and menacing he can be. Still, now it is apparently sufficient enough— some of them don't dare to approach his gigantic figure. Liam, with his Alpha instinct, is not holding back his growling, either. I can't fear his Alpha aura, but I can tell it's here, and pretty intimidating, too, as no one approaches him either.

I'm the only one keeping my calm, and not impressed by all this. So, I speak out for the three of us. I address the woman who spoke first. "We did not come here as Blood Moon Clan representatives. I don't even belong to them; I don't have any marking. Those two just came along."

"A rogue, then? Do you think that is any better, young lady? Do you know how we treat strays here?" Says a young guy on the side.

"I don't care if you consider me a rogue, but I just came to have a peaceful talk with your leaders. I have questions."

This really doesn't look good, despite my attempts to look as harmless as possible. About a dozen people and wolves are circling us closely already. I can't have us attacked now, so I ignore Bobo's efforts to shield me and address the woman. "Please let us through, that is all we ask."

"You don't get to make requests, girl. You should go back to where you came from and be glad we are letting you go alive!"

Gosh, this is getting nowhere, and I'm starting to get really annoyed, too. This gathering is not intimidating me the slightest, and all those growls are giving me a headache. So, I deliberately step forward, provoking a new wave of angry growling around me. My inner wolf, pissed at their disrespectful attitude, starts growling, too. "*That's right, girl.*" I click my tongue at them, directing my stare to anyone who is acting hostile.

"Enough! I asked to speak to your leader. Let us through right now," I enjoin them.

Most are surprised by my imperious tone, stop growling or take it down a bit. Some exchange looks, lost at what to do. I'm pretty sure a couple of wolves even took a few steps back. The woman has lost a bit of her confidence, too, and seems to be re-examining me with caution. She probably is struggling to know how to react.

Liam mind-links me at this very moment, his eyes going all around us to evaluate the situation. *"They hadn't realized you were an Alpha, too. You surprised them."*

"You... Which Clan's Alpha are you?" Asks an old man.

"None. I said it, I don't belong to a pack as of now. I was raised within the Gold Moon Clan as a child but got lost. The Jade Moon Clan picked me up, but I never belonged to them, either. Now, the Blood Moon Clan is protecting me, but I have yet to join them."

"An Alpha without a pack?"

I nod, hoping she will believe me. She is frowning hard, and her eyes go from one member of her pack to another. They are all mind-linking to decide what to do next.

Liam is not acting as anxious as before, either. He is observing them, looking interested but calm, analyzing the situation with cold eyes. Bobo hasn't moved an inch.

After a minute or two, the woman turns to me again. "What are your current relationships with the Clans you mentioned before?"

I'm getting tired of all this questioning. It's cold standing here, and I only have this much time before Damian knows where I am. My wolf agrees, and growls louder, giving them a new scare, enough for more of them to retreat.

"I already said it earlier! Now, let me through. None of you are Beta or Alpha, and I need to speak to a man named William Blue. That's your Alpha, right?"

While talking, I take out the business card and hold it high enough for all to see. They recognize it immediately. The woman finally walks up to me, up until Bobo starts growling, warning her not to come closer. She is only a few steps away now.

"My name is Gloria. You can follow me, but the car stays here. Can I get a name to give to my Alpha, at least?"

"My name is Nora, Nora Bluemoon."

As soon as I say those words, a lot of them get agitated all of a sudden. People start whispering, and the wolves are fidgeting, too. Gloria looks at me in shock. "Bluemoon? Is that a joke?"

I remain silent, leaving her to believe whatever she wants. Does my last name mean something to them? Anyway, I don't have time for this now. Can't we just go already? I don't have all day! Gloria is lost in her thoughts for a while, but she eventually turns around and starts walking.

As we follow her closely, a few wolves from the Sapphire Moon follow us, too. A lot of them are growling at Liam, but he simply ignores them. He is more focused on our silent conversation.

"Well done, but I wouldn't say we are fine. They were impressed by your Alpha aura, and your name is intriguing them, too. You probably just made them doubt whether they should kill us or not."

"I know, but at least now we have a chance at meeting their Alpha, and Damian isn't looking for us yet."

"Nora, I think I'm more scared about one angry Damian chasing after us than hundreds of Sapphire Moon wolves trying to kill us."

Honestly, I'm pretty much the same. No matter how many people are growling and circling us, I don't feel intimidated, thanks to my Royal Blood. But Damian? That's another story.

It doesn't take long until we reach a vast house. I expected a company building, but instead, this is more of a family house. Not your average household, though. More like the old colonial house, all white, a large romantic garden, and a terrace. I count four floors, and so many windows, I bet ten full families could fit in there. How many millions is such a house worth? I feel out of place just by standing in front!

Gloria stops at the front door and a few of the wolves who were still following and watching us scatter around. She doesn't even knock—an elderly man comes to open before that. He lets us in without a word, and Gloria takes us upstairs. Right before entering a room, she turns around to address Bobo and Liam.

"Just the girl."

"Hell no," immediately says Bobo, growling.

"Bobo, it's okay."

"Are you sure?" Asks Liam, looking concerned for the first time

I nod, but Bobo is obviously unhappy about this.

"You shouldn't go alone. I'm coming."

I see him take off his shirt, and he suddenly shapeshifts in front of us into his large wolf form. I roll my eyes, and Gloria gasps at his enormous size.

"Bobo! How stubborn can you be!"

"Never mind. As long as this one stays here, you can come in," says Gloria, pointing at Liam.

I guess this is all because of him being a Black Brother. Liam and I exchange a look, but he seems okay with it. I don't feel good about leaving him alone, though. I turn to Gloria. "You do realize that if anything happens to him, the Blood Moon Clan will react, right?"

She stays silent, but Liam sighs.

"Same for you, Nora. Let's both stay safe, all right?"

I nod and glare one last time at the woman, using my wolf to make her feel it. If anything happens to Liam, I won't stay still, either. She avoids my eyes and opens the door for me.

I step into a large office, Bobo behind me. It smells like old books, ink, and dust in here. It lacks sunshine, too, so much that the place is a bit suffocating. Half of the walls are actually covered by bookcases, filled with many more old books than I've ever seen in my whole life. The place is so large and dark, I have to keep walking in until I finally see a large leather couch facing a wall. When I turn around to see what that couch is facing, I almost fall on my knees.

A portrait. A large portrait of a woman sitting with a white wolf. I stay stunned in front of her, unable to speak. Moon Goddess mother, I can't believe it. Why does that woman resemble me so much?

I keep staring at the painting, at a loss for words. That woman is sitting straight and fierce like a queen, a hand on her white wolf. Is that wolf meant to be her other shape? Or just a pet? Her dress is as white as its fur, sparkling and spotless. More than that, I am mesmerized by her eyes. The very same color as mine, a very peculiar night blue shade. If the portrait wasn't so large, it might not have been as obvious, but this one is covering the whole wall. I can very clearly see each and every detail of her face. A face so much like mine.

The more I look, the less I can believe it. If it wasn't for a few details, this could even be taken as my spitting image. However, that woman doesn't have any scar, and a few of her traits are different, too. Her nose is a bit more crooked, and her lips are fuller. My hair is a dark brown, almost black, while hers is a bit lighter, of a caramel brown, but just as curly. Is that a... tiara on her head? Now that I'm thinking about it, her dress doesn't look from this area, either. More like something from the previous century. This portrait looks quite old, as well. Nothing on the background can give any clue— that woman sits alone against a dark blue curtain. I don't understand.

Who is this woman, and what is this portrait? It's so imposing, with a gold frame like the one you would see hanging in some old castle. That woman looks important no matter how you look at her. Her expression is hard to decipher. She looks very fierce, but I feel like she could be very gentle, as well.

Bobo suddenly starts growling, and I finally look away from the painting. I didn't notice the desk hidden in a corner. An old man is sitting behind it, staring straight at us. He looks about fifty, maybe older. His hair is white, but long and scattered on his head, giving him an odd look. I don't like the way he is staring. My wolf starts growling, too, feeling threatened.

"Who are you?" He asks in a very annoyed tone.

No one told him? I thought the Sapphire Moon wolves had given him information. Or is he testing me? His Alpha aura is quite imposing. Not as much as Damian, but quite close, I would say.

I breathe in and turn towards him. "My name is Nora Bluemoon. I came to talk to the Sapphire Moon Alpha."

"What do you want, child?" He talks with a scorched and drawling voice that gives me the chills. This man has something scary about him. Next to me, Bobo won't stop growling, his whole body bent around me in a protective stance, so close I can't take a step without pushing him.

What do I say now? The Witch guided me here, and until now, I was so focused on getting here that I never stopped to think about what I would actually say or ask once I did. Think, Nora. The Clans, the war.

"I came to ask for the peace," I blurt out.

This sounds so childish and stupid, even for me.

"...The peace?" Repeats the old man coldly.

"That's right. I know you hate the Blood Moon Clan, but we cannot afford any inner battles right now. Something much worse is coming, something dangerous and threatening our city."

I realize how real this is as I speak. It's as if the danger was at our doors and ready to hit us like a hurricane. As she said, that other Witch will strike again, and we should be prepared. A war among the packs is not something we can afford now.

Facing me, the old man scoffs. "Is that all you have to say, child?"

"Don't you believe me? This is serious, if—"

"I do not care for anything you have to say. Why would you actually dare to come here and plead for that wretched, vile, obnoxious group of mutts?"

What the...? I just can't believe how much hatred and disgust he just spat those words! I can feel my skin crawl hearing that! Calling Damian's pack a group of mutts? How insulting can this old man be to my mate! My wolf is outraged, and I have a hard time staying calm, too. I need to keep a clear mind, but that man is not making things easy.

I breathe in. "The Blood Moon Clan is not looking for trouble. Every pack can remain in their own territory, and we can keep things as they are. If you do not seek war, we—"

He suddenly slams his hand on the table, making me jump in surprise. Bobo growls even louder and uses his body to push me back, putting more distance between the Sapphire Moon Alpha and me.

"Those dogs started it! They are constantly looking for war, oppressing the other packs! Why should we submit once more to their tyranny!"

"What tyranny? Damian has never oppressed anyone!"

"What do you know, child! You come here, on our territory, and have the nerve to talk to me about peace? Do you have any idea of the suffering we went through? You have no right to order us! You have no knowledge of this world and no right to order me to do anything! Make peace with the Black Moon? Never!"

His yelling glues me to the ground, and I have to listen to him all along. It's like facing a wall. A wall built of hatred and anger that started long ago and has gotten stronger and thicker for an awfully long time. He called them the "*Black Moon*," too, but that was when their father was the leader. Can he really not accept the difference now?

So many emotions are going through me right now that I can't even decide how to react. I'm so confused and angry! And sad, too, because all of this seems so pointless! What do I do now? I try to think about his words, of how I can try to sort this out. A part of what he said is right. I have so little information! I am barely starting to learn about the Clans, but I wish I had been more aware of it earlier! All I know is what Bobo and Liam explained to me. Dealing with the Sapphire Moon Clan cannot possibly be as simple.

"What has their father done to you that you would hate the Blood Moon Clan so much? What kind of grudge would be enough for you to not care about war? Enough that you would leave other werewolves to die for it?"

He suddenly starts laughing. His laughter gives me the chills. It reminds me of how Alec broke down once Damian had captured him. Something insane that makes one feel uncomfortable. I could tell there is not a single trace of joy in that man's loud laugh. So, I wait for him to stop, despite how bad I feel about this. This is not good.

Once he stops and looks at me, his eyes look empty, like some puppet. A scary, crazy puppet. "A war? Why would they fear war? This man was death personified! A god of madness and violence, a demon! And the one he didn't do with his hands, he caused himself! Peace? He destroyed it, any hope of peace, he tore to shreds!"

As he yelled, he stood up, his voice echoing loudly in the whole room. I won't step back, but my whole body wants to run away. I want to run from here, from this man. Something about him is really unsettling and hard to look at.

"I do not care for any of his bastard sons! Those filthy mongrels should be exterminated and sent back to the gutter they belong to!"

"Enough!"

I couldn't hold it in any longer. That man may insult the former Black Alpha, even insult me, but there is no way I'm letting him speak about Damian or his brothers that way! My wolf is growling furiously, exhorting him to submit.

"Don't you dare speak about my mate that way! Not in front of me!"

His eyes suddenly spark a new light, and a sinister smile curls his lips. "Your mate, child? Could it be you actually are this mutt's partner? Really?"

This is not good. I step back this time, subconsciously. The old man is getting closer, and I do not want this madman anywhere near me. I gasp, and Bobo is growling furiously while shielding me, all fangs and claws out. My bodyguard is ready to attack the old man any second. This is not what I came for!

"You said you are his mate, right? Black's mate? His real mate?"

He keeps repeating his question, and I don't answer. This man has lost it. His intentions are written all over his face as he keeps stepping closer very slowly. His legs are so weak, actually, that it looks like he could fall any minute. Is this really the Sapphire Moon Alpha? An old man, driven by madness? So old and weak? This isn't right.

Even if he clearly means to hurt me somehow, no matter what, I don't even think he could. My wolf agrees. We can beat such an old wolf without a problem! But what can I do? He is not listening to me, and I won't let him hurt Damian or me either. What should I do?

"Father!"

Suddenly, someone barges in the room. A young man runs in, exchanges a look with me, and walks up to the old man. He supports him but brings him back to his chair with an annoyed look. The old man tries to push him away and resist him, but he is clearly no match.

"Out of my way! Out of my way, William! This child is Black's partner! I will—"

"You will do nothing, Father! Enough of this! Gloria!"

To my surprise, the woman we saw earlier runs into the room as soon as she is called. Was she right behind the door all along? She totally ignores us and runs to the old man. The young man that just called him father looks annoyed at her, too.

"Take him back to his room, make sure he stays there until I am back!" He says with an angry tone.

I realize the chair is actually a wheelchair when Gloria starts pushing him. As ordered, she takes the rambling old man out of the room with her, slamming the door behind them. With the three of us here, the situation has completely changed. Neither Bobo nor I have moved, but I have no idea how to react to the guy that just came in. He seems pissed when he turns to face us.

He is frowning, but I am more concerned about something else. This is the same feeling I have when Elena is around. That familiar, invisible sensation down to my stomach. He runs his fingers in his curly hair, taking it off his face.

"I am William Blue, the Alpha of this Clan. Who the hell are you?"

I keep detailing him, trying to grasp this feeling I get. My eyes wander to the portrait again, and back to this man. Those blue eyes, the same as mine, the same as this portrait. How come he has them, too?

"Nora Bluemoon."

"Bluemoon? You..."

His eyes run to the portrait and back to me several times. He doesn't hide his confusion but stays silent for a while.

So, I speak first, trying to get to him as I did with the man earlier. "Please. I came here to talk about your grievances against the Blood Moon Clan. I thought that man earlier was the Alpha, I—"

"He is the former Alpha. That man is my father, Alcott Blue. He's no longer the head of this Clan, I am. Are you saying you are from Black's pack?"

This guy is younger than I thought, maybe around Damian's age, no more than thirty. I hope he will be more reasonable and listen to me.

"Not exactly. I am his fated mate. I came to—"

"His fated mate? Isn't this guy engaged to that slut from the Gold Moon Clan!"

I can't help but roll my eyes. I wish he hadn't brought that very annoying detail up...

"He will no longer be! That is what I came to talk about. An Oath of Peace with the Sapphire Moon Clan."

He raises an eyebrow and crosses his arms, surprised. Even I am a bit surprised by my own words, but it just came out on its own. What am I thinking? An Oath of Peace? The Sapphire Moon Alpha seems to take it rather seriously, as he observes me very intensely.

"Why would his fated mate come to seek peace with us? Why should I trust you, or that man?"

For a few seconds, I was feeling better seeing that he was willing to listen, but now, I have no idea what to answer to that. He is right. I came here totally empty-handed, with nothing but my thoughts and no way to prove my good intents. I sigh. Why does all of this as to be so complicated? Come on, Nora, think of something. This man doesn't seem as harsh as his father earlier.

"I'm concerned. Not only about the Blood Moon Clan, but about everyone in Silver City. A Witch is threatening all of our packs. This is all linked to the attack. We have confirmed that those vampires were controlled by a Witch, and she will try again. I came here because if inner conflicts arise within the packs, we might be too weak to defend ourselves next time, and that is something no one wants."

He stays silent for a while, and leans on the desk, staring straight at me. I can't decipher what he is thinking or if he believes me or not. I want to ask him about many things. Why does he have the same eyes as me? Who is this woman? Yet I can't, for now. This is more important.

After a while, he sighs. "We already know a Witch was behind the attacks. She was nice enough to send us multiple threats over the past few years."

What? The Sapphire Moon Clan received direct threats? This is totally new!

"What kind of threats?" I ask.

"Dead birds, mostly, and some of our sources of water were poisoned. It started a few years ago when I was not even ten. We handled it as we could, so far, but the vampire attack was a first."

"Why didn't you tell the other packs? They could have—"

"Helped us? Should I tell you how the Sapphire Moon Clan was treated for years?"

Right... Back then, Damian's father was still the Alpha King, and the other packs were all struggling for survival. None of the neighboring clans, even if they had been willing, would have helped. This is sad, but he is right. They were on their own until now.

"So, this is why you didn't help when the vampires attacked?"

"Not exactly. My father forbids our warriors to go help the other packs, but I was mostly concerned about the vampires' aim. See, all these years, that Witch tried to steal something we never had in the first place, attacking our territory only. Yet now, she suddenly sent vampires on several turfs away from ours. I was curious to see what her aim really was, so I let it be."

"Wait, so you already know what she was after?"

He slowly nods, looking serious.

"We knew it, but we never believed it. For years, we thought she just wanted something she thought we had. Turns out, what she wanted was really there, but she was looking in the wrong pack all these years."

My head is buzzing as I start to understand what this all means. Pieces are falling together, and I look at the portrait once again. I remember the attack, what those vampires said. What the Witch wanted, she thought the Sapphire Moon Clan had it. Why would she have thought that in the first place? And as to know why she suddenly understood she was wrong, the past few weeks made it all too clear, too.

I feel my legs going numb, and for a while, I need to lean on Bobo to support myself. William is watching my reactions, too, and we both already grasp what is going on. However, we are still missing some clues.

A silence of a few seconds follows, but the thoughts are too loud in my head. He sighs, and his eyes go to the portrait as he starts talking again. “You said you were the Blood Moon Alpha’s fated mate, right? Is this the truth? The Moon Goddess paired you with Damian Black?”

“Yes. Damian knew of our bond ten years ago, but I only learned it very recently when we found each other again. I have been staying with his pack ever since.”

“You are not mated or marked yet.”

I shake my head. At another time, another place, I might have been embarrassed, but not now. I push my curls onto my shoulder, not caring about exposing my neck.

“That’s right. But we are fated mates, I swear.”

William Blue scoffs, shaking his head and muttering to himself. “Moon Goddess, sometimes she is playing cruelly with our fates... Or is this her way to show us the way, I wonder? “

Those questions are not addressed to me, and moreover, I don’t know what he means to say, so I stay silent. He takes a few steps, walking past Bobo, and sits on the couch. Elbows on his knees, fingers crossed, he raises his eyes to the portrait. He observes the woman for a long while, completely ignoring us. I don’t feel any threat coming from him anymore, and Bobo has stopped growling. We observe his lonely figure facing the painting.

“I’ve seen this portrait a million times since I was born. She has been here for fifty years, in the Sapphire Moon Alpha’s office. Yet I never get tired of watching her.”

I step away from Bobo a bit to come closer, watching the painting, too. William Blue keeps talking, his eyes never leaving the woman.

“Her name was Diane. Queen Diane, my great-aunt. She died long before I was born, but my father talked about her so often, I feel like I know her better than I knew my own grandmother.”

Queen Diane. I have heard that name before. Some unknown man I came across at Damian’s hotel called me that. How could he confuse me with a woman that passed away so long before I was born?

The answer is now clear. Queen Dian does look a lot like me. Or should I say, I’m the one that resembles her? I thought so the second I saw this painting.

“My family is a descendant of Royals. The Alphas before me were always so proud of their Royal Blood, but I always thought this didn't mean much nowadays. Just a few droplets, how much more of the Royal Blood could have been conserved after centuries? But that woman..."

He points at the portrait, with a faint smile.

"Queen Diane is a living legend for our Clan. I don't know how much of what I heard about her life is true, but if half of it is real, she was a living deity for our kind."

"A living deity?" I ask, a bit confused.

He nods. "They say Queen Diane was a doctor, but she could heal people just with her hands. Her wolf form was as represented here, white as fresh snow, with blue eyes like a newborn. A blessed child of the Moon. She feared no Alpha, and any wolf obeyed her words. She never had to fight a single fight, all she had to do was talk, and it was as if the Moon Goddess herself spoke."

All of this sounds all too familiar, and I start shaking unconsciously. I feel Bobo's fur pressing against me, but no warmth can help me. He keeps talking, unaware of my present condition.

"Everyone thought the Moon Goddess had been reincarnated, but she just wanted the life of a simple she-wolf. Her younger sister, my grandmother, adored her, too. She had Royal Blood and was called Princess Cynthia, but compared to Diane, that was nothing. But those two were as close as sisters can be. My grandmother was much, much younger than Diane, but her older sister aged very slowly. When Cynthia turned thirty, with a husband and children, Queen Diane was almost fifty years old. However, she still looked exactly like this painting: young and beautiful."

My eyes are fixated on the painting, trying to imagine the life of that woman. As I listen, a feeling grows inside me, and I say it out loud without thinking. "She must have felt lonely."

He looks at me, a bit surprised, and nods before turning his eyes to the painting again.

"That's exactly what my grandmother said. Diane was always alone. She dedicated her life to others, to her pack, but she never let anyone in, as if she had some secret she could never share. Yet one day, she suddenly revealed to her sister that she was pregnant."

William suddenly gets up and steps closer to the painting.

"When people asked about a father, Diane said there wasn't one, no matter how many times she was questioned. Queen Diane was preparing her last miracle, a pair of twins growing in her womb without any father. Do you believe it?"

No father? How could this be? She couldn't have conceived them on her own... right?

"She had a boy and a girl. DNA tests didn't exist back then, so I guess there was no way to know if they had no biological father or not. I guess we will never know. Back then, everyone knew about what Queen Diane could accomplish, so when she said she carried children all by herself, they believed it. Children conceived as if Moon Goddess had carried them herself, about fifty years ago."

"What happened to them?"

William sighs, and turns to me.

"When Queen Diane had her children, she said this birth would endanger the whole pack. According to her, her children would have the same characteristics as she did, but that meant they would also become prey for some dangerous people. Sadly, it turned out to be true. As the children grew, more and more attacks came. From vampires, witches, dark creatures lurking after the power of Moon Goddess' blessed children. Queen Diane, worried for her children, asked my grandmother to seek somewhere safe, somewhere her children could grow in the middle of werewolves, and be protected. My grandmother, Cynthia, listened to her and left, taking half of the pack with her. This is the story of how we came here. Looking for a new place to live, we came from the North, as the Sapphire Moon Clan. As sisters, Diane and Cynthia had equal Alpha ranks, but Diane was the oldest and a blessed child of the Moon Goddess. She was the one with the purest Royal Blood. So, when my grandmother came here, with half of the pack, she was not the Alpha of the main Clan. So, naturally, this pack that had come with her became a branch Clan, the Sapphire Moon."

I close my eyes. Something indescribable is growing in my stomach, and I can barely breathe. When I open them again, William is waiting for me to ask, as if he could read my mind.

"What was the original name of your Clan?"

"...The Blue Moon Clan."

I almost lose balance. William Blue's words float in my head like an echo that won't stop. The Blue Moon Clan. So there really was a Blue Moon Clan. It was real. I came here to stop a war, but now I suddenly learn about something I was not prepared to hear. Something about me, about where I come from. My legs are shaking.

I breathe deeply, but William Blue just calmly walks past me to go back to the desk.

"I really didn't think I would one day meet someone wearing the name of Blue Moon. My grandmother gave up that name when she came here. If you're the real thing, you are a survivor, miss Nora. So, I really hope you have a good story to tell me."

A good story? Does he mean about my origins? I don't know anything! Aside from what Alec said, I'm at a loss. Whether it's about my mother or my birth, I don't know a thing. Shouldn't he be the one to tell me more? And why would I be called a survivor? He can't mean... I stare at him again, confused.

"What happened to the original Clan?" I ask. "To Queen Diane and her children?"

I want to ask what happened to my mother, but those words won't come out. This truth hasn't fully sunk in yet.

He shrugs. "You tell me. You came all the way here to introduce yourself with that name, so I want to know what you know."

"I don't know anything!" I yell out of frustration.

All I could do was gather pieces about my birth that always turn out to be fake or wrong one after another. Now that I finally meet someone who could finally tell me where I really come from, who my birth mother really is, he suddenly wants to hear from me? Moon Goddess, this is impossible to bear!

"I initially came here to ask why you resent the Blood Moon, my mate's Clan, so much. I had no idea I was related to your pack at all! All I wanted was to find a way to stop the war between the Clans, and a way to stop that Witch! I never imagined this…"

At some point, I start crying, and I feel Bobo worrying about me. He pokes me gently with his nose, but the tears won't stop. All the stress and the emotions are overflowing right now, and I can't stop it.

"Nora, where the hell are you?"

Oh, Moon Goddess. Damian. I completely forgot! How long were we gone? He is already looking for us, and I didn't manage to do anything yet! He must have felt my distress, too.

"I am fine."

"Stop it, neither you nor your wolf sound fine. Tell me where you are right away!"

"What is it?"

William Blue noticed my expression and can't understand why I suddenly held in my tears. I wipe them away and shake my head. "My mate is looking for me."

He frowns. "Damian Black? How can you know if you are not part of his Clan?"

"That is an ability of mine. I can communicate with other Alphas as long as I've physically met them before."

"Or you lied about not belonging to him yet..."

"If I was lying, could I do this?"

I use my wolf's inner voice, but I don't bother to hide how annoyed I am, and he subconsciously steps back in surprise as soon as I mind-link him. It takes a few seconds for him to get it, but he regains his composure quite quickly.

"Interesting... This ability must be quite handy, I imagine."

"You still haven't said a thing about the Blue Moon Clan!"

He shakes his head. "I don't trust you just based on a physical resemblance and a name. Even if I do, there is no way I would trust the partner of a man like Damian Black."

"Damian is not his father."

"It still doesn't mean I can trust him. Why would he willingly work with us?"

"Because Damian would do anything to protect me!"

My words echo in the room for a while, leaving a heavy silence after them. I used my inner wolf without noticing, but I don't care who heard me. I'm running out of the time, and this man is so stubborn!

I try to calm down and ignore Damian's angry voice in my head to turn to face William.

"If I am right, and if what you said is right, then this witch might be after me. My father gave me the name Bluemoon; he knew who my mother was. I am a child of the Blue Moon Clan. Those twins, Queen Diane's children, were born fifty years ago, you say. Look at me! I look like her, and I have some of Queen Diane's abilities! I even have the same wolf form! And I am eighteen, the twin girl must definitely be my mother! My birth mother, my real mother..."

I catch my breath, trying to regain my composure, and step forward as I keep talking to him with a pleading voice, trying to convince him.

"That means I'm probably a descendant of Queen Diane, her

grandchild. A blessed child of Moon Goddess. The Witch attacked you because she thought I would naturally be with the Sapphire Moon Clan, but now she knows I'm not. I showed my wolf form in public weeks ago while fighting another Alpha. Right after that, vampires attacked, coming after me. She knew where I was. She won't go after your pack anymore; you guys are safe. I promise I will make sure Damian doesn't fight with you, either."

"Even if everything you said is right, didn't your mate promise an alliance with the Gold Moon Clan? Forget the Witch, what is their aim, other than ganging up against us? When two powers out of three allies themselves, what do you think happens to the last one?"

I have nothing to answer to that. I know Damian feared an attack from the Sapphire Moon Clan most, but what can I say? The Gold Moon Clan probably sought this alliance first, and now it does seem like the Blood Moon was getting ready to get rid of their pack.

I shake my head. "I don't trust the Gold Moon Clan. I don't want to see any fights arise right now."

"We hate the Black family, but we never started a fight in the first place. I am not my father, either. I'm not one to hold grudges either, and I won't look for a fight when nothing's happened since I became the Alpha of this pack. The ones who have been a thorn for months are those annoying puppets of King," growls William.

Wait, what does that mean? Does William mean to say they are not after Damian's pack, but after the Gold Moon Clan? How come? I'm lost.

"What do you mean by that? The Gold Moon Clan?"

"We share our Northern border with the Gold Moon. They keep making intrusions into our territory, testing our reactions, and behaving like they own the land. They even hinder our businesses and help the Rising Moon Clan in taking over our shops in the city. We established ourselves after lots of effort, and I don't like giving up. But if King and Black keep this going on, I will not—"

"What do you mean, King and Black? Damian hasn't taken any part in this!" I cut him off, annoyed.

William Blue stays silent, but it's obvious he doesn't believe me. What is going on? From what he says, it looks like the Gold Moon Clan has been bullying them for months! And why would Damian's name be associated with this? Gosh, I really hope he is wrong! I try to think of something, but Damian's voice is echoing like the thunder in my head.

"Nora! Nora tell me where you are right now!"

I see Bobo's head lowering more and more, and Damian and Neal are probably giving him hell right now. I sigh, and my wolf faintly growls at our mate, a bit annoyed, too.

"Stop yelling! I will meet you in fifteen minutes, at the Sapphire Moon Clan border. Bobo is with me, I'm fine."

"What the hell are you doing there?"

"Just come and get me."

After that, I ignore him again, turning to William.

"How can I convince you?"

"Convince me?"

"I need you to trust Damian and me. I don't care about the Gold Moon Clan, I don't want anything to do with them, but the Blood Moon Clan is not what it used to be. Damian has no desire to fight with others."

He observes me silently for a while, then tilts his head. Wow, with his curly hair falling on his temples, it makes it so obvious he has some of my features. His skin is darker, though, and he has some differences, like his square jaw and larger chin.

"You are not going to convince me you are our Princess?"

I roll my eyes. "Honestly, I don't really care about being a Royal or not. I only learned a couple of weeks ago that my birth mother wasn't the one I thought. All I want to know is where I come from, and what happened to my mother, who she was, and why did she have to give me up. But at the moment, I'm more worried about a fight between the packs, and calming Damian down. I will ask more later."

"I see... Well, I heard you, but I won't make any decision yet. So, you're free to go."

That's it? He heard me, and that's all? Why do I think this is all a bit too easy? William just stands there, composed.

"Thanks..." I say, a bit hesitantly.

With Damian's voice echoing in our ears, we really have to go. As Bobo and I go to exit the room, I take one last look at the portrait. To think this woman is probably my grandmother... I can't think too deeply now, though— we have to go. When I open the door, to my surprise, the corridor is empty. Where the hell is Liam! I turn around to William, but he is still nonchalantly leaning on his desk, staring straight at me.

"Oh, I forgot to mention, we are keeping the young boy Black."

"What! Why?"

"Liam! Liam, where are you?"

"Hi, Nora. Hm, well, you are not going to like it, but I'm pretty sure I've just been kidnapped. They gave me some cookies, and well, I got pretty drowsy after that..."

"Liam Black, are you telling me you just let someone poison you?"

"Not poison, sleeping drugs! I still feel drowsy, actually."

"Where are you?"

"No clue... It's all dark in here. It smells nice, though."

Who cares if it smells nice! This idiot just got captured and he doesn't sound alarmed at all! And we just left him alone for barely twenty minutes or so! How careless can he be?

"Liam, I'm so going to kick your—"

"Wow, language, Princess. Plus, my brother has already been yelling in my head for five minutes straight, and he's still scarier than you. Hey, are those brownies?"

"Stop eating the damn food, Liam! Damian is coming in ten minutes! You have to come with me!"

"Release Liam. Why would you keep him?" I ask William.

"As a token of goodwill from Black. The oldest brother, I mean."

A token of goodwill? He just literally captured Liam! This is bad, not funny, and giving me too big of a headache right now. How will I explain this to Damian? The three of us came here secretly, and now Liam is supposed to stay there? I can't let Liam be captured now!

I unleash my exasperation at William. "What goodwill! We never agreed to this!"

William frowns and walks up to me. When he is close enough, he reaches out his hand to me, and Bobo growls, but there is no animosity in his gesture. I wait to see what he will do, but to my surprise, he just takes one of my curls between his fingers. He stays silent and looks at me eye-to-eye.

I can tell he is detailing me, looking for any facial feature that may betray me. I don't have anything to hide, I'm not fake. I look like Queen Diane, and that's not a trick. I even look a bit like William.

After a while, he sighs and whispers, so low only I can hear it, "Consider it an exchange, then. Our princess against his brother."

I look at him, surprised. So, he acknowledges it? That I am from the Blue Moon Clan? It's... I don't know what to think of it now, but this is big. His blue eyes don't leave me, and I can tell he has made his decision. He really does think the same. That, wherever I came from, I am a descendant of Queen Diane.

I slowly step back and get ready to leave. I'm too choked up by my emotions to add another word right now. I grab Bobo's fur, pulling him to come with me so he will stop growling at William. We have to leave this place for now, before Damian causes havoc.

"Nora."

I stop and turn around, surprised. William is standing at the door of his office, his hands in his pockets. He's staring at me with an indecipherable expression. Gosh, he really does look a bit like me, with his curly dark hair that stops at his shoulders, and his blue eyes. He waits for a few seconds and suddenly blurts it out.

"Lilyan."

"...What?"

I look at him, confused. What is he talking about?

He sighs. "Your birth mother, Queen Diane's daughter. Her name was Lilyan."

I'm speechless.

Lilyan. My mother's name was named Lilyan. I finally know who she was! At least... I think I do. If this woman really was my mother. I suddenly remember Elena— Daniel said our parents had to be siblings! Which means... I turn to William.

"What about the boy? Her twin?"

"Gabriel. Lilyan and Gabriel Blue Moon."

So, I have Elena's father's name, too. Our parents. Lilyan and Gabriel Blue Moon, Queen Diane's miraculous children. Did they really have no father? It's so hard to believe... I nod. I'm too shaken up to even utter some thanks. Bobo pushes me, and we leave this place in a hurry.

As we exit the mansion, I try to calm down and think of what to do next. We are supposed to leave the Sapphire Moon territory to find Damian, but what about Liam?

"Don't worry about me, Princess, I'm pretty sure I can escape just fine on my own. I'll catch up with you guys later. Just let me know when Damian's done with the yelling."

"You really shouldn't be so relaxed, Liam. And stop eating whatever they give you!"

"Yeah, yeah..."

Sometimes he is so childish, I can't believe him. I'm pretty sure he is staying here on purpose just to avoid Damian's scolding. It's not like I can do anything about it for now, anyway. Moreover, if Liam says he can get out of here on his own, I trust he can. After all, he already is an expert at avoiding his brothers and sneaking into other packs' territories.

Bobo and I run back to where we left the car, and no one stops us on the way, though a lot of eyes are following us. Did William order them to leave us alone? Thanks to that, we reach the border without any issues a few minutes later.

Once we get there, however, there is an unusual assembly of wolves. A lot of them I don't recognize, but two groups face each other, and Damian is leading one of them. Nathaniel is in his wolf form right beside him. Oh, Moon Goddess, I can hear people yelling from here, and that doesn't sound good. Furious growling and insults are flying from both sides, both Clans' wolves are on edge.

I try to sneak in, and thankfully, the Sapphire Moon Clan wolves let Bobo and me through as soon as they notice me. When he finally sees me, Damian runs to me without consideration for the border or the bunch of wolves furiously growling at him. His large hands catch my waist first, and my feet leave the ground right away.

"Nora!"

As soon as they hear him, a few of the wolves stop growling to stare at me with curious eyes. Some of them still in their human forms whisper among themselves, but I can't hear what they say.

"Nora! What the hell are you doing here? You—"

He stops and turns his head around. A young werewolf that was still growling at him a bit too closely is suddenly faced with my annoyed mate. Damian growls at him twice as loud and without holding his Alpha power back. There is no way to compare. The Black Alpha's anger can be felt all around, and every wolf steps back in fear, including a few of the Blood Moon Clan. And he is not even in his wolf form.

"Truly impressive."

All heads turn. To my surprise, William is standing there, among the Sapphire Moon wolves, hands in his pocket, looking very calm. Did he follow us all the way here? Damian frowns and puts me down, but his hand is still around me, keeping me close.

The two Alphas stare at each other, and all eyes are on them. I notice some wolves are going back and forth between William and me, noticing our physical resemblance. Damian doesn't seem to care, though; he is just glaring at William.

"William Blue..."

"Mr. Black. I believe this is our first time meeting."

Is it, really? It seems unreal those two Alphas would have never met before. They exude the very same kind of aura, powerful and fearsome. It's like seeing a confrontation between fire and ice, or a tiger and a snake. Everyone around us is feeling the tension, too.

"I see you really did come to retrieve Nora. How surprising."

"I don't see my brother, however," growls Damian.

"Right. He's staying with us for now."

Despite William's calm, Damian and the rest of the pack immediately start growling furiously at him. The Sapphire Moon Alpha doesn't flinch.

"You better hand him over right away." Damian's eyes have turned ice-cold, and he is speaking with that terrifying, low voice of his. I see a couple of Sapphire Moon wolves' step back a little, frightened.

William shakes his head and points his finger to me. "No. As long as you have her, I'm keeping him here. Safe and unharmed, but on my territory."

Damian frowns, and addresses me, still glaring at William. "Nora, what is going on?"

"Damian, the Sapphire Moon Clan is—"

"Her rightful pack."

William cut me off in the middle of my sentence, and I look at him with shocked eyes. What does he mean now? My rightful pack? I don't have any rightful pack as of now!

Damian glares at William. "What does that mean?"

"I don't have the time or patience to explain this to you. Anyway, I would advise you to retreat back from our territory and take the time to discuss this with her if she wishes to. I promised her I would think things over, but while doing so, I need to guarantee nothing will happen to her. As such, I took your brother."

"Wait! When will you release Liam?" I ask, worried for him.

William stays silent for a long minute, then suddenly goes to unbutton his shirt. What is he doing? To my surprise, he turns around and shows their Clan's marking, a full blue moon, tattooed on his back.

"This is your clan. This should have been your marking, but

instead, you walk around unmarked like some stray. We can't have that. I want you to join our pack, Nora, the one you belong to."

I stare at him, speechless. To join the Sapphire Moon Clan? I never thought of this, but William's eyes are resolute. He is serious...

Damian glares. "No. Nora will join the Blood Moon Clan. Soon."

"Why would she? Aren't you engaged to another? Are you supposed to keep her as your mistress?" Asks William.

"Hell, I hope not!" Suddenly yells a voice.

Everyone suddenly turns heads. This has to be a joke. Alessandra King, now?

She is standing a few meters away, sided by a few of her own wolves. Were we that close to the Gold Moon Clan's territory? My wolf starts growling just at the sight of her. I hate that woman. What is she even doing here? No one is pleased to see her, as both sides start growling, too, but she doesn't lose her self-confidence one bit. She is standing with her arms crossed, looking at Damian like a cat preying on a bird. My wolf and I are both outraged by the looks she gives him.

"Hello, Damian," she says with a little hand gesture that annoys the hell out of me.

Damian doesn't reply; he keeps glaring at her with a very pissed look. I slightly shift my position to stand between the two of them, by pure instinct.

"King, are you that bored that you have to come to peek at the border so often?" Asks William without even looking at her. His eyes are still set on me, despite all of his wolves growling at both Damian and Alessandra.

She giggles. "Maybe. Well, my dearest fiancé bothered to come all the way here, I should at least say hi, shouldn't I?"

"Is that so...?" Whispers William.

I'm sure he is waiting for Damian's reaction right now, judging the relationship between the three of us. While Alessandra is clearly acting as if I'm not here, Damian pulls me closer to him, glaring at her with all his might.

"I've made things clear, Alessandra. Our engagement is canceled."

She starts playing with her golden necklace, absentmindedly. "Oh, I've heard something like that. Father is pretty annoyed at your attitude, you know. You are making things difficult, but I persuaded him it was just a matter of time before you changed your mind."

"I won't," Damian replies without thinking.

I am a bit proud of him, but Alessandra stops smiling, and suddenly glares at him. "Oh, you will. Do you know how many millions are hanging in the balance right now? Do you think you can actually afford this little tantrum of yours? Don't forget, Damian, I'm the one with the money. You might be powerful, but you need back-up. Who is going to give it to you if not me? Hm? This little tramp?"

"Watch your mouth!"

Not only Damian, but even William suddenly started growling at Alessandra at the same time. I have to hold back my mate; Damian is on the verge of shapeshifting to give Alessandra a piece of his mind. While holding Damian's arm, I also have to calm my own wolf, which more than pissed by Alessandra's attitude. If I let her, she would violently rip her face off in seconds.

To my surprise, William talks in an ice-cold tone that reminds me of my mate. "A tramp...? Aren't you one to speak, Gold? Your kind is nothing but a down-the-gutter breed of slum dogs."

Surprised, Alessandra looks at him, violently offended by his words. "What did you just call me? How dare you..."

"I call you whatever I please, you slut. Tell your wolves to back off from my territory right now, before I send you back myself!"

The Gold Moon Clan is clearly overstepping. However, Alessandra doesn't move an inch. Instead, she sends a deathly glare to William.

"Really? Your territory? Aren't you the ones who shamelessly took the scraps the Snow Moon Clan left behind? Don't talk to me about territory when this should have been ours from the beginning."

William snorts. "Is that what you guys think? Do you own this land? You are nothing but a mass of dogs playing around. Don't come to me and talk about your rights. You're merely a pack of stray dogs acting like vermin and thieves..."

Alessandra's face changes color upon hearing this, but she can't come up with any answer besides furious growling. It seems like William hit a nerve. Instead, she decides to ignore him and turn to Damian once more. "Are you really going to keep this stupid little act?"

"I have made things clear already," growls Damian.

"Oh, please! Shutting us out, nullifying business deals? Are you that blind that you would lose millions for the sake of that little... girl?"

She clearly hesitated on the last word, but I guess she ran out of insults, or Damian's glare shut them up.

Either way, she finally looks at me with a sneer. "Wake up, child. I don't care if you're an Alpha or whatever. You are nothing. I stand by what I said last time. No Clan, no family, no money, no power. Fated mates? Whatever. Damian will marry me, because I am the right partner for him, and for his Clan, to stand as his Luna."

I hate that woman. She's not just arrogant, she is also a greedy bitch. Greedy for my mate. Moon Goddess, I hate those conspicuous eyes of hers. I don't care about the Clans or those struggles of power and money. All I feel is hatred for this other woman who wants my mate, my Damian. My wolf is on the verge of coming out to kill her, and I must say, my human self has the same frightening thought.

Unaware of my anger, she keeps talking. "Whatever you do, you will never be enough, Bluemoon. Do you think you can afford it? Oh, sure, they might like you. You will be the adorable little doll. But his Clan will lose it trying to protect you. No financial support, no business deals, no allies. Watch it. It's only a matter of time before they all disappear because of you. All because of you."

I clench my fist, trying hard to hold it in. Damian is holding me tighter, angry. I can tell a lot of eyes are on me, worried or curious, but I don't give a damn right now. I'm fighting to contain my wolf, and my urge to silence this woman the hard way. I can't lose control now... This would launch a war between the two packs...

"I guess it's not too late. If you recognize right now that you were wrong to defy me and acknowledge that I will be the only right one to mate with Damian, I can talk to my—"

"NORA!"

I jump into my wolf form and aim straight at her. I ignore Damian's voice behind me.

This woman asked for it.

Chapter 12

"This is what I call a mess, miss Nora."

I ignore him. Sitting on Damian's desk, still as furious as before, I'm not impressed at all by Neal's lecture. Arms crossed, I look at him walking in circles in Damian's office. I don't care that he is annoyed at me; I'm annoyed at them, too.

It took Neal, Bobo, and Damian to stop me. I was that close to finally giving that woman what she deserved! I will remember for a long time the terror in her eyes when I jumped at her in my wolf form. I was that close to scratching her! But after escaping Damian's grasp, Bobo and Neal jumped at the same time to hold me back, and my mate caught me back a second later. Apparently, it took a while to calm my wolf down, but it's kind of blurry for me. I was so blinded by anger that I let my wolf take control entirely.

I do feel sorry for Bobo, though. I accidentally scratched his jaw with my claws while trying to escape them, and now he has a large compress on his face. I give him an apologetic look as he is standing against the wall, but he just seems bored by his brother's nagging.

"Not only this could have ended in conflict with the Gold Moon Clan, but on top of it, the Sapphire Moon was right there watching!"

"I'm pretty sure the Blood Moon Clan is already in conflict with the Gold Moon Clan," I growl.

"Not in the open! And it doesn't give you the right to kill their Alpha's daughter!"

"Well, the Sapphire Alpha was applauding..." Mutters Bobo.

Neal gives him a glare.

To be precise, William was even laughing out loud after they caught me. Whether it was because of my fury or because Alessandra and her followers ran away, he liked the show and made it clear. What a ruckus for that wretched woman...

I go back to ignoring Neal's litany about how reckless I was and stare outside. A mix of rain and snow started pouring right after I exploded. William took it as his excuse to leave, though he deliberately ignored the matter of Liam. Plus, Damian and the Betas were too busy trying to calm me down to argue any further. In the end, I was dragged back to Damian's office. I'm still angry, even after going back to my human shape and changing. I'm stuck with the Mura brothers, while Damian left to discuss what happened with the Gold Moon with his Lieutenants. Nathaniel is there, too, but he ignores us. I'm pretty sure he is busy mind-linking Liam.

"This is highly problematic, Miss Nora. None of us like Miss King either, but you can't attack other packs in the open like that! This is the perfect excuse for them to get back at us, and now is certainly not the time for this."

"So, what, I'm supposed to swallow her insults like it's nothing?" I ask angrily.

"No, you are supposed to act smarter than her! Don't stoop to that woman's level!"

Oh, I have an excellent idea about which level I would want to bring that woman down to...

"Is Damian done rambling?"

"Neal Mura is the one me to death right now. When are you coming back, you chicken?"

I hear Liam laugh in my head. How can he find fun in a situation like this...? I hope he stayed behind for nothing.

"I'm serious, Liam. When are you coming back?"

"Pretty soon. The Sapphire Moon Clan is kind of boring. They don't like people coming in, but it is quite easy to go out. I might have to beat some of their fighters' asses, though."

"How come you get to have fun while I have to be scolded for hours for trying to scratch that woman?"

"You just pick the wrong fights, Princess."

I roll my eyes before realizing Neal saw that. He probably thinks I'm annoyed at him and did this on purpose, but I really didn't. He clicks his tongue, and I look somewhere else, anywhere. Bobo is yawning like he couldn't care less. I wish I was as carefree...

The door suddenly opens, and Damian enters, followed by several people. Tonia is there, with Isaac, Vane, and Sean, too. The office suddenly feels crowded, but I stay on Damian's desk when he walks up to me. He goes to put his arms around me, but I ignore him. I'm too angry right now; I don't want to be hugging and acting sweet.

"Isaac. Tell us again what you just said," he says.

Isaac nods. "The situation with the Gold Moon Clan remains stable for now. Basically, they still act like nothing is wrong, despite us shutting them out. Most of the contracts we were working on have simply been signaled as 'on hold,' and they still make use of our name whenever they can."

He walks up to us, going around the desk, and uses the phone, dialing in some number. After a while, we can hear Thaddeus' voice. They exchange a few words, and Isaac puts him on speaker.

"We are about halfway into transferring the funds, but the Gold Moon Clan is greatly objecting. Miss Nora, I reached out to your Jade Moon Clan as you suggested, and their alliance with the Pearl Moon is valid. They have been giving us a hand with the financial aspect for transfer of funds, though the progress is quite slow."

I'm surprised, but happy to hear that. Did Vince really help in this? I knew he had a great relationship with the Pearl Moon Alpha, but I never imagined he would really be willing to use it for the Blood Moon Clan or me. So, they are transferring all the Blood Moon accounts from the Gold Moon Clan establishments to Pearl Banking?

I'm shocked at how Damian already put everything in motion. Isaac cuts off the phone and turns to us. "It's a slow process, but we are getting there. I think the hardest part will be the aftermaths of having so many breaches of contracts and accords nullified. Basically, the Gold Moon Clan will try to play dead the longest they can and try to grab as much as they can while trying to prevent us from cutting ties."

"What about your side?" Asks Damian to Vane and Sean.

"Everyone is following your orders, Boss. It's gotten lively, but the guys are happy to chase outsiders off our territory. The Gold Moon got quite complacent, our wolves were waiting for it, anyway," says Vane.

"We chased most of them off overnight. It got a bit physical, but we reminded them who has the better fighters. No killings, but a few broken bones," adds Sean with a smirk.

Damian nods.

So, this is really happening. The Blood Moon is cutting ties with the Gold Moon Clan. How will the other Clans react? I keep thinking about the dynamics between the packs in Silver City. It's a very fragile peace with have going on.

"What do we do about Liam?" Asks Tonia.

Nathaniel rolls his eyes. "He doesn't want us to help him, so leave him be. Knowing Liam, they might even beg us to take him back within the next three hours..."

Nobody contests that. I would think Liam tends to get himself out of these situations just fine. I just wish he wasn't basically hiding from this mess.

Isaac gives me a faint smile. "You scared us, miss Nora. Going to the Sapphire Moon Clan territory like that was a bit dangerous..."

Great, I am really getting to get scolded by all the Betas now?

Damian seems to be suddenly reminded of the matter, and his angry aura almost explodes in the room. "What the hell were you thinking? Going with those two again! Nora, you could really have been killed! And with what happened yesterday, what if this sicko had found you? You didn't even tell me a thing before going!"

"You would have never let me go if I had asked you!"

"And for a good reason! The Sapphire Moon hates us, they could have killed you on the spot, and this isn't like the Jade Moon Clan or the Sea Moon! This is damn serious, Nora, we are enemies! What the hell were you doing there!"

"I went to try and help you!" My yelling seemed to shock a lot of people, aside from Bobo. "I know canceling your engagement with the Gold Moon Clan will bring a lot more issues than you tell me! Liam told me about how things were with the Sapphire Moon Clan, and whatever it is, this doesn't look good! I couldn't leave it at that, so I went there to try and negotiate an Oath of Peace with them."

"An Oath of Peace? Nora, we are not even on speaking terms with those people! One single step on their territory could have gotten all three of you killed!" Yells Damian.

"Now that you mention it... How did you guys manage to go this far?" Asks Nathaniel.

I sigh. "That's the thing. It turns out I have a lot more in common with the Sapphire Moon than the Jade Moon."

Damian frowns again, and I can tell he is thinking hard right now, probably reminiscing everything William said earlier. All the others look concerned, too, so I breathe in and start to explain. I tell them everything. How I met William's father, his hatred for the Black

Brothers' father. I describe the painting the best I can, how much Queen Diane and I look alike, and all of her story William told me. When I stop, after explaining how William decided to keep Liam as an exchange for myself, the room stays completely silent, each of them in awe.

Tonia shakes her head as if she's trying to wake up. "You're saying... you are the grand-daughter of this Moon Goddess reincarnation, Queen Diane? And the Sapphire Moon Alpha's... cousin?" She asks, bewildered.

"His second cousin, supposedly, yes."

"Well, that would explain how you are so pure as a Royal..."

"It also explains why they let miss Nora on their territory so easily. The Sapphire Moon wolves' instinct probably prevented them from attacking. She is Royalty to them, it would be even harder than attacking their own Alpha," explains Isaac.

"So, what, now they want to have her as a part of their Clan?"

That is a good question. William's attitude was confusing on that part. He called me their Princess, and did say I belonged there, but... I feel like there is more than that. He is really mysterious and cunning. He was watching our interactions with the Gold Moon Clan, too.

"I don't like this," says Nathaniel. "Even if Nora is their Princess, that doesn't change the fact that they hate the Gold Moon Clan and us. King is probably going to play with that until one of us actually starts a war. And now they want Nora and are ready to capture Liam for that. We can't leave it at that, Damian. If the other Clans learn about this..."

Nathaniel is right. The tension at the border was no joke. If I wasn't there, they probably wouldn't even have bothered with words. I feel like we only won a short reprieve because I happened to be there.

"I still don't get why they hate you guys so much! I couldn't get anything out of William about that..."

"William? You are on a first-name basis with him now?"

I turn to Damian, surprised by his pissed-off tone. A bit annoyed, too. "What? Don't you dare start acting jealous, Damian, because I'm so not in the mood for this right now!"

All the others look at us, a bit awkwardly, but I don't care. I'm angry and exhausted, and I really can't take any more from Damian right now. I'm about to explode.

"I don't care if you're mad because I'm mad, too! I had to listen to that woman's crap for the second time in two weeks; that's enough! I'm tired of trying to sort things out, tired of all those secrets, and tired of you getting mad at me whenever I take a step out without telling you!"

"You're the one who said no more secrets!" He yells back.

Great, now we are both mad and yelling at each other! I see Nathaniel gesturing for the rest of the group to leave us alone, but I couldn't care less. I just need to get it all out right now.

"I don't want to have to lie to you, but you would never have let me go to William's territory if I didn't sneak out! And I couldn't stay behind, I had to try!"

"Why the hell do you think you have to solve everything! You're just a teen, Nora! You may be a Princess, but you don't have to carry the whole fate of Silver City! Why do you feel like you have to go and save the situation on your own!"

"Because I'm damn scared, Damian!" I yell, as I start crying, too.

"Why are you so scared? Nora, I told you I will protect you no matter what!"

"I'm scared of losing you, you idiot!"

I burst into tears.

Gosh, I've been crying way too much these days. All these emotions bottled up inside, and I can't hold them anymore. I may act tough, I may be doing my best in front of others, but I just break all of my armor when it's just Damian and me.

"Nora..."

"I've lost too many people already, Damian, I don't think I can take it, anymore. My dad died when I was young, the mother who raised me, too... Even Alec... I even lost my former pack! I'm so scared I'm going to lose you, too, because I'm so selfish..."

I try to wipe away my tears, to breathe in the middle of it, but it pours, and I can't seem to stop. Damian looks at me, all trace of anger dissipated already. He looks worried and unsure about what to do. I keep talking, with my voice hoarse and breaking.

"You know why I got so mad earlier? At you? Because that woman was right. She's right, Damian! I don't have anything to support you as a Luna should! I'm all the things King said! A powerless orphan! I don't care if I'm a Princess, what good is it? I know you love me, I get it, but this is never going to be enough! When William was talking about Queen Diane, all I could think of was how she was unable to protect her own children! My mom died, Damian, she died before I could meet her,

I don't even remember her! What if I lose you because I'm not strong enough to protect you? If this war really happens? What if...?"

Before I can finish, Damian grabs my wrist and forces a kiss on me. It's not like any of our previous kisses. This one is more brutal, imposing. I can tell he's mad. His lips pressed against mine, I have a hard time catching my breath. It's still passionate and enticing. I feel my body going numb while the fire roars inside. I can't escape his grip, and he keeps kissing me savagely until my legs give up. When he feels me falling, he suddenly stops and hugs me tight.

Trapped in his arms, I feel his breathing against my skin. We need to catch some air. He slides down against his desk until we are seated on the ground. He rubs my back gently, allowing me to calm down.

"Nora, listen, my Love. I'm sorry I let you feel like this. I know you went through all that, and I'm glad that you finally stop acting tough. It's okay to be scared, my Love. You can tell me everything."

I put my arms around his neck, holding him close. Only Damian can find the words to reassure me right now. He caresses my hair and keeps stroking my hair gently.

"Nora, I'm scared you'll get hurt trying to protect me or anyone. If there is something that worries you, tell me. If something scares you, tell me. Nora, you're the one who said no more secrets, so don't keep any from me, too. Don't close yourself to me. I can't read all of your emotions, and sometimes I have no idea what you are thinking about. I want to know my Love, everything about you."

I nod against his shoulder and raise my head up to face him. My eyes must be red and all teary because I see him frowning a bit. I don't care. I put my hand on his cheek, feeling his warmth under my fingers.

"I hate her... I hate that woman, Damian, and I'm scared she is going to take you away from me. If I don't have you, I don't have anything. I want to be your Luna, the only one for you. I don't want another woman to look at you or touch you. I want to be selfish."

He chuckles and comes to kiss between my eyebrows gently. "Welcome to my world, my Love."

So, this is what he feels, too? Who is he jealous of, then? I don't want to think about it. I just want to keep Damian as close as possible.

"Be jealous, then," I say. "If you are jealous, I'll know you still love me as much."

"I hope you'll remember saying that next time—"

Before he can finish his sentence, I take him between my hands and kiss him fiercely. I am still a bit clumsy and hesitant, but I let my emotions guide me.

I just want him. I don't care about a bond, or anything else. This is just me, and the man I fell in love with. We keep kissing intensely, and I put my arms around his neck. My heart is beating so fast, I feel like I could faint any second. Damian's grip around me tightens, and I know this is all too real. He kisses me frantically, and I join him. I want him, I want Damian so badly, I feel like I've been missing him my whole life, like a thirst only he can quench. Only him. Only Damian.

He interrupts our kiss, and we are still both out of breath. Taking my face between his hands, he looks into my eyes, his silver irises mesmerizing me. I know what he is looking for: an answer, my consent. He wants to be sure. But I am sure. I really do want this, I want him. I put my fingers through his jet-black hair, observing my mate. Gosh, this man is really too handsome... I gently come back to him, pressing my lips against his once again, giving him what he wants.

The next second, I feel his arms under me, and I'm carried away. His hands are firm, but his caresses are more rushed, a bit hastier. I don't hold back, either. I caress his neck, any part of his back I can reach, and I help him get out of his shirt. He carries me like I don't weigh anything and takes me to the bedroom before I even realize it.

My legs wrapped around his waist, I'm not ready to let go until I feel the satin sheets under me. We keep kissing like crazy, and I hear my own heartbeat in my ears. I hear Damian, too, whispering my name endlessly as his lips leave mine to go down my neck.

"Nora, Nora..."

I gasp and open my eyes, trying to catch my breath. Damian halts a second, looking at me and panting. Oh, Moon Goddess, his eyes are driving me crazy. I'm becoming someone else, and that girl is eager for more. The silver diamonds are shining with lust, too. Hungry like a wolf. I feel the last strings of my reserve snapping. I'm half-wolf and half-woman, striving for my mate, following my instincts and desire. My whole body is burning with wildfire, but gosh, I like it.

Damian is half-naked on top of me, and not holding back his desire either. He puts his head in my neck, his hand under my top, and keeps whispering words to drive me crazy between the kisses.

"Nora... Nora, I want you so bad..."

"Damian..."

He helps me take off my shirt, and I suddenly blush when his eyes fall on my bra. I'm grateful because Tonia got me something actually decent and a bit sexy, but...

"What is it?"

I blush even more because it seems so stupid to be covering my chest at this moment, but Damian is waiting for me. I try to avoid his eyes to confess. "Because... they're... small..."

It takes him a second to understand, and he chuckles. This is not funny! Now that my mate is about to see it all, I'm embarrassed at my small chest. But Damian ignores me and mercilessly pushes my hands away to see them.

"Nora, you're so cute..."

Cute? I don't want to be cute; I wish I was more of the sexy type! Why did I have to be on the petite side? I barely have any curves! But obviously, Damian doesn't care one bit. He keeps exploring my body, his fingers reaching everywhere. I feel the passion firing up inside again, and my cheeks become redder again when he takes off my skirt. I only have my panties left under him.

Damian stares at me, one hand on my leg and the other one supporting him. I love the way he is looking at me, making me feel beautiful. But this is a bit embarrassing, too, so I grab his face to resume our kissing, while my other hand goes to unbuckle his pants. I shouldn't be the only one staying naked, right?

We sit up on the bed, and Damian helps me. While he is getting out of his pants, I kiss his torso. I have seen him half-naked a lot of times already, but I never get enough of it. How does he achieve this Greek-sculpture body? So muscular, too. I silently promise myself to work more diligently on my diet and workout from now on.

I hear him exhale loudly under my kisses, and his fingers run over my back, grabbing my hair gently. He finally gets out of his jeans and takes me into his arms.

I know he is deliberately going slow for me. I feel my mate tensed up by desire, yet his hands are gentle. We go back to lying down next to each other. His lips go for my neck once again, his hand caresses my thighs. He is looking out for my reaction, trying to see any flaw, anything that might suggest a refusal from me. But Moon Goddess, I've never felt so ready. I undulate slowly, inviting him to explore more of my body. I want him to touch me more! Damian understands, and something lights up in his eyes. His hand slides all the way to my last piece of cloth, and I gasp as his fingers start playing underneath. Oh, gosh, this is... The fire seems to concentrate on this location while he keeps this going. He wants me fully ready, and I hear my own breathing changing minute after minute. I struggle to keep up with Damian's deep kiss. I want more, I want more of this, but he suddenly stops.

Damian stands on the side of the bed, staring at me. Those silver eyes make me feel so many things... His stare is so intense, I start burning with excitation again. He doesn't stop fixating on me while he takes off his boxers, and his hand reaches out for something from his drawer. When he comes back to the bed, he is entirely naked, and I feel him against me. All of his warmth and skin pressed on mine makes me crazy, and I grab him for a new long kiss.

I want him, I want my mate... I struggle to take off my panties until I'm finally naked, too, under him. Damian interrupts our kiss to stare at me once more, and I put my hands around his neck, keeping his silver eyes and breathless lips close to me. I'm panting, burning with desire. I don't know what happened to the previous Nora, but this one is perfectly synched with her wolf and ready. I hear the sound of paper being torn, and Damian takes my hand, kissing its palm.

"I love you, Nora, I love you so much..."

"I love you, too...So bad..."

He smiles, kissing my cheek. "So bad?" He repeats with a smile

"Mm..."

He kisses me again, so passionately, until I lose track of time, and suddenly, I feel him move inside. I let out a faint cry. Damian showers me with kisses, whispering gently in my ear, taking it slow for me. I catch my breath, slowly getting used to him, indulging myself in this pleasure. I love him. Damian loves me, and he makes love like he is pouring all of his feelings into me. This is it; this is all I needed.

Becoming one with my mate.

When I wake up the next morning, I still feel tired, and I don't want to move an inch. My whole body is practically melting on the bed, and I'm drowsy. I probably woke up because of this latent pain on my neck. I close my eyes a few seconds, trying to ignore it.

Damian's breathing next to my ear makes me smile. I remember the details of our night and how I finally had sex with my mate. We really did it. Damian undid all my insecurities, making me feel better than ever before. This one night unveiled so much for the both of us... It wasn't painless, but it was still great, and fulfilling.

I hear Damian's breathing change behind me, and I know we are both awake. His hand grabs the bed sheets to hold it tighter around me, his arm covering my bare chest. We both slept with only our underwear on, and the room is a bit cold, but Damian's warm chest is covering all of my back, and the balance between his hot skin and the cold air is perfect. He puts a kiss on my shoulder, another one on my neck.

"Good morning, my Love."

"Good morning..."

"How do you feel?"

"...Like your woman."

I hear him chuckle against my hair. I love the sound of his deep voice when he has just woken up, still a bit husky. Apparently, neither of us is willing to get up, as we lie in bed cuddling for a long time. Thank Moon Goddess I don't have work today, so I can stay in Damian's arms as long as they are there.

My mate gently kisses my shoulder again, and I feel the short spikes of his morning beard against my skin. Is it normal that I'm so sluggish? I don't feel like getting up at all.

"How is your neck?"

I raise my hand to touch it, but Damian grabs my wrist before I do.

"Don't. It's still a bit fresh."

I realize the faint scent of blood comes from the red stains on our pillows. Damian bit me a little on the lower left side; I can even feel the shape of his marking. It's not really painful, more like tingling.

"It's okay. How is yours?"

I hear him laughing against my hair again. What is so funny?

"I'm fine, too, despite my mate's eagerness..."

My eagerness? What does he mean? I struggle to free myself from his embrace and get on my knees while still holding the blanket around me. Once I'm sitting, Damian gets on his stomach to let me see, and I gasp. Oh, my gosh. This isn't biting, it looks like he was attacked by some wild animal! Did I really do this? Despite my bite marks being smaller, there are several on his neck, and they look like a mess, too. I turn red immediately, completely ashamed. I want to run away, but I'm more worried about my mate.

"Oh, Moon Goddess, I'm so sorry... Does it hurt?"

He laughs in the pillow, but I don't find this funny! I'm so ashamed right now! How could I bite him like a... an animal! I lean on his back and kiss the little injuries gently. I don't even remember biting him so fiercely! I was so into our... our intercourse last night, I lost track. This idiot just keeps laughing! I slap his back, annoyed.

"Damian, stop it! It's not funny! It's embarrassing!"

He doesn't stop, and he grabs my wrist to push me down on the mattress. I pout, but he doesn't care and starts kissing me, smiling against my lips. I try to fight him off playfully, but despite my annoyance at him, I eventually laugh and start answering his kiss.

This feels so much better now that we have gotten more intimate. I don't have anything holding me back anymore, no apprehension or fear. Damian is obviously enjoying it, too. Actually, his kiss gets more intense, and I feel a specific part of him getting more excited, too...

About an hour later, I exit the shower, drying my hair with a towel. Thankfully, with what happened last time, Bobo left some of my clothes in Damian's apartment. I pick up an off-shoulder striped top and a short velvet skirt. It's a bit sexier than I would usually wear to work, but I like it. When Damian exits his bathroom, I'm checking my phone. I notice his glance on my legs and the thin black tights I chose. Now that I think of it, he did mention he liked my legs... When he is busy putting on his jeans, I throttle to him and pick a shirt before him in his wardrobe. It's ninety-percent black shirts, so I just pick one randomly, and then look at his neckties until I find one I like. I settle for a silk silver one with two black stripes and hand it to him with a smile.

"You want to put it on me?" He asks with a smile.

"I have no idea how to make the tie..."

He looks a bit disappointed, so I give him a quick kiss before heading to the bathroom. When I am done, some light makeup on, he is waiting for me in the bedroom, frowning at his smartphone. I walk up to him, and he naturally puts an arm around my waist.

"What is it?" I ask, trying to take a peek at his phone.

"The Gold Moon Alpha is quite unhappy... He's harassing the secretarial office to schedule a meeting. And my mailbox, as well..."

I frown. So Alessandra really went ahead to complain to daddy... I really wish Damian and the others had let me scratch her face. At least she would have had something really worth complaining about.

I sigh. "You haven't seen him since the party?"

"He didn't attend, and I was more focused on you. Neal and Thaddeus are the ones to usually meet him. It seems like I won't be able to escape it this time."

I click my tongue. I don't care about the Gold Moon Alpha, but if I see Alessandra again, I'm really going for that woman's throat. Thank Moon Goddess, now Damian and I are finally officially mated, and well, I made it quite visible. Even with his shirt collar, my marking is still pretty noticeable. I'm torn between the remorse of injuring my mate and the proudness of showing off my territory. I get on my toes and give him a quick kiss. When I step back, I suddenly remember something I noticed yesterday, too.

"I wonder why my kissing is not healing this?"

"I thought about it, too, but I suppose a marking is different from an injury... You would never be able to mark me, otherwise. And I don't want to have to stop kissing you in the middle of having sex."

I blush immediately. "Damian! Don't say such stuff out loud, it's embarrassing..."

He chuckles and gives me a quick kiss. Is it me, or is he more playful these days? He is acting a bit like Liam... Liam! I forgot about him! I try to reach out to him with my wolf, but for once, I can't. What does that mean? Is he okay?

"Damian, any news of Liam?"

He shakes his head and takes my hand as we exit his apartment. So, he doesn't know either. I can't tell if he is worried or not, though. He just takes me down to his office, where once again, Neal is waiting for us. Bobo is there, too, and he walks up to me immediately. I put my hand in his fur, saying hello. Sometimes I wish Bobo was an Alpha, too, so we could mind-link easily...

I ignore Neal's gaze, however. I know he is still angry after me for trying to attack Alessandra, but I'm not the slightest remorseful. I feel like a guilty daughter trying to avoid her father's scolding.

"Boss, miss Nora..." He says, his eyes focused on me.

I mutter a "hi" while pretending to play with Bobo's fur. Damian, however, walks up to him with a sigh, showing him his phone.

"I see you saw my messages, Boss."

"You didn't need to give me a headache for that, Neal."

"You were obviously too busy to answer."

He says that while staring at my bite marks on Damian's neck. Why did I have to make it so obvious! Now I look like a very territorial woman. It might be necessary, though, if that woman comes around again. Damian rolls his eyes and goes to sit behind his desk, in a leather chair that suits him perfectly. Looking like this, with his black suit and the city's scenery behind him, he looks like one of those classy villains from an action movie. A very sexy villain.

"Anyway, we need to come up with a response. Obviously, the Gold Moon Clan is getting more and more agitated. The broken engagement is also agitating the other packs. Though King is doing everything he can to not disclose it, they're not blind. Some of the other Clans are already raising concerns."

"What are they worried about?" I ask.

"About the future, miss Nora. Some of them are happy that we won't be joining forces with the Gold Moon Clan, but they also wonder if we will create more conflicts that way," explains Neal.

"You think they will put pressure on the other packs?"

"Not only the other packs but all of Silver City's economy," sighs Damian. "Knowing King, he will try to use this to his advantage. They own half of the banking establishments in Silver City, which means every Clan's economy mostly depends on them. If they start cutting off the funds and holding all the money, the other packs will be starving and get agitated."

That seems logical. If the packs are unable to use their money, and the Gold Moon closes all of the banks, it will be difficult for them financially. At some point, the Clans won't be able to survive on their own and will take action.

"Won't they put the blame on the Gold Moon Clan?"

"Not directly. First, they are too big for other Clans to take on, and secondly, they are the ones with the money. You don't want to get on bad terms with the guy who has the key to your banking account. So, if they can't blame the Gold Moon directly..."

"They will hold the Blood Moon responsible," I whisper.

Neal nods, while Damian has a dark expression. This is the worst scenario, but unfortunately, Neal is right. Damian is the Alpha King of Silver City. If the other packs hold any grudges and they can't direct it at the Gold Moon Clan, it will all fall on him. I bite my lip nervously. I don't want to give in to the Gold Moon Clan, but is there any way to get out of this? They will most likely pressure them until Damian gives up, but this alliance would include him marrying Alessandra, and this is no longer a possibility since last night. He is now mine, no matter what.

Neal and Damian start talking about the recent moves of the Gold Moon Clan, and how to handle some business deals that were on hold with them, but I'm not listening anymore. I try to think of a solution.

Yesterday's meeting with William Blue was necessary, I know it. But what now? Damian and William obviously won't partner up anytime soon! And even if they did, the Gold Moon still holds half of Silver City's economy. How are we supposed to oppose them?

"Hey, Nora?"

I jump, surprised to hear Elena's voice after all this.

"Elena? What is it?"

"We have to talk, fast. I think the Opal Moon Clan is about to do something really, really stupid."

"What do you mean?"

"You are not going to like it. Our Alpha had a secret meeting with Taaron King last night."

Chapter 13

"So, you and that woman, Elena Whitewood, are..."

"Cousins. She is the daughter of Queen Diane's other child, my mother's twin brother, Gabriel."

They look at me in awe, perplexed, but I went as far as I could with my explanation. I had no choice but to explain our relationship to them since Elena gave me the information about the Opal Moon Clan. I didn't want to hide it from Damian anymore, that would have been unfair. So, I told them everything.

"So, she's also part of this Blue Moon Clan?" Asks Neal.

"Right. And William Blue's second cousin, just like me."

"Nora, why did you never tell me?"

Damian looks lost, and I understand.

I sigh. "Elena asked me not to because of her relationship with Nathaniel. Their relationship is quite complicated, and I didn't want to mess things up."

He stares at me a few seconds and holds his hand out for me to take it. I walk around the desk to join him, and Damian makes me sit on his lap, giving me a kiss on the forehead.

"I understand," he whispers.

I didn't tell him about the baby, as Elena asked when I told her I had to talk to Damian. She probably has her reasons for keeping this pregnancy to herself. Moreover, that would be a big secret for Damian to keep from his brother. When will she tell Nathaniel, though? Elena avoids the question whenever I try to know where their relationship is at. Aside from Bobo, Daniel, and me, I think no one else knows yet.

"I won't tell Nathaniel; you can tell him directly later. He doesn't like talking about his relationships, anyway," says Damian.

I can only agree on that point, but still, I don't really like that he is mentioning Nathaniel's relationships. It sounds like Elena is only one of many, and that's not what I wish for my cousin... However, I'm not supposed to intrude in this, we have a lot to handle already.

I turn to Neal. "What do you think? From what Elena said, do we have to fear that the White Moon will betray the Sapphire Moon Clan?"

Neal scratches his beard with a complicated expression. "That's very unlikely, in my opinion. No, from what miss Whitewood said, I would believe the Opal Moon is acting on its own. The White Moon has a long history with the Sapphire Moon— they were the only ones willing to finance them back when the White Group was struggling."

"They are scientists, right?" I ask, trying to remember what Bobo taught me.

"That's right. They are an old Clan in Silver City, but their former businesses were not doing well. A few years ago, they decided to aim toward the sciences. It was a difficult start, but they made use of their proximity to the University and constructed new facilities. The Sapphire Moon was the only pack willing to finance them, while the Gold Moon Clan didn't see any use of investing in science."

"How could they not? It's essential for people's health, medicine, biology, environment..."

"Yes, miss Nora, but back in the '60s and '70s, it didn't sound so promising. The Sapphire Moon made the right bet, though. The White Moon Clan took off thirty years ago with several medical breakthroughs and enough success to become a much wealthier pack."

"It explains why they don't get along with the Gold Moon Clan..."

It probably came as a bitter surprise to the Gold Moon Clan, realizing they lost such an opportunity to a smaller Clan. I can see how different they actually are from the Sapphire Moon, as Neal said.

"That, and their constant fighting at the border. Anyway, those two hate each other, and I really don't see the White Moon Alpha betraying the Sapphire Moon," says Damian.

"The Opal Moon would be acting on its own, then?"

"Xavier Whitewood is known to be quite hot-headed. It is more likely than Clark Hamilton allying the Gold Moon Clan."

Elena actually said the exact same thing as Neal. That her Alpha was sometimes rash in his decisions, but the White Moon Alpha would never agree to him meeting with the Gold Moon. The problem is, this means the packs have already started shifting alliances.

"Taaron King and Alessandra trying to conceal the broken engagement is really working against our interests, right?"

Neal nods.

"Even if we work with the media, they still hold a great deal of power, enough to stop us. I'm afraid we won't be able to hold them back long enough to be able to stabilize things between the packs."

"So basically, their idea is to put as much pressure on the other Clans as they can until they start pestering Damian to marry that... woman, right?"

"Exactly."

"They won't agree to anything else?" I ask, desperate.

"Probably not, miss Nora."

A long silence follows. The situation does seem impossible... To think my relationship with Damian would make such a mess between all the packs! I try to think of something, but all I can gather are the cards already in my hands. The Jade Moon Clan, and my relationships with Elena and William Blue.

Maybe I already have the answers... I turn to Damian, but before I can say a thing, I see him frown and make his angry face. "No, Nora."

"You don't know what I'm about to say yet!"

"You want to meet with William Blue again."

Gosh... He is right. I sigh and get up to face him, arms crossed. I feel Neal watching with deep interest, but I try to ignore that detail.

"An alliance with the Sapphire Moon, Damian, think about it! The Pearl Moon isn't big enough to go through that financial crisis, but William's Clan can. I can negotiate with them, and Elena can help us talk with the White Moon Clan, too."

"First, your cousin can't move against her own Clan. Secondly, the Sapphire Moon Clan hates me and all of the Blood Moon Clan. And finally, there is no way I'm letting you go alone again."

"I wasn't alone!"

"Yes, and where is my brother now?"

He has a point... If only Liam could answer! Don't tell me something really happened to him?

I bite my lip. "What if... I got Liam back?"

"What do you mean?"

"If I can prove William will hand us Liam back safe and sound, will you trust I can negotiate with him?"

"Last time we talked about this idea, he mentioned an exchange. I am not giving you to them, Nora."

Here we go again with his possessive issue... This is really getting old. Not that I don't know the feeling, though. There is no way I would let him go meet with the Gold Moon Clan. However, William Blue is apparently my cousin, not my fiancé!

"I swear I will come back. With Liam."

"Nora, I said no!"

"Damian, they won't harm me! I don't see any other way to help!"

"Once again, there is no reason for you to meddle in this! You—"

"Enough!"

This is my first time growling at my mate, but this time, I am really irritated. Won't he let me take my own decisions for once? I use my Alpha voice, as he won't listen to me, otherwise, and I am done with watching from the sidelines. He doesn't want me acting behind his back, I get it, but there is no way he will keep me from acting at all.

I lean towards him and take his hand between mine. "Damian, don't tell me not to meddle. You are this city's Alpha and my mate. No matter what, I am to be the next Luna. This is my problem, too. I caused this, the moment I fell in love with you, the moment I decided I would mate with you. This is my city, and I will protect it from anyone who tries to mess with it. Werewolves, vampires, witches, I don't care. I'm an Alpha, your Luna, and no matter what, a wolf. Damian, you have to let me do this."

Once I'm done, he stares at me for some long minutes, and silence befalls on the room. I am done talking, but Moon Goddess, can't he say something? No matter what, I know I won't be able to go against him if Damian still says no!

He suddenly sighs and takes a strand of my hair to put it behind my ear.

"Moon Goddess, Nora, do you have any idea how much I love you right now?"

I can't hold back a smile. I know his voice when he is about to give up. I win, and I even get some more of his love. Damian closes his eyes to rest his head on the back of his chair. I glance sideways and catch Neal with a faint smile, too. Can the Beta forgive the Goldgate episode with this? I turn back to Damian, waiting for his answer.

"Fine, I will let you meet with Blue. But I want you to come back, and with Liam, too."

I nod and try to reach Liam with my wolf again. Why isn't he answering? This is quite worrying right now, and I have no idea how to fix this... Oh wait, maybe I do. I wake my wolf, and we try to look for William's inner wolf together. Is it easier because it is my kin? Like Elena, now that we've met, I can reach him almost instantly.

"Nora. An unexpected but pleasant surprise."

"Tell me Liam is all right. I haven't been able to—"

"Who is that?"

"Liam Black! The guy you came with me! Black hair, blue-grey eyes, my age! Don't play with me!"

"Oh, the little one... I wonder."

"What do you mean?"

"You tell me. That boy escaped our territory around midnight last night. Those Black Brothers are as annoying as ever..."

"Liam escaped? On his own?"

"Quite an achievement, and in such a spectacular manner..."

"What do you mean?"

"He literally made a door explode and fled the premises leaving twenty of my people sleeping like babies behind him. I'm still debating about being impressed or angry."

Moon Goddess, Liam, what did you do now? ...And how?

"Oh, right. He actually left the room full of butterflies. Is it supposed to be a joke?"

Wait... butterflies? I instinctively turn around to stare at the large blue butterfly, which is actually flying around me. Could it be that witch's doing? Did she help Liam escape from the Sapphire Moon Clan's territory? Why, and how? I mean, she even knew he was locked up there. Did she know because of this butterfly? And why would she help Liam Black? Is it another proof of our alliance, perhaps? I'm so confused, I stay speechless until Damian calls my name.

"Nora, what's wrong?"

He takes my hand, bringing me back to reality at the same time. I try to organize my thoughts, figuring how to explain all of this. Neal and Bobo are waiting to hear from me, too.

"Liam. He's already gone from the Sapphire Moon territory."

Damian frowns, surprised. "Did he contact you?"

"No... William Blue just told me."

I'm still probably not allowed to talk about the Witch to the Black family... I wish she would contact me again, so I would know what to say and what not! She stays in the shadows so far, and only seem to lend me a hand from time to time, like when she led me to William Blue and that missing piece of my past that was with him. That only comforts me with the idea that I have to work with the Sapphire Moon Clan.

"William, can we meet?"

"What would that be about?"

"The Gold Moon Clan. I'll help you settle your issues with them."

"That sounds promising... But on what basis? I have to remind you, I may acknowledge it myself, but we need proof you are indeed our Blue Moon Clan's Princess. Until then, you are only Black's woman."

"That I can prove. But we need to talk, in person, and on neutral ground."

"Alone?"

I take a breath in. This idea has been at the back of my mind for a while, and until recently, I didn't think this would be realistic, but... maybe now is the time to do something really unexpected.

"No, with a lot of people."

"Interesting..."

I turn to Damian and choose my words carefully. He probably guessed I was busy mind-linking William because he was waiting for me with his eyes going colder and colder. Now that my attention is back to him, that icy stare of his melts immediately.

"You don't want me meeting William alone, right?"

"Right..."

"Let's say I would invite a lot of people?"

Damian seems to catch on my attempt to bring my idea on the table right away, because he suddenly stands up to face me, looking wary.

"Who are you thinking about?" He asks.

I don't avoid his gaze, and answer looking at him eye-to-eye. I borrow some of my wolf's confidence for support because it's like I'm facing a wall right now. I take a deep breath.

"All our allies. The neutrals, too. I mean the Alphas, the packs. We can gather all of them, Damian, and let them know we won't go by the Gold Moon's rules."

He shakes his head. "Nora, you are too optimistic. Most of the Clans fear us or hate us. They—"

"Damian, you are the Werewolf King of this city! Even if you are ruling by fear right now, is it enough to keep the peace? Soon, that won't be enough anymore! So, use it before this war really breaks out. Call them, summon them. I can't take this whole game of alliances anymore. Street fighting and bickering is fine, but an all-out war between packs? This financial pressure or whatever it is, it has to stop! No matter what, there is only one Silver City!"

He stares at me, looking impressed, surprised, and undecided. I know this is totally unprecedented and risky, but we have to. No matter what, all those schemes between the packs can't go on anymore. He turns to Neal, still holding my hand.

"What do you say?"

His Beta takes his time to answer, looking just as surprised as my mate by my idea. After a while, he nods slowly.

"It would certainly be worth trying... It's never been done before, though. Also, we are headed toward a conflict with either the Gold Moon or the Sapphire Moon. In any case, the Blood Moon will be seen as the source of the problem unless we go... very public."

Damian stays silent for a while, and I'm really nervous. This would be a crazy, unprecedented, and perilous idea, but right now, I'm sure this is our best way of solving things. Or at least, to try to show our goodwill. I still remember Vince's anxiousness when Liam and Nate visited the pack, even if it was a dinner. He knew one step wrong, one word could end his Clan.

Maybe this is what a lot of packs will think. Damian is the Alpha King, and saying he is feared is quite an understatement. I am immune to his Alpha aura, but I am the only one, and Moon Goddess, I see it all too clearly whenever someone else is in the room. Even other Alphas respect him instantly. He is way too strong, which also explains why most of the other packs never meet him personally. His reputation is plenty enough. However, things are changing, and there is no way he can remain isolated anymore.

"All right... Let's try Nora's idea."

"Yes!"

I can't hide my joy and jump at Damian's neck, kissing him. He chuckles a bit and kisses my neck, pulling me to sit on his lap. Behind us, Neal clicks his tongue.

"Before engaging in your happy couple activities, can we talk about the details?"

I blush a little. That wasn't really serious of me, but oh well.

Damian growls at his Beta a bit, annoyed, but Neal is right. I try to regain my composure and think about this seriously.

"We'll have the meeting on neutral ground, somewhere no one will feel threatened."

"We could use the Silver Stadium. It's one of the most neutral spots, easy to access, and at the heart of the city," suggests Damian.

Neal and I nod. Good idea. Werewolves love sports, so everyone is used to going to the stadium to watch matches, and as he said, it doesn't belong to any turf. Every wolf can go there within an hour and exit it quickly if we leave all doors wide open. No one will feel trapped if they are outdoor, either.

"We can send invitations to everyone, even the smaller packs," I say. "I'll tell Vince will come, and he can convince the Pearl Moon Alpha, too. William already promised he would come, and Elena can talk the White Moon Alpha into it, too."

"Actually... There might be a more efficient way, miss Nora."

What is Neal thinking about? The Beta gives me a smile, which is kind of scary in his case.

"Miss Nora, how good have you gotten at using your Alpha voice?" He asks.

"Pretty fine, I guess? My wolf always responds, and I can use it whenever I want to mind-link any Alpha I know or Elena."

"Do you remember when you reached out to everyone?"

The battle against the vampires. Of course, I do. It wasn't on purpose at all, I was just totally panicking. Moreover, Elena told me I should not use it, it's... annoying for other werewolves. Bobo described it as having my voice buzzing into his head, like some forceful echo.

"Neal, I'm not sure if... "

"I think this would be a very efficient way to call out to everyone and introduce yourself at the same time."

"I am not going to mind-link all the werewolves of Silver City again just to tell them who I am!"

He remains silent. ...Really? No, I won't! I turn to Damian, but instead of being against it, my mate seems to consider Neal's idea.

"Damian, no!"

"Nora, that might be a good way to—"

"Startle or scare everyone! Damian, I may have this power, but it is annoying to others and forceful!"

"Didn't you say to use fear to convince them? What if they don't want to, or are too scared? A Luna's voice might be more convincing…"

I bite my lip. Damian has a point, but... I'm scared of people's reactions. I don't like the idea of being feared because I am a Royal, nor forcing people with my power. On the other hand, I do know this is important, we can't compromise at this point. If I reveal my lineage, it might really help Damian gather all the Clans together. William might even support this once I prove it. He did say he wanted me to join the Sapphire Moon if I really prove to be Queen Diane's granddaughter.

"All right... But I won't threaten anyone. Just use my Aura to reach out to everyone, okay?"

"You do it the way you want, my Love."

"Okay, so... The stadium?"

"The stadium, in three days. Each Alpha can bring fifty wolves at most. No weapons, but any form is okay," says Neal. "They have to come on foot; we will close all roads surrounding the stadium."

His professional attitude is back again, but it only makes me worry more. This is serious. It was my idea, but now I am kind of freaking out... Damian glances at Neal, and the Mura brothers leave us alone.

Once they're gone, Damian grabs me by the waist and makes me sit in front of him on his desk. His arms around me, he leans to put a kiss on my forehead. He looks at me in the eye with a solemn expression.

"Nora, once you do this, there is no coming back. Everyone will know who you are. You won't be hidden anymore— your identity will be out in the open."

I nod. I know. Isn't it ironic? Three months ago, I was no one. A girl hid in a basement, unaware of her own background. I had no idea I had a mate waiting for me, looking for me.

Look at me now.

I have friends, a mate, a job, and a future as a Luna waiting for me. I smile. This seems so unreal, and yet, I love it.

Damian frowns, confused by my happy expression. "What is it?"

"I'm just... I'm fine. Despite all this mess with the packs, the whole Witch issue, even Marcus... When I think about it, I'm happy, Damian, because you're here. All of you. You, Bobo, Elena, Liam, Nathaniel, Tonia... Months ago, I was always scared, I thought no one would save me. If I disappeared, it seemed like no one would care about it. Now, I know you're here with me, and I'm not scared of the future anymore;

even if Hell breaks loose, I will fight it with you. I want to fight. That's something I never thought of before. I never thought of fighting back. There was no reason for it."

I put my hands around his neck, looking into his mesmerizing silver eyes I love so much. I give him a quick peck on the lips, before continuing.

"Now I got tons of reasons. I want to find the truth about my mom, protect you and my friends. I want to know more about my cousin and get closer to her. I want to be a Luna for the Blood Moon wolves, one they can acknowledge. I want to be with you, have a future with you."

He slowly lets out a smile and kisses me too.

"I want this future, Nora. I waited for this future with you for ten years. I want it now."

I bite my lip. The word "future" seems to mean a whole lot of things now, in Damian's mouth. I smile and caress his hair. I want to know more about this.

"What kind of future do you want?" I ask.

He leans on my shoulder and starts kissing my neck.

"A future with you in it every day. Waking up by my girl's side, seeing your smile."

He gives me a kiss between each sentence, making me blush uncontrollably. Will I ever get immune to Damian being romantic like this? But the merciless Alpha Black keeps kissing me.

"I want to live with you. Find a nice place you'll like. I want to have a life together. I even want to fight with you sometimes, so we can reconcile. I want to see you love your job and cooking. I want to see you with our friends and be a Luna for others. I want to see you grow up, and I want to see you pregnant with our child."

Oh, my Goddess. I'm red as a cherry and push Damian back from my neck before I die from combustion. A baby! Why would he mention having kids now? Is he doing this on purpose? We barely started having sex together! He laughs at my confused and embarrassed expression.

"Damian, you want children?"

He nods. "Only yours. And not now. You're too young, and I'm not ready to be a father. But someday, yes. When we're ready."

Oh gosh... I get red again and hide my face in his shoulder. How can this man make me feel so... Moon Goddess, when did I ever gain the right to be this happy?

I take a deep breath, one, two, three times. When I open my eyes, I see my inner wolf, shining with confidence. Her snow-white fur, our sapphire-blue eyes. We can do this. We have to.

Chapter 14

"Hello, everyone.

My name is Nora Bluemoon. Until now, very few werewolves had any idea of my existence. I was born in the Gold Moon Clan and raised in the Jade Moon Clan, but my mother was originally from the Blue Moon Clan, a much older pack. If I'm able to mind-link all of you like this right now, it is thanks to her blood. My mother was a Royal, and so am I.

This is most likely the first time Silver City ever had a Royal, but I am only using this power because I need all of you to listen. Our city is threatened. It is serious, and nothing we will be able to fight if we keep acting separately. I am calling all of the Alphas, and all of the werewolf packs. As children of Moon Goddess, we need to stand together against what is coming. You all saw, heard, or took part in the fight against vampires a few weeks ago. It was a serious thing, and some lost their lives or friends. But that was only a beginning. Something much worse will come someday.

I know this won't be easy to listen to, but I am the future Luna of the Blood Moon Clan. My mate, Damian Black, and I are calling all werewolves today to join us in this fight. There will be no submitting, only alliances if you're willing to.

I ask of all Alphas to discuss this with their packs. Any pack can be represented. We do not care about how many you are, your wealth, or your strength. All we ask is for everyone to come unarmed and in small groups of fifty people maximum. We will all gather at the Silver Stadium in three days at dusk. No weapons, no vehicles. Wolf or human form doesn't matter, as long as we can communicate.

I promise this not a trap, only a way for all of you to be heard. I know a lot of you will be scared. But I promise the Blood Moon Clan means no harm in this. Only a chance for us to find the way out in a crisis. Thank you, and may the Moon Goddess bless all of you."

I stop and open my eyes. In front of me, everyone is frowning or nodding. We are in Damian's apartment, in the living room. They all heard my inner voice clearly. Elena smiles gently at me. She is sitting on a couch, Nathaniel standing behind her. I asked my cousin to be here as a guide, because I wasn't sure I could do it properly. We didn't tell Nathaniel about our relationship, just that we were friends for now. For some reason, she asked me not to tell anyone else about it for now.

Damian is facing me, and he was holding my hand the entire time. He gives me a smile.

"You did great, Nora."

A few steps behind him, Neal is massaging his temples.

"I have to admit, I didn't think you could really do it, but I guess this headache is my retribution for doubting you."

I laugh a bit. I feel sorry for the Betas and the others, as other than the Alphas, everyone probably didn't enjoy having my voice echoing in their head. After a few seconds, I'm submerged by voices.

"*Who was that? A Royal? Really?"*

"Blue Moon, what is that Clan? Who are you?"

"I heard it, too! I really heard her!"

"The Blood Moon Clan? Since when do they have a Royal?"

"How did you do this!"

"The Blood Moon Clan has gone mad!"

"What threat, anyway?"

"Who do you think you are, commanding us!"

I close my eyes and try to shut myself out. Gosh, I didn't expect to get all the answers at once... Guess the mind-linking opened way too many doors. Dozens of voices are using the link backward, and I need my wolf's help to shut them down.

"Nora, are you okay?" Asks Damian, concerned.

"Sorry... It's my head..."

He helps me sit down while I try to concentrate. My wolf is confused, and it takes me a while to shut the ones I don't know out, while only keeping the voices I do recognize.

"Long time no see, kid!"

"Grandpa Seaver?"

"*That's me! Great job, young lady. Anyway, we will be there. I would have said no to Black, but with you, that's a different story. I don't forget my debts. I still owe you for my daughter's life, so consider it done. The Sea Moon Clan will come."*

"Thank you!"

It might not be a big Clan, but I'm still happy to get at least one positive answer. When I'm about to tell Damian, I hear William's voice.

"So, you learned how to use your Royal voice. Impressive."

"Will you come?"

"I said I would, didn't I? But do not expect us to suddenly act friendly toward Black. We still have too many issues to settle..."

I bite my lip. I expected this, but I really hope this meeting won't turn into a big fight between all of the packs... I tell Damian and the others about at least two Clans coming. Meanwhile, Vince also confirms the Jade Moon will come, though a lot of them are concerned.

"We expect this, but this is how it always works between werewolves anyway, miss Nora. No matter what happens, you did what you had to. We know how risky this is," says Neal.

"Don't worry, baby girl. It's going to be okay. Even if only a few packs show up, it's plenty, okay? We just need to open up a dialogue," adds Tonia with a reassuring smile.

I nod. Honestly, I wish Liam were there. He probably would have said something to make me laugh and taken my anxiety away. Since the younger Black's disappearance, I feel uneasy. I don't know what happened to him or the witch. He was supposed to be the one to capture her! Why did she free him? I hope I was right to trust her...

"Anyway, we need to get ready. Three days is a very short time to get everything ready. Securing the stadium, informing the human police, and preparing the lieutenants won't be an easy job," says Neal.

He takes out his smartphone and gives orders very fast, though he already did as soon as I agreed to this. A real Beta's job, I imagine.

Damian gets up to talk to Tonia, and as he leaves me alone on the sofa, Bobo jumps on it to lie next to me. The giant wolf puts his head on my knee. I know he wants to comfort me, and I scratch his ear.

"A bit higher, please."

"Bobo! It's funny to hear your wolf voice!"

"You're the one who opened the link. But It's tough to maintain for me. Your wolf's too strong; it's like sending rocks in a waterfall."

"I don't care, you're the one always in your wolf form, it's hard to talk to you!"

"I can hear from you anytime."

I roll my eyes, annoyed.

"I mean, when you can actually answer."

"Daniel says the same thing..."

"See?"

"Can you keep scratching anyway?"

My gosh, is he a wolf or a dog?

Anyway, it's good to know I can talk to Bobo like this, but it's hard for me to concentrate on a single Beta's inner wolf. Damian, Tonia, and Neal leave for his office, but I guess this is not really something I should be concerned with. Instead, I get up and head to the small kitchen. At least he has what I need to make myself some tea...

When my cup is ready, I exit the kitchen to get back to Bobo. However, I hear voices before coming in. Nathaniel and Elena are having a heated conversation, and neither of them heard me. Unsure what to do, I stay at the door a few seconds and hear some of it.

"Talk to me! Elena, I can't go on like this!"

"I told you, I'm fine, Nate. Stop asking, please."

"I don't believe you! You've been avoiding me for days; I can't take it! Do you think I haven't noticed it? You're pale, you lost weight... Elena, are you sick?"

"What? No, I'm not, I swear, Nate. I'm fine, okay? I really am."

"Then why...?"

"I'll tell you later, okay?"

"Later? What later! Elena... When?"

"After the pack meeting. Once it's over, we can talk. I promise, but not now. It's not the right time, with all that is going on. Nate, please."

I hear him sigh.

"Okay, but... you have to stop avoiding me, please. ...I miss you."

My cousin whispers something I can't hear, and after a few seconds, I hear enough to know I can't come in now. I'm blushing, but I'm happy for my cousin... From what I just overheard, Nathaniel really does love her, right?

I feel a gentle push behind me. Bobo! So, he left the living room after all. I get to his level and sigh deeply while playing with my best friend's fur.

"Bobo, everything is going to be okay, right?"

"I got your back."

I smile, feeling a bit better. I'm about to suggest we go back to Damian and the others, when I hear someone running across the apartment. What is going on? Bobo and I both get to the entrance, and I almost run into Sean, who just barged in, panting.

"Sean? What is going?"

"Where's the Boss?"

"In his office, but what is it?"

"The rogues. A hell lot of them. They are gathering at the borders!" He yells while running to Damian's office.

Oh, crap. Why now...?

When I arrive, right behind Sean, Damian is already standing in front of the glass wall. I slowly walk to my mate, and he naturally puts an arm around my waist as I stand next to him. He probably already knows. I follow his stare, and indeed, he is looking at our borders.

Close to the East border, I see them. A large group of people and wolves. It's hard to tell from here, but... There should be about a hundred, two hundred people. What is going on? I have never seen so many rogues gathering...

"What are they doing?" I ask.

"For now, nothing. They all suddenly started gathering a few minutes ago, but now, they just stand at our borders. It's really weird, Boss. They are not doing anything," explains Sean.

Why then...? Is this a threat? But rogues don't usually wait, they just burst into territories and attack. They are not supposed to be organized at all, and never in such large groups. It doesn't seem normal at all... From here, they seem rather calm. I use the mind-link to reach Vince.

"Everything seems rather calm, but the scouts are looking out, Nora. They are a few meters away from our border. I think they are establishing some sort of camp."

"A camp?"

"Yeah. Actually, it seems like they have a few children among them, too."

Children? Families... Are those wolves really rogues? It feels more like... Strays.

"Nora? What are we supposed to do?"

"Nothing for now, but keep watching closely. Just let me know if there are any changes, and alert everyone if they show any sign of an attack."

As you wish.

For a while now, Vince has started behaving like this with me. Whatever I ask or order, he will do without discussion. Apparently, the whole pack is okay with that, too, though it is still all new to me. I feel like I'm a secondary Alpha to the Jade Moon Clan or something.

I turn to Damian, but he seems rather calm about this whole situation. Is he suspecting those are not rogues, as well? If not, the fact that they suddenly gathered...

"Do you think they came because of me?"

"We don't know how far your voice reached," simply says Damian.

"The calling of a Royal may have had a bigger impact than we thought..."

Neal's words scare me for a second. It's true, I never knew how this ability could work before, and obviously, I had no idea how far it would go. My only thought was to reach as many werewolves as I could, I didn't really figure how far. But to gather so many outside people? The question is... Why? These people are obviously not from Silver City, why would they suddenly come to my calling?

"Let them be," suddenly says Damian. "They will most likely move in three days. We will see, then. Just keep watching them and our other borders. We never know if that Witch might strike again."

"Got it, Boss. About the... other topic..."

Sean's eyes are going from me to Damian with a hesitating look. From his attitude, I can guess right away who this is about. I turn to Damian.

"You are still looking for Marcus?" I ask.

My mate just nods, his eyes turning colder than ice whenever that name is spoken. Sean shakes his head, looking annoyed.

"Apologies Luna, we haven't been able to find him yet. Our hunters are on the lookout, but the bastard is good at hiding."

It feels a bit unreal to hear him call me that... But after my words earlier, I guess that's a real thing for everyone now. Damian gently caresses my arm and leans in for a quick kiss on my forehead.

"He won't be able to approach you, anyway. He can only stay hidden until I can get rid of him..."

His angry voice makes Sean and Neal look down, but as usual, I'm unaffected by his Alpha aura. I just nod and sigh. If only this could be all over soon...

The next three days actually became quite busy for me.

I go to work as usual, but as soon as I get home, Neal takes me for what he thinks are necessary lessons for the future Luna. Mostly, it is about Silver City's History, the complex relationships between the Clans, territories, and the basics of the economy and businesses. For me, who has never even been to school and is only self-educated, it is really tiring. I am willing to learn, but Neal is a severe teacher, and we didn't have much time for me to know enough before the gathering. We only finish really late at night, when Damian comes home from work and basically chases him out.

However, I start living with Damian during that time, and I love it. Everything I possess is promptly moved to his apartment, and once he gave me a bit of space in his wardrobe, that was it. I really never possessed much, anyway, except for what he had bought me, and my birthday presents, so...

Even if we couldn't be together by day, my mate wouldn't let me go every minute of the nights we shared together. Any worry I had melted like snow under the sun as long I was in Damian's arms.

But the nights were way too short. When the sunrise hit me on the third day, I woke up with my heart filled with nervousness. I was alone in bed, but I could hear the shower running. Waiting for Damian to come back, I lie there, watching the sunrise with pink and orange shades over Silver City. My city.

Within those few days, the feeling of being a Luna became more and more real to me. In the lieutenants and Betas' behavior, they made it clear they already saw me as such. Even at the restaurant, almost every werewolf staff member's attitude changed towards me. I guess it must be a bit unusual to see the Luna washing dishes and taking orders...

I feel fingers caressing my arm, and Damian's lips on my shoulder.

"Good morning, my Love."

I chuckle and turn around to give him a long, deep kiss. This has gotten so natural between us now... I put my hands around his neck and enjoy the taste of his lips. Damian's beard is exactly the length I love, a bit scratchy against my skin. He looks older and more serious, but I like that. We keep kissing, and I don't want to let go. My mate groans.

"Nora... We need to go..."

I don't care, I want him now. I keep kissing him playfully and manage to take off his shirt he just put on. Damian laughs and starts attacking my neck, his hands reaching for my underwear. I smile because I know it's my win. I feel my mate already excited above me, and as usual, he catches my hand to intertwine our fingers together. I feel his member against my thigh, and my body temperature rises immediately. His fingers reach for my most vulnerable part and start caressing me, making me feel good. I start breathing harder.

How did we get used to each other's bodies so quickly? I don't know, but gosh, this is the best feeling in the world when Damian finally enters me. I give out a sound my voice couldn't possibly make otherwise, and my mate kisses me passionately. We start moving, the oldest dance in the world. I reach for his skin's warmth, ask for more kisses, and let out my voice as I please. Damian's gentle, yet passionate. I relax under him, indulging in that pleasure as he keeps going. I love his erratic breathing against my ear. His voice makes me crazy, and I close my eyes to concentrate on those sensations. He accelerates, and I can't hold it in when it overtakes me. A wave of heat and pleasure, hitting me, blowing me away. Damian joins me, too, and groans loudly.

We both calm down, catching our breath. My mate puts his head in my shoulder and kisses my bare skin before letting out a sigh.

"Damn, Nora, you really make me crazy..."

I chuckle. Who knows how long Neal will scold him for being late...? As an apology, I kiss him on the corner of his lips.

"I know. But you love it, and I love it, too."

"You do?"

This time, it's his turn to give me a sneaky glance. Stop teasing me like this! I blush a bit and try to grab my panties, but Damian catches my hand first.

"Damian! Enough, I need to dress up, too!"

"Oh no, you need a shower!"

Without warning, he suddenly puts me over his shoulder. What is he...? Moon Goddess, why is he getting up, I'm totally naked! I try to protest, but he gets up and carries me like a potato sack to the bathroom. I can't believe him! He is still laughing when I finally chase him out of the bathroom to shower. Gosh, I know I started it, but still!

I take my time to shower, washing my hair and all, and when I exit, wrapped in my bath towel, I'm surprised to find a full outfit ready for me on the bed, brand new. I check it. A white woolen dress, a black leather belt, and laced booties?

"Tonia prepared it for you. She thought you might want something Luna-like..."

In her mind, it must have meant expensive! Though I have to admit, the dress looks gorgeous and very chic, with the back open and a lot of embroideries. I try it on, and indeed, I look very... respectable and pure in this. I definitely get a princess vibe from the long skirt, too. When I add the belt, I notice there are actually shiny stones embroidered in it, matching my diamond necklace. I add one of my pairs of black tights, and Damian helps me put my hair up with a hairpin.

My mate is already all dressed up, with his usual jet-black suit. I pick a black silk necktie and put it on him, as he taught me, and finish with a quick kiss on his lips.

"Ready?" He asks.

I nod. "Ready."

He takes my hand, and we exit his apartment. We meet Bobo and Neal downstairs and take the elevator to go a few stairs down. It's still early, but the Blood Moon lieutenants are gathered in the meeting room. I recognize Sean, Vane, Thaddeus, and Joshua, as well as Isaac, Nathaniel's Beta, among the people present. When we enter, they all bow, but this time, it's not just to Damian, but to me, as well. Wow, this is definitely new...

Sadly, the youngest Black Brother is still absent. We still haven't heard from Liam at all, and everyone is starting to get nervous about it. According to Tonia, he's never gone missing for so long, it's getting serious. Yesterday, Damian sent scouts looking for him, and we tried mind-linking him again without success. I even tried asking the witch's butterfly, still hanging around me, but nothing happened. Could something have happened to him? I almost told Damian about the Witch yesterday. Still, even if I did, I'm not even sure she had anything to do with him escaping the Sapphire Moon Clan...

Damian faces the whole group, and everyone listens in total silence as Neal starts talking.

"So far, the following Clans responded positively to the Invitation: The Jade Moon, the Pearl Moon, the White Moon, and the Sea Moon Clans. If we add the Sapphire Moon Clan, that makes a total of five

Clans, two hundred and fifty people. Seven smaller packs also announced they would show up: The Ruby Moon, the Flower Moon, the Asphodel Moon, the Lotus Moon, the Ivy Moon, the Twilight Moon, and the Winter Moon packs."

So many? I don't know how many small packs Silver City has, but seven seems already like a lot, though this is my first time hearing those names.

"They're not big?" Asks Vane.

"Not really. About thirty to fifty adults, at most. Most of them only have a couple of properties or businesses," explains Thaddeus.

"Not that important..." Says a guy I don't recognize.

"Any pack that is willing to come is important," I say. "Any willing werewolves will be welcome, regardless of their wealth or strength."

The guy looks down and apologizes right away for his words. Neal resumes talking about the security measures this time. I notice Nathaniel is absent, too. Why isn't he here? I ask Damian, but my mate shakes his head. Where could he be? I feel some fur against my leg.

"Bobo, do you know where Nathaniel is?"

"With Elena. He knows... about the baby."

Gosh, so she finally told him? Why now? I hope it goes well...

The rest of the day is spent talking about security measures, emergency situations, and how to organize the gathering. Everyone is getting tenser by the hour, including Damian. Neither of his brothers shows up, and soon, it's the end of the afternoon and time to go...

Black cars are all lined up outside of the building, and Damian and I take the second one, with Vane driving us. A lot of the lieutenants shape-shifted to follow us in their wolf forms— the others are going by car or motorbikes. It's really intimidating to be moving along such a vast group. Damian doesn't let go of my hand a single second. As agreed, only fifty of the Blood Moon Clan members are going, and Isaac left us about an hour earlier to meet with Nathaniel.

It takes half an hour to get to the stadium, and we left only a little before sundown. I try to reach out to Liam again, without success. I really hope he is okay...

When we arrive, Vane parks away from the gathering point, and we start walking towards the stadium, followed by fifty men and wolves altogether. To my surprise, the Jade Moon Clan, led by Vince, appears as soon as we approach. They only give me a quick bow of respect and move along.

As we get closer to the stadium, my nervousness rises. Not only that, but I also hear a great hubbub, coming from a large crowd. How many people came? I knew a few Clans were willing to come, but... It's still early, and I hear a lot of voices.

For the occasion, all fourth gates are wide open, allowing us to walk into the stadium easily. When Damian and I finally come in, I can barely believe my eyes. This is such a large crowd!

Did Neal say we should expect a few hundred? More like a few thousand! The stadium's benches are literally full of people! With the Blood Moon and Jade Moon packs arrival, a hundred more people add to the number. Despite the number, it is quite organized, though. Each pack stays as a group, sitting together and keeping their distances from the others. This way, it is easier to differentiate the bigger packs, with their leaders in front of them, from the smaller ones. Still, I have never seen so many werewolves gathered in one place. It is both impressive and scary.

Even with my Alpha features, I can feel the tension in the air. A lot of it. Everyone is eyeing each other. Those who haven't shape-shifted are ready to jump into their werewolf form at any moment. Moon Goddess, can this really go well?

Our arrival is actually the main point of focus for most of the people present. I have never felt so many eyes on me, and if it wasn't for Damian holding my hand tightly, I would be petrified. However, I can tell they are eyeing the both of us. No one can look at Damian directly in the eye. However, people are still intrigued by the Alpha King, who only rarely appears in public. Whispers come from all around, but Damian is perfectly indecipherable. His stone-cold expression, dark allure, and tall stature are enough to impress. Still, most of all, his Alpha aura is radiating, intimidating everyone around us.

"So that's him..."

"Is that the Luna who contacted us? She looks like a child!"

"He really looks like his father..."

"Hey, don't stare. Show some respect."

"I've never seen that girl before! The Jade Moon, she said?"

"You really think she is a Royal then?"

"I was wondering if they would really come..."

"He is really marked? What about the Gold Moon daughter, then?"

As we walk toward the center of the stadium, where a large stage has been installed, I look around, trying to find out which packs actually came. I notice Nathaniel, standing with Isaac on one side. What's wrong with him? He seems impassive, but I can tell he seems... annoyed? His eyes look a lot like Damian's when he is unhappy. Is it about the meeting? I hope this has nothing to do with his conversation with Elena earlier. I try to look around, but I don't see my cousin anywhere. Is the White Moon Clan there, as promised? Suddenly, I catch Marina and Grandpa Seaver's eyes, in front of the Sea Moon Clan. They both salute me in a very discreet but respectful gesture.

Next to them, to my surprise, is Lysandra Jones. So, the Purple Moon Clan came, too! Moreover, the other pack on their left must be her father's, the Violet Moon Clan. The man in front looks a lot like her, with his dark skin and amber eyes. His name is Andrew Jones, Neal mentioned him during our lessons.

I don't recognize any other group, though. But a lot of them are smaller, meaning they are smaller packs like the ones Neal mentioned earlier. But as I try counting, I found there are roughly twenty-five different groups around us. Even if not all of them brought fifty members, it's still a lot of people... A lot more than we expected. And the number keeps growing with the arrival of other groups behind us. I notice no one from William's Clan is here yet, but we still have time.

Damian helps me up to the stage, and we are now literally standing at the center.

This is... impressive. Hundreds of pairs of eyes are on us. I don't feel as intimidated as I thought I would, though. My wolf feels confident enough, especially with her pair right by her side.

"This is great, Boss. A lot more people than we thought come," says Neal.

"They are wary of us, though. Most of those wolves are warriors..."

They look at me, surprised. This is a bit new, but my wolf is observing our surroundings, and can quickly find which wolves are actually warriors or not. I can't say I'm surprised, though. With the Blood Moon Clan's reputation, we shouldn't have expected people to react any differently. Its obvious people are here to hear what we have to say, but do not trust us for a second.

The sun slowly comes down, and everyone awaits. There isn't as much noise as people lowered the chattering to listen to what the Alphas have to say. All of the leaders are standing in front of their packs, within a reasonable distance from each other.

I only recognize a few of them for now, but it doesn't really matter. Suddenly, I see Sean running to us.

"The rogues, they started moving."

"Nora, the sentinels said the rogues are coming."

I get the information from two sides, and I answer both out loud and through the mind-link, so they can know what's going on.

"Vince, what are they doing?"

"Just walking, they are not menacing. ...One of them asked to talk to us."

Next to me, Damian is frowning, listening to this with concern.

"Nora, he wants to talk to you."

I give Vince my phone number, and within a minute, I get a call from an unknown number. I put it on speaker for Damian to hear.

"Respects, Luna."

"Hello. Who am I talking to?"

"My name is Ryan. I represent all of us who came. We all heard your call, so we came looking for the Luna."

"...Where are you from?"

"The Western territories, but we were chased out by a Witch. First, she sent vampires to weaken us, then she poisoned all our water and food until we had no choice but to leave our home. There is nothing left back there, so we became strays looking for a new place to settle in. When we heard there was a Royal, we had to come. We encountered a few rogues on our way here, Luna, and we only have this many fighters. We have families, children. We are seeking Asylum."

The Witch. So, she came from the West. Not only that, but she already used the very same pattern somewhere else. This is serious. But that could also be an opportunity for us.

"You are one whole Clan?" Asks Damian.

"Yes. We are called the Steel Moon Clan. There are about two hundred of us. When we heard the Luna's call, that there were many packs assembled in one city, we thought that might be our chance to start over."

I exchange a look with Damian, but we already are thinking the same thing. My mate nods, giving me what I need.

"I give you permission to enter our grounds. Leave your pack outside the Jade Moon territory and gather fifty people at most to join us."

"Thank you, Luna!"

I hang up and leave Vince's men to deal with them.

Next to us, Neal is nodding slowly. "For now, this is fine. That way, we will have witnesses about the Witch's threat."

"But this might be an issue later, right?"

I understand right away. Even if we choose to welcome this new pack for now, there will be another issue sooner or later: We don't have any empty territory for a new Clan, especially such a large one.

"...That was an interesting display of generosity."

I turn around, and a man I've never met before is facing us. He is tall, with completely white hair, despite looking in his forties. He has a very clean-shaven beard and is wearing an elegant dark blue suit. Very politely, he bows slightly to Damian and me.

"Pleased to meet you. I am Clark Hamilton."

The White Moon Clan's Alpha! I was wondering if they were coming at all. William did say he would try to convince them. Does he know about the Opal Moon, their branch Clan, meeting with Taaron King? And more importantly, is he really on William's side?

We introduce each other, both parties staying extremely polite and expressionless before he leaves us to take his pack into an empty spot of the stadium. Right after him, William Blue comes in, followed by fifty people from the Sapphire Moon Clan. Gosh, I hope he and Damian can stay respectful toward each other...

He addresses me first. "Hello, Nora. How have you been?"

While he asks, his eyes are on the marking on my neck, but I act like I don't notice.

"I've been fine, thank you. How about you?"

"Well, I did have a couple of fights with my father about coming here. But after all, I do happen to have a few things to say, too..."

I really don't like the way he says that while glaring at Damian. What does he have to say? I'm afraid things will get ugly if those two argue. Damian doesn't say a word despite William's stares. His ice-cold silver eyes are just glaring all their might at my cousin, and his arm tightens slightly around my waist.

Those two look ready to jump at each other's throats. How are we supposed to negotiate alliances like this? Thank Moon Goddess, William soon leaves to go back to his pack.

When it's finally time, every wolf or man stands up. All the Alphas are in front of the packs, on the grass, all around us. There are a few empty spots, but from Neal's estimation, we have gathered over ten thousand people... Damian and I exchange a glance, and I step forward to address all of them.

"Thank you all for coming. I am Nora Bluemoon, who called you here today. Most of you probably came with a lot of questions in mind about that threat I mentioned. As I already said before, the vampire attack was only a beginning. Silver City is about to face someone much more dangerous: A Witch."

Right after my words, a lot of people start talking. This comes as a shock for most people, and I hear a lot of questioning in the ranks. They've faced vampires before, but a Dark Witch?

"How do we need this was really a Witch's doing?" Ask someone. "We only saw vampires in that attack."

"Something was definitely off about this attack. Any nearby water source attacked us," states Clark, the White Moon Alpha. "Some of my guys died from poisoning, not from their injuries."

"At least four packs witnessed it," says Nathaniel. "And we may have not had any Witch around for a while, but we do know how they work."

"That's right. Witches can subjugate other species and use their elements. Trust me, I've lived long enough to see a couple," adds old man Seaver. "A Water Witch, that's what we were facing!"

A lot of people nod in agreement. Grandpa Seaver may not be from a big pack, but he is well-respected.

"So what? Even if there is a Witch, who says she will attack again? We gave those vampires a hard time..." Says an Alpha with a strong accent.

"Great idea, Gregorovitch. Let's stay on our lazy asses in case nothing happens!" Scoffs Lysandra.

The man doesn't let the insult go, and both packs start growling at each other. Damian and I growl too to have them stop.

"Enough!" I yell. "We came to talk, not to fight!"

The man named Gregorovitch turns to me, looking annoyed. He points the finger at me with a disdainful look.

"Why should we believe you? You may call yourself a Royal, but who says you are? What proof do you have?"

Almost immediately, not only Damian starts growling furiously at him, but the whole Blood Moon Clan, too. I try to calm Damian down, but to my surprise, the next one to speak is William.

From where he is, my cousin turns his head toward the man who spoke with his eastern accent, looking even more cynical.

"Do you think anyone can summon so many packs like this? Are you able to mind-link other Alphas as you please, too? Anyone here who has seen Nora Bluemoon shapeshift into her white wolf form, with blue eyes, knows she is a blessed child of Moon Goddess."

The Alpha named Gregorovitch seems a bit reluctant to believe William. Still, he doesn't dare talk back and just crosses his arms. I was afraid we would lose time tracking my family history to prove myself capable, but William stepping in certainly helped. However, we need to resume to our main topic.

"As I said, a Witch is threatening Silver City. A Water Witch, according to Alpha Seaver and the White Moon Clan. She will attack again, but we can't know where and when. In any case, it will be a bigger blow, and we won't be able to handle it if we are not prepared for it."

People start talking between themselves again after my words, and mostly they seem concerned or anxious. Some are still staring at Damian and me with suspicion in their eyes, but at least they heard us. I turn to my mate, but before I say a word, Sean runs to us.

"Boss, Luna, they are here. The ro— I mean, the Steel Moon Clan."

"Let them in," orders Damian.

Soon enough, fifty members of the Steel Moon clan enters, agitating all the other packs present. The arrival of a different and unknown Clan raises a lot of suspicions, and I hear people calling them strays, protesting against their presence here.

"Who are those people?" Asks Lysandra.

"Strangers. Another Clan, chased from their land by the same Dark Witch that is now targeting us," I explain. "We called them here as witnesses."

I turn to the man who came forth, probably Ryan, the man I heard on the phone. He bows in a very respectful manner to Damian and me, all of the people behind him doing the same. Gosh, those people do look exhausted... A lot of them are quite thin, and some even have visible, fresh scars and injuries. I show him the crowd, and he nods, understanding what I'm asking of him.

Once again, he addressed to everyone present, telling them their story, in more details. How the Witch first sent vampires, killing almost half of their pack, then poisoned them little by little until they had no choice but to leave. With all the packs listening, he made sure to be as detailed as possible, and by the time he was done, most of the audience appeared to be shocked, some even look sorry for them. All the Alphas stayed silent, listening to him with deep concern.

"We heard the Luna's calling, and thought this might be our last chance at settling somewhere decent. Our pack is only a third of what it used to be, and our people are exhausted. We don't have any wealth left, only our people. But we would be more than happy to help you fend off that wretched Witch if we can," finishes Ryan.

"Why did the Witch target you?" Asks Andrew Jones.

"We still have no idea. We only saw her from afar. But anyone she killed, she kept their corpses. We couldn't even bury our people as we kept losing them to her."

Oh, Moon Goddess, she kept the bodies? I exchange a look with Damian. Why would she take dead werewolves' bodies for? My man just looks as confused as I am, and so does Neal. On the side, Nathaniel looks at a loss, too. This is too scary and disgusting to think about! Behind Ryan, a few of his people can't hold their tears. I can't even begin to imagine the nightmare they went through. Even the Alphas present seem truly sorry for them.

"May Moon Goddess protect her children and save their souls," says Tiffany Pearl.

I didn't see the Pearl Moon Clan Alpha arriving. But I recognize their Alpha instantly, she is one of the most beautiful women in Silver City. From what I've seen of her previously, Tiffany is not only pretty, she's also extremely smart. If she could be on our side, it might be easier to convince others...

"Princess, while gathering us all, you mentioned a plan against that Witch?" She asks, looking directly at me.

I feel a bit awkward being called that, but this is not the time to be embarrassed. Especially since I feel she is giving me more legitimacy this way.

"That's right. Most of you know that last time, we survived because a few packs helped each other. The White Moon Clan was supported by the Blood Moon and Blood Moon, and the Purple Moon helped the Sea Moon Clan, too."

I notice Andrew Jones gives a glare at his daughter, but Lysandra ignores him. Grandpa Seaver is nodding. Meanwhile, Clark Hamilton, the White Moon Alpha, gives a glance towards Nathaniel.

"This wasn't part of any alliance, yet they helped each other because they knew everyone's safety was at stake. I know some of you already have alliances, new or old. What I want to ask you all today, is to consider a global alliance. All of the packs present, working together against whatever that Witch will throw at us."

Immediately, a hubbub of shouting and talking raises from the benches, despite the Alphas attempts to moderate their own packs. From what I can hear, most of them are already against it. Why would they help other packs they have fought with countless times before? Why should they help smaller packs? My wolf is annoyed at all the jabbering, and so am I.

Suddenly, after a while of all the Alphas trying to calm them down, Damian lets out the most terrifying growl, and all the attention is on him once again. As if his Alpha aura had suddenly exploded in the middle of the stadium, the benches suddenly go totally silent again. Some people even fell from their seats or retreated by instinct.

My mate is so close to shape-shifting, his pupils turned black like an animal, and his teeth grew longer. He isn't the King of Silver City for nothing. I can tell a lot of the people present are totally scared, but I don't care if that's what it takes for them to listen. For a while, the whole stadium goes as silent as a cemetery as everyone calms down.

"...Why should we accept an alliance?" Asks a female Alpha. "We have been fine on our own so far, and the other Clans never lifted a finger to help while we were in trouble!"

"I know this won't be easy. Many of the packs here are used to cohabitating with others but also being on your own. However, if we act separately next time, we might all lose everything. If each pack only sticks to defending their own territory, the Witch will wipe us all one by one. You heard the Steel Moon Alpha. They were such a big pack, yet they couldn't do anything against her. Even our biggest Clans won't be able to act on their own this time," I explain.

"That's easy to say for you. But allying with the Blood Moon Clan?

Do you know how crazy that sounds?" Says another Alpha.

Damian stares at that man, who seems to shrink under his glare, and for the first time, addresses the crowd. "I know many of you still have in mind the crimes committed by my father. You all referred to him as the Mad King, and he deserved it. I am not him. I haven't sought to expand my territory, nor have I attacked other packs before. Most of you see my face for the first time today. Why would I go ahead and betray you now?"

"What about your alliance with the Gold Moon Clan, then? We are all aware of the financing issue that is going on. They have been closing off the banks, cutting us from our funds, and threatening us to use your very own name when we rebelled. Are you telling us you haven't been pressuring the other Clans through them?" Asks the Asphodel Moon Alpha.

"That's right. Was this a way to ensure we would obey to you today? Isn't it a bit too much to ask for alliances when you are using another Clan to threaten us on the sidelines?" Asks someone from the Lotus Moon Clan.

I knew the Gold Moon Clan issue would come back sooner or later... And everyone really thinks Damian is still allied with them. On the side, I spot William smiling. He was obviously waiting for this topic to come up.

Damian stays very calm and addresses everyone. "The Gold Moon Clan has been using my name to act on their own. The engagement is not real anymore, nor is our alliance with them. I know the rumors, but the Blood Moon Clan has had nothing to do with them ever since Nora had me cancel it."

Me? He is making it look like I forced him to do it! Well, I did make him choose between Alessandra and me, but still!

"I am now addressing you all as the King of Silver City. I took over a position my father didn't deserve because I had to. Our pack needed a new Alpha, and I became that man. Killing him also gave me the position as the King, with an even bigger Clan than the one my father led. I am the strongest werewolf; I am the King Alpha. Yet, I am mostly the Blood Moon Clan's Alpha. I haven't acted any differently since the Blood Moon Clan rose. I am not looking to submit anyone, but as Nora said, to find allies. Enough to protect Silver City. My brothers and I won't be able to do it on our own."

"you are only trying to raise an army!"

Everyone turns their heads to see who yelled that. Oh, Moon Goddess. Walking towards us is Alessandra King and her father.

The Gold Moon Clan just arrived.

As soon as I see that woman, my wolf and I want to attack her. How the hell does she dare to come here with that smirk on her face! Neal holds me back, a hand on my arm. He does well because otherwise, I might seriously go for her throat this time. In front of me, Bobo is growling like crazy, too.

Damian is glaring all his might at them, and they have no choice but to look down as they approach. Yet that doesn't stop the Gold Moon Alpha, who ignores him to address the rest of the packs.

"Do you really believe this would be an innocent alliance? Damian Black is here to have you submit to him!"

All the Alphas look at each other. Some seem surprised or confused, but others, like Grandpa Seaver or Lysandra, are obviously exasperated by his words. Tiffany Pearl and Vince are glaring at the Gold Moon Alpha.

"You have guts to show yourself, Taaron. After the mess your people put us into," says a man I believe to be the Celtic Moon Alpha. "Half of my businesses are about to go bankrupt because of you!"

Taaron King is a small man, with the exact brown hair as his daughter, and tiny black eyes. He is wearing an oversized coat and a golden chain that both look too big for his size, walking confidently like he owns the place. A trait Alessandra inherited from him, apparently... I glare at those two, like half of the people present in the stadium. Ryan and the rest of his pack look lost at what is going on, but they still positioned themselves between the Gold Moon Clan and us.

"Do you believe me to be responsible for this? You all know Damian Black is the King in this city; all I did was obey him! I did tell him, cutting off any funds to the other packs would be a bad idea, but who am I to oppose him?" Says Taaron with a pitiful voice.

How can he lie so blatantly? Don't tell me people are going to believe that? I should tear off this snake's tongue! A lot of werewolves are now looking at Damian with dubious or angry eyes. They can't believe this nonsense! He is so obviously lying! Before I can find any words, Alessandra starts talking, too, trying to act like a victim.

"My fiancé made use of our relationship as soon as he could. He said we should act quickly to prevent the packs from moving their money somewhere else, like the Sapphire Moon Clan he hates so much. This way, everyone would promptly consent to this alliance."

I'm going to spit blood if this bitch says another word!

"How dare you! Damian broke off his relationship with the Gold Moon Clan weeks ago!" I yell.

She turns towards me, but my wolf is standing on all fours and growling furiously, she can't even meet me in the eye. Instead, she pretends to look a little lower. "We held our engagement party not two weeks ago. Why would it make any sense for him to have broken if off now?" Says Alessandra.

"Because I am his Luna, you bitch!"

Alessandra laughs at me. Moon Goddess, if it wasn't for Neal holding me back, I would kill that woman. How dare she!

"You are no one! Suddenly, a little girl comes out of nowhere, claiming to be a Royal, and you become his Luna overnight? Who will believe that? Isn't it obvious he just picked someone to play the part and give him more power? I couldn't have pulled the Royal pretense off!"

"She really is a Royal, we saw her shapeshift," says Clark Hamilton. "They cannot fake the marking either."

Alessandra glares at him. "Royals mean nothing. They have been extinct for ages! Who cares about the Royals, anyway? It's all about wealth nowadays, and the Blood Moon Clan made sure to have both!"

William's pack starts growling furiously, as they hate for anyone to show disrespect to the Royals. Clearly, the Gold Moon Clan did not expect that from them. Both packs start yelling and growling at each other, but Damian silences them with a growl.

Then, he turns to Taaron King and addresses him with his deadliest glare. "I never asked you to put an embargo on any Clan, and our business relationship ended two weeks ago, as Nora stated. This gathering was my mate's attempt to protect all of Silver City, not for me to submit anyone."

"Really? Isn't it what you are doing right now?" Asks Taaron, without lifting his eyes.

"He is teaching you to show some respect, you damn mutt..." Growls Lysandra.

I see her father tell her to shut it silently, but she ignores him. So, the Purple Moon Clan also has a feud with the Gold Moon. Next to her,

I catch Clark Hamilton and William exchanging glances, too. I wish I knew what my cousin is thinking, but for now, I really have to shut those liars up if I want to have a chance at unifying the Clans.

"You are just spouting nonsense, King. Is that all you came for? What's your aim?" Growls Damian.

So many wolves from the different Clans are growling, that he has to speak louder and use his Alpha aura. King and his daughter are avoiding eye contact with Damian and gaze at the audience instead.

"I don't have any wrong ambition aside from enlightening our fellow citizens about your actions, Damian Black. A Witch's attack? Vampires? Why should we believe that?"

"Are you deaf? We witnessed it ourselves!" Yells Marina Seaver.

Taaron King shrugs. "What you saw were vampires. There isn't any proof anyone witnessed a Witch, or that those vampires will come back! Who can tell if this wasn't a one-time thing? Are you all willing to surrender to the Blood Moon out of fear? Black is just using this as an excuse to have you all submit to him!"

"We are seeking alliances, not a submission!" I growl.

"Isn't it the same? The Blood Moon Clan is too powerful! Any smaller pack will have to obey you once they accept this alliance! They might as well surrender their territories and wealth right now! Is there any Alpha here would believe they will be able to oppose any command from the Alpha King, Damian Black?" Asks Taaron King.

All around, despite the hostile faces, no one says a word. Of course, Damian is the strongest werewolf miles around. Now he is making this look like it's all a conspiracy!

"You're wrong," I say. "We will not submit the other wolves..."

"Why seek a stronger Luna, then? If you really are a Royal, as everyone here believes? Aren't you only another tool to make him powerful? No wonder he changed his mind and left my daughter!"

This time, Alessandra glares at her father. It seems like she didn't appreciate that reminder.

In the sidelines, I hear Andrew Jones click his tongue. "So, he did leave the King daughter..."

"No wonder," laughs Tiffany. "Isn't it obvious that miss Nora is a better Luna? That woman can't even hide her nasty jealousy."

Alessandra is red with embarrassment, serves her just right!

"A man with the most power, the biggest territory," her father continues, "and a powerful Luna. And now, not only that, but he brings an army here?"

While talking, he is pointing at Ryan's group. Seriously? He is even using the Steel Moon Clan now?

Ryan growls, outraged. "We only answered the Luna's call!"

"Oh, really? How convenient is it that a full pack showed up right before this gathering? How many did you say you were? Strange, isn't it? How Damian Black seems to be gathering more and more people?"

"We are refugees! The Luna spoke to us for the first time not even an hour ago!"

"And what right did she have to let you in Silver City, hm? Did Nora Bluemoon ask other packs while letting you in? The Blood Moon Pack is in the middle of Silver City, so which territory did you cross on your way here?" Asks Taaron.

"They crossed the Jade Moon Clan territory. Nora was raised in our pack, and she has every right to say who can come in or not!" Growls Vince.

Taaron King seems a bit surprised by Vince's reaction. The Gold Moon Clan probably had no idea of my ties with the Jade Moon Clan or did not expect it would still be relevant. But since Vincent submitted to me, I don't believe he would oppose me in anything.

However, King just decides to ignore Vincent's words. "Anyway, they did bring an extra pack here. Isn't it too much? Asking other packs to bring only fifty people, and bringing more wolves on their own?"

"Where did you go to school, King?" Asks the Asphodel Moon Alpha. "There's only fifty wolves of the Blood Moon here."

"You don't believe me? The Jade Moon Clan is backing off their Luna! If I add this new pack, they found who knows where, doesn't that seem a lot already? Who knows how many more Clans here are already on their side?"

Suddenly, people start muttering. I see William Jones and Lysandra argue, too, and now even Clark Hamilton is watching our group with suspicion. This can't be happening!

"We allowed any official pack to come! Every Clan here knows there are already alliances ongoing, don't you? All we ask for is to unite bigger!" I claim, trying to convince everyone.

"So, you admit it! You are already seeking to grow an army inside Silver City! And what of those who don't go along with your plan then?

Aren't you going to use brute force to submit them? Or will you leave them to die once this Witch attacks?"

"Enough!"

I've had enough of this! I used my wolf's Alpha Voice, silencing everyone. Taaron King just crossed a line there, and I won't tolerate it. Stepping away from Damian's grasp, I step forward. The whole Gold Moon Clan actually retreats a few steps back right away.

"I've had enough of you accusing my mate! We gathered everyone here to seek alliances against a threat that could be the end of all of us! Yet you come here, acting like you know anything! Where were you when the vampires attacked? Only defending your own territory! Now, you dare to say Damian manipulated anyone? You are the one playing around with business deals and finances until the packs can't take it anymore! You act like you own everything and use his name to get what you want! Alessandra comes uninvited to the Blood Moon territory, to the Sapphire Moon territory, and you dare to accuse me of inviting people in? At least I know where my place is!" I yell.

Taaron King look like he lost a few more inches under my Alpha voice and my wolf's growling, but Moon Goddess, I needed to put it out. In the assistance, I see William and Tiffany smiling, and Lysandra even applauds loudly.

After hearing me, some of the crowd seems confused, not knowing who to believe. I see Clark Hamilton exchanging glances with William, and Andrew Jones isn't showing any expression at all. Some of the smaller pack Alphas are glaring at Taaron King, but others are also giving Damian suspicious glances, too.

"Anyway," says Alessandra, "we will never agree to this alliance. All of those who think Damian Black cannot be trusted are welcome to join, us as well. Of course, there is no way we will keep any form of financial pressure on our allies."

Oh, Moon Goddess... So that was their aim. Having their own alliance, using people's distrust towards Damian, and the financial struggles for that. I look around, and some of the smaller pack Alphas seem hesitant. I can't believe this is happening.

Suddenly, a group goes to their side, led by an Asian woman. The Rising Moon Clan. Of course, they had to show they have allies, too. I bite my lip. This isn't going as planned at all. I wanted to form alliances, not to have one against us!

"I have to say..."

Surprised, I turn towards the voice. It's Andrew Jones, from the Violet Moon Clan, speaking. Everyone stops to hear him.

"I would be curious to hear the Sapphire Moon Clan's opinion. From what I know, you are enemies with both the Gold Moon and the Blood Moon, but this new Luna changes the odds, doesn't she?"

I turn around and find William staring right at me with a smile. Oh no, I do not like that expression of his. What is he thinking now...?

"That is right, Andrew, she could indeed change my mind towards the Blood Moon Clan... If Nora was willing to marry into our Clan, for example."

...What the hell did he just say?

I stare at William, totally speechless. What is wrong with him? Why would I ever agree to marry him, when Damian is right there!

"Who is going to marry who? William, are you crazy!"

"You say that one more time, and I'll put you to shreds!" Growls Damian.

He is ready to jump at William's throat any second. I've never seen Damian so angry before, and I must hold him back with both hands. But what game is William playing at? Around us, everyone is acting confused or surprised, waiting to see what will happen next. Due to Damian's sudden burst of rage, some people even shape-shifted out of fear.

However, my cousin looks perfectly calm. "It's not unheard of before. Especially for Royals— that's a way to strengthen the pureblood within our family."

"You know I don't care about the Royals' blood, William," I protest.

"But I do. And as far as I know, you are the only one left carrying so much of Queen Diane's pureblood."

"Wait a minute. The Sapphire Moon is related to Royals?" Asks Tiffany.

"That is right. The Blue Moon Royal family are our ancestors. The Royal blood had gotten so thin that the Blue Moon family was almost ready to give up that name. However, we were blessed with a Moon Goddess' reincarnation two generations ago, Queen Diane. And Nora Bluemoon, here, is that reincarnation's granddaughter."

A lot of reactions are heard around us. People are stunned by this revelation; some are looking at me in astonishment.

I shake my head. "Stop this nonsense, William. I'm already Damian's fated mate! Don't you respect Moon Goddess' will above anything?"

"Fated mate? With the Blood Moon Alpha?" Says someone.

"That would explain his sudden change of mind..."

"Anyone can pretend to be fated mates!" Yells Alessandra. "Isn't it obvious this is all just an act?"

I give her a deadly glare, making her shut up. All around us, people start talking again, raising suspicions about my relationship with either Damian or William. But I don't really care what they think.

I turn to William, annoyed. "I won't marry anyone else, William. I don't want to be with anyone but Damian, and you know that."

"...One of you may change your mind, you know."

I shake my head. Damian's arm grabs my waist, and he holds me against him while growling furiously at William. There is no way Damian will ever agree to that, even William knows that, so what's his aim?

"Enough, Blue. Nora is already my mate. What's your game?" Asks Damian, still growling.

My cousin sighs and puts a hand through his curly hair. Everyone can see his blue eyes and our physical resemblance. Funny how I look so much more like him than Elena, to whom I am closer in blood... I guess she took after her mom mostly.

"Maybe... I could consent to an alliance between us," says William. "If Nora was willing to come to my Clan."

"That's still a no," replies Damian right away.

My cousin raises an eyebrow, a bit surprised. His eyes go from Damian to me, but he soon addresses my mate again. I have a hard time figuring out what William is thinking, but I don't like what is happening.

"Really? Not even for the sake of your Clan? This might be your only chance..." Whispers William.

"Fuck you, Blue. I will never give up Nora."

Damian is in a defensive position, almost hiding me from William. Yet my cousin doesn't move an inch or seem impressed in any way.

Everyone is listening, to see if the Blood Moon and Sapphire Moon are going to fight or reach an agreement. This would be a first, and for the Gold Moon, a fatal blow. I look around. From what I've seen so far, aside from the Jade Moon, I'm pretty sure Lysandra and Grandpa Seaver are on our side, too. Lysandra's father, however, will most likely follow William, and I suspect Clark's White Moon, too. This puts both sides on equal grounds, though I'm not sure about the Pearl Moon Clan. Their Alpha Tiffany Pearl has been listening very closely, but aside from her disdain toward the Gold Moon, she hasn't taken any sides yet. Moreover, all the smaller packs appear to be torn and paying attention to whatever we say.

No matter how I look at it, everyone is already picking sides or making up their minds about it. Moon Goddess, this is not what I had hoped for... I turn to William, and I see my cousin smile.

"Do you understand, Nora? I may be able to forgive your mate and agree to an alliance with him if only you joined us."

I just don't get it. William has nothing to win in this. Me joining the Sapphire Moon has no benefit for him! The only thing is that he would tear Damian and me apart.

"That's the place you belong to from the start. You are not part of the Blood Moon yet; you can still join us."

"I am mated, William! Are you insane?"

"Aren't you going to consider it? This is what you wanted, Nora. Returning to your family, avoiding war, and unifying the Clans."

That's true, but not at the cost of my relationship with Damian! I look at my mate, but his eyes have gone ice-cold with hunger. If a single glare could kill, William would be reduced to ashes by now.

"Nora is not leaving me," growls Damian.

William turns to him with a smirk. "Are you so sure, Black? Wouldn't it be best for the both of you, anyway?"

Damian doesn't move an inch, still glaring at him with eyes full of resolve. I know there is nothing that could make him change his mind. My mate's arm is holding me tightly against him. Yet, William's smirk won't go away. Bobo is growling at him, and Neal is frowning. The Beta probably also thinks there is more to it.

"Blue, are you talking seriously? You could forgive the Black Brothers?" Asks Clark Hamilton.

"Why not? As Nora said, they are not their father," says William, very calmly. "After all, out of all of us, Nora should be the one who hates them the most."

What does that mean? Why would I hate Damian, Nathaniel, or

Liam? I was never involved with their father in any way, either! I spent my childhood in the streets before Vince picked me and Alec up to raise us in the Jade Moon Clan. Even before that, my roots are linked to the Sapphire Moon and Gold Moon Clans, I have never had any chance to even get close to Damian's father, the Black King.

William tilts his head, with a little smirk on. "You look confused, Nora. Maybe I should have told you everything from the start, it would have been less cruel. Didn't you want to know why we hated your mate's Clan so much to begin with?"

That's right. William never explained that to me. Why all of his pack had this deep hatred towards Damian's father, to begin with. Aside from his father's anger, we never really got close to the subject. To be honest, I sort of forgot this issue, things got too tense on other matters...

"The Mad King, Judah Black... Everyone hated him so much. He was a violent, crazy, only empowered by his brute force," says William.

Nathaniel shakes his head. "We already all know what kind of man our father was, Blue! That's the reason we went against him. Damian killed him to put an end to that madness. The Black Moon Clan ended that day, and our father's deeds, too."

"Really? Then tell everyone. Let Nora know what your father did," says William.

Nathaniel gasps. He is reluctant to say it out loud here. We all know this will bring nothing good, reminiscing about the Mad King. For most of the werewolves here, this is nothing pleasant to hear.

To my surprise, Damian starts talking, in a very calm tone, despite still glaring at William. "Our father was a monster. He killed more than a hundred wolves. He banished three Clans out and eradicated another one. He was a man who would fight with anyone who opposed him, including his own sons. Our father was mad, ruthless, and paranoid. He chased any witches and vampires that lived here away from Silver City."

Many people lower their heads. They all remember the darkest age of Silver City when it was ruled over by fear. No one knew when the King would unleash his wrath, where, or to whom.

What does this have anything to do with me? I was born far from there, in the Blue Moon Clan, in the North. After that, I lived hidden among the Gold Moon Clan and the Jade Moon Clan! What is William not telling us? When my cousin resumes talking again, I feel some uneasiness growing inside my heart.

"My pack parted with the Blue Moon Clan many years ago. As I told you, Nora, we were supposed to find a new place to settle in, somewhere our Royal Family's children could grow in peace, far from any threat. It took years to find it, and when we did, it took many more years for us to properly settle down in Silver City. We lost contact with the Blue Moon Clan along the way."

That's not so surprising... Fifty years ago, the means of contacting another pack weren't the same, and the original Clan stayed far in the North. William is continuously staring at Damian while talking, and my mate is doing the same with him.

"Do you know what happened to the Blue Moon Clan, Nora?"

I nod slowly. William never told me, but Elena did. When we met, she said someone had found her as a baby in the middle of a slaughter. No one from our original Blue Moon Clan had survived whatever attacked them.

"They were all killed," I answer.

"It couldn't possibly have been our father," interrupts Nathaniel. "He never went that far outside Silver City, not even when he..."

He suddenly stops talking, and his face goes white. Damian and Nathaniel exchange a look as if they both suddenly understood something. I see William smirk, and Damian seems in shock. Moon Goddess, what is it? I feel my heart sinking, and for some reason, it's harder to breathe. What is it they not telling me?

"Nate! When he what?" I ask.

After a few seconds, his eyes shift from Damian to me, and he answers with a blank voice.

"...When he chased all the vampires to the North."

It takes me a while to process what he just said. Their father chased their vampires to the North. That very same North where my original Clan was living? So, this is what William was aiming at from the start...

"Those vampires... killed the Blue Moon Clan?" I ask.

"That's right," says William.

Damian grabs my hand. I can't decipher his expression right now. My mate seems lost between anger, confusion, surprise, and... resolve. I know this hand just won't let go of me. I look at those silver eyes, and despite everything, they bring me some sort of confidence. My wolf agrees with me, too.

William is watching my reactions, and so are Nathaniel and Neal.

Even Bobo stopped growling and is just standing between my cousin and me in silence.

"You should have told me earlier, William. What happened to my mother."

"Yes, I apologize for that. We had other matters at hand. I wasn't sure of your identity, either."

"And now you are?"

He nods but turns to Damian. "Don't you have anything to say?" He asks. "About what your father did?"

"...I stand by my words. My father was a monster, but I'm different from him. However, I am truly sorry for your pack and what your Clan went through. I cannot undo his wrongdoings."

"What do you think you can do, then?"

"Be a better King."

Without adding another word, both of them stare at each other in silence. I try to understand William's intent behind his cunning expression. Around us, people are holding their breath, waiting to see what's next. A few of them are talking about what was just revealed.

"The Mad King was even responsible for another Clan's death... A Clan with Royals, no less."

"The Black family has no shame. Shouldn't they be taking responsibility for their father's actions?"

"He already killed his father! Isn't it obvious they never were on his side?"

"So what? A man who murdered his own family, who knows against whom he will turn his fangs next?"

"It's not the same. We were all glad the Mad King died..."

"The new Luna is there, too."

"I don't trust the Black family. With them being already so strong, who will stop them if they turn to be like their father?"

The chattering gets louder among the ranks, but I don't see any of the Alphas talking. Instead, all of them have their eyes on Damian and William, gauging them. Are some of them changing their minds? The atmosphere is so tense, some more people shape-shifted just in case. My own wolf is restless, too.

"Don't tell me you are going to overlook this!" Yells Alessandra. "The Blacks are a family of power-hungry, bloodthirsty murderers! Remember the Snow Moon Clan? They didn't survive, either! Are you going to push that one on the Black father, too?"

Both William and Damian turn towards the Gold Moon Clan, but I'm the first one growling. Can't someone make her shut up already? I wish I could do it myself!

"The Snow Moon Clan was—," says Neal.

"I'm not talking to a damn Beta!" Interrupts Alessandra.

Neal sighs, but I can tell a lot of people from the Blood Moon behind us are now even more pissed. Who does she think she is to disrespect a Beta like this!

"Watch your tone, King..." I say, warning her with a growl.

"I don't take any orders from you, either. Stealing my fiancé, pretending to be an innocent girl, a Royal? You're the one who should watch it! I am the Gold Moon's heiress! I say we will not stand by your lies!" She yells.

I growl at her even louder, until she has to lower her head. Her father suddenly stands up and addresses the other Alphas.

"Respectable Alphas, it is obvious this is all a well-thought scheme from the Blood Moon Clan! Think about it. A Witch? Why would a Witch attack now, after what their father did to her peers and the vampires? How convenient would it be that Damian Black would suddenly find a Royal mate? Right after ditching my daughter, too? They are the ones who ordered to cut all the other Clans' funds! Don't be fooled! That man used my daughter, and now he is using this Witch attack that will never happen to force you to submit to him!"

"We never sought to bind other Clans! We only asked for alliances!" I talk back.

Why is this man so stupid? Does he really think what he's saying? This is ridiculous! I am the very reason that Witch attacked us, and there is no way Damian could pull off something as wicked as that!

"It's no use talking, Nora. This idiot mutt has already made up his mind..." mutters William.

I'm not sure if Taaron King didn't hear him or decided to pretend he didn't. Either way, the packs are agitated now. It's obvious they don't know if this is going to end well or not, but everyone is expecting the worse if it doesn't. Even my wolf is ready to attack at any moment.

In the middle of all this, Tiffany Pearl, on the side, appears exceptionally calm. Playing with the long sleeves of her pale pink dress, she speaks in a clear voice. "Do we understand that you will release all control on the withheld funds, King?"

This time, Taaron King seems a bit flustered. He hesitates for a few seconds and tries to regain his composure. "Of course, we don't hold any hostility towards the other packs. However..."

He turns to point at Damian.

"I believe it would be dangerous to let this man hold any more power than he already has. It would be my duty to ensure this doesn't threaten anyone with the financial pressure of some sort. Of course, it would also require close attention to his relationships. If, after careful consideration, there is no way to—"

"In other words, you intend to retain any money that belongs to the Blood Moon Clan and those who associate with us," I growl, annoyed.

"This is only as a preventive measure! To protect the lesser Clans from this man!"

"Who is putting pressure onto the others, now, King?" Growls Lysandra.

He turns red from embarrassment and anger as the packs suddenly get even more agitated. Moreover, a lot of them are now growling at the Gold Moon Clan. Tiffany just put in the clear the Gold Moon intents.

"You're wrong! There is no Witch attack, and no one should trust Black! I am only doing what is necessary! Who needs an Alpha King, anyway? The Clans are doing just fine, why would we suddenly provide this man with any more power?"

"He's right!" Suddenly yells Gregorovitch. "Each pack for itself, that's how it should be!"

"We are all cohabitating in one city, you idiots! How do you think we can live together without fighting if there is no King to oversee all the packs?" Growls Lysandra.

"Just hand the woman over to the Sapphire Moon! We don't need a Royal to support Black!" Yells a female Alpha.

"That's right! The Sapphire Moon should take over! If they are Royals, they should be the ones to preside over us!"

"Are you crazy? They don't have any rights to rule Silver City! Black is the most powerful Alpha; he is the one who should be our Alpha King! Even our Moon Goddess gave him a Royal Luna!"

"Enough!"

My yelling shuts everyone down for a few seconds. I use my wolf's Alpha voice to address all of them. I've had enough of all this childish bickering!

"We are not here to discuss a new King or not! The threat is real; we don't have the luxury to fight each other! I don't care if you doubt my status as a Royal. I won't marry into the Sapphire Moon Clan and I won't acknowledge anyone but Damian Black as King!"

"Stop lying!" Yells Alessandra. "There is no Witch, no threat, you are just lying. Even your status as a Royal is—"

Before she can finish her sentence, a rumbling rises suddenly. What is this? Where is this noise coming from? Everyone looks around, and before I can understand what's going on, the ground starts shaking under our feet.

"What the...?"

Creaking noises are heard all throughout the stadium, and the packs start spreading in panic despite the Alphas trying to yell orders. The sounds are growing like something is coming closer. Damian starts growling, his eyes on the ground, where the soil starts tearing apart. Wide cracks are spreading fast, and tree roots suddenly come out at an incredible speed. I hear people screaming.

"A Witch! It's a Witch!"

"Don't stay on the ground! Climb the stairs!" Yells Damian.

Finally listening, most of the werewolves start running to the stadium's stairs, the Alphas trying to lead their packs. Suddenly, Damian pushes me into William's arms.

"Take Nora away!"

Wait, what? Before I can say a word, William starts running, forcefully taking me along with him.

"Damian!"

My mate is already running in the opposite direction, towards the crowd still downstairs. Moon Goddess, he is going to help the others!

"William, let me go! I have to go with him!"

My cousin isn't listening at all, pulling me with him up the stairs. I'm not leaving Damian! I struggle until I finally free myself from William's grasp. I hear him yell my name, but I don't slow down one bit. I feel another wolf right behind me, and Bobo arrives even faster than me to Damian's side.

"What...? Nora, go back!"

"No way, I'm not leaving you!"

He growls, but we both know this has no effect on me. Around us, the field is not cleared yet, but the ground is now totally invaded by roots. Still, a lot of werewolves that couldn't run fast enough are trapped by the roots and calling for help. I even spot Taaron King, lost under a large trunk that's pinning him face against the soil.

A few steps away, Lysandra Jones, too, is fighting to free her leg from some mud in one of the cracks. The roots keep progressing, and some of them even reached one side of the stadium, running between the benches and capturing more people. How do we stop this! I hear screaming, but aside from Bobo and Damian standing next to me, I can't recognize anyone else I know. Ten thousand people are running in all directions, and I suddenly notice all the stadium entrances have been barred by branches.

We are trapped.

"The Witch! Catch the Witch!"

I turn around. Right in the middle of a stadium, a woman is standing alone. No doubt possible— this is not a werewolf. She has crimson hair, and strange dark symbols are covering her arms. But...

Before I can say a word, I see Damian jumping into his wolf form and running straight at her. Moon Goddess, no!

"Damian, no!"

I scream, but it's too late— he's already jumping at her. A split second before my mate's fangs can catch her throat, a black shadow jumps in. I hear loud growls, and Damian is pushed back by another wolf.

The large black wolf growls at him and stands in front of the Witch, obviously protecting her from my mate. I recognize him immediately.

Liam.

Chapter 15

I finally reach Damian's side, and I think it takes him a few seconds to realize the other wolf is no other than his younger brother. Even I am still shocked to see this witch. She has a familiar butterfly flying around her. The very same blue butterfly that was with me these last few days!

She's younger than I thought, maybe her mid-twenties, with gentle emerald eyes and fair white skin. While I'm staring at her, I realize all the roots have stopped moving, and silence befell the stadium.

"Liam, what are you doing!"

Nathaniel, from one of the benches, is perplexed. He runs toward us, approaching his brothers, still facing each other. Some of the Alphas come back down, too.

The Witch turns to me, looking very calm.

"Hello, Nora."

"Hello..."

She smiles softly at me. I was right. She is not the Dark Witch, but the one who sent me the letter and the butterfly. Damian growls, and I know he wants his brother to push aside. However, Liam growls back, not moving an inch. I put my hand in my mate's fur, trying to calm him down a little for now.

"Damian, it's okay."

"What is the meaning of this, Nora?" Asks Nathaniel.

"She's on our side, I think..."

William arrives at my side, too, frowning.

"What do you mean? Why is the Black boy standing for her?"

"It's all right," says the Witch. "No need to fear me, I don't want to harm you in any way."

"Are you kidding me? You just did!"

No, she didn't. As everyone starts to look around, it becomes quite obvious, no werewolf was actually injured. Despite the panic, all the tree roots did was capture some people and trap them on the ground. Maybe about two hundred wolves. Even Lysandra is still growling at some branches, trying to free herself.

"What was that, then?" Asks Nathaniel.

"A little reminder."

She makes a little movement of her fingers, and the branches suddenly untighten their grip to release Lysandra's arm. The Purple Moon Alpha growls and massages her wrist with an annoyed look.

"Listening to all this nonsense, I thought it would be good for you all to witness how powerful a Witch can actually be."

She's right. As soon as she attacked, most of the werewolves panicked. It took us a few minutes to understand what was going on and look for her. Even the Alphas had a hard time holding their packs together until Damian intervened. This was only a warning... If she had intended to kill, this would have been much worse.

All of the Alphas have now come down and are staring at her with shocked eyes. Tiffany Pearl and Andrew Jones lost their composure.

"I thought all Witches had left Silver City..."

"Indeed, I'm the last one."

The werewolves around us all start whispering. I hold on to Damian and try to take him back.

Damian, it's really okay. She's on our side.

I feel my mate hesitate, but after a while, he shape-shifts back to his human form. Nathaniel hands him a pair of pants, and Damian dresses up, still staring at the Witch and Liam with doubtful eyes. Actually, Liam shape-shifts back, and the Witch gives him his shorts.

"Hi, guys..."

Both his brothers and I glare at him.

"Liam, you idiot! You should have told us you were fine!" I growl.

"Sorry about that. Syl needed me, so..."

"Syl?"

He suddenly takes the Witch's hand, and the smile she gives him makes no doubt about their relationship. I did not expect this…

Nathaniel is livid.

"You've got to be fucking kidding me, Liam..."

"I told you guys I had a girlfriend."

"You never said it was a Witch!"

Liam acts as if it was nothing, he probably expected this kind of reaction from his brothers. Actually, he's almost standing in front of the

Witch, as if ready to shield her at any moment. Nathaniel looks like he can't even believe what he sees, while Damian frowns and turns to me.

"...You knew?" He asks.

"I... She contacted me a week ago. She said she could help."

"You believe her?" He asks.

I hesitate a bit. Do I? I look at the Witch, but no matter what, my wolf isn't the slightest worried by her. My instincts tell me she is not an enemy, I don't feel any animosity coming from her. I slowly nod.

Damian takes my hand to keep me close to him and turns to face Liam and the Witch. "What should we call you? And why would you help us?"

She smiles. "My name is Sylviana. I come from an ancient and long line of Witches; my ancestors lived in Silver City long before werewolves came. We have always lived in peace with both werewolves and humans. Sometimes in secret, when the situation called for it like I was until now, but we never had any conflict with your kind."

"That doesn't explain why would help us against one of your own..."

Sylviana shakes her head and takes on a solemn expression. "Witches aren't like werewolves. We are solitary individuals; we do not feel the need to interact with our peers or get along with them. On the contrary, we are territorial creatures, and don't usually enjoy sharing."

"Silver City is a city of werewolves..." Says Nathaniel.

"I meant that we do not like to share with other Witches. Werewolves, humans, or animals do not have the same needs as we do, neither do you perceive a territory like us. To you, a turf is a land your pack has rights on. For me, it is a source of life, a way to draw more power and energy. I don't need buildings or money. The same way you wouldn't argue with humans or animals about your turf, I do not need to dispute my homeland with you."

"Then, this Witch is a threat to you as well, isn't it?" I ask.

Sylviana nods, and makes some movements with her hands, calling back all the roots under the ground.

"That's right. As I said, Witches don't share territories. If this Witch seeks to gain control over Silver City, she will eventually become a threat to me as well. We do not have any special feelings towards other Witches, though we usually respect each other's boundaries. The woman who attacked a few weeks ago is looking for more power, and she won't stop because I'm here. So, I believe we could find a mutual agreement and work with each other to keep her out of Silver City."

That sounds quite reasonable, indeed... The same enemy, a reason to work together and protect Silver City. Nate and Damian exchange looks, probably mind-linking each other, as well. Liam is eyeing his girlfriend, but they gently smile at each other. They do seem like a genuine, loving couple...

Meanwhile, Bobo appears at my side, standing against my leg. I wonder if Daniel is there? No news from Elena, either... After a while, Nathaniel looks pissed, but Damian turns to Sylviana again.

"You said that other Witch, the Dark Witch, was looking for more power... If our land and wealth are of no interest to her, what is she attacking Silver City for?"

Sylviana nods and takes a few seconds before answering, looking a bit unsure. "Witches divide into two categories: Light Witches and Dark Witches. I belong to the first group. I draw my powers from my own life energy and my relationship to nature."

She shows us her arms and the dark markings I had noticed earlier. Now that I can see them from up close, they are not black, but dark red... Those are burn scars! Moon Goddess, does that mean she has to injure herself to use her powers? Next to me, Damian is frowning too.

"As you can see, light magic comes at a cost... I can heal myself, of course, but the more powerful my spell is, the bigger is the cost."

"Sylviana could really die if she was to face that Dark Witch alone and directly," explains Liam.

Now I understand why he is so adamant about protecting her... As well as why she did stay hidden for so long. That attack from earlier was impressive, but now her arms are covered in severe injuries... And there might be more under her clothing, as well.

"Wait a second."

I turn around. Clark Hamilton, the White Moon Clan Alpha, just joined us. The Jones and Seaver are there, as well. I try to decipher Grandpa Seaver's expression, but the elder Alpha is just frowning behind his white beard.

"You... you helped us, didn't you? Last time... During the vampire's attack, the water kept turning on us and poisoned some of us. We were losing ground until the trees suddenly moved, too, and the water stopped. The branches shielded the injured wolves and tore vampires apart. That was all you, wasn't it?" Asks Clark.

Sylviana smiles. "Well, vampires don't mix so well with wood... And that Witch didn't want to face me directly, either."

"What does a Dark Witch do, then? How is she different from you?" Asks Nathaniel.

"As I said earlier, I sacrifice my own life force and body to use powers... Dark Witches do the same, but with other bodies."

I gasp. "You mean... like sacrifices?"

"Exactly. What's worse is, while a Witch's body is made for this hence can heal fast and recover, other species can't withstand powerful magic. Not only does she need bodies, but she also needs a lot of them, and living ones too."

Moon Goddess, this is... disgusting! How can someone be as evil as that? Injuring other people to be more powerful! I was wondering why Sylviana would go through the pain of injuring herself, but this other Witch is so hateful!

"Light Witches give their lifeforce to others, while Dark Witches take it. This is our fundamental difference. This also why we don't usually cohabitate: We have very different mindsets," explains Sylviana.

"Wait, who would be more powerful then?" Asks Andrew Jones.

Sylviana sighs. "I think... for now, that would be me. I won't get into the details, but in terms of brute magic, mine is much more powerful than hers. However... she is very aware of that and working to change that. She will keep gathering as much as she can until she can overpower me."

"How?" Asks Damian. "Is that why she is attacking us?"

"She was gathering bodies. Some from our pack," says Ryan.

"That's right. The more, the better. However, corpses aren't nearly as... good as living people for a Witch. Werewolves are filled with Moon Goddess' power, and the best..."

Damian and I exchange a look. I see horror and anger on my mate's face. Which means...

"That's right. A living Royal would be exactly what she needs. The perfect prey..."

A few seconds of silence follow her words. I feel several gazes on me, we all understand what that means. This Dark Witch is after me. She wants to use me as a way to enhance her powers, enough to be able to take on Sylviana and overpower her.

Since my grandmother was a reincarnation of Moon Goddess, a lot of her power resides in me, making some sort of... vessel for this Witch to use. How frightening. I shiver, and Damian immediately puts his arm around me in a protective way.

"She is not touching Nora," growls my mate.

"You're saying, as long as this Dark Witch can't get to miss Bluemoon, she won't be able to cross our border?" Asks Andrew Jones.

"Nora, or any other Royal..."

While she says that, Sylviana is looking right at me, with a mysterious look in her eyes. Oh, Moon Goddess! She knows about Elena, too; she knows I have a cousin who's also a Royal. We are both in danger.

"What are we waiting for, then?"

Everyone turns around. I had forgotten about the matter of the King family... Alessandra is standing next to her father, arms crossed, a few meters from us. What is she up to now? I start growling instinctively. I know whatever this woman is thinking, I'm not going to like it. Damian also. My mate shifts his position, putting himself slightly in front of me. Even William is growling and frowning.

"What do you mean, King?" Asks Lysandra.

Alessandra lifts a finger, pointing towards Sylviana.

"Isn't this woman what this Witch wants, anyway? Why don't we just hand her over?"

Immediately, I growl furiously, but Liam's reaction is way angrier. He shape-shifts in a split second and jumps at Alessandra. She lets out a scream of terror, but before the black wolf can get to her, Nathaniel steps in. I see his hand dive, and he grabs Liam's fur before trapping him in his arms. I always forget how strong he is, even in his human form… Liam furiously struggles to free himself.

"Liam, stop it!" Yells Nathaniel.

He is not listening. I have never felt Liam's wolf so angry before, but his murdering intent is real. Despite Nathaniel's attempts to calm him down, it's actually Sylviana who steps forward, putting her hand on his back and whispers something to his ear. Liam is still growling, but he eventually stops trying to fight off his brother after hearing her, and Nathaniel sighs.

Damian, who observed the whole scene in silence, turns to

Alessandra. His eyes have gone ice-cold again, and we can all feel his wolf imposing his Alpha aura to her. It's as if Liam's anger had added to his own. Alessandra, intimidated, has no choice but to look down.

"We are not handing anyone over. This is our city, and we will not answer any threat from that Dark Witch. That goes for anyone."

While saying that, he looks around at all the Alphas present, and each of them avoids his chilling stare, except for me.

"We have now confirmed that this threat is real," I say. "We should—"

"On the sayings of a Witch?"

I growl at Alessandra. Why is she still daring to speak? Will that damn woman ever learn to shut up! Yet she ignores the Black brothers and me on purpose and keeps talking to the other Alphas.

"Why would we believe her so easily? Isn't it obvious this is all a scheme? Suddenly, a random witch appears as a witness to concur with everything they said, and you don't find it suspicious in any way? They are lying! No one saw this Witch before in Silver City; they just brought her here to have her say that! She even bewitched them! Now she wants us working for her? I will not listen to the orders of a witch!"

I see a few people exchanging looks. Don't tell me some of them will be stupid enough to actually believe this would be all part of a scheme? Andrew Jones clicks his tongue, marking his annoyance at her.

"Enough. I don't know what game you're playing, King, but this is not a joke. I do not care for the Royals, but a witch's threat is not to be taken lightly."

"I have lost too many wolves already to think this is only a scheme from Black," growls Clark. "If you have anything actually useful to say, say it, or learn to shut up!"

Both Alphas growl at Alessandra, and it is now clear more and more people are exasperated by the Gold Moon Clan's actions. That doesn't stop them. Her father, Taaron King, steps forward, pointing his finger at us. Before he can even speak, however, Damian growls at him in warning, and his index goes back down right away.

"In any case, our Gold Moon stands by its words! We will not follow the Blood Moon's ruling any longer! Enough of their schemes! They should not try to overtake Silver City or pressure the Clans!"

People look at him with surprise, but most are just tired of his speech. How can such a pathetic guy be an Alpha? Except for the Rising

Moon Alpha, none of the other Alphas seem bothered enough to listen to him anymore. The only ones who are still hesitant are the leaders of lesser Clans, but none of them seem daring enough to speak up.

So, King keeps talking as if he was giving some grand speech.

"The Gold Moon will stand by its words and oppose the Blood Moon!"

"So, you really are as stupid as you look..." Sighs William.

Surprised to hear him, Alessandra gives him an annoyed look.

"Aren't you one to speak, Blue? You hate the Blood Moon as much as we do! You should side with us and—"

William suddenly burst into a dramatic laugh, echoing through the stadium. What is so funny? Even Alessandra looks uneasy after that. When he stops, he stares at her with disgust. "Side with you? I may not be on Black's side, but I still have better to do than to hang out with some bottom-of-the-barrel mutts."

Oh, Moon Goddess, he can really be insulting when he wants... Alessandra puts on an outraged expression, and Lysandra laughs out loud despite her father's glare.

"Serves you right, King! You really should learn how alliances work, because there is no way anyone here will ally with the likes of you!" She says.

"You are wrong! Many would follow us, even—"

"Because you hold their money? The small packs are just going to be taken hostages by you, and that's it," growls Nathaniel.

"The Rising Moon Clan shall side with—"

Before the Asian woman, the Alpha of the Rising Moon Clan, can finish her sentence, both Damian and William give her a thunderous growl. Having both Alphas using their auras against her, her words get lost in her throat, and she looks down.

"You may be young, Mari, but you should really learn your place before it gets you killed," mutters William.

The woman goes white, but Taaron King, ignoring her situation, scoffs. "The Rising Moon Clan is proud and respectable! And the Opal Moon Clan will follow us, too!"

Clark Hamilton, the White Moon Alpha, is now the one growling at King. Moon Goddess, did the Opal Moon Clan really plan to side with the Kings? Does that mean Elena's Clan is in trouble, then? Is that why she's not here? I glance at Nathaniel, but his gaze is on Clark.

"Say that again, King."

"I mean it! They are tired of your tyranny; they will rise as their own clan and—"

"Tyranny? The Opal Moon is our branch Clan! They won't dare to move behind my back!"

"Oh, they will! They—"

"They didn't even dare to come here!" Yells Clark. "Did this idiot, Xavier, say he would side with you? He wouldn't even come here to face me for that! I hope you are not counting on them, King, because I would rather slaughter the Opal Pack myself than let any of my wolves side with you!"

King looks at him, speechless. He probably didn't expect the Opal Moon wouldn't dare to oppose the White Moon in such an obvious way. Clark is burning with anger, but Nathaniel suddenly turns to him.

"Clark, you—"

"Shut up, Black! I may hate the Gold Moon, but don't you think I trust you, either! Do you think I don't know what's going on? Do you really think I'm that blind, Black?"

Oh, Moon Goddess... He is glaring right at Nathaniel, not his brothers. From Nate's surprised expression, I immediately guess what's going on. Clark knows about his relationship with Elena.

I didn't think the White Moon Alpha would know! He doesn't seem happy about it at all, either. Nathaniel doesn't dare to say a word after that and glances down, almost looking guilty. I've never seen Nathaniel like this, so nervous. What's Clark Hamilton's relationship with Elena? I thought the White Moon might side with us, but this makes it clear they won't.

Damian is staring at his brother, visibly surprised to hear this, too. I forgot he doesn't know much about his brother and Elena's relationship, either.

Taaron King, on the side, looks pleased by their argument, though he obviously has no idea what this is about.

"See? The Blood Moon Clan can't be trusted!"

I bite my lip. I don't like where this is going. We need alliances, but at this rate, we won't be able to do anything anytime soon. Putting the Gold Moon Clan's scheme aside, it is obvious they made it hard for any other Clan to trust Damian. The lesser packs look worried, and William will not change his mind, either. And the White Moon and

Violet Moon Clans won't act with us, either. Nothing has changed, despite our efforts. The only thing is that most Clans are now convinced that the Dark Witch is a genuine threat.

"The Black family should have stepped down years ago when Judah Black was murdered by his own son! Why should a family of murderers rule over Silver City? We are—"

"You don't think anyone would be stupid enough to choose you as the next King, do you?" Asks Lysandra with a growl.

"If anyone is fitting, it should be Blue, right?" Ads Tiffany.

"That is not the issue!" Says Nathaniel. "We need to take care of that Witch first!"

"That problem could take years, Black. And I have no intention to submit to you, meanwhile," growls Clark.

Why is everyone suddenly tensing up! They don't seriously think anyone will fight over the Alpha King position, do they? Even Damian is pushing me to stay behind his back, but I ignore him to face my cousin.

"William, tell them it's not what this is about!"

My cousin shakes his head. "I won't stand by your mate's side, Nora. You're asking me to help the man whose father murdered our family. I cannot do that."

"Enough of this! Damian is not his father; I've said it already! None of this is about some petty revenge! We could all be in danger if all Clans stay as they are!"

"You're blinded by your bond with him, Nora. This man—"

"I'm not blinded by anything! You are the ones all acting like children, closing your eyes on the real issue here! Didn't you hear Sylviana? That Dark Witch will keep making victims! As much as I can resent what happened to my mother, I also don't want to see more people die! I am a Luna, it is my duty to protect others! As long as I believe Damian is the most entitled to do that, I will stand by him! Hasn't Silver City been in peace since he took over? You are all arguing about what happened in the past! Does anyone here have anything to blame him for since then? Are you willing to sacrifice your families, our city's future, just because you're afraid of making the wrong choice? Well, you want to know what an awful choice is? Wait until this Witch gets to us, and just see who is scarier between Damian and her then!"

An interminable silence follows my words. The Alphas exchange glances, meditating on my words. I am staring at William, waiting for his reaction. Before either of us adds anything, Sylviana suddenly walks up to him in silence, making William step back, a bit surprised. But very calmly, Sylviana smiles at him and gently puts her fingers on his temples.

My cousin looks surprised, but after a few seconds, his eyes get blurry, like he is looking at something we can't see. Sylviana's hands let go after a few seconds, and William stands there, totally immobile.

I see a tear run down his cheek. Moon Goddess, is he... crying? What's going on?

He gasps and raises his eyes towards Sylviana. "Was this... real?"

"Yes. I'm sorry, but you needed to see the truth."

He shakes his head and wipes his tear away. Everyone is looking at the two of them while William breathes in, trying to hold back his emotions. Did Sylviana show him something just now? It looked like she was only slightly touching his head, though.

My cousin regains his composure after a few seconds and turns to Damian. "It seems like I owe you an apology, Black."

An apology? What is he talking about? William isn't looking at Damian with eyes full of anger, anymore. Instead, he looks calmer and resolute. I exchange a look with Liam, but he doesn't seem to know any more, either.

My mate frowns and turns to Sylviana.

"What was that?"

"A glimpse of the past... About what truly happened to their family."

"You can do that?" I ask, surprised.

Sylviana nods with a smile, but she doesn't explain anything else until my mate asks.

"...What happened?"

"Your father did chase the vampires to the North, but... It only led them into the Dark Witch's hands."

I gasp. So, the vampires didn't attack the Blue Moon Clan because of Damian's father, but because the Witch used them to get to my family? Precisely the same way she tried to do so a few weeks ago here, in Silver City...

"You're saying... she killed them?" I ask.

"She most likely instigated it. Judah Black only was wrong for sending her more vampires to use. Still, she would have attacked the Blue Moon Clan sooner or later, because of the Royal family."

That means my mom, Elena's father, and the two of us... I can't believe they met such a terrible and sad end. How did our grandmother feel, trying to protect us until the end? And what happened to our parents? I wish I could ask more from Sylviana, but we have more pressing matters at hand.

At least William isn't showing any animosity towards Damian or his brothers anymore. The Jones, too, watched the whole scene with deep interest.

"Are you saying... the Sapphire Moon might consider an alliance with the Blood Moon?" Asks Andrew Jones.

William seems hesitant. This could be decisive. If William is willing to stop this fighting with Damian's Clan, we could actually get closer to an alliance. Moon Goddess, this would be enough. If the Sapphire Moon decides not to ignore the Blood Moon Clan anymore and actually work with us, most of the packs will follow. The Jones would, for starters. Even Tiffany Pearl is looking with interest at Sylviana and standing right next to Vincent.

Next to William, a man is already discussing with Lysandra, probably his Beta. The Purple Moon Clan Alpha has her eyes set on the Kings, and so do I. Because if William agrees to a peace truce with the Black Brothers, this would be terrible news for them.

Alessandra is staring at Sylviana with eyes full of hatred, but the Light Witch doesn't seem affected at all. Are witches unaffected by werewolf auras? It looks like it. Sylviana is staring back, her hand slowly caressing Liam's back.

"Liam, are you okay?"

"I will be once we get rid of those Gold Moon suckers..."

"Why didn't you tell me before? About Sylviana?"

"A lot of reasons. She said this is how things needed to happen."

"Wait, do you mean she—?"

"Can foresee the future? Yeah, somewhat. But it's not all crystal clear, you know. A grain of sand can totally change it all, so... got to be careful."

I nod slowly. I can't totally grasp all the details, but it does explain a lot of Sylviana and Liam's previous actions. I glance towards Nathaniel. I still haven't been able to contact Elena at all. That's odd.

"Nathaniel?"

He turns his head towards me.

"Have you heard from Elena? I can't reach her at all..."

"I told her not to come here. Not in her condition. Her friend Daniel is watching her."

Oh, so this is about pregnancy. Indeed, I wouldn't have wanted Elena anywhere near here. Things are way too tense for her pregnancy, and if it ends up in a fight... Nathaniel's face is expressionless, I wonder what he really thinks about this baby. He doesn't seem so happy, either. Don't tell me something went wrong between him and Elena?

"You've got to be kidding me..."

All heads turn to Alessandra, who is staring at William with disgust. Did I miss something? My cousin is ignoring her, but he obviously just said something I missed. Damian, too, is glaring at the Gold Moon Clan.

"Now would be a good time to shut up," growls Lysandra.

Alessandra ignores her and points her finger at Damian while glaring at William. "Don't tell me you're going to let this go!"

Sylviana is smiling, but I am not. My guts tell me things are about to get ugly. The Gold Moon Clan was counting on William's hatred against Damian to work in their favor. A truce between the two would mean they cannot attack the Blood Moon or count on any other support. No pack would follow them against both the Blood Moon and the Sapphire Moon. Now, not only William won't fight Damian, but he might even side with him if they were to do anything. Andrew Jones and Tiffany Pearl look like they are okay with it, too.

Behind Alessandra, several Alphas look restless. They probably are reconsidering their options... She suddenly turns to me. Her eyes are full of hatred.

"You little whore... I should have killed you last time!" She yells.

"You're welcome to try!" I growl back at her, and half of the other people present are growling as well behind me.

Damian is the most furious one, but he's also the one holding me back. He addresses Taaron King and his daughter with a voice as cold as death itself. "This is the last time I hear one of you insult my mate. The next time, I will have your whole Clan dead."

"See! This man is threatening us! He does not deserve to be—"

"For someone who has insulted the city's Luna more than twice to his face, you should even be lucky to be still standing on your two feet, King," growls Nathaniel.

Alessandra almost chokes up from hearing him. "The city's Luna? Who?"

"The Luna Nora Bluemoon, granddaughter of Queen Diane, blessed child of Moon Goddess. She is a Princess to you, swine," mutters William, angered too.

Alessandra looks like she's about to go insane from anger. Her eyes go to the other Alphas, but no one will contradict them. Most aren't showing any expression. Lysandra is smirking while looking at Alessandra, and Old Man Seaver is shaking his head. The Rising Moon Alpha looks a bit scared, hesitant, and she is staring at Alessandra like she's crazy.

"If you do not wish to ally with anyone else here, you are welcome to leave. However, that embargo on the financial system hindering the other packs has to end by tomorrow, or we will take action," threatens Damian.

"Take action? You think you can take action, threaten us?"

Alessandra's tone suddenly changed. From craziness and anger, she suddenly went strangely calm. I glance towards Sylviana, but the Witch is frowning, visibly confused too. Damian's eyes are on the Gold Moon Clan.

"You really think you're the strongest wolf, Black? You think no matter what, you can take us on?"

What is she thinking? Damian is indeed strong, but her speech is mocking him. I exchange a glance with Liam and Nathaniel. Both brothers are on the look-out, too. I hang onto my wolf, ready to shapeshift, but what is she thinking? Only the Rising Moon and lesser packs would support the Gold Moon, why would she act boldly right now? Alessandra and her father but might be manipulative, but they are definitely smarter than bluntly provoking Damian... Especially when most of the packs are now supporting him!

On the sidelines, the other packs are getting agitated as well. They can sense something's not right in Alessandra's attitude.

"I don't know what game you're playing, King, but you better leave now," growls Damian.

She smiles in contempt. "I don't think so. Do you think I'm actually that stupid, Damian? That I would have come here without some back-up plan? Sure, I had hoped things would go smoothly, and you would have lost the Alpha King's spot in a peaceful manner, or with the Sapphire Moon's pressure, but... "

Every werewolf starts growling— something's about to happen. Alessandra is way too confident. Damian pushes me behind him, and William and Bobo both get closer to us. Nathaniel decides to move to the side, shielding his little brother and Sylviana.

"Damian..."

"Stay behind me."

"Alessandra... This is my last warning."

She laughs at him and suddenly smiles. "Too bad, mine is already over."

The next second, an explosion suddenly bursts from one side of the stadium. All heads turn in horror to witness wolves flying in flames, and screams are heard from all sides. Alessandra is still laughing when a second explosion bursts, closer this time. Bombs! They put damn bombs!

"Damian!"

I turn my head and see my mate, already in his wolf form, running towards Taaron King. I realize the whole Gold Moon clan started attacking the nearest wolves. Moon Goddess, this is hell!

I start running, too, Bobo right behind me. Another explosion bursts a few meters from us, and the blast pushes me back, making me lose balance and fall to the ground. I need to get up, I need to join Damian! I struggle to get back on my feet and start running again. Ashes and smoke are quickly invading the stadium, making my eyes sting and cry horribly. I hear werewolves growling and yelling absolutely everywhere around me. The whole stadium has become a war scene.

"Nora, we need to help Damian!"

"I know!"

I have no idea if Liam's voice came from my head or somewhere near me, but I don't have a second to stop. Where is Bobo? I lost him!

I suddenly spot Alessandra, fighting fiercely with Lysandra. Both shape-shifted into their wolf forms, and I jump between them as I let my wolf take over, too.

"Back away, Bluemoon, this whore is mine!"

I don't know why Lysandra is so keen on killing her, but I can't leave! Alessandra is the mastermind behind this; she has to die!

My wolf is so full of anger and hatred, the fierce fight is merciless. Alessandra is defending herself against the two of us, but she's definitely going to lose. Lysandra is not leaving her any way out, and I'm fighting like never before. My wolf is scratching her skin and biting her without any mercy, going wild. Lysandra suddenly yelps. Another wolf got her leg, and she's poorly injured. She turns away to fight him off, but Alessandra lost focus thanks to that, and I go right for her throat.

I feel her blood on my fur. She's suffocating, but my wolf fangs are not letting go. I bite harder, and her breathing is nothing but a little hiss.

"You... think you... won, Blue?"

"Do you think I'm not going to kill you? I won't have mercy for you!"

"I don't... care... You will pay. He... will..."

I feel her wolf die before she finishes her sentence. What? What did she mean? Who will what, who was she talking about? Lysandra returns, limping, and bites Alessandra's dead body out of anger. I let go of the corpse.

I need to get to Damian. Alessandra was about to die, but she seemed so sure... I start running, looking for my mate with a growing fear inside. There are fighting wolves everywhere, but the Gold Moon is losing. Some werewolves ran away, and others are injured. I come across corpses, but I can't stop to check. I'm terrified by what I could see. I've lost Bobo, even Liam. Everything is too confusing, and the smoke is so dense, I can only see a few meters ahead.

"Damian!"

"Nora! Where are you?"

I follow his wolf's aura, and finally spot him! Damian's fine! I run towards him, and I feel his relief. Something shines from a corner. I'm almost at his side.

I keep running. Damian's right there, in front of me. I see his wolf run towards me, but something's wrong. He looks terrified.

"Nora!"

I hear a gunshot, and something red suddenly covers my vision.

The blood splashes on my face before I even realize what's going on. I just heard a bang, and Damian stopped running. He's just in front of me, but I see the black wolf stumble and fall on his flank.

"Damian!"

Another gunshot is heard, but I couldn't care less. All I see is my mate lying on the ground with blood flowing from a hole in his chest. I run to his side, unable to think of anything else. Damian is injured!

"Damian! Damian!"

I keep calling his name, my wolf howling after her mate, but he is barely moving. Oh, Moon Goddess, no, no, no, not him, not Damian... I try to look for the bullet's location, and shape-shift to use my fingers. His jet-black fur is getting all sticky from so much blood, no, no... It can't be. I finally hear him breathing, but it's faint and erratic. Thank Moon Goddess, he's still alive, but the blood is still pouring out…

"Help! Nate! Liam!"

I mind-link anyone I can, I don't care who I reach or not. My mind is so confused right now, I can't even understand what's going on around me. We're in the middle of a mist of ashes, with smells of fire and blood all around. Those who haven't run away are busy fighting, nobody has time to pay attention to an injured wolf.

What do I do? Should I kiss him? I don't know if I can heal an injury this size! Damian had me promise not to use it again, and if I pass out here, in the middle of the fight...

I realize I'm crying, but Moon Goddess, who wouldn't? My fingers are still in my mate's fur, I'm not leaving him. I've never felt so helpless! Suddenly, something grabs my wrist, pulling me with sharp pain, and another gunshot is heard.

"Nora! Don't stay there!"

Bobo! It's Bobo, who just grabbed my wrist between his fangs.

"Bobo! Bobo, Damian's injured, we have to—!"

"Someone is shooting at you! Don't stay there!"

"But Damian, he..."

"Nora, you have to move!"

I try to fight Boyan off. I don't want to leave Damian alone, I can't! He might die if I leave him! Bobo won't let go of my wrist, even as I start bleeding. He keeps pulling me away with him. I don't want to leave Damian!

Suddenly, another gunshot resonates. Bobo whimpers and lets go of my wrist.

"Bobo!"

I see red blood running down his head, all over his brown fur. Oh, Moon Goddess, not Bobo, too!

"I'm fine! It just grazed me. But Nora, you have to move, you're the target!"

What? I look around, but I can't see who is firing at us. I look at Damian's body. Moon Goddess, I don't want to leave him, but if I'm the one they are shooting at... I stumble to get up, trying to find my senses. Tears are pouring down my cheeks. Damian, Bobo... I see him stumble to walk to Damian's side. He is really injured; a trail of blood is following him.

"Bobo..."

"Nora, just get away from here!"

I nod and turn around to run away. My heart is heavier and heavier. Moon Goddess, I don't want to leave them... I can't even breathe, my crying and running are making a mess of me, but I can't stop, either. Damian, Damian, please, someone save him...

I have no idea where I'm headed, but I don't slow down. Suddenly, I trip over something. It's a body... Taaron King! The Alpha is in such a bad state, his throat torn open, I can't bear to look. I don't know who killed him, but I can't stop. I get back up and start running once more. I try looking for a familiar face, anyone who can help me. Where is Liam, where is Nate? The gunshots have stopped. I run into someone, and some unknown wolf attacks me. A grey shadow and his fangs suddenly grasp my leg. I let out a cry of pain, but the pressure's suddenly gone.

"Nora!"

I turn around. William! I grab my cousin's collar, still in his human form and start screaming everything my lungs have left.

"William, Damian's hurt! He's hurt! Someone was shooting at us, and he... he got in between, he... He was losing blood, a lot of blood! William, please, you have to help him! I beg you, please!"

My cousin puts his hands on my face, looking horrified. "Nora, you're injured, you—"

"I don't care! Just help Damian, please, William! Please!"

He hesitates, but I'm just begging and crying like crazy. He quickly nods, and suddenly turns around while taking off his jacket, looking for someone.

"David! Nicki! Pierce! ...Lara!" He calls around.

He puts his jacket on my shoulders, and two wolves suddenly emerge from the black smoke. William pushes me toward them, but I ignore him.

"William, Damian, Damian he—"

"Nora, I swear I'll go find him, but you have to get away from here! Stay with those two, they'll escort you out! Okay?"

I can only nod, a bit numb to whatever he's saying. But his words and Bobo's resonate in my head, and I get it. I have to get out of here, run away. My wolf is begging me to go back to Damian, and I want to listen to her so, so badly. The only thing I'm scared of right now is my mate. I don't care about the explosions around us, the raging battle between all werewolves, or the corpses we run across.

The two wolves run in front of me, and I follow them like I'm in some nightmare. My legs are going numb, but I just can't stop. My heart stayed behind, where Damian was lying. I can't believe this is happening...

The stadium is invaded by smoke, and fires started after the explosions. Ashes are flying all around us, spreading so much smoke that I have no idea where we are headed. I just follow the duo blindly through the chaos.

Suddenly, a new gunshot bursts. The wolf that was running next to me stops running mid-air and rolls on the ground. Moon Goddess! Her head is covered in blood. She's dead. I gasp, and the other wolf turns around, facing a silhouette running towards us.

Another bang and he falls down like a dead weight. I scream in horror. Moon Goddess, they are both... I turn around, trying to look for the culprit. Who did this? Who shot them?

"Nora, Nora..."

A chill runs down my spine. That voice... Oh, Moon Goddess, no, no, not him, not now... I start running in the opposite direction. My legs take full speed, and I shapeshift in the middle of it without slowing down. My wolf takes over, and she's braver than me. Fear doesn't stop her; she keeps running as fast and as far as she can.

Why is he here? How the hell did he get here! This nightmare is getting worst by the minute. I can hear him running behind me. Can I outrun him? Can I? I have to!

"What the...? Nora?"

I turn my head, and I suddenly bump into someone at full speed. I fall on him, but he helps me up right away.

"Nora? Moon Goddess, you're covered in blood! Who—?"

"Run!"

"What?"

"He's here! He—"

I see his eyes finally spot the silhouette behind me. In a split second, Vince's expression changes, and he pushes me away from him. I hear another gunshot, and Vince's eyes suddenly go blank. I scream uncontrollably. He falls on his knees like a puppet. Moon Goddess, Vince! I can't stop looking at the Jade Moon Alpha's corpse, lying at my feet. A loud crying echoes in my ears, making me go insane. Moon Goddess, please make it stop...

A flash of pain suddenly tears my leg apart. I scream again, from the pain this time. I barely heard the gunshot. I fall, the pain bursting through my whole body. I suffocate. The bullet's silver is killing me, making my whole body spasm. I try to gasp for air, but a slap across my face throws me down.

"Finally! Finally, I can give you what you deserve, you little whore!"

His voice disgusts me the most, despite whatever else I'm going through. I spit some blood and raise my eyes to look at him, ignoring the pain.

Marcus.

He's disfigured by horrifying bite scars, and his face shrank. He looks like a monster, sweating and breathing hard like some savage. He steps closer, and I struggle to move away. My leg is so painful, my whole lower body is numb from the pain. I try to push with my arms, but my desperate efforts are useless. I can only grab a few meters before he catches me. I suddenly scream in pain. He's deliberately stomping on my injured leg!

"How pathetic you look... Look at you. A Luna? A Royal? You're just a little slut, crawling in dirt..."

I have to get away from him! Marcus points this gun at me, but my arms are moving on their own. My instincts act before I think— my wolf knows we have to. My leg is a whirl of pain... Like ice running through my veins, paralyzing me.

"You should have seen all this coming, Nora. Running away from me? Hiding in Black's shadow? Did he have fun with you? Did you become his bitch!"

This tongue of his is spilling words like poison. I don't want to hear Damian's name in his filthy mouth! Another gunshot bursts through the air and I stop moving. He shot a hole right in front of me.

"No bodyguard, no Black left to protect you, Nora... Do you have any idea what I'm going to do to you?"

"Don't... fucking touch me," I growl.

He laughs, like the insane monster he is. All of a sudden, I feel a violent pain in my stomach, and his foot kicks me again. I lose my breath.

His hand brutally grabs my hair, and I try fighting him off. He starts dragging me around, my bloody leg leaving a trail behind me. Moon Goddess, it hurts! I feel my body going numb again, losing strength.

"What the...? Let her go!"

Nate's voice. Yelling. Growling. Gunshots.

I try to open my eyes. A body on the ground is getting further from me. I see the light blue eyes closing, and I lose consciousness...

Chapter 16

My head hurts...

Something cold, heavy, and painful is lacerating my wrists. I feel heavy myself, almost numb. Where am I? It's so dark... Something reeks, too. What happened to me? I feel so weird. Like I've been... drugged.

I can't see a thing, but it's horribly cold, and my instincts tell me I'm underground... a basement? There doesn't seem to be any window or any air circulating. It feels like a small room, yet I can't hear anything but my own breathing. No wait, something's dripping... Some water?

I'm so cold. I struggle to remember, but with this headache... How long have I been there? What about Damian? Where is my mate? Is he fine? There was... so much blood... Did someone help him? I want to ask my wolf, but I can't feel her at all! This is so weird like she's... asleep or gone. I've never felt so utterly alone. I feel like I was a few years ago. It terrifies me.

The battle... The explosions... Who did this, and why? So many people died or were severely injured. Moon Goddess, I hope the highest number possible survived this. What was the Gold Moon Clan thinking? Did they lose it when they understood William wouldn't side with them against Damian?

Suddenly, I hear a ruckus. What's going on? Footsteps? Someone is approaching. Gosh, my leg and head are so painful already...

"So, you're awake, you whore!"

The next second, a violent kick in my stomach radiates pain through me. I gasp for air, unable to breathe, struggling. Before I can come to my senses, I feel someone stomping brutally on my leg. I scream, unable to hold it. This is unbearable! I suddenly remember I was shot right there, and I can feel the blood running on my legs—a sharp, shrilling pain where the bullet is still located. My own voice screams in my ears, and I can only hear half of what he's saying.

"...should have died... What you... Lost everything because of Black... Pay for it..."

I don't care, I don't care about anything that bastard says. I ignore him and bite my lip, unable to take the pain. His foot on my leg is crushing me, pressing so hard until I hear something actually breaking, and a new wave of pain takes me out.

I wake up again, and there's a taste of blood in my mouth. I'm alive... But still in pain, too. Is he gone? I try to move, but Moon Goddess, my leg... It still hurts so much; I can barely believe I was unconscious with this pain. And this cold, too. I'm shaking. Oh, Moon Goddess, my stomach, too... Marcus is crazy and even more dangerous. Next time, he might really kill me... How long have I been there? Are they looking for me? I can't even reach out to anyone; whatever he gave me is strong enough to keep my inner wolf in some sort of coma... I can barely stay awake, myself. I hear footsteps away and something glass-like breaking. It smells like... Alcohol. Is that whiskey?

"You... slut! You think they will ca-catch me? They can... nev... never get me! I'll send your... your corp... corpse back to him! B... Black should die, too!"

Moon Goddess, I can't see him, but he is so drunk... I try to move and feel broken glass under my fingers. Crap, this is so dangerous... I need to do something to get out of here. How do I make him talk?

"Wh... Why Damian? He did nothing to... you," I mutter, almost unable to talk.

"Black, t-took everything from me! He took my... my dignity! A s-slut like you is just... j-just a whore!"

Whatever he's saying doesn't make any sense, but I don't care. I feel him getting closer, and I try to move or crawl away, anyway I can. I feel sharp little pieces of glass pierce my skin, but this is the least of my problems right now. Moon Goddess, he reeks of alcohol!

"Stay away from me!"

"You scared? You should be my toy! You..."

"I'm no one's toy! Get the fuck away from me, you rapist!"

I suddenly hear him laugh, and a new kick bursts my stomach with pain. Moon Goddess... I don't know how much longer I can take this.

"Rapist? After what you did to me? You whore! Assassin! S-slut! You almost kill... killed me!"

...Killed him? I try to remember it again. It's so cloudy in my memories… Gosh, Nora, come on, remember… That night, in that apartment... Alec left me with him, and... He tried to touch me. A surge of fear invades me when I recall, but I have to fight this. I have Damian now. I'm fine, I'm fine. I can do this.

I remember the struggle. Marcus' hideous breath on me, his greasy hands on my legs. Him trying to tear my dress away. I fought him, I screamed, even. I remember the echo of my own voice. At one point, I think I hit him hard enough for him to let go for a second. That's right, I remember now. I pushed him with all I had and ran. I didn't recall where the entrance was, but I went to... Was it a kitchen? I saw those... I saw knives on the counter.

I took one, I remember that feeling between my hands. My fingers clenching on it. It was a long and large kitchen knife, very sharp. When Marcus came at me, I didn't have a second for hesitation. Just panic, guiding each of my movements.

My arms went forward until something blocked me. A weird sensation. A gasp and cold air running down my spine. I remember Marcus' face, frozen in a shocked expression. A whimper of pain, something so miserable and ridiculous. I didn't let go of the knife. I couldn't. As if my fingers were a part of it. So, I stepped back, keeping it with me, in front of me to defend myself, the blade drenched in red.

He screamed. In pain, in terror. I was still scared and panicked. I thought I was going to die, all of me was trembling. I couldn't see the injury, just his face. Like I was in a trance. He ran at me, and I raised my hands, trying to protect myself, forgetting what I was holding on to. I wanted to scream, but even my voice was muffled.

The blade went along his face, in a red, vivid, gross line.

I stabbed him, scarred him twice.

...Is it the reason he's not approaching me now? I try to think again, hard. Marcus had no problem touching me before, but he only used his feet this time. Is he...? Wait. More memories come back again.

"Don't you approach me! Don't touch me!"

I screamed that. I screamed that with all my might... With my Alpha voice. I just remembered it, but for him, it was... An order.

That's right. Marcus can't touch me. Moreover, I'm an Alpha, and he's nothing but a renegade now. His wolf has to obey me. He can't control me anymore.

"You little slut, you..."

"Shut up."

"Don't tell me to shut up!"

I don't have my Alpha voice right now. Moon Goddess, what did he drug me with? Enough to keep my wolf unconscious! I have to hold on, to stay alive. Until I can wake her up, or they can find me, some way. I breathe in. Gosh, my head is spinning so hard... I can faint at any moment again, and I hate that.

Marcus keeps insulting me, but I don't listen to him anymore. The worst he can do is kick me, and as long as I don't anger him, he should stay away... Or so I hope.

Damian, Damian... Moon Goddess, please let him be fine. I hope he can make it, at least until I get back to him...

I'm fighting to stay awake. My head is so heavy... I can feel his presence, somewhere in the darkness of that room. He is mumbling something, reeking of alcohol. That monster. I try to keep my eyes open; I look for my wolf. What happened to her? Marcus must have drugged me again because I can't feel her at all. How many hours have passed?

Besides my wolf, I'm scared because I can't feel my bond with Damian anymore. Moon Goddess, I hope he is okay. I miss him so much already... Why did I ever think this could be only a wolf thing? I love him. I love him so much, so, so much...

The memories of our time together, in his bed, warm my heart. His arms around me, his fingers caressing my skin... The way he stares at me, with his silver eyes filled with tenderness. His firm kisses, the spiky beard he kept because I told him I liked it...

Moon Goddess, I miss him.

I need to find a way to get back to him. I open my eyes again, trying to find Marcus, but without my wolf, it's too hard. That psychopath can go mad at any minute. He is staying away for now, but his kick earlier was not mere luck; he may try to go at it again and kill for good in the process. No way I'm letting him get close to me.

My wolf, I need my wolf...

I try to remember what Elena taught me. Tonia taught me how to fight, but Elena was the one to give me the clues to get closer to my inner wolf. She compared it to seeing myself in a mirror, reaching out for differences in my own reflection. My inner wolf is a reflection of myself, but getting to her is... No, she has to be there somewhere.

I need to reach her, in my... subconsciousness. I think I need to get unconscious again, that might help... Like some hypnosis. It might work.

It's not too hard. I've been fighting this urge to sleep all along, but what I am worried most is... will I wake up again after that? I feel the pain in my stomach and the blood drying on my leg. I'm self-aware of my current state. Alec beat me before, but never this badly. I know this might be my last time closing my eyes, but... This is my only chance to find my wolf and reunite with Damian. I have to.

It only takes a few seconds. I fall into a slumber...

In a white room, I'm sitting in front of a great mirror. I breathe in and approach it slowly. Why is it that I have two reflections? On my right is my wolf, standing proudly, her perfect white fur shiny brightly. I walk towards her, but when I get close, she suddenly starts growling furiously. I can't approach her? Why is she rejecting me? I... Wait, is this really my wolf? She... Something feels wrong about her. The scar! I realize she doesn't have my scar on her left eye. She is perfect, her sapphire blue eyes glaring at me. She's different but... I still feel she is my wolf. I try to get close again, but she growls, warning me not to come closer. She will really attack, so I step back.

I turn to look at the other reflection. This isn't a wolf... I take a few steps closer. It's a little girl, curled up, hiding her face in her arms. It's as if she's crying, yet I can't hear any sound coming from her. I approach, and she lifts her face. She's... me. Me, when I was a child. I stare at all her bruises, cuts. She looks just like I used to, malnourished and weak. Her hair is a mess, and the scar on her face is slowly bleeding.

"Who are you?" She asks.

"I am you."

She shakes her head. *"You can't be me."*

"I am you, in the future, I think."

"I don't have a future," she whimpers.

"You do. You are... my past."

"Wrong."

She's not? But she looks exactly like what I used to look like... I turn around, and the wolf is glaring at us, still growling. So, I address the little girl again.

"Who are you?" I ask

She shrugs.

"Who are you?" She asks.

"I..."

How do I answer that?

"My name is Nora."

"You're just a name?"

"No, I am... a werewolf, too."

She stares at me in disbelief. What else can I say? Who am I...? Does she mean my past or my identity? My family? What do I do?

"I am you," I say.

"You're not me!" She yells.

"I am your future."

"I don't have a future."

"You do," I insist.

"I can't. I'm dead, you know."

She... wait, what? I shake my head. "You are not dead! You're just... The past, my past."

"No, I'm the one you killed. Look at me. You're not me anymore. So, I'm dead."

What she says is right, in some way, but... Why doesn't it feel right? I look at her again. The fresh cut on her face... Is she me from when I was seven, after my parents' death? It's when Alec and I lived in the slums...

"...I'm sorry," I whisper.

This time, she looks surprised. *"Sorry?"*

"Yes. Because I should have been stronger."

"I'm not strong... I'm hungry," She frowns.

I remember. Every day was a struggle back then. We didn't find enough for both of us to eat and went many days without having anything. I hate those memories... Striving to survive, looking for scraps among the trash... My scar, too, probably wouldn't have been so wide and visible if it had been appropriately treated.

"It gets better," I say.

"Not for me. I'll stay here, hungry. I've always been here."

I don't get it. Isn't she a memory...? Why is she there, why would my wolf show me that? I turn to look at the white wolf again. She is glaring. Is she another memory, too? I never was in that form without a scar... What is she, then? I turn to my younger self again.

"Why don't you go to the wolf?"

"What wolf?"

She can't see her? I point to the wolf's direction, but she just looks confused. Why can't she see her? Oh right, I couldn't feel my wolf yet back then... Is this the reason? What can I do? There is no food here.

"What do you need then?" I ask.

She suddenly starts crying. "You should know! Why don't you give it to me!"

I shake my head, helpless. "I don't have any food..."

"I don't want food! I don't care about food! You never give it to me!" She cries, tears overflowing.

She doesn't want food? She said she was hungry! I look at her crying, lost at what to do. What is it she wants, then? I don't have anything. Behind us, the wolf is calmly sitting down, staring at everything I do. Is she waiting for something too...?

The little girl keeps crying, but I have no clue what she wants... What did I want back then? I was only starving... Day after day, it's only a blur now. I was lost after my parents' death, and Alec suddenly closed himself to me; I was all alone.

I was so lonely... I look down at her, and all of a sudden, my emotions go back to who I was. I start crying, too, my heart breaking from that loneliness. It was so hard... Cold, hungry, and lonely. There was no one to help me.

I crouch down facing her, and start caressing her hair gently. "It's going to be okay... We will make friends later. We will have so many people around us, you'll see! Damian, Liam, Nate, Bobo, Tonia..."

"You're lying!"

"No, I'm not! I promise. We have so many people caring for us in the future."

"It can't be. No one wants me."

"You..."

She won't believe me. Why would she? I never believed anyone would want me back then. Suddenly, I feel awfully lonely, too. I want Damian... I want him to take me in his arms.

"I hate you," she says.

"I'm sorry..."

"You hate me, too!"

"I don't hate you!"

She keeps glaring at me. She's wrong, I don't hate her... I don't hate my past. I learned to live with it, even the worst of it, even the saddest memories. What is she craving then?

Suddenly, I realize. I was so lonely back then, I had no one. No one wanted me, no one loved me. ...Not even myself. I stare at her again. She's the me I never loved—the weak, pitiful me. I remember Damian's words... He said it's okay for me to be scared, and it's okay for me to be sad. Did I ever allow myself to cry like this as a child? I convinced myself I had to be quiet... I had to live as if I was invisible. Alec convinced me I didn't deserve anything. Even worse, I convinced myself of that too.

I bow down and hug the little child against me. I caress her hair, trying to think of how I wanted a simple hug back then.

"I'm sorry... I'm sorry I didn't even love myself. I will learn, I promise. Forgive me."

She starts crying again, bawling out while holding on to me too. The more she cries, the more relieved I feel. Behind her, I look at the wolf, not wanting to go to her anymore. That wolf isn't me. She is the one I've always wanted to be—the perfect, fearless, beautiful, and strong white wolf.

I am not perfect, and I will never be. It's like Damian said. I have to allow myself to be weak sometimes and to cry, too. I have to learn to rely on others and to have faith in my friends. I need to accept their love and love myself. I don't need to be a perfect Luna for Damian. He probably wouldn't love me if I was. I think he said it before. He loves how fragile I can be and how I make him doubt and wonder. I can be that girl. I can be... me.

"Thank you..."

As she whispers that, she suddenly vanishes from my arms, and a wave of warmth washes over me. I glance at the wolf again. This time, she has changed. My scar is there. She looks a bit thinner too, and not as mighty as before. Now, she's my wolf. That's the real me.

She gently walks to me, and I pat her.

"Sorry I didn't listen to you earlier... And sorry I wasn't gentler with myself... With us."

She puts her head under my arm, and I keep caressing her for a while before she retreats to look me in the eye.

"We need to go back now... To Damian. I need your strength."

She nods, and we put our foreheads against each other. I finally feel her... All of her. As if I had only been hearing an echo all this time. This is me; this is my wolf. She starts growling, louder and louder. I feel a rise of power, something strong and beautiful coming from within.

I wake up to Marcus' yelling.

"What are you doing? You slut..."

I suddenly get up. I don't know where I get the strength to. I am a she-wolf, I am *her*. I growl, ready to attack.

Marcus grabs his gun, but I jump first. I go for his wrist and bite it as hard as I can. His screaming echoes through the walls, but I don't care. If I back off now, I'll be dead. I bite again, and again, and again while he swears and struggles. Blood flows down all sides. I hear a gunshot, and suddenly he stops moving.

I stop and let go. What a scene... I'm not sure if I killed him or if he unintentionally shot himself, but... Marcus is dead for good. His revulsed eyes and open injuries are gruesome, and I stumble away from it. I struggle to shape-shift back for what feels like an eternity. My body has gone past its limits. My leg is so painful... and I can barely see anything. I try to find my dress in the dark and clumsily put on whatever's left of it. I'm tottering to the door. I feel so horribly sick; every step is a fight in itself. I use all of my weight to push against it, and while doing so, notice something bright bouncing on my shoulders.

Moon Goddess, is that... my own hair? I turned completely white! I check again, doubting my eyes, but every dark curl has really turned into a pure white, like my wolf's fur. What is this? I don't notice any other changes in this darkness, but my hair is almost glowing. I will wonder later— I need to get out of here...

I finally open the door and fall into what looks like the inside of a cabin... It's barely enough for one person, but Marcus made this place a mess. And it reeks of drugs, too. I ignore it, and fight to stay awake, use what strength I have left to make it to the door.

When I finally open it, I see a silhouette running to me.

"Nora!"

I don't really understand what is going on around me. I think my legs just gave up. I hear steps running to me, and scrawny hands grab my arms. It takes me a few seconds to recognize that face, those shivering hands holding me.

"Oh, Moon Goddess, no, no… I'm so sorry, Nora... Forgive me, please..."

"…Alec?"

I want to push him away, get away from my brother. What is he doing here? Instead, I feel him hugging me. I don't have any strength left to push him away…I lose balance.

"You have to hold on... Nora..."

I hear his voice. Calling my name, again and again.

"I'm sorry... I promise I'll do things right, this time. I'll save you..."

Everything is blurry, and I'm so tired... I fight to stay awake, but I know myself how bad my state must be at that moment.

Why him? Why would my brother come to save me, of all people? How did he even get here...?

I smell him, but it's different from before. Something has changed. I can feel he's skinnier under his ragged clothes, too... I close my eyes for a second and struggle to open them again.

"You have to stay awake... I'll get you there..."

"A... Alec...?" I manage to whisper.

"Nora? You're awake? Y-You must hold on, I... I'll bring you there, and..."

Alec? Why would Alec save me? Am I dreaming again? Is this really my brother? I'm so confused... His hair's longer. His voice's raspier than I remember... What happened to him?

"I'm so sorry, Nora... When I heard he had you... I knew... I knew I had to come and..."

He keeps talking, most of it doesn't even make sense, and… I'm too tired... I struggle for a bit, but the darkness wins again...

Chapter 17

I slowly wake up to the beeping of machines. Everything is so white... It's blinding me. I close and open my eyes several times, making sure I'm awake. It feels like I've had a very long dream...

Something smells good. Flowers... roses? I turn my head slowly and notice several pastel-colored bouquets all around me. This hospital room... I have a strong impression of *déjà-vu*. About the pain, too. It's a quiet pain, though, like from behind a wall. I recognize the effects of some painkillers... My leg and stomach feel the worst, but it's bearable. What I can't endure, though, is this hole I feel inside my heart.

"Nora?"

I turn my head. Bobo is leaning on my bed, looking very worried. He is using crutches, and his usual braids are undone. He looks so tired... I feel his big hand on mine.

"Can you hear me? How do you feel?"

"I can... Bobo, where is Damian?"

He lowers his head and avoids my gaze. "You... You should rest, Nora. You've been in the coma for four days. It's probably best if..."

"Bobo."

I use my Alpha voice. I want to know where my mate is, right now. Why can't I feel him? Is he too far? I've never felt this horrible void since I met Damian. I need him.

Bobo hesitates and slowly makes a head movement, gesturing behind me. I turn around to my left and finally notice the other bed. Oh, Moon Goddess, Damian...

I start crying as soon as I see him. He's so horribly pale! For a second, I even think the unthinkable, but a slow beeping is echoing next to him—a very slow beeping. My mate looks like he's in a deep sleep, not moving an inch; I can't even see his breathing. Machines are surrounding him, one helping him breathe, others linked to his arms, tubes going through and through. I can't believe what I'm seeing. How did Damian become like this? How is he even alive? And why can't I feel him at all!

Tears are pouring down, and I breathe erratically, unable to calm down. I want to move, to want to go to Damian, but Bobo's hands grab my shoulders, keeping me down in bed.

"No, no, Nora, you have to stay put, please."

"Bobo, why is he like this? Why is Damian like that?" I ask, desperate.

"He... he was shot, Nora, remember?"

Shot? The gathering... Now I suddenly remember everything—the Gold Moon's bombs in the stadium, the surprise attack. I remember the gunshots, each one of them. My Damian, lying on the ground, bleeding. Bleeding so much...

"I can't feel him at all..." I whisper, in shock.

I can't. My wolf is going nuts. Damian is right here, I can see him with my own eyes, so why can't I feel him at all? I look at him, and it's like I'm staring at an empty spot. I can't accept it, I can't.

"When will he wake up?"

A long silence follows. I notice we are not alone. Liam is sitting right next to Damian's bed, his head on the mattress. He's sleeping, but his eyes are red, and he looks like a mess... He's holding his brother's hand tightly. It breaks my heart to see the usually smiling Liam like that. I reach for Bobo's big hand again, but I can't stop looking at Damian.

"Bobo, when will he wake up?"

Once again, no answer. I try to hold back my tears.

"Bobo, when!" I scream. I can't take it: this heavy silence, this awkward and wary atmosphere.

Bobo raises his head to meet my eyes with a somber and sorry look. "Nora, the doctors said he will... probably never wake up."

"You're lying," I retort right back.

Damian has to wake up. I can't imagine, for a second, that he will stay like this. I gasp, trying to catch my breath. I just can't understand, I can't believe there is a world where Damian would die like that.

"He's right there, Bobo, he's alive."

"Nora, his body is... They did their best with the surgery, but his wounds are too great. He... he didn't wake up after they operated on him. He's in a deep coma, and all those machines are keeping him alive, but..." His voice breaks.

I don't get it... I can't process what he's saying. All I can think of is this horrible, insufferable sensation in my chest, ripping my heart apart. I close my eyes, leaving my tears to flow out because I need to break right now; I can't contain it. What's going on? What is this nightmare I woke up into?

"Nora?"

Liam just woke up. Moon Goddess, he looks so miserable... His messy hair, the dark circles under his puffy eyes... He bites his lip and breathes in. "Good to see you up... How do you feel?" All the while, he doesn't let go of Damian's hand.

I shake my head. I don't feel anything but terrible right now.

He frowns. "It's... it's going to be okay, Nora. He... he will make it, I'm sure of it."

His voice sounds so weak and sorrowful, I know he wants to believe it. I want it, too, so I just nod. I can't imagine... So, I try to keep it together.

I breathe in, take time to calm down my tears. Bobo is caressing my hair gently. He pushes a button, and my bed gets me on a sitting position. Now that I can look around, I notice I really am back in the hospital's VIP room... Only that there's an additional bed and lots of flowers.

"What... what happened? What's going on right now? Bobo, you said... four days?"

"Four days and a half, actually," says Liam. "It took us a while to find you. You remember?"

I do, or just enough, I think. The cabin, Marcus... Right, he's finally dead. It's a blurry memory, but I'm sure of that, at least.

"Alec..." I whisper, suddenly remembering I saw my brother... Or I thought I saw him.

Liam sighs. "We found you with your brother Alec, in the woods... He was carrying you here; we found him half-way. You were taken in surgery right away. It took hours... You had a bullet lodged in your left leg and internal bleeding."

I look down at my leg. Indeed, I have a thick bandage all around my leg, and a strap holding it up. I vaguely remember that, too... But I can still feel the pain a bit. It doesn't really matter for now. I ignore it and turn to Liam again.

"What... what happened then? And Alec?"

He shrugs. “Your brother disappeared right after he brought you here, so I’m not sure. We tried to look for him, but honestly, you were our top priority... We did our best. Once you were out of surgery, they said it would take you a while to come back, so Bobo, Tonia, Sylviana, and I took turns watching you two. Somehow, I think your new... look helps Damian, so...”

My new look? I look down and finally notice white, curly hair. What happened to my hair? It went from jet black to a silvery-white. It looks totally unnatural...

“Yeah, it shocked us, too. No idea how you pulled that one off.”

“That’s the only change we noticed about you,” adds Bobo.

“Sylviana said you’re all charged up with Moon Power if that makes any sense to you,” says Liam. “Anyway, you and Damian were out, so Nate and William somewhat took over. With the Gold Moon out, everyone started working together.”

“What happened? Back at the stadium. I saw... bodies...”

I’m sure of that. People died—a lot of werewolves. Everyone was fighting, some were fleeing the scene, but I can’t forget the sight of dead bodies I came across. No face I recognized, but I can’t imagine they were only the Gold Moon Clan’s people.

Liam sighs and massages his neck, looking tired. “Yeah, it was a mess... Most of the Gold Moon people died, but all the packs had casualties. We lost people, too. Andrew Jones was killed, and Vincent Greene, too.”

“Marcus shot Vincent. I remember now... I was trying to run away, and I ran into Vincent...”

He shot him dead right in front of me. How could I forget that?

Liam slowly nods. “So, I guess now we know who killed him... Taaron King probably killed Andrew Jones. People saw them fighting right before. Greene’s new Beta died, too, by the way. And... Old Man Seaver passed away, too. Two days ago.”

Oh, Moon Goddess...

“So, it’s been a bit... complicated. People are trying to pull it together. Lysandra took over the Violet Clan, and Arthur Seaver did the same with the Sea Moon Wolves... The Jade Moon people are listening to us for now, and the Rising Moon surrendered, too. A couple other packs lost their Alphas, so... And there are still people in severe conditions.”

Moon Goddess... I remember the stadium; it was a war scene. It's been a few days, but how can we expect things to go back to normal so soon? With so many people dead, injured, or grieving...

And Damian. The Alpha King, being in a coma...

"What... what did Sylviana say?" I ask, full of hope.

Liam frowns. "She's helpless. His injuries are... "

His voice breaks again, and he lowers his head. I see a couple of tears falling. Oh, Liam... I choke up, too, and a long silence follows. Neither of us wants to speak. I can only contemplate Damian.

Even when William or Elena come to visit, I don't really react. All that time, I'm thinking. I'm thinking about Damian and me. About us. I'm so weak, but I don't want to sleep a single second I might miss with him.

I feel calmer every second that passes by, and more resolute. Bobo notices the change in me but doesn't say a thing. He can't possibly know. He probably thinks I'm in denial, but that's wrong. I can't ignore the obvious.

He told the truth. Damian is dying.

My mate is in a deep coma right now. Tonia comes to visit me with the surgeon, but we talk more about Damian's state than mine. The doctor explains it to me, but all I can remember is that his injuries are too great. It's a miracle he's still holding on, and Liam thinks it's because of me, but… I can't feel him. To my wolf, Damian's already in a place where I can't reach him, and I can't have that. I just can't.

Every one of our friends visits us. All of them, and the Alphas that made it out too. They're glad I woke up, but it's impossible to ignore Damian's fate. Those visits have a bitter taste, no matter how much we try to keep it in. Me, too. I don't want to pretend I'm fine. I'm dead inside. This black hole is eating me up, destroying me as my mate is fading away.

When nighttime comes, I'm perfectly calm and waiting.

Liam never left his brother's side a single second, neither did Bobo leave mine, even when the nurse came to change his bandages. Now, they are both dozing off on their chairs. I'm sitting up, looking at Damian.

A smell of wildflowers enters the room, one I've been waiting for.

"Good evening, Nora," she whispers.

I smile gently to Sylviana as she approaches. She takes a quick stop to caress Liam's hair, looking sorry for him and walks up to me. She sits on my bed, on the side where she can face Damian.

For a while, we both silently look at him.

"...Are you sure?" She asks.

I knew Sylviana would understand right away. I don't know why I was so sure of it, but there wasn't any need for me to explain anything—she just knew.

I slowly nod.

"Nora, you will most likely... Even if you've never been so powerful, his injuries..."

"I'll do it anyway."

She turns to me, but I keep speaking in a soft voice, not wanting to wake up the guys.

"I know, Sylviana. I will probably... not wake up, but it doesn't matter. I just can't let him die like this."

"He wouldn't want this..."

I shake my head. "It's my choice. I'm probably acting selfish right now, but... I can't live without him. And there's Liam, Nate... The Blood Moon Clan, the other packs... So many people need him."

"He needs you."

I smile softly. That's probably what Damian himself would say. I know that, but my decision is taken.

Sylviana understands and sighs. Her eyes shift to Liam. "Did you... say goodbye?"

I feel a tear rolling down my eye.

"Not really… It's always too late for farewells, anyway," I mutter, choking up a bit.

She silently starts to cry, too. I know she doesn't want to do this; she doesn't want to be the one to see me go. I'm leaving her with a heavy burden, but no one else but Sylviana would have helped me, and we both know that.

She takes my hand. Around us, the flowers silently start growing out, branches crawling all around us on the floor and walls. It's actually pretty... Roses are blooming all over as the branches keep progressing. They get to my bed and softly carry me to Damian's bed while Sylviana steps away. They gently set me right next to him. My heart suddenly warms a little as I can finally caress his check.

"Hello, my Love..." I whisper softly to him.

He can't hear me, but it doesn't matter. I take a while to look at him. My Damian, my fated mate... Moon Goddess, I love him so much... I don't want us to part yet, but if I don't do this, he will leave me into a world I can't live in...

I have a long thought for everyone who loved me. Liam, Bobo, Nate, Tonia, Elena, William, Daniel... It's hard. It's hard to leave them, without saying goodbye, without even apologizing for this. But it's too late for that now.

I lean towards Damian, look at him for the last time, and give him the longest, the most loving farewell kiss of our lives.

I'm floating. I'm numb, drifting in a world of unknown colors: no smell and no sensations, nothing but emptiness around me. I'm a whisper in a sea of emptiness. I'm free, in a place that's nowhere. ...Is this what dying is like?

It could be a second, it could be a year. I could be an instant mixed with eternity. Time makes no sense here; I wait without expecting anything. Where, When, Who... No questions make any sense to me. I'm just there. Free and... trapped. An ethereal space, a dive in emptiness. My soul on a lock, my mind in a blank. Slowly drifting apart, losing anything I gathered.

There's no light or warmth to accompany me; there's no one here. I'm trapped in this mute world, a deaf world. A lonely place, peaceful and scary at the same time, a black hole of emptiness. A long, long thread of loneliness.

I'm so numb and so tired. I'm asleep. I try to fly, I try to soar and climb, to find myself again. I want to go back to them... back to *Him*.

Ghostly memories echoing on my mind, striving to come back to me. Who am I? What have I lost...? The whisper of a forgotten voice, the shadow of a touch... Something I've long forgotten, something I yearn to remember again—memories barricaded behind an invisible wall, a lock keeping me a thought away.

I hear... sounds.

A prolonged wind... Someone's soft breathing. A little, regular beeping sound. The rumbling of something soft. Footsteps, soft voices... Life. I'm alive.

Or... almost.

I can't feel a thing, nor my own body. Just hear those sounds, like an echo reaching me—a glimpse of life from behind a heavy veil. Something I can't touch, but I can gather. Finally, a peek at life.

It comes and goes like a wave that never dares to approach. Sometimes it fades away, sometimes it's brighter than ever before. I wait for it, I'll be patient. Please, please come back to me. Wait for me. Forgive me. I'll be back. No matter how long it takes. I'll come back to you.

I hear them again.

It's a long road, a long way up. Wait for me. I'll come to you, I'm coming.

A ghost of mist holding me back, losing me again. I'll try again, I'll find my way back. I'll catch my breath, I'll grasp my life again. Wait for me. Give me some time, give me a chance.

The voices come back again. Calling my name, a name I can't recall. I'll listen to what I can't hear. Catching a thread, following it back. How do I get back?

Listen, listen to them. I need those voices. Guide me. Show me the way back home. I'm coming home, coming back to you.

I'll come back into my life. I'll get it all back, I will be with you. Wait, wait just a little bit.

One more time, and one more chance. One more breath.

"...Something changed?"

"I think so... Her heartbeat, it's faster. Look. Even her breathing looks more natural."

"Check again. We need to be sure this time. We can't give him false hopes again after so long."

I'm fighting my way back.

Sensations crawl back in, one after another. The gentle caress of the air on my skin. The heaviness of unconsciousness. The inner echo of my breathing. My heartbeat pulsing in my ears...

"You think she can... hear us?"

"Maybe. I always feel like she can. I talk to her a lot, just in case."

"I miss her, too. It's weird..."

"I know. Like, she's there, but... An empty shell. Even her wolf's gone, too. I miss her voice."

I miss you, too, and I want to come back... I must keep going. No hesitation, no looking back. Just this long, blind search for a way to return. A fog of unconsciousness, trapping me then and again. When will I finally wake up?

"I need you... I'll wait, Nora, no matter how long. I miss you, I miss you, Love... Can you hear me? ...Or maybe you're dreaming? I want to join you in your dreams. I miss you so much... I... I..."

A silence breaks and something painful holds my heart. A memory choking me, overflowing me with emotions. Did I lose you? Will you be able to wait a bit more, when you've already waited so long? What are you going through?

"I'm so sorry, Nora. I wish you were here... I wish I could tell you goodbye in person. I... I hope you'll be back soon. They all miss you. I'll miss you the most. Do you know how much you're loved, Nora? He is coming every day to see you... Liam and Bobo, too. Everyone loves you. They are all waiting for you... I hope you will be back soon. I'm so sorry we have to part this way. I hope you'll understand, Nora. We will see each other again, I promise. Forgive me."

Lips softly press against my forehead, and there is a gentle caress in my hair. Footsteps going away... Where are you going? I need you again. Where are you leaving? Why are you leaving me alone...?

The smell grows stronger. Fresh roses.

"Hey, Nora... Done playing sleeping beauty yet? We miss you, you know. Don't worry about us, but you got to come back. Damian misses you. Again. My poor brother deserves the price for most patient boyfriend, don't you think? Well, he's not your boyfriend anymore now, but still. I can't wait for when you'll be back... I'm bored here. I miss Sylviana, and Nate is..."

"Do you have no one else but her to talk to behind my back?"

"What are you doing here, mister blockhead?"

"Fuck you, Liam."

"In a good mood again, I see. What are you doing here, anyway?"

"What, I can't even visit Nora now?"

"As if. You don't give a shit about Nora; you were hoping to know about them. Well, I don't know a thing, and as you can see, Nora's not giving you a hint either, so fuck off, Nate."

Trapped in darkness again, I breathe slowly. When will this be over? It's getting more and more painful now... A heavy sleep catching me, a consciousness it's hard to come to. Words coming back to me, and sounds reaching my ears again.

"I know I said I'd wait but... it's hard without you... Can you hear me, Love? As long as you're not suffering again... I don't know how I'm getting by every day like this... I just wish you'd wake up... I miss the color of your eyes, Nora. The sound of your voice, too. I don't know how they keep going with their lives while I'm stuck here. I want to be by your side every day, every minute. I think of you every second. I..."

Fingers running through my hair, and something gently brushing the back of my hand. A smell I love. A familiar warmth, and that voice... A deep sigh.

"I just keep going. I wake up, go to work, talk to people, live every minute... And I come back to you. I'm the Alpha they want me to be, but... Everyone's waiting for you. For the Luna. They never mention you when I'm in the room. Do they think I'll break if they call your name out loud? They don't get it. I'm waiting for you, my Love. I'll wait, Nora, as long as it takes for you to come back."

How long will it take? How long has it been? I feel like I've been here forever... I have no idea. Days? Weeks? Months? Years? I'm so sorry... I keep fighting, looking for my way back, trying again. Why is it so hard? Why am I so weak...?

Moon Goddess... How did I lose my way? How do I go back to them? I'm scared I'll be too late, I'm afraid I'll be trapped in here forever. Eternity isn't for me. I want to feel again. Life is waiting for me, but I'm a step aside from the world, in-between.

Tell him I love him. I'll be back. Tell them I love you, I love you so much. I'll tell you when I'm scared again, I'll let you know when I'm in pain. I'm coming back.

I'm tearing down the wall, I'm screaming again. I'll let you feel my pain, Damian, I promise this time I'll share it all with you. I'll be a wolf again, I'll be your mate, forever.

I will cry, I will laugh, and I will share it all with you. Your Luna is coming back to life, your Luna is finding her way back.

I'm right there, where Love was waiting for us.

Where you're waiting for me.

I'm back. I love you.

Chapter 18

"Are you sure?"

Liam's voice. He sounds so impatient...

"Hundred percent. She's definitely waking up. I can feel her wolf again. Can't you?"

"Nope. But then again, I don't have your bond, so..."

Our bond. I can feel him, Damian's wolf. A magnificent jet-black wolf, waiting for mine to come back. She's waking up slowly, reaching out to him. *I* am waking up, slowly, steadily; It's like reaching the surface and catching my breath.

I open my eyes.

"Holy Moon Goddess Mother!"

I'm facing the ceiling. When I turn my head slowly, the first thing I see is... Him. Damian, so close and smiling to me. I smile back to him, feeling overwhelmed. He leans over me, gently kissing my forehead.

"Good morning, my Love."

I've never seen him look so overjoyed... It's contagious, I can't stop smiling at him, even though I'm feeling so drowsy. I hear footsteps running, and suddenly Liam comes in the room, panting, followed by people in white coats.

"Damian! Damian, is she still awake? Oh, Moon Goddess, she really is! Doctor, she's really awake, right?" He asks without catching his breath.

What's going on? I recognize Granny Ariana, smiling at me, and people start patting my wrists, checking my condition, and discussing my vitals. A doctor shines a small flashlight in front of my eyes and moves his finger.

"Miss Bluemoon, can you hear me? Can you follow my finger, please?"

It's a bit annoying, but I nod and do as he says. I'm a bit confused and overwhelmed by all those people in the room asking me questions.

Still, Damian and Liam both look thrilled. My mate isn't letting go of my hand and stays by my side as long as the medical team keeps examining me.

"Her vitals are normal; she is indeed completely awake... This is amazing. Miss Bluemoon, are you feeling discomfort in any way? How do you feel?"

"I am... drowsy."

Behind the doctor, Liam squeals, totally excited. Why won't he calm down? The man examining me nods while taking some notes.

"Well, that is perfectly normal in your condition. But your reflexes are fine for now, and your vitals, as well. We will have to work on your reeducation, of course, but overall, this is... A positively great return. Welcome back, miss Bluemoon."

Welcome back? I turn to Damian, a bit lost. I feel like I've been sleeping, but now I'm a bit confused again. He raises my hand to his lips to kiss it, and I realize I have trouble moving my fingers. I frown and try to move my limbs again. It's like my whole body has gotten twice as heavy as I remember it.

Granny Ariana gives me a reassuring smile. "Don't worry, sweetheart, it's going to take a while. Your body will need some time to readjust, but it will."

"Who cares? She's back! Damn, Nora, I've missed you!"

I take a look a Liam, smiling from ear to ear behind Granny Ariana. He looks... Different. He's visibly slimmer, a bit more muscular and taller, and his hair is a bit longer, too. He has a new piercing on his left ear. It's like he's lost all the teenage attitude to look more like his brothers...

I turn to look at Damian.

My mate, too. His hair is cut shorter, and he's not wearing a beard anymore, either. His eyes look darker and more profound. He looks thinner than I remember, too... How did they change so much?

"How do you feel, Love?" Asks Damian in a soft voice.

"I'm okay... What happened? You look different. Liam, you, too. I... How long was I...?"

Liam sighs and nods. "Nora, you saved my brother's life with your Moon Power, remember? He was dying, and you did that whole kissing thing. Next thing we know, you were unconscious, and he was completely fine!"

I turn to Damian, who's still caressing my hand.

"You healed me, Nora. You used your power, but it put you into a very deep sleep. You stayed in some sort of coma for a long time."

I gradually remember everything from before now. At least, my farewell to Damian, and the sight of his injuries... But a lot of my memories are still blurry. I have vague images of a big battle, a forest, a hospital... It's gradually coming back to me. My whole life here. My childhood, life with the Jade Moon Pack, my life with Damian...

A long time? That would explain why they changed. I take a second to process and look at the window. It's snowing outside... I turn to them again to finally ask.

"What day are we?"

"December 23rd..."

I try to remember vaguely.

"The fight... It was last Thursday, right? The 20th..."

Damian looks at me and sighs, a bit surprised and uneasy.

But Liam laughs awkwardly. "Nora, that Thursday wasn't two days ago but two years ago! You stayed in the coma for 23 months and over three weeks, girl."

Moon Goddess... Two years? I was asleep for two whole years? I'm in shock. It did feel like awakening after a very long time, but... I turn to Damian. He waited for me to wake up for two whole years? Oh, Moon Goddess... I open my mouth to apologize, but he shakes his head and holds my hand against his cheek.

"It's okay, Nora. I don't care how long it took. Don't apologize, Love. I'm just happy you're back..."

"Everyone will be happy you're back! Holy shit, I have to tell everyone!"

Liam takes out his phone and walks out of the room in a hurry, but I don't care. All I'm focused on right now is Damian. No matter what, I can't hold back a tear.

"Two years..." I whisper, still astonished.

"727 days," he says. "I counted every single day without you... That's a long time to catch back up, Love."

I slowly nod, smiling at him. I realized how much I've missed him now that I can contemplate him. The warmth of his skin, and his lips against my palm. His beautiful, unique silver eyes. He's even more handsome than I remember, with his new haircut and clean-shaven face. I concentrate on moving my fingers and caressing his smooth chin.

"…What happened to your beard?"

He smiles. "I was waiting for someone to grow it again. I'm happy you're back. It was a pain shaving every day..."

I giggle and nod again. "All right, you can start growing it again, then. I miss it. You..."

I stop talking, suddenly noticing something shiny on my hand. This is new... Damian realizes I noticed and smiles proudly while holding my hand up for me to see. I gasp. A gorgeous ring is placed on my finger, mesmerizing me. It's a thin ring, but I can't miss the shining sapphire stone on it, flanked by two moon-shaped diamonds.

"Damian, this..."

"Your engagement ring. ...You like it?"

I can't ignore his mischievous smile. He's obviously enjoying my surprised reaction, playing with my fingers, and waiting for my answer. I smile, too, but I'm just overwhelmed by emotions right now. Eventually, I can't hold back a little laugh.

"Damian Black, when did I ever get engaged to you?"

"Since you saved this stupid man twice, miss Bluemoon. I thought that you had paid a huge price for my life, so... It might as well be all yours."

He shows me his hand and the matching ring he's wearing, too, a simple platinum one. Oh, this man... I can't believe him. Damian has changed. He looks more peaceful now, not as restless as when I met him. His eyes have this gentle warmth to them, too.

"So?" He asks.

I smile.

"I like it... Mr. Black. I'm glad I woke up before we had our wedding ceremony, though."

He laughs and leans in to kiss my forehead.

"It was high time you woke up, Nora. I don't know how much longer I would have waited for that, too."

Right after he finishes his sentence, someone suddenly bursts into the room. Oh, Moon Goddess, my Bobo! I smile like a child, and he looks at me in disbelief, like he can't believe his own eyes. My best friend has changed, too. His hair is way shorter and arranged in neat little braids instead of his former dreadlocks. He seems bulkier, too.

Moreover, a pale scar is visible on his left temple.

"Nora!" He exclaims, before running to me.

"Hey, hey, easy, big boy!" Says Liam, holding him back. "Don't knock her out!"

Bobo stops right on my bed's side, and grabs my free hand gently, holding it tight.

"Seriously, Nora... I can't believe it..."

"Hey, Bobo... I missed you, too." I say. "How are you? That scar..."

He shakes his head. "It's nothing. Danny says it makes me look cooler."

"Hey, we got cool scars, too, okay?" Says Liam.

"What are you talking about? You barely had any scratches..."

I turn my head. Sylviana just entered the room behind Bobo, and she gives me a soft smile, sitting at the end of my bed. She's the only one that hasn't changed a bit, surprisingly, even looking a bit younger than I remember.

"Hi, Nora. We all missed you a lot..."

"Hi, Sylviana. Looks like I made it, after all."

"Yes, with a lot of luck. Moon Goddess obviously loves you too much to let you go..."

I can only agree to that, though I feel the weight of those two years. I turn to the guys as Bobo is pushing a button that puts my bed in a sitting position.

"You're going to have to fill me in."

"What do you remember?"

"Not everything. Until a few days before the fight, and after that... It's a blur. I vaguely remember us taking the car to the meeting, I think. And the Alphas came... And we started talking... I remember bombs exploded, and there was a huge fight."

Damian nods, and Bobo starts talking.

"We lost you in the confusion. I think The Gold Moon was targeting you from the start to weaken the Boss. Some wolves jumped at me right after the first explosions, and you were taken away."

"They isolated Damian and me too," adds Liam. "So, Damian was badly injured, as you know, but Nate and I made it through the first attack thanks to Sylviana. We had to participate in the fight, but we were worried about Damian and couldn't reach out to you. We realized something was wrong when the fight stopped with the Gold Moon wiped out and the Rising Moon surrendering. But you were nowhere to be found, and William told us the people he had sent to protect you had died. None of us could reach you."

"I… I was taken…"

Boyan nods.

"We realized that soon. Witnesses said they had seen a man taking you out, but they thought you were being evacuated, not kidnapped."

"Someone gave a description that was exactly that of… Marcus Sickels," says Liam. "We soon understood what must have happened, and we looked around for clues. But Damian was taken here in critical condition meanwhile. We didn't have many people to send to look for you that were not already helping evacuate the Stadium…"

"William helped," explained Damian. "The Jade Moon, too, looked everywhere for you…"

"Believe I or not, it was Alec that found you."

I turn to Liam, shocked.

"A-Alec?"

"Yes," he nods. "It turns out your brother was in the hospital, and when he saw all the werewolves coming in, he had somehow heard everything about you being missing. He knew about Sickels having a secret hide-out somewhere in the Jade Moon forest, so he went first to look for you. The Jade Moon Clan spotted him, so Sylviana and I ran there as fast as we could right after that."

Sylviana nods.

"You were in a critical state," she says. "Alec was arrested, and we took you to the hospital. You went several hours under surgery to stop your internal bleeding and save your leg."

The more she talks, the more it all comes back to me. Marcus' voice, his kicks in my stomach, stomping on my painful leg. Just the memory feels so painful… And Alec's hands taking me out of there. He carried me to safety. So, it wasn't some faraway dream. My brother was really there, he took me out of there.

"Why…"

I can't understand why Alec went there to help me. I still can't understand how he appeared out of the blue to help me. He felt different, too…

"Your brother had been in rehab for a while, Nora," explains

Sylviana. "Since the last time you had seen him, he was… thriving to get better, to get out of drugs."

"Sylviana actually helped, too," adds Liam.

"I didn't do anything he didn't want," she says. "Alec was… remorseful of what he had done."

I choke up a little bit, hearing those words. Alec did? Are we talking about the same person who abused me for years? That Alec, my brother? The one who tried to sell me to a rapist? It is still a bit too hard to believe.

I don't want to think about that now. I turn to Damian.

"Then?"

"Liam and Sylviana brought you back here," he says. "You were in critical condition like she said. Yet, when you woke up, you decided to do something even more dangerous."

Yes, I remember that too.

I remember the sad memories. How people died in the attack or succumbed to their injuries. Damian was one of the first to fall, but my mate was still alive when I came to. I remember my discussion with Sylviana, and my eyes naturally go to the witch.

I decided to use my Moon Power to save Damian. My mate was on the verge of dying when I woke up from my first coma, and I just couldn't have that. Sylviana nods, reminding me of what happened, but it's all coming back to me now.

Once she's done talking, Damian sighs. "That was a crazy thing to do, even for you."

"I wouldn't have lived without you," I answer.

He nods. "I said the same... If you had died in the process..."

He frowns from the thought, as we all know the result of my bet could have taken my life instead of those two years.

Liam claps his hands, taking us away from any depressing thinking, and smiles. "Anyway! Our princess is back now, for good! Right, Nora?"

I smile. "To be honest, I feel awfully sleepy..." I whisper, playing a bit.

Liam shakes his head. "Oh, hell, no! Girl, you are not going to play sleeping beauty again! You're back to the living now, so get ready, because you have a lot of people waiting for you and a whole bunch of things to catch up on, too!"

I nod to Liam's words. He's right, I missed two whole years! Those two years I will never get back… It saddens me a little bit, of course. I look at Damian, Liam, and Bobo, my three men, all looking a bit older. I smile and turn to Damian, with a mix of curiosity and apprehension.

"So, what did I miss?"

"Well first, it took a few days to settle everything after what had happened... Surprisingly, the events served as a lesson for everyone. All the remaining packs finally agreed to your idea of a Peace Treaty between the Clans. Sylviana used her magic to seal it, so no Alpha can break the peace vow as long as their turf is located in Silver City."

"Oh, come on, Damian, tell her about the Liege," says Liam, visibly excited.

I frown. The Liege?

Damian nods. "They also... agreed to recognize me as the official Alpha King of Silver City. It's more of a title than anything else, but everyone thought it would be best to make it... official. That way, no one would dare to raise up any more conflicts or take advantage of others under my name again."

"You should have seen it, Nora. Even William agreed to it, and all the Alphas discussed in one room, like equals."

"Anyway," resumes Damian, "there was a month of mourning, and then we began the reconstruction of the stadium. We also had to reconsider all the packs' territories and sort out the situation of the ones who had lost their Alphas."

"The Jade Moon is all yours, by the way," says Bobo. "They didn't have any Alpha or Beta left, so they just agreed you were their legitimate leader now. Until now, they answered to Damian while you were in the coma."

"Most importantly, we abolished the physical boundaries between the territories within Silver City," explains Damian. "No more frontiers between the turfs. Anyone is free to go wherever they want. Each pack still has its own establishments and properties, but when it comes to the streets, no more fighting."

Moon Goddess, that's amazing... Before that, any wolf was constrained to their own pack's territory, and would go anywhere else at their own risk! It also kept Damian from finding me all those years, as he couldn't go everywhere freely. This is such a huge change; I can't believe everyone agreed to it so quickly!

"This is great… Is it really happening?" I ask.

Damian and Liam both nod.

"Yep! It made things easier for a lot of people, actually, and reduced the fighting by an awful lot. I mean, there's still some bickering here and there, but trust me, it's nowhere what it used to be. And now we have a lot of new couples from different packs, too! Do you remember Marina Seaver? She got engaged to a guy from the Violet Moon!" Says Liam, looking all excited.

While listening to him, I suddenly remember another couple, much closer to us, that was struggling about being from different packs and turn to Damian. "What about Nate and Elena? And their baby? It must be born by now!"

As soon as I ask about them, Damian's expression suddenly goes dark, and Liam's smile drops. Both brothers look sorry, and I'm scared of their lack of answers. What? What's going on?

"Damian? What about them?"

"Love, Nate and Elena... They aren't together anymore."

I stay stunned for a few seconds.

"Wait... What? How come? What about their baby?"

For once, Damian stays silent, and Liam is suddenly the one looking angry. Since neither of them is talking, I turn to Bobo.

"Bobo! Tell me!"

"Elena left Silver City, Nora. A few weeks after you fell into a coma, she... she and Nate had a big argument. I think she had issues with her pack, too, and she… she left while still pregnant."

What...? She just left? Months ago? How could this happen? And the baby, too, did she decide to give birth to her child alone? I can't believe it...

Sylviana moves over and takes my hand, softly smiling at me.

"Nora, don't worry. I went with her when she left and made sure her baby was fine. I helped her find a place and give birth. They are both doing great. I came back a few weeks later."

I sigh in relief. So, Elena is fine... Elena and her baby are okay. Although, that doesn't erase the rest. I turn again towards Damian and Liam, angry.

"You do realize I'm going to kill your brother once I'm better?"

Liam, looking pissed off, nods. "Trust me, we both did it for you already. Nate is a fucking idiot, and he knows it, but he's one damn stubborn dog."

Damian's hand tightens around mine, and he gently caresses my cheek.

"Nora, you'll get angry at Nate later. You just woke up, I don't want you thinking about anything but getting better for now, okay? And Elena and her baby are fine, I swear. So, you can scold Nate all you want, but later, Love. Later."

I frown, but I don't have the energy to face Nathaniel about his attitude now, anyway. Despite all the medication I'm probably on, I'm well aware of my sore muscles and drowsiness. I sigh and push my head back on the pillow. While doing so, I realize my hair is back to its dark black color.

Sylviana sees my expression. "It went back to black right after your kiss, although it turned white again a few weeks later. Turns out, it changes color into a pale white at night, when the moon rises."

"So, I'm..."

"I would say you're harvesting Moon Power every time the sun sets. Whatever happened two years ago, your power unleashed completely. You can use your aura again and somehow recharge it as long as the moon rises."

Damian lets out a low growl. "She won't use it again. I'm not risking Nora going back into the coma."

"You should have been dead, and Nora used way more power than her body could handle to bring you back. No wonder she had to pay for it. I doubt she will ever fall into such a state again unless you are severely injured. Her power probably works just like mine: Too much power has to be paid at a high cost..."

I exchange a look with Damian. Sylviana's probably right about this, but I think it will take some time for my mate to accept it. He decides to ignore her and turns to me, kissing my hand again.

I want to chat with them some more, hear what else I missed, but before that, the medical team returns. They have even more people and has most of my friends leave as I need to go through a few more medical examinations.

For the whole afternoon, I pass several tests, checking my memory, control of my limbs, and cognitive response. As the hours go by, it's obvious I retrieve all my memories and mental faculties back, but my body is still in a weak state. Though the doctors explain that it's natural and expect a quick recovery, I must adapt to sitting in a wheelchair and being taken everywhere like this. My legs can't hold me at all and moving my arms ask me a lot of energy and focus.

When the head doctor comes to explain everything, Damian is sitting with me. "Your results are great, miss Bluemoon. As predicted, you were not in a regular coma; hence, your cognitive faculties all returned within a few hours. Your body, however, will need longer to readapt."

"How long are we talking about?" I ask.

I feel like a puppet, some doll that can't stand on her own.

"I don't usually give optimistic estimates, miss Bluemoon," he says. "But judging from how you can already move your head and arms, I would confidently say a few weeks. With a good therapist and efforts, it shouldn't be an issue."

"Can I go home, then?"

I just want to leave the hospital, breathe some air, and go back to a normal life as soon as possible. I miss it so much already. The doctor exchanges a look with Damian. My mate gives him his imposing glare, until the poor man clears his throat, coming back to me with a weak smile.

"Well, I will ask you to stay for the next 24 hours, at least, so we can prevent any unforeseen issue with your awakening. However, this is clearly a magic issue linked to your... wolf, miss Bluemoon, and a grey area for us. If you can have a proper caretaker and constant surveillance, going home tomorrow shouldn't be an issue, miss Bluemoon. I would still request you come back within the next few days for a couple more check-ups, though."

I smile brightly and turn to Damian. I can go home tomorrow! I don't even have to spend Christmas there! My mate smiles back at me and kisses my forehead.

After that meeting, I insist on Damian to take me to the inner garden of the hospital. It's covered in snow, but Moon Goddess, it's beautiful. Damian pushes my wheelchair on the little road. He wraps me in a thick blanket, but I lean back and enjoy the cold air on my face. It feels amazing... Being alive.

He finally sits down on a bench, next to my wheelchair, facing me.

"It's good to be back," I say.

He nods, taking my hand in his, playing with my engagement ring. "I've missed you so much..." He whispers. "I came here every day to see you. Before and after work. I knew you weren't there, but I just wanted to see your face, remember that you were still hanging on somehow. I slept so many times on the chair in your room, and Neal and Liam dragged me to work countless times. Nora..."

He takes a deep breath.

"I bought us a house a few months ago."

I stay speechless for a moment. Did I hear that wrong?

"...A house?"

"Our house. Your home. I didn't want to keep living on my own in my apartment at the Company building. I wanted... A place I could look forward to living in with you. A place where we could be together, a place we could call our house."

I look at him, speechless, as my heartbeat accelerates. He really bought a house. For the two of us, for when I would come back? I take another look at the ring. He really was preparing everything for when I would come back, no matter when it would be. I feel a little tear running down my face, my heart tightening at the thought. My poor Damian... How lonely must he have felt for those two years I made him wait... I cross my fingers with his.

"Tell me about it. The house."

He smiles. "I'll take you there tomorrow. It's a big white house with a little garden. I took my time choosing it. I wish I could have given you a choice in the matter, too, but... I picked one on an uphill, with a view of the east forest. There are five bedrooms aside from the main one, and a big kitchen, fully equipped—everything you could possibly need or want when you cook, Love. I didn't take a big house, but one you would feel home in. With more bedrooms, and enough space to welcome our friends... And our children, later."

Gosh, I love the idea. I lean in for a long kiss. Whichever house Damian picked, I'm sure I'll love it. I really want to see that house he got us and resume my life with him. Damian even thought about our future children... We had that talk before, so I know it's for a later future, but I already look forward to it.

"Damian?"

"Yes, my Love?"

"I... really want us to get married. Soon."

"Soon?"

"Yes... I'm now twenty-years-old, right? I already missed two years we should have spent together... I don't want to be late for anything else. I want to start living with you, I want to catch up on the time we have lost. I don't need a big ceremony, just to be yours as soon as I can."

He stays silent for a while and smiles. "Anything you want, Nora. We can even have the papers signed today if you want. The mayor is not really in a position to say no..."

I laugh a bit and give him a quick kiss. "Maybe not that fast, my Love. Let me be able to catch up on everything I've missed first. Also, when I can stand up again. Plus, I want all of our friends to be there."

He frowns a bit. "That's a lot of people. You know your cousin will harass me if I want to marry you?"

"William? I thought you two had solved your differences already, two years ago."

Damian makes a sour face.

"I thought so, too, but I clearly underestimated his... overprotective instinct towards you. He opposed strongly to our engagement."

"Don't tell me he still wants to marry me!"

Damian shakes his head. "That was just an empty threat to test me, Nora. Sylviana said that the whole thing about Royals being able to change mates was a total lie. And William doesn't feel that way about you; he sees you as a little sister, that's it. He's annoying enough as it is..."

I laugh. Imagining William and Damian bickering about me is a lot funnier now that the tensions between all the packs have eased up.

"He already got engaged a few months ago, anyway."

"What, really? To whom?"

"Remember Tiffany Pearl, from the Pearl Moon? Well, it seems like those two had never actually met face to face until the gathering..."

"You're kidding!"

I'm in shock, but Damian laughs. Oh, Moon Goddess! I would never have imagined... Tiffany is indeed the most beautiful she-wolf I've ever seen. I don't know her well, but from what I've seen, she's smart and beautiful. Yes, those two are probably a good match.

Around us, snow slowly starts falling, and we contemplate it a long time, my head resting on Damian's shoulder and his arms around me. From time to time, his lips reach for my forehead, as he whispers how much he's missed me...

"I can't believe you're really awake."

Daniel is holding my hand, giving me a big smile despite his teary eyes.

"We've missed you."

"Thank you, Danny. It's good to be back."

It's Christmas Eve, and I couldn't be happier. As promised, I left the hospital a few hours ago after another round of check-ups, and Damian took me to our brand-new home. I love it.

It's an old traditional family house, with wooden floors, a fireplace, and stone brick walls. The decoration is the opposite of his cold apartment. Damian picked warm tones and wooden furniture, with Tonia and Bobo's help. The more I visited, the more I fell in love with it. He thought of everything, even to include a little library where I could relax and read my books on a comfy sofa by the window.

Tonight, it's especially welcoming with all the Christmas decorations. I don't know how they managed to do so much in such a short time, but Bobo, Sylviana, and Liam made it all happen, just like one of those old Christmas movies. Tonia pushed my wheelchair in the salon, in front of the fireplace and Christmas tree. As the doctor said, I can still only move a little, but I know my muscles will remember their former strength soon enough.

For now, I don't really mind. The house is crowded with our friends and family. Sylviana is in the kitchen cooking with Neal's wife, an adorable woman named Angela. Neal is chatting with Damian and Sean. Being an orphan, I learned earlier that Sean doesn't have anyone to celebrate Christmas with, so we invited him over as well.

Next to us, on the couch, Tonia and Bobo are busy keeping the children entertained. Bobo's nieces, the twins Juliet and Phoebe, are six years old, and Isaac, Nathaniel's Beta, just had a baby boy. As I watch them playing with the kids, I wonder when will Damian and I have our own children. Somehow, as soon as we became a couple, I always knew we would have children someday. Daniel catches my glance towards the children.

"So, this wedding?"

I chuckle.

"Probably in May. We would have had it sooner, but everyone around us insists we have a proper ceremony, so..."

"I bet so. Everyone missed the Luna; how can they not have a proper occasion to celebrate your return?"

I turn towards him and whisper, even if only Tonia and Bobo can hear us. "Do you have news?"

He smiles and nods. "She calls from time to time. She's fine, Nora, I promise. What happened with Nathaniel... really was hard, but her baby girl is more important to her. I think it's for the best, really. She will come back when she's ready."

"…but why did she have to leave?"

"I advised her so," replies a feminine voice.

Sylviana just joined us, and she takes a seat next to Daniel. I notice that despite playing with the twins, Bobo is listening, too.

"Her baby was in danger if she remained here, Nora. The Dark Witch knows or will know that there is another Royal in Silver City, and she would have targeted Elena just as much as you. Even more so, if she had known she was pregnant. So, I helped her find a place to hide for the time being."

"So, the Witch will continue to target us?" I ask, worried.

Sylviana sighs and nods. "She is weakened for now, but in a few years, she will probably try again, though I have no idea how. I will try to keep her away for as long as I can, Nora, but my power isn't unlimited, and her thirst for power will keep growing. She will look for more targets."

From her eyes, I know what she's thinking about.

"You mean our children. Like Elena's baby."

"I fear so... Your children will be of Royal Blood, Nora, just like you. They will inevitably become her targets, as well."

"You think we shouldn't... have children until we stop her?"

Sylviana smiles and shakes her head, putting her hand on mine.

"No, Princess. Nothing should stop you from living your life. After everything you've gone through, you more than anyone deserve it. I promise I will do anything I can to protect you and your children, and all of Silver City, for as long as possible. Get married, Nora. Have the children you want with Damian, and when the time comes for a battle, we will be ready."

She looks so confident when saying this... I don't want to think of another war coming up. Behind Sylviana's shoulder, my eyes meet Damian and Liam, who have probably been listening. While Damian is gently smiling at me, Liam has a frown on while staring at his companion. He looks... worried.

"Did you try calling him again?" I ask Damian.

But he shakes his head. So, Nathaniel is still not answering... I can feel his wolf, but he's obviously ignoring us. Isaac did say he was in bad shape since Elena left.

Liam clicks his tongue. "I don't give a damn about this idiot, Nora. After what he—"

"Liam, not tonight."

Sylviana gets up and goes to him to talk, but he still looks annoyed and walks out of the room. I sigh. I miss Elena, and I wish I had been there when all this happened. Daniel gets up to join Bobo and the kids, while Damian takes his spot next to me, taking my hand.

"Don't worry about Elena. My brother is an idiot, but he's really in love."

I can't help but smile. "You three brothers are so alike... When it comes to love."

Damian laughs a little and kisses my temple. My eyes follow Liam and Sylviana, who are still talking a bit further. They seem to be disagreeing on something, but I can't hear what this is about.

"I think Sylviana is right."

"About what?" Asks Damian.

"About that witch. This is only a break we should enjoy before she comes back. Once she does, we will probably have to face a war… A worse one."

My mate nods.

"I agree. I've talked about it a few times with Sylviana, she's... She knows a lot. About the future, but she won't say anything. I think that's why Liam is so worried about her."

He stays silent for a while, observing the little twins, who have decided to play with Bobo's hair. Or more like mess with it. Next to my giant best friend, his nieces look like adorable little dolls. Daniel is carrying Isaac's baby and laughing at Bobo's new hairstyle. I like having the laughter of children resonating inside the house...

"Let's have children," I whisper.

Damian turns to me, a bit confused.

"I thought that was already in our plans?"

"I mean... Soon."

"I thought you wanted to put your work first? I don't mind, but Nora, I don't want you to rush because of the Witch or something else."

"It's not about the Witch, it's... I already missed two years of work, anyway. And I really want to enjoy my time with you. Talking about the future, I suddenly feel that what I want to see most is not a career, but raising our children. Starting a family, here. I don't want to worry about the Witch until then, I just want to live our lives as we would have."

Damian observes me for a while, then slowly nods. "I understand what you mean. To be honest, since I saw Neal's children, I've been thinking I really want to have a family with you. I've focused on work only before we were reunited, but now I want to focus on you, on us. Getting you better first, then our wedding, and having kids."

"What? Who is taking a break from work?"

Neal just entered the room and is looking at us with panicked eyes. Damian laughs, but his Beta is not really happy.

"No, no, no, don't you dare! Do you have any idea of the mass of work that we have? You already took a couple of days off, and the Company is going nuts!"

"Nate can take over for a while. As I recall, he's drowning himself in work these days— you may as well have him use his position as my second for once."

They start to argue about Damian leaving his position for a while, and Isaac jumps in to protest against Damian switching position with Nathaniel as well. Funny enough, everyone else finds their argument amusing since both Betas are almost begging Damian not to do it. While they keep bickering, Sean comes to a seat next to me, looking a bit awkward.

"Luna, I wanted to thank you for inviting me."

"No, it's nothing. I wanted to thank you, too. I've heard that you've been... looking after my brother Alec."

"Yes, he sends his… best wishes to you."

"Thanks, Sean."

He nods, a bit awkward, and doesn't dare add anything else.

Alec is probably the one which, surprisingly, changed the most during those past two years…

According to Sylviana and Tonia, my brother is now totally clean from drugs. After he was done with rehab, he kept up his psychological evaluation while trying to repair his past mistakes. That will probably take a while…

Alec chose to leave the Jade Moon pack, and Damian welcomed him in the Blood Moon Clan, under Sean's command. My brother is now working in the slums and entirely devoted to taking care of the orphaned children, who, like we did ourselves years ago, end up in the streets without a family to care for them.

I have yet to face him, though. He sent me two letters that I have yet to find the courage to open and read. I think I'm going to need time to be able to forgive him and face him again. Even if he saved my life two years ago, my brother has left scars behind that won't heal so quickly. No one here asked me about anything about it, but I think they already understood.

Sylviana and Angie finally bring the argument to an end when everyone joins for dinner. I wish I had been in a condition to help with the cooking and enjoy all the equipment my brand-new kitchen has to offer. Still, our good witch and Neal's wife did a terrific job by themselves. Everyone around the table eats and chats happily.

I find myself thinking that I want to have this kind of Christmas every year. Next year, maybe, Elena and my niece will be joining us, as well as my own child with Damian...

A few hours later, the children are happily playing by the fireplace, and all the adults are enjoying coffee or tea in the living room. It's a heart-warming sight. Sylviana comes back from the kitchen and comes to sit by my side. She has a mysterious smile on, intriguing me.

"Nora," she whispers. "Liam and I will be going home soon, but before that, I have a little gift for you."

I frown. A gift? But before I can even ask, she suddenly puts her hands on my temples and closes her eyes. I don't even realize I'm in the dark until a second later.

When I open my eyes again, a woman is suddenly above me, smiling at me. She looks young and tired. I can't move, I'm... wrapped up in something smooth and warm. I try to say something, a bit confused, but the only sound that comes out is a baby's squealing. The woman smiles, and I notice her beautiful sapphire eyes.

"Hello, my little princess..."

The more I look at her, the more I see how much she resembles me. She's younger than I am, but her sapphire eyes, her pale skin, and those soft traits are the same as mine. I notice her freckles and long chocolate brown hair when she leans to kiss my forehead gently.

"Oh, you're so beautiful, my baby... My little Eleanora..."

She hugs me tenderly, her eyes shining with infinite love.

"Nora?"

I suddenly come back to my senses. Sylviana is facing me, smiling. Damian is holding my hand, looking worried.

"Love, are you okay?"

"I'm... fine..."

I look at Sylviana, still in shock from what I just saw. I realize I'm crying, flooding with emotions.

"That... that woman... That was my..."

"Your very first memory I could find," explains Sylviana. "She was beautiful."

Oh, Moon Goddess.

That was my mother. My real, my birth mother. Princess Lilyan. I try to control my emotions, but the tears keep coming.

"Nora, what is it? Sylviana, what did you do?" Asks Damian, worried.

"I'm okay, she just... gave me a very beautiful present."

"I'm happy you liked it, Princess," whispers Sylviana.

I can't believe it... I just saw my mother! My mom, when she had just given birth to me. Oh, Moon Goddess... I'm just so happy right now, I can't describe it. Her eyes were radiating with love. She loved me so much. I'm trembling with emotions, Damian hugging me to calm me down while I explain what I saw to him and the others. After a while, I turn to Sylviana, still a bit shook up.

"She... She called me Eleanora."

"Yes, I heard it with you. It's a really pretty name for a Princess."

Damian smiles. "I like it, too..."

We discuss a bit more about my mother, and the revelation of my real name. I had no idea. I like it, but I think it's a bit late now, I've gotten too used to just being called Nora. Eventually, that's the name I've grown by. I'm just grateful to Sylviana for giving me a glimpse of my origin.

That night, when everyone goes home or picks a guest room, Damian carries me to our bed. I don't really feel sleepy yet. This is the best Christmas of my life, and I'm still thinking about my mother.

My mate helps me change, and we lie facing each other in the bed.

"I've waited so long to be able to sleep beside you like this..." Whispers Damian.

"It feels good to be in your arms again. And I really love our house. Thank you, Damian, I love this Christmas present."

He smiles softly, and we lie for a while, just staring at each other. His fingers are running through my hair. As Sylviana said, it turned a shiny white again. It's still a bit odd to me, but Damian is used to it, though he prefers it black.

After a long while, I hear him breathe in deeply, and I wonder if he's asleep. But his eyes are wide open, and still on me.

"Nora... I was thinking. Sylviana's present... There's something I have yet to give you, too."

"What is it?"

"A story."

I smile. "A story? A book you mean?"

He chuckles and gets closer to me. "Not a book, my Love. A memory. The beginning of our story."

I gasp? Really now? Damian smiles, and I feel his breath as he softly starts talking.

"Twelve years ago, I was fourteen... Liam already told you about it, but life with our father was a nightmare, even more so after our mother died. He came and went as he pleased, not giving a damn about us. When he did come home, he was just a violent drunkard. He hit anything or anyone he could until he fell asleep or went out again. We were barely getting by. I had dropped out of school to work, but I made sure Liam and Nate still went.

"I tried to provide so they wouldn't suffer from it, even if they obviously did. Nate had to get a night job, too, at some point. But we made it work, somehow. We had the apartment to live in, and enough food and supplies for the three of us. I didn't really care about anything else. As long as my father didn't hit Liam or Nate."

"But he was beating you instead..." I whisper.

"You know, I wasn't as strong as him, but I could handle it. My mom had left us, and my brothers were the only ones I cared about. I would rather suffer a thousand hits from my dad than let him touch a strand of Liam's hair. Or Nate's. Well, Nate did get hit, too, while trying to defend me."

"He loves you. They both love you so much."

He smiles tenderly at me. "I know, Love. That's how our mom raised us. She was the sweetest woman, all she wanted was for the three of us to get along. Raising three boys, three Alpha brothers, she probably feared we would end up fighting each other, but we actually only sided against our dad."

Now that I think about it, we might have the same issue with our children, since they will most likely be Alphas only...

Damian sighs and gets closer to me. Now, my head is resting against his arm, and his fingers are gently playing with my hair. I close my eyes, listening to the familiar deep voice of my mate.

"The first time I shape-shifted, I was ten. I was in a rage after my father and just jumped into my wolf form without even realizing it. He beat me up good that day. Even in his human form, I couldn't even stand up to him. I never did, for years. Honestly, it was... hard. Being an Alpha that never wins. Every time, I had some hope I could finally fight off my father, chase him out, but no, it ended only when he decided it or when I was out. I knew he was the strongest Alpha of the city, but I woke up in my own blood so many times, beating him became an obsession, as much as protecting my brothers. As the years passed, every time made me angrier. I don't think someone else can hate like I hated my father at that time. He knew it, and that made him more and more violent every time. Until one day."

I hold my breath and grab his shirt. I know I'm not going to like what comes next...

"That night, I had come home late, and Nate and Liam were in our bedroom. My father suddenly barged in, so drunk he was yelling like a mad man. He hit me before I could even say a word. I tried to fight back, but he didn't leave me a chance. I barely remember what happened, honestly, except that it was the most violent fight we ever had. We both let our wolves take over, but…"

Damian shakes his head.

"When he was sure I couldn't fight back anymore, he took me outside. I was half-conscious, but I felt his grip on my hair. He dragged me down like a bag of dirt through the streets. I think he really wanted me dead. He took me to the slums and beat me again until I passed out."

What a monster. Damian was already unable to fight back or defend himself, and he really tried to kill his own son...

"It was December, and freaking cold, too. When I came to my senses, it was still the middle of the night. That's when you appeared."

Me? I don't remember this...

"I remember every detail. You were thin and dressed in rags, but you were the prettiest little girl I had ever seen. You ran up to me from across the street. All the snow around me was red, but you didn't seem to care. You were almost crying, and you asked me if I was in pain or cold. I could barely talk. You kept asking if I was hurt, but you were just a kid. Moreover, you had your scar, and it was obvious it was fresh. You didn't want to talk about it, you just kept asking and asking about my injuries."

"Sounds like I was annoyingly stubborn..."

He laughs. "Right... You refused to leave me alone, no matter who many times I told you to. You just stayed with me. You even cried for me, you said you were sorry you couldn't heal me. You kept repeating that while crying. I lost consciousness again at some point. When I woke up, you were gone, but your scarf was around my neck, and a pile of blankets was on me. I probably survived a few more hours, thanks to that. My healing had begun, but my injuries were... serious. I honestly thought I was dying. I had never been in such pain or lost so much blood. But you came back a few minutes after I had woken up. You were crying again, and had that bruise on your face..."

Probably Alec... He started hitting me after our parent's death, and he was the only one I lived with, in the slums.

"You were crying because you thought I was dead. You said you had gone to seek help, but your brother rejected you. So, you stayed with me. You said you had a brother, and that the next day would be your birthday... But you refused to give me your name."

"Why?"

"You said I might kidnap you."

I laugh. Oh, Moon Goddess, what a stubborn girl I was! Talking for hours with a stranger but not giving my name so he can't kidnap me? What a unique idea! And Damian was too injured to move, anyway!

Damian laughs, too, and kisses my forehead briefly. "You were so adorable. Stubborn but caring and sweet. You said if I fell asleep again, you would give me a kiss, like the princess from your book."

"I said that?"

"You did. You laid next to me in the snow, and you said you would watch me so I couldn't sleep again. You were... Moon Goddess, I remember it so well. You were laying just like this, facing me and smiling at me. At some point, I closed my eyes a few seconds, and you suddenly kissed me."

Oh, Moon Goddess, how could I be such a shameless seven-year-old brat! I blush, even though I can't remember it, but Damian is smiling from ear to ear.

"It was like a fire suddenly took me. My wolf went crazy. I felt... better than I had ever been in a very long time. Even my injuries suddenly stopped hurting. I knew you were my fated mate right away, but I couldn't believe it. We were just kids! It was so unbelievable... Even now, it feels like it was a dream. Laying in the snow, somewhere lost in the slums, with you. I... I had never known or even imagined something like that before. That was the very moment you became so, so painfully and beautifully precious to me. Because you were just you, caring for a total stranger and worried he might be cold or in pain, even though you were injured yourself."

Damian hugs me tightly in his arms, and I hide my face against his shoulder. I wish I remembered any of this...

"I knew we were fated mates, but I had never imagined we would be separated so quickly... I lost consciousness again, and you gave me a little kiss. Every time, I would wake up instantly, and I realized my injuries were healing incredibly fast, so I understood. That you were, somehow, healing me with those. What I hadn't realized was that you were getting weaker each time you did. At some point, you totally lost consciousness. I freaked out, but you wouldn't wake up. You stayed like this for a whole three hours, but I couldn't do anything. I had never, ever felt so powerless in my life. When you came to your senses, I told you never to do it again. Of course, you didn't listen. You kept going. Until I woke up, and you were gone. I was completely healed, but there was no trace of you. I looked for you. In the slums, and after that, I kept looking after I went back to my brothers. You saved my life and had vanished... but we were still linked."

"So, you knew I was alive."

"Alive and suffering. I could tell anytime you were in pain, and that made me feel worse about not finding you. So, I kept looking. Month after month, years... Nate told me so many times to reject you, to cut our bond, but I never wanted to. I loved you too much already, I couldn't give up. Until we found you."

I smile. I know what happened after that... Thank Moon Goddess, he did. I sigh. I can't imagine how different our lives would have been if I was still in the Jade Moon basement, abused by Alec.

"I think I know why the Moon Goddess paired me with you," I whisper.

"Why, Love?"

"Because you're strong, and never afraid to fight. I am... Or I was, the opposite. I don't care about suffering, but I avoided fights at all cost, while you never backed away from one, even if you knew you would lose. You taught me that."

I hear him sigh, and he kisses me softly.

"Nora, you're the bravest, strongest wolf I know. I don't think I've seen anyone able to endure as much as you endured, yet still deeply care for others. Even after everything he did to you, you never betrayed Alec, because you still had some love for him, and for your pack, too. You're gentle and forgiving. I could never forgive my father, I only hated him to the core. I think... I'm the one who needs you. I can't care or be as patient as you are towards others. I would be as cold-blooded as my father if it weren't for you. ...I'm always terrified you might hate me, that you might get scared of that violent part of me. So, I learn, every day, how to be a better man, a better wolf, because of you. I want to be a fair King. Not someone that is only feared like I used to be, but someone people can think of as a protector, someone you can truly love, a real Alpha King."

"You already are. People look up to you."

"This is all because I have you, Nora. They have seen the best of me because I have a Luna as gentle and caring as the Moon Goddess herself. You bring out the best of me. You're the one everyone in this city really needs."

His words bring me to tears, and I hide my face against his shoulder. I'm needed. The girl that used to hide in a basement, the weak, pitiful wolf. They need me.

Damian soothes me, caressing my hair and my skin gently, covering me with tender kisses on my neck, my cheeks, my lips. When he stops, his silver eyes look at me with a gentle gaze.

"I love you..." I whisper.

"I love you so bad, too..."

He resumes kissing me again. I kiss him, too, and we get lost in each other's embrace in this long, long night of December...

Epilogue

Two Years Later

"Mama!"

I open an eye. A baby's giggle runs to me, and I suddenly feel a small, chubby hand grabbing mine. Gosh, that was a short nap.

"Mamaaa!"

He gets impatient quickly, so I sit up, waking up completely to look at the little toddler reclaiming my attention. The little boy, balancing on his two short legs, is pulling on my skirt and looking at me with his two bright blue eyes.

"Where is daddy, baby?"

He ignores my question and pulls on my skirt again.

"Choco?"

"It's not the time for your snack, honey."

"Choco!" He insists, suddenly getting teary.

I sigh. My son is such a glutton... I still can't believe how much an Alpha baby boy needs to eat. He keeps insisting, pulling on my skirt again. Suddenly, Damian walks into the room and spots our toddler and me right away.

"James Black! I told you to let mom sleep!"

Our son, jumping at his father's angry voice, runs out in a hurry, completely forgetting to cry. I laugh, and Damian walks up to me with a sigh, putting a knee down before me, as I'm still sitting on the couch.

"Sorry, Love, he ran out when I wasn't looking... Did you sleep enough?"

He puts a hand on my tummy, with worried eyes. My first pregnancy was exhausting, and Damian is scared this one might be as well. I smile.

"I'm fine, don't worry. James is—"

"Right here."

Bobo walks in the room, carrying James by his overall. Compared to the giant wolf, our little boy is no match. However, our son is laughing from being carried that way. He has fun on his own until Bobo drops him at his dad's feet.

Damian sighs and takes James into his arms.

"I told you to let mommy sleep, didn't I?"

"But... my Choco..."

Damian tries to scold him, but our baby boy is just interested in his chocolate snack.

Moon Goddess, I love them so much... James is his dad's copy, except for his blue eyes and chubby cheeks. He's almost two years old now. I didn't expect to get pregnant so fast, but it happened right after Damian and I decided to try. A fated pair's luck, I guess. Bobo comes to sit next to me on the couch, while James is still arguing in his baby gibberish with Damian.

"Daniel is still at work?"

"He's got crazy hours this week. I'm bored... so I came to keep you company, but I didn't think the Boss was at home, too."

"He was worried James was tiring me out, so he's been working from home again these days."

"You do look tired. How's baby number two doing?"

"He or she is well behaved and fine. I'm not as exhausted as I was with James."

It took us a while to realize I was pregnant, but I kept suddenly falling asleep anywhere, any time of the day. Damian thought I was overworking, but Sylviana was the one who told us I was expecting. The whole pack went a bit crazy after that, everyone was overjoyed.

Everyone insisted I take a break from my work and Luna obligations to focus on our baby, and that was the best for me, too. Bobo started watching over me again, and Damian reduced his work to spend time with me also.

Silver City is doing better than ever.

The packs are all helping each other, in good relationships, and a lot of new couples appeared at the same time. Of course, our wedding was a big deal, too, even if we tried to keep it low-key. Which was almost impossible, thanks to William and Tonia... We got married six months after I woke up from my coma in June, and I was pregnant already. All our close friends attended, even the Alphas from other packs, and a lot of people from Damian's pack, too. I also needed to join the Blood Moon. I now have a little black crescent moon tattooed on my wrist.

Our wedding was perfect, though, and one of the best memories I will ever have. Especially when Liam helped us flee from it to have our alone time...

"Mama!"

James finally escapes from his father and comes running back to me. He is all teary again, doing his puppy eyes.

"Mama... Choco, please?"

I sigh and get up to head to the kitchen. James follows me, still holding onto my skirt. I take out the brownie I made yesterday and give him a bit. I offer a bigger portion for Bobo, as well. Damian puts an arm around me and watches James trying to steal some cake from the big brown wolf.

"Let's have a girl next," says my husband with a sigh.

I laugh. We still don't know what's the gender of our next child, though Sylviana could probably tell us. She told Elena her baby's gender when she was only ten weeks pregnant.

Thinking about my cousin makes me a little sad. I miss her... So many years have passed by already; I wish she would come back to Silver City soon. I do get to call her every week, but she is so far, we can't mind-link. And James should meet his cousin, too.

We barely talk to Nathaniel anymore. Damian's brother has become so gloomy since Elena left... I wish they could sort things out. Other than him, everyone is doing fine.

Bobo and Daniel are more in love than ever and even engaged, despite Daniel's busy schedule since he got a job at the Children's Hospital. Tonia has decided to get back with Lysandra, though it apparently follows their fifth break up... William and his new wife just had their first child a few months ago, a baby girl. Neal just had his sixth kid, too! Apparently, his wife wanted a big family.

For us, I think two babies will be enough for the time being. I miss my job, and raising Alpha children is seriously no joke, even if Damian is helping me a lot with James.

"Mama!"

My son comes running to me, his eyes full of tears. Bobo probably didn't let him take his cake. He's such a crybaby... I'm about to crouch down to soothe him, but a voice suddenly echoes inside my head.

"Nora!"

…Oh, Moon Goddess.

That was Elena's voice!

-The End-

The Silver City Series continues in

His Sunshine Baby

About the Author

Jenny Fox is a French author, born in Paris in 1994. She reads alone for the first time at 6 years old, Harry Potter and the Philosopher Stone, and writes her very first story at 9 years old. Her teacher reads it in front of the whole class, and from then on, she will never stop writing, from short stories to fanfiction.

His Blue Moon Princess is her first story to be entirely written in English, inspired by her experience overseas and her love for Fantasy Novels.

Follow her at **@AuthorJennyFox** on her Facebook Page.

CPSIA information can be obtained
at www.ICGtesting.com
Printed in the USA
LVHW112354050820
662482LV00001B/1